Wendy Holden grew up in Yorkshire and was a journalist before turning to full-time writing. She is married with a baby and lives in London and Derbyshire.

Praise for Wendy Holden's bestselling writing:

'Fantastic fun . . . witty, high-speed satire . . . I've lost count of the times I've laughed out loud. Hugely enjoyable' *Daily Mail*

'Hilariously outrageous' *Cosmopolitan*

'Delicious mayhem. With this updated version of *Cold Comfort Farm*, Holden has pulled it off again. Simply divine' *The Times*

'Sparkling' *You* magazine

'Wonderfully high-spirited . . . formidable' *Sunday Telegraph*

'Devilishly witty' *Elle*

'Holden writes with delicious verve and energy. Lie back and enjoy it' *Mail on Sunday*

'Witty, frothy, dancing with excess . . . irrepressibly joyous' *Good Housekeeping*

'Fiendishly witty' *Marie Claire*

'Hilarious' *Mirror*

'So funny and readable you worry about the calorie content' *The Sunday Times*

Also by Wendy Holden

Pastures Nouveaux
Fame Fatale
Azur Like It

Simply Divine
Bad Heir Day

Wendy Holden

headline

SIMPLY DIVINE first published in Great Britain in 1999 by HEADLINE BOOK PUBLISHING

BAD HEIR DAY first published in Great Britain in 2000 by HEADLINE BOOK PUBLISHING

First published in this omnibus edition in 2004 by HEADLINE BOOK PUBLISHING

A HEADLINE paperback

10 9 8 7 6 5 4 3 2 1

ISBN 0 7553 2252 5

Typeset in Garamond by Avon DataSet Ltd, Bidford on Avon, Warwickshire

Printed and bound in Great Britain by Clays Ltd, St Ives plc

Papers and cover board used by Headline are natural, recyclable products made from wood grown in sustainable forests. The manufacturing processes conform to the environmental regulations of the country of origin.

HEADLINE BOOK PUBLISHING
A division of Hodder Headline
338 Euston Road
London NW1 3BH

www.headline.co.uk
www.hodderheadline.com

Simply Divine

To my husband

Chapter 1

The organ swelled as Jane approached the altar, light-headed with happiness and not eating. It had been worth it – the tiny waist of the wedding dress now fitted her with ease, and she was blissfully aware of her slender form moving gracefully beneath the thick satin. The air was heavy with the scent of white roses as, smiling shyly beneath her cathedral-length veil, Jane drew up alongside Nick. Looking at her with a gratifying mixture of awe and wonder, Nick's face lit up in a tender smile . . .

The organ swelled and made Jane, fast asleep and revelling in her favourite dream, wake up suddenly. A dead, heavy weight was dragging itself across her chest. Realising it was Nick, Jane groaned more with discomfort than relief as her boyfriend groped clumsily to get his bearings before starting to saw away at her like a lumberjack. She barely had time to let out more than a couple of dutiful moans before, having galloped past the finishing post even faster than normal, Nick dismounted and rolled, grunting, back to his side of the bed.

As usual, Jane was left to lie in the wet patch.

She sighed as she stared out into the darkness, feeling vaguely violated. Quite literally, a rude awakening. She'd never get back to sleep now. Still, perhaps she ought to be grateful. She and Nick rarely had sex at all these days, and when they did, Nick preferred entering from behind, lying on his side, usually semi-conscious. It was, apparently, too much effort for him to get on top any more. A clear case, Jane thought ruefully, of Missionary Impossible.

It had not always been thus. They had met as students at Cambridge, a city which had afforded ample opportunities for thrillingly spontaneous lovemaking. The shelf stacks of the university library had quite literally been pressed into service, as had the backs of bike sheds, the Backs at midnight; punts, pubs, teashop loos and even the Master of Magdalene's garden. Most memorably of all, Nick had once pulled out all the stops in the organ loft of King's College Chapel. The Festival of Nine Lessons and Carols had never seemed quite the same after that.

Trying to anchor her head more comfortably in the pillow, sleep still as remote as the stars, Jane recalled the moment she and Nick had met in the campus cafe. His brusque Northernness had struck her as rather thrilling, as did his rugged handsome face and the fact that he seemed Terribly Politically Committed. Besides, as an

English student specialising in Hardy, Jane quite fancied the idea of a horny-handed son of toil.

The horny part, unhappily, had recently made its excuses and left. As she lay dozing in the dark, Jane tried to pin down the exact moment when she realised Nick didn't fancy her any more. If she was honest, it was about six months ago. Around the time she had moved into his flat in Clapham.

The bedside table exploded into frantic sound as Nick's irritating Mickey Mouse alarm clock announced six thirty. Oblivious of Jane deeply asleep beside him, Nick swore loudly, swung his legs out of bed and yanked back the curtains. A weak sun struggled through the dingy windowpanes and illuminated the pile of dirty washing over which he leant to switch on the radio.

Jane groaned inwardly as the quarrelsome tones of John Humphrys flooded into the room. Not *more* current affairs. It only seemed five minutes since Jeremy Paxman had been switched off the night before. But, just as Nick could not sleep without having seen both the nine and eleven o'clock news and *Newsnight*, he seemingly could not rise without having the *Today* programme reverberating through the flat from dawn onwards.

Jane's conspicuous failure to be as obsessed with current affairs as he was drove Nick to distraction. 'Your idea of political awareness,' he once accused her, 'is the length of Cherie Blair's skirt.' Jane had bridled at the unfairness of it. Had she not, over the years, helped

Nick canvass his way on to every committee from the college JCR to a seat on the local council, all landmarks along the course of political achievement Nick had set for himself? She knew more about politics than most. But she *was* interested in the length of Cherie Blair's skirt. Very much so. And what was wrong with that?

Nick's small blue eyes were screwed up with concentration as he listened to John Humphrys mauling a minister.

'How can they get so cross about things so early?' moaned Jane, sticking her fingers in her ears.

'Shush,' said Nick, flapping his hands like an irritable dowager and glaring at her as the minister's voice came on again. 'He's interviewing James Morrison, the transport minister. My boss, in case you've forgotten.'

Jane rolled her eyes. Forgotten? If only. In the two months since Nick had started working as a special adviser in his office, she had learnt more about the transport minister than he probably knew about himself. None of it remotely interesting.

'I put it to you, Minister,' shouted Humphrys, 'that if caravans were only allowed to travel between the hours of two and five in the morning, the world would be a happier place.'

'Quite right,' muttered Jane, who had been stuck behind more swaying beige mobile homes hogging the middle lane than she cared to remember.

'Look,' growled Nick, 'it may be a joke to you, but the caravan debate's a political bloody hot bloody potato of the first bloody order. Caravan owners have rights too, you know. James Morrison's been under a lot – a hell of a lot – of pressure to champion them recently.'

'Should start calling himself Van Morrison, then,' said Jane flippantly, diving back under the duvet as the interview ended.

'Hilarious,' said Nick, crushingly, stomping out of the room as best he could in his bare feet. His sense of humour, Jane reflected, had been another casualty of their cohabitation.

Minutes later, she heard the shower crank reluctantly into action and hoped he wouldn't take all the hot water. It was a vain hope; he usually did. Her standard of living had never been lower. Moving in with Nick may not have been a good idea.

'Are you sure it's a good idea?' Tally had cautiously asked at the time.

'Of course!' Offended, Jane had rebuffed her best friend's obvious conviction that it wasn't with all the brio she could muster. 'Nick needs me,' she had explained. Tally looked unconvinced.

'Are you sure he doesn't just need you to pay half the mortgage?' she asked gently.

Jane winced. Nick was not exactly famous for his generosity. Tighter than a gnat's arse, if she was to be frank. Last Christmas she had bought him a Ralph Lauren bathrobe and a Versace shirt. Nick had reciprocated with a twig pencil and a teddy bear which had been a free gift from the petrol station.

'Honestly, Jane,' Tally went on, exasperated, her big grey eyes wide with sincerity, 'you've got so much going for you. You're so pretty, and funny, and clever. I just don't understand why you're throwing yourself away on him. He's so *rude.*'

Tally was right. Nick *was* rude, especially after a few drinks, and especially to Tally. The fact that she was grand and had grown up in a stately home brought Nick out in a positive rash of social inferiority.

But it was all very well for Tally to be censorious, she thought defensively as she burrowed yet further beneath the duvet. It was just fine for Tally to declare she was holding out for Mr Right. Or Lord Right probably, in her case. She didn't understand that relationships simply weren't that straightforward. They didn't just *happen.* You had to work with what you had, particularly if you were twenty-four and didn't want to be a spinster at thirty.

'You'll be saying you want to marry him next,' Tally had almost wailed. Jane judged it injudicious to confess that this was the whole point of her moving in. Not that it had worked. On the contrary, judging by present form, Nick's plighting his troth looked more unlikely than ever. Plighting his sloth, however, had been the work of seconds.

Once Jane was on site, Nick had seen no further point in squandering both time and money on trendy restaurants when there was a perfectly good TV at home to eat Pot Noodles in front of. Similarly, all trips to cinemas, bars, concerts and parties had come to an abrupt end now that they no longer needed to leave the flat to meet each other.

Jane's evenings consequently divided themselves between working out how to fit her clothes into the minute amount of wardrobe space Nick had allocated her and scenting and oiling herself in the grubby little bath that no amount of Mr Muscle made the faintest impression on. She, at least, was determined to keep up her standards.

Nick, on the other hand, now picked his nose with impunity, refused to shave at weekends and after she'd been living with him a month, no longer bothered to hold the farts in. From French kisses to Bronx cheers, Jane thought miserably, as Nick's sex drive wound down to a sputter. Her own, by contrast, had revved up alarmingly. Practically sex-starved except for the occasional middle-of-the-night grope, Jane had lately begun to fantasise about everyone and anyone who so much as smiled at her.

Especially that gorgeous man who had just moved in upstairs.

With a guilty thrill, Jane thought about last night's encounter. The man upstairs had been sticking his key in the lock of the outside door of the building just as she had been opening it from the inside. Talk about Freudian. She frowned, trying to wrench her thoughts away from the hulking figure with the tumble of fair hair that had greeted her when the door opened. She could still recall the enormous size of his . . . grin.

Jane sighed and yawned, knowing the water would

certainly be cold by now. She peered over the top of the duvet into the chilly, dusty air. The scant warmth from Nick's storage heaters – turned permanently down to low – went straight out of the ill-fitting windows. Even in summer you could practically see your breath.

Not that Nick was around much to notice the Arctic atmosphere of his flat. Now he had finally realised his dream of working at Westminster, he came home later and later. Night after night, he stayed in his office, doing Jane knew not what. Taking phone calls from furious caravan owners, apparently. She sighed. Perhaps she should invest in one herself. It would be a way of attracting his attention.

Nick may have been bitten by the Westminster bug, Jane reflected, but it could have been any one of the insects in his flat. The place was crawling, and it was the discovery of a new itchy lump on her leg that finally drove Jane from under the duvet into the chilly embrace of the morning. They simply had to move out of here. Finding a new flat, Jane felt sure, would cement their relationship, as well as heat it, roof it and supply it with windowboxes. So far she had not had much luck.

'We found a lovely first-floor flat in Kentish Town,' she told Tally, 'but Nick was worried about the carpet glue. He was afraid it might bring out his asthma.' She did not voice her suspicions that he was afraid it might bring out his wallet. Nor, to her credit, did Tally.

Shuddering, Jane stood before the wardrobe mirror and stared at her naked body. Her legs, at least, were reasonable, even if her waist was too thick, her breasts too small and that stubborn spare tyre spread like a swag across the front of her tummy. The plump tops of her arms also gave her cause for concern. Still, Nick had never said he wished she was thinner. Then again, he'd never said he wished she was anything.

She wrapped Nick's Ralph Lauren bathrobe round her and went into the freezing kitchen. Something about Nick's appearance caught her eye. She stared at him covertly over the top of the paper he was reading. He had obviously been spending at least some of his time in the bathroom squeezing a stubborn spot above one of his eyebrows, and his efforts had left an angry circular red weal that made him look as if he had been shot through the forehead. Jane could imagine how this had wounded his vanity.

'I'd put some toothpaste on that,' she said helpfully. 'Dry it up a bit. It's what all the supermodels do.'

Nick tutted and continued his perusal of the *Telegraph* leader column. 'Trust you to know that,' he said scornfully.

Jane shrugged and started to examine the *Sun*. Most of the inside page was taken up with a picture of some ragged-looking, wild-haired environmental protesters at a planned bypass site. They were surrounding, and apparently arguing with, a tall, rather debonair figure whom Jane recognised as the transport minister, James Morrison.

There was something oddly familar about the protester pictured closest to Morrison. With his high cheekbones and funny little snub nose, he looked astonishingly like Tally's brother, Piers. He even had her small, thin lips and the same large, sloping eyes which, in that patrician fashion peculiar to inbred aristocratic types, looked as if they were about to slide away down the side of his face. The resemblance was extraordinary. It just showed, Jane thought, dwelling on one of her favourite theories, that there really were only so many facial types in the world. There must be, if some wild crusty could look so like someone who, at this moment, would be sitting in the chapel at Eton with his hair plastered down and looking as if Matron wouldn't melt in his mouth.

'Bloody crusties,' Nick exclaimed, his attention drawn by the amount of time she had spent staring at the page. 'Drug-crazed hippies. All sponging off the state. Too busy making trouble for everybody else to do any work.' It was not, Jane saw, the time to start arguing the case for conservation. Clearly, the official view from the transport minister's office was that his press coverage that morning was not all it might be. Jane swiftly turned over the page.

A huge colour photograph of an extremely glamorous blonde girl sprang out at her. So pneumatic were her lips, so vast and plunging her cleavage, so huge and confident her smile and so contrastingly tiny her dress that one almost didn't notice the handsome but ineffectual-looking young man with her, who was gazing into the camera with vacant eyes. 'Bubbling Champagne!' proclaimed the headline. 'Society girl

Champagne D'Vyne, snapped last night at the Met Bar with billionheir escort the Hon. Stretch von und zu Dosch,' said the caption.

'Oh, Christ, it's that stupid Sloaney tart again,' exclaimed Nick, looking over and seizing on another target for his ire. He took a swig of tepid tea from his Houses of Parliament mug. 'She's absolutely bloody everywhere,' he snorted in disgust. 'And why's she got such a bloody stupid name?'

'Apparently she was conceived after her parents drank a bottle of champagne,' said Jane. She'd read it somewhere or other, and, having offered the information, felt acutely embarrassed as Nick razed her with a withering glare.

'The things you know,' he remarked in mock astonishment.

Jane flushed. It was true. Her ability to retain unfeasible amounts of trivia was ridiculous. Against her better judgement, she could remember all the words to 'Bohemian Rhapsody', and recall every contestant in *The Wacky Races* but had forgotten her own telephone number on more than one occasion.

'It's a good thing her parents weren't into Newcastle Brown, then,' snorted Nick in his grating voice. 'Or Horlicks. Anyway, why's she so sodding famous?'

Jane looked at Champagne D'Vyne's lithe, athletic form, a riot of curves gloriously set off by her practically nonexistent clothing. She wore no bra. Her gravity-defying breasts seemed to be of that elastic variety that needed no support other than their own exuberance. 'I can't imagine,' she said, her light tone laced with sarcasm.

'Well, there must be some reason,' Nick insisted, Jane's irony utterly lost on him.

Jane stared. Could he really not see? Or perhaps it was because Champagne D'Vyne had a cleavage like the Grand Canyon that she, acutely conscious of her own rather more Cotswoldesque *embonpoint*, had no difficulty pinpointing the root of Champagne's attractions. 'She's famous for having huge tits,' she said finally. 'And for being fantastically posh. A lethal combination, wouldn't you say?'

'Well, you should know,' Nick sneered. 'That's your department, all that frothy, titsy, celebrity stuff. Great campaigning journalism, I must say.'

Jane flinched. Her career wasn't all it might be but did Nick *have* to be so nasty about it? Working on an upmarket glossy magazine might not be the socialist ideal but it was undoubtedly something a lot of people would kill for. The problem was, after six months at *Gorgeous*, Jane rather wanted to kill herself. Commissioning endless in-depth investigations into the contents of celebrity fridges and the dinner party games of the rich and famous was a soul-destroying business.

The sound of footsteps in the kitchen overhead derailed her train of thought. She wondered what the man upstairs was doing.

As she had passed him in the doorway last night, her all-quivering senses had caught a whiff of his aftershave – a delicious, clean, sharp scent the other end of the smell spectrum from the aspirational, peppery Jermyn Street potions Nick seemed so fond of.

By now, Nick had disappeared into the bedroom to get dressed. Jane could hear him rattling through the rail of expensive Egyptian cotton shirts that he had recently wheedled out of her for a birthday present, any one of which cost almost as much as her best office jacket. He emerged eventually, his bullet-hole smeared over with what looked suspiciously like her expensive new MAC spot cover.

'Good luck with celebrity underwear drawers,' Nick sniped as she went to kiss him goodbye at the front door. 'I wouldn't ring up Champagne D'Vyne about those,' he added. 'I can't imagine she has much use for knickers. She's obviously dropping them for every chinless wonder in town.'

Lucky old her, thought Jane as the door slammed in Nick's wake. She heard the click of his Church's shoes receding down the path as she headed towards the bathroom. Time to get ready for work. Make herself *Gorgeous*. There must be some hot water now.

Jane went into the bathroom and shot out again instantly. The air was filled with an ear-splitting shriek which she realised, after a few seconds, was her own. To accompany it, a series of crashing thuds from upstairs shook the flat above. But Jane hardly noticed. The last thing to register with any of her senses was the huge spider crouched in the bottom of the bath. Vast, malevolent and murderous-looking, with terrifying markings on its back, it had evidently marched in from the garden while they were reading the papers.

Still screaming, Jane bolted through the hall and out into the entrance passageway, leaving the door of the flat wide open. As she paused for breath, she heard it click shut behind her.

'Need any help?'

Head spinning with fear of the hideous beast in the tub and the dawning, dreadful awareness that she was locked out of the flat, Jane stared wildly up the stairwell to the next floor. *The man from upstairs was leaning over the banister. Grinning at her*. Grinning, it had to be said, more widely than the circumstances merited.

Jane gasped as she remembered she was wearing nothing but Nick's bathrobe. As she looked down at it, lolling off her shoulders and gaping open, she realised she wasn't even really wearing that. Mortified, she clutched the edges of towelling tightly to her and felt a warm tide of embarrassed crimson flood her face. How much had those knowing racing-green eyes managed to see of her? Had he spotted her spare tyre? The way her unsupported breasts scraped the floor? He must think her a loose woman in every sense of the word. Talk about the woman who put the common in Clapham.

'Well, aren't you going to tell me what's happened?' asked the man upstairs on the stairs, by now slowly descending the stairs. His faded burgundy bathrobe, stopping at his knees, revealed long, finely-muscled golden calves. 'I think it's the least you can do, personally,' he added, flashing her a smile so brilliant it could have been spotted from the moon. 'I was just in the shower myself, and you gave me such a scare screeching like that that I lost my balance and fell over. Face down on the taps, as it happens,' he said, arriving on the ground floor and raking her with a rueful glance from beneath his thatch of damp, butter-coloured hair.

Despite herself, Jane sniggered. Falling face down on the taps was *too* ridiculous.

'Glad you find it funny,' remarked the man from upstairs, raising an eyebrow. 'I'll have a couple of shiners by the morning. Guaranteed.'

Contrite, Jane realised she wasn't giving him the best of incentives to assist her. 'I'm terribly sorry,' she stammered. 'Perhaps if you rub some steak on them?' She had a vague idea from somewhere that this helped.

'I'd rather eat it, frankly,' he replied. 'Anyway, what *were* you yowling about? What's the problem?'

'Well,' Jane muttered, suddenly feeling silly. 'There's, um, there's a rather large spider in my, um, bath.'

'Spiders won't hurt you,' said her neighbour breezily. 'It won't even move unless you make it. The whole point of a spider is being a spider. They don't go in for sightseeing or aerobics.'

'Well, this one's got a leotard on, actually,' flashed back Jane, remembering the nasty markings and determined to claw back some dignity out of the situation. She turned on her heel to re-enter the flat, only to encounter the closed door. 'Oh, and I'm locked out as well.' She banged her fist on the door in frustration.

'Hang on a minute.'

As if she had much choice, Jane thought, slumping against the door and watching the long legs lope back upstairs. She was hardly going to rush out and catch a bus dressed like this, was she? Not that it stopped some people.

Two minutes later, he had bounded down again, opened the latch with a credit card, entered the flat and flipped the spider out of the bathroom window. 'Thank you so much,' said Jane, stiff with embarrassment as well as cold. She had noticed by now that her legs were not only blue with the chill, but needed a shave. Her standards were beginning to slip after all.

'It's a pleasure. I'm Tom, by the way.' He flashed her another knee-trembler of a grin.

'I'm Jane.'

'Yes,' he said. 'I know.'

'You *know*?' Her heart swooped in a somersault. He knew her name. Jane surrendered herself to the thrilling thought that he must have more than a passing interest in her to bother finding out what she was called.

'Yes. There's a pile of bills with your name and address on them by the door.'

Chapter 2

'I want *ideas*. Big ideas. *Huge* ideas. Circulation-rocketing, magazine-of-the-year-award-winning ideas.'

The editor of *Gorgeous* put the tips of his manicured fingers together, pursed his lips and glared at his staff. Jane shifted uncomfortably on the sofa between the art director and the fashion assistant, both of whom were gazing vacantly into space.

Josh flicked an invisible bit of dust off the lapel of his Prince of Wales check suit and stared through his monocle at his features department. In other words, Jane. There had been talk, when Jane started, of recruiting a crack ideas team to help her, but it had so far failed to materialise. Nor, Jane knew, was it now likely to. *Gorgeous* operated on the principle common to most publications, that keeping staff costs down was as important as keeping the circulation up. The standard belief that the overworked staff would feel elated by the enormous responsibility and positively revel in the lack of support also applied.

'What I particularly want,' Josh continued, 'is some really *brilliant*, original, ingenious, attention-grabbing *gimmick*. I'm *sick* of seeing *The Sunday Times* stealing a march on us with Tara Palmer-Tomkinson. She should be writing for *Gorgeous*. She's done wonders for their figures.'

No mean feat considering she had a chest flatter than an airport runway herself, thought Jane, who was no fan of the celebrated sybarite.

'And *Fabulous* is snapping at our heels,' continued the editor testily. It was true that *Gorgeous*'s great rival, the society magazine *Fabulous*, was putting on readers at an alarming rate. 'We *can't* let them overtake us in circulation.' He banged his fist dramatically on his desk. A collection of silver-framed photographs of Josh with Princess Diana, Josh with Karl Lagerfeld, Josh with John Galliano and Josh with Kate Moss fell over with a crash. 'What's *new*?' he demanded, wiping Kate lovingly with his sleeve as he propped her up again.

His staff quaked. Everyone was terrified of Josh. Impeccably dressed and sharply good-looking, he had the reputation of being one of the most gifted and competitive editors in London. He was devoted to *Gorgeous* and expected everyone who worked there to be as obsessed with it as he was. He had, after all, taken it from a mumsy rag to a glittering social glossy in the four years he had been editor. No one could doubt his talents or his commitment. But his management skills were from the Darth Vader school.

'I see Champagne D'Vyne's all over the tabloids again,' ventured the chief sub. Her voice trailed off as she waited for Josh's reaction.

'Yes, doesn't she look wonderful, bless her,' said Josh, exposing his exquisitely-capped teeth in a dazzling white smile. He shook back a lock of hair that had had the impertinence to detach itself from its smoothed-back auburn fellows and stared thoughtfully at the chief sub. She blinked at him through eyelashes so thick with make-up they looked more black leaded than mascara'd. 'Ye-e-es,' said Josh, slowly, a gleam appearing in his eye. The chief sub blushed and put up a self-conscious hand to further tousle her moussed-up hair. She'd had a crush on Josh for ages. Had her moment finally come?

A stream of breathless excuses announced the sudden arrival of Valentine, *Gorgeous*'s deputy editor who, despite his lofty title, received almost as much flak from Josh as Jane did. 'Oh, you won't believe what happened to me on the way here,' he gasped.

'You're right, I won't,' Josh cut in rudely. 'So don't bother.' Valentine visibly slumped. But Josh hadn't finished with his unfortunate number two. He picked up a page proof from his desk and waved it at Valentine. 'Have you had these interior pages legalled?' he asked.

'Legalled?' echoed Valentine. One of his responsibilities was to make sure every page in the magazine had been through the in-house lawyers before publication. 'Why ever would the lawyers want to read "That Sinking Feeling: How To Choose an Amazin' Basin", or "Pale and Interesting: Picking the Right White For

Your Home"?' he demanded. His chest swelled defensively, straining the hard-pressed buttons on his suit still further. His eyes bulged.

'Well, you never know, someone may have slagged off a scatter cushion,' said Josh. 'Better talk it through with the lawyers, there's a dear.'

Valentine snatched the proof from him and rushed out in the direction of the legal department.

The meeting was dismissed and Jane settled herself behind her desk which, as usual, was a sea of last week's newspapers and possibly last century's page proofs. Her heart sank at the mess of it all. The entire office was piled up with old papers, envelopes, post nobody bothered to open, unwanted faxes from unwanted contributors and, worst of all, boxes of everything from Tandoori burgers to savoury ice creams sent in for review to the food editor, whose rare appearances meant they rotted and stank in the office's overheated atmosphere until someone (usually Jane) had the sense to throw them away.

The last of all the staff to arrive was Lulu the fashion editor, who had never seen a morning meeting yet. As always, despite being over an hour late, she gave an impression of great speed and industry, bustling in as quickly as her combination of tight black leather skirt, impenetrable dark glasses and vertiginous heels would allow.

As Lulu sashayed past her desk, Jane noticed she was dragging something odd behind her. And this time it wasn't one of her exotic collection of photographer's assistants. 'What's that?' asked Jane, staring at something long, black and rubbery trailing in Lulu's wake.

'It's a symbol of Life,' declared Lulu theatrically. 'It represents woman's struggle on earth.'

'It's an inner tube, isn't it?' asked Jane.

'No,' said Lulu emphatically. 'Only if you *insist* on perceiving it that way. The circle is also a representation of the cyclical nature of Womanhood and the fact it is made of rubber refers to the eternal need to be flexible. Woman's inheritance, in short.' She sighed and rolled her eyes. 'All that juggling of priorities.'

Jane snorted quietly. The only juggling of priorities Lulu did was forcing her breasts into an Alexander McQueen leather bustier.

'Women should think themselves lucky then,' drawled Josh's voice from his office where he was, as usual, listening. 'All I'm going to inherit is Parkinson's.'

Jane grimaced. It wasn't as if Josh needed to inherit anything. His salary, she suspected, ran well into six figures, he received more designer suits than he could wear and was courted by so many PRs he probably hadn't paid for his own lunch for years.

'Fancy a cup of tea, Lulu?' Josh's light, sarcastic tones floated across the room.

'Josh, darling, I'd just *die* for one,' breathed Lulu with her usual understatement.

'Off you go and get one then,' said Josh. 'And get me one while you're at it.'

Lulu grinned. 'Oh, you really are *ghastly*, Josh.' She always took his jibes in good part. Jane was unsure whether Lulu simply didn't get half of them or tolerated them because she realised she had an ally in Josh. Did Lulu, after all, know what side her sushi was wasabi'd on?

'She's a few gilt chairs short of a Dior front row, that one,' muttered Jane to Valentine, who had by now returned from the lawyers, as Lulu wobbled out of the office.

Josh overheard. 'It's so wonderful to have *someone* round here who knows about clothes,' he purred, shooting a loaded look at Jane. 'They're a very important part of Features.'

'Look,' said Jane, exasperated, 'I admit fashion's not my area but I pull my weight, you know.'

'Considerable weight it is too,' said Josh, who prided himself on his lack of political correctness.

'You could have him for sexual harassment, you know,' murmured Valentine in an undertone.

Josh's sharp ears twitched once more. 'I assure you,' he said silkily, taking his monocle out and polishing it, 'there's nothing sexual in it.'

Christ, and it's only Monday, Jane thought. Four and a half whole days to go before the weekend. And not an enormous amount to look forward to then. Nick was going to Brussels for a ten-day Euro transport summit, which put the kibosh on flat-hunting. On the other hand, there was always the delicious possibility of another on-the-stairs encounter with Tom . . .

Jane frowned. Just forget it, she told herself. There was no point, having worked away at Nick for the last few years and finally succeeded in moving in with him, to risk the bird-in-the-hand reality of a permanent relationship by having a crush on the upstairs neighbour. The thought of two in the bush with Tom remained a delicious fantasy nonetheless. But fantasy, thought Jane, was as far as it was going to get. Tom probably had millions of girlfriends anyway. And *she* had a boyfriend.

Around lunchtime, the telephone on her desk shrilled.

'Hello, *Gorgeous*,' said Jane, gritting her teeth, as she did the fifty times a day she had to give this absurd salutation.

'Jane, it's Tally,' came a distant, muffled voice from what sounded like the bottom of a mine shaft. The phone system at Mullions, the rambling manor in Gloucestershire where Tally's family had lived for four centuries, had not been rewired for the last two reigns at least. 'Please say you'll be around this weekend.' Even through the ancient and twisted phone lines a certain desperation could be detected. 'I'm coming to London. I need to see you. We have to talk.' Then, like a crumbling and decrepit actor who yet retained a fine sense of dramatic timing, the Mullions line abruptly cut itself off.

Talk about what? Was Tally in trouble? Surely not pregnant? Jane ran through a mental line-up of the workers on the Mullions estate and quickly dismissed the suggestion. There were two, and only one was a man – Peters the gardener who also, and often without washing his hands too thoroughly, doubled as butler.

Still, all would be revealed at the weekend, if Tally ever managed to reconnect to suggest a rendezvous. Feeling more cheerful, Jane went to the fax to send a second proof of his page through to Freddie Fry the restaurant reviewer. She prayed that this time it had no mistakes in it. Her ears were still burning from their recent conversation.

'It's preposterous,' Fry had blustered. 'Look at the second paragraph. Where it says "my newt's livers"?'

'Mmm?' said Jane mildly, looking at the offending line. It seemed perfectly properly spelt to her.

'My newt's livers?' boomed the notoriously brusque Fry. 'What the fuck are newt's livers? It should say "minute slivers", you bunch of morons.'

As the missive beeped and screeched its way through to Fry, Jane idly scanned the pile of faxes in the tray beside the machine. Near the top was a letter from Josh. She picked it up with interest but had not read five words before panic gripped her heart. 'No!' she gasped.

The fax was a letter commissioning a column and promising the writer not only all the editorial help they could possibly want, but £1,000 a shot into the bargain. It was addressed to Miss C.O.W. D'Vyne.

So this was the brilliant new gimmick. The circulation-soaring, award-collecting Great Idea.

'You're not serious!' protested Jane, shooting into Josh's office with the fax trembling in her hand. 'Champagne D'Vyne!' she exclaimed. 'But she's just a dumb Sloane. Tara Palmer-Tomkinson can at least write. Rather well, too,' said Jane, much as it pained her to admit it.

'Quite,' said Josh. 'And Champagne will write even better. With a little help from *us*, of course.' He grinned at her. 'But I don't just want a measly old Tara-sized column. No point just repeating what she does. I want something much bigger and bouncier.'

'Well, you've certainly got that,' said Jane.

'I want a whole double-page spread of sparkling social froth.' Josh's eyes glowed. 'A good fourteen hundred words of witty, polished copy every month, Maybe two thousand words. Make it four pages, even. You'll easily manage that.'

Jane blinked. 'Me? But how can I? I'm not the one with the glamorous social life.'

'Well, you said it, dear,' said Josh, yawning and stretching his long perfectly-tailored arms to the ceiling. 'No, but seriously, as we comedians say. Champagne and I have discussed it. It's just a simple matter of you talking to her every now and then. Keep on to her. Ask her where she's been, who she's seen, what she's bought and, best of all, who she's slept with. Then just jot it all down. Keep her diary, in other words.' He paused. 'Brilliant, isn't it?'

'Fantastic,' said Jane sourly.

'I thought you'd jump at the opportunity.'

'Yes. Out of the window,' snapped Jane. She could tell she had no choice in the matter. She groaned inwardly. Nick was going to have a field day when he heard about this.

'I've already thought of a name for it,' Josh continued, triumphantly. 'Champagne Moments!'

'We'll be the laughing stock of Fleet Street,' Jane mumbled miserably.

'Nonsense! It's just what *Gorgeous* needs. It'll knock *Fabulous* into a cocked tiara. How can it go wrong?' Josh clapped his manicured hands, with their faint hint of clear nail polish, together in delight. 'Champagne's fantastically posh and has huge tits. A lethal combination, wouldn't you say?'

The very words she had said to Nick that morning. Jane's heart sank.

Much as Nick might – and did – sneer at the triviality of Jane's latest project, tracking down Champagne D'Vyne turned out to be investigative journalism of the highest order. Jane was initially encouraged by the fact that Champagne was signed up with a vast international public relations outfit called Tuff PR. But this turned out to be a false dawn, as brokering Champagne's deal with *Gorgeous* and banking the cheques seemed to be the limit of Tuff's interest. Even less concerned was a snappy and extremely camp-sounding creature called Simon whose responsibility Champagne apparently was.

The two telephone numbers Simon gave Jane for Champagne both turned out to be useless. One was an incomprehensible answerphone message which cut off halfway through and the other the full mailbox of a mobile phone.

'So how do you suggest I get hold of her?' an exasperated Jane finally demanded of Simon. 'Telepathy?'

'Look, I'll do you a favour, OK?' was Simon's miraculous response. Blistering rage, apparently, was the only thing that made an impact. When the going got tough, Tuff, it seemed, got going. 'Champagne's doing a fashion shoot this afternoon for a magazine. You'll have to go along to that. It's a bore, because I don't want any strangers making her nervous on her first big job.'

Jane was surprised. She had not had Champagne down as the shy type. In her tabloid appearances, at least, Champagne seemed to have the front of a hundred Moulin Rouge dancers.

The photographic studio where the fashion shoot was to be held was in a converted warehouse in Docklands. As an entry into the glamorous world of Champagne D'Vyne, the building seemed unlikely. A poky, strip-lit, hospital-like corridor issued into a tiny office where someone with their back to Jane and almost completely hidden by a vast, battered leather chair was talking very loudly into the telephone. From the voice, and the pair of white-jeaned legs visible on the desk in front, Jane assumed it to be the studio secretary. She sat down on a shabby black plastic sofa to wait for her to finish her conversation, and wondered where in the building Champagne was. She felt faintly apprehensive at meeting a real life bombshell in the flesh. Particularly when she felt such a bombsite herself.

'What do you mean, hang on a sec?' the girl suddenly screeched. The back of her chair wobbled violently. 'No one tells me to wait for secs.'

Jane blinked. She'd dealt with some uppity secretaries at *Gorgeous* in her time, but this was a whole new ballgame. Models and photographers were, she knew, a notoriously imperious breed. She hadn't realised their secretaries were as well.

'Yes, I should bloody well think I'm connected.' As she got angrier, the girl's voice sounded increasingly like the honk of an extremely patrician goose. But not for long. Having reached the person she wanted to speak to, her voice suddenly dissolved into a syrupy, lisping, Sugar Kane wheedle.

'Is that you, Rollsy?' she gushed. 'Darling, I've been thinking about our trip to Paris tonight. It's just *too* wonderful of you to take me in your private plane but *could* we *possibly* take that glorious red Gulfstream instead of the blue one? I know I'm a silly, darling, but it's just that my nail varnish is the wrong colour for the blue . . .'

Jane swallowed. Clearly, studio secretaries moved in more elevated circles than she thought. Literally.

'The *red* one, darling, yes.' A hint of the imperious honk was creeping into the girl's breathy tones. Rollsy was obviously having trouble recalling which of his hundreds of Gulfstreams she meant. 'You know, the one with that divine little inglenook fireplace . . . Yes? Fabulous, darling. Big kiss. Bye-ee.' She slammed down the phone. 'Fucking idiot.' With a push of her long leg, the chair swung round.

Jane found herself staring at an arrogant-looking blonde with indignant grass-green eyes and a petulant, full mouth big enough to seat a family of six. She had cheekbones like knuckledusters, cascades of shining hair and a tight white jersey top through which her nipples could clearly be seen. Jane realised it wasn't the studio secretary at all. She was looking at Champagne D'Vyne.

'What the fuck's going on?' a voice behind them demanded suddenly.

A small, profoundly tanned man with intensely blue eyes, tight jeans and stack-heeled boots was standing in the doorway of the office. Three cameras, all with enormous lenses, were slung round his wrinkled brown neck, as were a number of thick gold chains. Jane recognised him instantly as Dave Baker, a well-known fashion photographer who had launched more models than NASA had space probes. He waved furiously at Champagne, tapped his huge, expensive-looking watch and frowned. 'For fuck's sake, we haven't got all day,' he shouted at her. '*Scusi* my language, darling,' he said to Jane, his Italian sitting oddly with his Cockney. 'We've been here three hours already and Her Blondeness has only just turned up. Only just got out of bed, apparently – though *whose* I wouldn't like to speculate.' He turned on his stack heel in disgust and minced back in the direction of what Jane imagined was the studio.

Champagne took absolutely zero notice. Her entire attention was focused on the telephone, which had just rung again. She listened intently, then let out an indignant yell into the receiver. 'I don't *believe* it, Rollsy,' she shouted furiously, completely abandoning her sugary tones. 'You've lent it to Prince *who*? Well, can't you get it back? No, the blue's simply *not on*, darling. *Nada*. I'd have to have a whole new manicure and you *know* how busy I am, angel.'

Jane's fingers crept towards her pad and pen. May as well make a few notes. You never knew.

'Oh, I *suppose* I could bear BA first class, if you simply *can't* get it back,' Champagne lisped petulantly. 'But *must* we go to boring old Paris *yet* again? Another weekend at the Crillon and I'll *kill* myself.'

After a few more minutes in this vein, Jane was stopped mid-scribble by a touch on her arm. It was Dave Baker again.

'Look, I'm sorry to bother you, *carissima*,' he said, the muscles in his wrinkled cheeks working like galley slaves as he cast a furious look at the still-chatting Champagne. 'But would you do me the most *enormoso* favour? I need to find out *urgimento* whether the light is OK for these pictures. Would you be a complete *cara* and sit for some Polaroids so I can check everything before we start shooting on film? Sorry, we haven't been introduced. Dave Baker, *fotografico*.'

'I know,' said Jane, touched by the modesty and friendliness of one at the top of a profession not noted for its humility. 'Of course. I'd be delighted. If you're sure I won't break the camera.'

Dave laughed. 'You're a very pretty girl, dear.'

Jane packed up her notebook and followed him into

a large, light room where snake-like black cables writhed over the floor like the inhabitants of a reptile house. A beautiful make-up artist, arms folded, awaited Champagne's pleasure beside an array of pots and brushes while a wide-eyed young man wearing very tight white trousers busily altered the angles of the photographic lamps and measured their strength with a light meter.

'*Molto bene*,' said Dave, sitting Jane in front of a huge backlit white screen and encouraging her to suck her cheeks in. '*Bella, bella*. Amber, *carissima*, a spot of make-up if you please, and *una piccola* tweak with the hair perhaps?'

Amber breathed mintily and absorbedly while she dabbed Jane's face with a bit of powder and lipstick and pinned her hair loosely up behind her head.

'Gosh,' said Jane, gazing at herself in the mirror Amber held up when she had finished. The soft, shadowy light made her face look fragile, her blue eyes huge and her hair a soft haze of piled-up gold. Amber had also done all sorts of clever things with a lip pencil so Jane's thin mouth, while not quite rivalling Champagne's six-seater, at least now provided respectable room for two.

'You've got lovely bones, you know,' Amber said matter-of-factly, snatching away a stray eyebrow hair with a pair of tweezers. 'You should wear your hair up more often. Or get it cut short to show off your face a bit.'

'Do you really think so?' asked Jane, settling back

into the chair happily. She was beginning to enjoy being a supermodel. She hoped Dave would give her a Polaroid shot to take back to Nick. He could keep it in his wallet. On the other hand, as he so rarely opened it, that might not be the best place.

'What the fuck's going on?' It was Champagne's turn to sound indignant. Her demanding tones echoed round the studio.

'I didn't realise this was a shoot for Evans the Outsize,' Champagne snarled, striding up to Jane. Her heels clattered furiously on the wooden floor. 'Who the fuck are *you*?' Her brilliant green eyes homed pitilessly in on the greasy roots of Jane's hair. Nick had taken all the hot water again that morning.

'I'm Jane from *Gorgeous*,' Jane stammered, terrified despite herself. Being sneered at by someone so beautiful was an intimidating experience. 'I've come to write your . . . I mean, I've come to discuss your, er, column.'

'Well, what the hell are you doing in front of the camera then?' Champagne's drill-like gaze moved from Jane's scuffed shoes to the sagging bra beneath her not-very-well-ironed white blouse. Jane's cheeks burned with shame.

'Jane very kindly stepped in to help us with the light reading since you were so *busy*,' said Dave.

Champagne seethed. Pausing only to throw a glance as green as a glassful of Chartreuse at Dave, she flounced out of the studio, muttering a stream of invective of which only 'fucking old poofter' could clearly be heard.

There was a short silence.

Dave sighed. 'Go and sort her out, Fabergé,' he murmured to his snub-nosed assistant. Fabergé started eagerly forward. But his services, it seemed, were not required.

'I'm ready.' Husky tones had replaced the honk. Turning round, Jane saw Champagne standing in the doorway wearing nothing more than a challenging gaze.

There really was, Jane saw, nothing holding those breasts up. Full and glorious, they soared onwards and upwards like helium balloons, each topped with its rosy nub of nipple. Champagne grinned at her astonished and silent audience. She strode forward, long muscles sliding up and down her slender thighs as she moved. She walked up to Dave and, thanks to the disparity in their heights, thrust her nipples practically in his face. 'Dress me,' she said in her huskiest tones, running both hands down the sides of her body. 'If you want to, that is.' She shot a searing glance from beneath her thick lashes and pouted at the room.

Jane sighed. Champagne had turned a tantrum into a triumph simply by taking her clothes off. Satisfied at the sensation she had caused, Champagne swung on her heel and began to sashay up and down the room like a supermodel. Watching her prance around, utterly uninhibited, it struck Jane that nakedness was a concept that only really applied to those with less than perfect figures. People with bodies as stunning as Champagne's were always dressed, in the sense that there was never anything embarrassing to conceal.

Delighted to be the centre of attention, Champagne

now dazzled the assembled company with a radiant smile.

'She can certainly turn on the charm when she wants to,' Dave muttered grudgingly.

'She can turn on more than that,' Jane whispered. 'Look at Fabergé!'

Dave turned round to see his assistant bending over some boxes. He was clearly trying desperately to conceal an enormous erection in his tight white trousers.

'*Well*,' said Dave delightedly, raising both eyebrows and grinning widely. 'I had no idea he was such a talented boy.'

Dave's good humour restored, the shoot proceeded. Champagne was in her element, posing, pouting and slinking about in a succession of tiny, tight evening dresses that Jane could barely imagine getting her own right leg into. As Champagne's grudge against her seemed to have completely dissolved under the hot studio lights and the attention, Jane bit the bullet and suggested, after the shoot was over, that it was time to talk through the first instalment of Champagne Moments.

'Well, it had better not take long,' Champagne snapped, looking at her diamond-studded Cartier watch. 'I've got a colonic at three,' she announced. 'Then a leg wax. Then Rollo's picking me up.'

'Fine,' said Jane briskly, fishing out her notebook and flicking the ballpoint release mechanism of her pen. 'Let's be quick then. Talk me through your week. What have you been doing?'

Champagne, slumped on an orange box in the studio with her elegant legs wound round each other, fished a cigarette out of her snakeskin Kelly bag. She lit it and frowned. 'Ah,' she said, addressing the far wall. 'Um,' she added. 'Er,' she finished.

Jane felt panic rising slowly up her throat. Of the many difficult situations she had imagined Champagne Moments might involve, the one in which Champagne was unable to remember anything she had done had never occurred to her.

'Um, I saw in the *Sun* that you had been out with Robert Redford when he came to London earlier this week,' Jane prompted.

A slight pucker appeared between Champagne's perfectly-plucked eyebrows. Robert Redford, Robert Redford, her bee-stung lips mouthed silently. Robert Redford. After a few minutes of profound frowning, a faint glow of remembrance irradiated her face. '*American!*' she pronounced triumphantly.

Jane nodded eagerly, encouragingly.

'*Actor!*' Champagne added a few seconds later.

Jane nodded again.

'Oh, *yah*,' pronounced Champagne eventually, her face glowing with the promise of full recollection.

The promise remained unfulfilled. Champagne could remember nothing more.

'I suppose I had a lot of QNIs last week,' Champagne concluded. 'Quiet Nights In.'

Heart sinking, Jane realised this was not going to make four sentences, let alone four pages. And if she returned to the office without the fourteen hundred words of sparkling copy Josh wanted, it wasn't going to be Champagne D'Vyne who got the blame. Why, if he'd wanted an It Girl, hadn't Josh simply signed up Tara Palmer-Tomkinson, Jane seethed to herself. She, at least, had the two vital skills Champagne lacked – the ability to string a sentence together and some idea of what she'd been doing all week.

Sighing, and sending up a silent prayer to the god of ghostwriters, Jane took her mental pickaxe and determinedly and repeatedly attempted to break the surface of the substance which lay like impenetrable rock between Champagne and her ability to recall anything whatsoever that had happened to her in the past few days. Thank goodness she had taken those notes when Champagne was on the phone.

It took several increasingly frantic phone calls a day for the rest of the week before Jane managed to extract enough information to make up the first column. The latest *Gorgeous* had been about to hit the printing presses, but Josh insisted the issue was held until Champagne Moments was written and slipped in at the last minute. At the end of the week, Jane staggered, utterly drained, into Josh's office and handed over four pages of print-out to her boss. Heart hammering, she sank on to the sofa and folded her arms to await the verdict. It was always nerve-racking showing Josh a piece. Few things ever seemed to come up to the standard he demanded. She crossed her fingers so hard that it hurt.

Josh read. He clapped his hands and rocked with mirth. He laughed so much at the Gulfstream stories that his monocle fell out. 'It's hilarious,' he gasped, dabbing his streaming eyes with the handkerchief from his top pocket. 'It's fantastic. A star, my dear, is born.'

Damn, thought Jane, uncrossing her fingers.

Chapter 3

Whatever it was Tally desperately wanted to discuss, she wasn't going to break the habit of a lifetime and arrive on time to do so. Sitting waiting in the corner of the local wine bar on Saturday night, Jane had got through one glass of house white and half a bowl of peanuts already. Not that she was too annoyed. No one could hold a candle to Champagne in the irritation stakes. And anyway, it was impossible to be angry with Tally. She was much too sweet and awkward. With her funny nose, large eyes, long legs and towering height, Tally had reminded Jane irresistibly of a startled ostrich the first time they clapped eyes on each other at Cambridge.

'Do you remember,' Jane often said long after she and Tally had become friends, 'that first English tutorial on Memory when we were asked what our earliest recollections were and you said yours was of the line of servants' bells ringing in the breakfast room at home. I thought you were the most ghastly snob!'

'I suppose I should have said they were ringing because the window sash had broken again and there was a howling gale blowing through the room.' Tally sighed. 'And that I was in there because my bedroom ceiling had collapsed and I was sleeping on the breakfast room floor.'

Tally, Jane soon realised, was not your typical upper-class girl, despite having had almost a textbook grand upbringing. From what Jane could gather, her mother had wanted her to ride but Tally was almost as scared of horses as she had been of the terrifyingly capable blondes strapping on tack at the Pony Club. Lady Julia had managed to force her daughter to be a debutante, with the result that Tally was now on intimate terms with the inside of the best lavatories in London. 'I was a hopeless deb,' she admitted. 'The only coming out I did was from the loo after everyone else had gone. I once hid in the ones at Claridge's for so long I heard the attendant tell the manager she was going to send for the plumber.'

Tally did, however, live in a stately home, Mullions, and was the descendant of at least a hundred earls. The earls, however, had done her no favours as far as the house was concerned. 'Trust' was the Venery family motto. 'I *so* wish it had been Trust Fund,' Tally sighed on more than one occasion. For the heads of successive generations had, it seemed, trusted a little too much in a series of bad investments and their own skill at the card table. A sequence of earls had squandered the family resources until there was nothing left for the upkeep of a hen coop, let alone a mansion.

'It's embarrassing really, having such hopeless ancestors,' Tally would say. 'These wasn't a Venery in sight at Waterloo or Trafalgar, for instance. But once you look at the great financial disasters, we're there with bells on. The South Sea Bubble, the Wall Street Crash, even Lloyds; you name it, we're there right in the middle of it, losing spectacularly, hand over fist.'

Tally's own father, who had died in a car crash when she was small, had tried to reverse the situation as best he could while saddled with a wife as extravagant as Lady Julia. But without much success. The result was that Mullions had been more or less a hard hat area for as long as Jane had known it. Nonetheless, Tally had, after Cambridge, decided to dedicate herself to restoring her family home to its former glory, continuing the work of her father.

Highly romantic though all this sounded, in practice it seemed to consist of Tally rushing round the ancient heap doing running repairs to stop it falling down altogether, and using any time left over to apply for grants that never seemed to materialise. As time had gone on, Tally seemed to have gently abandoned hope of getting the place back on its feet. She had confessed to Jane frequently that getting it on its knees would be a miracle. 'Although I suppose it possesses,' she sighed, 'what *House and Garden* would call a unique untouched quality.'

Jane scooped up another handful of nuts and looked

forward to what was always a plentiful supply of stories about Tally's insufferably grand mother. Lady Julia was as determined as her daughter that Mullions should go on – as long as someone else did all the work. She was markedly less willing than Tally to struggle into waders to drag weeds out of the oxbow lake or crawl along the Jacobean lead gutters pulling leaves out to stop blockages. Even more useless was Tally's brother, Piers. He seemed to prefer spending all his time – including holidays – at Eton. She must remember, Jane thought, to tell Tally about the crusty in the paper who had looked so like her brother. Tally would be amused.

Tally did not look amused, Jane thought, as the tall, grave-faced figure of her friend finally appeared in the wine bar. But she certainly looked amusing. What on earth was she wearing? Tally had never exactly been a snappy dresser but even by her standards this was eccentric. As Tally threaded her way between the tables, Jane saw she had on what looked like an ancient, enormous and patched tweed jacket worn over an extremely short and glittery A-line dress.

'You look amazing,' Jane said, truthfully, leaping up to kiss Tally's cold, soft, highly-coloured cheek. 'Is that vintage?' she asked, nodding at the dress which, at close range, looked extraordinarily well-cut and expensive, if a little old-fashioned.

'Mummy's cast-offs, if that's what you mean,' Tally answered, slotting herself in under the table and stuffing what was left of the nuts into her mouth. 'All my clothes have fallen to bits now, so I've started on hers. I must say they're very well made. The stitches don't give an inch. When I was scraping the moss out of the drains yesterday—'

'You surely didn't scrape them out wearing *that*?' gasped Jane. 'It looks like Saint Laurent.'

'Yes, it is, actually,' said Tally vaguely. 'But no, I wear her old Chanel for outdoor work. Much warmer. This glittery stuff's a bit scratchy.'

'How is Mullions?' asked Jane. This usually was the cue for Tally to explode into rhapsodic enthusiasm about duck decoys and uncovering eighteenth-century graffiti during the restoration of the follies. This time, however, Tally's face fell, her lips trembled and, to Jane's dismay, her big, clear eyes filled up with tears. The end of her nose, always a slight Gainsborough pink against the translucent whiteness of the rest of her face, deepened to Schiaparelli. This, clearly, was what Tally wanted to talk about.

'Whatever's happened?' Jane placed her warm hand over Tally's bony cold one. Tally swallowed, pulled it away and tucked her thin light-brown hair behind her ears before lifting her reddened eyes to Jane.

'Mummy,' Tally whispered. 'She's gone mad.'

Jane frowned slightly. Was that all? But surely Julia had always had a screw loose? She had more than once, Jane remembered, sent Tally back to the new term at Cambridge with instructions to 'drive carefully back to Oxford, dear'. After her father had died, the horses in the carriage block had been the nearest Tally seemed to have to a stable family background.

'How do you mean, mad, exactly?' asked Jane carefully.

'Don't ask how it happened. I've no idea. But she says she spent a night sitting naked on top of a mountain in the Arizona desert and it changed her life,' choked Tally. Julia had, she explained to an amazed Jane, recently flown off on holiday in all her usual first-class, chignonned splendour and had returned a bare-foot New Age hippy with her hair around her knees. 'And now she wants to go round the world and enlarge her horizons with Big Horn,' Tally finished.

'What's that?' said Jane. 'A New Age travel company?'

'Her new boyfriend.' Tally closed her eyes as if to block out the horror of it all. 'He's a Red Indian she met in Arizona. Only now he's living at Mullions. And he never says anything. Ever.'

'*What?*' said Jane. It couldn't be true. Lady Julia Venery, a New Age hippy? A woman whose idea of crystal therapy was looking at the window display of Tiffany's. And a Red Indian boyfriend? Julia, whose only previous experience of reservations was the kind one made at The Ritz. 'I can't believe it,' she said. 'What does Mrs Ormondroyd make of it?' The powerfully-built, raisin-faced housekeeper at Mullions was in a permanent state of outrage as it was.

'Big Horn's causing havoc,' sniffed Tally. 'Mrs Ormondroyd put his prayer flag in to wash with a red jumper and it came out streaked like a sunset. He was furious, in a silent sort of way. And now he's trying to build something called a sweat lodge in the rose garden. Mr Peters is not amused.'

The sour old butler/gardener had never been amused the entire time Jane had known him. Neither, come to that, had Mrs Ormondroyd. Unsure what to say or do in the face of such disaster, Jane ordered two more glasses of wine, and another bowl of peanuts.

'Can't Piers do anything?' she asked.

Tally sighed so heavily the top layer of peanuts rolled on to the table. 'Gone AWOL,' she groaned. 'No one at Eton has seen him for ages. Apparently he's—'

'Joined a gang of environmental protesters?' Jane leapt in as the photograph of the crusty clicked into place in her head. However unbelievable it seemed, it was only half as unbelievable as the Julia story.

'How on earth do you know that?' gasped Tally, shocked out of her misery to look quite her old self.

Jane explained about spotting his picture in the paper. 'Nick was furious,' she added.

A wintry smile crossed Tally's strained features. 'That makes me feel better at least,' she said ruefully. 'Piers was last heard of a hundred feet beneath a runway at Stansted, glorying in the name of Muddy Fox. He seems to be rather notorious. Been arrested at least twice, apparently,' she sighed. 'Still, he's not the first of the family to do that. My great-great-great-grandfather was thrown into jail three times for running up gambling debts. By my great-great-great-grandmother, apparently.'

They lapsed into silence. It struck Jane that the conversation was getting surreal. Two glasses of wine on an empty stomach plus Tally's mad family history was a potent brew – even without the week she'd had.

'Never mind,' she said eventually. 'Look on the bright side. If Piers goes on making headlines like this he'll get his own chat show. Then you'll really be able to put Mullions back to rights.'

But instead of cheering up, Tally's face fell even further. She took a deep swig from her glass and coughed violently.

'Now I have to tell you the worst thing of all,' she stuttered, after Jane had banged her on the back and her eyes had stopped streaming. Jane looked at her apprehensively. Short of Mrs Ormondroyd and Mr Peters opening a Tantric sex workshop, it was difficult to imagine what that might be. 'Mummy wants to sell Mullions.' Tally's voice was as tight and dry as her face.

'*No!*' Jane gasped. This really was a disaster. Nick at his most scathing and Champagne D'Vyne at her worst paled by comparison. '*Why?*'

'To pay for her travels. It's her right, she inherited the house in Daddy's will. And she can do what she likes with it – there's no title to hand down anymore since the Ninth Earl, my grandfather, lost it on a hen race in 1920.' Tally paused and swallowed. 'Mummy says the place is an old wreck and we'd be best advised to get shot of it while it is still worth something. She s-s-s-says,' Tally gasped, her self-control deserting her, 'that she suddenly realised she'd spent her entire life [gulp] perpetuating [sniff] an outmoded feudal system.' Tally clapped her bony hand to her mouth as the tears spilled down her long, thin cheeks.

'Well, she took a long time to work that out,' said Jane. 'Did she never get any clues from the fact she lived in a stately home with servants' bells and a stable block?'

Tally said nothing. Both red hands were covering her face now. With a twinge, Jane saw the signet ring with the Venery family crest shining dull and gold on Tally's little finger.

'But you've had that place for four hundred years, for God's sake,' Jane raged, feeling suddenly furious. 'You can't let go of it now. Can't you stop her?'

Tally shook her head. 'Not unless I can come up with some brilliant plan for it to make money. But as I can't even get grants to repair the place, I very much doubt I'll get them to start building restaurants and things. And quite frankly, Mrs Ormondroyd's cooking is hardly a draw.'

'You could always marry someone rich,' Jane suggested. 'Then they could buy the place off Julia.'

'Fat chance,' said Tally miserably. 'Who's going to want to marry *me*?' She raised her thin face hopelessly to Jane. 'It's not as if I'm pretty. Or rich. I'm going to die a spinster in a council house at this rate.'

'Hang on, hang on,' said Jane, seeing Tally wobbling at the top of the Cresta Run of self-pity. 'What about all that stuff about Lord Right? What about finding the perfect man?'

'Forget it,' said Tally, flashing her a hurt, how-could-you-mention-that-now glance. 'At the moment, I'm trying to hang on to the perfect home. Not that anyone thinks it's perfect except m-m-m-me.' She started to snivel again.

'Now look,' said Jane briskly. She was, she knew, at her best when she was trying to help other people out of trouble. Unable to solve any of her own work or Nick problems, she nonetheless felt completely confident she could sort Tally out somehow. The most appalling messes always had ingeniously simple solutions. Didn't they? 'There's got to be a way out of this,' she said decisively, sitting up straight and giving her slumped friend a challenging look. 'We need to get you a knight in shining armour. Sir Lancelot. Or Sir Earnalot, more like.' She grinned. Tally remained hunched and hopeless.

'He doesn't even have to have shining armour,' Jane added. 'You've got plenty of that standing around the Great Hall.'

'Well, it's not very shiny,' sniffed Tally, 'but Mrs Ormondroyd does her best. You know what she's like.'

'Half cleaner, half demolition squad,' grinned Jane. 'Well, a knight on a white charger then. Or, even better, a gold chargecard. A multi-Mullionaire.'

'But where am I going to meet someone like that?' asked Tally dismally.

Jane had to admit it was a good question. 'Let's have another glass and think about it,' she said.

After an hour more of lamenting the situation at Mullions, Tally suddenly decided she couldn't bear to be away from it another second. 'After all,' she said mournfully as Jane poured her into the train at Paddington, 'I might not be living there much longer.'

'We'll think of something,' said Jane, clunking the train door shut like a capable nanny. Tally was the only person who could make her feel in control. The only person more hopeless than she was.

Jane returned to the flat. As she opened the front door, she saw Tom and a fair-haired girl going slowly upstairs. His hand was spread tenderly across her back and he was talking to her. They seemed to be much too absorbed in each other to notice Jane crossing the hall beneath them. Anaesthetised by alcohol, Jane blinked, pursed her lips and nodded slowly and exaggeratedly to herself. Of *course* she was not disappointed. She had only had one conversation with Tom, and that had been in far from ideal circumstances. And of *course* Tom had girlfriends. When someone looked like that, it was only to be expected. Good luck to him, in fact, she thought, stabbing furiously at the Chubb with the key and a trembling hand.

Inside, Jane collapsed on the sofa with a cup of camomile tea which Nick always said looked like pee but which she hoped might do some overnight super-cleansing of her system and save her from the hangover she undoubtedly deserved. With an effort, she forced herself to think about Nick and what he was doing in Brussels. He had left this morning so early she had not even said goodbye to him.

She gazed vaguely at the bookshelves opposite the sofa and smiled fondly at the fat spines of Nick's vast collection of political biographies. The sudden need to find a man for Tally had helped put Nick into perspective, albeit the perspective given by several large glasses of dubious house white. There was no doubt that, at his worst, Nick was rude, unsupportive, mean and selfish. But she wouldn't be without him, Jane assured herself. She loved him. She lived with him. Occasionally they even had sex.

Poor old Tally, was Jane's last waking thought before passing out on the sofa. The only man who made the earth move as far as she was concerned was Mr Peters with his shovel.

'It's fantastic,' trilled Josh as Jane entered the *Gorgeous* offices one morning a week later. 'Blanket coverage,' he yelped, gesturing at the newspapers which lay scattered about the desktops. The new issue of *Gorgeous* had obviously hit the publicity jackpot.

'They've all picked up on her column.'

Jane grabbed a pile of papers. It was true. Only the *Morning Star*, it appeared, had resisted the temptation to carry a picture of Champagne D'Vyne on its front page.

'Eat your heart out, Tara,' crowed Josh. 'The party's over.'

Jane gazed in fascination at a vast picture of the multiple-Gulfstream owning Hon. Rollo Harbottle in the *Sun*. To say he was far from handsome was an understatement. Rollo looked as if his features had been thrown on from a distance by a group of near-sighted darts players. Teeth like tombstones and a receding hairline hardly improved matters; it was a face, in short, that only a bank manager could love. Most gruesome of all, it was gazing with lascivious appreciation at Champagne's barely-there knickers, clearly almost not visible beneath the near-transparent material of her dress. Talk about heir and a G-string, thought Jane. According to the caption, the Hon. Rollo Harbottle was poised to inherit a vitreous enamel fortune.

'He looks horribly pleased with himself,' observed Valentine. 'Flushed with success, in fact. But he *has* done quite well, I suppose. Considering he looks like something you'd find on a fishmonger's slab.' He gazed at the photograph in awe. 'I've never seen an overbite like it,' he said, shaking his head. 'They should preserve it for dental science after he's dead.'

'Well, she's obviously not with him because of his looks,' said Jane.

'Yes, the vitreous enamel fortune probably has something to do with it,' Valentine agreed. 'What you might call a chain reaction. He probably bowled her over.'

'And we mustn't forget his title,' grinned Jane. 'Champagne's obviously a sucker for the class cistern. I wonder whether he's taken her to the family seat yet.'

Josh, ignoring them, was flicking busily through the centre sections of the newspapers. 'Look at all these inside spreads,' he crowed.

It was true. The *Daily Mail* had run a line-up of every man Champagne had ever been out with and had calculated their net worth in a facetious paragraph beneath. The Hon. Rollo Harbottle, Jane noted, was the richest. Second was Giles Trumpington-Kwyck-Save, an equally ill-favoured supermarket heir Champagne had apparently dumped a couple of weeks before.

'That's market forces for you,' observed Valentine. 'Wonder how long it'll be before Harbottle's been passed on to the next gold-digging party girl. I'd give him a week.'

'Oh, I don't know. After all, do you love anyone enough to give them your last Rollo?' snorted Jane.

Even some of the quality broadsheets had made features of the story. The *Daily Telegraph* had lined up a collection of the most eligible bachelors in Britain for Champagne's consideration and headlined the piece 'Sparkling Possibilities'. The *Guardian*, meanwhile, had run a pious piece by some former millionaire's wife headlined 'Why I Prefer Poor Men'. Josh fell about laughing when he saw it.

All morning the phones rang with requests about *Gorgeous*'s new star columnist. 'Richard and Judy want her,' reported Valentine, putting the phone down after one conversation.

'So does Chris Evans,' smirked Josh. 'But I've told him TFI's got a long way to go to beat the Big Breakfast offer.'

'I can't quite believe what I've just heard, but I think that was the *Today* programme,' said Jane, putting down her receiver in horror. Surely people weren't taking Champagne seriously? 'It's a nightmare,' she moaned to Valentine. 'That column's going to run and run now. What have I got myself into? All these papers calling her the It Girl. Which makes me the Shit Girl, I suppose. The nearest I get to a trust fund is Sainsbury's loyalty points.'

'Keep your chins up,' said Josh, overhearing as usual and giving Jane the broadest of grins. 'You'll grow to love her in the end. You'll be twin souls soon. Sisters under the skin.'

But why, thought Jane miserably, do I have so much more skin than she does?

Tracking Champagne down for the second Champagne Moments column proved even more exasperating than the first. Her mobile was switched off and her home answerphone was full. Simon at Tuff PR was just full of himself

'Look, Champagne's very busy,' he barked. 'She worked very hard promoting a new club last night. She's at home. I don't think she's even up yet.'

Jane saw red. 'I'm going round there,' she announced. Phoning was obviously useless. It might be good to talk, but only if the other person picked up the receiver. 'What's the address?'

Trust Champagne to live in one of the most exclusive squares in London, Jane grumbled to herself as, half an hour later, she piloted her battered red 2CV into a row of porticoed palaces, their white stucco gleaming in the afternoon sun. The vehicles parked outside resembled an al fresco luxury car showroom. A futuristic, white open-top sports model lounged decadently alongside a vermilion Corniche more brilliantly scarlet than Vivien Leigh with a double first. My love is like a red, red Rolls, thought Jane enviously, conscious of the dent in the side of her own door and the flotsam and jetsam of rubbish on the floor.

Appropriately enough for one of her probable bra size, Champagne lived at number 38. Standing like a shrunken Alice in Wonderland before the colossally oversized black-painted door, Jane dithered between bell pushes marked 'Visitors' and 'Tradesmen'. Which, she wondered, was she? Trade, certainly. Or perhaps both. She pushed first one and then the other, but there was no reply from either. Eventually, she pushed the huge door itself with her fingertips. Unexpectedly, it swung open.

Jane entered a vast, white-painted hall where a curving wrought-iron staircase mamboed its way up to a huge Edwardian skylight. A white door stood slightly ajar to the right. All was silent. Even the traffic outside was stilled, lost in the high-ceilinged space, the all-absorbing quiet of wealth. It was, Jane thought jealously, a far cry from Clapham, where Nick's windows practically cracked if Tom dropped a peanut upstairs. She did not, however, want to think about Tom just now. Especially, she did not want to dwell on the niggling feeling of betrayal after seeing him with the blonde girl.

Without warning, the quiet erupted into ear-splitting noise. It reverberated off the floors, resounded off the pillars, flashed back sharply from the huge chandelier that hung in the centre of the ceiling. It turned out to be a small, grey poodle with spiteful little black eyes, which had shot out of the door on the right and was now engaged in skidding round Jane in circles on the marble. It was a ghastly creature. Its high-pitched, hysterical bark was, Jane thought, the most irritating sound she had ever heard.

'Gucci, what the fuck's the matter?' Jane instantly revised her opinion. The second most irritating sound she had ever heard.

'Champagne?' called Jane.

'Who's that?' bawled Champagne.

'It's Jane. From *Gorgeous*. I'm here about the column.' Silence followed. Jane pushed the glossy white door further open.

'Hang on,' yelled Champagne. 'I'm coming.' From the giggles that followed, Jane deduced Champagne was not alone. Nor was her last remark necessarily addressed to Jane. Did she have a man in there?

Jane picked her way between the piles of clothes, shoes and shopping bags that formed islands in the sea of cream carpet on the sitting room floor. The room was so enormous that even the huge, black Steinway grand filled little more than a corner. From the piles of dresses slung over the piano stool, Jane deduced its ivories had seen little tinkling of late and that its main function was to support the collection of silver-framed photographs which, in the best Belgravia tradition, crowded its gleaming surface.

Champagne had still not appeared. Jane crossed the room towards the photographs, waves of pale carpet ebbing about her feet as she moved. Although most of the pictures featured Champagne holding gum-baring contests with a string of celebrities, there were a few more personal ones as well. Jane peered closely at a large picture of two children: a blonde girl and a boy in front of a well-kept country house. There was no doubt that the girl was Champagne – the knowing smirk and the self-conscious pose were all there even then. As was the rest of it, Jane saw jealously. At the time she herself had been a pudgy-kneed child with a pot belly, Champagne already had a neatly-cropped mane of white-blonde hair (it must be natural after all) and the long, slender limbs of a thoroughbred. But, Jane comforted herself, if Champagne had the legs of a racehorse, she had the brain of one too. And her boyfriend, Rollo Harbottle, had the teeth of one.

Jane felt rather sorry for the pleasant-looking boy she imagined must be Champagne's brother. It was bad enough having to talk to Champagne for a few hours a week. Growing up with her was something she couldn't begin to imagine.

She picked up another photograph of a white-haired baby being pushed in a pram by a fierce-looking woman in a dark blue uniform. There was no time to put it back as the mistress of the house suddenly bounced into the room and strode quickly up behind her.

'Oh, that's me and Nanny Flange,' Champagne declared in her ear-splitting rattle. 'Sweet old thing really. Left after I bit her leg.'

'Did what?' asked Jane.

'I bit her leg,' said Champagne matter-of-factly. 'Mummy was furious.'

'Well, I suppose it was a bit naughty.'

'Yah, Mummy went ballistic. "Oh, darling," she said. "How *could* you have bitten Nanny's *filthy* leg?" ' Champagne put back her head and roared with laughter.

Her bare, brown flesh was scarcely covered by the tiniest pair of knickers Jane had ever seen. A tight, cropped, pink T-shirt evidently made for a two-year-old struggled to cover her exuberant bust. Her hair was a bird's nest, a cigarette dangled from the corner of her lipstick-smudged mouth and her mascara had run, but this, Jane was irritated to observe, only made her look more beautiful than ever.

As Gucci exploded into more high-pitched yapping, Jane realised they were not alone in the room. Slinking his way along the back wall was the snub-nosed photographer's assistant whose trousers had been so excitable at the Dave Baker shoot. Matters had evidently developed since then. He stood, twisting his hands, by the door into the hall.

'Weel I see you again?' he mumbled to Champagne in a heavy French accent.

'Yah, course you will,' said Champagne, drawing on her cigarette as she bundled him out of the door. 'Buy *Gorgeous*, there's a good boy,' she added, closing the door firmly and padding back into the sitting room.

'Phew,' she said. 'Just in time. Rollo'll be here in a minute. He'd go ballistic if he bumped into Fabergé.'

Quite, thought Jane. Rollo probably had a vitreous temper. Nonetheless, disappointment flooded through her at the news that he and Champagne were still together. On the evidence of what she had just witnessed, she was beginning to wonder if she might bag Rollo for Tally. Whatever his shortcomings, he was at least rich.

The poodle's yapping continued unabated. Jane's head started to spin with the volume. 'Gucci, darling,' cooed Champagne, falling gracefully to her knees to pet him. 'You're hungry, aren't you?' Scooping the shrill scrap of noise into her arms, she left the room.

Jane followed her into a brilliant white kitchen where Champagne was rummaging in a vast metal techno-fridge much taller than she was. Like her, it had evidently not seen any food for several days. The only evidence of nourishment anywhere were the empty bottles of Krug thrust neck down in a Fortnum's box in the corner.

'Bingo!' Champagne, who had been throwing open a succession of empty cupboards, finally produced a tin. As she placed the scraped-out contents before the dog, Jane realised it wasn't Pedigree Chum. 'But that's foie gras,' she said.

'Yah, absolutely,' said Champagne, not batting an eyelid. 'Gucci adores it. Can't stand the stuff myself. *Bloody* fattening. And so cruel to the geese as well, forcing all that food down their throats. Worse than an anorexic rehab centre.'

Jane's antennae began to twitch. She fished out her pencil and started to scribble. 'Better mention my really cool new car,' Champagne honked, noticing.

'What car?' asked Jane.

'Parked outside. White sports car?'

Jane recalled the menacing machine lurking alongside the kerb. 'Hey, big spender,' she said, mock-chiding but envious.

'Oh, it wasn't that much,' Champagne said silkily. 'Rather a bargain in fact. Amazing after-sales service as well,' she added coyly, looking at Jane from under her eyelashes. 'So I'd love to give them a mentionette in the column, if possible.'

'Fine,' said Jane, wondering what sort of after-sales service Champagne had required. After all, the car was brand new. Perhaps someone had had to come and show her where the ignition key went. Or . . . It suddenly dawned on Jane that Champagne had probably been given the car for free. Bargain indeed, she thought furiously, breaking the stub of her pencil on her notebook.

There was an abrupt ring at the front door. 'Oh fuck, it's Rollsy,' groaned Champagne, leaping up. 'Sorry, have to run. Got to dash off to New York. But we've done the next column now, haven't we?'

Jane found herself being shown to the door just as the Hon. Rollo Harbottle manoeuvred his teeth into the hall. Up close, he was even more repellent than he appeared in the newspapers. How on earth could Champagne bear to touch him? Nick may be grumpy, but at least he didn't have a face like a basket of fruit. And he was, Jane thought happily, finally back from Brussels tonight. Hopefully with a vast box of Belgian chocolates.

Chapter 4

Jane put the phone down, feeling numb with disappointment and fury. She'd spent all lunchtime buying, and all evening preparing, dinner for Nick's return. And now he'd called to say he would be late. Not by a few hours, though. *By another whole day*. 'There's a Caravanning League of Belgium Fringe Pressure Group fondue I can't afford to miss,' he informed her via a crackling mobile phone.

Depressed, Jane returned to the kitchen. The pasta had taken advantage of Nick's phone call to weld itself to the bottom of the pan, while the putanesca sauce, which she had hoped might set a spicy and whorish tone to their reunion, was starting to burn. Cooking, Jane knew, had never really been her forte. But then, what was?

At least, she thought, poking the flaccid, off-white mass of pasta, she could always beat Tally into a cocked cacciatore. No one this side of Macbeth's three witches was as bad a cook as her. Jane would never forget the evening at Cambridge when Tally had invited her round for supper.

'What's this?' Jane had asked, staring at a burnt-looking lump of bread running with sticky sweet goo. 'Sixth Form Special,' Tally had replied proudly. 'Toasted Mars Bar sandwich. You stick a couple of slices in the Breville and put a Mars Bar in the middle. Close and cook for two minutes. Delicious. We lived off them at Cheltenham.'

Jane felt a stab of guilt at the thought of Tally, Mullions and the missing multimillionaire. Locating one had sounded so simple after a bottle of wine on an empty stomach. In the cold light of day, it had presented certain logistical difficulties. Thumbing through her address book, Jane realised she didn't know a thousandaire, let alone a millionaire. The nearest she could manage was Amanda, an old friend from Cambridge who had married a merchant banker and swapped bedsit life for six-bedroomed, domestically-aided splendour in Hampstead. Jane wondered if she should get in touch.

The telephone rang again. Jane dashed to answer it. Had Nick changed his mind?

'Hi there,' said Tally mournfully.

'I've just been thinking about you,' said Jane, hoping she didn't sound too disappointed.

'Probably because Mullions has become one huge psychic energy transmitter since Mummy's come back,' said Tally grumpily. 'As I speak, my mother's making ritual fire towards the waxing moon and Big Horn is ceremonially constructing a mercurial harp in the paddock.'

'A what?'

'You don't want to know. Suffice to say, it is based on the ground plan of Stonehenge and the geometry of the magic square of Mercury. And, to top it all, quite literally, is a stone from the ancient Cheesewring site in Cornwall.'

'*No!*' said Jane.

'Oh yes. Apparently it is meant to bring harmony and peace to the house, but I can assure you that from where I, Mr Peters and Mrs Ormondroyd are standing, it's war. *Damn!*'

'What was that?' asked Jane.

'I'd better go. Billiard room door's just fallen off.' Moral support wasn't the only kind Tally needed at the moment.

She could do with a boost herself, come to that. Nick's no show had hardly got the evening off to a flying start.

Wandering into the tiny sitting room, Jane stared at the candles on the table guttering in the breeze which swept under the door. The carefully wrapped little welcome home present (a pair of cuff-links) lying on Nick's plate suddenly looked pathetic. The polished wine glasses, shining in the candlelight, stood ready for the bottle of champagne and the bottle of Pouilly-Something she'd dithered over for ages at Safeway's, unable to decide between Fumé or Fuissé.

Pouring herself a stiff gin and tonic, Jane decided to spend the evening lying on the couch with an old bonkbuster. After all, snuggling up with Jilly Cooper was probably the nearest she was going to get to a sex life for the moment.

Ten minutes later, lost in the adventures of a raunchy TV executive and her well-heeled brute of a lover, Jane was suddenly brought down to earth. By something on her ceiling. She sat up and listened. A series of loud clatters from the flat above made her wince. All hell seemed to be breaking loose. It sounded as if Tom was playing Twister with a herd of elephants in platform shoes.

Jane tried to concentrate on her book. The TV executive and the brute were now indulging in some steamy bedroom scenes. She followed the bumping and grinding avidly, vicariously. The banging on the ceiling kept pace, a faint thump of music accompanying it.

Jane gripped Jilly hard by the spine and glared at the words. Five seconds later, she flung Mrs Cooper to the floor in despair, flew out of the door and up the stairs and banged her fists on Tom's door.

The door opened to reveal Tom naked from the waist up and rather red in the face.

'Hi, there,' he grinned, shoving back a clump of hair from his glowing forehead. Something around Jane's lower pelvis ignited like a gas stove at the flash of armpit revealed as he did so.

'Hi,' said Jane, shifting from foot to foot. 'Er, you're making quite a lot of noise, actually, and . . .'

'Am I? God, sorry. I'm just packing up a few things. I'm moving out, you see.'

'Moving out?' Jane looked up at him as he filled the doorway. His smooth, tanned torso suddenly struck her as eminently *lickable*.

'Yes. I'm going to New York. Tomorrow, in fact. So you won't have any more noise problems. I've just finished in any case.'

'Oh. Right.' Jane was suddenly filled with the wild desire to drop to her knees and beg him to make as much noise as was humanly possible. 'Well, good luck,' she said, starting to back away from the door. 'Goodbye.' This was beginning to sound like *Brief Encounter*. If only it was. An encounter with his briefs was just what she needed.

'Bye then,' said Tom, and closed his door.

Jane re-entered the flat. It was now frustratingly silent. Absolutely no reason to go upstairs again at all. She walked over to the window and, sighing, started to clear the table. She looked out. The sky was still light outside, the usual grey, featureless fading evening oddly characteristic of Clapham.

She gazed up beseechingly at the patchy ceiling, stained by generations of overflowing baths, broken-down shower units and rising damp. She willed Tom to break out into a foundation-shaking series of crashes, but there was silence. Except – Jane's ears pricked up – a slight, insistent tapping at the window behind her, which could have been a branch.

Only there were no branches near her window.

Nothing grew in the scrubby, slimy apology for a back garden that Nick had neglected for as long as he had lived here. A rapist, then. A Jehovah's Witness? Jane whipped round, and drew her breath in sharply, her hand shooting automatically to her throat. Something huge, dark and misshapen was visible at the window, tapping gently against the pane.

She approached cautiously. The object seemed to be hanging from some sort of string. As Jane got closer, she realised it was a trainer. Poking out from inside it was a white slip of paper. Jane scrabbled frantically to open the peeling, scabby, moss-streaked window frame. She grabbed the piece of paper with a shaking hand and smoothed it out on the half-dismantled table, upon which one of the candles still flickered.

'Apologies for noise,' a decisive hand had written in blue-black ink. 'Can I take you out to dinner to say sorry?'

Jane's stomach plunged through the floor. Her knees shook. Should she ignore Tom out of loyalty to Nick? But Nick had let her down with his wretched caravanners' fondue. And what was the point of going out for dinner, piped up a Sensible Voice in her head, when there was a dinner all ready down here? She knew from experience that the putanesca sauce would respond well to treatment; if she added a little more tomato puree, only an interesting hint of smokiness would suggest how near it had come to disaster. The pasta was, well, just pasta. And there had never been anything wrong with the tomato ciabatta, the rocket salad and the Pouilly-Something.

Jane rushed upstairs before she could change her mind, knocked on the door and issued the invitation. 'It'll be ready in half an hour,' she said.

'Half an hour, then,' drawled Tom. 'Want me to bring anything?'

'Just yourself,' grinned Jane, instantly feeling mortified for sounding so cheesy. She was filled with a sudden terror that once he was across the threshold she'd be overcome with a form of socially maladroit Tourette's syndrome, telling him to 'sit ye down' and 'take a pew'.

Back in the flat, Jane threw herself against the door in an ecstasy of knotted-stomach guilt. Honestly, said the Sensible Voice. Anyone would think that you'd swung naked from the chandeliers, licked cream off his entire body and committed triple-chocolate adultery, the way you're reacting. You've only invited him to dinner. Jane pulled herself together. Half an hour, she thought, panicking. Five minutes for the food and twenty-five to make herself look more stunning than a 2,000 volt charge.

Twenty minutes later, Jane was standing despairing in the bedroom, having tried on and abandoned every outfit she possessed. He might think it odd she had changed, anyway, she thought, prising herself back into her jeans and white linen shirt. Ten minutes. She brushed her hair furiously, cleaned her teeth manically, re-applied her worn-off lipstick and gave herself another coat of mascara. As usual, it took longer to unclog her handiwork with a lash comb than it did to put it on in the first place. Five minutes. 'Aagh,' squealed Jane, giving herself a last slick of perfumeless Mum and a powerful blast of Chanel No 19. Three minutes. She rushed into the kitchen and uncorked the half-bottle of champagne for Dutch courage. Shame I never got round to the food, she thought, eyeing the reproachful mass of pasta as she knocked back an entire flute in one.

Right on cue, there was a knock at the door. Heart thumping, Jane opened it to find Tom waving a bottle of Moët. 'By way of apology, as you wouldn't let me take you out,' he grinned. 'And it's cold, so we can drink it now.'

As Jane sloshed it unsteadily into two glasses. Tom went straight to the bookshelves. 'What's this like?' he asked, selecting *Callaghan: The Man and The Myth* and *The John Major I Knew*.

'Not what you'd call a racy read,' said Jane. Even Nick had struggled with the Major book.

'But then,' she added, 'I'm not the one to ask. Politics isn't really my thing. Nick gets cross with me because he says all I care about are Cherie Blair's skirt lengths.'

'Cherie Blair's skirts are a crucial issue,' said Tom gravely. She had no idea if he was teasing her. 'Nick's away, I take it?' Was that a gleam in his eye?

'How did you know?'

'Elementary, my dear Jane. After you'd been up – and rightly, too – to complain about me, I simply put my ear to the floor and listened.' He grinned at her and emptied his champagne glass down his muscular throat.

'Yes. He's in Brussels.' She explained about the caravanners' fondue party. Tom raised an eyebrow.

He moved on from Nick's books to her own. Jane sent up a rare, silent prayer of thanks to her absent boyfriend for not allowing her room for her collection of bonkbusters. Those had been relegated to piles on the floor beneath the shelves while Nick had conceded a few inches of the shelves themselves to the battered old volumes of Keats, Yeats, Eliot and Shakespeare Jane had studied at university. Books that she still opened now and then to remind herself that she had once had a brain.

'It's when I read Yeats that I realise how hopeless it is to try and be a writer,' Tom sighed.

'Are you a writer, then?' Jane gasped. 'How *romantic*. What are you working on?'

Tom looked amused. 'I'm not sure it's all that romantic.'

Jane mentally kicked herself. How could she have sounded so jejune?

'It's about this serial killer driving around the Aberdeen ring road,' Tom elaborated. 'He's had a few lines of coke, his necrophiliac Alsatian's asleep in the back, and the man's bored, so he suddenly decides to follow this car and see where it's going. When the car stops at a service station, the killer gets out and does the business, as does the dog. This seems quite fun to them, so they start following another car at random, then strike again when it stops, then start following a van to see where that's going. And so on and so on until the man and the dog eventually drive off the Humber Bridge.' He stopped, and looked triumphantly at Jane. 'It's a sort of metaphor for our violent, haphazard society and the random nature of the choices we make in life. And death.'

Jane's heart sank. It sounded horrible.

'It's sort of *On the Road* meets *In Cold Blood*, so I thought I'd call it *Cold Road*,' said Tom, beaming. 'What do you think?'

Jane screwed up her courage. 'To be honest, not much,' she said. 'Ghastly, actually. I can't bear books like that.' She regretted it the moment the words left her.

Tom turned back to the bookshelves. Jane noticed his shoulders moving up and down. He was evidently struggling with his feelings.

'I'm so sorry,' she gasped, touching him on the arm. 'I didn't mean . . .'

Tom whipped round. His eyes blazed and his mouth quivered. Jane realised he was laughing.

'That plot,' he grinned, 'was suggested by my agent the other day. He told me that that's the sort of thing I would have to start knocking out if I ever wanted to make any money.'

'Ugh,' said Jane, relaxing a little. 'Well, I certainly wouldn't buy it.'

'Shock value equals publicity value apparently,' Tom said. 'Frankly, I'd rather write a bonkbuster. I see you've got quite a collection.'

So he'd noticed the Jilly Coopers after all. Tom

grinned as Jane poured him another glass of Moët foam with a wobbling hand.

'Yes, of course. I can see the plot now.' Tom stared theatrically at the ceiling. 'Impecunious writer takes flat for a few weeks above beautiful blonde who lives in basement with boyfriend who doesn't realise how lucky he is.' He paused. 'Writer meets girl over romantic dinner, falls in love but has to leave for New York the next morning.'

Jane buried her reddening face in the champagne.

She'd read about sexual tension before, although all it had meant with Nick was that she wanted it and he didn't. But here it was now, the real thing. The air between Tom and herself felt thick with energy. Jane imagined a white flash of electricity if she touched him, like the opening credits of the South Bank Show. By now, Nick had receded to the far outback of her mind. Not waving, not even drowning. Not, for the time being, at all.

She stole a glance at Tom from under her triple-mascara'd lashes. He had all the careless glamour of one of those singlet-clad models in the Calvin Klein ads, except that Tom's seemed genuinely effortless. His hair had obviously not seen a comb for at least a day and his jeans were ripped at the knee. The most convincing testament of all to his lack of vanity was the T-shirt proclaiming 'Some Idiot Went To London And All I Got Was This Lousy T-shirt'.

'I always wondered who actually bought those,' Jane said, breaking the crackling silence.

Tom looked down at his chest, surprised. 'Got it from a jumble sale,' he said. 'Quite like it, actually. I find the implication that people come back from London laden with exotic gifts unobtainable elsewhere rather romantic really.' He grinned.

'Er, would you like to eat?' Jane asked. After all, it was the whole point of the evening. Wasn't it?

Tom nodded politely. 'Love to. But can we talk a bit more first? I find it practically impossible to have a conversation over food. I'm always shoving my fork in my mouth at the exact time someone is asking me a question.'

It was amazing. He wanted to talk to her. Jane racked her brains to recall the last time she had had a proper conversation with Nick. Or, come to that, the first time.

'We were talking about my bonkbuster, I believe,' Tom said lightly, igniting a Marlboro and gazing at her from between the slits in his narrowed eyelids. 'Now, where had we got to?' He stared at the ceiling again. 'Ah yes.' He blew a sequence of perfect smoke rings. 'Writer comes down for dinner with beautiful blonde, falls in love, but realises that as he is going away next morning and she has a boyfriend, it can never be.' He stopped, pulled a face and looked at Jane. 'Pity.' It was impossible to tell if he was serious. Nevertheless, disappointment flooded her.

'So.' Tom slipped from the armchair on to the floor and crawled across the rug to where Jane perched on the edge of the sofa. He looked into her eyes, took her face in his hands and touched her lips with his. 'So he steals a kiss anyway.' Jane's back locked rigid with excitement.

With a light finger, Tom traced the outline of her cheekbones and lips before slowly, deliberately, lowering his mouth again to hers.

Jane's brain flew round her cranium like a flock of disturbed sparrows. He couldn't do this to her. But, as his tongue gently slid between her acquiescent lips, she felt very glad that he had.

'Do you do this to everyone you've only just met?' she stammered as he came up for air.

'No, of course not. Anyway, we've met before.'

'What about your girlfriend?'

'Don't have one.' He was lying, Jane knew. So the girl on the stairs had been his agent, had she? 'More to the point, what about your boyfriend?' asked Tom wickedly. By now his hands had slipped inside her shirt. They were cool and dry, unlike Nick's, whose were always the temperature and moistness, if not the cleanliness, of the hot towels served in Indian restaurants. Tom's tongue, too, was miraculously free of the rivers of saliva that accompanied Nick's rare attempts at tonsil hockey.

'He's not here,' said Jane. Having decided that she would sleep with Tom, she felt quite calm now. What possible harm would one empty, brittle, mad, impetuous and utterly meaningless fling do? It was, anyway, Nick's fault for throwing her in temptation's way. Wasn't it?

Jane looked boldly into the clear eyes a few inches from her own. 'Let's just get something straight, shall we?' she said, as Tom's hand gently pushed down her jeans zip and started investigating her knickers.

'What?' mumbled Tom. 'I've got some condoms.'

'There's something else.'

Jane made no attempt to resist as he pushed her gently down on the rug. Thank goodness she'd hoovered it reasonably recently. And thank double goodness she'd shaved her armpits. As Tom's mouth moved down to her stiffening nipple she breathed in the heady scent of him – top notes of basil with a dash of salt.

'What?' muttered Tom. His tongue flicked thrillingly about her nipple. Jane gasped as every nerve in her body started singing the Hallelujah Chorus and her insides dissolved into molten metal.

'This is a one-night stand, isn't it?'

'Of course.' Tom looked up at her and grinned through his tangle of hair. 'This is far too much fun to last.'

'So you won't respect me in the morning?'

'I sincerely hope not.'

'That's all right then.'

Chapter 5

'Wore that yesterday, didn't you?' Josh asked as Jane came into the office the next morning.

Jane ignored him. Who cared if she'd rushed out of bed at the last minute and thrown on the clothes still lying on the floor from the night before? Josh was lucky she'd got them on the right way round. She sighed as her eye caught the clock. Tom would soon be leaving to catch his flight to New York. She would never see him again. Parts of her – very particular parts of her – regretted this intensely. But it was just as well, obviously. Last night had been a meaningless, mad and utterly shallow fling. But as meaningless, mad and utterly shallow flings went, it had been a good one.

Tom had made her feel more beautiful and desired than Kate Moss, a World Cup win and the National Lottery jackpot all rolled into one. He had been the gentlest as well as the most skilful of lovers, although admittedly her field of comparisons was limited. He had made her laugh. He had astonished her by his gentleness and sensitivity. And she had never seen such an enormous penis. It had looked big enough to pick up Channel Five. The World Service, come to that.

Nick would finally be on his way back from Brussels now. He'd probably pass Tom in the air. Jane swallowed to combat a rising and recurring nausea, unsure whether it was an excess of champagne or guilt.

Two Nurofens later, Jane stood on the strand of the morning's news, preparing to wade through the tide of tabloids. 'Wondered when you were going to get on to those,' came Josh's voice out of his office. 'Then again, you should know everything about the big story already.'

Please don't let it be another transport minister disaster, prayed Jane. She couldn't cope with the thought of Nick sulking all week like he had after the run in with Piers and the crusties. Trembling, she scrabbled for the *Sun*.

'END OF A LAV AFFAIR', read the headline, breaking to an astonished world the shattering news that Champagne had swapped the vitreous enamel heir Rollo Harbottle, whom the tabloid unkindly dubbed 'Loo Rollo', for a more glamorous model. The paper revealed Champagne's latest consort to be 'brooding bad boy of rock Conal O'Shaughnessy, lead singer of moody Mancunians the Action Liposomes, whose "Make Mine A Large One" single, taken from their *Seven Deadly Cynics* album, was last summer's chartbusting sensation.' O'Shaughnessy's unsmiling face glowered from Champagne's side in the *Sun* photograph. His hairy eyebrows lay along the top of his brows like a draught excluder.

'She'll take to being a groupie like a rock chick to water,' observed Valentine. 'Although I imagine the only kind of rock that gets her going is the sort Burton gave Taylor.'

This new, although not completely unexpected, turn of events made the phone call Jane received later that day all the odder. There seemed to be no voice on the other end, just a series of agonising gasps and sobs.

'Who is this?' asked Jane anxiously. Had Nick somehow found out about her infidelity and collapsed into tears, realising how much he loved her? Her heart raced with guilt-fuelled panic.

'It's Sha-Sha-Sha-Champagne,' the voice on the other end managed to wail before dissolving into another round of sniffles.

'What on earth's the matter? What's happened?' Jane was alarmed. Her interlocutor seemed distorted by agony of the most unimaginable nature.

'I've just got [gasp] a crisis on my hands at the moment [gulp],' stuttered Champagne. Then followed some words Jane could not quite catch. Something about slashing. About cuts. Jane froze as the line went dead, visions of Champagne bleeding to death in the bath crowding in on her.

She immediately telephoned Simon at Tuff. 'Has someone died?' she demanded. 'Has,' she asked, crossing her fingers behind her back, 'Gucci been run over?'

'Leave it with me,' rapped out Simon, sounding concerned for once. If Champagne was hurt, Jane realised, the Tuff PR bank balance would hardly escape unscathed either. 'I'll call you back. Relax, I'm sure it's fine.'

But Jane could not relax. Listening to what had sounded like Champagne's last few minutes on earth had not been a pleasant experience. The surprising realisation that she didn't wish Champagne any real harm dawned on her. It was not, after all, Champagne's fault that they had been thrown together in this bizarre fashion. Christ, thought Jane, giving herself a thorough mental shake. I'm almost starting to feel sorry for her.

When the phone rang again, Jane dashed to answer it.

'Hello,' said Nick.

'Hello,' stammered Jane, wondering if he could tell by the timbre of her voice what she'd been up to. 'You're back.'

'Yes and no. I'm actually calling to say I'm not *coming* back. To the flat, I mean.'

His voice sounded distant. But then again, it was, thought Jane. Being in Brussels.

'Oh dear, what a pity,' she said. Damn, and she'd been shopping for dinner again, too. 'Have you missed your plane? Do you have to go to more meetings?'

'No,' said Nick abruptly. 'I'm leaving you.' The silence that followed his words reared up and buzzed in Jane's ear.

'*What* did you say?' She clutched the receiver,

stunned. Had he, could he have, found out about Tom?

'You heard me,' Nick said calmly. 'There's no nice way of saying this, so I won't. It's over. I just don't think it's working any more.' Hang on, this wasn't in the script, thought Jane, her mind racing. He's dumping me and he doesn't even seem to realise I've been unfaithful. It was almost insulting.

'I feel we've grown apart,' Nick said. He could have grown all sorts of parts, Jane thought bitterly. It had been so long since she had seen him naked he could have developed an extra leg for all she knew.

'How long have you been feeling this?' Or rather, who, Jane added silently. It was obvious now what he was trying to say.

'Well, I've actually been seeing Melissa for a while,' Nick said, understanding her perfectly. 'She's in the same office. It's being going on for about five months.' Roughly the time she had been living with Nick, Jane calculated swiftly. So that's why he had been staying so late at Westminster. He hadn't been lying when he told her he was working on briefs. Jane scowled. Had whips been involved as well? No doubt there had been plenty of pairing. No wonder it was called the Mother of Parliaments.

'Was she with you in Brussels?'

'I, um, haven't been to Brussels,' Nick said, at last having the grace to sound slightly shamefaced. 'I've been in London, trying to decide what to do. About us. And now I have. I'm moving out.'

'Moving out? But it's *your* flat.'

'Ye-e-es. I'm moving in with Melissa. But there's no need for *you* to leave. Stay as long as you like. As long as you keep up with the, um, mortgage payments, of course.'

'Of course.' How magnanimous of him. With one bound he was free and had gained a tenant with a doubled rent cheque. 'Right, then,' Jane said, feeling thoroughly out-manoeuvred. 'Um, OK,' she added slowly, uncertainly. Suddenly, quite unexpectedly, a mist veiled her eyes and a warm flush spread across her face. A sob caught in her throat.

'Look, I'm sorry—'

'Don't.' It wasn't the loss of Nick that tore at her heart. It was his criminally appalling timing. Why hadn't he done this to her yesterday, before Tom had, well, done what Tom did? Their fling needn't have been quite so meaningless and shallow after all.

'I'll be round to pick up some things,' Nick said uncomfortably. 'I'll understand if you're not there.'

Jane put the phone down as hard as she dared without drawing Josh's attention.

It rang again immediately. 'I can explain everything.'

'What do you mean?' asked Jane.

'Nothing's wrong at all. I don't think you quite understood.'

'What?' asked Jane, too confused to place who was speaking.

'Champagne. When she called you. She's upset because the manicurist cut her nails the wrong shape, that's all. Got a bit emotional about it.' With an effort, Jane recognised Simon's voice. He had evidently recovered his sang-froid. 'She's fine now, though. Emergency over. Thought you'd like to know.'

Bugger Champagne and her manicures, thought Jane. Crisis on her hands indeed. 'Fantastic,' she said heavily.

Wishing the accelerator pedal was Nick's head, Jane shot over Waterloo Bridge like a 2CV out of hell. He had discarded her like yesterday's newspapers. Only even yesterday's newspapers had a longer lifespan with Nick. Some had hung around the flat for years.

The scales had fallen from her eyes to such an extent that she could no longer see straight, and completely missed her exit off the Elephant and Castle roundabout. The things she had done for Nick, she raged, shooting down the Embankment in the opposite direction to the one she had intended. The support she had given his career, particularly. When he was trying to get elected to the local council, en route to his goal of working in Westminster, was it not she who had stuffed endless envelopes for him? Wandered devotedly around in the pouring rain canvassing for him? Even stood in for him at his Town Hall surgery when he had been unavoidably delayed. Unavoidably delayed doing what? Jane now fumed, curling her lip with fury. It was not a surgery she wanted to see Nick in at the moment. It was Accident and Emergency.

She had stuck with him through thick and thin. Not that she had ever been all that thin. But she had certainly been thick. Stupid beyond belief, in fact. She ground her teeth as she remembered the answerphone choked with messages from Nick's constituents, all of which she had diligently noted down for him. People complaining to the councillor about stains on their bathroom ceiling. People whispering suspicions that their neighbours were beaming death rays through the wall at them. People railing about hospital waiting lists, including the never-to-be-forgotten Cypriot matron whose swollen legs had bulged and snaked hideously with fat varicose veins. She had arrived in person in the end, choosing a morning when Nick was particularly badly hungover to come and show him exactly how much she needed an operation on her calves. It had worked. Once he had forced down his nausea, Nick had been on to the hospital like a flash.

Then there had been Nick's many meannesses. The way he always forgot his credit card in restaurants; the way he always had his ear clamped to his mobile when the taxi needed to be paid for; the day he had claimed to have no money to pay the window-cleaner and Jane had subsequently found his wallet stuffed with notes. But far worse than any of this was the fact that he had not dumped her earlier.

If she got home in time, might Tom still be there? It was a vain hope, but Jane pressed the accelerator further down anyway. As she parked outside Nick's flat, now her own, she looked up. On the first floor, Tom's crumbling bay windows were in darkness. He had emphatically, definitely, undoubtedly gone.

So that was that then. No point in thinking about him any more. It was time to pick herself up, dust herself down and start a lover again. And her newly single state held certain compensations, Jane tried to tell herself as she let herself into the flat. For a start, she could run herself a bath since Nick was no longer around to take all the hot water. His dirty underpants would no longer litter the floor. The tide of foamy scurf encirling the basin each morning would be a ring of the past. John Humphrys would no longer shatter the early morning silence. But it *was* silent. Absolutely, ominously silent. When, later, she turned the squeaking bathroom taps on, the thunder of water sounded like Niagara Falls.

Lowering herself into the hot embrace of the tub, Jane was shocked to see the bathwater rise further up the sides than usual. She'd got fatter lately, there was no doubt about it. She stared down the length – or was it the width – of her body, plump, white and slick with moisture under the electric bathroom light. Little, shining, blancmange-like islands of tummy, breast and thigh rose above the foaming water line. I look like the Loch Ness monster, Jane thought in panic.

Her breasts lay along her torso, white and pointed like a couple of squid heads. Her waistline, never a strong point, lay conclusively buried under layers of spare tyre and water. All waste, no line. Jane stretched a leg out of the water and scrutinised her cellulite as calmly as possible, before despairingly concluding there was more orange peel there than an orchard in Seville.

Somewhere inside me, determined Jane, there is a thin woman waiting to get out. She dared not contemplate the possibility that somewhere outside her was an even fatter woman trying to muscle in.

She stared at her face in the mirror in the bath rack. The overhead lighting minimised the blue of her eyes and emphasised the bags beneath them. They looked bigger and blacker than a Prada tote. Her lips were dry and looked thinner than ever and the spots on her forehead seemed of Himalayan proportions. Her crow's feet were at least size ten.

No wonder Nick had left her. Tom was probably glad to see the back of her as well. Which is more than I am, thought Jane, catching sight of her reflected rear in the mirrored cabinet as she heaved herself, pink and steaming as a fresh-cooked prawn, out of the bath.

Wrapped in a towel, she felt like a sausage roll, a stuffing of soft pink meat. She felt disgusted with herself. She was too fat to live. She could just stick her head in the oven and it would all be over. Easy. Except for the disgusting thought of all that gluey takeaway pizza cheese which had stuck to the oven bottom. She pulled a face, imagining the stench from the ancient slop of the pineapple and peperonis Nick had been so fond of. No, she wouldn't put her head in the oven.

She'd put it in the fridge instead.

It's at times like this that a girl needs her sense of hummus, Jane decided, shovelling in the remains of a Marks and Spencer's Greek dip selection that wasn't too far past its sell-by date.

She wandered through into the gloomy living room and switched the lamps on. One bulb pinged defiantly back at her and conked out. Jane slumped on the sofa and stared at the very rug where, barely twenty-four hours before, Tom had done all those unimaginably wonderful things to her. She clenched her fists and screwed up her eyes. She wanted Tom, desperately. But she had no number, no idea where he was. They'd been ships that passed in the night. That had been the point of the encounter. Then.

If she couldn't have Tom, she'd have to make do with Gordon, Jane decided, reaching for the bottle. This called for extreme measures in every sense of the word. Anaesthetising. Comforting. The deep, deep peace of the double gin.

Chapter 6

One of the bitterest pills to swallow, Jane considered, was not just that her love-life and work life were on the kind of downward trend not seen since the Wall Street Crash. Much worse was the fact that Champagne seemed set on an endless upward trajectory. For, if the first Champagne Moments column had been a sensation, the second almost caused riots. Within hours of *Gorgeous* appearing on the news-stands, it had sold out. People, it seemed, simply couldn't get enough of her. Champagne's combination of stunning beauty and astounding vacuousness seemed to have struck some kind of chord with public and media alike. The Lost Chord, a despairing Jane supposed.

Champagne, naturally, was well aware of her popularity. 'If there's no beginning to her talents,' Jane sighed to Valentine, 'there's certainly no end to her demands.' Only yesterday Champagne had called insisting *Gorgeous* hire a Learjet to fly her to a polo match, a request that followed hard on the Blahnik heels of a recent demand for a helicopter to take her to a shooting weekend.

'Doesn't she ever use roads?' Jane had marvelled aloud.

'Well, you always said she was an airhead,' Valentine reminded her. Josh then amazed them both by revealing he had promised Champagne a company car as a compromise, which left Jane wondering who was compromised, exactly. Josh had then played his trump card by saying he'd thrown in a chauffeur too.

'She's worth it,' Josh said shortly. 'Our circulation is on the up.' But it wasn't just her own magazine that Champagne dominated. International heavy-hitters from American *Vogue* to Russian *Tatler* were rushing to profile her. Her increasingly frequent appearances on TV translated straight into column inches in the tabloids. When she appeared on *Have I Got News For You*, Ian Hislop, after asking Champagne how she kept her figure, had been rendered unprecedentedly speechless when Champagne had said she worked out 370 days a year. The press had gone wild.

'What would you say to those who call you an egomaniac?' Bob Mortimer had asked her on *Shooting Stars*. 'Oh, they're completely wrong,' Champagne had replied. 'I absolutely *loathe* eggs.' This became Quote of the Week in every paper from the *Daily Mail* to the *Motherwell Advertiser*.

Most notorious of all was Champagne's appearance on *Newsnight* when Jeremy Paxman asked her whether it was true she spent each and every night out partying. 'Absolutely not,' Champagne had replied, apparently deeply affronted. 'As a matter of fact, I spent last night finishing a jigsaw puzzle.'

'A jigsaw puzzle?' Paxman had asked sardonically, raising one of his famously quizzical eyebrows.

'Yah, and I'm bloody proud of myself,' Champagne had declared. 'It's only taken me ninety-four days.'

'Ninety-four days? Surely that's rather a long time for a jigsaw,' Paxman bemusedly replied.

'Well, it said three to four years on the box,' said Champagne triumphantly.

On the strength of this performance, negotiations to give Champagne her own chat show were well advanced.

It was odd, Jane thought, that a public, not to mention a press, that had already endured years of Caprice, Tamara, Tara, Normandie and Beverley could possibly have the stomach for yet another pouting party girl, but stomach it most certainly had. Perhaps it was, Jane mused, because Champagne seemed somehow to combine all of them. She had Caprice's looks, Tara's class, Tamara's chutzpah, Beverley's shopping obsession, and probably now close to Normandie's money as well.

Oddly enough, Champagne never seemed to encounter any of her rivals. Jane had two theories as to why. Either they all avoided her or, as was far more likely, Champagne spent night after night with them in Brown's, Tramp and the Met Bar but could recall absolutely nothing of it afterwards. Champagne's memory, Jane considered, made a goldfish look like Stephen Hawking.

Not that this in any way held her back. No breakfast TV programme was complete without at least a reference to her; there was talk of her kicking off at Wembley, and rumours were beginning to circulate of a planned tribute in Madame Tussaud's. 'I hope that's true,' Jane said to Valentine. 'I might get more information for the column out of a waxwork.'

'What we need,' said Josh, 'is the new sex.' The Monday features meeting had begun.

'You're telling me,' simpered Valentine, examining his cuffs and pursing his lips in his best John Inman fashion.

'You know what I mean,' Josh snapped. 'I'm talking about what's the latest hip thing. The new rock and roll, the new black, the new brown, the new whatever. What's really, really hot just now?'

'Well, this office for a start,' said Valentine huffily. 'The air conditioning is a joke.' He flapped a plump hand about in front of his perspiring face.

Josh took no notice. 'Is being common the new smart?' he wondered aloud. 'Are men the new women? Is staying in the new going out?' He looked round the table. 'Where's Lulu? There must be something fashiony we could do. Are low heels the new stilettos? Is short the new long? Is underwear the new outerwear?'

'Lulu's still in bed,' said Jane, who had received a telephone call from the absent fashion editor to this effect a few minutes before. 'Her alarm didn't go off.' She paused. 'So,' she asked tartly, 'is absence the new presence? Is staying in bed the new getting up?'

'Poor Lulu needs her rest,' said Josh, leaping, as usual, to the fashion editor's defence. 'She needs to rest. She gets ill very easily, poor dear.'

'You're telling me,' said Valentine. 'She's certainly the only person I've ever known claim they had bunions in their ears.'

'Oh, shut up,' said Josh. 'Let's concentrate on the matter in hand. What's hot, what's hip. Is death the new life? Is being fat the new thin? Is,' his eyes widened as if knocked sideways by the brilliance of his own train of thought, 'rock and roll the new rock and roll?'

As she entered the sandwich shop at lunchtime, trying to psych herself up to a mayonnaise-free, butter-free and most of all fun-free lettuce leaf roll, Jane spotted Valentine. He was muttering darkly in a corner with Ann, the deputy editor of *Blissful Country Homes*. A monthly celebration of Agas, appliqué screens and City bankers downshifting to barn conversions in Bicester, *Blissful*, as it was known, was a stablemate in the same magazine company as *Gorgeous*.

Meeting her gaze, Valentine rolled his eyes and beckoned Jane over. 'I've just been telling Ann about Josh. How he can be so rude to me, considering the strain I have been under, I can't imagine.'

'Strain?' asked Jane, relieved that she wasn't the only one suffering at the moment. There was nothing like someone else's woes to take one's mind off one's own.

She looked at Valentine's shining, agitated face. 'Why, what's the matter?'

'It's Algy, my cairn terrier,' wailed Valentine. 'I went away last weekend and put him in a kennel where he got in with all the wrong dogs. He now refuses to come to heel and poos all over the house. It's very upsetting.'

'I know just how Valentine feels,' Ann said sternly to a nonplussed Jane. 'One of my tabbies isn't well at the moment. It's dreadful. I have to inject my poor pussy twice a day.'

Never had a day been so designed to test Jane's patience to the full. She returned from the sandwich shop to find a letter from the BBC asking Champagne to go on *Desert Island Discs* and recommending she choose a mixture of contemporary and classical music. Jane snorted. Probably as far as Champagne was aware, Ravel was a shoe shop, Telemann someone who came to fix the video and Handel something that her bulging designer shopping bags were suspended from. None of this improved the fact that top of her list of jobs this afternoon was getting more column inches out of Champagne.

Jane delayed the evil moment as long as possible, rummaging about her desk and returning telephone calls, sometimes to people who hadn't even called in the first place. Eventually, however, she bowed to the inevitable.

'What the *fuck* are you doing calling this early?' barked the sleepy, furious voice at the other end. Jane looked at the clock. 'It's ten past three, Champagne,' she said with exaggerated patience. 'In the afternoon, that is.'

'Is it? Oh. Had no idea. Bloody late night last night,' honked Champagne.

Jane hardly dared breathe, let alone say anything that might knock Champagne off this particular train of thought. Like a truffling pig, she had caught the first tantalising whiffs of that rare and precious commodity Anecdote. 'Really?' she asked gently. 'What were you doing?'

'Went to the races with Conal. Bloody good fun, actually.'

'Which ones? Sandown? Kempton Park?'

'No, the East End somewhere.'

Jane frowned. Which of the racecourses was actually in London? None, as far as she knew.

'Bloody funny horses,' Champagne continued. 'Really weird and small-looking. Went bloody fast, though.'

The penny dropped. 'Do you mean you've been to Walthamstow?' Jane gasped. 'The dog track?' Conal O'Shaughnessy had clearly been attempting to inculcate Champagne into working-class culture. Jane was not sure how successful he'd been.

'Yah, and then we went for supper,' Champagne recalled after a few minutes' hard thought. 'Conal tried to make me have a green Thai curry but I told him no way was I going to eat anything made out of ties. Particularly green ones. Hermès ones I might have considered.'

'Have you seen this?' asked Valentine as Jane stopped scribbling and put the phone down. He flopped an open copy of *Vogue* on her desk. Jane coughed as the powerful smell of ten different scent inserts filled her nostrils. Below her on the glossy page Champagne sprawled across an advertisement spread for an after-shave called Leather, her ice-blonde hair spilling over a clinging leather catsuit and her nose hovering above an improbably large and clumsy frosted glass bottle. 'My favourite scent is Leather,' ran the slogan.

'Well, it would be,' said Jane. 'Essence of wallet.'

'On the other hand, it's great to see her getting a good hiding,' said Valentine.

'It's absurd,' grumbled Jane. 'Champagne's endorsing practically every product there is. Talk about a legend in her own launch time. Even that ridiculous poodle of hers is doing a dog food ad, for which I expect it gets paid more than I earn in five years.'

'Never mind,' said Valentine, putting a hot, damp palm on her shoulder. 'Just remember this. She may have the looks, the wealth, the boyfriend, the ad endorsements, the national newspaper columns, the TV appearances, the talk of film deals, the world at her feet . . .' His voice trailed off.

'Yes?' prompted Jane, fixing him with a beady eye.

'But she can't possibly be happy,' Valentine finished valiantly.

'Can't she?' asked Jane tightly.

Valentine was saved from answering by Jane's phone ringing. He scuttled across the room and disappeared behind the pile of newly-arrived gold lamé oven gloves heaped on his desk for review.

'I was just calling to say,' Champagne boomed, 'when you call me to read my column back to me, call me at the Lancaster.'

'The Lancaster?' echoed Jane. The Lancaster was the most expensive luxury hotel in London. A former office block off Piccadilly, the new, all-suite hotel had swiftly upstaged the Metropolitan's chic. Each suite famously boasted extensive views over its own butlers, hot and cold running individual fax lines and an outside temperature gauge in the wardrobe so you could choose exactly the right clothes to combat any hostile elements encountered between leaving the hotel lobby and stepping into the limo. 'But why?' asked Jane. Was Champagne's huge flat in Eaton Square no longer good enough?

'My cleaner's resigned and the flat's an utter tip,' drawled Champagne. 'So I called the Lancaster and they're giving me a suite for free. Told them I'd mention them in the column, so stick them in somewhere, will you? Oh, and mention the beauty treatments. Gucci and I are having the time of our lives. He's having a sauna and a seaweed wrap at the moment, in fact.'

'Is Conal with you?' Jane asked, quietly grinding her teeth. If he felt moved to trash the suite in rock-star fashion, please let him throw the TV at Champagne, she prayed silently. Followed by the minibar and the breakfast trolley.

'No idea where he is,' Champagne barked. 'Haven't

seen him for ages. Not since he asked me if I wanted to go to Latvia with him the other day.'

'Latvia?'

'Yah. But I told him not bloody likely, he could go on his own. I mean, I haven't read a review of it anywhere. Might be awful.'

'Oh, I didn't realise it was a restaurant,' said Jane, embarrassed. Another trendy eaterie that had passed her by.

'Why, what else is it?' bawled Champagne, sounding surprised. 'A country? Oh. Well, I suppose that explains why Conal's been away all week. I thought there must have been some trouble over the bill or something.'

Weeks passed. Returning to the empty flat and seeing Tom's darkened first-floor windows got every evening off to a bad start for Jane. She had no doubt that Tom was now holed up in a TriBeCa loft with a long-limbed blonde, tapping out a bestseller between trips to Dean & Deluca. Even though she knew he was thousands of miles away, she still saw him everywhere. The world suddenly seemed to be full of tall men with tousled blond hair and deep-set eyes. It was rather like living in Stockholm.

Nick, meanwhile, had faded from her life almost as if he had never been there. He had shuffled round a couple of times to pick up such essentials as his peppery aftershaves, his Queen albums and the set of wooden coathangers that had fitted Nick's up-market self-image better than they had ever fitted into the wardrobe. They had muttered to each other from behind the barrier of a cup of tea. But that was the limit of their contact. It was incredible to think they had ever lived together. And it was terrifying to think she had ever wanted to marry him. Tally, she knew, would sympathise with that.

It was while pondering this that Jane realised she had not heard from Tally for ages. Guilt swamped her. To think she had been spending all this time moping over the loss of a man, when her best friend might have lost her house. She had, Jane realised, agonised, done precisely nothing about finding Tally her Mullionaire.

'Nick's left me,' she told Tally when, at last, the telephone was answered at Mullions. She felt relieved. At least the family, or what was left of it, was still in residence. Jane waited for Tally to whoop with joy. But whoop came there none.

'So we're both young, free and single,' Jane pressed, eagerly. 'Both in the same boat.'

'Yes, except that your mother doesn't keep writing "Go For It" in lipstick all over the Venetian glass mirrors,' sighed Tally. 'Nor does she run up and down the Long Gallery with a net saying she's catching dreams.'

'Oh dear.' Jane's stomach knotted with guilt. 'Listen, why don't I come up? This weekend?'

Tally seemed to perk up at this. 'That would be wonderful,' she said with feeling. 'Then you can see what I'm up against. Can you remember the way?'

'Of course,' said Jane, reeling off a few directions.

'Just round the first bend past Lower Bulge, isn't it? Sharp right or you'll miss it?'

'You can't miss it now,' Tally said dolefully. 'There's a huge, glaring, red For Sale sign plastered all over the front of the gatehouse.'

Having put the phone down, Jane switched on the news and dug a fork into her pasta. She almost choked as Champagne immediately sashayed across the screen, on her way to some premiere with Conal O'Shaughnessy. Foaming at the mouth as best she could with a mouthful of pesto sauce, Jane hurriedly switched over, only to find herself staring into the face of James Morrison the transport minister, taking on the bypass protesters once again.

Jane squinted over her pasta at the screen, hoping to spot Piers. It certainly looked lively. Nick would be furious, she thought gleefully. Hordes of muddy, wild-haired creatures were rushing about the site shouting abuse at the hapless politician. Some were even throwing things at him. It was really rather exciting. Jane could almost hear the thuds and bangs.

She *could* hear the thuds and bangs. She turned down the TV and listened carefully. Above her head, a series of abrupt thumps followed by a crash confirmed that someone was in the first-floor flat. Her insides plunged suddenly downwards like a hi-tech lift, leaving her stomach with a curiously empty and airy feeling. Had he, was it possible, could she entertain the wild hope that Tom had come back?

Swaying on her weakening knees, Jane let herself

out of the flat and walked slowly upstairs. Her palms were sweating, her back felt hot and her intestines were surging like a geyser. Her heart thumped with excitement as she tapped at Tom's door.

It was opened by a tall, spotty youth with an unfeasibly large Adam's apple and huge, smeared spectacles. He blinked shortsightedly at Jane. She felt almost sick with disappointment.

'Um, hello,' she mumbled, after a few seconds' shocked silence. 'I'm, er, your downstairs neighbour. Just come to say, er, hello.'

'Hi,' mumbled the youth, avoiding her gaze and tangling black-nailed fingers in strands of greasy hair. He looked a bit like Jarvis Cocker, but ugly. A sweet, fusty and greasy smell hung about him.

'I was wondering,' Jane gabbled, glancing fitfully into the flat behind him where several vast cardboard boxes filled up the sitting room, 'whether you knew anything about the person who used to live here. I'm trying to get hold of him. He, er, left a few bills behind, you see.'

'Dunno,' mumbled Jarvis vaguely. 'Landlord might, but I think he lives in Spain. Want his number? It's somewhere in there.' He waved a white and emaciated arm in the direction of the boxes, piles of clothes and upended furniture heaped in the room behind.

'No,' said Jane, clearing her throat aggressively as she retreated back down the stairs. 'No, it's all right.'

But it wasn't.

Chapter 7

Heading west for the weekend at Mullions, Jane derived a brutal satisfaction from making the poor old 2CV go far faster than it could really manage. It soon beat her at her own game, however, by obstinately refusing to stump up the horsepower required to overtake a man who was a Caravan Club Member, had a Baby On Board, believed Campanologists Did It with Bells On and as a consequence could see nothing at all out of the rear window. Which, thought Jane, furious but impotent, explained his snail-like pace but not the reason why he steadfastly and unstintingly stuck to the middle lane.

As a result, Jane arrived at Mullions not mid-morning, as she had planned, but at lunchtime. Tally was right about the For Sale sign. Subtle it was not. As she swung in under the crumbling gatehouse that announced the beginning of the park, Jane profoundly hoped lunch might be over. Mrs Ormondroyd was the kind of cook who believed all vegetables should be boiled to a gluey mass and regarded pastry that rose with profound suspicion. It was no surprise that Tally had considered toasted Mars Bar sandwiches a culinary breakthrough.

It had always seemed odd to Jane that no one in the Venery family seemed to expect their cook to be able to cook. The thinking appeared to be that generations of Venerys had got by on watery Brown Windsor soup and bony cutlets and hadn't come to any harm beyond delicate digestions and a generally fleshless appearance. And what was bad enough for them was certainly bad enough for their descendants. Given what she was expected to eat, it was no wonder Tally was so tall and thin. Looking like a beanpole was certainly the nearest she was likely to come to fresh greens.

And what went for Mrs Ormondroyd certainly went for Mr Peters the gardener, Jane was reminded, as the car bounced over the potholes in the drive. Like his colleague in the kitchen, Mr Peters was a retainer whose prime function, as far as Jane could work out, was to be retained irrespective of what his skills were. Or weren't. A generous critic might assume that Mr Peters' criterion of excellence was what would look good in the park in five hundred years' time as there was no evidence that he was interested in the contemporary landscape at all. His idea of a formal garden was distinctly lax.

Tally's hair-raising descriptions of the state of Mullions had prepared Jane for the worst. So, as the first view of the house slid along her windscreen, she was surprised and relieved to see it still seemed to be standing, more or less in its entirety. Across the shimmering oxbow lake, the pile of mellow stone glowed yellow as butter in the soft sunshine. The leaded glass in the eponymous mullioned windows glittered like slices of diamond, and over the crumbling stable block, the weathercock that pointed the same way no matter what direction the wind came from shone in what was almost a spirited fashion.

As she drove past the rose garden, heavy with overblown, un-deadheaded blooms, Jane looked hard for the sweat lodge Tally had mentioned, and the mysterious mercurial harp. But there was no sign of either. She turned into the stableyard, which backed on to the kitchen wing. This, for the last hundred years at least, had been the main entrance to Mullions, ever since the massive front door had come off its hinges while being opened to admit Queen Victoria – who, on that occasion, had apparently been amused.

Mrs Ormondroyd came out to greet her, dressed, as always, in a checked nylon overall of violent turquoise blue, her massive calves covered with tights the colour of strong tea. Her large-nosed face with its uneven eyes and spreading ears was, as usual, the deep-creased picture of disapproval and suspicion.

'You're just in time for lunch,' she grumbled.

'Great,' said Jane bravely. 'I was hoping I would be.'

'Well, you might change your mind when you see what it is.' Mrs Ormondroyd scowled, leading the way back into the kitchen. Jane followed, bewildered at this unexpected flash of self-knowledge on Mrs Ormondroyd's part. Had she finally accepted there were limits to her cooking skills?

Inside, the welcome was warmer.

'Jane!' shrieked Tally, clattering over the stone flags like an excited five-year-old. Jane found herself enveloped in a dusty, mothball-scented hug. 'It's so nice to see you,' Tally gasped. 'You look wonderful. Much thinner.'

'Do I?' Tally always said the right thing, but this really was the rightest thing of all. Hoping she meant it, Jane stole a swift look down at herself. Her stomach was a bit flatter, largely thanks to the steep drop in her wine consumption. Opening a bottle just for herself, alone in the flat, made Jane feel like an alcoholic. However, she permitted herself the occasional gin and tonic because she needed the lime slices to counteract the risk of scurvy from her unvaried diet of pasta and pesto.

'You look so smart,' Tally said, holding her at arm's length.

'It's only my jeans,' said Jane. Her white shirt wasn't even new. Yet it was newer by a generation than anything Tally had on. Her sharp, bony elbows protruded from a tiny, shrunken pullover. A pair of half-mast trousers ended halfway up her skinny calves. 'Amazing trousers,' Jane said with perfect truth, unable to tear her eyes away from the dark, wide-pinstriped creation that, like the dress Tally had worn to the Ritz, had a faintly antiquated look about them. 'More of your mother's Mainbocher?'

'Oh, these.' Tally looked down. 'No, Daddy's. They're his old school trousers. I found them when I was looking for something to wear in bed the other day. They're very warm. A bit worn out on the bottom, but I expect it was all that caning.' She flashed Jane a strained grin. Her fine, mouse hair was scraped haphazardly back in a rubber band, and there was a more anxious expression than usual in her clear, almost lashless grey eyes. Tally's pale cheeks with their dusting of patrician high colour seemed thinner, which made her snub nose with its red-tinged tip look odder than ever.

Mrs Ormondroyd had stomped off a while ago, but Jane suddenly realised they were not alone in the kitchen. A large, silent figure was standing at the back, making almost imperceptible sounds and movements at the large stone sink. Jane started in shock. It wasn't any old large, silent figure standing there. It was a Red Indian in the finest spaghetti Western tradition.

'Jane, this is Big Horn,' said Tally, following the direction of her astonished gaze. 'He's cooking lunch,' she added hastily, as if this somehow explained his appearance. Big Horn turned from his labours and walked slowly towards them, his large, bare feet moving soundlessly over the worn flagstones.

About seven feet tall, and naked from the waist up, he was impressively muscular, with a tan the same strong terracotta colour as Mrs Ormondroyd's tights.

Above his deep-set, brilliant dark eyes, his centre-parted hair was thick, black and long, tightly plaited and wound with brightly-coloured thread. Across his torso he sported an impressive array of complex tattoos as well as several necklaces of shells and beads. From the waist down, what looked like a fringed apron of embroidered chamois leather seemed to be all that protected his modesty. Yet he was silently impressive, ready to take on General Custer at a moment's notice, despite being armed with nothing more than a slotted spoon.

'How do you do,' Jane said, smiling.

Big Horn inclined his large-featured head slightly. A faint smile thawed his thick, beautifully-cut lips and he raised one eyebrow a fraction of a centimetre.

'Big Horn and Mummy are on the Ayurvedic diet,' Tally explained, shepherding Jane out of the kitchen. 'They eat to suit their personality. By that reckoning,' she whispered, once they had reached the kitchen passage, 'Mummy's is all mung beans and Chinese worm tea. At least that's what Big Horn's been making all week.'

'How very unflattering,' said Jane. 'If someone was cooking to suit my personality I'd expect lobster and foie gras at the very least.'

'Well, Mrs Ormondroyd tried to cook a chicken,' said Tally, 'but as soon as Mummy saw it, she picked it up and started waving it about over everyone's heads. According to her, raw poultry absorbs negative energy.'

Jane giggled. 'And what about negative smells? All

those beans must have had an effect.'

'Yes,' confessed Tally. 'I suppose there have been some rather ripe odours about.' She screwed up her snub nose.

'I suppose you could call it,' chortled Jane, 'the Blast of the Mohicans.'

Tally giggled, just as the housekeeper came back down the passage and swept past them, her face as stony as the floor. The sound of her thighs swishing together in their tea-coloured tights faded into the kitchen. 'And Mrs Ormondroyd's been driven to distraction,' whispered Tally.

'I imagine she finds that mini-apron thing of his very distracting,' grinned Jane. 'I bet Big Horn's the most exciting thing to hit the Mullions kitchens since the days they had naked boys turning the spits.'

'I think you're probably right.' Tally pushed back the tattered green baize door at the end of the kitchen passage and stepped out into the Marble Hall, the freezing, lofty space at the heart of the house. The black and white chequer board Carrara which gave the hall its name stretched away beneath their feet. A number of dusty statues on plinths stood desultorily about, while a massive, carved Jacobean oak staircase climbed wearily up to the house's upper floors, sagging slightly as if the effort was too much for it. Which, in some places, it evidently was. Jane spotted, beneath the treads nearest the hall floor, several piles of books that were evidently supporting the whole structure. She had no doubt that some of them were first editions, grabbed haphazardly from the Mullions library.

Adding to the atmosphere of weight and weariness were the Ancestors – Tally's name for the collection of heavily-framed oil portraits whose subjects' red-tinged nostrils identified them as Venery forebears. Two loomed from each of three walls, and another four accompanied climbers of the staircase up to yet more portraits in the Long Gallery on the next floor. There was, in fact, scarcely anywhere one could go in Mullions without contemplating the snub-nosed, thin-lipped visage of a long-dead member of the family. The Venerys as a dynasty had cornered the market in bold, unsmiling poses centuries before the likes of Conal O'Shaughnessy had smouldered on to the scene.

Suddenly, a terrifyingly loud and utterly anguished scream from upstairs shattered the brooding silence of the hall. Bits of plaster started to drift down like snowflakes. Jane's hand leapt to her throat as she stumbled towards Tally in terror. It sounded as if someone was being disembowelled, dying in childbirth and being burnt at the stake simultaneously.

Tally, however, looked oddly calm. Bored, even. 'Mummy, doing her primal screaming,' she explained, rolling her eyes in exasperation. 'She does it every lunchtime. It helps expel the tensions of the morning, apparently. But it doesn't do much for the roof.'

As the frantic beating of her heart subsided, Jane raised her trembling vision to the painted ceiling far up in the gloom above. Painted in the Italian Renaissance style by a pupil of Verrio, the ceiling's once-writhing congregation of plump gods and goddesses was indeed looking distinctly patchy.

'Only this week, Triton lost his trident and both wheels of Phoebus's chariot peeled off,' sighed Tally. 'Nymphs and shepherds are coming away all the time. It's falling apart up there. You can barely walk across the floor without causing some disaster among the deities.'

Jane shot a speculative glance at a wobbly-looking piece of the egg-and-dart moulding which seemed about to detach itself from the frieze which ran round the walls below the painting. One more shriek of Julia's might easily result in its leaping for freedom.

'Primal screaming?' Jane struggled with the concept of the former steely lady of the manor bawling her head off. Almost as amazing was the fact that it was before lunch. The Julia of old rarely stirred from bed before two.

'Yes, it's ghastly,' Tally said. 'The Ancestors are horrified,' she added, waving a long white hand in the direction of the portraits.

'They look it,' said Jane. And there did seem to be a certain, barely perceptible, alteration in their faces. Each painted eyeball, previously passive, now bulged slightly with what might have been horror, and each formerly straight, tight mouth had acquired a definite downward turn.

'Yes, the Ancestors are very shocked,' Tally said sadly. 'The ones in here are appalled enough, but the ones in the Long Gallery practically need counselling. They're nearer to the noise, you see. And it's not just the screaming that's upsetting them. Mummy's been round the whole of Mullions feng shui-ing it, and decided the chandelier in the drawing room was covered in bad chi.'

Jane stared. 'Still, I suppose Mrs Ormondroyd doesn't handle a duster like she used to,' she said.

Tally looked at her sternly. 'Really, Jane, this isn't all some huge joke, you know,' she said. 'Believe me, there's nothing funny about it.'

Jane determinedly turned down her irrepressibly curving lips.

'What is bad chi?' she asked, trying to keep her shoulders from shaking; a challenge as they were shuddering from the cold anyway. However mild the climate was outside, inside Mullions the atmosphere was so icy you could skate on it.

'Sort of bad luck, I think,' said Tally. 'Anyway, she's taken the chandelier down and replaced it with a piece of nasty old dried buffalo skin that smells cheesy and looks very odd with the Grinling Gibbons. But the worst is what she's doing in the bedrooms. She's moved the eighteenth-century bed that Queen Victoria slept in and replaced it with a piece of carved bark to counteract what she calls the negative energy of colour chaos emanating from the Gobelins tapestries.'

Jane blinked. Tally was right. It wasn't funny. It was hilarious. Her lips started to quiver again at the corners.

'But at least they haven't built a sweat lodge in the rose garden yet,' she said comfortingly.

'No, but only because they're going to build a yurt on the parterre,' sighed Tally. 'And Big Horn's practically worn out the lawn with his ritual dancing at dawn. All the telephones in the house stink of Mummy's essential oils, which Mrs Ormondroyd hates. And when Mummy destroyed the vacuum cleaner the other day, Mrs Ormondroyd almost handed her notice in. It was only Big Horn's coming past at the crucial moment with his apron flapping that changed her mind.'

'Why, what was Julia doing with it?' asked Jane, genuinely curious. 'I didn't know your mother knew what a vacuum cleaner was, let alone how to use one.'

'She was trying to hoover her aura,' Tally confessed. 'According to Mummy, hoovering your aura – which is apparently a sort of spirit force surrounding you – draws out all the impurities in your soul.'

'Like a sort of spiritual spot wash?' Jane was worried she would laugh if she didn't say anything. It was, she could see, truly awful for Tally. Julia had obviously gone completely mad this time. More barking than a pack of hounds, in fact.

'Yes, but in Mummy's case the dustbag burst and she ended up with far more impurities than she started with,' said Tally. 'Including a contact lens she'd lost in the seventies, apparently.'

There was a rustle above them, accompanied by a faint tinkling of bells. Jane looked up, and gasped. 'Julia?' she exclaimed in amazement.

Nothing could have been further removed from the

perfectly turned out Lady Julia of old than the pair of brilliant eyes Jane found staring down at her from a tanned, lined and completely unmade-up face. Julia's wild hair looked as if she had been dragged through a hedge backwards, and then dragged through it forwards again. What looked like bits of foliage were stuck in it for good measure.

Only Julia's voice was still the same – more cut glass than a factory of Waterford. It took more than a few months' New Ageism, it seemed, to make an impact on a lifetime's Old Money. 'Jane, darling!' declared Julia, as she descended the stairs amid acres of flowing white robe. 'So it *was* you!'

'What do you mean?' asked Jane, almost overwhelmed by the clouds of essential oil scent that floated in Julia's wake. She was aware of Tally squirming in embarrassment at her side. Julia took no notice. Her full attention was trained ecstatically on Jane. The intensity of it was unsettling.

'When I looked at the chart at midnight last night, I noticed that Mercury was sextile with Venus,' breathed Julia, dramatically. 'Emotional change was in the air. It was *you*!' As Julia patted her cheek, Jane felt her toes curl.

'I see,' she said awkwardly. How exactly did one reply to this kind of greeting? 'Well, it's very nice to see you, Julia. You look very well.'

'*I feel* well,' said Julia, clasping her hands in apparent ecstasy. 'I have never felt *quite* so well before. My life was empty and unsustainable and now it's full of truth and spontaneity. Would you like some lunch?' she added.

'Er . . .' Jane prevaricated, remembering the mung beans.

'We're going out,' said Tally hurriedly.

'That's nice,' said Julia absently. 'Well, if you'll excuse me, I have a lot to do this afternoon. Mr Peters is very worried about it not having rained for a while on his roses, so Big Horn and I are going to appeal to the Great Earth Goddess on his behalf and perform a rain ceremony.' She wafted off through the door into the kitchen passage.

'Now do you see what I mean?' asked Tally.

Jane put an arm about her shoulders. 'Let's go for some lunch at the Gloom,' she suggested, leading Tally back down the kitchen passage to the door. The local pub, the Loom and Bobbin, or the Gloom and Sobbing as Piers had once dubbed it, owing to its mausoleum-like Victorian atmosphere, provided unmatchable therapy for depression. However miserable one was, one couldn't possibly be as dejected as the hatchet-faced regulars draped over the bar.

They drove along in a silence punctuated only by the 2CV's bouncing and jolting over the potholes in the drive. As they passed the lake, Jane glanced over at Mullions. Seen from across the water in the mellow afternoon light, it seemed to be floating serenely atop a great expanse of pearl. The rose window in the dining room, rescued from the ruins of a nearby abbey, flashed cheerfully as the sun passed across its ancient panes, and the oriel window by the entrance door bulged happily. The balustrade of Jacobean stonework, which formed the edge of the terrace in front of the house, undulated merrily along the wall and the turrets stood clear-cut and golden against a blue sky. Seen from this distance, it looked the epitome of the power and style of the landed gentry. No one could possibly have imagined that it was collapsing and that the cash-strapped family was having to sell it after four hundred years of ownership. No one, thought Jane, could possibly have imagined there was a Red Indian in there, either, not to mention a New Age lady of the manor. The depressed silence continued as she and Tally passed under the For Sale sign.

'Why will no one ever give you grants?' Jane asked, realising she had never raised the subject before. It did seem odd, though. From this angle, Mullions looked such a jewel. More idyllic even than those posters of sun-soaked castles amid undulating emerald downs that the English Tourist Board put inside Tube trains to upset commuters. 'Surely the National Trust or someone can help out?'

Tally sighed, and made an odd, scraping noise that sounded suspiciously like the grinding of teeth. 'Do you really think I haven't *tried*?' she asked testily. 'But Mullions is too run down for someone like the National Trust to take on. And even if they were interested, they would want enormous endowments to help with the upkeep. But they're not interested. Apparently it's not important enough a building.'

'Isn't it?' asked Jane in surprise. 'Why ever not?'

'Oh, something not quite right about the groin vaulting in the antechapel,' said Tally wearily. 'And apparently our spandrels are below par. The Jacobean strapwork's been found wanting, and the neo-classical columns in the hall were, it turns out, made by one of Adam's less gifted pupils.'

'Alas, poor Doric,' said Jane, drawing up outside the Gloom and Sobbing.

Tally frowned.

Tally slammed the car door shut and following Jane into the pub.

Inside, the usual funereal atmosphere prevailed. A sullen fire spat in the cavernous hearth and a collection of locals who might have been there since Jane's last visit sat slumped over their pints of Old Knickersplitter, the Gloom's sour, home-brewed ale. Apart from gin and tonic, the pub sold practically nothing else.

'So Julia's still really set on selling it?' Jane broached the subject as she pulled open a bag of cheese and onion crisps so ancient they could well have been the prototype for the brand.

Tally nodded miserably. 'Yes. And the estate agents are egging her on. Even though the place is hardly in a state to sell. The electricity supply is totally erratic – the state of our connections would horrify Mr Darcy. The heating is a joke. You can hear the pipes banging and creaking for miles, but nothing ever makes it to the radiators. And the entire water supply is plumbed with lead.' She shifted uncomfortably on the hard bench they were sitting on.

'Doesn't that drive you mad?' asked Jane.

'No, I suppose it's what everyone in similar houses did at the time . . . oh, I see what you mean,' said Tally. 'Yes, lead piping was supposed to be one of the reasons behind the fall of the Roman Empire. You do go insane in the end, apparently.'

'Maybe that's what's happened to Julia,' suggested Jane.

Tally shook her head. 'She doesn't even use water any more. She washes her face in pee.'

'No!' exclaimed Jane. She had raised her glass halfway towards her lips. Now she put it down again.

''Fraid so,' said Tally. 'She says that, apart from doing whatever wonders it's supposed to do, it's quick, cheap and warm. Unlike anything that comes out of the Mullions bath taps, she says.' She gazed despairingly into her smeared glass. Old Knickersplitter was an even less cheerful prospect than her mother. 'The fact remains,' Tally finished, 'a damp-proof course and a new roof would do more good than all the feng shui in China.'

Jane frowned. 'We've got to find you this rich man fast,' she said firmly. 'Someone loaded and sexy.'

But the eyes Tally turned to Jane were utterly devoid of sparkle. 'Sexy? It's so long since I slept with someone I've practically sealed up'. Tally sighed. 'And it's too late for the house, in any case. The first person is coming to look round next week.'

'Who?' Jane asked. 'You never know,' she added, determined to see light at the end of the tunnel, even if it was another tunnel altogether, 'it might be someone gorgeous who'll fall for you.' If Tally had a radical makeover in the next few days, got her hair cut and stopped wearing her father's school trousers, there might well be a chance.

'Doubt it,' said Tally. 'He's a pop star, apparently. I can't imagine I'm his type.'

Jane was forced to admit this was not untrue. Tally's idea of contemporary music was probably 'Greensleeves'.

'Still, let's be thankful for small mercies,' Tally sighed. 'At least Mummy and Big Horn won't be there when he comes. They're off for a few weeks, to some ashram in California. Apparently Big Horn's going to lock himself in a dark shed for a month and contemplate his inner child while Mummy looks for the wise woman in herself.'

'Well, that'll be a fruitless search,' said Jane.

Chapter 8

'What's bitten you?' Jane asked. She had just arrived in the office to find Josh with a face like thunder.

'Only that Luke Skywalker's had an accident skiing,' Josh grumbled. Luke Skywalker was the *Gorgeous* astrologer. Or, rather, the astrologer for *Gorgeous*. Even the most flattering of byline pictures had not succeeded in making Luke's unkempt, stringy hair, large nose and doleful eyes appealing. And he probably looked much worse now.

'Oh, poor Luke,' said Jane. 'Is he OK?'

'Not really,' said Josh irritably. 'The clumsy bastard smashed into a rock and now he's got amnesia. Can't even remember the past, let alone predict the future. You'd have thought he'd have seen it coming.'

Jane raised her eyebrows as she sat down and started to poke about her desk. In an attempt to impose some order on the chaos of her life, she had recently taken to noting down the next day's most important tasks on a

Post It before she left the office the evening before. This morning, she gazed at the little primrose sticker and sighed. Top of the list was ringing Champagne.

She tried the mobile last. It ground away, unanswered. Jane had just decided to put it down when someone at the other end picked it up.

'Yah?' barked Champagne, over what sounded like loud banging and sloshing sounds in the background.

'It's Jane. How are you?' asked Jane, trying to sound enthusiastic.

'Fine. Just got back from shooting, in fact,' honked Champagne. 'With the Sisse-Pooles in Scotland. Bloody awful.'

'Oh, I hate blood sports too,' agreed Jane, starting to scribble down the conversation for the column. 'So dreadfully cruel.'

'Hideously cruel,' Champagne agreed, much to Jane's surprise. 'Making people stagger over the moors in the peeing rain wearing clothes the colour of snot is absolutely the worst, the most inhuman thing you can do to anyone. Let's face it,' Champagne added, in the face of Jane's stunned silence, 'I'm just not an outdoor type of girl. The only hills I care about are Beverly.'

And the only kind of shoots you care about are movie ones, the only Moores you're interested are Demi and Roger and the only bags that grab you are by Prada, thought Jane, working up the theme for the new column and scribbling furiously. And we all know whose butts you're most interested in at the moment. Unless, that is, you've been poached by a loaded gun.

That, at least, was a thought worth probing. 'Who were you shooting with?' Jane asked. It didn't sound like a very O'Shaughnessy activity. Perhaps Champagne had dumped him for some vague, weatherbeaten blond lord with a faceful of broken veins, a labrador and vast tracts of Yorkshire. Tim Nice Butt Dim.

'Well, Conal, of course, who the hell do you think?' came the booming honk. Slosh, slosh went the mystery background noise. 'The Sisse-Pooles asked him along as well. He had a blast, actually. Haw haw haw. God, I'm funny.'

Jane gritted her teeth. 'How did he do?' she asked, trying to imagine the determinedly working-class O'Shaughnessy stumbling around a moor with a collection of portly patricians in plus fours.

'Only thing he shot was one of the beaters,' boomed Champagne. 'But that didn't matter. Bloke was as old as the hills anyway. Oh yes,' hollered Champagne over the noise, 'Conal had a great time. He likes a good bang as much as the next man. Haw haw haw.'

'So you're still together?' The relationship with O'Shaughnessy had now lurched past the fortnight mark. In Champagne's book, that was practically the equivalent of a diamond wedding.

'Bloody right we are,' bawled Champagne. 'More than that, we're getting married!'

Jane's pen dropped with a clatter to the floor. 'Married?' Despite being separated from the conversation by the glass wall of his office, Josh's head shot up like Apollo 9.

'Yah, Conal asked me last night,' screeched Champagne excitedly. 'At least, I *think* that's what he said. Might have said "Will you carry me" as he was a bit out of it at the time. But by the time he came round, I'd dragged him into Tiffany's. Couldn't go back on his word then!' She roared with laughter.

The banging and swishing seemed to reach a climax. Champagne's voice was now barely audible over the terrific sloshing noise, as if she was caught in a terrible storm. Jane finally decided to voice the suspicion that had been building for some time. 'Champagne,' she asked, 'are you filing your column from the shower?'

'Not exactly,' bellowed Champagne. 'I'm just test-driving my new whirlpool bath. It's amazing. Some of the jets do frankly thrilling things.'

Jane put down the phone feeling sick. Champagne's wedding was a nauseating prospect. Day after day, Jane realised, she would be forcibly reminded of her own single status as Champagne banged on relentlessly about what would most certainly be the Media Wedding of The Year. The only bright side to it was the fact that if her wedding was splashed all over *Hello!*, even Champagne might be able to remember something about it for the column.

Still, when life failed, there was always food to fall back on. At lunchtime, Jane headed for the supermarket, deciding to buy herself something glamorous and comforting for supper. She headed automatically for the dairy counter, with its wealth of sinful lactocentricity. But here lurked disappointment.

Disillusionment, even. Scanning the shelves, Jane couldn't help noticing the number of products that seemed to exist to mock the solitary, manless diner. Single cream, drippy and runny and the antithesis of comforting, luxurious double. Those depressing, rubbery slices of processed cheese called Singles.

Feeling self-conscious, Jane shuffled over to the more cheerful-looking Italian section, where she plumped for a big, squashy, colourful boxed pizza. Something about its improbable topping – four cheeses, pineapple, onion, olives, chicken tikka, prawns, peperoni, tomato, capers and tuna – struck her as amusing, and its mattress-like proportions looked intensely comforting. And Italians liked large ladies anyway.

Once the pizza box was in her basket, however, Jane felt racked with embarrassment. She was, she told herself, at least a stone too heavy to wander around in public carrying such a blatant statement of Intent To Consume Calories. Hurriedly retracing her steps, Jane slipped the pizza box back on the cooler shelf and replaced it with a nutritionally unimpeachable packet of fresh pasta. No one needed to know she intended to eat it with eggy, creamy, homemade carbonara sauce.

Having secured the bacon, Jane went into a dream by the eggs, confused by the vast variety on offer. Was barn-fresh grain-fed more or less cruel than four-grain yard-gathered? Spending so much of her time in her own dreary office building, Jane was intensely sympathetic to the plight of battery hens. She picked up a cardboard box of eggs and shoved them vaguely in the direction of her basket. Only it wasn't hers.

'Oh, I'm so sorry,' Jane gasped to the tall, dark-haired, leather-jacketed man standing right next to her. 'I seem to have put all my eggs in your basket!' She retrieved them and giggled. 'I'm sorry. I was miles away.' But the man did not smile back. His handsome face didn't even crease. After staring at her hard for a second or two, he walked swiftly away. Jane gazed after him. Really, people acted very oddly in supermarkets. They were the strangest places. Some, she knew, were cruising zones. Some even held singles evenings.

Rounding the corner, hoping to happen upon some garlic bread, Jane bumped into Mr Leather Jacket again. 'Sorry,' she muttered again. He stared at her even harder. Annoyance flooded her. What was his problem?

Then a thought struck her. Jane flushed deeper and redder than a beetroot. Oh Christ, she thought. He thinks I fancy him. He thought I put my eggs in his basket on purpose. It's probably accepted supermarket flirting code. Eggs probably mean something very intimate and reproductive. Christ. How embarrassing. She looked round in panic at the contents of the baskets around her, suspecting the existence of an entire alternative universe of shopping semiotics. What, for example, did carrots mean? Or sausages? She hardly dared think about cucumbers. And meat? Were there such things as pick-up joints?

Even more embarrassing was the fact that her advances had been rejected, even though they had been unconscious. Or had they? Had there been some subliminal attempt to attract the man in the egg section? Had she been screaming out 'Fertilise Me' as she plonked her Size Twos into his basket? They had, she remembered been free range as well.

Jane returned, shamefaced, to the office. Mercifully, the day passed without any more interruptions from Champagne. Jane's relaying of the wedding news to Josh resulted in a six-foot-plus bunch of flowers and a six-pack of Krug being whizzed round to the Lancaster double quick. Josh was evidently putting in an early bid for a place on the invitation list.

At home, Jane put the pasta on to boil and opened the low-cal tomato sauce which she had eventually bought and which promptly spattered all over her. She gazed miserably at the sauce spots staining her new white blouse. Damaged goods. Shop-soiled. She may as well face it, she was, Jane decided, starting to snivel, on the shelf, and the one marked Reduced For Quick Sale at that.

She poured herself a stiff gin and tonic and felt pleasantly weak as the spirit flowed through her veins. So what if she didn't have a boyfriend. Plenty more fish in the sea, she thought encouragingly, raising the glass to the light. Even if they were probably sharks. Or, worse, tiddlers. Even worse, plankton. She'd clearly boarded the wrong train of thought here, Jane decided, finishing the glass. And now she'd upset herself. If depression was a black dog, she was currently presiding over a whole kennel full.

The telephone rang. Torn between the always lurking

hope that it might be Tom, and the always lurking dread that it might be Nick, Jane decided to screen the call and hovered as the answering mechanism clicked loudly on. 'Oh, Jane, it's Amanda,' floated out the serene, clear and confident tones of a woman evidently at the other end of the coping-with-life universe from Jane. Amanda? Amanda who? Surely not Amanda-from-Cambridge. Amanda-with-the-vast-house-in-Hampstead. Rich-Amanda-she-had-meant-to-get-in-touch-with-about-Tally.

Since Cambridge, Jane and Amanda had seen each other only sporadically. The last time, Jane remembered, blushing, was when she and Nick had gone round there for dinner and Nick had attacked Amanda's merchant banker husband Peter for being a running dog capitalist. His opinions, Jane toe-curlingly recalled, had gathered force if not coherence from the gallons of Veuve Cliquot that Peter had provided, and Nick had soaked up like it was going out of fashion.

'Amanda!' Jane snatched up the receiver, hoping her words didn't sound too drink-sodden. 'Just got in through the door,' she lied. 'How *are* you? Haven't heard from you for ages.' She decided not to refer to the circumstances of their last meeting.

'Nor I you,' said Amanda smoothly; she had evidently reached the same conclusion. 'Which was why I was getting in touch. I thought you and Nick might like to come round to dinner Saturday week. Should be quite fun. If you can bear another tableful of City types, that is.' She gave a glassy giggle.

Jane blinked. Amid the clutter of her gin-fogged brain, three clear possibilities gradually emerged: Amanda was very forgiving, Amanda had lost her memory, or Amanda had a *placement* problem. The latter seemed the most likely. Two guests had obviously dropped out of her dinner party and Amanda needed bodies quickly. She must, Jane thought, be *desperate* to consider having Nick back. She obviously hadn't heard they were no longer an item.

'I'd love to, but . . .' Jane started to explain about Nick. Then she stopped. A thought had struck her. What about Tally? A big dinner party at Amanda's would be full of City bankers. Men with money. The kind of men Tally desperately needed to meet. Jane's brain fizzed. Amanda didn't need to know about Nick. Hopefully she wouldn't find out, either. Jane would simply turn up with Tally, and break the change of partner to Amanda at the last minute. Fantastic. At last she was able to do something to help her friend.

'Actually, I think that might be OK,' Jane said slowly, shoving the receiver under her chin and making jabbing-frantically-at-the-Psion movements into thin air. 'Mmm, yes. It's fine. We'd love to. About eight thirty?'

Breaking the scheme to Tally would be simple, Jane decided. She would just tell her the two of them had been invited together. She hoped she could rely on Amanda not to make it awkward.

That decided, Jane went to bed, and dreamed of Tom. As she did at least twice a week, she recalled in vivid detail as much as she could remember of their night together. Frequent reminiscence would, she hoped, like water on a garden, keep the memory green. But she was already beginning to forget exactly what he had said to her. Admittedly, there had not been much. The sex, however, she could remember perfectly. Jane was reliving a particularly delicious moment, right down to the moans and sighs, when she realised that she was actually not asleep, but awake, and the moaning and sighing was happening directly above her head.

Jane opened her eyes wide and sat bolt upright. The moaning and sighing was more regular now, and was accompanied by rhythmic thuds. As the noises climbed the decibel scale to ecstasy, Jane realised that, in the flat above, Jarvis was apparently grinding some willing female into the shagpile.

The irony of it. Jane threw herself face down into the pillow and bit hard to prevent herself from screaming. Should she go up there and ask them to stop? Should she go up there and ask to join in? Jarvis and his partner were making so much noise now, moaning and sighing, panting and gasping, that Jane wondered what more they could actually do to mark the crucial moment. Blow a horn, perhaps? On the other hand, that was probably exactly what was happening now.

'Cheer up,' said Josh. 'Why not do some work to take your mind off things?' He flung a handful of A4 sheets across the room. 'There's a piece here to edit. Needs a bit of restructuring, I think.'

Shocked out of a delicious daydream in which Tom appeared in the office with a pair of first-class Eurostar tickets to Paris, Jane came abruptly down to earth. Or, even more depressingly, to sticky, stained carpet as she scrabbled to detach the pages from the floor. She scanned the opening paragraph. The appalling grammar, dreadful spelling and sentences looser than seventies Monsoon smocks made any kind of argument impossible to decipher. 'Restructuring?' snarled Jane. 'It needs scaffolding. It needs a whole team of builders with their bums sticking out.'

Oh sod it, she thought, half an hour later, looking at her watch. I'm going to lunch. Even the prospect of a lettuce roll in the local sandwich bar wasn't as depressing as staying in the office under Josh's baleful eye and the increasingly powerful aroma of rotting Thai prawn ready meal samples wafting over from the food editor's desk.

As it was early, Jane managed to grab a table. She bit into her roll, which tasted, as usual, of cotton wool, and allowed herself to daydream about Tom again. They were aboard the Eurostar now, stretching out in First, and she was just taking a crisp, chilled sip of a particularly rich and golden vintage champagne.

'Hi, there,' chirped a cheery, familiar voice. 'All alone, are you?' Jane did not look up. She didn't want to be disturbed. At least, she didn't want to be disturbed by fat Ann from *Blissful*, now bearing down on her with a plate full of pasta, a full-fat Coke and a bright chatty smile. Oh no, thought Jane in alarm, clutching her roll in panic. I don't want to spend all lunchtime hearing about her sick pussy.

'Actually, I'm glad you're on your own,' said Ann, plonking a pile of tomato goo that smelt strongly of sick on the table. That makes one of us, then, thought Jane. 'I've been meaning to have a chat with you for *ages*,' Ann continued. 'You see,' she stretched out an arm and placed it on Jane's, the thick hairs on her upper lip quivering, 'Valentine told me you split up with your boyfriend. And I wanted to say I was sorry.'

Thanks, Valentine, thought Jane. Then, as Ann did not immediately remove her clammy hand from her arm, the panicked thought that Ann might actually be trying her luck seized her. 'Thanks, Ann,' she said uncertainly.

'Welcome to the club!' said Ann, raising her Coke to the level of her thick, shiny nose.

Jane felt a rush of panic. 'What club?' she asked quaveringly. Could Ann see something she, Jane, had never been aware of? Maybe this was why she had never managed to make relationships with men work. 'The singles club,' beamed Ann, loading a forkful of goo into her mouth.

'Oh, I'm okay,' Jane said unsteadily. 'I'll put a Lonely Hearts ad in *Time Out* or something.'

'I'd be careful where you put your ads,' Ann said, with her mouth full. 'Personally, I've had very little luck with *Time Out*.'

'Really?' whispered Jane, wishing she hadn't bolted her sandwich so quickly. She could feel it lying like a slug at the bottom of her stomach. Her digestive system was in far too much of a tiz to let it progress any further. It lurked there, unmoving and uncomfortable.

'Yes, first there was the man who had inherited land.' Ann cocked her head to one side and frowned at the ceiling. 'But it turned out to be his grandfather's allotment in East Ham, which wasn't quite what I had in mind . . .

'Then there was the man obsessed with his mother. Then the man obsessed with his ex-girlfriend who picked his spots all the time.' Ann ran a ruminative buttery finger over her own far from flawless complexion as she spoke. 'Then I decided I'd have more luck going for the older man market, you know, the more mature, sophisticated sort.'

Jane nodded, fascinated, unable to speak.

'Which was when,' Ann finished, shoving the rest of her tomato mush in her mouth, 'I found myself having a night out with a retired brigadier from Basingstoke. Who didn't show the slightest interest in my pussy.'

Say what you like about Champagne, Jane thought a few days later. You couldn't deny she had the gift of the grab.

'It's *too* marvellous,' Champagne yelled excitedly with the eardrum-shattering tones she seemed to reserve exclusively for Jane. 'Everyone's being just *too* generous. Alexander McQueen's already offered to do my wedding dress and darling Sam McKnight's doing my hair as a favour. Plus the sweet Sandy Lane and the angel Hotel du Cap are fighting over giving me a free honeymoon!'

Hope it's the Sandy Lane, thought Jane bitterly. But only if Michael Winner's there.

'And,' Champagne added with what was meant to be a happy sigh but which sounded like Arnold Schwarzenegger giving artificial respiration, 'Mario Testino's agreed to do the wedding photographs! Such a darling. Just beyond *heaven*, don't you think?'

Champagne's neck wasn't merely brass, thought Jane. It was solid platinum. 'So where are you actually getting married?' she asked.

'Can't believe you're asking me that. It's so *obvious*,' Champagne bawled. 'Where on earth do you think?'

Jane's mind raced. Westminster Abbey? St Paul's? A beach in Bermuda? Underwater? The moon? San Lorenzo? Prada on Sloane Street? 'Er, no idea,' she admitted.

'St Bride's, Fleet Street, the journalists' church, of course,' barked Champagne. 'After all, it's my trade!'

Jane leant back on her chair and gritted her teeth. 'What will the dress be like?' she forced herself to ask.

'Oh,' trilled Champagne with what was meant to be a light tinkle of laughter but sounded like someone smashing up several industrial-sized conservatories. 'I can't remember anything apart from something about an eighteenth-century fantasia, inspired by Madame de Pompadour. Darling Alexander is stretching his ingenuity to the limit.' Not to mention his stitches, thought Jane. There was only one definite thing about what Champagne would be wearing. It would be tight.

'What about music?' asked Jane.

'A musical friend of Conal's is going to arrange some Action Liposomes hits, including "Hot To Trot", so everyone can sing them as hymns. And I've also asked the choir of St Bride's to sing "Wake Me Up Before You Go Go" by Wham, which is one of my favourite songs ever.'

'And where will you live?' Jane asked, wondering what Madame de Pompadour would have made of it all. Not much, was her guess.

'Well, a socking great mansion in the country, of course,' honked Champagne. 'Where the hell else does any self-respecting rock star live? I'm going to be lady of the manor. Opening fêtes, local hunt, that sort of stuff.'

'I thought you said you weren't the hunting type,' said Jane.

'Yah. Loathe it,' bawled Champagne. 'All that effort to look like a place mat. But they look rather sweet milling about the lawn. We're going to see a place tomorrow, s'matter of fact.'

'Where?' asked Jane, scribbling away. This was perfect column fodder. 'I mean, what county is it in?'

'Dunno. England, I think. Place has a very odd name. Called Millions. Very appropriate for Conal, I must say. Haw haw haw.'

Jane put down the telephone, feeling numb. So Conal O'Shaughnessy was the rock star Tally had been talking about. Poor old thing. She had no idea what was about to hit her.

Chapter 9

Tally sloshed the whisky into her mug. She felt in dire need of a stiff drink. 'I know it's not six o'clock yet,' she said to herself. 'But it must be six o'clock somewhere in the world.'

It was, in fact, just before twelve. Conal O'Shaughnessy and Champagne D'Vyne were coming to view the house at noon. Pacing backwards and forwards over the black and white squares of the Marble Hall, Tally's mind dwelled on every ghastly detail Jane had told her about Champagne. She could hardly believe such a person existed. Yet, sighed Tally, if her mother was forcing her to sell her home there was no use crying over spilt ilk. Money talked, although she wasn't entirely sure she liked what it said. Breeding, these days, was something Japanese people did when they cut themselves.

Tally took another sip. The whisky helped calm her jangling nerves. She gazed at the mug as she raised it to her lips. It depicted a strange-looking creature with what looked like an upside-down coathanger protruding from its head and bore the legend Tinky Winky. The mug had been a present from Piers and Tally had never understood what it represented.

There was a lot Tally had never understood about her brother. Least of all why he seemed to think some rotten old scrubland outside an airport was more worth preserving than four centuries of family history. But to be fair, Tally thought, gasping as the iodine taste of the whisky blazed a trail down her throat, it was entirely possible that Piers, uncontactable and out of reach, didn't have the faintest idea what was happening at Mullions. She sniffed at the remaining alcohol in the bottom of the mug. Was it peaty island malt or TCP? It wasn't the first time she had suspected Mrs Ormondroyd of adulterating the bottles.

Tally gazed despairingly out through the vast and dusty floor-length windows of the Marble Hall. It was raining, as it had been ever since Julia and Big Horn had performed their rain dance for the benefit of Mr Peters' roses. That had been over a week ago. Big Horn and Julia had now jetted off in search of their inner selves, leaving behind them a swamp that was once a rose garden and a soggy hole where the ceiling of the Chinese Bedroom used to be. Tally had spent the morning trying to clear up the mess.

She sighed. Never had getting Mullions back on its feet seemed such an utterly hopeless prospect. She was getting tired of the struggle, not to mention cold and wet of it. Jane, on the other hand, had been firing on all cylinders when she called her about Amanda's dinner party, which she seemed convinced would provide the answer to all Mullions' problems. Jane had even urged her to get a facial. 'Oh, and go and buy something new to wear,' she had instructed. 'Something sexy.' Tally sighed again. Jane had to be joking. Shopping, in Lower Bulge, was Shangri-la if your idea of sartorial heaven was American Tan tights. And she couldn't even afford those. Still, there seemed no reason not to go to the dinner. It meant an evening away from Mrs Ormondroyd's cooking at least.

Spring had yet to make an impact on the naked trees in Mullions' park, which looked miserably bronchial, their bunched, vein-like branches black and lumpy against the sky. The mangy grass looked even patchier when wet and Tally could see that the bulrushes in the oxbow lake were getting out of hand again. Why didn't Mr Peters do something about it? she fretted. Well, he never had before, so he was unlikely to start now, especially after Julia's parting request was to ask him to make her a didgeridoo out of one of the Elizabethan bedposts. Unlike Tally, who had been beside herself at the casual vandalism of the idea, Mr Peters' objections sprang from his misapprehension that a didgeridoo was a sex aid. He had stormed off in high dudgeon and had not been seen since.

Suddenly, a long, white limo with blacked out windows glided into view and proceeded swiftly up the drive towards her. Tally knocked back the rest of whatever brew was in her mug and realised, panicking, that it was now too late to change clothes. The combination of her father's hunting pink, one of her mother's old tweed skirts and a pair of wellingtons would just have to do. She ran a hand hastily through her hair, hoping it was still reasonably presentable. She had brushed it yesterday, after all.

Giving herself a hurried spit wash, Tally rounded the corner of the house from the kitchen door, rubbing her forehead furiously. She was just in time to see a spoilt-looking blonde struggling out of the back of the car, her progress impeded by a tiny green miniskirt and perilously high heels. Tally gasped. Jane had warned her that Champagne was a beast but not that she was a beauty. The girl now swaying slightly on stilettos on the gravel had the rippling blonde mane, large eyes and full lips of a Botticelli angel. Tally blushed for her own red-tipped nose and scraped-back hair.

Champagne's tiny skirt stopped at a point obviously designed to make her beautiful, tanned, finely-muscled legs look longest. Her minuscule blouse was made from a matt material Tally had never seen before, with a rippling, liquid, milky texture that clung to Champagne's bronzed and rounded breasts, exposing a wealth of golden if goosepimpled flesh. She certainly wasn't dressed for looking round a cold and draughty country house. Tally, who was, shifted uncomfortably in her ancient and mud-stained wellingtons. She felt like a cross between the town crier and the village idiot. And, from the way Champagne was staring rudely at her, she obviously looked that way too.

'Christ, what an old *dump*,' Champagne honked, lighting a cigarette. Her brilliant grass-green gaze swept pitilessly over the crumbling, wet bricks and soaked window frames which looked at their most irredeemably rotten in the rain. 'Could you tell whoever is in charge here,' she ordered in loud and patronising tones, 'that Miss Champagne D'Vyne has come to look round the house.'

'Actually, that's me,' muttered Tally, embarrassed. 'I live here. I'm Natalia Venery. How do you do.' It was only after she had stuck her hand out that she realised her palms still carried a fair proportion of the Chinese Bedroom with them. Champagne recoiled.

'I didn't realise you were coming alone,' Tally said, feeling rather disappointed. She realised she had been secretly looking forward to meeting the famously sexy rock star Jane had told her about. There hadn't been such a high-profile musician at Mullions since Thomas Tallis had dropped by in 1580.

'Yes, well, can't be helped,' snapped Champagne. 'Conal can't come this morning, and as I'm in charge of spending his money anyway, I thought I might as well give the place the once-over myself.'

'I suppose he must be very busy,' Tally said brightly.

Champagne frowned. 'I'm pretty bloody busy *myself*, actually,' she said indignantly. 'I've got ten parties, three premieres, a dress fitting and a skin peel to cram in before the end of the week. Conal's only got the Brit Awards and a court appearance.'

'A court appearance?' asked Tally, before she could stop herself. 'Oh dear.'

'Yah,' drawled Champagne, her heels scraping on the mossy stones as she tottered in Tally's wake round the side of the house. 'It's very boring. Some ghastly drummer the Action Liposomes had long before they became famous has crawled out of the woodwork. He's saying that *he* wrote "Hot To Trot" and has the rights to all the profits from it. So he's suing Conal. Can you bloody *believe* it?'

'How dreadful,' said Tally, grateful to Jane for her crash course in popular culture, thanks to which she knew 'Hot To Trot' was the Action Liposomes' mega-selling hit and not a racehorse, as she would otherwise have assumed.

'Oh, it's all a fuss about nothing, of course,' Champagne said dismissively, pausing theatrically by the back door. 'Conal says the guy's just trying it on. Jealousy, you see. People can't cope with other people's success. It's just one of those ghastly things that happens to you when you're famous. Believe me, I *know*. People have no *idea* how hard you have to work to be successful. The *sacrifices* you have to make. Oh no, they just try and put you down. People want to put *me* down all the time.'

'Really?' said Tally mildly.

'Yah,' howled Champagne, whipping herself into a frenzy of self-pity. 'I mean, people think I have the most *amazingly* glamorous life. But I don't. I get parking tickets on the Bentley just like everybody else. *I've* had to wait for delayed Concordes as well.'

There was a silence. Tally shifted from wellington to wellington, not quite knowing what to say. 'Would you like to see round?' she ventured nervously.

Champagne nodded and took another drag of her cigarette. 'Bit remote out here, isn't it?' she barked, suddenly, as if the thought had only just occurred to her. Under her thick eyeliner, her eyes snapped suspiciously around. She cocked her head in the direction of the few desultorily twittering birds that could be heard. 'Very quiet,' she boomed. 'Where's the nearest Joseph?'

Tally looked blank. 'Um, in the village church, I should imagine,' she said, puzzled. Champagne had not struck her as the pious type.

'What?' honked Champagne, her face contorted with contemptuous amazement. 'I mean Prada, Gucci, Joseph. Where do you go for retail therapy?' she shouted, as if to a moron. 'Shopping!'

'Oh, um, there's the village for milk and stamps and things,' Tally stuttered, panicked. 'Lower Bulge, it's called.'

Champagne threw her head back and laughed. 'Lower Bulge! Definitely my kind of town. Is there an Upper Bulge as well?'

Tally nodded, trying not to look too offended. 'Yes, there is, as a matter of fact.'

Champagne laughed so much she almost lost her balance on the mossy, cracked path. To hide her blushes and confusion, Tally started to force open the door of the kitchen entrance, which had swelled and stuck again with the damp. It took a few minutes.

'What time do you have to get up to milk the pheasants round here?' Champagne demanded as she strode ahead of Tally into the kitchen only to collide with Mrs Ormondroyd carrying a big bowl of evil-looking slop towards the back door.

'Ugghh!' shrieked Champagne.

The housekeeper looked thunderous.

'This is Mrs Ormondroyd,' stammered Tally. 'She's the housekeeper here. Mrs Ormondroyd, this is Miss D'Vyne. She's come to look at the house.'

'Charmed, I'm sure,' muttered Mrs Ormondroyd, sounding anything but. She took in Champagne's scanty clothing with a single, withering stare. Like a threatened peacock, Champagne immediately pushed her cleavage out still further and looked contemptuously at the housekeeper's nylon overall. The standoff ended only when Mrs Ormondroyd, who was still holding the slop bowl, moved off with massive dignity through the back door, where she could be heard emptying it down the drain. Tally let out a silent sigh of relief. The slop wasn't supper then, after all. 'Christ,' said Champagne. 'What a dragon.'

'Her heart's in the right place,' said Tally loyally.

'Shame nothing else is,' remarked Champagne. 'She looks like someone's driven over her face.'

Tally prayed Mrs Ormondroyd hadn't overheard. She would, she knew, be lucky if tonight's Brown Windsor was even tepid. Or brown, come to that. She led

Champagne down the kitchen passage into the Marble Hall.

'It's *freezing*,' bawled Champagne 'Haven't you got any central heating?'

'Just one old and rather unreliable boiler, I'm afraid,' faltered Tally.

'We just met. Back there. Haw haw haw,' honked Champagne. There was a distant crash from the direction of the kitchen. Bang go the chops as well, thought Tally. She realised, guiltily, that the prospect wasn't too disappointing. 'We have some wonderful statues,' Tally said quickly, gesturing at the marble figures surrounding them. 'They're considered very fine.'

Much to her amazement, Champagne gazed at them. 'Talk about a six-pack,' she exclaimed, running her hand over the muscular stomach of Mars.

'It's a copy from Praxiteles, actually,' corrected Tally.

'You trying to be funny?' Champagne snapped.

Tally swallowed. She decided to try and interest Champagne in the portraits. 'These are all Venerys,' she said, waving an arm in the direction of the Ancestors.

Champagne looked at them with interest. 'Filthy bastards,' she pronounced delightedly, after peering at them for a few seconds. 'On the other hand, it's pretty obvious from their weird red noses.'

'I'm sorry?' said Tally, taken aback. The Ancestors' eyes were visibly bulging. More blue veins than the painters had ever intended stood out from the canvases.

'You just said they were all venereal,' honked

Champagne. There was a visible frisson of fury from the pictures on the wall.

'No, no, not at all,' said Tally, horrified. 'Venery is the family name.'

Champagne raked the portraits over again with her brutally frank gaze. 'Oh,' she said. 'Still, who on earth would want to have sex with that lot anyway?'

'Would you like to see some other paintings?' Tally said brightly, aware of the Ancestors' painted pupils boring furiously into her back. 'We have a very important Dutch School in the Green Drawing Room.'

'How *boring*,' Champagne boomed. 'Who on earth wants to look at a painting of a *Dutch school*?'

To say that Champagne held the treasures of Mullions in low esteem was an understatement. Fifteen minutes later, Tally was close to despair. When shown Queen Victoria's corset, which lay in a display case in the Green Drawing Room, Champagne had expressed disgust that the Queen-Empress wore such filthy old underwear. She had been interested in the Library until she realised it contained no videos. Tally's offer to show her the Grinling Gibbons elicited enthusiasm until she proudly brought Champagne before the carved Blue Room fireplace and was asked where the monkeys were. Tally's explanation that the tapestries were by Gobelins met with blank disbelief. 'But how could they reach?' Champagne stormed.

Nor had she been impressed by Tally's self-deprecating explanation that the nearest Mullions got to an indoor pool was the parts that the fire buckets dotted about to catch the rainwater could not reach. What Champagne really wanted, Tally realised, was not a country house but a country house *hotel*. And, probably, the more overheated, overstuffed, overdecorated and overpriced the better.

There seemed scarcely any point in showing Champagne the bedrooms, but she insisted. She also insisted on grinding out her fifth cigarette in the ancient oak of the staircase. And it was as a near-desperate Tally led the way up to the first floor that disaster struck. As Champagne staggered by, her high heels sinking into the soft old oak, one of the biggest portraits of the Ancestors suddenly broke free of the wall, swung drunkenly on one nail and fell. The heavy frame containing the Third Earl crashed just inches from Champagne's feet. Another nanosecond and her skull would have been smashed. Oh, for another nanosecond, Tally thought. After all, Champagne's skull wouldn't have made much of a mess. It wasn't as if there were brains in it.

It took almost a full minute for Champagne to realise she was still alive. Her green eyes widened and her vast red mouth opened in a roar that brought down an avalanche of plaster and almost the rest of the portraits as well. 'Get me out of this hideous dump,' she screamed at Tally. 'Now! It's *disgusting*. I *hate* it. I don't want to live in some old *shithole* with walls covered in venereal disease and *goblins*! We're going to St John's Wood like everybody else. If it's good enough for Liam and Patsy, it's good enough for Conal and me.'

When the white limo finally disappeared from sight, a hugely relieved Tally examined the fallen picture. Miraculously, the heavy Jacobean frame had hardly a scratch, and the stairs had not sustained too much damage either. Tally sank to her knees on the damp marble floor and gazed around her. The Ancestors, their equilibrium apparently restored, gazed at her with approval. She could have sworn that there were twinkles in some of their painted eyes.

She pulled a face at them and sighed. Selling Mullions was going to be even more difficult than she had first thought. Particularly now the house seemed to have taken matters into its own hands.

Chapter 10

'Oh dear,' said Josh, devouring the front page of the *Sun*. 'He's been knocked off the number one spot and is plunging down the charts.'

It was a week later. Jane looked up from the papers in which she, too, was reading the sorry tale of how Conal O'Shaughnessy had lost his case against his former drummer. 'Hot To Trot' had after all been ruled to be the creation of one Darren Diggle from Wigan, to whom the humiliated heart-throb had been forced to pay a multimillion-pound compensation package.

'And you know what that means,' crowed Josh. 'Goodbye, Champagne. Farewell, my bubbly.' He was clearly thrilled. All stories about Champagne were good news for *Gorgeous*, as, Champagne being their columnist, the magazine always got a mention.

'That's nice,' said Valentine. 'Dumping him just before they were about to get married. What about for richer, for poorer? The poor sod needs her support.'

'Champagne would certainly have had the "for poorer" bit written out of the marriage service,' said Jane. 'And I don't think support is her strong point. You can tell that from looking at her underwear.'

When Champagne rang, Josh was proved right. She had had absolutely no scruples in dropping O'Shaughnessy like a shot. 'Rather a pity, really,' she honked to Jane. 'I never liked his music all that much, and quite frankly he was a bit common. But he really had the most *enormous* willy.'

Jane's thoughts instantly flew to the other person she knew who was similarly equipped. She swallowed, but looked determinedly on the bright side. At least Champagne wasn't getting married now. She would be spared the details of bridesmaids, luxury Portaloos, honeymoons and the rest of it. And all for a marriage that probably wouldn't have lasted five minutes anyway. Jane had little doubt Champagne would have dumped O'Shaughnessy without a qualm the moment a better prospect presented himself. Champagne's idea of emotional baggage, after all, was being fond of her Louis Vuitton.

It was more than enough to make even Elizabeth Taylor feel cynical about marriage, Jane decided. And to think she had so fervently wanted a wedding herself. To Nick, of all people, who still rolled up at the flat with almost weekly regularity, ostensibly to unearth another armful of embarrassing albums and a mouldering jumper or two. Jane, however, suspected the real reason was to check she had not moved somewhere else. If only she had the energy to, she thought sadly. But at the moment the last thing Jane felt like doing on a Saturday was trailing miserably around the type of peeling, smelly South London prison-cell bedsits her single salary could afford.

Spending Saturday househunting would, however, have one distinct advantage. It would keep her away from the shops. Jane had always known life as a single woman was a social minefield. But it was not until the eggs-in-wrong-basket incident at the supermarket that she had realised it was a shopping one as well.

Saturday shopping, Jane had come to realise, actively conspired against the single. A recent visit to Heal's had almost resulted in a nervous breakdown as she found herself alone amid a sigh of blissed-out couples testing out vast, comfy sofas with names like Figaro and Turandot and bouncing up and down on enormous beds called Renoir and Picasso. As she fled from the mass of the young, beautiful and sexually fulfilled, Jane wondered vaguely what Thackeray would have made of the CD rack his name had been so freely given to, and also which of the Brontës the elegant silver wine rack was honouring. The alcoholic Branwell, perhaps?

There was no escape in John Lewis, where Jane found herself at close quarters with yet more cheerful couples weighing up the rival claims of seagrass and seisal. At Harvey Nicks, beautiful thin girls with perfect bottoms and unstructured-linen-clad boyfriends compared brands of aubergine crisps in the food hall, while at Selfridges dreamy twosomes dithered over duvets.

Sainsbury's check-out queues were nothing less than a conspiracy of besotted lovers with trolleys full of rocket salad, parmesan, vine-grown tomatoes and champagne. Usually, Jane made her way home from these excursions with nothing but M&S knickers and a huge single-woman-sized chip on her shoulder.

Still, hope was in sight. There was Amanda's dinner party to look forward to. At least that should sort out Tally. Jane was beginning to realise she was rather counting on a result from it herself.

Champagne, by way of profound contrast, lasted barely twenty-four hours without a new man on her arm. Jane opened the papers two days later to find the centre spreads of the tabloids devoted to a shot of Champagne, skirt riding up to her waist and apparently innocent of underwear, snogging someone in the back of a limousine. The snoggee, according to the practically identical accompanying reports, was 'one of London's most eligible bachelors, dashing millionaire property developer Saul Dewsbury'.

'She's certainly met her match this time,' Valentine remarked. 'So to speak. Because from what I hear, Saul Dewsbury's responsible for more burnt fingers than the Spanish Inquisition.'

According to Valentine, Dewsbury had a reputation for being as ruthless in the bedroom as he was in the boardroom. Valentine accordingly suspected his liaison with Champagne was as much about business as it was about pleasure. 'It usually is,' he said. 'My father's in property, so I've heard a few stories about Dewsbury.

His last girlfriend's father was leader of a council where he was apparently trying to get planning permission for some Princess Diana-themed wine bars. Dewsbury dumped her as soon as it was granted. And I think he got about five hundred acres of prime Sussex countryside out of someone else, which apparently he's made into a Space Experience.'

Jane sighed. 'That column's going to have more plugs than the John Lewis homes department. Not that it doesn't already.'

Her fears were justified. Suddenly Champagne, followed by the ever-eager paparazzi, seemed to be spending her entire life in one or other of the businesses in which Dewsbury had an interest. These ranged from a West End theatre which Dewsbury was converting into luxury flats with individual lifts and plunge pools, to a disused medieval City church he was transforming into a nightclub. A Georgian townhouse had just been demolished in all but façade to accommodate a gym for the twenty-second century, whose colour-sensitive walls would reflect the collective mood of the gym-goers.

'Talk about making hay while the *Sun* shines,' remarked Valentine one day, scrutinising a picture of Champagne in a sparkling leotard bicycling for all she was worth while the wall behind her loomed an ominous black. 'It's ridiculous. The column's practically a prospectus for Dewsbury at the moment.'

In the end, Jane lost her patience. 'I've told her we're not running another word about him,' she told Valentine a day or so later. 'I absolutely refuse ever to plug him again. Champagne's furious. She says she couldn't think of anything else to say. Claims to have writer's block.'

'Well, I'd agree with the block bit,' said Valentine.

Champagne, however, seemed to be utterly in Dewsbury's thrall. And looking at the pictures of them that appeared almost daily in the papers, Jane didn't find it too hard to see why. Extremely handsome, and with cheekbones so sharp you could cut cigars on them, Dewsbury looked as cool and dangerous as a Smith & Wesson on ice. Thrillingly ruthless, thought Jane, feeling herself going emerald with envy. Damn Champagne. It wasn't fair how men came buzzing round her like bees to a honeypot. Or, in Dewsbury's case, a moneypot.

On the day of Amanda's dinner party, Jane finally screwed her courage to the *placement* and called her to say Tally would be replacing Nick as her partner that evening. Amanda's voice had been acquiescent, but tight. 'So up herself she could practically tickle her tonsils,' Jane giggled to Tally over a pre-dinner party departure gin and tonic in the flat.

'And her husband's so boring,' whinged Tally, who seemed to be going off the whole idea.

'He definitely puts the Square in Square Mile,' said Jane. 'But just imagine his incentive package. More to the point, think of those of his friends.'

Amanda cast a satisfied glance around the bathroom. She was particularly proud of the fleur-de-lis lavatory paper. To most people, the Balkan war had meant mass graves and Radovan Karadzic. To Amanda, watching the highlights on breakfast TV as she lunged backwards and forwards on her rowing machine, it meant that attractive Bosnian fleur-de-lis shield.

The hall was faintly scented from the light bulbs dabbed with essential oils. Not for the first time, Amanda congratulated herself on selecting precisely the right shade of paint for the walls. Biscotti, with the dado and picture rails picked out in Etruscan. She looked round brightly as she descended the stairs, the half-smile on her face fading as she noticed the morning's copy of *La Republicca* loitering unread on the doormat. She hated being reminded that, having decided to take the paper to practise Italian for their Tuscan holidays, neither she nor Peter ever bothered to look at it.

She bent over the banister to look down into the basement kitchen. Yes, there was Peter, by the Aga, chopping chillis as requested. He looked distracted, as usual. The dinner party would, if nothing else, be a chance for her to catch up with whatever was going on in his head at the moment. Peter was always too tired when he came home to tell her anything. But at table, he would have to regale their guests with something of what had happened in his life for the past month or so. Really, dinners were quite useful in that way if you thought about it.

She trotted into the sitting room (or was it drawing room, she never could decide) to plump up the Kettle

Chips. 'Peter,' she called. 'Peter, darling. Have you remembered to slice the lemons for the gin and tonic?'

There was no reply from the kitchen. Amanda returned to peer down over the banister. Her husband was nowhere to be seen. Panic shot up Amanda's gorge. It was almost eight sixteen. People would be arriving any minute. She hated it when everyone came en masse, requiring one to perform the feat of taking coats, pouring drinks and making small talk simultaneously.

Dashing inelegantly up the elegant, sweeping staircase to the first floor, Amanda banged on the bathroom door. A faint gasping could be heard from inside. Amanda shoved it open. She screamed.

Towering over the washbasin, her husband had his trousers down and his penis flopped into a sinkful of cold water. 'Peter,' she stammered, realising that, subconsciously, this was the moment she had always been expecting. The reason for his distraction. The moment when Peter confessed that his suppressed passion for Fish Minor back in the fourth form was why he could never love her as a woman needed to be loved. Amanda gazed at him in wide-eyed, speechless anguish.

'Sorry,' Peter said matter-of-factly, straining a watery-eyed smile in her direction. 'Just had a pee and forgot I'd been chopping chillis. Dick feels like it's on fire. Talk about a red-hot poker.'

Amanda descended in disgust. As if she hadn't enough to put up with. First there had been that wretched Jane Bentley ruining her *placement* by saying she was turning up with Natalia Venery instead of her boyfriend. Please God they weren't going *out* with each other, thought Amanda, sending up silent prayers in the direction of the decorative baskets suspended from the oak-effect kitchen beams. Merchant banks were hardly bastions of liberalism. A couple of lesbians at table could scupper Peter's chances of promotion until well into the next century. Then there had been that arrogant bastard Saul Dewsbury who had called at the eleventh hour – quite literally, at eleven o'clock that morning – to say not only would his girlfriend and Amanda's star guest, Champagne D'Vyne, not be coming, but he doubted he could make it himself.

Amanda stole a look through the glass oven door. There sat the boeuf en daube and the luxury coquilles St Jacques warming beneath. Thank goodness there were some things, Harrods Food Hall for instance, that never let you down.

She shuddered. It had been a close-run thing with Dewsbury; for a few minutes, her numbers had hung precariously in the balance. He had agreed to come in the end, though only after Amanda had gone through the rest of the guest list with him. He'd made an abrupt volte-face after that – there was obviously someone he wanted to meet.

But who? Amanda racked her brains as she circled the dining table, making sure the forks were tines down in the French style. Probably it was the deeply dishy Mark Stackable, the unfeasibly young head of investment with Peter's firm Goldman's. Through the medium of Peter, Dewsbury had often tried, without success, to get Stackable to underwrite his projects in the past. He was probably trying again. At the thought of Stackable, Amanda felt a frisson in her gusset. It wasn't just out of politeness she'd placed him next to her at table.

She scattered the cushions a little more, and gave a final ruffle to her artful-casual arrangement of glossy magazines. Then again, Dewsbury might well be wanting to catch up with Nicola Pitbull, Goldman's head of development. It was unlikely he had any interest in meeting her useless and deeply embarrassing artist husband Ivo who everyone thought must have got something on Nicola, otherwise she would never be seen dead with him. Not for the first time, Amanda wondered what that something was.

Apart from herself and Peter, that only left Sholto Binge, a financial journalist who was an old school friend of Peter's, and of course Jane and Tally. None of whom Dewsbury would give two hoots about.

'Everyone here now, darling?' Peter hissed half an hour later, as, firebucket style, he relayed the gins and tonic from the kitchen to Amanda in the hall.

'Apart from Saul,' said Amanda through clenched teeth. 'Honestly, the *cheek* of the man. I practically had to *beg* him to come, and now he's late. *Christ*,' she added, glancing through the sitting-room door at her guests. 'Ivo's eating the potpourri. He must think it's vegetable crisps. I'd better go.' She snatched up a bowl of Japanese crackers and dashed to the rescue.

'Ivo, my darling,' said Amanda, gliding up to him with the bowl. 'Do try some of these. They're delicious.'

Ivo stretched out a hand and stuffed one into his mouth. 'Hmm,' he said, after chewing for a few seconds. 'Not mad about peanuts, actually. Think I prefer the other things.'

'Have you met Natalia Venery?' Amanda interjected hastily, before Ivo could resume his consumption of Elizabethan Rose.

Tally, draped on a piano stool next to Ivo, nodded. 'Yes. We're having a lovely chat,' she said, gazing at Amanda with large and pleading eyes. Amanda, either unable or reluctant to realise that this was SOS code for Tally's having failed utterly to light the conversational blue touchpaper and wanting help, moved complacently on to the large navy-blue damask sofa where Jane was trying to put as much space as possible between herself and an edgy, skinny blonde wearing a bright red suit. The blonde was smoking furiously, a deep frown creasing the space between eyebrows so plucked they were practically nonexistent.

'Oh, I see you've met Nicola, Jane,' smiled Amanda. 'Works with Peter. Married to Ivo, who's sitting down over there next to Tally.'

'Yes,' said Jane. She was furnished with all the information already. Nicola had rapped it out before lapsing into a sullen silence. She had pointedly not asked Jane any questions at all. Jane cursed herself for having let Amanda plonk her down here. Her hostess had seemed determined she should stop talking to the dark-haired American still standing with Peter over by the piano. They'd arrived at the same time and he'd introduced himself as Mark Stackable, a banker from the same firm as Peter.

He was so handsome she hadn't even sniggered at his name. She stared over the room at him now. He was gorgeous. *And* smart. His expensive-looking suit gave way to a crisp white shirt which set off a tan just the right side of improbable. He looked, Jane thought, as if he could show a girl a good time. Though which girl, if it came to a choice between herself and Tally, remained to be seen.

She looked across at Tally, still valiantly trying to kick-start a conversation with Ivo. As instructed, she had made an effort, and as a result her usual eccentric appearance was so toned down it could even pass for classic-with-a-twist. The classic was the perfectly-cut black dress which looked like one of Tally's more successful raids on her mother's wardrobe. It showed off her long legs to perfection, and played down the broadness of her shoulders so that her bare arms looked elegant and endless. The twist was the battered fuchsia feather boa that Tally clutched and tore at nervously with her long thin fingers, but this, Jane noted approvingly, actually reinforced the bohemian-aristo air of Bloomsbury that hung about her milk-white skin, piled-up hair and huge grey eyes. Tally looked, in short, unprecedentedly presentable.

Jane shifted uncomfortably in the black silk shirt and narrow cigarette pants she had hoped trumpeted to the world her recent weight loss. She had looked positively svelte in the full-length mirror (a first), and had felt sufficiently emboldened to slick on a mouthful of Mon Rouge. Now, compared to a Tally bordering on the beautiful, she wondered if she'd made enough of an effort. After all, it was a two-horse race now.

'Nicola's the top woman at Goldman's.' Amanda yanked her back from dreamland and deposited her next to the blonde again. 'She's *terrifyingly* successful!'

Why not just give me her CV and have done with it? thought Jane, expecting to hear Nicola's bra size next. Not that she looked like she needed one. Nicola was so flat-chested, Jane thought waspishly, her only possible use for bras would be for the identification of sex in the event of an accident.

'What do you do?' asked Nicola languidly, obviously already uninterested in the reply. Jane stared regretfully at her empty gin and tonic glass and prepared to address the heart-sinking question. In her book, 'And what do you do?' came second only to 'Have you discovered the love of Jesus?' as a conversational show-stopper.

'Jane's a journalist,' said Amanda brightly. 'Be careful what you say to her,' she added gaily as she strutted off across the carpet towards Sholto. 'You know what these wicked journalists are like.'

Sholto, catching the end of the sentence, beamed at her. 'You *are* a tease,' he said admiringly.

'I work on *Gorgeous*,' Jane admitted, blushing. She could imagine the contempt with which Nicola, who had probably smashed more glass ceilings than the Crystal Palace demolition gang, would regard a society glossy.

Nicola stared at her. Jane shrank from her gaze.

'The one with the Champagne D'Vyne column, isn't it?'

Jane blushed again and nodded, embarrassed. She was surprised Nicola had even seen Champagne's column. Surely she was too busy being a Mistress of the Universe to read anything other than the share prices.

To her amazement, Nicola melted. 'Oh, but I *love* that column,' she gushed. 'It's wonderful.'

'So do I,' piped up Amanda, making a return circuit with a bowl of pistachios in one hand and the rescued bowl of Elizabethan Rose in the other. She proffered the pistachios. 'I *adore* it. And *so* interesting you should be talking about that, because tonight someone who knows—'

'It's true that she doesn't *write* it, isn't it?' Nicola interrupted.

Jane jolted with shock. Did people actually know then? Was recognition round the corner at last?

'I heard she doesn't write a word,' Nicola persisted.

Jane nodded, feeling months of pent-up frustration prepare to pour itself out to a sympathetic audience. 'Absolutely,' she began.

'Not as much as a full stop,' added Nicola, inhaling half her cigarette in her excitement.

'Not even a comma,' Jane agreed. 'I—'

'No, her agent does everything,' said Nicola gleefully.

'What?' Jane felt the ebullience drain out of her, slide over the sofa cushions and disappear under one of Amanda's original-feature Georgian doors.

'Yes, I go to the same gym as her agent,' panted Nicola. 'Guy called Simon. Says he writes every word. Gets absolutely no thanks from Champagne either. Bloody ungrateful, I call it.'

'*Bloody* ungrateful,' added a voice from the doorway. 'But I think you'll find the agent is prone to exaggeration.'

Everyone stared at the newcomer. Black-haired and handsome, he lounged confidently against the door-frame wearing a suit as sharp as a razor. His glittering, black eyes were fixed on Nicola, whose furious expression said louder than words that she wasn't accustomed to being argued with. His sensual lips were pursed in an amused, dangerous, Tybalt-like smile.

'This is Saul Dewsbury, everyone,' said Amanda, proudly. Dewsbury moved across the carpet like a panther, his eyes sweeping the guests. Did Jane imagine it, or did his glance, impenetrable as a tinted limousine window, linger on her a second or two longer than it did on the others?

'I'm *terribly* sorry about Champagne,' Dewsbury said, turning his back to the fireplace and addressing Amanda across the room. 'She was *desperate* to come but she just had to stay in and write her column, I'm afraid.' He shot a look at Nicola. 'Deadlines, you know.'

Amanda nodded eagerly. 'Oh, I'd hate my little dinner party to deprive the rest of the nation of their monthly treat,' she twittered. An explosion of choking filled the room. 'Are you all right, Jane?' asked Amanda, concerned.

'Oh, f-f-fine,' gasped Jane, conscious of Dewsbury's glitter-eyed interest. 'Just went down the wrong way. I'm fine, really.'

'*À table*,' announced Amanda in her best French accent, motioning everyone to head next door into the canteloupe-coloured dining room. Jane looked apprehensively at the thin, grey iron chairs, complete with finials and fragile-looking strips of purple crushed velvet running over the seat and up the back to serve as both backrest and cushion.

Sitting down, she found they were every bit as uncomfortable as they looked. Particularly the prime slot Amanda had waved her to, next to the barking Ivo. There was an empty place between herself and Amanda. Would she hit the jackpot and get Mark Stackable? Or the booby prize, the scary Saul? A flock of butterflies rose in Jane's stomach as she saw Stackable come towards her, and settled down again as he was steered firmly to a seat the other side of Amanda. 'And you're here beside me, Saul,' Amanda called coquettishly, patting the ribbon of velvet between herself and Jane.

Mercifully, Saul was assigned to Amanda for the coquilles St Jacques. Jane, meanwhile, prepared to dig for victory with Ivo. Fortunately, her long apprenticeship getting conversational blood out of a stone with Champagne had its uses.

'What do you do?' She hated herself for asking the

dreaded question, but this was an emergency. She was even prepared to ask him about discovering the love of Jesus if it didn't work. Across the table, Tally flashed her a grin. Jane half scowled back. It was all very well for Tally to look so jolly. She'd landed the coveted seat on the other side of Mark Stackable, and they were already chatting away like old friends. Even more annoyingly, Tally now looked positively gorgeous. The alchemy of the candlelight wiped the redness from her nose, gave her eyes a velvety depth and threw a halo of soft gold about her hair. As she moved her elegant fingers about the stem of her glass, the Venery gold signet ring caught the light.

'I'm an artist,' Ivo said, or sputtered, simultaneously revealing a cavalier attitude to oral hygiene and more plums in his mouth than an orchard of Victorias.

'What sort of an artist?' asked Jane.

'I work with kens, mostly.'

'Kens?' Visions of Barbie's boyfriend and Mr Barlow from *Coronation Street* segued rather confusingly before her.

'That's right,' said Ivo. 'Coca-Cola kens, baked bean kens, tomato kens, you name it. I collect them, crush them and make pictures out of them.'

'Do you wash them first?' asked Jane.

'Not always, etcherly,' said Ivo. Really, his voice was ridiculous, thought Jane. He was so grand he could barely speak. 'You can git some very interesting iffects when the kens are still full. For instance, I orften put a bean ken in the road, wait for a car to run over it and spletter it, then scrape it up and stick it on the kenvess.'

Amanda placed the daube on the table, along with a bowl of what looked like grey mashed potato. Jane's heart sank. Oh no. Of all things in the world she could never digest.

'Artichoke, Jane?' asked Amanda, digging into, and lifting, a huge chunk of the mixture and dolloping it in a heap in front of her. Fartichoke, thought Jane. They never had agreed with her. She looked warily at the grey pile on her plate. It had all-night stomach problems written all over it.

'So you're the famous Jane,' came a silky drawl at her side. 'I'm very glad to meet you at last. I've heard a lot about you, from Champagne.'

Jane looked into Saul's sharp, handsome face. His hooded eyes stared steadily back at her. He raised a single, elegant eyebrow and twisted his full, sensual mouth into the widest and most charming of smiles.

'Yes, well, I suppose I could say the same about you,' Jane said guardedly. She noticed he wore a watch chain. A sharply-folded handkerchief protruded like a knife blade from his waistcoat pocket. Jane took an enormous sip of nerve-steadying wine. 'You're very busy, from what I hear,' she blurted. She found the stillness with which Saul held himself intimidating, like a snake about to strike. 'What do you do to relax?' she added, trying to sound casual. It seemed wise on the whole to get him off the subject of his businesses, given that she had recently tried to ban Champagne from ever mentioning them.

'Oh, this and that,' said Saul, watching amusedly as Jane gulped back more of Peter's best Domaine de Vieux Télégraphe much too quickly. 'I'm quite keen on racing. I have an interest in a couple of racehorses, as a matter of fact.'

'Really?'

'Yes. One's called Dogfood so it knows what's in store for it if it loses. The other's called Knacker's Yard for the same reason.' Saul grinned wolfishly at her. Jane tried to suppress a shiver. He was so cold. She felt like the *Titanic* to his iceberg, but without the warmth and humour the word iceberg normally implies.

'I'm also quite keen on fishing,' said Saul.

He was not the type Jane could easily imagine standing for hours on a riverbank. 'You are?'

'Yes, I'm very fond of getting my rod out,' Saul enlarged. 'At the moment, as it happens, I'm trying to develop the ultimate fly.'

Despite herself, Jane's gaze flashed involuntarily to his crotch.

'Fishing fly,' said Saul, sounding amused. His eyes were curiously expressionless beneath their hoods. 'I'm developing a type of fly which always catches a fish.'

Jane was still not sure if he was teasing her or not.

'The secret,' said Saul, locking her gaze with his own, 'is to attach a female pubic hair to each one.' Embarrassment coursed through her. Ivo, on her other side, was riveted.

'Fish can't resist the female pheromone,' Saul continued. 'And oddly enough, different colours of pubic hair attract different types of fish.' He paused, and raked Jane's fair crown with a meaningful look. 'Salmon, like gentlemen, apparently prefer blondes.'

Ivo sniggered.

Jane became aware that, the other side of Tally, Sholto's interest had now been engaged.

'I say, is that really true?' Sholto asked, his rather Hanoverian, bulging blue eyes protruding even further. His spongy scalp flushed pinker with excitement.

'How very interesting,' Jane muttered, thrusting her fork savagely into the pile of abandoned and cooling artichoke mash.

'Yes, isn't it?' Saul purred. 'I was trying to persuade Champagne that she should mention it in the column, as it must be of interest to a great many readers.'

Something interesting in Champagne's column, thought Jane, would be a first in itself.

'But I understand from Champagne that, how shall I put it, that her column is subject to a certain amount of, er, *censorship*.' Saul gave Jane a dangerous smile.

'You edit Champagne's column rather, er, *enthusiastically*, from what she tells me,' Saul continued glassily.

Jane took an indignant swig. 'What do you mean?'

'I mean,' said Saul softly, his relentless gaze holding her own without blinking, 'that you sometimes even *remove* things she wants to put in.'

'You mean I don't let her plug your flats and gyms the whole time?' Jane snapped, conscious of a churning in her stomach that had nothing to do with the artichokes. 'Well, I'm sorry, but we have a readership to consider. I think they deserve slightly more than just an extended commercial for *your* business interests.'

'Since when did anyone give a toss about the *readers*?' drawled Saul, a sardonic smile playing about his lips. 'There are more important interests to consider. Champagne's, for instance. Not to mention yours.'

'I don't follow,' said Jane.

Saul raised his eyes to heaven and gave her a patronising smile. 'Put it this way,' he said, as if talking to the profoundest idiot. 'I happen to know quite a few things about Champagne.' He pressed his face conspiratorially closer to Jane's. Her nostrils filled with the scent of discreet but expensive aftershave. 'You wouldn't believe what she gets up to in the bedroom, for example,' he whispered. She gazed, fascinated, into his hypnotic eyes. 'Not the sort of things nice girls do at all. I've got photographs, naturally. Think what a shame it would be if they found their way into the, ahem, gutter press.' He paused, and calmly took another sip of wine.

'You *wouldn't*,' stammered Jane. It never occurred to her to doubt that he had the photographs he spoke of. He probably had the soundtrack as well.

'Of *course* not,' Saul smiled. 'Depending, of course, on the sort of, um, *editing* that Champagne's column receives from now on.'

'You mean if I don't plug your businesses you'll give the pictures to the tabloids?'

'I see we understand each other perfectly.' Saul pressed a cool, slim hand on her own hot one.

'What on *earth* are you two whispering about?'

boomed Amanda, trying to sound jolly but feeling rather strained. For the past ten minutes she had been struggling with the realisation that Saul Dewsbury had apparently been persuaded to come to dinner to see, of all people, Jane Bentley. '*Do* tell the rest of us,' she shrilled. 'We're dying to know.'

'Oh, nothing,' stammered Jane.

'Change places for pudding, everyone,' ordered Amanda, piling the plates together and cursing under her breath as she remembered too late her recently-acquired new rule that plates should be taken out individually to the kitchen, as stacking them makes it look as if one is not used to having servants.

Saul was now sandwiched between Nicola, who lost no time in berating him about the colour of the towels in his new health club, and Tally, who began to tell Amanda the latest dramas from Mullions. Jane was hugely relieved to escape the Siege Perilous next to Saul and sit herself next to Mark Stackable who, anticipating the Inevitable Question, immediately started explaining in great detail exactly what it was he did at Goldman's. As she listened, Jane noticed that Saul had stopped listening to Nicola. Much to the latter's annoyance, he was now blatantly eavesdropping on Tally's conversation with Amanda.

'How old did you say your house was, Natalia?' he suddenly asked her. He then launched into so many questions about periods, ageing and background that the place began to sound positively menopausal.

'Is Mullions listed?' he asked Tally lightly.

She shook her head. 'Too run-down and patched up,' she said, 'and we can't get grants to restore anything unless we can raise half the capital ourselves. So selling's the only option, really.' Tally sighed. 'Some more people are coming to look around tomorrow, in fact. Jane's coming up to lend moral support.'

'It's not listed as much as listing,' supplied Jane, who by now had drunk four large glasses of Télégraphe and was feeling wittier than Oscar Wilde. 'I always told Tally it would be the ruin of her.'

Beside her, Mark Stackable sniggered. Jane looked at him in delight. He was young, handsome and no doubt extremely rich. It seemed unbelievable that he had a sense of humour too. Amanda, meanwhile, seemed to have lost hers. She was passing round the petits fours with a face like a cat's bottom. Jane leant towards Stackable trying to expose as much of her cleavage as possible.

'Tell me more about yield curves,' she breathed.

Chapter 11

'So what happened?' asked Tally. 'What did you do after I left?' They were standing in the kitchen at Mullions, which, thanks to the absence of Mrs Ormondroyd and the presence of a number of dusty sunbeams, was looking uncharacteristically cheerful. The light, albeit muted, flooded like headlights on full beam into Jane's leaden eyeballs. It wasn't merely the mother of all hangovers she had. It was the mother-in-law.

'You don't want to know,' said Jane, slumping at the sink. 'Have you any Nurofen?' She wondered miserably if Mullions' plumbing was up to the demands she might be about to make on it.

'But I *do* want to know,' said Tally, gently but insistently. 'You looked near to death when we left this morning and you haven't said a word apart from the occasional "Stop the car, I need to be sick." Now fess up, do.' She placed her mug lightly down on the kitchen table. The noise reverberated round Jane's hypersensitive brain like a thousand slamming doors. She groaned.

'Did anything happen with Mark Stackable?' pursued Tally. 'You were getting on like a house on fire after I left.' She looked hurriedly around at the beamed ceilings and acres of oak kitchen table and quickly touched wood. 'Or perhaps I shouldn't say that. Anyway, you were both shouting your heads off during the Hat Game.'

'What about you and Saul Dewsbury then?' Jane retaliated weakly. 'He gave you a lift back, didn't he?' She must be feeling vaguely better. Until now it had not even occurred to her to wonder what had happened after Tally had taken her flat keys and disappeared with Champagne's saturnine lover.

'Yes, well, I couldn't wait all night for you to leave,' said Tally. 'And Saul drove me to the door. That's all,' she added firmly. There was no question that she wasn't telling the truth. Tally never lied.

'Well, nothing happened with Mark Stackable either,' Jane muttered, pressing her hot hands to her throbbing head. 'At least, not what you think.'

'But you didn't come back to the flat,' Tally murmured. 'I left the window open for you, like you said.'

Jane felt her salivary glands working overtime. Was she about to be sick? And was there a dignified way of telling gentle, strait-laced Tally the ghastly truth? That Mark Stackable had not as much driven but lurched her back to his flat, taken her up into his bedroom and . . .

'Ugh, no, no.' Jane pressed both hands to her temples in an attempt to literally squeeze out what had happened next. Remorselessly, the pictures reeled fuzzily past on the blood-red screen at the back of her eyes. They had even edited themselves down to the most gory bits. The bits where Mark flopped her on to his bed and peeled her clothes off one by one. The bit where he had slowly pushed her legs apart. Then, the crucial moment, the bit where what wasn't supposed to happen had happened. It could not be held back. It had spurted everywhere.

Jane shuddered at the memory. She had practically *exploded*. First she had vomited all over *him*. Then all over his extremely smart Liberty waffle-cotton duvet. Then all over his sisal matting, which Jane knew from experience wasn't easy to get normal dust out of, let alone undigested artichoke mash. '*Nothing* happened,' she wailed to Tally. 'I threw up *everywhere*, fell asleep in a stupor and then snuck out and came home before Mark woke up. It was chaster than a night with the Pope.' It was true. A plateful of Amanda's artichoke mash had turned out to be the ultimate in safe sex. I should, Jane thought bitterly, recommend it to Marie Stopes.

'Oh dear,' said Tally sympathetically. Her eyes drifted faintly towards the back of the kitchen. Had she heard a faint thud? She prayed it wasn't Mrs Ormondroyd smashing yet more of the Sèvres. Then she remembered it couldn't be. Mrs Ormondroyd was away for a few days visiting her ailing sister. Briefly Tally's thoughts seized on the idea of Mrs Ormondroyd coming to one's sickbed. 'How ghastly,' she added.

Jane nodded. Still slumped against the sink, she was beginning to grasp the enormity of what she had almost loved and certainly lost. She'd got within a Y-front of a night of wild passion with a glamorous and sexy man and it had all gone more pear-shaped than a skipful of Conferences. She hadn't been in a fit state for a one-night sit, let alone a one-night stand. And there wouldn't be a second chance, as she could never face Mark Stackable ever again. Jane hung her head in self-disgust. The run of bad luck with men that had started with Nick and hit its lowest ever point with Tom showed no sign of ending. She was, and looked set to remain, officially the most hopeless single girl on the planet.

The faint banging sound continued. 'Oh,' said Tally, light suddenly dawning. 'That must be the managing director of that gourmet sandwich company coming to look at the house. I'd better let him in.'

Jane greeted the news with an unpleasant swirling at the back of her throat and a nauseous lurch in her stomach. She hoped the visitor hadn't brought any of his wares with him.

Several hours later, after poking in every room and cupboard in the house, the captain of the sandwich industry told Tally that Mullions was a tad too small for the global staff incentivisation centre he had in mind. 'On the other hand, "The Mullions" could be a marvellous name for one of our products,' he remarked.

'It could be the flagship sandwich of our new Heritage range. I can see it now, roast pork with apple stuffing in sun-dried aubergine ciabatta with parmeggiano shavings and the merest hint of rocket and pecorino pesto. A real taste of Old England.'

'I'm not sure he was quite the right person,' Tally said after the sandwich Czar had left.

'On the other hand, he certainly wasn't short of bread,' observed Jane.

'Whatever is pecorino?' asked Tally. 'It sounds like a minor Italian painter.'

'Who did you say the next lot were?' Jane asked as a vehicle rounded the last bend and approached the house. Tally peered at the sheet of estate agents' notes on a marble-topped side table in the hall. 'Um, Mr and Mrs Hilton Krankenhaus,' she said. 'Americans,' she added.

'You don't say,' said Jane, as they left the back door and dashed round to the front.

At the foot of the terrace steps, a plush and gleaming hi-tech people carrier was just disgorging its contents. The vast, sports-jacketed man had a head as shiny, pink and moist as boiled ham, whilst at least a third of the height of the fur-swathed, thin-faced woman with him was a mass of sculpted and teased hair. Not so much big hair, thought Jane, as skyscraper. Of a determined auburn, it looked as delicate and brittle as spun sugar.

As they approached, it became obvious that Mrs Krankenhaus's face had more lifts than the Empire State

Building. 'She's had so many tucks she probably farts out of the back of her neck,' whispered Jane. Mrs Krankenhaus's skin was stretched as tight as a drum across the bones of her face; it looked as if it would split if she laughed, although judging from her surgically fixed expression, there didn't seem much danger of that. Vast, knotty gold earrings the size of quails' eggs dragged down her wrinked lobes, and her eyes stared out like glass marbles beneath eyebrows that were a perfect, surprised semicircle of bright orange pencil.

The Krankenhauses evidently expected their arrival to be marked at the very least by the appearance of Anthony Hopkins and Emma Thompson in best *Remains of the Day* fashion. They looked at Jane and Tally with undisguised disappointment. Perhaps we should have put on Elizabethan costume, thought Jane. Then I could have looked as ruff as I feel.

'Hello,' said Tally, stepping forward towards the visitors and holding out her hand. 'Natalia Venery. How do you do?'

'Hilton P. Krankenhaus the Third,' bellowed the man, thrusting forward his unpleasantly clammy palm and almost yanking Tally's arm off. 'Well, let's not hang around, let's git going. Ah didn't git where Ah am today hanging around.' Neither Tally nor Jane had the faintest idea where Hilton P. Krankenhaus had got today. But they guessed they were about to find out.

'Y'heard of Krankenhaus's Catflaps?' Hilton drawled as Tally began to lead him up the Ancestors' staircase. 'Biggest catflap providers in the Yewnited Stites.'

Tally was saved from replying by a commotion at the foot of the stairs.

'Hey! There no elevator here?' shouted Mrs Krankenhaus, wobbling perilously on her high heels as she clung to the newel post.

'Sorry, no,' said Tally.

If Mrs Krankenhaus could have frowned, she would have done so, but the relevant muscles had long since been removed. She hauled herself up the steps one by one, clinging to the banister as she went, with Jane hovering behind in case of disaster. 'These goddam stairs,' cursed Mrs Krankenhaus furiously, an expression of amused surprise fixed permanently on her face. As they passed the Ancestors, Jane felt their painted pupils contract in horror.

'I'm afraid I haven't heard of your catflaps, actually,' said Tally. 'I'm not much of a cat fan, you see,' she added apologetically.

'Doesn't like cats!' Hilton boomed over his shoulder to his wife who, having hauled herself to the top of the stairs, stood there open-mouthed. Not with surprise, however. She was busy checking her lipstick in a clouded, mould-spotted eighteenth-century mirror.

'Can't see a goddam thing in this,' she was muttering to herself, utterly ignoring her husband.

'Well, that's a darn' shame,' Hilton declared to Tally and Jane. 'Cawse the old place would sure liven up with a few moggies around.' Terrifying visions of Ann from *Blissful* and her poorly pussy sprang to Jane's mind.

'This is the Long Gallery,' Tally said, leading the way.

'Uh-huh,' said Krankenhaus noncommittally, casting a cursory glance over the great carved oak double doors that formed the entrance to the passage. Suddenly he stopped and peered at them more closely. Then he slapped his knee. 'Ma!' he exclaimed, sticking his snout-like nose against the wood and beckoning over his wife. 'You'll never guess what these goddam carvings actually say. HK! HK for Hilton Krankenhaus.'

Tally cleared her throat as politely as she could considering the outraged hammering of her heart. 'Actually, it's HK for Henry and Katherine,' she said, rather shrilly. 'Henry the Eighth and his first wife, Katherine of Aragon. The doors were carved for their state visit. In fact, the whole Long Gallery was built for it.'

'King Henry the Eighth of Britain came here?' exclaimed Mrs Krankenhaus, her expressionless marble eyes and immobile forehead belying the amazement in her voice.

'Well, no, as it happens,' Tally confessed. 'He was supposed to, but then the Third Earl, who lived here at the time, caught pneumonia and so the entire royal party went somewhere else. Rather bad luck, actually. But then the Third Earl was known as the Unlucky Earl.'

'I'll say,' said Hilton. 'What a bummer.' He returned to his scrutiny of the carvings. 'These here doors have given me an idea though,' he said to Mrs Krankenhaus. 'Imagine a scaled down, catflap-sized, miniature version of these. In oak. With my initials on them just like this. Classy, huh? They'll go down a storm in the Hamptons. The VIPs'll snap 'em up.'

'Hilton,' said his wife in an irritated voice. 'You know as well as I do that there are no VIPs in the Hamptons.'

'What ya say?' Hilton looked puzzled. It didn't make much sense to Jane either, and Tally had no idea what the Hamptons was.

'There are just Ps, remember?' finished Mrs Krankenhaus magisterially.

Hilton nodded. 'Sure, honey,' he said distractedly, his mind crammed with catflap possibilities. 'Or,' he added excitedly, walking forward into the Long Gallery, 'we could do a catflap that's like a picture, all scaled down in miniature, with a little gold frame round it and all. That miserable son of a bitch over there would do.' He pointed at the age-blackened portrait of a consumptive-looking man in a Regency striped waistcoat.

'That's Lord Vespasian Venery,' said Tally, stung on her ancestor's behalf.

'Yeah, so what's eating him?' asked Krankenhaus, temporarily diverted from the subject of feline exits and entrances.

'Well, he was always rather sickly, and died in a duel in the end,' said Tally, gazing sympathetically into her antecedent's sad eyes with their drooping lids.

'Doesn't look like a fightin' kinda guy to me,' said Krankenhaus dismissively.

'No, he wasn't,' said Tally. 'It wasn't his duel. He

stumbled across someone else's by accident. He had very bad eyesight, you see.'

But Krankenhaus wasn't listening. His attention was now fixed on the linenfold oak panelling which ran the length of the Long Gallery. Tally hoped desperately he had noticed the woodworm. Surely he wouldn't buy the place if he had.

'Come to think of it, this old panelling along here would make a great showroom,' Hilton said, gazing speculatively along the length of the dusty, dark wood corridor with his bulging, boiled-egg eyes. 'You could just cut into the sides here and fix the flaps on. It's a sin to waste a great long room like this. Just imagine,' he added, as the idea took hold, 'fifty Krankenhaus Catflaps lined up all the way down this room, from one end to the other, and cats wandering in and out of 'em all, demonstrating 'em, all day long!'

Tally almost doubled over in horror. She looked at Jane in anguish.

'Ah disagree,' declared Mrs Krankenhaus. Tally and Jane looked at her gratefully. 'Ah think we should rip the lot out,' she pronounced, devastatingly, sweeping a bird-like, ring-encrusted hand through the dusty air. 'These filthy old cushions, for a start,' she said, stabbing with a gleaming red talon at a seat which had once supported Charles I.

Jane caught Tally's agonised glance. Desperate measures were needed. She took a deep breath. 'Quick, look,' she gasped, pointing into the gloomy far corner of the hall. 'Did you see it?'

'What? What?' said both the Krankenhauses.

'A mouse?' squealed Mrs Krankenhaus.

'The Queen,' said Jane in a low whisper.

'The Queen of *England*?' said Mrs Krankenhaus, as if she expected to see the familiar grey-haired, bespectacled figure of Elizabeth II trot briskly out of the shadows with her corgis at her heels.

'Queen Katherine of Aragon,' hissed Jane. 'She never got here in life, but . . .' Her voice fell away dramatically. She could not, in fact, think of anything else to say.

'She haunts Mullions,' Tally hastily joined in, knowing full well that the most the house held by way of apparitions was an occasional wailing from the cellar around Christmas which could have been anything from wind to the seasonal village help whom Mrs Ormondroyd didn't get on with.

The Krankenhauses looked doubtful. 'You mean Her Majesty – her ghost – walks here? In this corridor?' stammered Mrs Krankenhaus.

'Yes,' said Tally cheerily, now safely on the home straight.

'With her head tucked underneath her arm, naturally,' chimed in Jane helpfully, remembering too late that, of Henry VIII's wives, Katherine of Aragon was one of the divorced rather than beheaded or died persuasion. The Krankenhauses did not notice but Tally gave her an icy look.

'Well, isn't that kinda cool, though?' asked Hilton, clamping one huge, reassuring pink hand over his wife's tiny wrist. 'Ah mean, what's an old British home without a ghost? You gotta have one, it seems to me.'

Tally looked horrified. Was defeat to be snatched from the jaws of victory?

Jane's brain raced. 'Er, yes,' she ad-libbed heroically. 'But I think you need to think carefully about the *implications*.'

The Krankenhauses looked at her, puzzled.

'The cats,' Jane explained, as inspiration suddenly, brilliantly, struck. 'Animals react very oddly to supernatural phenomena, as I expect you know. Cats are especially terrified . . .'

Five minutes later, the Krankenhauses had gone amid much scrunching of gravel and grinding of gears. Relieved, Tally watched them depart, her long, lean frame slumped against the floor-length hall windows and her lanky shadow thrown back across the black and white tiles by the fading sun. Jane, also gazing out over the park, admired the way the light was so soft and low you could almost see every blade of grass.

'I love this time of the day,' Tally said. 'It's almost the only time when the light doesn't show what a wreck the poor old place is. And it's so quiet. Nothing and no one else around.'

There was silence for a few minutes. The sun sank further behind the conifers at the edge of the park, which stood as upright as a row of feathers. Red Indian feathers, thought Jane, wondering vaguely what Big Horn and Julia were doing. She gazed out into the gathering darkness so hard that her vision began to swim.

'Tally,' she said suddenly. 'You know what you were just saying about nothing or no one else around?'

'Mmm?'

'Well, it's just that . . . I can see someone coming.'

Tally's drooping eyes snapped open. It was true. A figure, just visible in the misty, milky distance at the bottom of the park, was coming slowly towards them up the drive. Fear gripped Jane's heart. Had Katherine of Aragon finally decided to drop in for a fino before dinner? Most terrifying of all, had Hilton P. Krankenhaus III changed his mind?

The apparition did not pause. It kept moving directly towards them. Neither Tally nor Jane dared stir. Their attention was fixed on the approaching figure, as if merely by staring at it they could somehow deflect it. But it was not to be deflected. Across the bridge and over the ha-ha it came. Round the bend and past the rose garden. Up the steps to the terrace. Hearts thundering, Tally and Jane dashed outside to meet it.

As they approached, they saw that the visitor was neither a coachman nor a headless queen. It was a man in modern dress. Very possibly Gucci.

'Good evening,' he said in a light, well-bred voice that nonetheless held a hint of steel in it. He held out a well-manicured hand to Tally. 'Saul Dewsbury. We met last night.'

Tally flushed. 'Yes, of course.'

'Lovely to see you again,' said Saul, nodding to Jane. His stark impeccability contrasted profoundly with the rioting decadence around him. Absolutely every hair was in place. Even his eyebrows looked groomed. 'It completely slipped my mind last night that I would be in this area on business today,' he said. 'It seemed rude not to drop in. From what you said I thought Mullions would be very beautiful, but it's even lovelier than I expected.' He looked fixedly at Tally as he spoke. To Jane's mixed horror and disgust, Tally actually blushed.

'How is Champagne?' Jane asked pointedly.

'Champagne is very well, thank you,' Saul replied. Jane looked fiercely at Tally to make sure she was taking this in. 'At least, she was the last time I saw her. You see our relationship, unfortunately, is over. As of this morning, in fact.'

Jane stared. Over? So suddenly? She gazed at Saul, who looked back at her boldly, one eyebrow inquiringly raised as if daring her to ask why. Champagne had seemed *terribly* keen on him. Was it possible he had finished with *her*? Could it be that for the first time in her life, Champagne was the dumpee, rather than the dumper?

'Look, I realise it's getting late,' Saul said, giving Tally another of his melting looks, 'but I wonder whether it might be at all possible to see round Mullions. I'd love to see inside what is obviously an exceptional sixteenth-century manor house.'

And could it possibly be, thought Jane, her head buzzing with more wild surmise than Cortes's men in Darien, that Saul had dumped Champagne because of Tally? Throwing over the famous and beautiful Champagne D'Vyne for the plain, flat-chested, decidedly eccentric-looking Tally seemed rather unlikely, admittedly, but what else was he doing here? She didn't believe for a minute his claim to be here on business. Whatever was going on? She had no idea but she knew she didn't like it.

'Oh, yes, of course, I'd love to show you round,' said Tally, beaming at Saul. 'I'd be delighted to. And you must stay and have some supper. Jane's just about to go back to London for work tomorrow, you see, so I'd be glad of the company.'

'No, no, I'm in no hurry,' said Jane, stretching her eyes warningly at Tally. 'I can stay for a while.' Until Saul Dewsbury is safely out of the place, she added to herself.

'You'll need to set off now to miss the Sunday night traffic,' urged Saul. Jane flashed him a furious look. 'Don't worry,' he added, giving her his most charming smile. 'I'll look after Natalia.'

Jane seethed. 'Well, if you're sure?' She made a final, direct appeal to Tally, who nodded and smiled reassuringly.

'I'll be fine,' she said eagerly.

She can't wait to get rid of me too, thought Jane miserably. Barely twenty-four hours after meeting Saul, she's completely under his spell.

Jane felt uneasy all the way back to London and not merely because the 2CV's petrol gauge had rocketed into the red zone. The image of Saul standing proprietorially with Tally on the terrace alternated with last night's ghastly scenes at Mark Stackable's flat. Damn

Amanda. If she hadn't insisted on annexing Mark all the way through dinner, Jane would have established that he was single some considerable time before she was two gins and tonics, a bottle and a half of wine and three ports the worse for wear. At that randy, fuzzy-headed stage even Sholto was beginning to look promising, so Mark's whispered revelation during the coffee that he was still looking for the girl of his dreams had naturally had an electric effect.

Jane had accepted his offer of a lift home with alacrity and, after ten minutes' exposure to the low, thrilling purr of his Porsche Carrera, had jumped at the chance to come up and admire the mosaics in his bathroom. His flat had been extremely glamorous, Jane remembered dimly. It had been more of a loft, with a very fast lift that opened straight into the sitting room. Or perhaps that was just how it had felt.

Jane groaned. The whole ghastly, embarrassing experience could not have been more different than her night with Tom. She sighed, as she always did, at the thought of her by now completely imaginary-seeming lover, so utterly without a trace had he vanished. Recently, she'd even tried tracking him down through his work – if she found his publisher, she thought, then surely she could get his address. She had combed the shelves of every bookshop she came across for writers called Tom, and scoured their book jackets in the hope there might be a photograph of him. There wasn't.

Tom knew where *she* was, of course. But he thought she was living with her long-term boyfriend. Jane's heart sank as she pulled up outside the dingy Clapham flat.

Sliding her key into the lock, Jane felt more of a sense of doom than usual. For starters, some thrash metal band seemed to be playing loud and live directly above her sitting room. Damn Jarvis, she thought, coughing so loudly it hurt her throat, in the hope he would hear her and turn it down. He didn't.

In the corner, the answering machine was winking like a lecher with a twitch. Someone had been leaving a lot of messages. Jane's heart sank as the first one crackled on. It was Champagne.

'Help me. Oh God, help me.' Jane froze to the spot. The familiar, patrician tones sounded weak and desperate. Racking sobs boomed out of the machine's microphone, followed by several loud sniffs and choking coughs. 'Help me. For fuck's sake,' gasped Champagne, 'get over here, quick.' The suspicion that it might be another nail crisis crossed Jane's mind. Failing that, too deep a fake tan? A botched bikini line? On the other hand, did Champagne's desperate state have anything to do with the fact that the relationship with Saul Dewsbury was apparently over and he seemed to be quite happy about it?

The agonised sobs started again. The situation did not sound promising. Jane checked the time the last message was taken – fifteen minutes before. She picked up the phone, called 999 to give them Champagne's address and rushed back out to her car.

Chapter 12

It was not, Jane thought, exactly unusual to see Champagne in the arms of a muscular man. The difference this time was that the man was a paramedic. Draped helplessly across his broad, green boiler-suited chest, Champagne's tiny frame looked infinitely fragile and vulnerable.

'Na, 's all right. She don't weigh *nothing*,' said the paramedic, refusing offers of help from his colleagues. As he lowered Champagne on to the stretcher in the columned entrance hall, Jane felt tears prick the back of her eyes. Her throat ached from suppressed weeping. Champagne, admittedly, had had her irritating side, but not even her worst enemy would have wished her to die like this.

Champagne's head lolled back as the burly paramedic settled her body carefully on the stretcher. He pressed a freckled hand over Champagne's breast and began pumping her chest. Then he gave her mouth-to-mouth resuscitation. Watching his capable, businesslike actions, Jane reflected sadly how having one hand clamped on Champagne's bosom while their lips were locked on hers had once been the stuff of most men's fantasies. It didn't look like a dream come true from where she was standing.

'Well, you called us just in time, love,' said the paramedic, finally seizing the end of the stretcher and preparing to shift Champagne into the ambulance outside. 'Another ten minutes and I reckon she'd have been a goner.'

'You mean she isn't?' asked Jane, who had been convinced she was looking her last on her one-time tormentor. As relief swept over her, she realised how numb she had been feeling before.

'Well, she's taken a massive overdose, but if we get her stomach pumped in time, there may be a chance.' The paramedic looked up at Jane without smiling. 'Well, better get 'er down to A and E. Coming? You 'er next of kin?'

'Er, no,' said Jane, flattered despite the circumstances that anyone could think she and Champagne were related. But then again, looking at Champagne's exhausted, bruised and make-up-less face, perhaps it wasn't such a compliment. 'I'll follow in the car,' she said.

As the ambulance wailed off through the square, Jane did an automatic tour of the flat to make sure doors and windows were shut against burglars. Stooping to check that the curling tongs on the floor beneath the hall mirror were turned off, it struck Jane that any activity in the interests of Champagne's safety should be filed, at least for the moment, under Stable Door, Late Closing Of.

In the stuffy, airless bedroom, the entire contents of Champagne's wardrobe lay scattered about, although whether this was evidence of recent turbulence or Champagne's usual idea of orderliness, Jane could not be sure. Jimmy Choo shoes lay caught in Agent Provocateur underwear; Chanel suits were heaped upon piles of screwed-up pashminas. Selina Blow had fallen, Blow on Blow, and a rainbow tide of shoes ebbed and flowed around the edges of the pile. *Anyone who says money can't buy happiness doesn't know where to shop*, read an embroidered cushion lying amid the unmade bed. It sounded a hollow assertion now. As if in confirmation, a Coutts chequebook lay open on the floor, empty apart from the unfilled-in stubs.

A high-pitched squeaking noise was coming from the unhooked telephone which lay across the bed. Jane softly replaced it. As she did so, her eye was caught by the empty bottle of Krug which had rolled into the corner, its last drops soaking into the carpet. Beside it, a battered childhood teddy bear stood drunkenly on its head. An image of the laughing, blonde, pampered child Champagne had once been flashed before Jane's eyes. How sad that all that had come to all this. And how much sadder, Jane thought, that Champagne apparently had had no one to ask for help apart from herself. If, when in extremis, the only person the It Girl could turn to was the Shit Girl, things had come to a pretty pass. And not a celebrity backstage one at that.

Sitting in the hospital waiting room, Jane tried not to stare at the array of oddly-twisted limbs, bleeding heads and hanging-off fingernails hoping to be treated this side of Christmas. She buried herself instead in a creased and greasy issue of the local freesheet whose main source of stories seemed to be the local police station. Accordingly, the editorial consisted almost entirely of reports of attacks on pensioners, murders, robberies and fights, and did not make for particularly cheerful reading. Looking again at her companions in the waiting room, some of whom seemed to have clashed with something big and angry, Jane realised that she was probably getting a preview of what would be in next week's edition.

When she was finally ushered in to see Champagne, hidden behind bilious green screens in a narrow hospital bed, Jane stifled a gasp. Champagne looked dreadful. Seen in the harsh light of a hospital ward, the emerald eyes looked sunk and defeated and the famous six-seater lips were no more than a camp stool. The even more celebrated breasts looked saggy and deflated, apparently incapable of filling a trainer bra.

'Hello,' Jane whispered as the doctor pushed the screens back together behind her. There didn't seem much point asking Champagne how she was. Jane had often seen Champagne with a drip on her arm, but had never before seen her with one in it.

Champagne opened her eyes and looked straight into Jane's. There was, Jane was relieved to see, a hint of the old boldness there, but something else besides, almost anger, as if Champagne had finally come to realise what a sham her life was and how short-changed she had been by glamour and fame. Their relationship was going to be interesting from now on. Jane tried to imagine life with a chastened Champagne being grateful to her for saving, as she almost certainly had done, her life.

'What the *fuck* took you so long?' rasped out Champagne suddenly. The voice may have been weaker, but its imperiousness was not diminished one jot. Jane almost jumped a foot in the air with shock. It's the drugs talking, she told herself. Whatever were they pumping into her?

'Well, they kept me in the waiting room,' faltered Jane, surprised. 'It took a long time to get whatever it was out of you, the doctor told me. You could have died, you know.'

'Almost bloody did, thanks to you,' Champagne barked. 'Rang you hours ago, but you didn't bother to turn up until I'd practically snuffed it.'

'I don't understand,' Jane stammered. 'You tried to kill yourself. I saved your life. It's not me you should be blaming, it's that bastard Saul Dewsbury. He's the one who dumped you. He's the one who brought you to this.' She was, she knew, jumping to conclusions. But what other explanation was there?

It was Champagne's turn to look amazed. 'Kill

myself?' she echoed. '*Him* dump *me*? You must be joking. I dumped *him*. Yesterday morning, in fact.'

'Dumped *him*?' stammered Jane, struggling to comprehend. Her head was already spinning with lack of sleep and the pitiless strip lighting. So Dewsbury had been lying.

'Too right I dumped him,' rasped Champagne, rolling her eyes. 'He's been boring the arse off me with his ghastly yawnsville businesses for weeks now. I'm sick of the sight of him. Anyway, I found out he hasn't any money. In debt up to his eyeballs. Especially now he's been running *me* for a month.' Her cackling laugh dissolved into a hacking cough.

'So why did you take an overdose? I don't understand.' Jane stared at her.

'For Christ's sake, you don't think I took those pills because of *Saul*, do you?' Champagne looked incredulous. 'They were *sleeping pills*,' she snarled. 'It's an exhausting business, being me, you know. I'm worked into the ground and I need my eight hours' beauty sleep. How the hell was I supposed to know how many pills you should take?'

'How many *did* you take?'

'No idea. Loads, I suppose. Just kept stuffing them in until I felt sleepy. But then I started to feel a bit weird so I rang you.'

Jane stared at the chipped vinyl floor. To think she had actually imagined, even for a second, that Champagne had any capacity for despair, any self-knowledge whatsoever. She should have known. The only deep thing about Champagne was her cleavage.

'But now you mention it,' said Jane, 'why did you ring *me*? There must be lots of other people you, er,' she groped for a phrase, 'um, know better.'

'Oh, yah, quite,' said Champagne airily. 'Stacks. Loads, in fact.' She looked calmly back at Jane.

'So why didn't you tell *them*?'

'I can't *believe* you're asking me this,' Champagne spluttered. 'Surely you don't think I'm stupid enough to risk anyone I know *socially* seeing me zonked out of my head? I didn't even have any *make-up* on. I'd never get asked anywhere again.' She shot Jane a withering look. 'I couldn't have called them anyway,' she added. 'Everyone I know goes out in the evenings. Apart from you.'

'I see,' said Jane, getting to her feet before the urge to pull the drip out of Champagne's arm overwhelmed her. 'I'm afraid I have to leave now,' she muttered.

'Oh, well, thanks for dropping by,' said Champagne sarcastically. 'Eventually,' she added.

'Yes, well, I'll try and be earlier next time,' said Jane with suppressed fury, trying not to think of the wasted six, no, seven hours she had just spent in the hospital and for which she would pay dearly at work tomorrow. Later today, in fact.

'I'll talk to you later this week,' Champagne said airily, by way of farewell. Insulting Jane seemed to have done her the world of good. 'Lots to report. New man, for a start. Met him last night. Footballer, Welsh international who plays for Chelsea. Thighs so huge he can't cross his legs.' Champagne looked pointedly at Jane's far from perfect thighs.

Outside, Jane leaned briefly against the wall and took a deep, shuddering breath before attempting to find her way back down the maze of corridors to the exit. Blundering amid the blinding brightness of the shining vinyl floors, she became dimly aware of a voice calling, 'Excuse me.'

She turned. It was the weary-looking, clipboard-laden houseman who had taken her to Champagne's bed.

'Don't worry, she's going to be fine,' he assured her. 'She'll be out in a few days. She's recovering very well, and should be back to normal in no time.'

'Wonderful,' said Jane dully.

Saul, thought Tally, was a revelation. A miracle, no less. Holed up in her remote, crumbling manor house, she had, after the succession of disastrous would-be buyers, almost given up on ever being rescued. She had started to feel like Tennyson's Mariana of the Moated Grange. Marry Anyone of the Moated Grange, come to that.

What was most gratifying was how much Saul seemed to appreciate the house. 'This place is just *wonderful*,' he said as Tally started her tour. He clasped his hands and gazed around, shaking his head slowly in apparent amazement. 'It has such history. Such atmosphere.'

Such bloody *potential*, he thought to himself, keeping his eyes downcast to disguise their avaricious shine.

He'd had a feeling about this place as soon as Tally had started to talk about it at the dinner party. And what a bonus that had been. He'd gone to Amanda's to warn that uppity bitch Jane to stop cutting him out of Champagne's columns, and come away with an entree into the best deal of his life. Which was just as well considering Champagne had dumped him the next morning. But, if he was honest, that had been something of a relief.

What a lucky dog I am, he reflected gleefully. To lose one golden goose might be seen as careless, but to find another within twenty-four hours was damn near miraculous. And what a golden egg Mullions was. Once you knocked the whole pile down and built a commuter estate in its place, of course. There were *bazillions* to be made here. But he had to be careful. Tally was obviously obsessed with the old heap. Softly softly catchee bulldozer, Saul warned himself, his head bubbling with plans.

'It has such atmosphere,' he repeated, pacing slowly round the drawing room, unable to think of what else to say. If he meant to be convincing, he'd have to work on his architectural vocabulary. Tally would probably prefer he admired her corbels to her cheekbones. He stole a quick glance at her. Not that she had very good ones. Her face was thin and concave, rather like the reflection in a spoon.

'You mean it's freezing and it smells of mildew,' Tally grinned, self-deprecatingly. But she thrilled inside. Saul's interest was a pleasant and profound contrast to the

Krankenhauses, the sandwich king, and most of all Champagne D'Vyne. Not to mention the fact he seemed, well, almost *interested* in her. She shrank from the full beam of his gaze.

Saul smiled at her with something approaching lust in his eyes. Tally really was a gorgeous sight. An estate worth several million standing before him in a baggy sweatshirt and the worst haircut he had ever seen. And, even better, showing signs of being mightily taken with *him*.

'Natalia . . .' he said.

'Call me Tally.' Her eyes shone and a blush rose from her neck to her forehead. It did not suit her, Saul thought.

'May I look in here?' he asked, approaching the doorway of the Green Drawing Room and almost cringing with veneration for Tally's benefit. He stared, with every appearance of utter fascination, at the portrait of the Second Lord Venery as a be-ruffed, brocaded child. 'Such a noble face,' he said in fascinated tones. 'Even at that age. Such breeding.'

'I think it was more a case of such bleeding,' Tally replied, ecstatic at the intensity of his interest. 'He was a very unhappy child. Got the strap a lot from his father.'

'Oh, a belted earl,' said Saul, grinning at her in the semi-darkness. Tally started, then giggled nervously, and proceeded to lead him from treasure to treasure. 'Miraculous,' declared Saul, apparently almost asphyxiated with admiration on being shown the decorative ostrich egg Queen Victoria had given to the Fifth Earl. What really struck him as miraculous, however, was the fact that Tally was still alive after having breathed in the dank and dusty atmosphere of the house for twenty-odd years. It was incredible she hadn't died of consumption. On the other hand, she wore a lot of clothes. All of them at once, by the look of it. Pretty odd-looking, as well, with that funny snub nose. Still, ugly girls were always easy. They were so grateful.

And Tally *was* grateful. She was thrilled to have someone in the house so interested in simply *everything*. Saul had even been fascinated by the large pieces of lava on the downstairs corridor floor brought back by the Fourth Earl from Pompeii. 'Hot stuff,' he had said wittily, trying to disguise his disappointment that the rocks on the carpet were not, as he had thought, bits of the house that had already fallen down.

'Splendid,' he had said, feeling a piece of brocaded curtain dissolve in his hands at the precise moment Tally invited his admiration of the Eighth Earl's stuffed bustards. It was more than splendid. The place was even closer to collapse than it looked. Some of the wooden floors were so soggy and worm-eaten they were practically sponges. He probably wouldn't even need to bring in the bulldozers. Just leaning vigorously against one of the doorframes should bring the whole place crashing down.

His stomach surged with excitement. If he could pull this off, it would be the biggest success of his life. He looked speculatively at Tally's layers of sweaters. He needed to pull *those* off, too. If he could make Tally fall in love with him, and even better, marry him, things could really start moving. Big metal things, with cranes and drills attached.

'Oh dear,' Saul suddenly announced as they mounted the staircase under the baleful eye of the Ancestors. 'I've been so fascinated by everything you've shown me that it's *far* too late to drive back to London.' He was speaking nothing less than the truth. He had been *enchanted* by the disastrous state of the house. And Tally had been even more of a pushover than he had hoped. He still needed to push her over *properly*, however. 'I would just *adore*,' said Saul, his eyes fixed meltingly on her, 'to see the Elizabethan Bedroom.'

'Oh, yes, of course,' said Tally, wondering vaguely where Saul might sleep. Beds as most people understood them hadn't been much in favour at Mullions lately. Her own tiny single bed which she had had since childhood was about the only serviceable one left. Tally doubted Saul would want to curl up in Julia's smelly old bearskins, still less spend the small hours standing in the garden as Big Horn had sometimes done. His idea of a good evening out, Tally supposed. But not everyone's.

She stopped short halfway down the Long Gallery. 'Here's one of our finest tapestries,' she said proudly, gesturing at a murky piece of cloth upon which Saul could discern practically nothing. 'Made to celebrate the wedding of the Fourth Earl and Countess. It depicts the legend of Jonah and the Whale.'

'Jonah and the Whale, eh?' smiled Saul. A mischievous glint stole into his eye. 'Not very flattering for the poor old Countess,' he remarked. 'Large lady, was she?'

Tally turned a horrified glance on him. Briefly, Saul felt his fate hang in the balance. He had dared to make light of the Mullions heirlooms. Then Tally's face split into a smile. 'You *are* dreadful,' she said and led the way onwards.

They reached the Elizabethan Bedroom door. Tally pushed but the door resisted.

'Here, let me,' said Saul, applying himself to the unrelenting oak, which immediately relented to such an extent that the door flew open and they both shot across the polished floor, narrowly avoiding a skirmish with a Georgian washstand.

'Wonderful,' said Saul, picking himself up and gazing upon the house's greatest treasure. The extent of the moth damage on the counterpane's embroidery made his heart sing. The heavy, carved bedposts were obviously as humming with woodworm as they were cavorting with semi-naked gods and goddesses, and his cup ran over when the electricity suddenly cut out. Tally fumblingly lit a candle whose flame sent Saul's profile, his nose curved and lengthened, jerking devilishly across the cracked, whitewashed walls of the room. He turned to look at her, his eyes gleaming. 'You're gorgeous,' he said, addressing not Tally but what he had by now estimated as the ten thousand acres of prime building land she represented.

Tally glanced demurely at the polished floorboards

and shivered. Less from the cold than the excitement of being completely alone in the proximity of a bed with the handsomest man she had ever seen in her life. And who had just told her she was gorgeous into the bargain. Her heart thumped and her throat felt dry in profound contrast to the distinctly moist feeling in her gusset.

'I want you,' said Saul, urgently, to the rolling, curving acres of the Mullions estate standing before him in human form. A slow smile spread across his face and his eyes glowed as he looked deeply and (quite literally) speculatively into Tally's. Surrender, he saw, was written there in capital letters. 'I'm desperate for you,' he told her passionately.

Chapter 13

'Out of hospital and flat on her back again, I see,' said Josh fondly, holding up the centre spread of the *Sun*. Under the headline 'SEE NIPPLES AND DAI' was a huge picture of a scantily-dressed Champagne with her new football star boyfriend. ' "Dancing the night away in a skimpy gold bikini top and matching hot pants",' he quoted.

'Ooh, lovely,' said Valentine. 'And what was Champagne wearing?'

Jane pointedly said nothing. She was sick of Josh, sick of Valentine, sick of the job. Most of all, she was sick of Champagne. Once out of hospital, Champagne had lost no time telling every tabloid editor who would listen about the exhausting, stressful pressures of fame that had led to her near-fatal encounter with sleeping pills. Sympathetic spreads about burn-out syndrome had resulted, along with fact boxes covering everything you needed to know about insomnia.

Insomnia, Jane snorted to herself. It was the first time she had heard staying up all night at Tramp and the Met Bar count as inability to sleep.

Since their encounter in the hospital ward, Jane had been unable even to look at a photograph of Champagne without foaming at the mouth. To be told that the person whose life you had saved was not only ungrateful but had actually hand-picked you to do it on the grounds that you were their social inferior was more than infuriating. It was devastating. Jane's self-esteem was currently lower than absolute zero.

Her telephone rang. 'Be quick with that,' Josh rapped out. 'We need to have a features meeting. Everything you've suggested to go in next month is rubbish.'

Jane thrust her middle finger up half-heartedly in the direction of her boss's temporarily turned back and picked up the receiver. 'Is this Jane Bentley?' asked a peremptory cut-glass voice, but one which didn't, mercifully, belong to Champagne.

'Victoria Cavendish here. I'm the editor of *Fabulous*, as you probably know.' Jane did know. Everyone knew. Victoria Cavendish had been around long enough to qualify for fully paid-up legend status. She had edited *Fabulous*, *Gorgeous*'s direct rival, for years, and was supposed to be every bit as shrewd and ambitious as Josh. She was also supposed to be the sort of editor who wouldn't even share a lift with you if you were wearing the wrong length of hemline that season. Rumours about her abounded. Whiplash thin, she reportedly existed on one rocket leaf a day, bathed in Badoit and sent her daughter's school clothes to be unpicked and recut by the Chanel atelier. She had, it was said, once resigned from a job because her office, while vast, was half a centimetre smaller than that of another of the company's editors. Size was also an issue when it came to Victoria's staff, some of whom, it was whispered, had been sacked for the ultimate crime of Putting On Weight. If true, Jane thought, it was certainly the most literal interpretation of gross misconduct she had ever come across.

'I'll come straight to the point,' said Victoria briskly. 'I'm looking for a deputy editor. I've heard great things about you and I wondered if you might be interested.'

Jane's eyes bulged. Interested? She was *fascinated.* 'Well, it certainly sounds like a strong possibility,' she said neutrally, conscious that Josh, who had a sixth sense where phone calls were concerned, was listening through his open office door with his ears out on stalks.

'Well, we'd better meet up then,' said Victoria briskly. 'Tonight? The Ritz? Seven?'

'Fine,' said Jane, echoing Victoria's monosyllabic style. She put the phone down with as much nonchalance as she could muster.

'So good of you to make it,' said Josh as Jane came into his office and sat down next to Valentine. 'Now, to work. We've got to get more celebrities in the magazine. Any ideas?' He looked round hawkishly.

Jane and Valentine shuffled uncomfortably, caught out again by Josh's favourite trick of calling meetings without notice when only he had had time to prepare for them.

'Well, fortunately, I've had one,' sighed Josh martyrishly. 'It's called Namesakes. We ask George Bush what his favourite bush is, Michael Fish what his favourite fish is, Mike Flowers what his favourite flowers are . . . geddit? Any other ideas?'

Jane blinked. 'You are joking?' she said. 'I thought we were supposed to be a sophisticated magazine.'

Josh raised an eyebrow. 'I happen to think it's a rather good idea,' he said, in a tone that brooked no argument.

'OK, how about asking Jean-Marie Le Pen what his favourite pen is?' said Valentine, the faintest trace of weariness in his voice. 'Sir Peter Hall his favourite hall? John Major and his favourite major?'

'Damon Hill and his favourite hill?' said Jane, reluctantly getting her brain into gear. 'Jon Finch and his favourite finch? Oliver Stone and his favourite stone? Joan Rivers and her favourite rivers?'

'Excellent,' said Josh. 'Now off you go and ring them all up.'

Jane looked hard at the clock, as if she could force it by sheer effort of will to move round to seven and her meeting with Victoria. It seemed too good to be true. Was she really being offered an opportunity not only to escape from Josh but also from Champagne?

'Right, fire away,' barked Champagne when Jane picked up her ringing telephone several seconds later.

'Sorry?' asked Jane.

'Ask me questions, so you, um, I can write the column,' shouted Champagne. 'I'm back with a bang and raring to go.'

'You've made a lightning recovery,' Jane told her.

'Yes, well, I've had my inner labia pierced,' yelled Champagne. 'That sorted me out, I can tell you.'

'Ugh, how awful,' grimaced Jane. 'Did you sit on something sharp?'

'Course I bloody didn't,' boomed Champagne. 'Cost me a bloody fortune. My acupuncturist did it.'

'Acupuncture!' exclaimed Jane. 'That's not acupuncture. That's S and M. Why on earth did you do it?'

'Labias are the bit where all your stresses gather,' Champagne informed her with exaggerated patience. 'Apparently it's the ultimate place to be pricked. As it were. Ha ha ha.' The receiver exploded with her window-shattering laugh.

Jane stared dully into space. George Bush and his favourite bush paled into insignificance as she realised that she was spending hours of her life transcribing, nay, *inventing*, the thoughts of a woman who paid large amounts of money to be stabbed in the front bottom.

Meeting the editor of a glossy magazine in The Ritz was definitely Jane's idea of journalism. Even if the editor had not yet arrived. Pastel satin sofas and low-slung chairs lurked invitingly in gilded corners. A pianist tinkled soothingly in the background, while penguin-suited waiters glided smoothly about bearing trays of champagne and bowls of fat nuts.

Refusing all offers of refreshment – she didn't want to commit herself to a mineral water and have Victoria roll up and order a champagne cocktail – Jane fished in her bag for the virgin copy of *Hello!* that lurked in its depths. She waded greedily through the glossy pages, wallowing in the usual smorgasbord of washed-up rock stars in stonewashed jeans, lovely homes with a firm emphasis on leopardskin, face-lifted film stars flogging autobiographies and, Jane's personal favourite, Euro-royal gatherings featuring dresses apparently designed by people who had heard about clothes but never actually seen them. Grinning to herself, Jane turned the page. Her good mood evaporated instantly as her eyes fell on a large photograph of Champagne and her latest lover gurning at the camera from the frilled and flower-printed depths of a large four-poster bed. 'Britain's Most Famous Party Girl Talks Frankly About Fame After Her Recent Illness And Introduces Us To The New Man In Her Life' ran the big red and white headline. Jane hesitated. She knew reading on could seriously damage her mental health. But she couldn't help herself.

Champagne, you're a model, TV personality and, most famously, a writer. How do you fit so many things into your life?
I'm fantastically well-organised, basically. And very self-disciplined. The early bird catches the modelling contracts, after all.

You're obviously ambitious. What drives you?
A chauffeur, mostly. Ha ha ha. No, but seriously, I love working. I have a very strong work ethic.
Champagne, what is the secret of succeeding in so many different areas?
Sheer perfectionism, I think. I also make it an absolute rule to be pleasant, patient and punctual at all times.

Jane gasped and stretched her eyes.

Your life seems very glamorous. Endless parties and celebrity premieres. Is it as glittering as it looks?
Not at all. Making small talk with famous people is completely exhausting, and I'd like to see the average builder manage five hours a night in my Gucci stilettos.
Did all this have anything to do with your recent illness?
Yes. I was burnt out, basically. People just don't realise the hard, hard work that goes into being a star. They think they'd like my money and fame but they wouldn't last two minutes with my timetable. Most of the time, it's unbelievable.

Unbelievable was the word. And two minutes, thought Jane, was about the longest Champagne spent on any item on her timetable.

Champagne, you have achieved so many things. Is there any ambition you would still like to fulfil?
I would love to be appreciated for my writing. Not for who I am. And I would love to develop my film and TV career. This morning, for example, I visited a beekeeper for a guest slot on a nature programme. It was amazing. So many bees. I told him I couldn't imagine how he remembered all their names. I would also love to do some charity work. I'm looking into doing something for the Centreparks charity for the homeless, taking over where the Princess of Wales, God rest her, left off.
Finally, Champagne, could we ask you about your relationship with Dai Rhys?
Dai is the first man in my life I would seriously consider settling down with. He's so supportive and, being so well-known himself, he completely understands the enormous pressures of fame and the endless demands.

Tell me about the endless demands, thought Jane sourly.

Are you a football fan?
I wasn't, but I am now. Dai's explained so much about it. I even understand the offshore rule – very important when you earn as much as Dai does.
Do you prefer rich men?
I really don't care about money. Love is the most

important thing to me. If Dai hadn't a penny in the world I'd still adore him.

Jane snorted so loudly that a couple of elderly duchesses on the next sofa almost dropped their glasses of sherry. They glared over their bifocals at her in fury.

Are wedding bells in the air?
Marriage is certainly on the cards.

You bet, thought Jane. Dai's credit cards.

Would you have a traditional wedding?
Yes. With my darling little pet poodle Gucci as Best Dog, of course.

Jane could read no more. As there was still no sign of Victoria, she decided to head for the loos. That would also get her out of the way of the hovering waiters. They probably think I'm a prostitute, she told herself, before realising that the prostitutes on this particular patch were probably better dressed than she was.

In the powder room, Jane stared at herself in the mirror, looking miserably at her shiny nose and forehead. Her crimson jersey brought out the red of her eyes beautifully.

When Jane returned to the lounge, a woman with a helmet of black hair, a slash of red lipstick and spike heels was occupying a minuscule area of one of the sofas. Jane had seen enough pictures of the *Fabulous* editor to know who it was. The woman was talking urgently into a mobile phone. Or was she? As Jane approached, she realised there was a mirror glued to the inside of the mouthpiece flap. Victoria Cavendish was evidently checking her lipstick the executive way.

'Hi,' said Victoria, holding out a cool hand clanking with rings. 'Two champagne cocktails, please,' she added, waving imperiously at a passing waiter. Jane felt relieved. At first glance, Victoria had looked dangerously like the skinny, self-denying sort whose idea of a racy drink was Badoit and Evian in the same glass.

Although probably in her mid-forties, Victoria had the figure and, perhaps less advisably, the clothes of someone half her age. That someone, however, was not Jane. Victoria's sharp suede jacket and matching miniskirt were far snappier and more costly than anything she had in her own wardrobe. Round Victoria's neck was a soft brown shawl, which Jane recognised as one of the wildly expensive kind which were, as far as she could remember, made from the beard hairs of rare Tibetan goats. Victoria's, of course, was probably made from the facial hair of the Dalai Lama himself.

Jane crouched on the edge of the seat, crossing her legs to minimise the spread of her flanks and wishing she had remembered to clean her shoes. Come to that, she wished she had had her hair cut, lost a stone and spent a day in Bond Street in the company of a personal shopper and an Amex card.

'Well, as you know, I need a deputy,' said Victoria,

lighting a menthol cigarette with a lipstick-shaped lighter. She crossed her bird-like black legs, the razor sharp heels just missing her bony ankles. Jane shivered. There was more than a touch of the Rosa Klebb about all this.

'You're very highly recommended,' said Victoria. 'Apparently you handle contributors very well and I particularly need someone I can trust with a very high-profile new writer we have coming on board.' A thrill ran through Jane. A famous writer. How wonderful.

'Who is it?' she asked.

'Can't tell you, I'm afraid, until you're all signed up,' said Victoria, taking another swig from her champagne glass. 'But someone who will hopefully send our circulation into the stratosphere.'

Martin Amis? wondered Jane. Iris Murdoch? She thrilled at the thought of day-to-day contact with a proper author. 'Sounds wonderful,' she said, reaching for her own glass, then realising it was empty. As was the dish of nuts. Jane realised she had shovelled in the lot in her excitement.

'So I take it you're interested,' said Victoria, clicking her metallic blue-tipped fingers for the bill.

Jane nodded. 'Yes please.'

'Good. I'll bang you a contract over tomorrow.' Victoria levered herself upright. 'Must run now,' she said, which struck Jane as no less than fighting talk, given her footwear. 'I'll be in touch tomorrow.' She shimmered away across the carpet in a cloud of the sort of delicious perfume Jane instinctively knew one didn't buy in Boots.

Jane wandered slowly out of the hotel and along the darkening street back towards the Tube station. The 2CV, which had not worked for several days now, lay languishing by the Clapham roadside waiting to be put out of its misery. It probably would not live to see another MOT. The potholes of Mullions had seen to that.

It was flattering though odd, Jane thought, as she wandered absently down the stairs into Green Park Tube, to be suddenly so much in demand. Odd, too, that Victoria Cavendish should be eager to sign her up without so much as asking for her opinion of *Fabulous*, let alone without a CV, references and especially without the reams of sparkling features ideas invariably demanded on these occasions and never referred to thereafter. Especially as Victoria, if rumour was to be believed, had her own special methods of selection.

Candidates for employment were, so it was said, generally invited to lunch with her so she could observe their table manners and satisfy herself that they didn't cut their salad with a knife or belong to what she designated the HKLP (Holds Knife Like Pen) brigade. Victoria, reportedly also used these occasions to ensure that any of her would-be co-workers were not prone to the verbal social *faux pas* that would condemn them without trial into what she called the PLT (Pardon, Lounge, Toilet) category. Jane could believe it all.

Victoria, as was well known, was completely unrepentant about both her magazine and the social aspirations it enshrined. 'Snobbery,' she was often quoted as saying, 'is merely an acute awareness of the niceties of social distinction.'

Even candidates who scraped through Victoria's restaurant tests were far from home and dry. They still risked one of the editor's celebrated spot checks in which she had a member of staff call the would-be employee's parents' home (the number, with address, was demanded on the *Fabulous* application form) to make sure that the person answering had a suitably patrician tone of voice. By these combined methods any social chameleons of humble origin were prevented from getting their plebeian feet under *Fabulous* desks. Some, it was said, were filtered out right at the beginning of the process simply by Victoria's casting an eye over the parental address. If it was a number rather than a name, the letters were filed straight in the bin, a process which had always struck Jane as somewhat unreliable, ruling out as it did any members of the Prime Minister's family, for starters.

Yes, it was certainly strange that none of the usual hurdles had been placed before her, thought Jane now, crossing the dirty platform to her Northern Line connection at Stockwell. Especially as she was not at all sure she could have jumped over any of them. The word 'toilet' had certainly passed her lips from time to time, and she had yet to see anyone, herself included, eat a Caesar salad without resorting to a blade of some sort. And, although thinner than she used to be, she was certainly not racehorse skinny.

There was, however, one highly plausible explanation for Victoria's keenness to get her on board, one quite detached from all the flattery about her superior editing skills. Josh. All being fair in love and circulation wars, it was entirely within the rules of the game for Victoria and her rival to poach as many members of each other's staff as possible. Bagging as key a person as the *Gorgeous* features editor was certainly a feather in the *Fabulous* editor's cap, and would be even if Jane's parents had lived at 13 Railway Cuttings and she ate her salad in the lounge with a saw held like a Biro.

The contract duly arrived next day. As Jane had expected, Josh affected utter insouciance when she handed in her notice. His casual acceptance, however, lost some of its conviction after Valentine spotted him half an hour later smoking furiously in one of the stairwells.

Yet Jane's bombshell was short-lived in its effects. Midway through the afternoon it was superseded by a bigger bang altogether – Valentine's news that Champagne was leaving Dai Rhys the footballer. He had overheard it being discussed at a neighbouring table at San Lorenzo that lunchtime.

'Surely not,' said Jane. 'She's just been all over *Hello!*. All over him.'

Valentine raised an eyebrow. 'Well, she's given him the red card now. Brought on a substitute.'

'But who?' asked Jane, faintly surprised at Valentine's apparently sound grasp of the argot of the terraces. 'Who could possibly be left?'

'Remember when she did the National Lottery draw a few weeks ago?' asked Valentine.

Jane shuddered. The memory of Champagne in a pink sequinned dress struggling before an audience of millions over a task as simple as selecting a set of numbered ping pong balls was still fresh. 'Mmm?' she said, wondering where this was leading.

'That young unemployed scaffolder from Sheffield won it. Wayne Mucklethwaite, wasn't he called? Biggest Lottery winner ever?'

'Ah, yes,' said Jane, light dawning. 'I think I see what you're getting at.'

At least, she thought, she would no longer be around to chronicle the inevitable demise of that relationship as well. Which reminded her. Champagne had not yet been told she was leaving. No point putting off the blissful moment, Jane decided, picking up the receiver.

She almost sang her news when Champagne answered. In reply there was a sharp gasp at the other end, followed by another, and another. 'Uh, uh, uh,' went Champagne. Jane's stomach contracted with concern. Was Champagne having a seizure with the shock of it? Or had she caught her *in flagrante* again? Jane listened carefully. Limited though her experience was, it didn't sound orgasmic to her.

'Champagne? Are you all right?' she asked, feeling vaguely guilty. Was Champagne, after all, capable of human feeling? Was she finally realising how much she depended on Jane?

'Uh, uh, uh,' went the dreadful, rasping gasps. 'Yah, I'm, uh, uh, fine. On the, uh, uh, Stairmaster, actually. I'm in the, uh, uh, gym. Leaving, are you? Oh well, good luck.'

And that, it seemed, was that. No 'Thank you for all you've done'. It would, Jane thought, have been unbelievable, had it not been so eminently believable.

'Um, well, good luck to you too. I, um, hope it works out with Wayne,' Jane said.

'Oh, yah. Absolute sweetie,' said Champagne smugly. '*So* generous. Just bought me a necklace with the most *humungous* diamond in it. I suppose I do rather deserve it though. After all, I *did* pick his balls on *National Lottery Live*.'

Chapter 14

Tally stared worriedly upwards as the embroidered canopy above her and Saul rocked alarmingly backwards and forwards. She was torn between praying that the Elizabethan bed wouldn't collapse, which it threatened to, and that Saul wouldn't stop. He was, she had discovered to her amazement, capable of making love to her for a whole hour, which was exactly fifty-seven minutes longer than anyone else had ever managed.

And that, Saul realised, about to collapse himself from exhaustion, had clearly been quite some time ago. Even Champagne hadn't required so much servicing. He should have known. The quiet ones were always the worst.

His spine felt twisted beyond repair from the lumpy old mattress of the Elizabethan bed. 'But Elizabeth the First slept in it,' Tally had told him indignantly when he had suggested it was less than comfortable.

No wonder she was called the Virgin Queen, then, it was on the tip of Saul's tongue to say.

'You're amazing,' he panted to Tally. 'I want to marry you. Now.' He was speaking no less than the truth.

A loud, sudden knock on the heavy oak bedroom door pre-empted Tally's reply. Saul's face dropped in shock. There had been no one in the house except Tally since he first came here, well over a week ago now.

Drained of all colour, every hair on his body erect, Saul clung to Tally in terror. As he watched, rigid with fright, the door creaked open and light from a guttering flame shone into the room, sending the shaking shadow of a bent and fearsome-looking creature wobbling terrifyingly across the walls. Saul gibbered hysterically as a huge and brutish face, its brilliant eyes shining and its lines and creases made more hideous still by the dramatic candlelight, shuddered slowly into view.

'What's *that*?' he shrieked.

'It's Mrs Ormondroyd,' said Tally calmly. 'The housekeeper. She must have come back from her sister's.'

Saul looked in horror at the fearsome expression plus nylon overall and ghastly lumpy legs now issuing through the door. He fumbled for his cigarettes with a shaking hand.

'Dinner's in an hour, Miss Natalia. Oh.' Mrs Ormondroyd's gimlet eye alighted on Tally, sitting up in bed with the sheets pulled over her breasts, and Saul, who wasn't making much effort to conceal anything.

'Didn't realise you had comp'ny. Very sorry, I'm sure.' She couldn't, Saul thought, have sounded more disgusted if she had discovered Tally in bed with her father, her brother and a couple of Alsatians.

Dinner was, for Saul at least, a revelation. He poked uncertainly at the rapidly-cooling surface of what looked like a chop. He tried to cut it, only to find that it was so well done you practically wanted to give it a round of applause. Saul frowned. He hated overcooked meat. He much preferred it bleeding. Badly injured, at the very least.

'What's the matter?' asked Tally, discerning his disgruntled face through the gloaming of the freezing dining room.

'It's cold,' Saul said. He had to shout it twice before she heard him at the other end of the refectory table. Saul realised in a flash why so much of the aristocracy had loud voices. Conversation in places like this would otherwise have been impossible.

Tally sighed. It was too much effort to explain that food always arrived cold in the dining room. The distance between it and the kitchen, not to mention the icy blasts encountered in the various corridors en route, meant that only the hardiest of dishes arrived at the table in a vaguely eatable condition. Over the centuries, the Venery cooks had refined their menus by a process of trial and error (which was certainly how those eating them saw them) down to the few items that could cope best with the adverse conditions. Those dishes were but two: the Brown Windsor that had already featured on tonight's menu, and which Saul had instantly christened Primordial Soup. The other was the cutlets he was staring at now.

Saul gazed down at the meat, an island surrounded by a sea of thick, greasy slop. The plate hardly set the ensemble off to best effect, being made of what looked like tarnished tin. Saul pushed it away, noticing as he did so some marks and scratches on its rim. He screwed up his eyes to examine them in the gloom. 'Tally,' he asked, 'are these plates solid silver?'

'Yes,' Tally called back. 'Mrs Ormondroyd's smashed all the Sèvres now, and this is all we have left. Even she can't manage to destroy metal, although I daresay she's made a few dents.'

Saul raised his eyebrows and took a sip of wine. It really was remarkably good. He groped towards the bottle and read the label. 'But this is Margaux nineteen forty-five!' he shouted in amazement.

'Oh dear, I am sorry,' yelled Tally. 'It's just that I can't afford to send Mrs Ormondroyd to the Threshers in Lower Bulge any more. I told her we should economise and see if there was anything left in the cellar. There are quite a few bottles down there, she says, so I suppose she can use it to cook with if it's too horrible to drink. It might help her cutlets.'

The only thing that would put Mrs Ormondroyd's cutlets out of their misery, thought Saul, was a controlled explosion. 'No, no, no need to do that,' he said hurriedly, thinking of the excitement an influx of fifty-year-old Bordeaux would make on the London wine markets. And the profit he could make out of it. 'I'll get rid of it for you,' he assured Tally. 'No problem.' She beamed at him gratefully.

Later, shivering by a sickly fire in the Blue Drawing Room over the mugs of thin, tepid Nescafe grudgingly produced by Mrs Ormondroyd, Saul returned once again to the attack. 'We could do such wonderful things here together once we were married,' he urged, trying not to stammer with the cold and clasping both her chill hands in his. Tally hesitated. It wasn't that she had any particular objections to rushing headlong into matrimony with someone she had hardly met. Her ancestors, after all, had done it for generations; the Fourth Earl, for example, had married a Somerset heiress to whom he had been introduced only once before, in the cradle. But there *was* something she wanted to know first.

'What happened with you and Champagne D'Vyne?' Tally asked, screwing her courage to the sticking place. 'Weren't you quite keen on her?' Tally was desperate to be reassured that Saul was not still in love with the bird-brained philistine who had been so rude about Mullions, still less the glamorous, blonde, and beautiful party-girl-about-town whom, if Jane was to be believed, every man in the universe lusted after.

Saul took another deep drag on his cigarette. It was true that on paper his liaison with Champagne had been an ambitious entrepreneur's dream come true. Yet he had soon discovered that the cost of running her far outstripped any business benefits she might bring.

Incidents such as being made to book an entire suite at the Savoy because she wanted a room service club sandwich hadn't helped. Nor had the time she demanded a Jacuzzi full of champagne because of all the extra bubbles.

Saul shuddered as the memories crowded in. Not to put too fine a point on it, going out with Champagne D'Vyne was one of the worst experiences of his life. She had been the most unstimulating woman he had ever met, which was odd when you considered she wanted seeing to at least three times a night. Then there had been her dreadful, loud, spoilt, braying voice. The people in the flat above had banged on the ceiling merely when he played back her answerphone messages.

'Um, it just wasn't to be,' he muttered eventually to Tally, not sure he wanted to relive the trauma by putting the details into words. 'We weren't quite, um, suited,' he added. 'She was a bloody nightmare,' he said finally.

'Was she *really* that bad?' sighed Tally, blissfully, thinking that Jane, who had frequently uttered those very same words, had more in common with Saul than she realised. 'I don't know her at all, you see.'

'Obviously you never read her column,' said Saul bitterly, 'otherwise you'd know everything about her including the colour of her knickers. When she bothered to wear them, that is.'

'No, I never read any of them,' confessed Tally, wondering what it would be like to wear no knickers.

Nothing short of dangerous in the winter at Mullions, she imagined. Mrs Ormondroyd, she knew, always wore at least four pairs in January. 'I don't buy magazines,' she added. She didn't admit that the real reason Mullions no longer subscribed to any publications was the cost. And the fact that she had hated to see the Lower Bulge newsagent's tiny, spindly son struggle the mile up the winding Mullions drive, his fragile old bicycle visibly sagging beneath the weight of all the papers and magazines Julia had once taken. 'So I'm afraid I haven't the faintest idea of what's going on anywhere.'

'In that case,' said Saul, dropping a kiss on her head, 'I think you and I are going to get on just fine.'

Suddenly, the telephone shrilled outside in the gloom of the passage.

'I think it might be for me,' Saul said, leaping up to answer it. 'I've got a couple of deals on the boil at the moment.'

'Who was it?' asked Tally, when he returned a few minutes later. 'One of your deals?'

Saul shook his head. 'Wrong number.'

In Clapham, Jane put the phone down in astonishment. Saul Dewsbury was *still* there. And what did he mean Tally couldn't come to the phone because she was having a shower? The only showers at Mullions were those that appeared unexpectedly through the ceilings during thunderstorms. Still, if Tally was having a fling with Dewsbury, on her own head be it. She had made her four-poster and now she could lie on it, Jane decided. She had more than enough to think about. Such as how to lose a stone overnight before she began her new job at *Fabulous* tomorrow.

Chapter 15

Beautiful, lissom girls with long blonde hair crowded the foyer of the *Fabulous* offices. Uncomfortably stuffed into her first-day-smart clothes, Jane's heart sank as she realised that everyone else was at least two sizes smaller than she was. And they all looked exactly the same, which was to say, different from her. Not only did they have identical clothes – tiny white T-shirts revealing brown navels, skinny black trousers and high-heeled boots – they had symmetrical features too. Waiting for the lifts, Jane decided, was like standing in the middle of an exceptionally glamorous multiple birth, twenty-two years on.

Everyone had a tan, a delicious little nose, cheekbones higher than the Andes, glossy hair and pert little breasts. They all wore minimal make-up and that type of dark nail polish that made their fingers look as if they had been trapped in the door. Talk about a clone zone, Jane thought. The people who thought Dolly the sheep was such a breakthrough should have come here first, where it had all obviously been going on for years.

There must be, Jane supposed as she entered the lift, an appearance-improving machine somewhere in the building, probably up by the managing director's office. She imagined it to be called the Glamourtron, a tall silver cylinder with sliding doors. It was here that Personnel summoned one on arrival, and into here one stepped, grey-thighed, mottled of face, split of end, stained of teeth, bloodshot of eye and bulging of waistline. One would stay inside the cylinder for ten minutes (possibly longer in extreme cases; Personnel to decide). There would be a mild humming and then the doors would spring back. Out one would step, tanned, blonde and glossy-haired, with a delicious nose, pert chest, and cheekbones as high as the Andes. Dressed in tiny white T-shirt, skinny black trousers and trapped-in-door nails. Jane felt excitement rise within her. Would Personnel call her today?

The lift finally arrived at the *Fabulous* floor and out Jane stepped, her nostrils filled with the same delicious perfume absolutely everyone seemed to be wearing, and entered the *Fabulous* offices. As at *Gorgeous*, about a third of the space was devoted to the large glass box denoting editor territory. Victoria's photographs, Jane could see through the windows, were blown up even bigger than Josh's. Victoria with Princess Diana, with Cherie Blair, with Karl Lagerfeld, with John Galliano, with Donatella Versace.

Jane wondered when Victoria herself would put in

an appearance. Or, for that matter, when anybody would. The office was empty. Jane busied herself in the familiar task of flicking through the papers, in which, as usual, Champagne and her lottery winner received radioactive publicity.

Today's shots showed Champagne and Wayne Mucklethwaite, the richest 24-year-old man in Britain, almost invisible under designer carriers in Bond Street. Talk about label dame *sans merci*, thought Jane, making out bags from Chanel and La Perla that could hardly have been intended for Wayne. Relief that her days of dealing with Champagne were at an end flooded through her. The thought of never hearing those arrogant, barking tones again was nothing less than utter bliss.

'Hello,' said someone. A gangly girl with big eyes, a short, lacy skirt and long blonde hair had appeared in the office. 'I'm Tish. Victoria's secretary. You must be Jane.' Jane nodded, feeling suddenly self-conscious as the rest of the staff finally started to trickle in. 'I'll introduce you to everyone, shall I?' offered Tish helpfully.

Just then, an extremely thin man with an extremely flat bottom came mincing into the office in a pair of extremely clean white trousers. His frail build looked incapable of supporting his vast black sunglasses, let alone the two huge and clinking bags of duty-free swaying from each beringed and wrinkled hand.

'Should keep me going until lunchtime,' he remarked, crashing the bags theatrically into the middle of his desk.

'That's Larry, the travel editor,' said Tish. 'He's just got back from holiday,' she added, rather unnecessarily.

'And who's this?' Jane asked as a glamorous older woman with violent purple lipstick, white cropped hair and a pair of extremely tight cream leather trousers made her entrance.

'Oonagh, the picture editor,' supplied Tish. 'She and Larry are a brilliant double act. Just watch them.'

'How are you, dear one?' cried Larry to Oonagh. 'Well, I hope.'

'Ghastly, actually,' replied Oonagh, checking her reflection in a black Chanel compact. 'My husband actually wanted to have sex with me last night. Can you imagine?'

Larry shuddered. 'Not with *your* husband, darling.'

'Precisely,' said Oonagh. '*Such* a drag.' She snapped shut the compact. 'Still, no *visible* damage. Anyway, how were the Bahamas, darling? Just beyond blissful?'

'Oh, beyond, beyond,' trilled Larry. 'Except that I nearly had a *very* nasty accident. I was putting on my bathers and there was a scorpion lurking in my crotch. Can you imagine?'

'Well, frankly, darling, I'd think yourself lucky,' sighed Oonagh. 'Nothing's lurked in my crotch for years. Apart from my wretched husband, that is. Right, now I need to talk to Jeffrey Archer, darling, *urgimento*. Any ideas how I can get hold of him?'

'Oh, just lean out of the window and shout, I should think,' replied Larry.

Jane's attention was distracted from this fascinating

exchange by the arrival of four girls who immediately went into a huddle over the newspaper horoscopes.

'No *way*!' the tall, chestnut-haired one in the centre exclaimed dramatically. 'I just can't *believe* what he's said about my star sign. It's just, like, *uncanny*. He says I'm struggling with an impossible dilemma. So true. I've been invited to a fancy dress party on Friday and I can't decide whether to go as Sharon Stone or Grace Kelly.' She closed her eyes and shook her head in amazement at the perspicacity of the astrologer. '*Unbelievable*. I simply can't work out whether I'm more *Basic Instinct* than *Rear Window*, do you know what I mean?'

Jane gazed at her discreetly. Rear End was nearer the truth. There seemed little outward resemblance between the ice-blonde, stick-thin Princess of Monaco and this frankly rather buxom brunette, but Jane was not going to jump to conclusions. *Fabulous*, even more than *Gorgeous*, was famous for its wealth of well-connected employees. The brunette was probably a duchess at least. The only comfort was that she plainly hadn't been to the Glamourtron either.

'That's Tash,' whispered Tish. 'She's the drinks party editor.'

'What about me?' exclaimed a thin blonde. 'I've been asked to go to Woggle Wykeham's tonight to play Boggle, as well as being invited for drinks at Minkie Rochester's.'

'That's Tosh,' whispered Tish. 'She's the weddings editor.'

'So you can't decide between Boggle at Woggle's or drinkies at Minkie's?' asked Tash.

'Yah, 'xactly,' said Tosh.

Jane cast eagerly about for any handsome men. There were none. Nor were there, as far as she could see, any men at all, apart from Larry, who hardly counted. Her heart sank. The office had the atmosphere of a girls' boarding school dormitory. She never thought that she would miss Valentine and Josh, but . . .

A few minutes later, a throwing open of doors and rustle of bags announced Victoria's arrival. She marched in frowning, distracted and impeccable, swinging a tiny handbag violently back and forth. Behind her staggered Tish under a heap of boxes, bags, newspapers and dry-cleaning. Victoria didn't need a secretary, Jane decided. She needed a Sherpa. Nodding frostily in Jane's direction, Victoria stalked into her office and slammed the double doors.

It was hardly an effusive welcome. Inside the huge glass box, Victoria was gesturing dramatically, the phone glued to her ear.

'Who is Victoria talking to?' Jane whispered to Tish. The important new writer, perhaps. Or Archie Fitzherbert, the magazine company's dynamic-sounding managing director who, so rumour had it, was reasonably young, reasonably charming and reasonably presentable. He sounded, thought Jane, distinctly promising. 'It seems to be someone terribly important.'

'It is,' said Tish, pushing her bottom lip out as she tried to choose from among the myriad bottles of nail varnish on her desk. They were, Jane noticed, the only bottles there. Tippex, or anything else one might expect secretaries to need in the normal run of events, was noticeably absent from Tish's desk. There were no staplers, no letter-headed paper, no pens. There was a Sellotape dispenser, but it was innocent of Sellotape. With its lipstick, mirrors and nail varnish, Tish's desk bore more resemblance to a dressing table than anything appertaining to a professional amanuensis. 'Victoria's calling the agency for a new nanny for her children,' said Tish breezily. 'She often does on a Monday. They tend to leave over the weekend, for some reason.'

The novelty value of hearing people saying '*Fabulous*' instead of 'Hello, *Gorgeous*' when they answered the telephone was already starting to grate. Jane was dreading the moment when her phone rang and she had to say it herself. It wasn't long in coming.

'Hi there,' honked horribly familiar tones.

'Champagne, hello,' said Jane, vaguely touched that her old adversary was bothering to call her in her new place of work. 'How are you?'

'Pretty bloody chuffed with myself,' yelled Champagne. 'Just signed the Superbra contract. Half a million notes for lying around on a beach in my underwear. They're going to shoot the ads in the South of France. Talk about Monte Carlo or bust. Haw haw haw. God, I'm funny. But it's bloody annoying to think I've been doing it for free all these years at Cap Ferrat.'

'Well, that's wonderful,' said Jane briskly. 'I'm really very glad for you, Champagne.' After all, she told herself, she could afford to be generous now.

'Yah, bloody marvellous, isn't it? I'll be on massive billboards all over the country,' honked Champagne. 'And all over the back of buses. I'll look like the back end of a bus. Har har har!'

'Marvellous,' said Jane. 'I *am* glad you're doing so well,' she added through gritted teeth. 'It's lovely to hear from you but I've got to go now.' Victoria had finally detached the telephone from her ear and was gesturing at her to come in. 'I have a meeting with the editor.'

'Haven't finished yet,' Champagne shouted imperiously. 'Wayne and I have just got back from the new villa in Marbella, the one I helped him buy.'

'Is it nice?' asked Jane, making coming-soon movements to Victoria.

'Fabulous. Three swimming pools and ten bedrooms, one with a two-way mirror so you can spy on the guests. Hilarious. My idea. Love to know what other people are doing in bed. Staff are morons though. No one speaks a word of bloody English.'

'Really? Oh dear.'

'Yah. Bloody nightmare, basically. *And* I've gone and lost the yellow sapphire ring Wayne gave me. He'll go ballistic if he finds out.'

'Oh dear,' said Jane, with exaggerated patience. 'What a shame.' *Get off the phone*, she thought, furiously.

'But I've thought of a brilliant way round it,' Champagne continued mercilessly. 'I'm going to claim it on my car insurance. All I have to do is blow up my Lamborghini and pretend it was in there.'

'But didn't he give you that as well?' asked Jane, incredulous.

'Oh. Yah. Think you're right there,' bawled Champagne. 'I'd forgotten that, actually. Oh well. You are writing all this down, aren't you?' she added suspiciously.

'Writing it down? But why should I? I've moved magazines, you know,' Jane said as gently as she could. 'I'm working for *Fabulous* now.' Champagne was obviously in denial. How sad. And yet, in a way, how touching as well.

'Yah, I know you are,' Champagne yelled. 'So am I.'

'Oh, I *thought* you'd be thrilled,' beamed Victoria as Jane rushed, panic-stricken, into her office. 'Seemed such an obvious thing for *Fabulous* to do. Champagne's exactly the same age and background as our ideal reader, as well as being *slightly* more famous and glamorous. She should send our circulation rocketing. Not to mention,' she added, almost as an incidental, gazing complacently at her perfect nails, 'being a death blow to *Gorgeous*.'

'But why didn't you tell me?' stammered Jane.

'No point until everything was signed and sealed,' said Victoria, silkily. She grinned. 'I was going to just now, but Champagne beat me to it. But I *knew* you'd be thrilled. Champagne never stops telling me how *brilliantly* you get on together. But we couldn't let you in on our little secret because Champagne, bless her, was *terrified* that wily boss of yours would suspect we were after you and try to stop it.'

'Champagne was?' asked Jane, stunned. 'But why? You mean she *knew* you had approached me?'

'Knew? My dear, she was the only reason I *did*,' said Victoria, smiling incredulously. 'She made it a *condition* of her coming here that *you* would edit her copy. You know how temperamental these famous writers are. Most of them hardly need *anything* doing to their work at all, but they think they can't do anything without their dear old editor.' Victoria smiled pityingly.

The photograph-crammed walls of Victoria's office began to spin round Jane. A cold sweat broke out on her forehead. So Victoria hadn't approached her for her legendary editing skills at all. She had recruited her solely at the whim of Champagne who had been cunning enough to see that her lucrative new contract would be of very short duration once Victoria realised how poor her raw copy was. Not only that, Champagne had persuaded Victoria to keep her own move to *Fabulous* a secret from Jane.

The extent to which she had been outmanoeuvred sank in. Champagne had succeeded in making her her pawn, dependent on her for her job. The roles had been reversed. Jane saw with awful clarity that she was far worse off than she had ever been at *Gorgeous*. She was now utterly in Champagne's power.

'It's marvellous,' Victoria said, dimpling and beaming at Jane as she sipped a cup of black coffee.

'Champagne's first job for us will be to cover the New York fashion shows next week. Should be quite a read!'

Jane felt the soles of her feet fizz with envy. Champagne, doing the fashion shows. Crammed between the stars and the fashionably starving in a little gold front-row chair, watching as Naomi and Kate sashayed languidly by in a variety of unfeasible outfits. Rushing from one show to anothe rin a whirl of limos; drinking in gossip and cocktails at the post-show parties. Jane longed with all her soul to go.

'I see,' she said dully to Victoria, forcing the corners of her mouth up into a semblance of a smile and trying to sound enthusiastic. 'Well, it should be quite a read, as you say.' If only she could go as well, Jane wailed inside because there were no prizes for guessing who would write the reports in the end. And the expense of sending Champagne to New York would be phenomenal. Even Josh, who had given her a Bentley and a chauffeur without a second thought, would never have gone this far. Jane wondered what personal transport arrangements *Fabulous* had offered Champagne. A Learjet, probably.

'Features meeting!' Victoria suddenly shouted through the open doors of her glass box. 'May as well see what rubbish this lot have come up with for the next issue,' she added *sotto voce* and with a conspiratorial wink to Jane as Tish, Tosh, Tash and co. filed in. 'Thank goodness we have Champagne's column, at least.'

Thank goodness, thought Jane, sourly, noticing, as she took her seat, that another man besides Larry had appeared. He had, Jane noted with interest, undeniably film-star looks. With his thin, pale hair, long nose, little round rimless glasses and quivering chin, he reminded Jane irresistibly of Charles Hawtrey. He was, it appeared, one of *Fabulous*'s freelance contributors.

'Right, let's get started,' rapped out Victoria, revolving in her executive swivel chair with a pen between her teeth. 'We need more *Fabulous* people, *Fabulous* homes and *Fabulous* lifestyles for the next issue. In particular, we need someone *Fabulous* for the cover. A real star. Any suggestions?'

'What about Lily Eyre?' ventured Jane. 'Up and coming actress. Going to be huge. Apparently Hollywood wanted her for *Full: Throttle* with Schwarzenegger, but she turned it down because she wants to do small, quality British films. I thought she sounded quite interesting.'

It was evident from the silence around her that nobody else did. Victoria looked as if she hadn't heard.

'Ugh, not her,' said Oonagh at length from the back of the room. 'Dreadful common ankles.'

Jane looked blank. What on earth was Oonagh talking about?

'Oh yes,' continued Oonagh. 'It's an absolute fact. Upper-class women have thin, elegant, bony ankles while lower-class women have big, thick, shapeless ones. You can always tell.'

'Any other ideas?' asked Victoria.

Lily Eyre, Jane realised, had been consigned to the dustbin. She felt uneasy, unable to understand why there wasn't a chorus of approval. Josh had been after Lily Eyre for months. She was not only an interview-shy rising star, in itself enough to make her intensely sought-after, but one with that delicate English pink-and-blonde prettiness beloved of upmarket glossy magazine editors. She was, in short, textbook-perfect cover material.

Charles Hawtrey suddenly roused himself. 'Well, what I'd certainly like to know,' he piped up in a high-pitched, reedy voice, his fists clenched in his lap, 'is where one can get a jolly good spanking these days.' A sudden, violent convulsion shook his weedy frame. He had, Jane realised, quite a bad twitch.

Victoria raised her eyebrows. Jane stifled a giggle.

'Apparently,' Hawtrey squeaked, by now purple-faced with exertion and indignation, 'there's hardly a single school in the county where they still have cold baths and corporal punishment. Now it's all warm beds and TLC. I've been to several dinner parties recently where people have been complaining about it. The fathers, in particular, are all furious. They don't see why their sons should have an easier time at school than they did. And speaking personally,' Hawtrey stammered, as a series of twitches threatened practically to throw him off his seat, 'it didn't do me any harm.'

'Well, there *has* been a certain amount of anti-bullying legislation passed,' ventured Jane.

Hawtrey shot her a withering look. 'I'm aware of that,' he spluttered, as another twitch convulsed him. 'What I'm saying is that it takes a magazine like ours to stand up and say that there shouldn't have been. We built an Empire on being flogged senseless by the Upper Sixth. We must campaign,' he said, now jerking up and down like a bucking Bronco, 'to bring back Matrons with warts and being chased around the quad by the randy Latin master.'

'No, surely not,' said Victoria, much to Jane's relief. 'Latin's a dead language. Being chased by the randy French master, perhaps. That's much better. It's a seriously brilliant idea, Tarquin. Make a great think piece. Look into it, will you?' She gazed sternly round the room again. 'Well, that sorts out our *Fabulous* Dinner Party Debate for this month. But we still need our *Fabulous* Lifestyle. Someone very rich and glamorous, preferably.'

'But weren't we doing that piece about that very beautiful actress, Sonia Svank, going back and discovering her family castle in Lithuania?' asked Larry. 'I thought that sounded marvellous.'

'It would have been, had the castle not subsequently been turned into a rustic hospital,' retorted Victoria. 'When the photographer turned up, there was a Lithuanian farmer having boils removed from his willy. *And* it was tiny.'

'Well, size isn't everything, you know,' smirked Larry.

'I'm talking about Sonia's *castle*,' snapped Victoria. 'In other words, I don't think she had one.'

'But that's impossible,' said Tash wonderingly. '*Everyone* has a castle somewhere.'

'Look,' said Victoria, looking determinedly at her

watch, 'I was due at the Caprice ten minutes ago. Everyone keep thinking about the cover interview. And keep an eye out for possibles at the Movers and Shakers party on Friday.'

Friday was four days away. 'Movers and Shakers party?' Jane asked Tish after Victoria had flounced out of the office.

'Mmm. *Fabulous* does it every year,' said Tish nonchalantly. 'It's a publicity thing really. We invite all the most happening people in London to a party and drown them in poo.'

'Poo?' stammered Jane, wondering why she had never heard of this extraordinary event before.

'Shampoo,' said Tish, looking at her in astonishment. '*Champagne*, in other words.'

Jane blushed deeply. She clearly needed a crash course in upmarket rhyming slang. Despite her embarrassment, a spasm of excitement gripped her intestines. A party full of happening people, some of whom had to be single and some of whom might even be men. So there was at least one advantage to this new job. 'It sounds wonderful,' Jane breathed, thinking excitedly that she could smuggle Tally in too. Then she remembered Saul Dewsbury and scowled.

'Yah, last year Bonkers Brixham was snogging Bruiser Baddeley-Byng for hours,' supplied Tash, overhearing their conversation. This intelligence left Jane none the wiser as to who was the female half. If either.

* * *

'Darling, must you wear that skirt *again*?'

Tally, buttoning her faithful old Black Watch tartan over two pairs of long johns and her grandfather's First World War army fatigues, turned in surprise to see Saul watching her from the bed.

'You have superb legs,' he said. 'Such a shame to keep your tights under a bushel.' It was true, he thought. Tally did have nice legs. But that was about the size of it. After the Himalayas of Champagne's exuberant physique, the foothills of Tally had been a comedown in every sense of the word. But there were compensations. Saul was not a religious man, but he still sent out a prayer of thanks for his deliverance every morning he woke gibbering to find his recurring nightmare was just a nightmare. He was not, after all, trapped with Champagne and a stream of deafening anecdotes in a taxi from London to Paris where she leapt out and left him with the fare. After Champagne's extravagance, it was refreshing to find that Tally's idea of luxury was a new bar of soap, a fire that managed a flicker and lights that did not fuse once all evening.

Saul, however, found it rather more convenient if they did. Under cover of darkness, he could turn on all sorts of useful little taps to do some nifty bits of damaging flooding here and there to speed up the decaying process, although rather irritatingly someone – he suspected Mrs Ormondroyd – usually managed to turn them off before too much damage was done. He was sure she was spying on him. He had come across her unexpectedly twice yesterday, once when he was gazing with admiration on the work of a particularly vicious and destructive colony of deathwatch beetles and again when he was staring speculatively at a fine Tudor fireplace in one of the upstairs bedrooms. She had looked at him long and suspiciously.

She had had good reason. Saul had recently bought a share in an architectural salvage company and Mrs Ormondroyd caught him in the act of calculating how much his target customer, an Islington film producer, would pay to install the Red Bedroom fireplace in his weekend home near Southwold. The less worm-eaten sections of the panelling in the Long Gallery would certainly be received gladly into one of Fulham's larger bathrooms and Saul had instantly earmarked the Jacobean staircase as a centrepiece for a second gym he was planning to open. Mullions' huge cast-iron baths, meanwhile, which probably hadn't been full or hot during the reign of the present Queen, were sought after for Georgian townhouses from Hackney to Harlesden. As for the pestles, mortars, toffee hammers, bone-handled knives and chopping boards scattered about the kitchen, there wasn't a theme pub in the country that wouldn't rush to stick them up on its wall for period atmosphere. The house's eponymous mullioned window frames, equally, would fit seamlessly and extremely profitably into the footballers' mansions currently being flung up the length and breadth of Cheshire.

Tally's breath, Saul noticed now, was clearly visible in the freezing air. It was little wonder they spent so much time in bed. Buried several feet beneath blankets and sheets was the only warm place in the house, and even then Saul half expected to wake up and find some of his frostbitten toes lying on the floor. It was like *Dr Zhivago*, he decided. Only Tally looked slightly less like Julie Christie than he himself looked like Omar Sharif.

Much as he dreaded flinging back the sheets and exposing his warm flesh to the cold, Saul knew he had to scowl and bare it. He had things to do, after all. Today he planned to walk the estate and make a rough calculation of the maximum number of houses that could be crammed on the site. And there were other decisions to make too. Herringbone or straight brick-work driveways? Cul de sacs or ovals? Video entry-phones or traditional enamel bells? Fitted kitchens or freestanding units? The penthouses, he had already decided, would have their own private roof terraces, but there was still the parking to think about. Would he really be able to drain the oxbow lake and build an underground multi-storey as he planned? There were a few more calls to make about the financial backing as well. And, of course, he still had work to do on Tally. He was within an ace of getting her up the aisle, he knew. But victory was not yet his. Tally hadn't quite given in.

He leapt off the bed and felt the usual twinge in his spinal column as he went striding, naked, over the splinter-ridden floorboards to kiss Tally. As the morning sun, struggling through the dusty diamond-paned windows, gilded his tautly-muscled body and haloed his tousled black hair, her heart did a forward roll.

'Don't you think it's too cold in the house to wear short skirts?' she asked.

'Well, that's one very good reason why we have to start thinking about ways to get the place warm again,' said Saul briskly, pulling his damp and chilly shirt over his head and belting his trousers round his trim waist.

He was aware that the log supply was running low, but he was damned if he was going to chop any himself. He'd sooner put the furniture on the fire; in fact he would, without a second thought, had not the oak refectory table had Hampstead basement kitchen written all over it. He'd get a fortune for that. Saul was confident a similar dazzling future awaited the pair of fine Jacobean chairs that had somehow escaped the attentions of the woodworm. Perhaps they were saving them for dessert.

Mrs Ormondroyd could get the logs, he decided. She looked as if she could fell entire forests before breakfast. Oh, for a few creature comforts, he thought, bracing himself for a Mrs Ormondroyd breakfast, normally prunes and burnt toast. Prunes were hardly the thing to get one firing on all cylinders. On the other hand, perhaps they were.

'Tally, I've been thinking,' said Saul, now glued to the looking glass where he was, ostensibly at least, tweezering out an ingrowing hair. 'I know exactly how you can get this place back on its feet. Imagine it. New roof, new wiring, new window frames and a brand spanking new heating system.' Tally gazed at him raptly.

'New paintwork,' continued Saul. 'Repointing the brickwork. New grass on the lawn.'

'Oh,' sighed Tally ecstatically, an orgasmic light in her eyes. He was reminded of when Champagne demanded he talk dirty.

'Meet me in the Blue Drawing Room after breakfast,' said Saul. 'Tell Mrs O I'm giving it a miss today. I have more important things to do.'

Mrs Ormondroyd's broad back radiated disapproval as Tally entered the kitchen. She crashed the kettle on to the Aga, banged a few pots about and in case Tally still hadn't got the message, the scraped, blackened and torn toast she was finally presented with spelt it out in Hovis of fire.

'What's the matter, Mrs Ormondroyd?' Tally asked innocently.

'Back's playing up,' muttered the housekeeper. She clamped a large, sausagey hand to the bottom of her spine. To the small of her back, if her vast back could be said to have a small.

Tally sighed. 'Mrs Ormondroyd, I think we both know what's really the matter,' she said. 'I just don't understand why you hate Saul so much. He truly loves Mullions and really wants to find a way to get the place going again. He has tons of ideas,' she ad-libbed in anticipation of the revelations awaiting her in the Blue Drawing Room, 'and we may as well see if any of them work. After all, the alternative is to sell the place to the type of ghastly person we've had looking round recently, and while Mummy's away we should explore every option before she comes back and turfs us all out.' She bit into her toast and grimaced. It was like buttered coal from the grate. She wondered vaguely whether a loaf of carbonised bread would burn in the Blue Drawing Room fireplace. 'Give him a chance, at least.'

Mrs Ormondroyd's back remained silent and impassive.

Outside in the hall, the telephone bell shrilled. Almost immediately, it was picked up. The low voice of Saul floated into the kitchen, although his words were impossible to make out. There was a ting as he replaced the receiver. Half-turning so Tally could see her massive profile, Mrs Ormondroyd heaved her Brezhnevian eyebrows upwards. Tally finished her toast in as much silence as was possible given the crashing of her jaws against the carbon. Then she left the kitchen.

Billows of smoke greeted Tally on her entrance into the Blue Drawing Room. Saul was crouched in the vast hearth, eyes streaming, trying in vain to persuade a smouldering, resentful pile of still-damp wood into warm, blazing life. 'Whoever said there was no smoke without fire was talking utter shit,' he snapped as Tally came up behind him. 'No wonder this is called the Blue Drawing Room. Look at the colour of my hands.' The patches that were not black with soot were, Tally saw, almost indigo with chill.

'Here, let me,' she soothed, taking the tattered bellows from him and trying not to mind that he had been thrusting their Elizabethan carved oak end straight into the burning embers. 'I'm used to it.' A few well-directed wheezes later, she had persuaded a respectable blaze into being.

Saul gazed at her pinched face in astonishment. How did she manage to be so thin and yet apparently immune to the worst the cold could throw at her? She really did have the constitution of an ox. Mrs Ormondroyd, on the other hand, just *looked* like an ox.

'Why do you never get colds?' he asked.

'We were never allowed to wear socks after March,' Tally answered. 'And we took cold baths every day. It was very good training for learning to live in an English country house.'

'We?' asked Saul.

'My brother Piers and I,' said Tally.

'Your *brother*?' gasped Saul, alarmed. He had not bargained for this. Visions of a patrician, urbane head of the family in a fifteen-piece tweed suit suddenly appearing brandishing a riding crop and grilling him in merciless detail about what he was up to loomed large and hideous before him. His heart thundered like the last furlong of the Grand National as all his carefully-laid plans swayed and shuddered in the balance. Penthouse balconies, herringbone brick drives and video entryphones swooped mockingly before his racing vision, then faded dramatically away. The figures on his imaginary bank balance morphed from the hoped-for brilliantine black to an angry, frustrated red. Tally had a brother. What a nightmare. Was the brother here? Spying on him? Concealed somewhere in this vast, rotting warren of a house?

'Where is he?' asked Saul. He had intended the query to sound insouciant, but it flew out in a high-pitched yelp.

'Oh, I'm not sure,' said Tally, sighing into the flames. 'He could be anywhere.'

Saul, having heard what he most feared, was somehow able to stifle the cry of panic that threatened to loose itself from the moorings of his throat. But he was able to do nothing about the shocked, colourless white of his blood-drained face.

'The last we heard he was underneath a runway at Gatwick,' Tally added.

Saul's head spun. 'Wh-what?'

'Under a runway at Gatwick,' repeated Tally. 'He's an environmental protester, you see. He went AWOL from school and the only time I see him now is in the papers if he's been throwing mud at a minister or something. He hasn't,' she ended sadly, 'been near Mullions or his family for months.'

Saul let out a sigh of relief so vast he feared it might extinguish the hard-won fire. His feet tingled with the joy of the reprieved. 'How fabulous . . . I mean, how dreadful,' he stammered. But Tally was too lost in her thoughts to notice. It made her sad to think of her brother. They had been close as children, had clung together in the face of their mother's more eccentric excesses and affectations. Tally had written regularly to him at school, bowled up frequently with picnics and chatter and advice about girlfriends and in between times had sent him money she could ill afford to spare.

Piers's current lack of communication was a disappointment she felt keenly.

'Who was on the telephone, by the way?' she asked, changing the subject. It hadn't occurred to her to wonder before, but the faint hope that it might be Piers struck her as she edged into a mice-dropping-free corner of the sofa.

'Wrong number again,' said Saul smoothly, after an infinitesimal silence. It was, too, he justified to himself. His business contacts had strict instructions from now on to call him on his mobile.

Feeling more in control again, Saul lit a cigarette and stood in as upright a manner as he could muster given that he was several spine-twisting nights on Mullions' mattresses the worse for wear. He felt gingerly at his left cheek. Shaving in wobbly Elizabethan mirrors had done nothing for the symmetry of his sideburns. No wonder the Tudors had always gone in for beards. Much safer. He cleared his throat; his ticklish cough was getting worse. Tally looked at him expectantly.

'You ought to be in pictures,' announced Saul.

Tally flushed. It was true that someone had once compared her to Celia Johnson. It was very sweet of Saul to try and flatter her, but really, one had to be realistic.

'I'm much too tall to be a film star,' she faltered.

Saul looked nonplussed. 'No, not *you*,' he said, in rather more astonished tones than Tally might have wished for. 'The house. Here.' He thrust a brochure into her hand.

Tally gazed at it. 'The ultimate location' read a line of mock Elizabethan script rolling across the front of a familiar-looking combination of golden stone and oriel windows, viewed from across a pearly lake. It looks astonishingly like Mullions, thought Tally, fascinated to see that some turrets of the gatehouse had fallen off to leave just the same gap-toothed effect as on the one at the end of their own estate road. She looked closer. It *was* Mullions. 'Where on earth did you get this from?' asked Tally, gazing up at Saul, bemused.

'From myself,' said Saul, turning up his hands for dramatic emphasis. 'I put it together, using a few of my contacts from the advertising world.'

'But what is it? What does it mean?'

Saul gritted his teeth. Some people really were slow. 'It's a brochure,' he said, with exaggerated patience. 'A brochure advertising Mullions to film companies.'

Tally looked at him blankly.

'It's a brilliant idea, don't you see?' Saul urged, a chilly touch of impatience creeping into his voice. 'The film world is crying out for locations like Mullions. Period dramas needing backgrounds. You know, *Sense and Sensibility, Pride and Prejudice*, that sort of thing. There are a few films that I happen to know are going into production at the moment. We can target them. They'd pay a fortune.'

'But wouldn't they need, oh, I don't know, electricity, loos, food and all that?' gibbered Tally, shrinking against the sofa back as she tried to think quickly. 'Wouldn't they wreck the house?'

'Oh, no, no, no,' said Saul, fingers firmly crossed behind his back. 'You'd never know that they'd been there afterwards. Film units bring their own jennies. That's filmspeak for generators,' he added, rather pompously. 'But you don't have to worry your pretty little head about any of it. All you need to do is pop out and say hi when Tom and Nicole roll up in their trailers.'

Tally gasped, feeling dazzled. Saul had obviously thought it through. 'I know so little about it,' she murmured. 'You're the expert. But it sounds harmless enough.'

Saul looked at her huffily. 'Well, don't overwhelm me with your enthusiasm.'

Feeling guilty as well as scared, Tally gave him a contrite and dazzling smile. 'It sounds a wonderful idea,' she said. 'Thank you so much, darling. We must,' she added, straining to please, 'get these brochures off as soon as possible.'

Saul grinned, a hint of triumph in his eyes. 'Actually, I sent them out yesterday.' In a lightning move, he grabbed both her hands and pulled her close, gazing into her face with heart-melting sincerity. 'I won't ask you again,' he croaked, reflecting as he did so that the combination of the bed, his cough and the freezing cold would probably see he didn't survive to, 'but now you have proof that I'm desperate to help you and Mullions, will you marry me?'

Chapter 16

Deciding what to wear for the Movers and Shakers party was a nightmare. Desperate, Jane had even considered asking Champagne if she could borrow one of her dresses, but thought better of it after realising they probably wouldn't fit over her head. Just as she was juggling the idea of her all-purpose black trousers teamed with an all-purpose black jacket, or all-purpose black jacket teamed with all-purpose black trousers, or perhaps a daring combination of both, the telephone on her desk shrilled.

Ten minutes later she put it down. Her ears were singing as she went into Victoria's office. 'I've just had Champagne's hotel in New York on the line,' she reported.

Victoria looked up from the card, personalised in neat serif capitals, on which she was writing in the thick, black-inked oversized hand developed at prep school to make sure it got to the other side of the paper.

'They say Champagne has checked out.'

'Why?' said Victoria, absently. 'I thought it was the best one in town. We even got her the Presidential suite.'

'It is and we did,' said Jane through gritted teeth. 'But it's not good enough for Champagne. She's just checked out in a fury because the lifts to the penthouse are too slow for her.'

Victoria nodded. 'Quite right too,' she said with the air of one who'd seen more penthouses than Bob Guccione. 'Slow lifts can be *very* frustrating.'

'There's something else,' Jane said, keeping the urge to scream and throw things just about under control. 'The photographer called me earlier and said he and Champagne were among those invited to the exclusive dinner Ralph Lauren held after his show. Apparently it was unbelievably lavish. Champagne, caviar, lobster, you name it.

Victoria nodded, looking bored. So far, so run-of-the-fashion-mill, said her face. 'Yes? And?'

'Well Champagne apparently decided in the middle of it all that she wanted lasagne,' said Jane. 'She stormed out of the dinner when she was told there wasn't any and went back to the hotel and demanded they found some for her.'

'Well, I jolly well hope they did,' said Victoria hotly. 'Those hotels are supposed to be able to get you anything. A white elephant steak at four in the morning if you want it.'

'Oh, they got it all right,' said Jane. 'It's just that

Champagne's exclusive at-home interview with Ralph Lauren, which we fought off all the competition to get, may now be in some doubt.'

Victoria breathed in deeply and exhaled, flaring her nostrils dramatically as she did so. She fixed Jane with a look of pitying patience. 'Sooner or later,' she said, in exaggeratedly patronising tones, 'even the most sophisticated and privileged among us gets the urge for something simpler. Many's the time I've come back from some A-list premiere or party, thrown off my heels and asked for nothing more than the maid to rustle me up a simple eggs Benedict.'

Jane sighed. OK, if Victoria wanted to play hardball, she'd got herself a game. She hadn't wanted to tell Victoria this, but . . .

'That's not all. I've had a call from the British Consulate as well. There's been some trouble with Customs. Champagne was held at Heathrow on the way over.'

Result, this time. The colour drained from Victoria's face. Jane saw her mind flicking swiftly through the Rolodex of possibilities, of which there seemed really only one. A drugs charge would mean the column would certainly have to go.

'Why?' Victoria croaked, the fingers of her right hand clenched into a white-knuckled knot round her Mont Blanc.

'She refused to hand over her passport on the grounds that the photograph in it wasn't flattering enough,' said Jane. 'They had to practically prise it out of her hand, apparently. She held up Concorde for half an hour. Joan Collins is talking about suing for the delay.'

To disguise the relief she felt, Victoria put on her most indulgent expression. 'Well, say what you like about Champagne, she's never boring.' Equanimity restored, her pen hovered over the card again. 'And, more to the point, she's certainly had an effect on the circulation.'

I'd like to have an effect on her circulation, thought Jane as she left Victoria's presence. Like cut it off completely.

She returned to her desk, just in time to answer the telephone which had been ringing for ages, ignored, as usual, by Tish who was otherwise occupied flicking through the latest *Vogue*. Jane's heart sank as the familiar honk blasted through the receiver. After the exchange she had just had with Victoria, Champagne choosing now to call – collect, naturally – from New York was like a blow upon a bruise.

'Four bangs,' squawked Champagne. 'I've managed four bangs so far!'

'What?' It sounded positively modest by Champagne's usual standards. So why was she boasting about it?

'Four crashes because people were staring at my underwear ads when they were driving!' Champagne boomed. 'One fatal.'

'Oh, I see,' said Jane. 'How awful.'

'No, it's brilliant. Proves the ads are really working. Superbra are thrilled!'

'I'm delighted for you,' said Jane. 'Is that everything?'

'Yah, think so,' said Champagne. Then, 'Oh, no, hang on, there *is* something else. I've packed in Wayne.'

Why aren't I surprised? thought Jane.

'Just too much of an oik, really,' declared Champagne, even though Jane hadn't asked. 'Hasn't a clue. His idea of a seven-course meal is a six-pack and a hamburger. Thinks Pacific Rim is something sailors get. The last straw was when we were in a restaurant and he pronounced claret claray. *So* embarrassing.'

'Quite,' said Jane, not sure how else to respond.

'But I've met some scrummy men in New York,' Champagne continued. 'The *sweetest* English politician at the Donna Karan show last night. *Bloody* nice guy.'

Jane had seen the coverage of Champagne at this particular fashion bash in the tabloids that morning. Coverage, however, had hardly been the word. Champagne's clinging silver dress had made her cleavage look like the San Andreas Fault.

'Yah, he was really interesting,' Champagne gushed. 'We talked for hours about politics.'

'Really?' said Jane faintly. Surely, as far as Champagne was concerned, Lenin was the guy who wrote songs with Paul McCartney. Her idea of a social model was probably Stella Tennant and dialectical materialism meant wearing a velvet Voyage cardigan with a leather Versace miniskirt. Champagne's concept of social security, Jane felt sure, was ten million a year, a country house in Wiltshire, flats in Paris and New York and a Gulfstream V.

'What's the politician called?' asked Jane, realising she hadn't thought about Westminster for what seemed like a lifetime. 'And what on earth was he doing at a fashion show?'

'James Morrison,' barked Champagne. 'Used to be the transport minister, apparently, and he's just been made Secretary of State for Pop. I told him I thought it was amazing that the prefects at Eton had their own minister, but I supposed it wasn't that surprising if you think that most of them end up in the Cabinet anyway. But he meant pop *music*. And popular culture in general, which includes fashion, apparently.'

'I see,' said Jane, vaguely wondering if that meant Nick, too, was now on cheekbone-crashing terms with supermodels. She had no idea whether Nick still worked for Morrison, and didn't care. She hadn't, she realised, thought about *him* for ages either.

'Well, must dash. My masseuse is waiting,' Champagne said by way of finale. 'Oh,' she added nonchalantly, 'tell Victoria I probably won't be back for the Movers and Shakers party. I know she wanted me there, but some producer wants to talk to me about a film part.' She stifled a yawn. 'He must be *desperate* for me. He's paid for a new Concorde return ticket so I can stay on an extra day.'

Jane felt weak with envy. Film parts were falling into Champagne's lap now as well. If only a *real* film part would. Like the lighting rig. 'How wonderful,' she said sincerely. 'I'd *love* to go on Concorde,' she added longingly.

'Terrifically boring the tenth time, I can assure you,' yawned Champagne.

'Oh, Tish,' wailed Jane after a lunchtime spent trailing despondently round Bond Street looking at dresses she could neither fit into nor afford. 'What *am* I going to wear to this party?' Everyone else in the office seemed to be pulling glittering garments out of plastic bags and exclaiming over them. 'Look at what the others have been buying,' she moaned.

'Buying?' said Tish. 'You must be joking. No one's bought a stitch. Everyone's had the fashion department call things in for them. Apart from *you*, that is.'

'Oh,' said Jane, feeling foolish. It had never even occurred to her to borrow.

'Follow me,' said Tish.

The fashion department was a riot of racks stuffed with brilliantly-coloured clothes. Emaciated long-legged girls bobbed between them like exotic birds, clutching armfuls of shimmering dresses. Shoes lay scattered all over the floor, spilling from boxes lined with brightly coloured tissue paper. Jane was reminded of Champagne's bedroom.

'This is what *I'm* wearing,' Tish announced, producing a tiny dress made of ivory silk embroidered all over with tiny pink roses. 'Isn't it pretty? It's amazing anything's left,' she added. 'Tash has already been up here and was trying to wear practically everything at once to make sure no one else got a look-in. Oh, Tiara, Jane needs a dress for tomorrow,' Tish called as the fashion editor, a willowy redhead with huge green eyes and a vague air, wafted in. 'Got anything?'

Jane flushed beetroot as she submitted to Tiara's scrutiny. She doubted anyone as huge as herself had ever been seen in the fashion department before.

'Mmm,' said Tiara, putting her hands on her non-existent hips. 'Mmmm,' she repeated, putting her head on one side and tossing her curtain of hair in a shimmering arc as she did so. Jane felt nervous. Why had she allowed Tish to put her through this? There probably *had* been something in M&S if she'd looked hard enough . . .

'Mmm. You're in luck. I've got just the thing. Bias-cut.'

Tiara thrust a scrap of cream-coloured fabric into Jane's arms and shoved her into the fashion cupboard. Wispy bits of sequins and feathers tickled Jane's nose as she struggled into the dress while bent double underneath racks of clothes. She felt like a contortionist. Bias-cut, Tiara had said. Hopefully not biased against her.

'Wow,' said Tish as Jane emerged a few minutes later. 'That's *incredible*.' Which, thought Jane, walking resignedly to the mirror, could mean practically anything. At first glance, through half-closed eyes, it looked fine. Up close it would probably look dismal. Good from afar, but far from good.

'It really suits you,' said Tiara encouragingly. And, looking at herself critically in the long mirror, Jane had to agree. The extreme plainness of the long cream satin dress emphasised every curve and, by means of clever boning, wiring and general wizardry, contrived to give her a bust to rival Champagne's. A long slit up one side revealed a long, miraculously slender-looking and for once completely unbruised length of leg. Delight and excitement fizzed in Jane's stomach. She certainly looked the party part now. My cups, she thought, looking at her *embonpoint*, runneth over.

But Tish hadn't finished yet. Next, Jane was frog-marched to Sash the beauty editor for a make-up lesson. It was astonishing how a few well-placed strokes of charcoal eyeshadow could transform her eyes from small and piggy to huge and mysterious. Sash also showed her how to fill out her lips, normally the only dependably thin parts of her body, to look plump and luscious.

'Remember to lick before you drink anything, so the lipstick won't come off on the glass,' Sash warned. 'And *don't* eat. Don't even nibble. Remember, little pickers wear bigger knickers.'

Jane grinned. She was planning to take a leaf out of Champagne's book and not wear any knickers at all. She was determined to avoid visible party line.

'Archie Fitzherbert's office called you,' Tash said casually when Jane got back to her desk. 'Wanted a word, I think,' she added vaguely.

'What, Archie Fitzherbert the managing director?' Jane's stomach was suddenly thundering with panic. 'A word with *me*?'

Tash nodded. 'You're to call his secretary.'

Jane fumbled for the phone. Visions of instant dismissal, unpaid mortgages and repossessed flats floated through her panicked mind. Had Champagne been complaining about her? 'Which secretary?' she asked. Archie Fitzherbert, she knew, had two. A dragon called Mavis and an angel called Georgie. Tash shrugged.

Jane dialled, tremblingly. She got Mavis.

'One mayment,' said Mavis sternly. 'I think Georgina is dealing with this.'

Jane caught her breath. *Dealing* with this? What on earth was happening?

'Sorry,' said Georgie, bouncing on to the line like a friendly dog. 'I know this is awfully short notice . . .'

'What is?' croaked Jane, her worst fears assuming hideous, three-dimensional reality.

'Oh, didn't Tash tell you? Tomorrow morning. Archie would like you to attend one of his staff breakfasts.'

Jane sank in her chair with relief only to sit bolt upright again with terror. Archie Fitzherbert's 'meet the people' staff breakfasts were famous throughout the industry. Or notorious. Ostensibly, they were informal meetings to discuss staff-related issues, but most people suspected their real purpose was for Fitzherbert to spot check how switched-on his employees were. Jane saw her planned evening of collapsing in front of the telly metamorphosing into a night of frantically ripping through every issue of every competing magazine in order to be able to discuss its strengths and weaknesses confidently should her opinion be sought.

As she left the *Fabulous* building that drizzling evening, Jane noticed with a pang that the road outside, as usual, looked like the most fantastic outdoor car showroom. It was filled, nose-to-tail, with the shining, glamorous vehicles belonging to the boyfriends of the magazine company members of staff. They revved impatiently as their lissom girlfriends came rushing out of the revolving doors, tossing their shining hair and throwing their expensive handbags in the back seat before sliding into the front and roaring off. Jane strode on, trying not to care that there was no one to whisk her away to cocktails and candlelit dinners. Trying not to care, too, that the rain was now smashing against the pavements like gobbets of wet, cold lead.

She dashed into a newsagent and bought every magazine she could lay her hands on. Clutching her slippery armful, she hurried through the downpour to the Tube station. A speeding bus spattered the contents of a deep and dirty puddle all over her from the thighs downwards. Looking with loathing at the offending vehicle, which screeched dramatically to a halt at a bus stop a few feet away, Jane saw that it bore on its side one of the posters of Champagne in her Superbra underwear. Her bra was the same level as the top deck, while the lower one lined up with her skimpy G-string. Jane watched as the men in the queue, office drones with overpadded shoulders dragged down by the straps of their laptops, gawped at the advert before clambering aboard the bus and sitting on the bottom deck. It was,

Jane realised, the nearest any of them would come to getting inside Champagne's knickers. Certainly for the price of a bus fare.

Chapter 17

It was over twelve hours later that Jane entered the fetid mouth of the Tube again, but it might as well have been twelve minutes. Her eyes felt as hard, dry and heavy as golf balls. She had spent half the night hunched over her pile of magazines, and had fallen asleep over them in the end. She had woken up at five in the morning to find her nose pressed against a pageful of advice on dealing with irritable bowel syndrome.

Still, no one could accuse her of not preparing, she thought. And once the ordeal of the Fitzherbert breakfast was over, there was this evening's Movers and Shakers party to look forward to. Jane thought happily about the creamy liquid perfection of the party dress hanging in the cool darkness of her wardrobe. She focused her mind firmly on it as more and more people surged into her carriage at the next station.

The stop after that brought an even bigger influx. As her head became wedged under the armpit of a plump, perspiring businessman, who was evidently very fond of garlic, Jane tried to divert herself by thinking about her party shoes as well.

She had laughed when Tiara first suggested she try on the tiny, gossamer-light silver sandals, doubting she could get one, ragged-nailed, unpainted, bunioned toe in them, and had been amazed to find that they not only fitted, but gave her feet a grace she had never thought possible. They had even encouraged her to paint her toenails for the first time in years. She was, Jane realised, entering dangerous, perhaps fatal waters. She was beginning to see the point of spending a fortune on looking good.

'Ow!' Jane growled into the businessman's armpit as someone stood heavily on her toe. She moved her head the fraction that was possible to glare at the offender, and instantly wished she hadn't. An extremely spotty youth, his yellow-tipped, angry red bumps shining hideous and near in the harsh overhead light, gazed fishily back at her. Clamped to his ears were a pair of cheap headphones from which a grinding, sneering sound, interspersed with a fizzing rattle, emanated.

Jane sighed, loudly, knowing she was far from being the only unhappy traveller. The sense of mass irritation was almost as palpable as the overwhelming heat. She tried to prepare a selection of choice observations about the magazines she had read for the Fitzherbert breakfast, but was distracted by the sensation of her carefully moussed-up hair melting in the moist, sulphurous fug. She wrinkled her nose. The carriage, frankly, stank. It was one thing to travel like a can of sardines. To smell like them as well was just too bad. Desperately seeking distraction, she gazed through the window in the door at the back of the carriage, into the next one.

There he was. About eight feet away from her, his blond head clearly visible above the mass that pressed about him. Was she hallucinating? Had she finally gone mad?

No, she hadn't. It *was* him. No doubt about it. Tom. Suddenly, incontrovertibly, unbelievably here. Not in New York. Not anywhere else in the world, but here, alive, in the flesh, in London, in the very Underground carriage next to hers. He looked well, tanned, the ends of his hair bleached by the sun. He also looked even handsomer than she remembered.

Jane stared urgently at him. Surely he must see her. But Tom was gazing vacantly out of the carriage windows, seemingly oblivious to his surroundings. Jane tried to move, to make a gesture. He would, he must, sense her presence. She struggled again, but she was packed too tightly between the armpit and the acne to move. She was trapped. Until the next station, that was. Please, God, let it come soon.

Between Leicester Square and Tottenham Court Road, the train ground to a halt in the tunnel. Jane twisted herself desperately about, but could have been no more securely pinioned if she'd been bound hand and foot. And gagged into the bargain. For there was no point shouting. Tom would never hear her through two panes of glass and a mass of people. Feeling dizzy with panic, Jane locked her gaze on to him, burning into his leather jacket like a laser, willing him with every fibre of her being to turn and look at her. He must. He had to.

He didn't. The eyes that had melted her heart looked blankly out of the window at the black tunnel walls. The hand that had played her body like a harp, plucking deep, throbbing notes that still resonated, hung limply from a ceiling strap. Jane wanted to scream. Her eyeballs ached with the intense staring. She felt her gaze to be a lasso, thrown round him, connecting him, an invisible thread that would break if she so much as blinked. As long as she was looking at him, she thought, he could not get away.

Eventually the train gave a juddering, shuddering lurch and moved on. Seconds later, it had drawn into Tottenham Court Road station and flung open its doors. Jane was forced to look away now. She had to get out. Desperately, she scratched, pushed and clawed her way out on to the platform and elbowed against the tide of people pouring out of the train. She struggled towards the next carriage. It was half empty when she gained it. And Tom had gone.

'Tom!' screamed Jane, turning desperately round in the midst of the raft of commuters and glancing wildly about her for the blond head and the leather jacket. The wide, unwieldy crowd moved with a pitiless shuffle up the stairs, making it impossible for her to move at more than a snail's pace. In the escalator hall, Jane scoured the length of the commuter-crammed moving staircases with her eyes, but Tom was nowhere to be seen. She pushed her way up, muttering apologies, attracting angry glances, crashing her shins painfully into the sharp, heavy edges of briefcases. Tom *couldn't* have disappeared into nothing. Not when she'd been so close to him.

Through the ticket gates the crowds moved, as thick, slow and dense as treacle. Finally, Jane rushed out into Oxford Street, panting, her head bursting and dizzy with hot, pounding blood. For the next fifteen minutes she dashed up alleyways, down dead-end streets, across busy roads and around squares, but with no success. Tom had completely vanished. Eventually she slumped on a bench in Soho Square and burst into tears. No one passing batted an eyelid. You got all sorts of nutters wandering around Soho, after all.

When Jane entered the Archie Fitzherbert breakfast, she was half an hour late and felt a hundred years older. The breakfast was practically over but she didn't care. Nor did she care that her hair was all over her face and her mascara, despite automatic-pilot efforts in the loo, hopelessly smudged. She had walked the half mile from Soho Square to the *Fabulous* offices in a fragile daze, trying not to let the dreadful truth hit her that she had been mere feet away from the man she had been thinking of almost nonstop since he had left her, and she had let him get away. *Again*.

'Jane! Good morning,' called the managing director, half bouncing up from his chair as she came in. '*So* pleased you could make it.' He appeared to speak without irony. Jane bulldozed a smile across her face as he motioned her to sit down, waving a tanned, square-fingered hand across the array of croissants and toast wrapped in linen napkins. 'Have some breakfast,' Fitzherbert smiled. Jane nodded and drew in the chair beneath her, noticing that no one else had taken up the offer so far. The food was untouched.

Jane was too distracted to notice much else. All she took in about Archie Fitzherbert was his rather theatrical lilac suit, fashionably jarring orange tie and air of focused enthusiasm. Motivation shone from his every pore. He radiated energy and success. He was, in short, a deeply depressing sight, and the last person on earth Jane wanted to see at that moment.

He introduced the others at the table to her, an assortment of deputy editors, managing editors and advertisement and promotions people from other titles in the group, whose names Fitzherbert was evidently proud to be able to recall from memory. In her frazzled state, however, Jane forgot them as soon as he said them.

'We were just talking about *Lipstick*,' Archie Fitzherbert said, training a polite but penetrating gaze on her. As she picked up her coffee cup, Jane heard the unmistakable sound of a gauntlet hitting the floor. She was expected to make a contribution. Well, she could. Launched by a rival publishing company, *Lipstick* was the latest women's magazine to hit the already gorged market. It had been judged a great success, but Jane had thought from the start that it was boring. She said as much now.

'*Really?*' said Archie Fitzherbert, leaning forward and looking utterly fascinated. He clutched at the tablecloth with his fingers. 'How *very interesting*. Why *is* that?'

'There's nothing original about it,' Jane said, conscious, for once, of not giving a damn what anyone else thought. 'It's derivative, it takes the successful bits of practically every other magazine and mixes them together, but it's got no soul of its own. It's less than the sum of its parts.'

There was a shuffling silence. Jane suspected that before she came in, *Lipstick* had been the subject of considerable praise. But she didn't care. She felt oddly clear-headed and detached, as if the shock of seeing Tom and the misery of losing him again had left her no energy for worrying about trivia. She took a sip from her coffee cup, aware that Archie Fitzherbert was still staring at her. As was everyone else in the room.

Fitzherbert suddenly looked at his Rolex. 'Well, thank you for coming, everyone,' he said, and stood up, smiling politely as his guests drained coffee dregs and stumbled to their feet. There were a few crashes as the more maladroit dropped cutlery. Everyone mumbled their thanks, grabbed coats and bags and hurried out of the room. As Jane prepared to leave, she suddenly became aware that Fitzherbert had glided to her side. 'I'd like a quick word,' he said, sitting back down and motioning her to do the same. A few of the last to leave gazed curiously over their shoulders as the doors swung shut behind them.

'May I ask, since you seem to have such strong views, what you think of your own magazine?' Fitzherbert inquired in carefully neutral tones, locking his eyes on to hers. He was, Jane noticed, really quite handsome. But she also noticed the wedding ring. Taken, then.

She hesitated. It was, she knew, her cue to say something flattering about Victoria, to laud her to the skies, to say what a great and inspirational editor she was.

'Fairly dull really,' someone said. Jane heard the voice ringing round the silent room and realised it was her own. 'I think,' the voice continued, 'that it needs to move with the times more. It's quite witty, which is important, and has a certain amount of glamour. But there's a lot that could be done with it nonetheless.'

'Such as what?' asked Fitzherbert, his light, pleasant tones still betraying nothing of what he thought.

Jane took a deep breath. She'd clearly talked herself out of a job anyway, so she may as well speak the truth. What had she to lose? Somewhere out there in the mockingly bright sunshine, Tom was wandering about London and she had no way of finding him. She had been given a second chance and had wasted it. What did anything matter now?

'Well, I think it could be better informed,' she heard herself saying. '*Fabulous* staff don't seem to think they need to read the newspapers, apart from the horoscopes, which is a pity. Which means that everyone else spots the big stories first and gets their interview requests in.

And big interviews and stories, as you know, are what sell magazines.'

Fitzherbert nodded. He seemed to be encouraging her to say even more. Probably because after this she would have to offer her resignation and it would be cheaper than sacking her. Oh well. Since he'd asked . . . 'It's also not very sexy,' Jane continued recklessly. 'Or perhaps as hip as its rivals.' That much *was* true – Josh had placed a far greater emphasis on predicting trends and spotting rising stars than Victoria did.

She stopped and took a sip from her coffee, feeling scared but strangely unburdened. Fitzherbert kept up a sphinx-like silence for a few seconds. Eventually, he cleared his throat.

'Well, I'm *very* interested in what you say,' he remarked. 'Very interested indeed.' The interview, such as it was, was evidently over. Jane scrambled to her feet, certain she would find her P45 on her desk that very afternoon. Once Victoria got wind of this, she would be out faster than a Porsche Boxster.

As she passed through the mirrored entrance into the Movers and Shakers party, Jane smiled. A beautiful stranger smiled back, dazzling in a clinging satin dress, perfect make-up and a Grace Kelly ripple of blonde hair curling down over her shoulders. She felt pure Hollywood. Or, looking down at the vast glass of champagne in her hand, perhaps pure Bollywood.

Jane planned to drown all thoughts about Tom in gallon after gallon of champagne. And all thoughts about her no-doubt-wrecked professional future. She had, so far, been spared the expected post-Fitzherbert tongue-lashing from Victoria, who had been out of the office all day having her legs dyed and her eyelashes waxed for the party. Or was it the other way round? There had also been something about a seaweed wrap, eyebrow reconstruction, mud treatment and cellulite-blasting. Victoria was, for all Jane knew, probably having a damp-proof course put in as well.

'Jane, darling, you look delicious,' cried Oonagh, bustling up atop a pair of high black boots.

'Wonderful boots,' said Jane.

'Thank you, my darling,' said Oonagh. 'They're my fuckits,' she added, unexpectedly.

'Fuckits?' said Jane. Did she mean fuck-me shoes? Or was it the new Patrick Cox label?

'That's right,' grinned Oonagh. 'Expensive things I treat myself to even though I can't really afford them. I just think, oh fuck it, and buy them.' Oonagh smoothed her heavily beringed hands down her body. Her clinging black dress showed off her tiny waist to perfection. For a fifty-something, she really had the most wonderful figure.

'How do you keep in such good shape?' Jane asked her, smiling gratefully at the waiter glugging champagne into her glass.

'Sleep in my bra, darling,' Oonagh said briskly. 'Always have done. Never take it off, except for gala occasions. Not that there are many of *those* these days.'

'Who's here?' Jane looked around at the sea of

braying, grinning faces and wondered who they all were.

Oonagh on the other hand knew everyone. Being the *Fabulous* picture editor, Jane supposed that she probably had to. Nonetheless, she seemed to know more about the guests than might be deemed strictly necessary.

'Busty Binge-Fetlock's over there,' Oonagh whispered, gesturing in the direction of a stout, shock-headed man in tartan trousers who seemed to be deep in conversation with a coat stand. 'Terribly well-connected. On first-name terms with most of Europe's royal families. Rather near-sighted, though, as you can see. Probably thinks that fur's Queen Silvia.'

'And who's that?' Jane asked, looking in the direction of an impossibly lithe brunette whose legs went up to shoulder blades which protruded like Cadillac fins. On her head was something that looked like a meringue with a feather in it.

'Oh, that's Fluffy Fronte-Bottom,' twittered Oonagh. 'Great girl. One of the Basingstoke Fronte-Bottoms. They say she eats nothing but chips and pizzas, but you can't believe *that*, can you?'

Depends if they ever reach her stomach, I suppose, thought Jane. The girl was so thin that in profile she was almost invisible.

'And who's that over there?' she asked. A stunningly arrogant-looking man with a riot of thick dark curls was looking over with an appreciative expression. A thrill ran through her.

'Careful,' whispered Oonagh. 'That's Sebastian

Tripp. Apparently has the most *enormous* you-know-what. Women have been hospitalised, I'm not joking. Don't touch him with a bargepole. He's a serial shagger.'

'A case of wham, bam and see you in Casualty, ma'am,' said Jane.

'Exactly,' said Oonagh. 'Oh, and that's the Hon. Barnaby Fender over there, talking to Princess Loulou Fischtitz.' She nudged Jane in the direction of a tall, gangly man stooping to talk to a very short, plain, plump girl. 'He's a very sought-after banker. Bonuses are quite beyond belief, apparently.' Oonagh gave Jane a dirty wink. 'But bats on the other team, they say. Friend of Dorothy. Shame, as Loulou's his perfect woman. Just the right height to give him a blow job. Standing up. Anyway, I'm off, dear. Must circulate. I'll leave you to your own vices.'

As Oonagh disappeared into the throng, Jane looked warily around for Victoria, whom she was determined to avoid at all costs. Thankfully, she was nowhere to be seen in the vast crowd. Time, Jane decided, to put her best front forward. The champagne was beginning to have an emboldening effect. Knocking back a third glass, Jane launched herself into what she hoped was a sea of possibilities.

Her progress was made hazardous by both her high heels and the waiters who, elaborately dressed in Nehru collars and turbans, also bore ceremonial swords which threatened to shred the material of any passing dress. They reminded Jane strongly of Kenneth Williams in *Carry On Up the Khyber*. Anyone planning to squeeze by them also had to take into consideration their huge and unwieldy platters piled high with curries and Indian nibbles. Bearing in mind Tish's warning, Jane declined all offers of food. There seemed little point in dressing up to the nines and then spoiling your chance with the handsomest man in London by having a samosa between your teeth at the crucial moment.

There really were some *extraordinarily* handsome men in the room, obviously all scions of families who for centuries had had the pick of the gene pool. And the deep end at that. Everywhere Jane looked there were cheekbones, golden tans and more floppy blond fringes than you could shake a silver-backed hairbrush at. None of the women seemed larger than size eight, or sounded older than age eight. 'Oh, Bunter, you shouldn't!' Jane overheard them squealing at their escorts in high, babyish tones as she pushed by.

She slinked towards the back of the room, feeling like sex incarnate. Feeling like sex with anybody, in fact. Never had her blood pounded so hard and fast in her ears. She looked down with awe at the unaccustomed sight of her wobbling Mansfieldesque cleavage. A little over the top? she wondered. Actually, there was rather a lot over the top. Oh well, she told herself. Men like breasts. No boobies, no rubies, as Zsa Zsa Gabor once said. And tonight was the best chance she was going to get of picking up some family heirlooms.

'Allow me,' murmured a voice at her elbow just as

Jane found herself gravlaxed between two braying members of the minor aristocracy. They were locking overbites like stags locked antlers. Jane gratefully allowed a cool hand to lead her into a relatively uncrammed spot at the back of the room.

'Thank you,' she gasped, looking for the first time at her saviour. 'Mark!' she exclaimed. 'Mark Stackable!' Deep, crimson shame filled her. The last time she had seen Mark Stackable was in the company of a large pool of artichoke vomit she had deposited all over him, his floor and his waffle-cotton bedcovers. 'W-what are you doing here?' she stammered.

'First things first,' said Mark. He lifted two brimming glasses of champagne from a passing tray and handed one to Jane with a dazzling smile. 'Nice to see you again. Your very good health.' Jane blushed as she sipped. He had more reason than most people to say that.

'Are you a Mover and Shaker?' she asked. It sounded graceless, she realised, as soon as the words were out. Because *of course* Mark must be. His bonuses could probably even give the Hon. Barnaby Fender's a run for their money. And she'd forgotten quite how handsome he was.

He, on the other hand, seemed to have forgiven her. His thick-lashed dark eyes, which may or may not have been midnight blue, were looking warmly, if not directly at her, then certainly at the area of her cleavage. He switched on a large and brilliant white smile and pushed back his thick dark hair. Jane's knees felt weak as the surging crowd suddenly pressed her closer to him. His skin was close-shaven and tanned. He smelt rich.

'Apparently, although I'm not sure which,' grinned Mark. 'It's good to see you.'

'I'm so sorry . . .' she began, not wanting to bring up, as it were, the subject of the artichokes but feeling it had to be broached.

'Don't mention it,' Mark said, making it sound more of an instruction than an act of politeness. 'Let's pretend it never happened?' He flashed another glimpse of his stunningly white tombstones. It was obvious that he bore no grudge. He seemed to have simply wiped it from his memory.

'You're looking very well,' Jane said. She felt surprised and relieved and grateful. Not to mention extremely randy. Her mind fumbled for some useful neutral territory that she might steer towards his asking her out for dinner.

'And you look wonderful.' He gazed appreciatively at her cleavage again. Jane, unsure whether he was addressing her breasts or herself, grinned. The evening looked more or less in the bag. She was about to start a conversation about restaurants but noticed, just as she opened her mouth, that his eyes had slid over the top of her head and had fastened themselves on someone behind her.

'Mark, *darling*,' honked a familiar voice. 'Here you are, you *naughty* poppet. I've been looking for you *everywhere*.'

Jane froze. Champagne, she thought in horror. But

how? She was supposed to be thousands of miles away in New York. How could she possibly be here? Jane could hardly bear to face her. Only the thought of Champagne getting a close-up view of her well-covered shoulder blades and random moles persuaded her. She turned round.

Champagne had never looked more beautiful. Her white-blonde hair streamed over her fragile shoulders. Her knuckleduster cheekbones glowed with the merest hint of blusher and, through the clinging folds of her thin Voyage dress, her nipples protruded like screwed-out lipsticks. Her brilliant green eyes raked Jane up and down like searchlights as she stretched out a chilly hand heavy with rings. Her wrist was so thin it was exactly the width of her Cartier watch face. You could not see the straps at all.

'I don't believe we've met,' Champagne said frostily.

'We have, actually,' Jane said boldly. 'I'm Jane from *Fabulous* magazine.'

Champagne's six-seater lips parted in astonishment. 'Well, you scrub up well, I must say,' she blurted. She looked pointedly at Jane's dress.

'I tried that one on,' she added sweetly. 'But it looked cheap and nasty on me.'

She paused.

'Suits you, though.'

Around the base of her champagne glass, Jane's fingers itched. She longed to empty it in that arrogant face. Instead she said, 'Aren't you supposed to be in New York? With your film director?'

'We flew back together in the end,' barked Champagne. 'Talked about the film idea on the way.' She reached towards a passing platter. 'Whoops! Oh dear. Clumsy me. *So* sorry.'

Jane felt a hot, slithering sensation down her front as a vast pile of chicken tikka masala streamed off the serving dish and slid down her front. Thick, greasy sauce of a bright orange hue spread slowly across the pristine cream satin of the dress. Gasping as the hot, smelly slime seeped between her breasts, Jane briefly contemplated bludgeoning Champagne to death with one of the passing bottles of Bollinger. She did not have the faintest doubt that the food had been tipped over her on purpose. Clutching her arms to her breasts, impervious to the shouts of Mark behind her, Jane shoved her way through the crowd to the door and a taxi, her only thought to get home and change. She had been planning to take her dress off, admittedly, but not in these circumstances. Her hot, spicy evening had suddenly turned very cold.

Chapter 18

The staff of *Fabulous* were rarely at their best first thing on a Monday morning. In common with the rest of the nation, they shuffled slowly and unwillingly into the office. It had taken Jane a few weeks to realise that their reasons for doing so were rather different than most people's.

The clue was in the fact that they all carried large, expensive-looking weekend bags into the office on Mondays, and they all had bruises on their foreheads. Their dazed appearance, Jane gradually gathered, was the result of practically the entire *Fabulous* workforce spending its weekends in Grade One listed buildings. She knew from Mullions that banging one's forehead repeatedly against low doorways was the occupational hazard of the country-house guest. So perhaps it was hardly surprising the staff weren't the quickest of thinkers. All that cranium-crashing was bound to take its toll on the brain.

This ingenious theory, Jane realised, also explained why everyone smoked like a kipper factory during those first few hours in the office. The fear that you'd only stayed at Chatsworth while the person next to you had been to Windsor informed all discussions. The exaggerated, laid-back drawls with which information about weekends was exchanged obviously disguised panic of the highest order.

The Monday after the Friday of the Movers and Shakers party, however, Jane entered to find the joint positively jumping. 'Wasn't Grotty *unbelievable*?' Tash was shouting as Jane came in. 'Taking off those knickers and putting them on her head. Shame they were Totty Fotheringay's knickers, though. She looked furious . . . And didn't Loulou look *completely out of it*? Apparently at least four Rolls-Royces' worth have gone up her nose since January . . . Wasn't Bumzo hilarious? Trying to stick his tongue down Victoria's throat. She looked as if she was quite enjoying it, actually . . . And isn't Mark Stackable a *dream*? Hunktastic or *what*? Champagne certainly seemed to think so. Did you see them go off together?'

Jane's heart sank. Another one bites the dust, she thought miserably. Mark must think her utterly mad anyway. As well as disgusting. Throwing up everywhere on the first date, getting covered in food the second. She was beginning to wonder if there was a curse on her.

'And did you see *Jane*?' Tash sniggered conspiratorially. 'Rushing out with CTM all down her front!

Talk about an *Indian takeaway.*' Various coughs and agonised stretching of eyes alerted Tash to the fact that Jane was sitting at the desk behind her. Jane derived some comfort from watching the tide of mortified puce that now rose swiftly up the back of Tash's neck.

'Uuurrggghh.' Everyone was suddenly distracted by a profound groan coming from Oonagh's direction. Head bent over the lightbox, she was examining a set of wedding photographs for the social pages. 'All that inherited wealth and not one of them seems to own a full-length mirror,' wailed Oonagh, holding one of the offending images between her finger and thumb as if it was something very nasty indeed. 'This poor woman's hat looks as if a poodle's died on top of her head. And look at all that jewellery. And that *food. Pork chops* for goodness' sake. Talk about swine before pearls.'

'Whose wedding was it?' asked Tish.

'Pandora Smellie-Lewes,' sighed Oonagh. 'She's married someone called Conte Juan Paz de Barcelona de Cojones de Soto.'

'Who everyone knows doesn't have a bean,' said Tash, 'but poor Dora was *so* desperate to marry a title. Talk about a wannabe.'

'You mean a Juannabe,' snorted Tosh.

Jane was relieved that Victoria, so far, had not made an appearance.

'I'm not sure we'll be seeing Victoria today,' said Tish as if reading her mind. 'Hermione's had a relapse.'

'Hermione?' asked Jane. 'That's not one of her children, is it?' Visions of a distraught Victoria bending over the bed of a sick child flashed before her. Her soft heart dissolved with pity, with a powerful slug of guilt. How *could* she have said all those things about poor Victoria to Archie Fitzherbert?

'No, Hermione's her daughter's kitten,' said Tish breezily. 'Had to be rushed to hospital with a suspected ingrowing toenail or something. But she's fine now. Has a private room with her own nurse. I've sent some flowers from all of us. A card is going round the office for everyone to sign.'

'I see,' Jane blinked. 'Well, anyway, Tish, perhaps you could give me a hand with this interview request. I need to get it out today. Could you type it for me?' She handed a scribbled sheet of paper to the secretary, whose attention was now focused on painting each nail a different colour. She looked up from the paper to Jane in astonishment.

'I don't do much typing, actually,' she drawled in what, for her, passed for surprise.

'She's not the type,' said Tash, standing at the fax.

Jane raised an eyebrow and opened a file on her computer to type the letter herself. It was a request to Lily Eyre's agent for an interview. Common ankles or not, Jane was determined that *Fabulous* should do something about the pretty actress before everybody else did. As she typed the opening sentence, her telephone rang.

'Hello,' said an American voice. Jane froze as she recognised the businesslike tones of Mark Stackable.

'Hi,' muttered Jane in astonishment. What on earth

did he want? Surely having seen her covered in undigested food for the second time was enough to put him off seeking her company for ever.

Apparently not. 'I wondered whether you might be free for dinner tonight?' he said. 'It strikes me that we haven't managed to have a proper conversation yet.'

'Er, yes, I mean no, we haven't,' Jane said, amazed. 'I mean yes, I'd love to.'

'I've booked a table at Ninja,' said Mark. Ninja was a wildly expensive new Japanese restaurant where only the eye-wideningly rich or universally famous had a hope of being admitted. Nonetheless, Jane was surprised at his choice. After the CTM fiasco, one might have imagined Mark would want to give exotic food a rest for the moment.

'Look, I've got to dash,' he said briskly. 'Bit of a salmon day. Meet you in the Ninja bar at eight thirty, OK?' The line went dead.

It was nice, Jane thought, to be in the hands of someone decisive for a change. But that, she determined, was as far as Mark's hands were going to get. At least, until the question of how well he knew Champagne had been satisfactorily explained.

Ninja was one of those irritating restaurants which didn't bother having a sign outside, presumably on the grounds that the people who mattered knew where it was anyway, and those who didn't simply didn't matter. Jane realised she must be in the latter category, after spending ten heart-stopping minutes rushing up and down the street before finally realising the stark, anonymous, utterly signless black glass doors that looked exactly like an office were in fact the portals of Ninja.

There was no sign of Mark in the bar, which was of the minimalist, understated persuasion that looked far better without people. Anyone, however smart, who dared sit on one of its perfectly-aligned beige-covered stools ran the risk of making the place look hopelessly untidy. Intimidated, Jane decided to powder her nose instead.

Signs, it seemed, were not Ninja's strong point. Squinting at the tiny sexless figure on the black marble lavatory door, Jane assumed it was the ladies until she suddenly found herself in the men's. Ricocheting into the women's room, Jane looked at her appearance in despair. The faithful old black jacket and trousers were showing distinct signs of wear and tear; she had realised too late that her only other suit, along with the remains of Tiara's ballgown, was at the cleaners. 'I don't even have any clothes of my own,' she grumbled to herself. 'I just rent them from Sketchley's.'

She had done her best with her floppy, insubordinate locks, but it was still less of a hair-do than a hair-don't. It collapsed in a vague bob about her shoulders, perfumed with the smell of the sandwich bar in which she had queued at lunchtime. Why was it, Jane wondered, that her scent faded into nothing only a few minutes after application, while the odour of fried bacon and chips clung on more determinedly than the Ancient Mariner's albatross?

It took her a good few minutes to find her way out of the loos. The doors were innocent of anything as cumbersome or unaesthetic as a handle, and Jane scrabbled at panel after relentless panel of shining black marble before finding the one that opened. When, red-faced and flustered, she arrived back in the bar, Mark was sitting in the corner, talking urgently into the smallest mobile phone she had ever seen.

'Look, I'll have to get back to you tomorrow,' she heard him say as she approached. 'I'm late for a meeting now, so I have to go. *Ciao*. Hi there,' he grinned, snapping his mobile away. 'Krug?'

'Yes, please,' Jane nodded, shifting her bottom on to one of the tiny beige stool cushions.

'Shame you had to leave the party,' Mark said.

'Yes, wasn't it?' said Jane, thinking that it was more of a shame Champagne had seen fit to throw a trayful of chicken tikka masala all over her.

'How do you know Champagne?' she asked. There seemed no point in beating about the bush.

'Known her for years,' Mark said breezily. 'Her family's been with Goldman's practically since it started. Nice girl. Knows an awful lot about money.'

A waiter of inscrutable Orientalness came to escort them to their table. Jane decided not to pursue her inquiries further. Why spoil the evening by discussing Champagne? Better stick to drinking it. And what did it matter anyway? What was Mark Stackable to her?

There was only one man she really cared about, and she could never find him now.

At some unseen signal from Mark, the waiter shimmied over with two more chilled glasses of champagne. Jane tried hard not to knock them over as she struggled to push aside with her knees the several layers of thick, white starched linen under the table. It was the type of restaurant where sitting down was like getting into bed.

Mark, buried in the menu, suddenly began to make a succession of noises of mixed agony and surprise which the waiter began to note down. He was, Jane realised, ordering in fluent Japanese.

'I'll have the same,' she smiled at the waiter, who looked back at her impassively.

'I've already ordered for you,' Mark said, snapping the menu shut. 'I used to work in Japan,' he added airily, 'so I like to get it out and dust it down every now and then.'

'Do you now?' grinned Jane.

Mark, however, did not smile. It dawned on Jane that perhaps his sense of humour was not his strongest point after all. Then again, he was so good-looking, it was probably greedy asking him to be funny as well.

A wooden board of sushi arrived and was placed on the table between them. Jane stared at the neatly arranged diagonals of cold fish and rolled rice and felt her appetite desert her. What she wouldn't give for a vast, steaming plate of spaghetti.

'It's very difficult to find food in London that doesn't destroy your body, don't you find?' Mark observed, plucking his sushi elegantly between tiny chopsticks and dipping it expertly into a bowl of soy sauce. Determinedly Jane nodded, shoved a piece of sushi in her mouth and swallowed it as quickly as possible.

'How was your salmon day?' she asked.

Mark raised his eyebrows and made 'I'm eating sushi' gestures. 'Oh, fine,' he said when his mouth was empty. 'Not too many CLMs in the end.' Mark glanced at her uncomprehending face a trifle impatiently. 'Career limiting manoeuvres?'

Jane noticed that everything he said ended with a strange, upward, interrogative note that made each sentence sound like a question, even when, as almost always, it wasn't.

'Best overcome and remedied by efficient blame-storming and arsemosis?' said Mark. 'Blamestorming,' he explained, rather tersely, 'is like brainstorming, but the idea is to find some other guy to blame for when everything goes wrong?'

Jane giggled nervously, hoping he wasn't going to do the corporate talk all night. She knew nothing about the financial world. Her idea of a bear market was the cuddly toy section at Hamley's.

Mark gestured to the waiter to fill up her glass again. 'I can see I'm going to have to teach you a thing or two about the City?' he remarked, reading her thoughts alarmingly easily. 'Do you, for example,' he asked, shoving in a mouthful of rice and seaweed, 'know about leverage?'

Mark's mobile phone shrilled just as she was about

to confess that she didn't. Flashing her a terse look which Jane interpreted as 'This is important so you'll have to excuse me?' Mark got up quickly and walked to the bar, his heels clicking on the marble like Fred Astaire.

After what seemed an eternity, Mark clicked back again. 'Sorry, but I'm afraid I'm involved in a pretty mega project at the moment?' he said. Jane was beginning to find his note of permanent inquiry maddening. 'Big bucks, if it comes off?'

Mark's eyes, Jane noticed, positively blazed at the mention of money. Perhaps the City was exciting after all. Being rich *must* be interesting. It struck her as strange that, although he ended each of his statements with a question mark, Mark had yet to ask her a single question about herself. She hadn't noticed before, being too drunk the first time she had met him, and not having had time the second, but his mind, she was beginning to realise, had a strangely incurious cast. The only thing he seemed to be interested in was interest.

She laid down her chopsticks and drank the rest of her champagne. The room was starting to spin faster than Alastair Campbell.

'I'm not too hungry either?' Mark said, noticing Jane had stopped eating. 'Too much at lunchtime?' he added, patting his perfectly flat stomach. 'Tell you what, why don't you come back to my flat for, um, a peppermint tea? It's just around the corner?'

A corner half an hour away by taxi in the depths of

Clerkenwell, as it turned out. Jane could have lived in the entrance hall of Mark's apartment block alone, she thought as she was ushered through the gleaming, concept-lit brick-lined space which seemed very different to the chandeliers-and-gilt-lobby she remembered going back to after Amanda's dinner party.

It was. 'Like it?' said Mark as they zoomed upwards. 'My new loft apartment. It's awesome. So cool. I've only been here a week or so.'

'When did you move?' asked Jane. She felt embarrassed. She had been meaning to move for months and hadn't done as much as look in an estate agent's window.

'Last week?' said Mark. 'I saw this place after a meeting and just had to have it. I had to get out of Cheyne Walk. There's no buzz there any more?'

Almost as soon as they had closed, the lift doors sprung open again, straight into a vast, light room which Jane realised must be the sitting room. 'Yeah, the lift opens straight into the flat?' said Mark. 'Cool, huh?'

It was completely empty apart from two colossal white sofas which faced each other, as if squaring up for a sumo wrestling match, over a huge expanse of polished, honey-coloured wood. Behind them, a spiral staircase of the same wood wound up and away into the ceiling, and, further back still, two huge windows covered with thin-slatted Venetian blinds stretched film-noir-like to the floor. On a glass coffee table between the two sofas, a single white lily rose from a huge glass flowerpot. It was the barest room Jane had ever seen.

'Space,' Mark said, spreading his arms and grinning at her eagerly. 'The ultimate luxury, don't you think?'

Jane managed a smile. The discovery that Mark's idea of a good thing was basically thin air was not encouraging.

'And this is the cuisine,' said Mark, leading her into a vast white kitchen illuminated by a sloping glass roof. Its expanses of stainless steel and smooth white surfaces were more suggestive of an operating theatre than anything to do with eating. The vast fridge, which Mark proudly opened to show how it was shaped like a huge mobile phone, was bristling with ice-makers and water dispensers. Definitely a fridge too far, thought Jane. The front of the stove had so many buttons and lights it looked like the flight deck of Concorde. 'Not that I use it?' Mark confessed, mock-embarrassed. 'Haven't eaten in for, gee, must be five years?' he added proudly.

Jane could believe it. Nothing looked as if it had ever been touched. It was all so clean she felt as if she ought to be fumigated, or at least slip on protective clothing.

'Drink?' asked Mark, trotting across the brilliant white space and returning with a bottle of red wine and two gleaming glasses. 'Nothing under fifty pounds a bottle is ever worth drinking, don't you agree?'

Jane nodded dumbly.

Mark took a tiny, restrained sip of the wine, then gave her a wolfish grin, evidently flossed to within an inch of its life. 'Want to see upstairs?'

As he led her out of the kitchen, Jane caught a glimpse of a bathroom beyond containing the biggest pair of weighing scales she had ever seen. Mark, Jane realised, was beginning to make Narcissus look self-deprecating.

'You've gotta see my bedroom?' said Mark.

Up the spiral stairs he went, into a room the size of a small airport terminal. Like downstairs, it contained the absolute minimum of furniture – a vast bed covered in a spotless white duvet and a huge mirror bolted to the wall opposite. It would almost have been kinky, Jane thought, were it not for the fact that the mirror was so far away from the bed you'd need binoculars to see yourself.

'Like my chandeliers?' asked Mark, pointing upwards to a ceiling as white and radiant as eternity. 'Cost a fortune. Specially designed for the loft. Great, aren't they?'

Jane looked up at the bright, twisted mass of cracked teacup, wine glass and coathanger, interspersed with the occasional bulb, which hung from the centre of the bedroom ceiling. It was, she supposed, witty. But she'd heard better jokes.

Mark picked up a small, slim remote control from the floor at the side of the bed and pointed it upwards. The chandelier immediately dimmed. 'Come and look at my million-pound view?' he smiled, clicking over to the floor-length windows. Jane walked over and stood beside him, gazing out as directed to the prospect of the City. The box-like buildings, centre of the world money trade, only reinforced Jane's feeling of unease. Mark's flat was so sterile. There seemed to be no books anywhere. Nor pictures. The only thing framed was mirrors.

Mark stretched out an arm and drew her to him. He started to kiss her neck, his mouth moving slowly up to her face. As he held her to him, Jane felt something big and hard pressing against her.

'Oh, excuse me?' Mark said, suddenly rummaging in his trousers and extracting his bulging wallet.

He began to kiss her again. The taste of the wine as he explored her mouth was now sour and metallic. Jane felt unable to respond. The truth was, she realised, that she could never really feel anything for Mark Stackable. There was nothing warm or witty about him. Nothing human. He was rich, but that really was about the size of it. Or was it? Something that was definitely not his wallet was rubbing urgently against her pudenda.

But it couldn't have been more different from Tom's tender caresses, and his thrilling subtlety. Jane stood as rigid as a statue as Mark grasped her breasts as eagerly as if they were fistfuls of banknotes, tears sliding down her face as he unbuttoned her jacket and roughly pushed it off. He stopped and looked at her in amazement as sobs began to shudder through her body. She shook her head, buttoned her clothes and squeezed his hand as she detached herself and went downstairs into the sitting room in search of her bag. After all, it wasn't Mark's fault that he wasn't Tom. Nor was it necessarily a bad thing he was obviously so obsessed with money. Some women, including, no doubt, most of the *Fabulous* staff, would kill for a man like him. It was just that, as far as Jane was concerned, Mark Stackable had feet of K.

Chapter 19

'Bollocks,' said Tosh to Oonagh.

'No, darling. Bollocks Beaufort-Baring wasn't *at* this wedding,' said the picture editor, bending over the lightbox and squinting at the pile of photographs she was examining with Tosh in her capacity as wedding editor. 'You're probably confusing him with Bruiser Aarss, who was there with the Hon. Bulymya yl Bowe.'

'Are you sure?' asked Tosh, picking up a photograph and scrutinising it closely. 'This looks like Bollocks to me. Don't you think so, Jane?' She held it up to the light.

Jane squinted at the image of a short, stocky young man with a novelty waistcoat and an alarmed expression. 'Complete Bollocks,' said Jane, who actually knew nothing about him save the fact that he had clearly emerged from the shallow end of the gene pool and was, as far as she could see, still dripping wet.

Oonagh sighed. 'I probably need a break,' she said. 'I've been wading through those pictures for so long I can't tell my Aarss from my yl Bowe any more.'

Jane's telephone rang. She gazed at it in terror. What if it was Mark? Three days had passed since she had left him with his expectations quite literally raised, and there had been much agonising in between. Had she done the right thing? Had rejecting the advances of the richest man she was ever likely to meet been a good idea?

Jane took the receiver with a shaking hand. For once, she was almost relieved to hear Champagne at the other end of the receiver. 'I've got some *brilliant* news,' came the triumphant honk. 'I'm going to be a film star. Marvellous, isn't it? I saw Brad again last night.' Naturally, she made no mention of, still less an apology for, the CTM incident.

'Brad who?' asked Jane. 'Pitt?'

'No,' came the outraged squawk. 'Brad Postlethwaite. The hot new British director I told you about. The one I met in New York. Anyway, we had dinner at Soho House last night and afterwards he offered me the most *amazing* part.'

I bet he did, thought Jane. 'A part in what?' she asked.

'He's making a really cool new film,' bawled Champagne. 'Sort of like *Four Weddings and a Funeral*, but it's called *Three Christenings and a Hen Party*. It sort of sends up English society christenings. He wants me to play myself. So obviously I've signed up for the best acting lessons money can buy. I'll be sending you the invoices, of course.'

'Playing *yourself*?' said Jane slowly. 'It's tongue in cheek, then?'

There was a silence. 'I'm not putting my tongue in anybody's cheeks,' blustered Champagne at the other end. 'It's a seriously challenging artistic opportunity. Brad says it's a cameo role,' Champagne gushed, 'but I do hope he lets me wear my diamonds.'

'When do you start?' asked Jane.

'Monday,' boomed Champagne. 'That's why I'm calling you. About the stretch limo. To take me to the set. Brad says the film hasn't got the budget to pay for one, so you'll have to sort it out for me. Want it big, black and shiny. Oh, and with a TV, telephone, fax, blacked-out windows, white suede seats and a cocktail cabinet.'

'You must be joking,' said Jane. 'We can't afford that.'

'Well, you'd better bloody *try*,' shrieked Champagne, slamming the phone down.

'Champagne's got a part in a film,' Jane told Victoria who was busy filling out her expenses slips in her office. 'She seems to expect us to provide a stretch limo to drive her to the set. As well as paying for her acting lessons.'

Victoria stopped stabbing her calculator and stared at her. Jane felt uncomfortable. She didn't know quite where she was with Victoria these days. The expected blow had not yet come. Victoria had not said a word about the conversation with Archie Fitzherbert. There must be a reason for this, as it was impossible that he had not told her. She was obviously biding her time. Waiting to strike. It made Jane nervous.

'Champagne,' Victoria explained patiently, a dangerous gleam in her eye, 'is our biggest asset. Whatever she wants, she can have. If she's in a film, great. Get her to write about it. Go on set with her. Do a big number. Come to think of it, let's put her on the cover.' Victoria's eyes blazed feverishly. 'Yes,' she breathed, like one witnessing an ecstatic vision. 'Let's put her in a director's chair, with her legs either side of it like Christine Keeler. What a great idea.'

Jane reeled out of the editor's office.

'By the way,' Victoria's voice floated out behind her, 'I've been meaning to have a word with you about this interview with Lady Dido Dingle, the interior designer.'

Jane blanched. The Lady Dido Dingle piece had been an editing nightmare. Like many of the *Fabulous* pieces which crossed Jane's desk it needed a rewrite so heavy she could have brought in a JCB.

'What about it?' Jane asked through gritted teeth. She had, she thought, done a reasonably good job on it.

'Well, it mentions her fifth home in St Tropez and her downstairs toilet,' said Victoria, putting her head on one side and looking questioningly at Jane.

'Yes that's right,' said Jane, nodding. 'With a solid gold seat and a diamond flush button.'

'*Fabulous* readers,' said Victoria, closing her eyes in

exasperation, 'do not go to toilets.'

Which explained, thought Jane, the expressions on the faces of some of the people on the party pages.

'They use *lavatories*,' said Victoria. 'Or *loos*.'

When Jane rang Champagne back to say she could have a car, and was next month's cover story into the bargain, she was as magnanimous in victory as ever. 'Yah, I should bloody well think so,' she honked indignantly.

'So where is this set?' Jane asked. 'Although I suppose we could travel up together in the limo.'

'We bloody well could not,' Champagne shouted furiously. 'I'm the star. I'm not sharing my limo with anyone. You make your own sodding way there.'

Jane called the film production company, where a squeaky-voiced girl called Jade said she'd have to get back to her about the location. She was more forthcoming about the cast. It turned out that *Three Christenings and a Hen Party* was to star none other than the up-and-coming British actress Lily Eyre. After an excited discussion, Jane shot back into Victoria's office. There could be no excuse now for not putting Lily on the cover.

'She'll be the next Andie MacDowell,' Jane pleaded. After all, she reasoned, Lily Eyre was the star of the film. Champagne was just a walk-on. 'And we could do her first. Have her exclusively, the film company says so. She's beautiful. She'd make the most brilliant cover.'

'Look, I'm sorry,' said Victoria sternly, sounding

anything but apologetic. She did not like being argued with the first time, let alone the second. 'Champagne's our cover, and that's all there is to it.'

'But . . .'

Victoria's eyes flashed fire. She stood up, her leather miniskirt creaking indignantly. 'I'm not discussing it any further. Have you the faintest idea how busy I am? How many things I have to do today?'

'What *is* she doing today?' Jane whispered to Tish after Victoria stalked out of the office clutching a make-up bag, obviously en route for the loos.

'Erm, lunch at the Caprice,' murmured Tish, flicking through Victoria's diary. 'Then she's having her high-lights done. Then she's going to her aromatherapist. Then she's seeing her dressmaker. Then she's off to Bali for a week on holiday. She didn't tell you? Oh. Do you want me to get that?'

Jane's phone had by now been ringing for some time. 'No, it's OK,' said Jane diving for it, thinking she'd rather have it answered this side of the millen-nium. It was the *Three Weddings and a Hen Party* film company.

'Sorry about the confusion earlier,' said Jade. 'It's just that we've been juggling locations slightly until we got the price we wanted. It's now definite that Champagne D'Vyne will be filming her scenes in the West Country.'

'How lovely,' said Jane. Visions of rustic, verdant bliss unfolded before her. 'Where, exactly?'

'Well, don't get your hopes up too much,' said Jade.

'The place is falling apart from what I hear. Rotting old pile called Mullions. The nearest village,' she paused and sniggered, 'is called Lower Bulge.'

The next day could not have been more beautiful. As the 2CV, given an unexpected stay of execution by a new garage down the road, backfired its way through the hedge-lined lanes leading to Mullions, Jane caught occasional glimpses of ploughed fields through which running pheasants lurched drunkenly from side to side. Placid ponies stood nibbling on green hillsides. A more soothing scene could not be imagined.

Jane was consumed with curiosity about what Tally had been up to. Guiltily, she realised it had been weeks since she had spoken to her. And what tumultuous weeks they had been. She had started a new job and she had found and lost once more both Tom and Mark Stackable, with varying degrees of regret. She had thought she had finally rid herself of the dead weight of Champagne, only to be proved hideously wrong. Tally, meanwhile, had hardly been idle. She had apparently converted Mullions into Ealing Studios.

Jane had thought at first that Jade was mistaken, but the directions she was given confirmed that Mullions was indeed where *Three Christenings and a Hen Party* was being immortalised on celluloid. It must be part of Tally's push to generate new business. An admirable and uncharacteristically enterprising effort, thought Jane, but it was a shame, nonetheless, that the production had Champagne in it. After her previous experience showing Champagne round Mullions, Tally had sworn on the heads of all the Venerys never to have her within a million miles of the place again. It was odd that she had changed her mind.

As the weather was so crisp and fine, Jane decided to leave the 2CV by the gatehouse and walk through the parkland to Mullions. She would be late for the arranged on-set meeting with Champagne, but not significantly. And certainly not later than Champagne herself. Champagne could be late for Britain.

After a pleasant ten minutes wandering along the estate road with the afternoon sun on her face and the sleepy church bells of Lower Bulge floating drowsily across the fields, Jane rounded a corner and stopped dead in her tracks. A scene seemed to be in full swing. Not wishing to disturb the filming, Jane slipped behind one of the bushes bordering the path, blessing Mr Peters and his slatternly pruning for such a convenient and copious screen. She peered out and watched.

The actors looked a decidedly scruffy bunch, all with straggling beards, metal-framed glasses and cagoules in every hideous fluorescent shade from violent pink to acid yellow. All wore hiking boots, were hung around with rucksacks and compasses like Christmas trees and were looking angrily in the direction of someone Jane could not quite see. She wondered where this scene fitted into the plot.

'What do you mean we can't walk across this land?' one of the cagoule-wearers was shouting, shaking his skinny fist. 'This is a right of way, this is. Marked on all the Ordnance Survey maps. Just look.' He waved a handful of much-creased cartography in the invisible someone's direction. 'You've no right to stop us, you haven't.'

'I have every right,' shouted a threatening, familiar voice. *Saul Dewsbury*, thought Jane in horror, shrinking further back into the bush. *Still around*. She imagined he had got bored of Tally and gone back to Chelsea ages ago. But no, he was here, larger and louder than life. This was obviously nothing to do with the film. This was another plot altogether.

'Don't want my land messed up by a load of wandering outward-bloody-bounders like you lot,' Saul was yelling, still out of sight.

His land? thought Jane in panic. Surely to God Tally hadn't *married* him. That would be a disaster. Not to mention insulting. They had always sworn to be each other's bridesmaids.

'Stomping around with bloody knapsacks,' continued Saul's echoing, contemptuous tones. 'Just piss off, will you? If you don't make yourselves scarce this minute, I'll horsewhip you off. I'll give you blisters where your boots have never been.' There was a cracking sound. Jane knew without having to see that Saul was slapping a riding crop over his thigh.

The ramblers' glasses flashed with impotent fury, but they decided not to call his bluff. Instead, they walked as slowly and defiantly as they could back along the path to the gate, muttering into their beards as they went. 'Won't get away with this,' the leader vowed as they passed Jane hidden behind the bushes. 'Breaking the law. We'll get him for this. Arrogant tosser.'

'Yeah. Who the hell does he think he is?' demanded another plaintively. 'Ruined our walk, he has. I'd just got into my stride and all. And what about all these egg sandwiches? I spent all last night making 'em.'

'Never mind the sandwiches,' said the leader, looking resolute. 'They'll come in useful, don't you worry. An army marches on its stomach. An' this is war. There've been some odd rumours about what that bloke's up to 'ere as it is. Time to get in touch with a few of our mates, I reckon.'

The little group stomped out of the gateway and disappeared behind the hedge along the road. Jane wondered who their mates were. And even more about the rumours.

She waited a few minutes until she was sure Saul had gone, then stepped out on to the path, almost colliding with Saul as she did so. He was passing the bush, presumably en route to the gate to make sure the ramblers had disappeared.

'Ow,' he shouted, as Jane's knee collided with that part of his thigh which still smarted from overzealous application of the riding crop. 'You!' he exclaimed, glaring at Jane. 'What the hell are you doing here? You're trespassing. I've a good mind to call the police.'

'I'm here for the filming, actually,' Jane said, trying to disguise how rattled she felt by his assumption of control. *Surely* Tally couldn't have . . . 'I'm here,' she continued lightly, 'to bring the sights, the sounds and if

I'm very lucky the scenes of Champagne D'Vyne's cinematic debut to the printed page for the benefit of the glossy magazine-reading public.'

Saul stared at her, the colour draining out of his face. 'Champagne?' he gasped, his lordly tones dropping several decibels. 'Is *Champagne* in this bloody film?' He gasped at Jane in horror before recovering himself rapidly. 'I haven't seen the final cast list yet,' he muttered.

'She's got a starring role,' said Jane, amused at his consternation. 'I'm surprised you haven't popped down to say hi. Although,' she added slyly, 'I don't suppose Tally would particularly appreciate that. Is Tally around, by the way? I was rather hoping to be able to stay at the house.'

'Tally's not here at the moment,' said Saul firmly. 'I'm looking after the place for her. She's gone to London.'

'London?' exclaimed Jane, not believing him for a minute. Tally's loathing of London was legendary. Had he, she suddenly thought wildly, got *rid* of Tally? Hidden her under the floorboards and taken control of the estate? Saul, Jane was quite sure, was capable of anything to get his own ends. And there was no one around to stop him.

'Yes,' said Saul, smoothly. 'She's gone shopping. Buying a wedding dress, as it happens. We're getting married next weekend.'

Jane gasped. Next weekend. Relief that it had not yet happened mixed with horror that it was going to.

'Where's Mrs Ormondroyd?' she demanded. If she could get any sense out of anyone about what had been going on she'd get it out of the housekeeper.

'Mrs Ormondroyd, alas,' said Saul, admiring the signet ring on his little finger and playing with one of his elegant cuff-links, 'is sadly no longer with us. We had to let her go.'

Jane stared. The ring on his finger bore the Venery crest. Tally's ring. 'What, you mean you've sacked her?' she gasped. 'But Mrs Ormondroyd's been here for years. Centuries.'

'Exactly,' said Saul, lighting a leisurely cigarette. 'Mrs Ormondroyd didn't fit in with the, well, *enterprising* spirit that Tally and I are trying to introduce at Mullions. Nor, for that matter, did Mr Peters, who has also sadly left us. And now,' he said smoothly, 'I'll have to leave myself. Regrettably I won't be able to put you up at Mullions tonight. None of the bedrooms is fit to receive guests, unfortunately.'

When, thought Jane, watching Saul's dapper form retreating, had they ever been?

Jane walked rapidly down the slope into the park. There was little more she could find out until Tally returned from London. If she had ever gone there, that was. Jane glanced up at the rambling old house and calculated that her chances of finding Tally inside that maze of rotting rooms if Saul wished to keep her hidden were nil. Mullions was the kind of place where people got up in the night to find the nearest lavatory, lost their way and were discovered forty years later as a skeleton in the Clock Tower broom cupboard.

Jane headed towards the film set. Even to her jaded and preoccupied eye it had something of the excitement and romance of a fairground. Caravans and lorries were parked haphazardly on the grassland, and ponytailed, T-shirted people bustled importantly about clutching clapperboards. On the grass immediately below the house, a gaggle of people with clipboards, cameras and loudhailers were concentrating on the scene about to be filmed.

As she approached, Jane saw that it was a scene between Lily Eyre and her co-star, a gangly young man with a tousled fringe and a disorganised air who was evidently meant to provide the Hugh Grant factor.

Lily was even more beautiful in the flesh than in her pictures. She had a vivid heart-shaped face in which two huge blue eyes shone like naughty sapphires, and a large, infectious grin. Her long, gold hair was as yellow and crinkly as spiral pasta and, as far as Jane could make out under the jeans, her ankles were slender and irreproachably upper class. As she waited for her cue, giggling with her co-star, she seemed to radiate charm and good humour.

'Take twenty-four,' shouted a red-haired girl with a clapperboard as Jane sidled in next to her at the edge of the set.

'A-aaa-aand ACTION!' shouted a shambolic-looking man in a baggy sweater and geeky glasses, evidently the director, Brad Postlethwaite. He looked too cerebral to be tempted by Champagne, Jane thought. Whatever state he had been in when he offered her whatever part he had offered, he was clearly regretting it now.

'CHRIST!' he yelled as a figure suddenly appeared and ran across the back of the scene being filmed. 'Champagne, you've arsed up the eyelines again. For FUCK'S SAKE!' He spoke, Jane thought, amused, with the acid vehemence of the truly bitter.

'What do you mean?' bawled back Champagne indignantly. 'There's nothing wrong with my eyeliner. I know a damn sight more about make-up than you do.'

'Not eyeliner,' yelled the director furiously. '*Eyelines.*' His voice dropped, suddenly weary. 'You're distracting the actors on set so they keep looking at you and not at each other.'

You could hardly blame them, Jane thought. Champagne was wearing a fluorescent pink minidress so tiny one wondered why she had bothered putting it on at all. Her tanned thighs were exposed in their entirety while her breasts soared outwards and upwards like a couple of moon-bound Apollos.

'That dress should win an Oscar,' whispered the redhead with the clapperboard. 'Best supporting role.'

'A couple of Golden Globes at least,' giggled her blonde companion, whose bag, bulging with brushes, pots and tubes, proclaimed her to be a make-up girl. 'Unbelievable, isn't she? Talk about star attitude. Have you heard, she's even been demanding her own trailer?'

'Yes. And Brad told her she could have the honey-wagon if she wanted,' grinned the redhead. 'She was thrilled until she found out it was the toilets.'

'She's not very good at the jargon, is she?' smiled the blonde. 'When she first came to have her make-up done she had a very odd idea of what touching up was.'

'She thought a dolly grip was some sort of sex position, apparently,' snorted the redhead. 'Ooh, I'm on,' she added, suddenly realising the filming had ground to a halt and the director was staring at her furiously. 'Take twenty-five,' she called, slamming down her clapperboard so hard it made Jane wince.

'Get out of shot, for God's sake,' bawled the furious director at Champagne. 'For the millionth time, and almost the millionth take, THIS ISN'T YOUR SCENE!' Brad pushed his glasses on top of his unkempt hair and rubbed his eyes. He looked utterly defeated. 'OK, OK,' he said. 'Let's do your bit, Champagne. Your big scene. You walk across the set, grin at the camera and walk off again. That's all there is to it.'

'That's all there is to it *now*,' grinned the clapperboard girl. 'She had a line to say at the beginning but Brad got so fed up with her fluffing it he made it a non-speaking part. Lily's been very good about all this, I must say,' she added. 'Most stars would have a major fit if they had Champagne to put up with.'

Indeed, far from being annoyed, Lily, now smoking a cigarette beside the cameraman, actually seemed to be enjoying it. Her eyebrow was raised and her face shone with suppressed laughter. It was, Jane realised with a pang, the most perfect, provocative expression for the cover of *Fabulous*. Really, she was beginning to be obsessed with the magazine.

'AACTION!' shouted Brad.

Champagne stood up, took a deep breath and tottered across the set on her high heels. 'Break a leg,' murmured the redhead as Champagne closed her eyes and started to flex her tyre-like lips in what was evidently some sort of pre-performance ritual.

'Well, she'd certainly rather break a leg than a nail,' observed the make-up girl. 'I should know, I spent about three hours painting them this morning in exactly the right shade of nude she wanted. If nothing else, there's no end to her talons.'

'Shush, it's her Moment,' cautioned the clapperboard girl. 'We don't want to miss a piece of acting history.'

Pausing for a good few minutes in front of the camera, Champagne stuck her chest out and flashed a prolonged and utterly plastic grin before sashaying slowly off set.

'Cut!' said Brad. 'Perfect, Champagne. Got it in one. Take a break, everyone. Lunch.' He passed a weary hand across his forehead, looking as if food was the last thing on his mind and strong drink the first.

The two girls exploded. 'That bit wasn't even filmed,' hiccuped the redhead. 'There's no one sitting on the camera.'

Jane smiled broadly. It was true. The seat behind the lens was empty.

'Is it a shawl?' honked Champagne, wobbling across the grass towards Brad.

'She means a wrap,' tittered the make-up girl.

Jane, giggling, suddenly felt the smile freeze on her lips. Champagne, looking furiously in the direction of the sniggering, had spotted her.

'Where the hell have *you* been?' Champagne honked, stumbling over, her green eyes flashing furiously. 'What about this story you're supposed to be writing about me?'

The clapperboard and make-up girls melted away, leaving Jane feeling alone and unprotected. 'I got delayed,' she said hurriedly.

'Well, you'd better catch up quickly then,' Champagne barked. 'I'll have to show you round, I suppose. I bet you don't know the first thing about a film set, do you?'

'Er, not much,' Jane admitted.

Champagne rolled her eyes and tossed back her white-blonde hair. 'Well, you'd better come with me,' she huffed. 'But first, you can take me to lunch.'

'Fine,' said Jane, looking at the queues of actors starting to form at the trestle tables some distance away. It would be fun to eat with the cast. And useful. She'd pick up lots of good anecdotes for the piece and it would be a chance to meet Lily.

'You surely don't think we're eating *on set*?' Champagne declared, looking at Jane in amazement. 'I'm sorry, but I think a star of my calibre has the right to expect something a bit more upmarket than the filthy crap they serve here. Can you see Demi Moore queuing up with that lot?'

'No,' said Jane, truthfully. Demi Moore was, indeed,

nowhere to be seen. Lily Eyre was though, chatting happily to a bunch of cameramen as her plate was loaded with what looked like the most delicious noodles. Jane's stomach rumbled. She adored noodles. And the smell was heavenly.

Suddenly, from somewhere close by, something started playing an irritating and familiar-sounding tune in high-pitched, tinny notes. Looking around without success to identify where it came from, Jane realised it was 'There's No Business Like Showbusiness'. To her surprise, Champagne suddenly put her hand down her cleavage and extracted a tiny gold mobile phone. She snapped it open. The tinny music stopped.

'Yah?' Champagne listened for a few seconds. 'Yah,' she said finally, closing the phone and shoving it back down her dress. She sniffed and tossed her hair. 'That was my New York acting studio,' she said loftily. 'Calling to tell me to make sure I'm projecting enough. Do you think I'm projecting enough?'

Jane's eyes dwelt briefly on Champagne's bulging bust, straining against the thin material of her dress like a dam about to burst. 'Oh yes,' she said with complete truth. 'You're projecting more than enough.'

'The food on that set is simply uneatable,' Champagne complained ten minutes later, her temper not improved by having to hobble all the way to the gatehouse where Jane had parked the car. 'Can you believe it,' she huffed from the front seat, 'Brad won't even let me have my own chef. I mean, it's the bare minimum a star expects on set. Julia Roberts would freak out. Tom and Nicole would go ballistic.'

'Brad should think himself lucky,' said Jane, starting the engine, 'that you didn't insist on a chef for Gucci as well.'

Champagne looked at her in contemptuous astonishment. 'Well of course I did,' she honked. 'I told him that Gucci needs a very special Russian diet. Can't eat anything but caviar at the moment, poor lamb. But of course Brad took *absolutely* no notice. Callous *bastard.* Can't think what I ever saw in him. Wouldn't even let me have a bodyguard, let alone a personal trainer. Stingy *bastard.*' She paused for breath. 'Still, he *had* to give me a trailer in the end. He actually thought he could make me stay at the local pub with everybody else. Can you *imagine*?'

Jane didn't bother to reply. By now they had reached Lower Bulge.

Lunch, in the event, was nothing more substantial than a bag of cheese and onion crisps each and a half of Old Knickersplitter in the Gloom. 'Can't believe no one in this town knows how to fix a lobster club sandwich,' huffed Champagne as, a mere half an hour later, Jane drove the 2CV back to Mullions as hard as she dared, hoping the piles of noodles would still be on offer when they returned. But when they arrived back on the set, not so much as a beansprout remained.

Champagne climbed out of the car in such a manner as to expose as much tanned bottom as possible. 'I'm back now,' she announced to no one in particular. 'You can carry on filming.' She staggered over the grass towards the girl with the clapperboard. 'Where's my call sheet?' she demanded.

Not batting an eyelid, the girl detached a piece of paper from a folder in her bag. 'Here you are,' she said, handing it to Champagne, who scanned it eagerly before looking up in fury.

'But I'm not in any scenes at all this afternoon according to this,' she shouted. 'What the fuck's going on? Where's Brad?'

'Filming the big love scene,' said the production assistant. 'The set is closed, I'm afraid.' How much full frontal nudity could there possibly be in a film called *Three Christenings and a Hen Party*? thought Jane. Could Brad be barricading himself inside the set for other reasons altogether?

'I *demand* to see him,' raged Champagne. 'What do you mean, big love scene? I'm the one who makes the big scenes around here.'

There was an acquiescent silence.

'Brad was so happy with what you shot this morning that he thought you probably needed the afternoon off to rest,' said the redhead quickly. Whatever was she doing in films, Jane wondered, when she obviously had a brilliant future in diplomacy?

Champagne tossed her head, faintly mollified. 'Yes, I was rather good, wasn't I? Oh well.' She turned and looked at Jane. 'Suppose I'd better fill you in on some of the jargon,' she declared. 'For the piece you're writing about me. Got your notebook ready?' She pointed at the lighting rig behind her. 'Lights,' she boomed, as if

Jane had never seen one before. 'Big ones are called redheads and the little ones are called blondes.'

'Er, other way round actually,' murmured the red-headed clapperboard girl.

Champagne ignored her. 'And that big machine they are slung up on is called the cherry popper,' she announced.

'Cherry *picker*, actually,' said the girl before beating a retreat under Champagne's furious glare.

Champagne wandered over to a group of men surrounded by wires, microphones and speakers. 'This is Nigel, one of the sound men,' she revealed, pouting at a handsome, bronzed six-footer with blond hair tied back in a ponytail. 'Nigel has a very large and hairy thing he waves around everywhere.' Champagne gave Nigel the most blatantly suggestive smile Jane had ever seen.

'I think Champagne means the boom microphone,' said Nigel, grinning back.

'And this is Chris, the chief cameraman,' Champagne continued, dragging Jane into the personal space of a tanned and muscular hunk in a New York baseball cap. 'Otherwise known as the gofer.'

'You mean the gaffer,' said Chris in a broad Australian accent. 'Rather a different thing in the pecking order,' he grinned. 'But that's not me, anyway. The gaffer's the chief electrician. And his deputy, that's Ian rummaging in that box over there, is known as the best boy.'

Champagne lowered her lashes and smouldered at Ian, who started to scrabble even harder in what looked like a case of electrical leads. 'The best boy, eh?' she repeated loudly. 'Best at what, I wonder?'

As a flush crept up Patrick's pale and somewhat pimply neck. Champagne returned to pouting at Chris.

'Chris and I have discovered we've got lots in common,' she honked. 'We've both got some Scottish in us, apparently. His name is McCrae, and my grandmother was from Edinburgh.'

'What an astonishing coincidence,' said Jane, ironically.

Champagne glanced suddenly at the Rolex weighing down her wrist. 'Look, can't stand here all day. Come and find me later,' she ordered Jane. 'Must dash. I've got the runs.' She staggered off over the field.

'She means the rushes,' said Chris. 'It's when what's been filmed during the day is shown. Hardly worth her turning up, really. I don't think she's going to appear on much of it, to be honest.'

'Never mind,' said Jane, turning round to see Champagne flirting wildly with Nigel some distance away. 'I'm not so sure she intends to go and watch it. She seems to be more interested in the sound.'

Chris grinned as he watched them. 'Well, she's wasting her time with Nigel,' he said. 'He may look macho but he's as gay as New Year's Eve. Fancy a drink later?' he added. 'Are you staying in the pub?'

Jane hesitated. She had not considered the question of her overnight accommodation since unsuccessfully raising it with Saul Dewsbury. 'Yes,' she said. 'I think I probably am.'

Chapter 20

Tally shrieked as the bright red bloodstain began to spread over the virgin white satin of the wedding dress. 'Shit,' she yelped. 'Bugger.' The needle had driven right into her finger. It had been a charming thought of Saul's that she should embroider her wedding dress with the Venery family mottos of deer and hares, but they had not come out as successfully as she had hoped. Her hares looked like hamsters, and the deers' antlers like TV aerials. Not to put too fine a petit point on it, her sewing was a shambles. And, boringly, it had kept her practically imprisoned in her bedroom throughout the first few days of the filming.

The bloodstain, fortunately, was less of a disaster than it first seemed. It was on the inside of a sleeve and if she kept her left arm to her side throughout the wedding, no one would be any the wiser. Not that anyone would be anyway. Saul's insistence on a speedy, private register office wedding meant the two of them would be practically the only people present.

As she plunged the needle once more into the satin, Tally determinedly tried to bury all thoughts of the traditional ceremony in the family chapel which she had always imagined she would have. With flowers by Mr Peters and serried ranks of Mrs Ormondroyd's quiches alongside knockout glasses of the Fourth Earl's punch. And her mother's veil, but not, alas, the family tiara. That had been sold long ago to cover one of someone's less fortunate evenings at Monte Carlo.

The family chapel, in any case, had been ruled out of the proceedings the week before, when the crested and pilastered Venery family gallery high up at the back of it had finally come crashing down. It was a tragedy, Tally had thought as she surveyed the damage with brimming eyes, that she and Saul could not marry on the same spot where so many of her ancestors had celebrated their union.

'Such a shame,' she said to Saul. 'The Fourth Earl married no less than three wives here.'

'What did he do with the first two?' Saul stammered as best he could between his chattering teeth. Like the rest of the house, the chapel, as always, even in the scorching height of summer, was freezing.

'They died in childbirth, I think,' said Tally vaguely. 'Then there was the Fifth Earl,' she added, brightening. 'He got married here. Quite a wild chap, by all accounts. Took his mistress on honeymoon with him and his wife.'

'What did his wife make of that?' asked Saul,

clutching his herringbone tightly round him.

'Went mad and died of diphtheria, I believe.'

'Well,' said Saul, still shuddering, 'looks like we're doing the right thing then. A wedding here sounds about the worst start to married life imaginable. Just as well the place has collapsed.'

If only it was just the chapel that had collapsed, Tally thought. The rest of the house seemed poised to come crashing down at any moment as well. Tally fretted about the fretwork every night as she went to sleep, and she felt guilty about the fading and black-flecked gilt everywhere, so desperately in need of renewal. The cracked console tables were no consolation whatsoever and the bas-reliefs were a source of deep anxiety. There was also nothing remotely amusing about the ha-ha. The only comfort for Tally was that she no longer had to face the increasingly baleful-looking Ancestors. A furious and shaken Saul had removed them from the walls of the staircase some weeks earlier after another leap for freedom by the Third Earl had narrowly avoided crushing him to death. 'Bunch of miserable old bastards anyway,' Saul had said, watching the then-still-employed Mr Peters heave the Ancestors' reproachful and indignant countenances into a storeroom.

Tally sighed. Where was Saul? she wondered, letting her sewing fall into her lap. He had dashed off a good half hour ago saying that he thought he had heard something suspicious downstairs. Something suspiciously like Champagne D'Vyne, she imagined jealously. She may have spent the last few days in thimble-wielding purdah, but Tally knew perfectly well Saul's old girlfriend was on the set. No one within a four-mile radius of that unmistakable voice could possibly be innocent of the fact.

Saul was definitely up to something, Tally was sure. He was practically nowhere to be seen these days. Once or twice she had rounded corners to find him muttering into his mobile phone and, despite his protestations that he was talking business, she had not quite believed him. Business with Champagne, maybe, she thought crossly.

It's just pre-wedding nerves, Tally told herself briskly, dismissing her demons. She knew from the ancient and dog-eared copy of *Brides and Setting Up Home* she had bought from the newsagents in Lower Bulge that engaged couples were often beset with doubts and fears about each other before getting married. The best cure for cold feet, she decided, was a brisk trot along the chilly corridors to the kitchen, where a ready-meal lasagne had been heating in the Aga for what seemed like hours.

The kitchen seemed impossibly huge, dark and empty without Mrs Ormondroyd. Her sheer bulk had somehow made it look smaller. The lasagne, meanwhile, was dried out and dead. Tally was prising it sadly from its foil coffin when Saul walked in.

'What's *that*?' he said, throwing a disgusted glance at the lasagne. 'Something Mrs Ormondroyd's left behind in the bottom of the oven?

'You're not in the Fulham Road now, you know,' said Tally furiously. 'You're not with Sha-Sha-Champagne D'Vyne now either,' she added, her scant bosom heaving. 'Though you ob-ob-ob-viously wish you were.' She dissolved into tears

The look of absolute horror on Saul's face was some comfort, at least. 'I can assure you I don't,' he said, with feeling. Understanding dawned in his face. 'Is *that* what's making you so baity?' he breathed, sending up a silent prayer of thanks that Tally wasn't, as he had feared, pregnant. 'Let me tell you,' he said, taking his fiancée's heaving form in his arms, 'that woman was the worst mistake of my life. She practically bankrupted me. I've been avoiding the film set like the plague rather than risk running into her. Oh, Tally,' he said, kissing the top of her head and trying not to mind she had not brushed her hair for what looked like a week at least. 'You mustn't. It'll all be fine, you'll see. You have to admit the film idea was a huge success.'

Tally sniffed and nodded, not quite daring to remind Saul that a condition of the film crew's coming had been that no shooting was to take place inside the house. To date at least one love scene had been filmed on the Elizabethan bed and a riotous party scene in the Blue Drawing Room had caused the room's great treasure, the precious Eagle chandelier with its delicate arms fantastically wrought with birds of prey, to rock wildly. A network of terrifying-looking cracks had since spread across the ceiling surrounding it.

Tally was about to tell Saul a few stately home truths

when, somewhere beyond the hall, the shattering sound of glass crashing on the floor stopped her. She sighed. The Eagle, it seemed, had landed.

Rather surprisingly considering the number of people on the film set, the Gloom and Sobbing turned out to have plenty of room to spare. Jane was as relieved to get a bed for the night as she was disappointed to find the promising-looking cameraman called Chris was nowhere to be seen. It dawned on her, as she sat in the deserted bar with a book and a half-pint of Old Knicker-splitter, that he was perhaps staying in another pub altogether. On reflection, it seemed more than likely that everyone else on the film had chosen the more cheerful if more distant Barley Mow in Upper Bulge to the lugubrious Gloom.

The Gloom's lumpy bed and scratchy sheets not being conducive to a lie-in, still less a good night's sleep, Jane was up and about on the film set by ten. Breakfast was being served and she headed gratefully for a plate of creamy yellow scrambled eggs and a mug of steaming tea.

'Looking for Champagne?' called the redheaded clapperboard girl who, despite her tiny size, was tucking into an enormous plateful of fried bread, tomatoes, sausages and bacon. Jane, who had in fact been hoping for a morning encounter with Chris, nodded anyway. 'Try her trailer,' said the redhead.

Jane looked around for a Demi Moore-style gleaming silver pantechnicon. 'Where *is* her trailer?' she asked.

'Over there,' said the girl, pointing in the direction of a tiny, battered, domestic caravan. 'We borrowed it for her from the continuity girl's parents. They live near here, thank goodness. They're invited to the world premiere of the film to make up for not being able to go to Skegness all summer.' She finished her sausages and gathered up her clapperboard. 'Tell Champagne she's on soon,' she called. 'There's a crowd scene coming up where she has to smile at the camera. If she gets on set now we might get it right by midnight.'

Jane knocked on the caravan door. A flurry of hysterical barks announced Gucci was within, but the expected accompanying growls from his mistress did not materialise. 'Champagne?' Jane called, rapping again. The top half of the door creaked reluctantly open to reveal the head of a tousled-looking Champagne who, maddeningly, looked more glamorous than ever with wild hair and sleepy eyes.

'You!' she said disgustedly. 'Why the hell did you have to come now? I'm busy, um, perfecting my technique.'

'Well, apparently they want you on set in a minute,' Jane said, 'I'm here to collect you.'

'Well, I can't come just like that, you know,' snapped Champagne. Was she hearing things, thought Jane, or was there a stifled guffaw from within? Her suspicions were confirmed when Gucci, scenting escape, threw himself against the lower door which swung open to reveal Chris the dark-haired gaffer lying on the floor, naked and in a state of supreme excitement. Completely unabashed, he grinned winningly at the astonished Jane.

'What's the matter?' he asked. 'Never heard of making love to the camera?'

'I'll, um, see you on set,' muttered Jane, backing away in embarrassment tinged with disappointment. So this was what Champagne had meant by having some Scottish in her. No wonder she hadn't seen Chris in the Gloom and Sobbing.

Jane walked away, trying to concentrate on the scenery rather than what she had just seen. It really was a beautiful morning. A powerful sun was burning the last mist off the lake to reveal a dazzling silver mirror beneath. Brilliant green grass swayed ecstatically in the rosemary-scented wind like a music and movement class, each blade shining as if Nature had not only washed it, but given it a squirt of hi-gloss conditioner as well. The leaves on the thick-trunked trees dotted here and there across the undulating parkland tossed and shimmered like a row of chorus girls' feathers.

Et in Arcadia ego, thought Jane as her feet swished through the grass. Well, she could vouch for the ego bit, certainly. She looked up to find herself approaching the tiny ornamental rotunda that stood on a gentle slope on the other side of the lake. She had walked further than she thought.

As she approached the little building, Jane realised she was not the only one pacing about the park that morning. Propped up against one of the encircling pillars was an ashen-looking Brad, smoking furiously. He was evidently a man with a lot on his mind.

Probably recharging his spiritual batteries for the day's filming, Jane thought, skirting gingerly past him so as not to disturb the creative process. She gasped as a cold and bony hand shot out and grabbed her by the wrist.

'I've just seen the rushes,' Brad blurted out. 'Couldn't face seeing them last night. And in every shot from yesterday morning that stupid tart's wandering around in the background flashing her tits and her knickers. The christening scenes look like they've been filmed at Raymond's Revue Bar.'

Jane looked at him, not knowing what to say. Much as she agreed with Brad, she had her professional responsibilities to consider. After all, if Brad threw Champagne off the set, *Fabulous* would be left without a cover and the deadline was looming. Once again, Champagne had her by the short and curlies. 'Her acting method is very, er, avant garde, isn't it?' she murmured.

Brad turned glittering and feverish eyes upon her. 'I think it's more avant a clue,' he hissed.

Deciding he was better left to himself, Jane continued on her way and walked up the slope behind the lake to the estate road and the old gateway. As the estate entrance came into view, Jane noticed a flash of silver turn off the main road beyond and come flying through the ancient archway like a Cruise missile. As it bounced over the potholes Jane stumbled out of the way on to the verge, expecting the car to plunge past her towards the house. It didn't. There was a mighty screech of brakes as the wheels locked and what looked like a hundred thousand pounds' worth of prime babe magnet shuddered to a halt a foot or so in front of her. Jane looked up at the windscreen. Sitting behind it, to her astonishment, was Mark Stackable.

The tinted driver's window glided electronically down to reveal Mark's stern, unsmiling profile. Jane stared at him, embarrassed, wondering what on earth he was doing here. Had he come to try and persuade her to give him another chance? If so, he looked very surprised to see her.

'You really didn't need to come all the way up here,' she stammered. 'We could have met in town.'

Mark stared at her in astonishment. 'Met *you*?' he repeated in tones that implied he would have crossed continents to avoid her. 'I'm afraid I'm up here on business. Nothing to do with you, I'm afraid. At all,' he added emphatically. It was the first time Jane had ever heard him not end a speech with a question.

Of course, thought Jane. Business must mean the film. The success of *Four Weddings and a Funeral* meant that no City investor worth his salt could afford to ignore the potential of a follow-up made in the same style. *Three Christenings and a Hen Party* was worth a punt of anyone's money.

'You know what I think,' she said to Mark eagerly, and wanting to make amends for her behaviour at his flat. 'You should have some male strippers from Sheffield as well.'

'Excuse me?' asked Mark, astonished. His fingers stopped their impatient tapping on the steering wheel.

'What the hell are you talking about?'

'Yes,' enthused Jane, swept away by the brilliance of her idea. 'You can't afford to ignore the success of *The Full Monty*. If you have a gang of unemployed Yorkshiremen getting their kit off at the posh hen party, you'll have both the top British hits of recent years in one. And,' she added, inspired, 'you shouldn't call it *Three Christenings and a Hen Party* either. You should call it *The Full Fonty*!'

'I haven't the faintest idea what you mean?' Mark said wearily, his fingers now drumming a tattoo.

'The film, of course,' said Jane. 'The film that's being made over there.' She gestured in the direction of the now-buzzing set from where the occasional loud bray could be heard. Champagne was obviously now up and about and ready for her close-up.

'I've got no interest in *that* whatsoever,' said Mark, casting a contemptuous glance at the straggling conglomerate of caravans and lighting rigs. 'That's small fry. I'm here to have a meeting about the house.'

'Oh, so you've come to see *Mullions*?' Now that made even more sense. What else, thought Jane, would a rich young banker about town be doing on a Saturday apart from buying himself a mansion in the country? It was odd, admittedly, that Mark's choice should have fallen on Mullions, but the house, as Champagne and the film set demonstrated, was proving to be the sort of place that attracted unlikely coincidences.

She wasn't sure, however, that Mark buying Mullions was altogether ideal. Jane shuddered at the thought of him making the ramshackle old house the same sterile temple to contemporary interior design as his Clerkenwell flat. Visions of Mark using the suits of armour as novelty linen baskets in his surgically precise bathroom and replacing the Elizabethan four-poster with a circular waterbed flashed before her. The only remotely appropriate thing she could imagine him doing was returning the ancient dungeons below the house to their original use as torture chambers and making them into a gym.

'Are you sure you're interested in Mullions?' Jane asked, alarmed. 'The place is collapsing, you know. Rotting on its feet. Practically rubble.'

'Yes, I know,' said Mark. 'That's precisely why I *am* interested. It's got *megazoid* potential?'

Jane blinked. He thought Mullions had potential? This was not what she had expected to hear. Perhaps she had got him wrong. 'Why don't you leave the car here and walk over to the house with me?' she suggested enthusiastically. 'That way you get the best view of it. Over the lake.' Mark looked at her doubtfully, then nodded and opened the door which ran the entire length of his gleaming vehicle. His jeans, Jane couldn't help noticing as his legs swung out on to the path, had creases so sharp they looked dangerous. He was obviously not a man who was used to casual dressing. 'Nice car,' she remarked, privately considering it flasher than a warehouseful of kitchen cleaner. 'New?'

'All my cars are new,' said Mark crushingly, grabbing a large black folder out of the passenger seat and pointing the car alarm key at the lock. There was a swishing, clunking sound as his security system came on stream. 'I change them every six months, or sooner, if the ashtray gets full?' He gave her a wintry smile. Jane was not entirely sure he was joking. But she was relieved he had de-iced a bit. As with the vomit episode, he seemed to be erasing her rejection of his advances from his memory. Part of the reason, she was touched to see, seemed to be his enthusiasm for Mullions.

'The place has had a bad time lately,' Jane began as they set off across the greensward in the direction of the house. She grinned. 'You can practically smell the dry rot from here.'

'Yes,' said Mark, clutching his folder to his chest. 'Wonderful, isn't it?'

Jane gave him a quizzical look. What was so wonderful about it? Still, perhaps he meant that the opportunities for sympathetic refurbishment were endless. Jane hoped fervently that Tally was somewhere in the house to show him round. Mark had arrived in the nick of time. He was just what she was looking for.

Chapter 21

Tally gazed forlornly round the rose garden. What once had been a civilised area for after-dinner strolling was now, with its rampant thorns, something that the Prince in Sleeping Beauty might recognise. The roses were not so much rambling as rioting.

Trowel in hand, Tally peered through the bushes at the park beyond. She could just about see the film set and the people moving about on it. Relief flooded her when she recognised the strutting figure with white-blonde hair, who, from the sound as well as the look of her, was enjoying a full and frank exchange of views with a tall man with a megaphone. Champagne D'Vyne was safely on set. So, wherever Saul had disappeared to again, it wasn't to be with her.

Really, I'm getting paranoid, Tally thought to herself as she poked half-heartedly with her trowel at the long-untended earth. Saul was doubtless making some arrangement or other for the wedding. Or the honeymoon, which she imagined must be a surprise, as Saul hadn't uttered a word about it. But try as she might, she couldn't quite quash a feeling of misgiving. 'Something's rotten round here,' she thought, feeling like a prophet as a bush bitten to death by blackfly collapsed into her lap.

As usual when she was not quite certain about anything, Tally decided to blame herself. Perhaps I feel, subconsciously, that I'm not good enough for him, she told herself. That I'm not pretty or stylish enough. This morning's events alone were enough to support this theory – Saul had been unimpressed when she had appeared at breakfast in her father's old shooting suit.

'You'll be wearing the suits of armour next,' he had snapped.

'But I've nothing else left,' said Tally, thinking that the suits of armour idea was not such a bad one. Once you got them warmed up, they would be very hard-wearing and perfect for walking, although fiddly tasks like washing up or gardening might be tricky.

She was also slightly worried about Saul's attitude to Mullions these days. His former awed respect seemed to have been replaced by something bordering on the cavalier. And not the Charles I variety at that. When, for example, she had shown him Mullions' other single remaining treasure beside the Elizabethan bed, a tiny sketch of the infant Edward VI thought to be by Holbein, Saul had observed breezily that he thought Holbein was a stop on the Central Line.

Perhaps, Tally reasoned with herself, sitting back on

her heels and letting the trowel slide from her lap, she felt uneasy because she was getting married without a single member of her family present; an unprecedented step for a Venery. Yet Julia and Big Horn were still away at their ashram with no definite date for their return. 'We'll come back when the time is right,' Julia had breathed enigmatically as she and Big Horn piled into the astounded minicab driver's back seat on their way to the airport. Piers, of course, had not been seen for months. Still saving the earth two hundred feet under some runway, Tally supposed wearily, wondering if she would ever see her only sibling again.

If only she could talk to Jane about it all. She had suggested to Saul that her best friend be witness at the wedding, but Saul had been so appalled at the idea she had dropped it without further ado. The very mention of Jane's name got him in a rage for some reason. It had seemed better, more loyal to him at any rate, not to get in touch with Jane at all for the time being. Passions were running too high. Plenty of time for everyone to make friends after the wedding. Nonetheless, Tally missed her. Jane was so straightforward. Her opinions came directly from her heart, and her advice was always sensible, except, of course, when it came to addressing her own love life. Tally wondered what Jane's romantic status was at the moment. Chaotic as usual, she imagined.

Or perhaps not. Tally, getting to her feet and stretching her back, stared in astonishment as she saw someone who looked rather like Jane walking rapidly down through the rose garden towards her, accompanied by someone, a man, whom Tally didn't recognise. She squinted at the couple. The man looked astonishingly handsome. With extraordinarily clean jeans.

'Tally!' called Jane, breaking into a run. She dashed up and caught Tally in a bear hug. 'Haven't seen you for ages,' she muttered into Tally's scratchy and rather smelly tweed shoulder. 'God, I've missed you!' She held her friend at arm's length and stared into Tally's hesitant grey eyes. She looks thinner, thought Jane. Strained, even.

'Natalia Venery, meet Mark Stackable,' she said with a flourish. 'He's come to look at Mullions. You must be expecting him.'

Tally frowned. Unreliable though her memory was, apart from when recalling the more recondite episodes of family history, she was sure the estate agents had stopped sending people to look round the house at least two weeks ago. After Saul had been to see them, in fact.

'They say the place is just too near to collapse to sell,' Saul had reported, the picture of regret. Tally had dolefully agreed, unaware that Saul's purpose in going to the estate agents was to take the place off the market himself. 'Don't worry, I'll think of something,' he had told her. She had given him a watery grin, unaware that he already had.

'Oh,' Tally now said to Mark, who was staring at her in the astonished way everyone who came to Mullions seemed to. 'I'm not sure I was expecting anyone actually. But you're very welcome. Would you like a cup of tea?'

She prayed not. The Aga had been playing up so much lately it was quicker to go on foot to the cafe at Lower Bulge than wait for a kettle to boil.

'I had an arrangement to see your husband?' Mark said crisply. He felt impatient with this obviously batty woman. He'd wasted enough time already. 'Mr Dewsbury? He and I have been discussing the estate quite a lot recently?'

Jane stared at Mark, puzzled. He'd come to see Dewsbury?

It made slightly more sense to Tally. 'Oh, I *see*,' she said slowly. So Saul had decided to take the matter of finding a buyer into his *own* hands, had he? There was, Tally supposed, no reason why not, although he *might* have discussed it with her first. 'Well,' she said to Mark, 'I'm afraid my, er, Mr Dewsbury's not here, but I'm sure I can tell you anything you might want to know.'

'Good,' said Mark. 'I just wanted to check that the bulldozers are still on schedule?'

Tally gasped and took a step back. 'B-b-bulldozers?' Jane shot to her side.

'What do you mean, bulldozers?' she demanded. This sounded serious.

'Well, Dewsbury should have arranged it all?' said Mark. Never had his ludicrously interrogative tones irritated Jane so much. 'They're coming in a fortnight to flatten the place?'

'*What*?' said Jane, taking over the role of official spokesperson. Tally looked too shocked to speak. One hand was clapped to a face more drained and grey than the Mullions gutters. She looked as if she was about to be sick.

'Yeah, though Dewsbury says if we wait three weeks the house will probably fall down on its own. Sooner if somebody sneezes?' Mark grinned.

Tally removed her hand. Her mouth opened and closed like a goldfish.

'Then,' said Mark, snapping opening his folder and riffling through its pristine white pages, 'we slap up the houses.'

Tally's face had now changed from grey to ripe tomato. She started to sputter something. Jane put a quieting hand on her arm. Here, at last, was the evidence she had been waiting for. She had *known* there was something fishy about Saul from the start.

'Houses?' she asked, trying to sound as calm and matter-of-fact as possible.

'Yeah,' said Mark, flashing his tombstone teeth. 'Hundreds of them. Making astronomical profits for everyone involved?' He looked at Tally. 'I bet you're thrilled, aren'tcha?' He licked his lips.

Tally made a choking sound.

'Astronomical? Really?' croaked Jane, squeezing Tally's arm warningly. Her head echoed to the thunderous sound of everything crashing into place. So *this* was what the marriage was all about. Saul had seen millions in Mullions the minute he clapped eyes on it, and seducing poor, batty, scatty Tally was the way to get his hands on it. He must have cooked up his plan almost immediately after Amanda's dinner party and had roped in Stackable to finance it.

'Astronomical,' Mark almost sang. 'So you haven't been filled in on the details, huh? Best left to the men, huh?' He paused and grinned at them.

Jane was by now almost breaking Tally's wrist, so desperate was she to keep her friend quiet. They needed Mark to tell them as much as possible.

'Well,' Mark drawled, gazing at his documents with love in his eyes, 'we thought three hundred and fifty K a time for the smallest two-bedroomed rabbit hutch? And, as you know, we're building four hundred of them? Only the best breeze block, and each house comes ready-equipped with satellite dish, herringbone brick drive, carriage lamps and automatic garage door?' He stopped and looked at Tally's and Jane's astonished faces. 'Dewsbury doesn't seem to have briefed you very well, I must say?'

'No need, now you've done such a great sales pitch,' said a smooth voice behind Tally. 'Couldn't have put it better myself.' Saul sauntered into view, his eyes glittering boldly. 'Sorry I wasn't here when you came,' he added easily to Mark, 'but I was in the loo and the door fell in on me. Took rather a while to lever it off.' He grinned widely all round.

Tally and Jane's mouths stayed as straight and flat as spirit levels.

'I think you owe me an explanation, Saul,' said Tally, in low, fierce tones Jane had never heard her use before.

The law of the Dewsburys was if in doubt, brazen it out. Saul now proceeded to apply that law to its last letter. 'But my darling,' he said, smoothly, 'just think of the advantages. The astonishing profits. With the sort of money we're talking about we can dismantle Mullions brick by brick and re-erect it in Arizona. On the moon, if you like. Just think of the . . .' His pleading voice died away. His expression widened and deepened into abject terror. It seemed to be reacting to something behind Tally. 'Oh God, no,' he gasped, as if the Grim Reaper himself was coming across the park behind them. 'Please. Anything but that.' Saul took a few steps backwards, then suddenly spun on his hand-tooled leather heel and shot off round the back of the house.

'Hey, hey, not so fast,' bellowed Mark, seeing millions, if not Mullions, disappearing before his eyes. He skidded after Saul across the gravel, the papers flying out of his folder as he went.

Both woman craned round to stare at whatever had so terrified Saul. Picking her wobbling, skyscraper-heeled way determinedly over the muddy grass in a pair of unfeasibly tight leather trousers and shades so profoundly black they looked opaque came Champagne D'Vyne.

'Where the bloody hell have *you* been?' Champagne brayed, looking straight at Tally as her metal Gucci heels dragged excruciatingly over the soft old stone of the steps. 'I've been all over this dump looking for you.'

Tally drew in her breath in a short, indignant gasp.

'Don't worry,' whispered Jane. 'I don't think she can see a thing in those glasses. She thinks she's talking to me.'

'I gathered that,' hissed Tally. 'I just object to my home being described in that way. Although I suppose,' she added ruefully, 'judging from what I've just heard, I'm lucky to have a dump left. I just can't believe—'

'What's the matter?' Jane asked Champagne hurriedly. Now was not the time for Tally to embark on an orgy of agonised heart-searching. That could come later.

'That bastard Brad has only *sacked* me from the *film*, that's all,' honked Champagne. '*Outrageous*. How *dare* he? Who the *bloody hell* does he think he is?'

'What happened?' asked Jane. 'Artistic differences?'

'Well, for some reason,' Champagne boomed, still addressing Tally, 'he seemed to think I was being unreasonable, asking for a double to film some of the party scenes.'

'Body double? I thought they were only used for stunts,' said Jane.

'Yah, but in these party scenes, we're supposed to be drinking champagne, and of course I never drink anything less than Krug,' Champagne spluttered indignantly. 'And Brad was actually expecting me – *me* – to drink filthy *supermarket stuff*. So I *insisted* on a body double because otherwise I'd probably be throwing up all night. But he refused and threw me off the set.' Champagne fumbled furiously for a cigarette. Her efforts to light it were so severely hampered by the restrictions the sunglasses placed on her vision that Jane took pity on her and stepped forward to help. Without muttering a word of thanks, Champagne stuck the cigarette between her blood-red lips and took a deep, rasping draw.

'Well, anyway,' she demanded, staring at Tally again, 'you've got to get down there *now* and tell that bastard Brad he's got to put me back in that film *this minute.*' She stabbed a red-taloned finger in Tally's direction. 'Tell him,' she declared grandly, 'that if he comes on his bended knees and gives me Lily Eyre's part, I'll reconsider.'

'Look, I'm sorry to interrupt,' said Jane suddenly, 'but something slightly odd seems to be going on over there.'

Tally and Champagne followed the direction of her gaze to the park entrance. Wending its way over the rise behind the lake was a strange little procession of about thirty people. Capering figures in flowing clothes and brightly coloured pointed hats led others brandishing flags and playing bongos and flutes. People were clapping, waving their arms and letting out little cries.

Tally peered in their direction. She hadn't thought the day could possibly get more surreal. She had thought wrong. 'It's like the Pied Piper of Hamelin,' she breathed wonderingly. 'There's even someone on stilts.'

How could she see that far? wondered Jane in awe. To her, the approaching figures were just a blurred and slow-moving block. But then, Tally always had had superior eyesight. This honing of the optics came, Jane imagined, courtesy of the genetic inheritance of generations of Venerys scanning the horizons of their vast acreage. Being grand, however, had its downsides too. Like the girls at *Fabulous*, Tally had always suffered the most agonising of periods. Blue blood was evidently more painful.

'They look positively *medieval*,' Tally breathed, gazing at the approaching ragged band and thinking that it looked like a scene out of Brueghel. 'Apart from those people in ghastly fluorescent cagoules at the back, of course.'

This rang a Saul-shaped bell with Jane. Sure enough, bringing up the rear of the procession, were the grim-faced hikers she had encountered yesterday morning. So this was who their mates were. But what were they here for?

A sudden shriek from Tally made her jump.

'Piers!' Tally screamed, dashing helter-skelter down the slope of the ha-ha. 'It's Piers! It's my brother! Piers!' she shrieked, rushing to the figure at the front of the crowd and launching herself upon him. 'Where on *earth* have you been?' She buried herself in his neck which, even from the distance of the terrace wall, Jane could see was far from clean. Blood, it seemed, was thicker than shower gel. She walked swiftly up to join them.

'Well, a hundred feet under it, actually,' Piers said good-humouredly to Tally. 'We've been living in a hole under the new runway site at Gatwick for the last two months.'

As she approached, Jane stared at Piers in astonishment. How on earth had Tally recognised him? His fair hair, once as smooth and shining as a gold ingot, hung in matted ropes about his shoulders. Gone was the pink and white schoolboy face Jane remembered, and gone, too, were the Eton coat tails, brushed to within an inch of their lives by Mrs Ormondroyd. Instead, Piers wore layer upon layer of mud-caked sacking that made him look like an Arthurian hermit. With studs through his eyebrow, nose and upper lip as well as through his earlobes, he was not so much Piers as Pierced.

'Oh Piers, how could you?' cried Tally. 'Why didn't you get in touch?' she wailed, half furious, half ecstatic. 'I've been *desperate* to see you. So much has happened. M-m-mummy's disappeared and M-m-m-mullions was nearly bulldozed, and it was all because of m-m-m-*me*. How could I have been so *m-m-m-mad*? Oh, *Piers*!' She buried her face in his neck again and shook with sobs.

'Shush,' said Piers, his braceleted wrist rattling as he patted her on the back. He grinned at Jane. His smile, she noticed, was as brilliantly white as ever, but then it probably took more than two months down a mudhole to undo a lifetime of expensive orthodontics. 'And by the way,' he added to Tally, 'I'm not called Piers any more. I'm Muddy Fox now. Muddy, for short.'

'Oh *Piers*,' gasped Tally, completely ignoring this and emerging from his dirt-crusted shoulder, her face swollen and red with tears, 'I nearly lost *everything*. Oh, *Piers*!'

As Tally flung herself on her brother once more, Jane looked nervously around at his companions. Next to Piers stood a tall, solidly-built figure with a long grey matted beard, a rough-woven cloak of mud brown fixed with a Celtic clasp, and greasy grey locks hanging almost to his elbow. He looked like something straight out of Malory, thought Jane, blanching as she noticed the long, dull-grey metal object in his hand. It looked terrifyingly like a weapon of war. Is that a broadsword in your hand or are you just pleased to see me? she thought nervously.

'Don't worry, it's only ceremonial,' said Piers, following the direction of her eyes. Jane wasn't sure how reassuring that was. After all, the Druids had held some pretty gory ceremonies. 'This is Merlin, my right hand man.' Piers waved a tattooed hand at the brown-cloaked figure.

Merlin bowed gravely. 'Good morrow, fair maiden,' he boomed.

Tally looked astonished.

'And this is Laughter,' said Piers, drawing to his side a hostile-looking girl clutching a baby. 'Merlin's wife. But the baby belongs to us all. Concepts of fatherhood are so limited and bourgeois. Not to mention,' Piers added, grinning, 'the fact no one really knows who the father is.'

Laughter looked thunderous.

'So what's been going on here?' Piers asked, waving towards the film set. 'I heard there was some strange dude around ordering everyone off the rights of way, which is why I thought I'd pop over. But I didn't realise it was Steven Spielberg.'

'It's not,' said Tally. 'Oh, don't ask.' She clutched her hair with her fingers and rolled her eyes. She took a deep breath. 'The film set is, or at least it was, an attempt to bring some money in to keep Mullions going. It seemed a better idea than Mummy's, which was to sell up.' Briefly, Tally filled Piers in on the events of the past few weeks.

Piers took the news, even the episodes concerning Saul and the bulldozers, with his impressive sang-froid. 'The Red Indian guy sounds pretty cool,' he remarked. 'Shame I missed him. And I wouldn't have minded meeting this Saul cat either. Merlin could have given him a good seeing to with Excalibur. Couldn't you, Merl?' Beside him, Merlin grinned, exposing blackened teeth in his beard. 'So what are you going to do now?' he asked his sister. 'Want to see what the crystals have to say about it?' He rattled a bag which hung at his belt. 'They're very wise.'

Tally tried not to shudder. 'Er, thanks, but no, I'll be fine,' she said nervously. 'I'll just get back to the drawing board. Think up some more business ideas. More films, perhaps.'

'What about a rock festival,' suggested Laughter, looking almost enthusiastic. 'Like Glastonbury. It'd be brilliant. You could have floating stages in the lake.'

Tally's eyes bulged. 'Well, I *was* perhaps wondering about a few classical music concerts,' she faltered.

Piers grinned round at his companions. 'Well, if

we're not needed here, we'd better get back to the runway,' he remarked to the assembled troops. 'We could catch that earth-healing ceremony at Avebury on the way back.'

'What? You're going already?' stammered Tally. 'Wouldn't you, er, like some tea?'

'No thanks,' grinned Piers, clapping her on the back. 'So many green belts, so little time. I'm at Gatwick if you need me. When you next need someone to throw themselves in front of a bulldozer, don't hesitate to get in touch.'

As she watched Tally once again launch herself on her brother, Jane saw something move out of the corner of her eye. She looked round to see another, smaller and altogether different procession snaking across the parkland in white vans, bearing what looked like satellite dishes and aerials. A cameraman and soundman, whose equipment sported the livery of the local news station, were already moving in on Piers, while a gaggle of other lens-laden and boom-microphone-waving types were swiftly approaching. Piers, Jane realised, must be rather well known. Famous, even, by the looks of it. On the outskirts of the crowd, young men and women with notebooks, obviously from local papers, were earnestly scribbling down vox pops. One unfortunate, whose career as a journalist Jane suspected might be shortlived, had hit upon Merlin as an interviewee.

'What can you tell us about today's protest, Muddy?' a grey-anoraked news reporter asked Piers eagerly, thrusting a fat black-tipped microphone at him.

'It's cool,' Piers replied, not batting an eyebrow stud at all the attention. 'It's over, in fact. We're heading back to Gatwick now.'

'Back to the runway protest?' asked the man. 'How's that going, Muddy? You've been down there quite some time now, haven't you?'

'Two months,' said Piers. 'And we're not giving up. We'll be down there for as long as it takes.' He turned to his followers and thrust a triumphal fist to the sky. They cheered and threw their caps and bells in the air. The stilt-walker waved a stilt. Piers, Jane realised with surprise, had real charm. He was a figurehead. The shy little schoolboy she remembered had grown up to be a charismatic leader of men.

She wasn't, it seemed, the only one who thought so.

'Filthy's just *so* wonderful, isn't he?' breathed a low, husky voice at Piers's side. The interviewer blanched and extended his shaking microphone to the stunning, pouting blonde in tight leather trousers who had suddenly appeared in the crowd and was snaking her slender arm round Piers's shoulders.

'Filthy, my hero,' simpered Champagne, grinning at the cameras as she ran a perfectly-manicured fingernail over his much-pierced countenance. 'Such a *stud*, isn't he?' she pouted into the lens. Piers looked astonished but not horrified. Beneath the dirt on his face, Jane swore he was blushing. Laughter, meanwhile, looked livid.

'Champagne D'Vyne, isn't it?' said the reporter, jostling with about ten others who had suddenly zoomed in, in every sense of the word, on the unexpected drama that was unfolding. 'The famous It Girl?'

'That's right,' breathed Champagne in her best Sugar Kane tones. 'At least, it *was*. But not any more. I've always been *fascinated* by preservation and conservation. I'm very keen on recycling.' She paused. 'I *always* get the maid to take my champagne magnums to the bottle bank.' She shot the bearded reporter a glance so sizzling you could have fried sausages on it, then grinned and ran a hand through her gleaming hair. As the movement rucked up her blouse to reveal an expanse of brown tummy, Champagne was rewarded with her favourite sound, a fanfare of whirrs and flashes from the cameramen.

'Who *cares* about films, parties and premieres,' pouted Champagne passionately, running a finger up and down Piers's mud-encrusted sleeve, 'when there are so much more *important* things like runway protests going on?' She tickled Piers under the chin with an alabaster finger. He looked both shy and delighted. 'From now on, I'm giving up the high life for life underground,' Champagne announced in ringing tones. 'I'm joining Filthy and his intrepid band. From this moment on, I'm no longer an It Girl. I'm a Grit Girl.'

There was a gasp from the reporters, the crowd and Jane most of all. 'Terrific,' shouted one of the newsmen. 'Britain's favourite party girl joins Britain's favourite environmental protester. Who would have thought it?'

Who indeed, thought Jane sardonically, watching Champagne, in her element once more as she held court to the TV cameras. Joining Piers and his band of high-profile crusties was, of course, a heaven-sent, if not heaven-scented, self-publicity opportunity. No self-respecting narcissist could pass it up. Particularly one like Champagne, whose latest venture, the film, had ended rather less gloriously than she had anticipated.

'Yah, I know Swampy really well,' Champagne boomed into a phalanx of microphones. '*Such* a sweet guy. I was on *Shooting Stars* with him once . . .' She had totally stolen Piers's thunder, Jane noticed. Not that he seemed to mind. He was gazing at Champagne with all the helpless fascination of a rabbit caught in the headlights. Which, Jane thought, probably wasn't all that far from the truth.

As soon as the interviews were over, the TV van raced away across the parkland in order to be first back in the studio with the great exclusive. Behind it, the young reporters, newsroom-bound, ran for their cars and careers.

Left alone at last, Piers's crowd began to pick up its bags, shoulder its children and get back on its stilts, ready for departure. Piers gave a thumbs-up sign to Tally by way of farewell.

Champagne did not so much as look at Jane as she tottered away, clinging like a limpet to the latest person to save her career. As Jane accompanied Tally up the steps to the house, she had the rare feeling of being able to predict the future with absolute accuracy. Give or take an adjective, she knew exactly what was going to be on the front pages of the tabloids next day.

Chapter 22

'What exactly *is* an integral, double-aspect utility room?' asked Tally several hours later, looking up at Jane and frowning. Sunk in a leather armchair so battered it could have been served with chips, she was looking wearily through the papers that had fallen from Mark Stackable's folder as he ran after Saul. 'Integral. Double aspect. It sounds rather philosophical,' Tally added.

'I think it's a sort of lean-to scullery with two windows,' said Jane. All those weekends trailing around flats with Nick had left her better versed than Tally in the argot of estate agents.

Tally gave another deep sigh. 'I just can't believe I was so stupid as to have been taken in by Saul.'

'Well, he's very charming,' Jane said heroically, even though she had never found him anything of the sort.

Tally nodded, grateful for the excuse.

'And you can't choose who you fall in love with,' added Jane. 'As I know only too well.'

'Yes, but Nick was *ghastly*,' said Tally, displaying none of Jane's diplomacy.

I wasn't thinking of *him*, thought Jane. She fell silent and gazed into the fireplace.

'Now I'm back to square one,' said Tally. 'I have to find a way to keep this place going.' Her despairing gaze took in the whole of the chilly, peeling, rotting, collapsing, ageing gloom of the Blue Drawing Room. She slapped the palms of her long hands down on the worn armrests of her chair.

'Well, we'll just have to think of a thriving business idea,' Jane said briskly, pouring herself another tot from the rapidly-diminishing bottle of Bowmore that Tally had discovered in one of the kitchen cupboards along with a litre of gin and a bottle of flat tonic. Mrs Ormondroyd, it turned out, had squirrelled away quite a stash. 'I know what I'd like to do. Not that it's much use to you.'

'What?' asked Tally, holding her glass out to Jane and rustling in a bag of stale peanuts which constituted the rest of the treasure trove from under the butler's sink.

'I want,' said Jane, raising her eyes to the mould-spotted and peeling ceiling, 'to set up a company that records the omnibus edition of *The Archers* for people who miss it on Sunday mornings. You know, people who are away, or on holiday, or forget that the clock's turned back or forward or whatever, or it's Armistice Day.'

'Yes. That's a brilliant idea,' said Tally, sitting up.

'Because if you miss the omnibus, you lose the plot for about the next six months. And then your life has no meaning.'

'Exactly,' said Jane. 'My company would provide a solution to that sad fate. And I know what I'd call it as well. *Ambridge Too Far*. Like *A Bridge Too Far*.'

Tally grinned. 'But it won't make a million,' she said. 'Not unless you branch out into recording *EastEnders* and *Coronation Street* for people as well.'

'No chance,' said Jane. 'I can't work a video.'

'I wonder what I could do,' mused Tally, pushing one of Mark's brochures away from her with the tip of a wellington. 'Piers always used to talk about opening a shop that sold nothing but bacon sandwiches,' she said. 'But that would hardly make enough to keep this place going. Even if Piers wasn't vegan now, which I expect he is.' She sighed. Her face looked suddenly older, and infinitely tired. Give it up, Jane urged her friend silently. Just abandon the struggle. It's a losing battle, and even Mullions isn't worth sacrificing your youth and life to. But Tally would never give in, Jane knew. 'I can't be the one to let it all go,' Jane recalled Tally saying once. 'I can't be remembered for all time as the one who lost the house.' Yet she had come close.

Jane gazed into her glass wondering why she was worrying about Tally so much. Her own prospects were, after all, hardly glittering. Personally, they were a disaster, and professionally they were little better. The disappearance of Champagne a hundred feet under the runway at Gatwick, which she would normally have greeted with joy and relief, also meant *Fabulous* would have no cover. Jane groaned at the thought of Victoria's wrath now the film story could no longer be run.

Tally sat up suddenly. 'Did you hear something?' she hissed at Jane. 'Something banging somewhere?'

Jane's ears strained in the singing silence. Tally was right. A faint noise could be heard from the Marble Hall. They gazed at each other in terror.

'It might be,' gasped Jane, her throat dry with fear, 'the wind.'

Tally shook her head. 'You can always hear that.'

It was true. The building had so many holes you could use it to drain pasta.

'Something's coming in,' gasped Tally, drawing her gangly legs into her chair and hugging them tightly. 'Look. The door.'

As they watched, terrified, the Blue Drawing Room door started to open slowly, revealing the hall beyond. A full moon was just visible through the top pane of one of the hall windows, a brilliant silvery pearl, positioned, as if by some celestial jeweller, on a bed of dark blue velvet. Tally gasped sharply. 'Not Saul come back?' she breathed, putting into words what Jane, too, most feared. 'Please don't let it be him,' panted Tally.

It wasn't. A figure in a white flowing robe slowly appeared through the door. Tall, dignified and slow-moving, it glided into the room as if in a trance. Even from across the distance and the gloom, the brilliance of its burning eyes could clearly be seen.

'Mummy!' exclaimed Tally, thrusting her legs back

out and sprawling in relief across the chair. 'You *terrified* me!'

'*Darling*,' breathed Julia, moving swiftly over to her daughter, and gazing intensely into her eyes. 'I have only one question to ask you,' she said dramatically, grasping Tally's thin shoulders. '*Have you?*'

'Have I what?' asked Tally, alarmed at her mother's earnest expression. Seen the light? Strayed from the path of righteous wisdom? Got a bun in the oven? Turned lesbian? What would have been an open-ended question for most people was practically limitless with Julia.

'Sold Mullions, of course,' gasped Julia.

'No,' said Tally apologetically. 'I'm afraid I haven't.' She braced herself for her mother's wrath.

'Thank Goddess!' proclaimed Julia dramatically, sinking to her knees in a billow of cheesecloth. 'I'm *so* relieved,' she said, in low, dramatic tones. 'There are great opportunities ahead for us all. Big Horn has had the most *wonderful* idea for Mullions.'

'Oh really?' said Tally guardedly. She had had quite enough brilliant ideas for Mullions for one day. Did this one, she wondered, involve integral double-aspect utility rooms?

'Yes. Yes,' breathed Julia, ecstatic. 'He's so *creative*, that man, I can't *tell* you.' She clasped her hands and gave a semi-orgasmic shudder at the mere thought of it. Around the base of Jane's stomach, something twinged with envy.

'Come here, my darling,' Julia called over her

shoulder. 'Tally's *dying* to see your wonderful plans.'

Something tall detached itself from the shadow of one of the windowledges. A pair of strong, tanned thighs glowed in the firelight as Big Horn, still sporting his chamois leather miniskirt, came slowly towards the group of women. In his braceleted, tattooed arms he carried a large black folder which he deposited ceremonially on the rug in front of Tally. She looked at it suspiciously. It was not, after all, the first one she had seen that day.

'Big Horn and I,' declared Julia, 'and, of course, the Mother Goddess,' she added, quickly glancing upward, 'have come up with a plan for Mullions which would cost us practically nothing and,' she added, dropping her ringing tones to a discreet, excited whisper, '*make us a fortune.*'

Big Horn, his face impassive, gave a slow, dignified nod of agreement.

'We want,' continued Julia, her face ablaze with excitement, 'to make Mullions into an ashram. A retreat.'

Jane and Tally looked at each other in mixed disappointment and incomprehension. 'A retreat?' asked Tally doubtfully. 'What exactly *is* a retreat? Isn't it something to do with monks?'

'Not necessarily.' Julia serenely ignored the bad vibes. 'It's somewhere to cleanse yourself spiritually and internally. *Not,*' she added sternly, 'to pamper yourself physically. A retreat is very basic, preferably with no heating, TVs, telephones or radios.'

'It doesn't sound much fun,' ventured Jane.

'It's not meant to be *fun*,' said Julia, almost pityingly. 'It's meant to be a place where you unlock your human potential. You spend hours meditating, fasting, chanting. Some people simply lock themselves away in isolation for days on end, visualising, learning to listen to their inner selves.'

So that was what Nick had been doing in the bathroom all that time, thought Jane. If only she'd realised.

'You take classes in yoga, go for long walks, tune into world harmony and learn humility by doing menial household tasks like cleaning the lavatories, fixing shelves and doing the washing-up. And, of course,' Julia cast her eyes modestly to the floor, 'paying really rather a lot of money for the privilege.' She beamed triumphantly and clapped her hands. 'Mullions,' she pronounced, 'could not be more suitable.'

Silence ensued.

'But surely,' said Tally, struggling to find a polite way to say what she thought. 'Surely,' she gabbled, failing, 'you don't really expect people to pay a fortune to eat practically nothing, lock themselves away for weeks in sheds, spend hours contorting themselves and clean the loos into the bargain? Only nutters would pay to do that.'

'Yes. Nutters like me and Big Horn, obviously,' said Julia, offended. 'We've just come back from doing it ourselves.'

There was an embarrassed silence. Then Jane, who

had been thinking furiously for the past few seconds, barged in. 'It's a brilliant idea, Tally. Don't you see? You *can* make a fortune out of ashrams. They're terribly nineties. I've read about them. They're springing up everywhere, even in this country. In California, all the film stars go to them and pay the earth to stay there.'

Julia clapped her hands and Jane blushed as Big Horn gave her a stiff nod of approval and curved his magnificent lips upwards in what might even have been a smile.

'That's right,' Julia gushed. 'Just look at the figures.' She opened the folder. 'It'll cost next to nothing to set up. Why, Big Horn and I are practically an entire ashram in ourselves. I can take Breathing for the Millennium, Workshopping Your Pain, Locating Your Inner Child and World-Harmony Yoga classes and Big Horn can do Group Hugging and Lacto-vegetarian Meditation. We don't need telephones or TVs, and the food is really basic. Even Mrs Ormondroyd can manage to chop up a few carrots and boil a few lentils for dinner.'

There was another silence. 'Um, Mrs Ormondroyd's not around at the moment,' Tally hesitatingly confessed.

'But I'm sure we can find her,' added Jane quickly.

Julia smiled absently. 'And people don't even need to stay in the house,' she said. 'In California, lots of them sleep outside in the woods for that extra back-to-nature experience. We can get Mr Peters to knock up a few teepees.'

Tally nodded. Wherever Mr Peters had got to, she

had better find him fast. Something told her that he had not been snapped up by another estate just yet.

'Some people pay up to fifteen hundred pounds a week to stay on ashrams,' said Julia, running her finger down a column of figures, and displaying a grasp of financial matters that would have impressed even Saul Dewsbury. 'We could undercut that by hundreds and clean up in this part of the country.'

'Gosh,' said Jane. 'It certainly puts the money in harmony, doesn't it?'

Chapter 23

Returning to London from Mullions, Jane found the capital an oasis of calm after the tumultuous events in the countryside. While life, admittedly, continued manless, it also continued Champagneless, and as the fashion season came round again it had the added bonus of being Victoria-less as well. After a week in Milan, Victoria was now in Paris. Left in charge of *Fabulous*, Jane for the first time was enjoying the freedom of selecting features and planning entire issues herself.

She had not, as yet, dared to move from her deputy's desk into the glass-windowed sanctum that was Victoria's office. This was less fear of hubris than the fact that Tish would be completely incapable of putting her calls through to another desk. But in any case, Jane did not want to tempt fate. Archie Fitzherbert had left her to her own devices so far. Her criticisms over breakfast about Victoria and *Fabulous* had, unbelievably, apparently been forgotten. Fitzherbert had, Jane decided, probably just dismissed her as mad. Which was probably fine by him. Mental instability, after all, seemed practically a requirement of the job for senior magazine staff.

It was wonderful to be left alone to get on with things. There was only one cloud on Jane's horizon: the question of who would replace Champagne on the magazine's cover. The printer's deadline was approaching and she would have to make a decision soon.

At least, Jane thought, she didn't have to worry about Tally any more. Any scars left by Saul had apparently healed quickly. Tally, indeed, seemed to have emerged practically unscathed. The extent of Saul's deceit and his true intentions towards her beloved home had evidently extinguished any feelings for him other than disgust. Not that there was time to dwell on anything anyway. Having finally accepted Big Horn's plan to convert Mullions into what amounted to a cosmic Center Parc, Tally, together with Julia, was now frantically preparing for an influx of stressed-out celebrities.

'It's amazing how many people have signed up,' Tally gasped excitedly down the telephone. 'Especially when you see the brochures Mummy's sending out.' She paused. 'Because they're not brochures at all, really. Just pebbles with the telephone number engraved on them. But they seem to be bringing in the business. Mummy says it's because the pebbles are lodestones and draw the person they are sent to towards Mullions. And you should see Mr Peters. Slapping up teepees quicker than you can say General Custer.'

'So you found Mr Peters, then?'

'Yes, he was wreaking havoc at the Lower Bulge bowling club,' Tally giggled. 'They'd had to cancel games for the first time since 1910 because Mr Peters had practically destroyed the green, and he'd cut the electrics off twice by running the lawnmower through the cables. They seemed rather glad to see the back of him.'

'What about Mrs Ormondroyd?' asked Jane. 'Did you track her down as well?'

'Yes,' Tally said. 'She was working in the local dentist's surgery. Apparently business was down by almost fifty per cent. People were frightened enough of going to the dentist, but the thought of having to see Mrs Ormondroyd as well just finished them off. She's having a wonderful time now, though. Giving huge simmering pots of chickpeas the occasional stir whilst gazing uninterruptedly at Big Horn.'

'How is Big Horn?' asked Jane, smiling.

'A revelation,' said Tally sincerely. 'He's running the place like clockwork. He's got more business acumen than the entire City put together.'

'He was probably a top fund manager in a former life,' said Jane sardonically.

'Well, funny you should say that, because it turns out that he was in this one. According to Mummy, Big Horn's originally a barrow boy from Bethnal Green who went to work for a merchant bank in New York. He used to get the biggest bonuses on Wall Street until it all got too much and he burned out and went to live on the reservation in Nevada where Mummy met him.'

'No!' said Jane. 'So Big Horn's a Cockney?'

'Yes, and he's a film star now as well,' Tally said. '*Three Christenings and a Hen Party* is finished but Brad decided at the last minute to reshoot some of the christening party scenes with Big Horn as a guest. Brad thought he would add a certain—'

'*Je ne sais Iroquoi*?' butted in Jane.

'Exactly,' giggled Tally. 'After all, as Brad said, look what a big, silent Red Indian did for *One Flew Over the Cuckoo's Nest*!'

Entering the *Fabulous* office the next Monday morning, Jane found Tosh shrieking with laughter at something a white-faced Tash had just said.

'What's the matter?' asked Jane.

Tosh screwed up her face, evidently unable to speak for mirth.

Tash looked agonised.

'Good weekend?' pressed Jane.

'No,' burst out Tash. 'I've had the most *ghastly* weekend actually. I was staying with the Uppe-Timmselves when my hostess came into my bedroom without knocking to have a bedtime chat with me and caught me *peeing* in the sink. It was *beyond* embarrassing.' She crimsoned at the memory.

Tosh exploded once more.

'You should have told her it was part of your yoga routine,' said Jane.

'Yes, well, sadly one never thinks of these things at

the time, does one?' said Tash. 'But as I said to her, if you don't provide en suite bathrooms for all your guests, what else can you expect? I mean, who wants to walk miles down a draughty corridor in the middle of the night in the pitch black looking for the lavatory?' She looked at Jane in anguish. Jane tried to appear sympathetic and not catch the eye of Tosh. The giggles bubbling up in her throat would certainly damage the fragile *esprit de corps du bureau* she had managed to establish in Victoria's absence.

'Speaking of outside lavatory arrangements,' drawled Tosh, rubbing a hand roughly over her streaming eyes, 'did you see Champagne D'Vyne at the runway protest on the news last night? She's *beyond*, isn't she? Said she was passionate about green belts, particularly the ones you get from Mulberry.'

'Yes,' Tash joined in, glad of the distraction. 'She's certainly the first environmental protester I've ever seen who gets her entire wardrobe from Voyage. And apparently Michaeljohn have to send a stylist down to Gatwick every week to give her hair that fashionably tangled look. Hilarious, isn't she?'

'It's all very well for her to try and save the planet,' remarked Larry, 'but I'm not sure she's on the same one as the rest of us in the first place.'

Talk of Champagne and holes reminded Jane again of the one she had left on the *Fabulous* cover. Jane had considered many options over the past few days, but no one seemed quite right. Except Lily Eyre, and Victoria had already vetoed her. Still, thought Jane defiantly, if

Victoria was going to go swanning off round the minibars of Europe and leave someone else to run her magazine, she would have to take the consequences. Deciding, for once, to act on instinct, and before she could change her mind, Jane picked up the telephone, dialled Lily Eyre's agent and offered her the cover and an interview.

'Lily Eyre's going to be our next cover,' Jane told the rest of the staff at a features meeting that afternoon. Lily Eyre's people had accepted with alacrity and Jane had briefed one of her best and wittiest freelance writers to interview the actress. Her stomach felt tight with mixed apprehension and triumph as she thought about it. It was a bold move, but there seemed no reason why it would not pay off.

'But what about her ankles?' asked Tash doubtfully. 'Aren't they supposed to be dreadful?'

Jane shook her head, trying not to stare at Tash's own distinctly solid lower calves. 'They're fine,' she said reassuringly. 'Right, ideas. Anyone got any?'

There was a silence.

'There's this artist I read about,' said Tash hesistantly. 'She's the daughter of the Earl of Staines and she makes papier-mâché lamp bases out of prostitutes' telephone box calling cards.'

Another silence.

'Well,' said Jane brightly, determined to be encouraging, 'we *do* need to beef up the arts side. You're certainly on the right track, Tash.' Albeit stuck in a siding on a branch line, she thought to herself.

But the message seemed to be getting through. The staff seemed to be trying a bit harder, and were even venturing into areas of the newspapers other than the horoscopes.

'Have you seen this?' said Tosh a day or so later, proffering a copy of a recently-launched literary magazine. '*The Scribbler*'s main interview this month is with a writer called Charlie Seton who they're raving about as the new James Joyce.'

Jane raised a sceptical eyebrow.

'He's sex on a stick, apparently,' sighed Tosh. 'I only know because a friend of mine works there. She says Charlie Seton's just *gorgeous*. Just *amazingly* good-looking. Oh, and really, really talented, of course,' she added quickly.

Amused, Jane looked closer at the piece. 'Eton, Oxford, bedsitter in Soho,' she read. It was, as Tosh said, great *Fabulous* material. Jane squinted at the picture of the author. It was very heavily art-directed, so much so that beneath the scribbles and pasted-on cutouts of lightbulbs and lips, it was impossible to see what Charlie Seton actually looked like.

'I thought I could go and interview him this morning,' suggested Tosh.

Jane looked at her sternly. Tosh knew perfectly well she had a mountain of beauty copy to rewrite. 'Sorry,' said Jane. Tosh's face went into freefall. 'You're much too busy. You've got that piece about the new blue lipsticks to tidy up.' Tosh pushed out her bottom lip.

Unmoved, Jane picked up the magazine and read

the piece again. Was it, she wondered, worth giving Charlie Seton a call? He might make an interesting piece. And the bits of his face that you could see looked reasonably promising.

Hell, I deserve it, thought Jane. I'll go and see him myself. I don't get to pull rank very often. In fact, I don't get to pull *anything* very often.

'Busty Models' read the badly-written sign on the shabby Soho door. Walking slowly up the other side of the street, Jane looked at the very young, sunken-eyed girl in a black PVC waistcoat and miniskirt lounging against the doorframe. She was chewing languidly and obviously waiting for business. She didn't *look* very busty, Jane thought. But then, with her scraped-back, lifeless blonde ponytail and greyish skin, she didn't look much like a model either. She was, however, looking suspiciously at Jane.

Jane couldn't blame her. She had been wandering up and down this street for the last ten minutes at least and still hadn't been able to locate Charlie Seton's flat. Because he was a writer, she had assumed that he would be in the garret. But as she peered up to the crumbling second-floor windows with their cracked windowboxes containing long-dead plants, it occurred to her that writing by the light of a red bulb might be difficult. Jane cleared her throat and crossed the litter-strewn street towards the girl in PVC.

'Does a writer called Charlie live round here?' Jane asked.

The girl carried on chewing her gum. 'No,' she said. 'There's no one called Charlie round here.' She spoke, somewhat surprisingly, in the pleasant, enunciated tones of a vicar's wife.

Jane turned away, disappointed. She was in the wrong place, obviously. Odd, because this had definitely been the name of the street. That, evidently, was that then. She began to walk away.

'But there *is* a writer round here,' the girl called after her. Jane turned. The girl was chewing her gum, grinning. 'Down there in the basement.' She pointed beneath her feet. 'Say hello from me.'

Jane quickly retraced her steps. She bent slightly and peered down into the lighted basement window directly below, whose top four inches were exactly level with her ankle. The room inside was lit by a single bulb. Cigarette stubs overflowed from an ashtray all over the desk below the window, and a rumpled duvet covered a mattress on the floor. Papers, both newsprint and manuscript, were scattered everywhere. Yes, it looked like a writer's room. If she inclined her head slightly to the right it was just possible to see the back of a T-shirted figure sitting at the desk. Charlie Seton was obviously hard at work.

Absurdly aware of her smart little herringbone suit and brand-new high-heeled ankle boots, Jane went through the open front door of the scruffy building and descended the stairs at the back of the passageway. She tapped at the battered door at the bottom. The paint on its ancient surface was so blistered and cracked it was possible to see every colour it had ever been. Jane counted burgundy, mustard, bilious green and diarrhoea brown before the door creaked open to reveal Charlie Seton.

Only it wasn't Charlie Seton. It was Tom.

'Tom!' croaked Jane. 'Tom!' she squeaked, fumbling for the right words to convey the explosion of excitement, confusion and hope that had just detonated within her. She gazed desperately from one to the other of his eyes. She felt like a bad actress in a straight-to-video romantic turkey.

'What an amazing coincidence,' she gasped eventually in strangled tones. The film seemed to have switched to *Brief Encounter*. 'You see, I've come here to interview you. Isn't it hilarious? From the magazine.'

'Oh,' said Tom. 'Of course. Right.'

So far he had conspicuously failed to gather her up in his arms and murmur 'At last, my love, I've found you' into her neck. Jane wasn't sure what film he was in. Something inscrutable, perhaps one of those tortuous coming-of-age-in-eastern Europe sagas that win all the Best Foreign Language Film Oscars. Still gazing intently into his face, Jane felt dizzy with the almost overwhelming desire to shout 'Do You Still Love Me?' from the rooftops.

What she actually said was, 'What are you doing here?'

'I came back,' Tom said simply. 'New York didn't work out exactly as I expected. Look, why don't you come inside?'

'Why didn't it work out?' asked Jane, following him into the room which looked even scruffier from inside than it had from the pavement. There was no furniture apart from the mattress, the desk, a rickety chair and a sink at the back with a shelf over it.

'I suppose you could call it a misunderstanding,' said Tom, smiling faintly.

Jane's heart started thumping with terror. A woman. She might have known the dead hand of the Manhattan blonde would be involved. 'Girl trouble?' she croaked bravely.

'No!' laughed Tom. 'Not at all. My agent here sent me over there to work on the script for the new *Godfather* film. I was thrilled. It sounded like a dream come true.'

'So what went wrong?'

'Well, when I got there,' Tom said, rubbing his hair ruefully, 'it turned out the agent had misheard and I was expected to write the script for a cartoon about a mafioso fish called the Codfather. Not *quite* Robert De Niro.' He lit a cigarette.

Jane giggled and felt sufficiently emboldened to probe further. 'But why have you changed your name since you came back? And why,' she was unable to stop herself blurting out, 'didn't you get in touch with me?'

'I haven't changed my name,' said Tom. 'Charlie Seton is the name I write under. Always has been. My *nom de plume*.' So that explained why she could never find him in the bookshops, thought Jane. 'And in answer to your other question,' he said lightly, 'I didn't really see the point in coming round to see you at the flat in which you live with your boyfriend. Cup of tea?'

'But . . . I don't. I mean, I do. But he doesn't. Any more. That is.' A slight frown furrowed Tom's forehead. Jane wondered if he had understood her. The second cue for him to gather her into his arms and whoop . . . passed. They were still, it seemed, in different films.

'Why did you move in here?' Jane asked awkwardly, feeling so *Brief Encounter* her throat ached. Of all the ecstatic reunion scenarios with Tom she had imagined, she had overlooked the possibility of this one.

'It's a good place to write.' Tom filled an old Russell Hobbs kettle at the sink. 'A real slice of old Soho. It's very stimulating.'

Jane's thoughts automatically flickered to Busty Models upstairs. She wondered *how* stimulating, exactly.

'Although,' Tom added, reading her thoughts, 'you have to be careful when you live below Busty Models. Looking up at the window is distracting. Most of the girls who work that pavement don't wear any underwear, and I can see straight up their skirts from here.'

'Really?' said Jane sourly. 'One of them sends you her love, anyway. The blonde in black plastic.'

'Oh yes. Camilla.' Tom dropped two teabags into a couple of chipped mugs that he held in one hand and poured on a stream of boiling water with the other. 'Poor thing. It's a dreadful story. Upper-middle-class family, promising student at Oxford, got fed up, ran out of money, came down here and became a prostitute. Doing well now, though. Runs that place like clockwork.'

'She runs it?' gasped Jane, amazed. 'But she only looks about ten.'

'She's nineteen,' said Tom. 'Going on ninety. And very funny with it. Some of the stories she tells are hilarious. You wouldn't believe who goes up there. Several MPs, for a start.'

'Really?'

'Oh yes.' Tom extracted the teabags from the mugs. 'Camilla has to be very careful. Not all of them are in the best of health. If she comes on too strong with the whips and masks, she could cause a by-election. When the Tories were hanging on to a majority by their fingernails she could have brought down the government. And the things she tells me about what she does you wouldn't believe.'

'Like what?' asked Jane, genuinely curious.

'Well, one of Camilla's favourite tricks, apparently,' said Tom, not quite meeting Jane's eye while she, for her part, wondered how apparently 'apparently' was, 'is to take a mouthful of Coca-Cola before giving someone a blow job. Apparently you get the most amazing sensation.'

Silence followed this astonishing piece of intelligence. They were not, Jane realised, in *Brief Encounter* any more.

'Look, shall we start the interview?' she asked, hoping to get the conversation out of the rather embarrassing siding it seemed to have got stuck in and remembering why she was here. She may as well try to salvage something, if not her dignity or the relationship, then at least a few hundred words of page-filler for *Fabulous*. 'I haven't got much time, you see,' she added. 'I've got an advertiser's lunch.'

Stepping into Victoria's Manolo Blahniks, Jane had discovered, involved more than just sitting in the office hammering out feature ideas. She had also to turn up to the ghastly events known in the trade as 'lipstick lunches' – launches of new beauty products by the magazine's advertisers. Jane's heart sank at the thought of the one that lay ahead – for a perfume called Orgasmique. Ghastly name for a scent, she thought. Who in their right mind would want to go round smelling of sexual activity all day? Who indeed, she thought, forcing herself not to gaze too longingly at Tom's invitingly rumpled mattress. Had someone spent the night there with him?

'Shall I sit here?' she asked, deciding to take charge and lowering her bottom on to the rickety chair at the desk. She felt absurdly formal standing up in her high heels and neat suit.

'I . . .' said Tom as Jane's tailored rump made contact with the chair, 'wouldn't sit there,' he finished as the chair seat slid away beneath and left her sprawled on the floor, skirt around her waist, giving Tom a gala performance of her underwear.

'Sorry,' said Tom, lingering rather longer than perhaps he should have done on the contemplation of her La Perla. 'Everything in this place is falling apart, I'm afraid. The only really safe place to sit is the deck, and even that's a bit dodgy in places. Tread softly, for you tread on my floor, as Yeats didn't say.' He sat down on the mattress.

Jane rearranged her legs. 'Well, you told me a bit about your career before,' she said determinedly, switching to interviewer mode to cover her embarrassment. 'What are you working on now?' she pressed. 'Did you ever get round to writing that bonkbuster?'

Tom raised his eyebrows. He shook his head. 'No. I never did, sadly.' His sexy, sleepy eyes crinkled with amusement. 'Still, it's not too late to start.' He looked at her speculatively. There was silence again.

Jane sighed. She knew that, despite her best efforts, she was going nowhere with this interview. She was wasting both her time and his. 'I'm afraid I've got to go,' she said, struggling to her feet and shoving into her bag the notebook in which she had only just started to write. 'I'm late for this dreadful, boring lunch, and it's all my fault because I got here so late. I'm sorry.'

'Don't be so hard on yourself,' said Tom easily, drawing on a newly-lit cigarette. 'It really doesn't matter.'

That much was abundantly clear, thought Jane, stumbling in her high heels up the rotting stairs on the way out. Tom could obviously take her or leave her. Leave her, preferably. She felt desperate with disappointment. Tom had been ambiguous to the point of incomprehensibility. Only the thought of Camilla loitering outside stopped her from dissolving into tears as she picked her way down the scruffy passageway.

Chapter 24

Fortunately, the lunch provided Jane with the opportunity to drown her sorrows in a great deal of champagne. She had hung on to every word the Orgasmique Nose had to say about the top and bottom notes of his new perfume. He had seemed the only stable thing in a whirling, Bollinger-fuelled world. Flattered by her apparent rapt attention, the Nose had been charmed.

Damn Tom. Who needs a man when you've got a career? were the alternate trains of thought occupying Jane as she lurched drunkenly from side to side in the taxi on her way back to the office. When she eventually, after much reeling, gained her desk, she noticed the office was practically empty apart from Larry.

'Wheresh everyone?' Jane asked. It was, after all, ten to four. Even *Fabulous*-length lunches should be drawing to a close by now.

'Tish has gone shopping,' said Larry. 'And Tash

and Tosh are seeing their psychics.'

'Their *pshychics*?' slurred Jane. 'What on *earth* for?'

'Well, psychics *are* the shrinks of the nineties,' said Larry. 'Anyone who's anyone goes to one, basically.'

'*Do* they?' said Jane.

'Absolutely,' said Larry blithely. 'I wouldn't be without mine. So *entertaining*, for one thing, hearing all about your future. Psychics are so *relaxing* in that way. They do all the talking and thinking for you and you don't have to bang on tediously about your childhood to a psychologist like we all did in the eighties. *So* exhausting, trying to remember whether it was Uncle Jasper or Uncle Henry who groped you in the gun room.'

Tish appeared with an armful of shopping bags to rival Champagne in her heyday. 'Uncle Jasper, definitely,' she grinned.

'I see,' said Jane, still wondering vaguely why girls on *Fabulous* were at all curious about what lay in store. If anyone could predict the future to within five pounds of their future husbands' bank balance, surely it was Tash, Tosh and Tish. From girls' school to upmarket former polytechnic to photocopying at *Fabulous* to marrying a suitable ex-public schoolboy, their lives had been programmed since birth. Her own future, on the other hand, might benefit from a bit of forewarning and forearming.

'Laetitia in the art department started it all off,' said Tish. 'Her psychic predicted that she would marry a tall, dark, handsome stranger whose name began with

D. And she was bang on, apart from the fact that Laetitia's husband's blond and his name's Caspar. *Strordinary*, don't you think?'

'*Amazhing*,' said Jane, knowing Tish would be oblivious to her sardonic tones. Tish was one of those people, to quote Julian Barnes, who thought irony was where the Ironians lived.

Jane stared down at her desk and began shifting papers from one pile to another, trying to stop her slowly-sobering thoughts straying back to Tom. There was no point dwelling on him any more. He had made it pretty obvious what he thought about her.

The telephone rang. Jane reached for it. 'Hello?' she said.

'Hello,' said a voice both familiar and unfamiliar at the same time. 'How did your lunch go?'

Jane caught her breath and tried to prevent her hands from shaking, her heart from giving out, her liver from failing and her feet from beating a tattoo on the floor.

'Tom! I mean Charlie,' she gasped.

'You mean Tom,' said the voice. 'So? How was it?'

'Oh, fairly ghastly,' stammered Jane, as her hangover now beginning to kick in. Her throat was dry and she felt slightly sick.

'We didn't seem to get very far with our interview,' said Tom breezily.

'No,' said Jane. 'We didn't.'

'Perhaps you'd like to finish it,' said Tom, utterly matter-of-fact.

'Ye-es.'

'Well, if you want to meet up again,' said Tom briskly, 'tomorrow evening would be best for me. I've got a short story to finish during the day.'

Jane's stomach shot to the floor, bounced up and hit the ceiling and continued yo-yo-ing between the two for almost half a minute. Was she imagining things, or was Tom asking her out to dinner?

'I'd *love* to,' she breathed passionately. 'Er, I'd like to very much,' she repeated stiffly, aware that she was in danger of scaring Tom off completely.

'Well, I hope you like pasta,' he said. 'If you do, I know a great little place called San Lorenzo.'

Jane's eyes bulged. San Lorenzo. The Belgravia headquarters of the ladies-who-lunch brigade, preferred pit stop of every passing international celebrity worth their hand-chipped sea salt. She had hardly thought Tom could stretch to that. Perhaps he was doing better than she thought.

She should have realised there was something odd when Tom suggested they meet outside Leicester Square Tube, rather than Knightsbridge. But the restaurant was indeed San Lorenzo, although not quite as Jane imagined it. This San Lorenzo was a tiny, old-fashioned Covent Garden Italian where the only ladies lunching – or dining – looked like ladies of the night. The menu was innocent of anything even approaching truffle oil and the waiting staff was made up of two elderly, boot-faced Italian waitresses who clacked around in sloppy mules with tea towels flung over their shoulders. The straw Chianti bottles on the walls were obviously there from the first time round and not as part of some post-ironic retro-kick. It was so traditional it practically got up and did a jig as they entered.

Having dressed for Belgravia, Jane felt slightly *de trop* in her new Joseph suit and cursed her extravagance at blowing a week's salary on a haircut at lunchtime. Tom, meanwhile, was wearing his usual uniform of battered leather jacket, tired jeans and another T-shirt from his collection of jumble-sale specials. This evening's one was emblazoned with the dates from a Whitesnake tour of 1981.

'Aaah, Meester Tom,' said the waitresses, their hatchet faces melting into expressions of starstruck charm as he led Jane into a tiled foyer of Barbara Cartland pink which, she noticed, clashed beautifully with Bob-Monkhouse-tan walls. 'Thees way,' fussed one, pulling out an oilcloth-covered table for Jane to get behind while the other arrived with a brimming carafe of black-red wine.

'Wonderful,' said Tom, grinning and rubbing his hands. The gnarled old waitresses had by now melted so much they were almost a puddle on the floor. They gazed at him adoringly as they handed over the menus.

'Wonderful fresh pasta tonight, Meester Tom,' said one. 'Bring back childhood memories. Like Mamma used to make.'

Tom smiled. 'You forget, Bianca, that I'm not Italian.'

'Ah, but Meester Tom you 'ave an Italian soul,' giggled

the old woman. 'Romanteek. Artisteek.' She waved her arms expansively.

'And I don't want to bring back childhood memories either,' Tom grinned. 'Can't think of anything more ghastly. I'd much rather bring back naughty adolescent memories.' He darted a teasing look at Jane, who blushed deeply.

'In that case,' said Bianca delightedly, 'you must 'ave the 'ouse speciality. *Pollo alla principessa*. Chicken for a princess. *Ecco!*' She gestured at Jane and beamed.

'Two of those then,' said Tom. 'I hope you don't mind me ordering for you?' he said to Jane after Bianca had gone. 'But I promise you it'll be delicious.'

Jane couldn't have minded less. Having Tom order for her in this cosy, candelit, unpretentious place could not have felt more different from having Mark squeaking and grunting in his show-Japanese as he ordered ostentatiously from the menu at Ninja. Nor could the food, when it came, have been more different. Instead of fish so raw it was practically still breathing, the chicken arrived roasted to golden perfection.

'Beakerful of the warm South?' asked Tom, proffering the carafe and crinkling his eyes at her in the candlelight.

As they talked, Jane could well believe he was a storyteller. His accounts of life on his Soho street were positively Dayglo in their luridness. He was a skilled listener too, she realised as he began delicately to probe her recent disastrous romantic history. Slowly and reluctantly at first, then willingly and eventually torrentially, Jane talked a lot about Nick and a little about Mark. Tom listened intently, rolling his large, candlelit eyes sympathetically now and then. For his own part, he said little about his love life. And Jane could never quite find the right moment or phrases to start asking.

'Coffee?' Tom asked, as the lovestruck waitresses loomed after the homemade tiramisu.

'No, thank you,' said Jane. 'Actually, I'd better go,' she added reluctantly as Tom produced a fistful of grubby notes out of his pocket.

'My treat,' he insisted when Jane started to scrabble for her purse.

'It's been lovely to see you again,' she said. Please ask me back for a drink, her eyes begged him.

'Come back for a drink,' said Tom right on cue. 'It's only round the corner, and you can call a cab from there.'

'All right,' said Jane, her eyes turned determinedly aside from the endless fleet of empty, available cabs clearly visible through the restaurant windows. Her legs trembled as she got to her feet.

Soho seemed a city of light as they walked through it. It was raining, and the neon signs of the restaurants and bars were brilliantly reflected in the wet pavements. Figures hurried by in the hissing rain, intent on their own business, silent and hooded as monks. Taxis honked and hustled their way through the traffic-crowded streets. Tom, apparently almost unconsciously and so delicately she could scarcely feel it, took her hand in his as they turned off Old Compton Street. Delirious happiness flooded through Jane's veins. She wanted nothing else in the world.

Someone else, however, did. The thin, desperate face of a young girl gazed pleadingly up at them as they passed the dark and rotting recess of an abandoned restaurant doorway. 'Here you are,' Tom muttered, stopping. Jane heard the rattle of change as he unearthed a handful of silver and put it gently into the dirty, proffered palm which protruded from the end of a plaster cast. 'Can I sign your cast?' asked Tom, smiling at the beggar.

'You can sign me wherever you like, darlin'.'

Camilla was on duty as they arrived at the flat. Her black plastic outfit shone in the street lights and a cigarette hung from between her wet, red-slicked lips. As they approached, Jane felt under scrutiny.

'You look very glamorous,' Tom said to her cheerfully. 'How's business?' He spoke to Camilla, Jane noticed, with as much courtesy and respect as if she had been a doctor or a barrister.

'Booming,' said Camilla, in her ironic, well-spoken voice. 'The good wives of Woking seem to have been having a lot of bedtime headaches recently. Not to mention,' she added, leaning forward conspiratorially, raising her eyebrows and shooting a loaded look at the red-lit window above her, 'the good wives of Westminster.'

Inside Tom's flat, Jane looked around in surprise. 'Tom! You've tidied up.' The papers were still there, but they were heaped rather than scattered. The duvet, although unrepentantly unironed, was actually pulled over the mattress and the pillows had a suspiciously plumped-up look about them. Had he expected her to come back with him? Oh, what did it matter anyway? It was a bit late to play hard to get now.

Jane avoided the chair and lowered herself on to the edge of the mattress while Tom lit candles and poured two tots of whisky into glasses. A low, calm swell of music swirled gently into the air. 'What's this?' Jane asked, gazing at the flickering flame through her glass and admiring the way the amber fluid turned to liquid gold.

'Vaughan Williams' Fifth,' said Tom, lighting a cigarette and settling himself against the pillows. Jane felt the space between them quiver. 'Preludio.' The haunting, insistent, plaintive notes increased in intensity.

Jane closed her eyes. 'It's lovely,' she said, aware it was a horribly inadequate description. She had, after all, said the same thing barely two hours ago about the San Lorenzo chicken. 'I'm afraid I don't know anything about music,' she added apologetically.

'Well, all you really have to know is whether you like it or not,' said Tom simply. 'I like this because it's very calm and relaxing. It's one of those pieces that puts into notes all that longing you could never put into words.' He said it without a hint of theatricality, as if merely stating a fact. Who or what was he longing for? Jane wondered. Gazing silently into the middle distance, drawing on his cigarette, Tom did not enlighten her.

As much to relieve incipient cramp as to break the tension, Jane got to her feet. For once, her knees did not crack like pistol shots. She crossed to look at the mass of books piled against the wall at the back of the room. It was her turn to examine his library now.

Suddenly, a finger lifted her hair from the back and she felt a warm mouth exploring the nape of her neck. Her spine exploded into shivers. She closed her eyes and gave herself up to blissful oblivion as Tom gently nibbled her ear.

'I didn't know what to say to you yesterday,' murmured Tom. 'You see, I had spent all this time persuading myself that you were living with your boyfriend and there was no point in trying.'

Damn, thought Jane, her fists clenching. What sort of deluded fool had she been to want to move in with Nick in the first place? It had ruined everything ever since.

'But then you came round here and I thought you'd come to tell me it was over with him,' Tom mumbled, 'that somehow you'd found me, but you said you had come from the magazine to do an interview, which, naturally, rather threw me, and then you *did* tell me it was over with him, but I didn't know what to think by then. If you understand what I mean.' Tom paused. 'I'm not sure that I do, though.'

Jane smiled and did not answer as his lips started nibbling round her cheekbones. She stood stock still, terrified to move in case he stopped. Tom gently turned her round and pushed her trembling lips apart with his own. He smelt of soap and tasted of salt, thought Jane, melting into his mouth and arms as her legs gave way beneath her. Pressing her gently to him, Tom pushed a warm hand beneath her Joseph and fondled her stiffening nipple.

'I've wanted you ever since that night,' he breathed. 'I just couldn't stop thinking about you. I thought you must have forgotten me ages ago, that you must have thought of it as just a one-night stand. Which it was, of course. Only it wasn't.'

'No, it wasn't,' Jane murmured, clutching his rough-soft hair in her fingers.

'But will you respect me in the morning?' Tom muttered as he slid the exploring hand into her knickers.

'I certainly hope not,' murmured Jane.

Chapter 25

Jane had not slept all night. It had seemed a good idea at the time; in fact, it had seemed a crime to do anything else. But now she was paying the price. Concentrating on the recondite detail of the next issue's fashion pages was almost more than she could manage. Just what was Tiara talking about?

'What do you mean, boars' pelvises?' Jane felt a migraine coming on. This meeting had been going on for an hour already and there seemed no end in sight.

'Boar's pelvises. Alessandro uses boars' pelvises in his hats. He's, er, the sort of Damien Hirst of millinery,' said Tiara, proffering some dim Polaroids featuring a pale, rickety, bony structure wearing another on her head.

'Don't tell me. He's the next pig thing,' sighed Jane, hoping it wouldn't catch on. There were quite enough boneheads around in fashion as it was. Tiara tightened her lips. Her sense of humour, thought Jane, had gone the way of her puppy fat and original facial features. Wiped away without trace. Perhaps that was what the Glamourtron did to you.

'We're planning a spread on the couture, of course,' said Tiara.

Of course, thought Jane. To justify Victoria's continuing absence at fashion shows, if nothing else. Yesterday Victoria had returned from Paris Fashion Week and declared it the most tedious experience of her life. Then she had promptly boarded Concorde for the New York shows.

Tiara produced more Polaroids and spread them on the big desk before Jane. 'These are the latest batch. Amazing, aren't they?'

In one, a topless, emaciated woman wearing what looked like a gas mask and the ripped bottom half of a ballgown was staggering up the runway with a Doc Marten on one leg and a moonboot on the other. In another, a woman was wearing what looked like a green hospital gown. Tiara was right. Amazing was the word.

'Couture really is astonishing, isn't it?' muttered Jane. 'I mean, all those customers at the shows paying upwards of fifty thousand pounds for something they'll only wear once.'

'What do you mean?' asked Tiara indignantly. 'Some of them wear it *twice*.'

After the fashion meeting, Jane wandered out into a features department more deserted than the *Marie Celeste* after a bomb scare. 'Where's Tash?' she asked.

'Gone to a wedding,' said Tish, as if this was the

most natural thing to do on a Tuesday morning. But then, at *Fabulous*, Jane supposed it was. No one here went to anything as tacky as a Saturday marriage. She looked at the clock. Half past twelve. Seven long, miserable, endless hours before she met Tom for the concert at the Barbican he had promised her to start her musical education.

Unclamping herself from his warm body that morning had been like leaving part of herself behind. Too happy to sleep, she had lain there wide awake all night, gazing through the gaping curtains to the dark blue sky in which passing planes glowed like slow-moving stars. Light-headed with tiredness, Jane closed her eyes and escaped into the inner world where she could see him, smell him, feel him again. How on earth did people in love manage to get any work done at all? she wondered. How did they fit anything else in?

She reluctantly dragged herself back to the film magazines and the burning question of her next front cover. Most of the 'ones to watch' sections seemed very excited about an American actress called Jordan Madison who was variously described as famously moody, notoriously uninterviewable, utterly beautiful and star of a string of indie films of which the latest, *Fish Food*, had been a huge critical and cult success.

'Oh yah, Jordan Madison,' said Tosh, passing Jane's desk en route to the fax. She rolled an over-made-up eye at the full-page pictures of the frail-bodied actress with her colt's legs and long, flat, black hair. 'You'll never get her. She *never* does interviews.'

Jane immediately picked up the telephone and began placing calls with and sending faxes to Jordan's LA press agent, New York press agent and the New York press agent's LA press agent. She knew a challenge when she heard one.

As the last note hung in the air, the tears continued to flow uncontrollably down Jane's cheeks. Tom, silent beside her, gave her hand a sympathetic squeeze. Jane cast a quick, blurred glance around and saw that almost everybody else in the concert hall was sitting ramrod straight with eyes as dry as the desert. Had they no souls? she wondered. Or, more likely, had she had one too many resistance-weakening gin and tonics before the beginning of the concert? 'It was so beautiful,' she gulped afterwards as Tom handed her yet another large gin and tonic from the bar. 'It was the saddest thing I've ever heard. What was it called?'

'*Pavane pour une infante défunte*,' said Tom. 'Pavane for a dead princess. Ravel used to make his students play it, and yell at them that he'd written a pavane for a dead princess, not a dead pavane for a princess.' He grinned and kissed her on the tip of her nose. 'Cheer up. Let's go and have that romantic dinner you promised me.' The lyrical moment was shattered in an instant as Jane remembered the mess her flat was in.

Having sent Tom round to the off-licence to buy some wine, Jane let herself quickly into the hall. Without even pausing to take her coat off, she rushed frantically around tidying up heaps of clothes, shoving her tampons and Ladyshave into the bathroom cupboard and spraying perfume liberally over the pillows.

Moving on to the kitchen, she emptied the prewashed salad she'd splashed out on in honour of the occasion into a bowl and threw the potatoes into a pan. Next she tackled the scarily exotic-looking red snapper in the fridge. She was relieved to note from the cooking instructions that it required no more attention than the cursory slick of butter she had been planning to give it. Just as she lowered the fish into their crematorium, Tom came through the door. Rushing to meet him, Jane noticed a pair of grey knickers on the bedroom floor and kicked them swiftly under the bed.

'Why haven't you taken your coat off?' he grinned, brandishing a bottle of Moët at her. Jane hurriedly divested herself.

'What's for dinner?' he asked, picking two champagne glasses from the kitchen cupboard and giving her his crinkle-eyed smile.

'Fish,' said Jane.

'Sounds brill,' grinned Tom. He shrugged off his battered leather jacket and lit up a Marlboro.

'I suppose you think that's very finny,' said Jane, twining her arms round his neck. 'But you're certainly a dab hand,' she added, as his warm fingertips slipped inside her knickers again. He certainly wasn't one to flounder, she thought, gasping as he rubbed gently at the warm, willing wetness between her legs.

'Cod we go to bed?' breathed Tom, grinding his

cigarette out with thrilling force in the base of the cheeseplant.

'Just give me time to mullet over,' said Jane, walking slowly backwards towards the bedroom and pulling Tom with her.

As he pressed her gently down into the perfume-scented pillows, Jane prepared to give herself up to pure pleasure as Tom began to kiss her slowly. Very slowly. In fact, he almost seemed to have stopped. Jane opened her eyes. Above her, in the semi-gloom, Tom had raised his head slightly.

'What's that funny smell?' he asked. Jane felt panic shoot through her. Perhaps she *had* been a bit heavy-handed with the Number 5.

'Scent,' she admitted, shamefacedly. Would he think she was irredeemably naff? Dabbing perfume on pillows like a twelve-year-old.

'No, not that,' said Tom, sniffing. 'A sort of burning smell.'

'Aaaargh!' Two nanoseconds later, a naked Jane had leapt out of bed with a speed that would not have disgraced an Olympic high jumper and raced into the kitchen where the red mullet was now distinctly black.

She pushed aside her tangle of hair and looked at Tom helplessly as, also naked, he loped up to the kitchen door. She was encouraged to see that the sickening smell of burnt fish, which she knew would linger around the flat for days, did not seem to have dampened his ardour one iota. A splendid erection rose triumphantly out of his abundant dark-blond pubic hair. He looked, she decided, rather like one of those fertility statues in the British Museum. 'Fancy a takeaway?' she asked with a weak grin.

'No, but I fancy you,' said Tom, giving Jane his slow-burn smile.

'Oh no,' wailed Oonagh.

Jane started reluctantly out of the most wonderful daydream at the crucial moment when she was just going up the aisle with Tom. As there was no further interruption, she lapsed back into it, to find herself fast-forwarded to their honeymoon in the sort of Caribbean luxury hideaway where you just stuck a flag in the sand when you wanted another cocktail. The daydream then changed scene to a sunny garden path down which she and Tom were walking with two merry, blonde, fish-finger-advert children.

'No. No. No,' cried Oonagh, burying her perfectly-coiffed head in her elegant arms. 'I don't believe it. It can't be true,' she moaned from the muffled depths of her cashmere. 'That has to be the most embarrassing thing that's ever happened to me in my entire life.'

'What?' asked Jane, looking up distractedly. 'What's happened?'

Oonagh raised a despairing head. 'The Duchess of Dorchester has just rung me,' she said in anguished tones.

'So what's the matter with that?' It sounded like a *Fabulous* dream come true to Jane.

'The matter is that she's an old friend of mine,' wailed Oonagh. 'Or *was.* I went to her daughter's wedding last week. Apparently there's a *video.*'

'Oh *no,*' chimed in Tash, looking outraged. 'I just *don't* believe it. I mean, how *naff* can you get? Only *common* people have wedding videos. You're *quite* right to be furious, Oonagh.'

'Not *that,*' spat Oonagh. Tash blinked. 'I'm more concerned,' Oonagh gasped, 'about the fact that quite a large part of the video features me making very loud and rude remarks about some of the other guests. Apparently my seat was practically *next door* to the video and sound recorder. Daisy Dorchester is *incandescent.*'

Jane looked quickly down at a pile of faxes on her desk before anyone could see her laughing.

Most of the faxes were refusals from Jordan Madison's seemingly limitless band of press agents. Refusing to take no for an answer, Jane had pursued them by telephone and had still ended up with no for an answer. 'She doesn't do innerviews,' everyone had snarled, leaving Jane wondering why Jordan Madison needed press agents at all in that case. On the other hand, what was the point of not giving interviews if no one knew you didn't give interviews?

Jane sighed. She had to get this piece in the bag somehow. Having one good cover simply wasn't enough. Two and she'd be home and dry. And she needed to do it soon, before Victoria swept back, as she must eventually, and took all the credit for her efforts.

Jane's heart sank at this most depressing of depressing thoughts. She was getting used to running the place on her own; more than that, she was enjoying it. Good ideas were finally starting to come out of the features department.

The telephone rang, providing a welcome excuse to leave Oonagh to her somewhat unsolvable problem. It was Tally.

'You won't believe how well it's going,' she exclaimed. 'People are just pouring in to the retreat. We even had a wedding here the other day.'

She spoke, Jane noticed, entirely without longing for her own near-miss nuptials. Clearly Tally had had enough of men for the time being.

'It's going to be in *Hello!* next week,' Tally twittered. 'It was some heir to a vitreous enamel fortune marrying his psychic, apparently.'

'Not the Hon. Rollo Harbottle, surely,' said Jane.

'Yes, how on earth do you know him?' Tally sounded astonished.

'Don't ask. Marrying his psychic, was he? Very trendy. I'm glad to hear he's finally got himself a relationship with a future.'

'You should have been there,' said Tally. 'It was hilarious. Mummy arranged it and you know what that means. A mad New Age ceremony where the bride and groom were naked and coated with mud and sang to each other at the top of a hill as the dawn rose. They were standing,' Tally added, snorting, 'in the middle of a giant representation in leaves of the male and female genitalia and exchanged oak saplings instead of wedding rings.' She giggled.

'What else is happening?' said Jane, trying not to look too amused for Oonagh's sake. The picture editor was still staring into space, contemplating the smoking ruins of her social life.

'Well, the retreat is full already and Mummy wants to build more tents,' said Tally. 'She says there's no more beautiful sight than the dawn rising over teepees.'

'Not my idea of a morning glory,' giggled Jane, thinking instantly of Tom. Really, she was becoming one of those people who thought about sex every six seconds.

'How's it going with you?' Tally asked.

'Fine,' said Jane, not wishing to start the Tom story now. She'd tell Tally when she saw her. 'Everything's fabulous, in fact. All I need now,' she muttered, almost to herself, 'is Jordan Madison and my world will be perfect.'

'Sorry?'

'Oh, nothing.' Poor dear Tally, stuck in what were quite literally the medieval backwoods of Mullions, was hardly likely to have heard of Hollywood's latest hip, hot and happening star.

'Oh, it's just that I thought I heard you say Jordan Madison,' said Tally.

'I did,' said Jane, surprised. 'Why, have you heard of her?'

'She's Hollywood's latest hip, hot and happening star, isn't she? I only happen to know because she's staying at the retreat at the moment.'

'WHAT?' yelled Jane.

Tash whipped round and stared.

'She's a great friend of Mummy's. Worships her, in fact. Mummy helped her to discover the goddess inside herself or some such guff while they were cleaning out the loos together at that ashram in California.'

'It's amazing what you find down a U-bend, isn't it?' Excitement rose in Jane like a geyser. 'Gosh, do you think you could get Julia to ask her . . .' Her voice dropped to a murmur as she explained the *Fabulous* cover situation. 'Having Jordan on the front would practically make my *life*,' she ended. 'Oh, and could you find out if we could bring a photographer?' Don't ask, don't get, she told herself, feeling cheeky.

'All right,' said Tally breezily. 'She's in a tree-hugging seminar at the moment, but I'll ask her the minute she's out. Call you back.'

Why did I bother going through the agents? wondered Jane. It seemed so obvious, in retrospect, that mad, hippy Julia would have an address book starrier than the Milky Way. Everyone knew that these days the real deals were done in AA meetings, drug clinics and holistic retreats, not the agents' offices. Why hadn't she thought of the New Age network before?

Despite this excitement, it didn't take long for her mind to drift back to Tom. What was he doing now? He wrote in the afternoons, she knew. She devoted a blissful few minutes to imagining Tom, sleepy of eye and furrowed of brow, scribbling furiously in longhand like a schoolboy taking Common Entrance.

Almost exactly an hour later, Tally called back. 'That's fine,' she said. 'No problem.'

'What? You mean Jordan will do it?'

'She'd love to,' said Tally. 'Anything for a friend of Julia's, she says. She's here for the next fortnight at least, so any time you want to come up is fine. And it's perfectly all right to bring a photographer.'

'Holy shit.' Jane crashed the receiver joyfully down, leapt up from her desk and danced wildly round the room. Never, never would she laugh at Julia and her New Age eccentricities again. 'We've got Jordan Madison for our cover,' she shouted. 'Thank Goddess,' she yelled, punching the air and running out of the office, feeling like a winning-goal-scoring footballer doing a lap of honour round the stadium. This would show Victoria, she thought. This would put a bomb under the opposition on the news-stands. This would confirm her position as a hot new editor who could make things happen. She was much too excited to stay in the office. She decided to dash out and tell Tom straightaway. How wonderful it was, she thought happily, running down the back stairs, to be in love and have someone to share good news with.

Scattering a giggle of camp-looking photographers and their assistants in her wake, Jane shot through the foyer, out of the doors and on to the street. Plunging straight through the crowds of improbably tall Scandinavian schoolchildren wandering impassively up and down Carnaby Street, she dashed across Soho, skipping down the narrow streets, dodging parking meters and people, running across roads in front of taxis, sidling through narrow spaces between cars. At Busty Models she bolted through the door without even tapping on Tom's window and narrowly avoided falling flat on her face on the stairs leading down to his flat.

'Tom, Tom,' she cried excitedly, bursting through the door. 'Tom?' she repeated, a nanosecond and a whole world of difference later. Because Tom was not writing. He was not even alone. Tom was standing in the middle of the room embracing a beautiful blonde. And not any old bog-standard, run-of-the-mill beautiful blonde either. The girl he held in his arms was Champagne D'Vyne.

Chapter 26

Huddling deep in the dark, warm, foetal fug of her duvet, Jane heard the answerphone repeatedly click on. Whoever was calling, she didn't care. She'd turned the sound right down, just as she'd switched off the entrance buzzer by the flat door. If only she could switch off her life. Her dehydrated brain throbbed from the entire bottle of gin she'd drunk the night before. But coping with a hangover was nothing compared to catching Tom in flagrante with Champagne.

Jane had no idea what time it was. She didn't care about that, either. She just knew that from now on, every second of every minute of every hour of the rest of her life was going to be utterly, painfully, blackly miserable. For a brief moment, the world had been her oyster. Now it was just a shell. She was back in the bad movie again. Or perhaps the bad oyster.

She stared at the ceiling and wondered how she could have got it so wrong yet again. Why hadn't she seen what was coming? Tom hadn't given her many clues, it was true, but she should have known it would end badly. It always did. With Nick, with Mark, and now with Tom. And all within a few weeks. True, married, trusting, hi-honey-I'm-home happiness was beyond her reach, now and for ever. If it wasn't for bad luck, Jane decided, she'd have no luck at all.

She was cursed, there was no doubt about that. But not just by a failure to pick the right man. Her life was blighted by a beautiful blonde, a glamorous albatross hanging round her neck with six-inch stilettos and a pressing appointment at Michaeljohn. Champagne was utterly inescapable. Try and move magazines and you found she'd come with you. Visit your friend in the middle of nowhere and you'll find her in the garden. Bury her two hundred feet under a runway and she pops back up with her arms round the man of your dreams. Jane screwed up her eyes in despair. It might be caprice on the part of Fate to bind her life up with Champagne's, but it wasn't her idea of a joke. Almost worse than Tom's betrayal was the contemplation of a future not only manless but clamped as firmly to Champagne's side as her Chanel handbag.

Jane could not blank out what she had seen in Tom's flat. The sight of him clasping Champagne seemed tattooed on the inside of her eyelids. For the millionth time, she ran and re-ran the fatal ten seconds of footage in the video machine of her brain, but still managed to make no sense of it. *Why* hadn't he told her he had a girlfriend? He had been so open about everything else. She had *trusted* him, for God's sake.

She got up and staggered, head throbbing, to the shower. But if washing Tom right out of her hair was simple, washing him out of the bathroom, or any other part of the flat, was impossible. Although he had only visited it twice, Tom's presence seemed now to permeate its very fabric. He had walked on *that* floor, sat in *that* chair, laughed at her cooking in *that* kitchen and, most of all, *slept in that bed*.

She could barely glance at a written word in case she thought of him. If she turned on the radio, the merest hint of classical music set off a waterfall of weeping. Even the soap powder in the kitchen cupboard reminded her of the blonde children that would never now run merrily down the pathway.

The day after the day after she had discovered Champagne and Tom together, Jane finally sought refuge in the *Fabulous* office.

It was a hideous mistake. Here, more than anywhere, reminders that she was the only single, betrayed woman in the world seemed brutally abundant.

'I'm having *just the worst* time with my boyfriend,' Tosh was drawling to Tash as she entered. Jane pricked her ears up. This sounded promising. 'He's being *such* a pig. He told me yesterday he was taking me to Bali.'

'Well, what's wrong with that?' asked Tash. 'Although,' she added, raising her eyebrows, 'I suppose Bali *is* a bit five-minutes-ago now that everyone who's anyone is going to Sardinia. Actually, I *do* see your point.'

'No, no,' said Tosh. 'The problem is it turns out he's taking me to the *Nutcracker*. To the boring old *ballet*! Can you imagine *anything* more *yawnsville*?'

Even in the loos, where Jane retreated frequently during the morning to indulge in some spontaneous weeping, there was no escape. The basins were, as always, positively blazing with the flowers that were sent to the *Fabulous* office. From hopeful PR companies, hopeful designers and, worst of all, hopeful lovers they came, a never-ending stream of fashionable bunches. Brilliant gerberas wrapped in brown paper; withered twigs in glass pots; vast, rope-bound sunflowers the height of a tree; massy bunches of heady lilies; they were all plunged unceremoniously into the basins waiting to be taken home by their recipients. Or, as often happened, forgotten and left in the loos to rot. Her own flower-receiving days having been cut off in their prime, Jane found the sight of these exuberant, neglected bunches almost too painful. She briefly considered patronising the men's loos instead.

Jane tried to take comfort in the Jordan Madison layouts stacked for approval on her desk. She signed them off almost without looking. The Madison coup now felt flatter than a week-old glass of Bollinger. What difference did it make to anything?

'Someone kept calling and calling for you yesterday,' Tish told Jane as the morning drew to a close. She had clearly only just remembered. 'A man. But he wouldn't leave his name. Um, and the advance copies have just come in. On the desk in Victoria's office.'

'Advance copies of what?' asked Jane dully. She did not comment on the mystery caller. She didn't care.

'*Fabulous*, of course,' grinned Tish. 'The Lily Eyre one. Remember?' she added, teasing.

'Vaguely,' said Jane. It seemed a lifetime ago. But she may as well look at them. Go through the motions.

Dragging herself into Victoria's glass box, she glanced cursorily at the new issues, gleaming beneath swathes of plastic packaging. She could barely bring herself to cut it open. The Jane who had edited that issue and sent it joyfully off to the printers was a different, younger and more hopeful creature altogether than the shattered wreck who stood looking at the finished product.

The cover was, indeed, a radical departure from *Fabulous*'s staple diet of demure debutantes. Dressed in brilliant red, her lips a slash of identical scarlet, Lily Eyre looked sexy and exciting. Inside, the interviewer had turned in a witty and incisive piece, with lots of hilarious quotes about the film business from Lily. When Jane had first read it, it had made her laugh. Now, looking at the cover, she wanted to cry.

She had no idea whether the issue was good or bad. Was it a bold departure from the norm or a disastrous experiment which might well backfire on the newsstands? What did she know? She couldn't even tell a good guy from a deceitful two-timing bastard.

Tish interrupted her reverie. 'I've just had a message

from Archie Fitzherbert's secretary,' she said. 'He wants to see you in his office this afternoon.'

That was that then, thought Jane numbly. Fitzherbert had obviously taken one look at the issue and hated it. He'd probably *retched* at the horrid *obviousness* of it. He'd probably tell her to go and work on *Penthouse*. She'd lost her man, now she was going to lose her job.

The telephone on her desk shrilled. Miraculously, as if aware there was a crisis, Tish actually went to answer it. Jane stood cowering by the magazines in Victoria's office. She didn't want to talk to anyone.

'It's a woman,' hissed Tish, covering the receiver. 'Very grand-sounding. Shall I put her through to Victoria's phone?'

Tally, thought Jane gratefully. If there was one sensible, kind, concerned voice she needed to hear just now, it was Tally's.

'Yes please,' she instructed Tish, sitting down heavily in Victoria's huge leather revolving chair. Her relief was shortlived. It was not Tally on the line. It was Champagne. The woman she had last seen all over Tom like a rash. Jane felt weak with hatred. She prepared to slam the phone down, but Champagne's opening remark caught her off guard.

'Where the bloody hell were *you* haring off to the other day?' barked Champagne. 'You didn't even say hello. *Bloody* rude, I thought.'

Jane gritted her teeth. *She* had caught Champagne with her arms round someone she had imagined was *her* boyfriend. Was she expected to apologise for it? Should she have stayed and chatted? 'I suppose I was rather surprised to see you there,' she replied, dangerously evenly.

'Why?' demanded Champagne.

She obviously thinks I'm even more stupid than I think I am, Jane seethed to herself. 'Because I thought you were at the Gatwick runway protest, of course,' she snarled, biting each word as it came out. 'With *Piers*.'

'Oh. Yah, well, actually, that all turned out to be a bit of a misunderstanding,' honked Champagne. 'Got myself in a bit of a hole there, to be honest. In fact, as far as Piers is concerned I'm afraid my name's pretty much *mud* at the moment. Haw haw. Christ, I'm funny.'

'Oh,' said Jane, sarcastically. 'It's all over with him, then?' Poor Piers. Champagne had probably dumped him in her usual subtle fashion. She hoped Laughter wouldn't be too hard on him.

'Yah, actually,' boomed Champagne. 'Shame really. He's a bloody nice bloke. Bit grubby, could use a shower now and then. But *triffically* sweet guy. *Great* guy, actually. But we rather fell out over the whole runway business. The *hole* runway business. Haw haw haw.' Her ear-splitting laughter rolled like thunder through Jane's aching head.

'What happened?' asked Jane. She felt too weary to be angry.

'The problem was,' Champagne honked, 'that we were there for different reasons. I thought they were protesting *for* a runway at Gatwick, not *against* one.'

Jane felt dizzy.

'Anyone normal would have thought the same,' declared Champagne remorselessly. 'I mean, the schedules to Nice are an utter *disgrace*. They need about four times as many flights as they're running at the moment. The times I've had to *slum* it in Club because First is already booked up. So when I heard that Piers and his gang were protesting about the runway, I thought, yah, *splendid* chaps. Those runways *need* protesting about. They need about four more of them, not to mention more planes.'

Jane opened and closed her mouth like a surprised flounder.

'But it turned out that Piers and co. were actually trying to stop the bloody runway being *built*!' exclaimed Champagne. 'Ridiculous. *Unbloodybelievable*. But then again,' she added, 'I suppose I can see their point of view.'

'*Can* you?' spluttered Jane, at last finding her voice.

'Yah,' said Champagne. 'I mean, none of them have ever been to Nice in Club Class, so they have no idea what a *complete and utter nightmare* it is. If they had, obviously they'd understand. It's just a question of education. Anyway, I'm not calling you to tell you all this rubbish,' Champagne barked imperiously. 'It's about something else. We need to meet. Now. Urgently. For lunch.'

'Why?' asked Jane. What could there be to say?

'Because I have some brilliant news for you,' honked

Champagne impatiently. 'An amazing offer.'

Jane frowned. Was it to be a *ménage à trois*, then? Or Tom-sharing, with Champagne having custody and Tom being allowed out for weekend visits? Or was Champagne about to offer one of her cast-off chinless wonders as a compensation package?

Jane's instinct warned her to steer well clear, but hard fact, in particular her impending dismissal by Archie Fitzherbert, seemed to suggest that, if she wanted to keep body and soul together for the foreseeable future, she was hardly in a position to turn brilliant news and amazing offers down. And Champagne, as Jane now realised, was in any case her destiny. No point in resisting her.

Jane was delayed leaving the office for her lunch with Champagne, because the inside of her jacket collapsed. She'd heard of unstructured linens, she thought crossly, sticking the lining back together with Sellotape, but this was ridiculous. She hoped it wouldn't flap open and reveal her handiwork during the lunch. Champagne may not be most people's idea of observant, but there was no doubt at all that she would notice that.

Even more stressed out after ten minutes in a gridlocked taxi, Jane announced her arrival at the restaurant by attempting to push the revolving door the wrong way. She was late, but Champagne had not arrived either. A supercilious and speedy waiter led Jane to their empty table. His sinuous form slid through the tight-packed tables with ease, while Jane found that presenting her bottom in a sideways shuffle to pairs of elegant lunchers was the only way she could get through the gaps herself. She threw herself into her chair, stared fiercely and unseeingly at the menu and wished desperately that she hadn't come.

After a few minutes she looked up and started to examine the eaters around her. They were mainly, she saw, emaciated women, ladies who lunch, although most of them looked as if they hadn't seen lunch for years. They were so thin that probably the only thing holding them together was their plastic surgeons' stitches. Jane shuddered as a tall, oleaginous man who she assumed was the restaurant manager made the rounds of the tables, planting ostentatious kisses here and there. Those surgery-raddled faces, she felt, might well come away on his lips.

Time passed. Champagne was now over half an hour late and Jane was beginning to feel vaguely mortified. She had polished off an entire bottle of sparkling mineral water and was desperate for the loo but, having no idea where they were, was reluctant to perform the required bottom-shimmy through the tables again in what would doubtless be the wrong direction.

Suddenly, a wave of perfume so strong it could have wiped out Barbados came crashing into her nostrils. The waiters wiped the sneers off their faces and goggled. Champagne had arrived, clutching Gucci and an armful of vast carrier bags emblazoned with the best of Bond Street.

Jane stood up so Champagne could smash both her

cheekbones into her face. 'Darling!' Champagne yelled. As intended, her look-at-me voice had the desired effect. There was a snapping of neck joints all round as everyone in the restaurant undid weeks of careful work by their masseurs and craned to stare. Once there were enough people looking at her, Champagne pushed her black lace microskirt up as far as possible and sat down.

Under her arm, Gucci stared out, his bead-like little eyes shining malevolently. 'Doesn't he look splendid?' gushed Champagne, lifting the poodle and dangling him towards Jane. 'Don't you just *adore* his collar?'

Jane stared at the row of diamonds glittering round the dog's skinny neck. Economics was hardly her strong point, but the collar was, she realised, probably worth more than the GDP of a smallish East European country.

'It's Guccigoo's birthday,' Champagne explained, setting Gucci on the table where he lost no time sticking his nose in the bread and his tongue in the butter. 'That collar's got forty diamonds on it,' she boasted. She leant towards Jane conspiratorially, displaying a cleavage deep enough to bungee-jump down to two passing, plate-laden waiters. Four first courses wobbled perilously for a few seconds. Champagne cast a sideways glance at Gucci, who by now was scrabbling furiously at the tiny dishes of salt and pepper and scattering their contents all over the tablecloth.

'It's worth a hundred thousand pounds!' Champagne whispered loudly. Jane's mouth fell open. 'Of course, the whole thing was the most *enormous* secret,'

Champagne continued, widening her eyes as if to convey the unimaginable subterfuge that had been involved. 'I didn't want Gucci to guess *anything*. It was the most *wonderful* surprise for him this morning.'

She leant back triumphantly in her chair and took a sip from the glass of chilled champagne from the complimentary bottle that had appeared as if by magic on the table. The oleaginous manager swept by, nodding and beaming. Jane wondered when Champagne would get to the brilliant news and amazing offers. She looked at her miserably. With her perfect, arrogant face unmarked by so much as a wrinkle, her white-blonde hair a shining mass on her shoulders and her tiny dress rucked up to show as much of her slender body as possible, it was not difficult to see why Tom had been tempted. Jane tried not to look at Champagne's perfect bare legs and tried to hide as much of her own stubby fetlocks under the table as possible.

Champagne was beaming at her. Her glossy lips parted to treat Jane to a smile so brilliant it could probably have been seen from Mir. Jane shifted uncomfortably in her seat. Being on the receiving end of Champagne's charm offensive somehow felt worse than when she was just being offensive.

'Darling! How *are* you,' Champagne gushed. 'It's *heaven* to see you. You're looking absolutely *wonderful*.' She raked Jane with her hard, green eyes. 'You're *so* lucky,' she declared. 'You *so* suit no make-up.'

Jane blushed deeply. Trust Champagne to zoom in on that. She knew she should have made time for a little mascara, at least. But lately she hadn't seen the point of putting it on. It scarcely improved the way you looked and it was a bore to have to clean it off at night. Besides, she thought miserably, it only streaked when you cried.

'You really do have the most *wonderful* cheekbones,' Champagne continued. Jane was aware that lack of sleep and general anguish had scooped great care-worn hollows from her cheeks. But she doubted they improved her appearance.

The waiter glided up. As she ordered, utterly at random, and barely glancing at the menu, Jane wondered if Champagne was ever going to get to the point.

'Christ, I'm absolutely *pooped*,' Champagne announced brightly, looking with deep satisfaction at the carrier bags crowding the floor. 'Signing all those credit card slips *really* takes it out of you. *Exhausting!*'

'What have you bought?' asked Jane. Everything, by the look of it, she thought.

'Oh, these aren't for *me*,' said Champagne, gesturing at the bags. 'No, all *my* things are in the limo.' She waved a perfectly-manicured hand in the general direction of the restaurant window and the shining Rover visible outside. 'These,' she announced, waving at the bags which lapped around their table like a tide, 'are for my brother.'

'Your brother?' said Jane, dimly remembering the photograph on the top of the piano in Champagne's flat. It was the first time Champagne had ever mentioned him.

'Yes,' barked Champagne. 'You know. Or you should. You've been shagging him for the past week, at least.'

'What?' said Jane slowly. This was too incredible. Surely Champagne didn't mean . . . 'You don't mean . . . Tom?' she croaked.

'Of course I bloody mean Tom,' said Champagne, draining her glass. 'Unless you've been shagging someone else as well.'

Jane's bowels felt loose with shock and her tired head was spinning as she struggled to get a grip. Tom was Champagne's *brother*? He couldn't be. No two people could *possibly* be less alike. Tom was an obscure, impoverished writer who lived in a basement below a brothel in Soho, while Champagne was a Belgravia-dwelling professional socialite whose dog had a £100,000 diamond collar. Tom wrote seriously, and every word himself. The same certainly couldn't be said for Champagne.

Tom wore battered leather jackets and jumble-sale T-shirts. Champagne wore head-to-toe designer labels with little or no clothing attached. Tom had dirty blond hair that looked as if it was cut with a knife and fork. Champagne's shining mane was professionally blow-dried every day. And yet, Jane thought, gawping at Champagne as if seeing her for the first time, there *was* something about the cheekbones, the green eyes, the sultry, naughty smile . . .

'But you don't even have the same name,' stammered

Jane. 'Tom's surname is Seton.'

Champagne drew on her cigarette and fired it out in two volleys from her nostrils. 'He *writes* under that name, sure,' she said. 'But his actual surname is D'Vyne. Tom's full name is, er,' she stopped and wrinkled her nose, as if preparing for a great feat of memory, 'Thomas Charles Gregorian Seton D'Vyne. Mine is,' she paused again, 'um, Champagne Olivia Wilnelia Seton D'Vyne,' she finished triumphantly.

Wow, thought Jane. Champagne's family had hardly held back over the font. Then again, there seemed to be an unwritten rule that the upper classes could have more names than everybody else. She remembered that from Cambridge. Along the corridor she had lived on, everyone but herself seemed to have three or more initials painted up above their door. Tally had had at least five.

'Tom dropped the D'Vyne because he said he thought it sounded too grand for a struggling writer,' said Champagne, a faint note of scorn in her voice. 'But I'm convinced the real reason is that he disapproves of my lifestyle. He hates socialites and the whole London party scene and didn't want anyone to connect him with my column inches. *Or* me. He's always been obsessed with money,' she finished, stabbing out her cigarette.

'*Has* he?' asked Jane, astounded. In the short time she had known him, Tom had seemed the most generous soul imaginable. He had practically emptied his pockets for the beggar they had met on the way back from San Lorenzo. He had not struck her as the mean type, still less the rich type.

'Obsessed with not having it, I mean,' honked Champagne. 'He refused his part of our trust fund because he wanted to make it on his own. And I was never allowed to mention him in the column, in case people stopped taking him *seriously* as a *writer*.' Champagne rolled her eyes mockingly. 'I mean, as if there was the faintest *possibility* that anyone could *not* take him seriously as a writer. He's hardly a laugh a minute on the subject, is he?'

Jane shook her head dumbly. If only she'd stopped a few more seconds and allowed Tom to explain. She'd blown it yet again.

She put her head in her hands and groaned. The horrible reality of the situation pressed in on her like a smothering pillow. And not just the dreadful misunderstanding, either. There was also the hideous fact that she had managed to fall in love with Champagne's *brother*. Of all the brothers in all the world, she had to fall in love with that one.

'Yah, he told me about this girl he's met,' Champagne said, eyeing Jane assessingly. 'Never thought for a *minute* it was *you*. Bit *odd*, though, I must say, the way you rushed off the other day. Tom was a bit cut up after you'd gone, actually. Dashed straight out after you, but you'd scarpered.'

'I, er, thought . . . I mean, I thought you . . . the . . .' She stopped and gazed miserably at Champagne.

'Oh, for Christ's sake,' Champagne boomed

suddenly, so loud that the entire restaurant stopped to listen. 'You surely didn't think I was shagging my own *brother*?' She shrieked with mirth. The clatter of dropped jaws and forks all round was deafening.

'Oh God,' said Jane, panicking. 'What am I going to do now? I've ruined everything. Tom'll probably never speak to me again. He'll think I'm a hysterical freak.'

Champagne patted her hand. 'Oh, *all* his girlfriends are. I wouldn't worry. Ha ha ha.' She giggled at Jane's horrorstruck expression. 'Just teasing. Can't you take a joke? Pop round and see him tonight.'

'I'll go round now,' muttered Jane, getting to her feet. The room whirled around her. She swayed, feeling as if she was about to faint, and sat down again.

'He won't be there,' Champagne said, examining her nails with satisfaction. 'I tried to get him to come shopping but he told me he was spending every afternoon this week researching in some mouldy library somewhere. *Not* my idea of fun. Now look,' she boomed, 'there's something *really* bloody important I need to talk to you about now, OK?'

The earth-shattering revelations about Tom, then, were obviously just an aperitif, thought Jane. She dreaded to think what was coming next.

'Tom's not the only writer in the family,' Champagne honked, her green eyes blazing triumphantly. 'I've been offered a vast sum to write a novel myself. Brilliant, isn't it? Aren't you thrilled?'

'That's nice,' said Jane, wondering why on earth *she* should be pleased.

Champagne stared at her in amazement. 'What's the matter with you?' Several heads turned their way. 'You should be dancing on the *tables*. They're offering me half a million, OK? Serious dosh. Big potatoes.'

'I don't understand,' said Jane with as much dignity as she could muster, 'why *I* should be pleased that *my* work on *your* columns has got *you* a big fat novel deal. I'm *not* thrilled.' Her voice had risen to a faintly hysterical pitch. 'If anything I'm *furious*.'

There. She had said it. And if Champagne resigned from *Fabulous* as a result of it, she didn't care. She'd had enough. Of everything. The last forty-eight hours had left her drained, weak, bewildered and exhausted. And rather drunk. The bottle, she saw, was now empty. She had had a lot of champagne on an empty stomach. In more ways than one.

Champagne stared at her with amused astonishment. 'You *idiot*,' she honked. 'You don't understand, do you? I'm asking you to write this novel *for* me. We split the money. Two hundred and fifty grand each.' She smashed her empty glass against Jane's. 'Yah?' she boomed. 'Brilliant, eh?'

A sudden vision of freedom flashed before Jane's eyes. Two hundred and fifty thousand pounds. She could pack in her job. She was about to be sacked anyway, she thought, remembering her date with Archie Fitzherbert that afternoon. And what was the point of staying at *Fabulous* when Victoria was likely to sweep back into her editor's glass box any minute and make Jane's life an utter misery?

'We've got six months to do it in,' rasped Champagne, 'so you pack your shitty job in right now and we'll get cracking. All we have to do is rehash the columns and sort of link them together in some kind of storyline. Money for old rope.'

Jane looked away from Champagne's commanding gaze. Was she sure she wanted to get into this? The money was good, certainly, but would it be worth risking her sanity? Knocking out a monthly column with Champagne was torture enough. Six months' solid novel-writing would probably reduce her to care in the community status. She didn't feel all that far from it already.

'Can I think about it?' she asked.

'*Think* about it?' barked Champagne to whom this was obviously an alien concept. She glared at Jane with all the impotent rage of someone who has never been refused anything. For the first time ever in her dealings with Champagne, Jane experienced the amazing sensation of being in charge.

'I'll call you this afternoon,' she said, getting up.

'Well, I've got a colonic at three and my acupuncturist's at four,' honked Champagne. 'I don't want any sudden shocks during those or I'll have to spend the rest of my life on the loo. Call me at five. Oh, and could you get the bill? I'd love to treat you but I don't think my plastic will stand it.'

Why didn't she just accept Champagne's offer? Jane wondered as she climbed the stairs to the managing director's office. Flying in the face of Fate seemed foolish, particularly when she stood to gain a large sum of money and the sort of freedom she had hardly dared dream about before. As she knocked on Archie Fitzherbert's door, she made up her mind to say yes. After all, she was not likely to hear anything in the next few minutes that would make her want to change her mind.

'He's ready to see you,' said Georgie. 'Just go straight in.'

Jane knocked timidly on the oak door with the shining gold handle, wondering why she was bothering. She didn't need to go through this. She could turn and walk away, call Champagne and accept the book offer. But she was here now, and anyway she'd always wondered what Fitzherbert's office was like. Perhaps the Glamourtron was in here. She pictured the managing director sitting in a vast white leather swivel chair like Blofeld in the Bond films, stroking a white cat with a malevolent glare. The floor would be glass, with piranhas gliding menacingly beneath it, ready to slash to ribbons any editor whose circulation figures had slumped.

At a murmur from within, Jane pushed the door open. A pale room the approximate size of the entire *Fabulous* offices stretched away before her. Just as Fitzherbert in person resisted the stuffy, pinstriped manager stereotype, his office, too, was innocent of all mahogany or heavily framed oil paintings. Full of fat white sofas the size of stretch limos, book-piled glass-topped coffee tables, and concept bookcases of undulating wood, it resembled a film star's penthouse. The only clue to its inhabitant's profession were the framed magazine covers on the cream-painted walls. There was no desk. Fitzherbert, it was said, hated them, preferring to do all his work on sofas, or on the move. And rumour, for once, appeared to be true. The managing director, clad in a shirt of his trademark lilac set off with baby blue braces, was sprawled with his feet up on a white day bed, holding the *Daily Telegraph* inches from his nose. On top of the skyscraper of magazines beside him on the coffee table was the latest issue of *Fabulous*. Jane's heart sank.

Fitzherbert held his position for a few more seconds before sitting up, swinging his long, spare legs on to the polished wooden floor and grinning at her. He was, Jane decided, clearly trying to lull her into a false sense of security.

'Jane! Thank you so much for coming to see me. Sit down, do.' Fitzherbert pointed at the sofa opposite him with one dayglo pink-socked foot. Jane sank gingerly into the deep embrace of the cushions and wondered if she could ever get up again. Fitzherbert's office seemed deliberately designed to confuse and confound expectation. Which, of course, gave him more power over what went on in there.

'I asked you to come and see me because I have an idea to put to you,' Fitzherbert announced in a voice almost as bright as his socks. 'It concerns a slight change of, er, um, career.'

Jane nodded. This was what she had been expecting.

'I had a long conversation with Victoria yesterday,' said Fitzherbert, a slight frown rippling his tanned forehead.

Doubtless because one of the new issues had been biked round to her and she had hated it, thought Jane. 'She's back from New York, then?' she croaked.

Fitzherbert nodded.

'She's *back*, but she's not, ah, very *well* at the moment.' Fitzherbert agitatedly tapped the coffee table before him with the thick bottom of his Mont Blanc pen. 'In fact, she's apparently on the verge of a nervous breakdown. Stress. Overwork. Whatever,' he said, waving his hand in a half irritated, half dismissive gesture.

Jane stifled a gasp and cast her eyes down to disguise their outraged expression. *Victoria*, stressed? To her certain knowledge, the most anxious-making thing in Victoria's life was deciding between the Ivy and the Caprice for lunch.

'She needs a break,' Fitzherbert stated, raising his eyebrows slightly. 'Needs to get the city out of her system and all that stuff, find herself again et cetera,' he continued in a swift monotone, tapping his pen again. 'So the company's er, um, booked her into this place she wanted to go to. New ashram in the West Country. Called Millions or something, and from what they charge for a month there, that's about right.' He flashed Jane a wide but rather mirthless grin. She looked back at him blankly, failing to see what any of this had to do with her. Poor Tally, she thought vaguely. She must tell her to slam Victoria in a shed to get to grips with her inner child as soon as she arrived.

'The reason why I'm discussing Victoria's, er,' Fitzherbert raised his eyebrows, 'um . . . *indisposition* with you is that we've decided she should take a year off.'

Jane said nothing. What was all this leading to? Why didn't he just get to the point and put her out of her misery?

'So, I wanted to offer you the position. Acting editor, of course. For the time being, at least. Interested?'

Jane gulped. Was she hearing right? She had come here to be sacked, and now she was being offered what sounded suspiciously like Victoria's job. Acting editor of *Fabulous*. Jane's heart soared up into the back of her throat. She wanted to squeal with delight, jump up and down on the spot, turn cartwheels all round the spacious room. But she did none of these things. Instead she said quietly, 'Yes.'

'*Great*,' said Fitzherbert. 'Really great. I've just seen the new issue.' He stabbed at the shining cover on the coffee table before him. 'I thought it was really *excellent*. Very fresh, energetic, enthusiastic. One of the best issues for years, in fact.'

'Thank you,' stammered Jane, blushing a violent, confused and very un-editor-like red.

'*Great* cover, this girl, too.' He bashed Lily's nose with the end of his pen. 'Great pictures inside as well. And what *fantastic* legs she has. Terrific ankles.'

Fitzherbert leapt to his feet. 'I understand you've got someone even better for the next. Well, that's *marvellous.*' Fitzherbert shook Jane's hand. 'Carry on the good, er, um, work. Personnel will be in touch about contracts and all that jazz.'

And the Glamourtron? Would Personnel be in touch about that as well? wondered Jane. Surely now, when she was poised to take over one of the house's glossiest titles, it must be her turn at last. It was on the tip of her tongue to ask Fitzherbert, as, wreathed in smiles, he ushered her out. But his door shut smartly behind her, and the chance was lost.

Outside, Jane hugged a puzzled Georgie and dashed downstairs to the foyer. She was captain of her own ship, finally. She had the job she had always wanted, and, at last, no doubt whatsoever that she could do it brilliantly. After all, did she not have Jordan Madison lined up for the next cover? Whatever mess her private life might be in, her professional one was shaping up just dandy.

Little did Victoria know, thought Jane, that she had no intention of relinquishing the editorship now she had her feet under the table. She had serious plans for *Fabulous.* They raced through her mind as she walked briskly along in the sunshine. More interviews. Better features. Funny pieces. Investigations. More sex. *Much* more sex.

Jane gazed joyfully up at the azure sky above the grimy buildings, a thank-you-everyone speech babbling through her head. Thank you, Josh, she thought, for being sufficiently horrid to drive me into the *Fabulous* job in the first place. Thank you, Champagne. If you had been one iota less nightmarish, I would have taken your book offer and never gone to see Fitzherbert today. And most of all, thank you, Victoria, for your blissful, hysterical self-indulgence. Thank you, everyone. I want to thank everyone I ever met, ever. Jane grinned ecstatically at a number of doleful passers-by. She buzzed with confidence. She felt brilliant with light. She radiated with energy. She felt like a human power station. Most of all, she was full of hope, which she needed, considering what she was about to do.

Rounding the corner, Jane spotted Camilla lounging, as usual, in the doorway. She raised an eyebrow as Jane crossed the street towards her. 'Hi,' beamed Jane, striding through the door and descending, sure and fleet of foot, down the stairs at the back. At the bottom, she paused just a second before throwing open Tom's scabby door.

He sprang up from his desk when he saw her, a half fearful, half hopeful expression in his exhausted, red-rimmed eyes. The bags beneath them were as big as suitcases. Caused by sorrow, or mere overwork? Thrown, Jane hesitated in the doorway, willing her confidence to come back. Tom had every right to be furious. She had judged and condemned him without a shred of evidence. Would he reject her? She scanned his strained face for clues, found none and decided to fling herself on his mercy.

Speechless with remorse, desperate for contact, Jane

dashed across the room and flung herself into Tom's arms. 'Oh God, what a mess,' she whispered, burying her face in his neck. 'I'm so sorry. It was all a stupid misunderstanding.'

'I'd have tidied up if I'd known you were coming,' said Tom brokenly into her hair. 'And, by the way, just before you vanish yet again, will you marry me?'

An hour later, snuggled under the duvet with her head on Tom's chest, Jane thought ecstatically that she would rather be in this dingy Soho basement than in the finest suite at the Hotel de Paris. She quickly revised this. Being with Tom amid the splendours of Monaco's finest might just have the edge on where they were now. Well all that would come with her glossy new job. She smiled dreamily and pushed her hips closer still to Tom. I want to melt into him, she thought, so that we can never be parted again. But then, that wouldn't be quite so much fun. And it would certainly make sex difficult.

Jane felt she might die and go to heaven any minute. She had won the double. She had the man of her dreams and the job of her dreams and there seemed little more to wish for. Only one nagging, unsolved problem remained. Champagne was unlikely to be thrilled at the news that she wasn't going to be able to write her book.

Jane hugged Tom closer, pressing one ear into his warm flesh to muffle the honking, furious tones that seemed already audible. All the wrath of the Eumenides, she knew, would have nothing on the fury of a

Champagne done out of half a million pounds. By her own sister-in-law, as well. Jane rolled her eyes at the thought of it. Josh had been right after all. Sisters under the skin.

She must have sighed, because Tom pressed her closer. He fumbled for another cigarette and lit up, drawing the smoke into his lungs with a happy sigh. Talk about the Duke of Marlboro, thought Jane worriedly. Tom smoked far too much. Not that she blamed him really. Even someone as certain of his own ability as Tom was must find it stressful to work so relentlessly on his writing without ever really knowing where his next rent cheque was coming from.

Jane had no doubt that Tom would eventually make it, but she worried about how he was going to support himself in the meantime. Or *themselves*, she corrected, half enchanted, half fearful. Her wages, even as an editor, would hardly be enough to set up a marital home from scratch. Oh, why had Tom turned down his trust fund? It would have come in so useful just now.

She corrected herself sternly, knowing perfectly well that if Tom had kept his trust fund and spent it on cars, cocaine and Krug like everyone else, she would certainly never have met him. Jane pondered again on the amazing differences between Champagne and her brother, a train of thought that returned, with a circularity far from satisfying, to the worrying question of the book. *Could* she do it? *Should* she do it? It would be easy enough, after all, a mere matter of rehashing some of the columns, as Champagne had said. It might not take up *too* much time. She could do it and work as well, she told herself. Just about.

On the other hand there was another matter to be considered. Through Fitzherbert's offer, through achieving her own editorship, Jane had finally been granted an opportunity to break free, professionally at least, from Champagne. She had at last been given responsibility, a grown-up job that gave her a real place in the world, a profile of her own, a chance to run her own ship, in her own way, with her own ideas. Did she *really* want to go back to ghost-writing now?

Jane turned on to her back as she weighed up the options. She decided to consult Tom. After all, it might be selfish to turn down the money when they both needed it.

An idea struck her. Perhaps, if she found the right person, she could persuade Champagne to get someone else to do it instead. Using the existing columns as material, anyone who could string a sentence together and had the vaguest idea about plot construction and editing could write Champagne's novel for her. *Anyone* could do it really. Anyone . . .

'Tom?'

'Mmm?' said Tom, pulling her to him in the crook of one strong arm.

'You know you used to talk about writing a bonkbuster?'

The organ swelled as Jane approached the altar, light-headed with happiness and days of not eating. It had been worth it – the tiny waist of the wedding dress now fitted her with ease, and she was blissfully aware of her slender form moving gracefully beneath the thick satin. The air was heavy with the scent of freesia and white roses as, smiling shyly beneath her cathedral-length veil and perfect make-up, Jane drew up alongside Tom.

Looking at her with a gratifying mixture of awe and wonder, Tom gave her a tender smile. He looked exhausted, thought Jane, but then again, so would anyone who had spent the last six months writing his own book in the morning and knocking off a novel with Champagne in the afternoons. In the end, though, it had been relatively painless. The editor from the publishing house had been thrilled with it, so much so that the more literary arm of the house had made a substantial offer for Tom's own first novel. The advance for his sister's, meanwhile, had ensured they had one hell of a honeymoon ahead of them. And if half what was being said about German rights, US rights and film rights was true, they'd be holidaying on Mustique for the rest of their lives.

Jane glanced behind her, catching Tally's eye. Tally raised a gloved hand and grinned, looking as if she might burst with happiness. The Dewsbury business was obviously all over now; Tally had not even commented on the recent tabloid pictures of her erstwhile lover snapped with some unsuspecting anorexic heiress in a nightclub. Sitting in what passed for a beer garden at the Gloom, Jane had turned the page over quickly.

Tally had merely smiled faintly and rolled her eyes, as if unable to believe any of it had ever happened.

Next to Tally, Julia blew Jane an exuberant, two-handed, bracelet-rattling kiss, almost knocking off Big Horn's headdress as she did so. Affecting not to notice, the majestic Indian remained as stock still as ever, his massive chest covered with even more feathers, bones and brilliantly coloured tribal beads than usual. It was obviously his gala outfit. As Jane's gaze passed to him, to her utter amazement he raised one magnificent dark eyebrow and tipped her the lewdest of winks.

Next to Big Horn, Archie Fitzherbert's attention was completely taken up by the person sitting on his other side. There, in a vast red hat under which her eyes burned smokily and her hair poured down as flat and black as tar, Jordan Madison, *Fabulous*'s most successful cover girl ever, sat in all her waifish glory. Her air of fragility was exaggerated by the fact that on her left sat the solid form of Mrs Ormondroyd, tissue clamped firmly to her nose. Jane shuddered at the memory of her most recent dealings with the huffy housekeeper. It had not been easy persuading her not to make the wedding buffet.

Jane turned her head back to the front, admiring how wonderful the restored Mullions altar looked now. Tally had insisted Jane's wedding should be the first to take place in the newly refurbished chapel. Even the eighteenth-century organ had been restored for the occasion and, as it struck up for the final hymn, the sound flowed out as confidently as when Handel, who was supposed to have inaugurated the instrument, first set finger to keyboard. It sounded, Jane thought, as smooth and strong as the well-aged brandy she had sipped to steady her nerves before the ceremony. As the quavering voices of the congregation struggled and failed to match the purity of the music, Jane felt Tom beside her fumble beneath her veil and squeeze her hand.

The service flashed by. Much to her relief Jane got Tom's many names right. She had spent a panicked night before whispering them into the dark surroundings of the Elizabethan bed, terrified that she'd get them all wrong like the Princess of Wales. She hadn't realised what a minefield this was. It would make a great problem for the *Fabulous* advice page. Only, on this day, her wedding day, she had vowed to try not to think of *Fabulous* once. She was, she knew, obsessed with the magazine, and thought of very little else except, of course, Tom. And *Fabulous* had repaid her devotion handsomely by soaring twenty per cent in circulation since she took over, leaving *Gorgeous* and Josh a very satisfactory distance behind.

Jane turned to walk back down the aisle with Tom. It was not difficult to spot Champagne's vast and violent magenta feather hat bobbing wildly as she waved at her brother. Beside her was her latest swain, an up-and-coming film actor in an electric-blue satin frock coat who had, it was said, ensnared Champagne with the promise of a cameo role in his next project. Jane wondered, noticing Brad at the back of the chapel with

Lily Eyre, if the actor knew quite what he was letting himself in for. His subdued expression, contrasting profoundly with Champagne honking (and looking) like an excited Canada goose beside him, suggested that it had begun to dawn on him.

It was amazing, Jane thought, as she passed serenely by the exquisitely refurbished Jacobean oak pew where Champagne was sitting, to think they were now relations. She would never have imagined this possible. The strange fate which had intertwined their destinies from the start had by no means given up its influence. She had not only married Tom in the chapel at Mullions; she had also married Champagne. Jane plastered a vast, shaking but hopefully genuine-looking smile on as her new sister-in-law tottered up in the receiving line outside the chapel door.

'Ow!' Jane winced as, attempting an air-kiss, Champagne speared her in the eye with her huge and sprouting hat. A few guests down the line, Jane spotted Big Horn eyeing up the feathers with interest.

'Darling, you look *wonderful*,' Champagne gushed. 'It's so *interesting*, isn't it, how not everyone suits white? And so sweet of you to wear what is obviously your *own* jewellery,' she added, before passing on in a cloud of Jo Malone.

Jane gasped indignantly, as if a bucket of freezing cold water had been thrown over her. 'She's amazing, isn't she?' she stammered to Tom. 'I mean, it doesn't matter that I'm actually related to her now. She'll always see herself as the glamorous society girl and me as the slave. She'll always be the It Girl and I'll always be the Shit Girl.'

'Oh, ignore her,' said Tom, grinning. 'Let's go and have a drink.' He bore her off in the direction of the party, held in the newly refurbished and almost unrecognisably smart Blue Drawing Room.

A few circuits of the room later, her face plastered in lipstick from all the congratulatory kisses, Jane bumped into her new sister-in-law once more.

'Wonderful party,' Champagne gushed. 'Rahly marvellous.'

Jane grinned. Champagne had clearly not been stinting on her namesake beverage. 'Thank you for saying so,' she said, beaming delightedly. Champagne *could* be pleasant when she tried. Jane was almost beginning to feel fond of her. 'That's a real compliment,' Jane said, warmly, 'considering you've been to more parties than I've had hot dinners.'

Champagne pursed her lips, lifted an eyebrow and slowly scrutinised Jane's body from head to toe. 'Oh, I don't think so,' she smirked. 'Not quite *that* many.'

Bad Heir Day

For my parents

Chapter 1

The bride had still not arrived. Beside Anna, Seb fidgeted, sighed and tutted, while the surrounding cacophony of wailing babies and coughing increased. There seemed, Anna saw as she glanced round the candlelit chapel, to be an awful lot of people there. All better dressed than herself. As she caught the haughty eye of a skinny and impeccably turned-out brunette, Anna dropped her gaze to her feet. Realising that there had been no time even to clean her shoes, she immediately wished she hadn't.

Everything had been such a rush. After breakfasting at his usual leisurely pace, Seb had glanced at the invitation properly for the first time and, after much panicked scanning of the Scottish mainland, eventually discovered the location of the wedding somewhere in the middle of the Atlantic.

'Fucking hell, I thought it was in Edinburgh,' he roared. 'It's practically in Iceland.' Seb thrust the *AA Road Atlas* at her, his stabbing finger a good quarter inch off the far northwest coast of Scotland. Anna stared at the white island amid the blue, whose shape bore a startling resemblance to a hand making an uncomplimentary gesture with its middle finger. She glanced at the invitation.

'Dampie Castle, Island of Skul,' she read. 'Well, I suppose getting married in a castle is rather romantic . . .'

'Castle my arse,' cursed Seb. 'Why can't they get married in Knightsbridge like everybody else?'

'Perhaps we shouldn't bother going,' Anna said soothingly. After all, she had met neither component of the unit of Thoby and Miranda whose merger they were invited to celebrate. All she knew was that Thoby, or Bollocks, as Seb insisted on calling him, was a schoolfriend of his. There seemed to be very few men who weren't. While his habit of referring to Miranda as Melons confirmed Anna's suspicions that she was one of his ex-girlfriends. Again, there seemed to be very few women who weren't.

Seb, however, was hell-bent on putting in an appearance. Abandoning plans to drive to Scotland, they flew first class from Heathrow to Inverness instead and drove like the wind in a hired Fiesta to the ferryport for Skul, Seb in a rage all the way. Being stopped by a highway patrol car and asked, 'Having trouble taking off, sir?' had hardly improved his temper. In the end, they had arrived at Dampie too late to be shown their room, too late to look round the castle, too late to *look* at the castle at all, as darkness had long since fallen. Too late to do anything but rush to the chapel, where the evening service would, Seb snarled as they screeched up the driveway, be halfway through by now at least. Only it wasn't.

Ten more brideless minutes passed, during which a small, sailor-suit-clad boy in front of Anna proceeded to climb all over the pew and fix anyone who happened to catch his eye with the most contemptuous of stares. Anna returned his gaze coolly as he bared his infant teeth at her. 'I'm going to kill *all* the bridesmaids,' he declared, producing a plastic sword from the depths of the pew and waving it threateningly about.

'I'm feeling rather the same way towards Melons,' murmured Seb, testily, when, after a further half hour, the bride was still conspicuous by her absence. 'Then again, she always did take bloody ages to come.' He sniggered to himself. Anna pretended not to have heard.

'Thoby should think himself lucky,' whispered a woman behind them as the vision in ivory finally appeared at the door. 'Miranda is only fifty-five minutes late turning up to marry him. She's always at least an *hour* late whenever she arranges to meet *me*.'

'There's probably a good reason for that,' muttered Seb.

'Shhh,' said Anna, digging him in the ribs and noting enviously that Thoby clearly *did* think himself lucky. His inbred features positively blazed with pride as Miranda, her tiny waist pinched almost to invisibility by her champagne satin bustier, drew up beside him at the altar on a cloud of tulle and the arm of a distinguished-looking man with silver hair and a second-home-in-Provence tan.

'Stella McCartney,' whispered the woman behind.

'*Where*?' hissed her companion.

'No, the dress, darling. *Achingly* hip.'

'Aching hips, as well, I should think. It looks like agony. Poor Miranda.'

'Still, it's worth it. Mrs Thoby Boucher de Croix-Duroy sounds *terribly* grand. If not *terribly* Scottish.'

'No. They're about as Scottish as pizza,' whispered the second woman. 'Hired this place because Miranda was *desperate* to get married in a castle. And I hear Thoby isn't quite so grand as he seems anyway. Apparently he's called Boucher de Croix-Duroy because his grandfather was a butcher from King's Cross.'

'*No!*'

'*Yes!* Shush, we've got to sing now. *Damn*, where *is* my order of service?'

As everyone vowed to thee, their country, Anna sneaked a proud, sidelong glance at Seb and felt her stomach begin its familiar yoyo of lust. His tanned neck rose from his brilliantly white collar, his tall frame, drooping slightly (Seb *hated* standing up), looked its best in a perfectly cut morning suit innocent of the merest hint of dandruff. His long lashes almost brushed his Himalayan cheekbones. He might make the odd thoughtless remark, but he was the best-looking man in the chapel by a mile, even – Anna prayed not to be struck down – counting the high-cheekboned, soft-lipped representation of Jesus languishing elegantly against his cross. Seb was *gorgeous*. And, source though that was of the fiercest pride and delight, it was also rather terrifying. Seb attracted women like magnets attracted iron filings – and in about the same numbers. If being in love with a beautiful woman was hard, Anna thought, it was nothing to being in love with a beautiful man.

After Miranda had got all Thoby's names in the wrong order and, amid much rolling of eyes in the congregation, promised to obey, everyone returned to the castle's tapestry-festooned hall for the receiving line and *vin d'honneur*. Anna looked admiringly around, drinking in the vast fireplace blazing with heraldry and a fire of infernal proportions, the latticed windows and the stag's head-studded stone walls along with her rather flat champagne. Seb, meanwhile, made a beeline for the newly-weds.

'Bollocks, you old bastard!' he yelled, slapping the groom so hard on the back his eyes bulged. 'Melons!' he whooped, pressing himself close to the bride whose chest, Anna noted, was flatter than pitta bread. Seb's idea of a joke, obviously; Anna wondered what, in that case, the significance of Thoby's nickname could be. She maintained a fixed smile as Seb nuzzled Miranda's neck and stuck his tongue down her throat. 'For old times' sake,' he assured a distinctly tight-faced Thoby as he and Miranda came up for air.

'Darling, you look marvellous.' The impeccable brunette Anna had spotted in the chapel was suddenly beside them, Silk Cut fumes pouring from her nostrils, gazing at Seb like a dog eyeing a bowl of Pedigree Chum. *My* pedigree chum, actually, thought Anna hotly, slipping her arm through Seb's, looking meaningfully at his profile and trying not to notice that the brunette's brilliant white dress accentuated her spectacular tan just as Anna's own black dress accentuated her spectacular lack of one. But Seb did not return her glance.

'Anna, have you met Brie de Benham?' Seb shook off her hand.

'We were in the same year at university,' Anna muttered. She did not add that they had actually sat next to each other throughout Finals and the girl had sobbed hysterically through each paper before eventually walking off with a First.

'We *were*? I don't remember,' countered the brunette. She raked Anna's figure up and down and, like a hurt-seeking missile, homed in instantly on the vulnerable area of her stomach. 'How *very* clever of you to wear your money belt under your dress.'

Anna went redder than a Mon Rouge lipstick. Come gym, come diet, come what may, the soft swag of flesh that clung around her hips had resisted all attempts to shift it. It had remained with all the knowing, grim relentlessness of the last guest at a party. She had been determined to lose it for the wedding. But it had been even more determined to attend.

Whipping round to display her fine-boned back, Brie de Benham began a lively conversation with a tousle-haired man in a velvet jacket of highlighter-pen neon green.

Seb had not heard the exchange. He had other matters at hand – quite literally. Anna turned to see one of his palms wedged firmly inside the dress of a curvaceous blonde, the back of which was slashed to the top of her bottom.

'So I'm flying back to Hollywood next week,' the blonde was saying in a deep, slow, seductive voice. 'Paramount are interested in one of my screenplays and I'm having lunch with Liz Hurley because Simian are interested in one of the others. Darling, you should come too. You'd be wonderful in films. The new Rupert Everett . . .' She traced a slim finger round Seb's lips.

'Just saying hello to Olivia,' Seb muttered to Anna. 'Old friend of mine. Liv, darling, meet Anna.'

The blonde's stare was the same chill blast as someone opening the lid of a freezer. 'Hi. What did you say you did?'

Needled by the haughty tones, Anna was tempted to declare she cleaned loos at Watford Gap Services but, still reeling from Brie de Benham's opening gambit, failed to muster the necessary nerve. 'Um, trying to do some writing . . .'

'Got an agent?'

'Um, no.'

'*Oh*. Gosh, there's someone I absolutely must speak to over there. Big kiss, Seb, darling. Catch you later.'

'Seb, how are you?' A girl so skinny that her eyes were quite literally bigger than her stomach had appeared in the blonde's powerfully scented slipstream. She did not even look at Anna. 'It's been ages.'

Since *what*? Anna wondered crossly, looking at the new arrival's puffed-up eyes, pneumatic lips and bed hair. Rumpled, rough-cut and a sexy, dirty blonde, it did not disguise in the least the girl's delicate face and air of fragile sensuality. Automatically, Anna sucked in her stomach and once more cursed the gene that had given her hair the colour of carrot soup.

'Strawberry!' Seb's eyes lit up. 'You look *amazing*. I hear you're modelling.'

'Yeah,' drawled the girl. 'A Storm scout just stopped me in the street . . .'

Typical, thought Anna. The only people who stop me in the street are tourists wanting to know where the Hard Rock Café is. She stood feeling utterly surplus to requirements – surplus, in fact, in every way – and listened to Seb chatting away animatedly to the exquisite newcomer. Strawberry was so thin as to be barely visible in profile; her perfectly flat front and back making Anna feel about as sexy as an overstuffed black bin-liner. She looked around wildly for the champagne tray.

A tall and slightly maladroit waiter was circulating uncertainly in her vicinity, looking as if he might shed his load at any moment. Among the many lipstick-smeared empties which formed its contents, Anna spotted a single full glass of champagne. The waiter caught her eye and started towards her; at precisely the same time, something very large and colourful bore down from the opposite side of the room. Before Anna knew what was happening, a portly figure in a suit of wildly clashing checks had made a surgical strike on the glass. She and the waiter stared at each other in dismay, during which time Anna registered that he was really rather good-looking. He had wide-apart dark eyes into which locks of thick, dark hair intruded, making his progress through the crowded room more perilous than ever.

'And you are . . .?' Anna tore her eyes from the waiter's to realise with horror that the portly checked suit was thrusting his heavy red face into hers. He was, Anna calculated, twenty-five going on at least fifty. The type of man who wore piglet print boxer shorts. For whom teddy bear ties and novelty cufflinks were invented; sliding her glance to his plump little wrists, she saw that, sure enough, a pair of miniature *Sun* front pages in enamel – one bearing the legend 'Up Yours Delors' and the other 'Gotcha' – were securing his French cuffs. As his glazed and lustful gaze slid slowly over her bare arms, Anna, out of the corner of her eye, saw Seb place a hand on Strawberry's naked back and steer her away into the crowd.

Chapter 2

'Er, I'm Anna. Anna Farrier.'

'Orlando Gossett,' boomed the check suit. 'How do you do. And *what* do you do?'

'I, um, nothing much at the moment, as it happens,' Anna stammered. As an expression of faint contempt seeped into the protruding blue eyes of her neighbour, she added, flustered, 'Trying to write.'

'Write, eh?' boomed Orlando. 'Well, you're in good company. You see that dark-haired girl?' He pointed a fat red finger in the direction of the skinny brunette. 'That's Brie de Benham. Works at the *Daily Telegraph*. Real rising star, they say. Does all their big interviews. And that chap with the white jacket on she's talking to?'

Anna nodded.

'Gawain St George. Works in Washington for *The Sunday Times*. One to watch, apparently.'

'Yes, I know Gawain,' Anna said. 'I know Brie too, as it happens. We all did the same university English course.'

'*Did* you now? Well, in that case I wouldn't be wasting time talking to *me*. I'd be over there, trying to screw some work out of them. Ever heard of *networking*?' Orlando Gossett raised his eyebrows and gave her a patronising smile.

Natural politeness – or rank cowardice – stopped Anna pointing out that she'd had no desire to talk to him in the first place. It was with great difficulty she resisted the temptation to dash his glass of champagne into his scarlet jowls.

'Actually,' she muttered, 'the kind of writing I want to do isn't really journalism. More novel-writing, really. Books.'

'Oh well, you'd better try and talk to Fustian Fisch. Chap with the very bright green jacket on? Got the most colossal book deal – well into six figures, I believe – before he'd even done his Finals. Something about a mass-murdering Welsh tree surgeon who's obsessed with Beethoven, apparently. Film rights went for a fortune . . .'

Anna glanced at Fustian Fisch. He was busily helping himself to three glasses from the replenished tray of the gangly waiter and looked astonishingly arrogant. *A six-figure book deal.* Anna sighed inwardly. So far, she had failed even to get a sentence published. And it wasn't for want of trying; before finally abandoning her attempts to write a novel she'd sent off screeds of manuscript to practically every magazine, agent and publisher in the *Writers' and Artists' Yearbook*. The response hadn't even been the sound of one hand clapping – more one letterbox flapping as the rejections trickled slowly back. Still, at least the diary she had recently started was going well. Writing for a readership of one, it seemed, was easier than trying to hit the spot for thousands.

'. . . now Lavenham, over there, he's got the whole thing completely sussed.' Orlando Gossett was gesturing at a group at the other side of the room. 'Father's made a fortune out of the sewage business – been made a life peer as well – and the son will be rolling in it for the rest of his life. You could s-s-say,' Gossett chortled, 'that Lavenham won't have to give a *shit* about anything, in fact. Haw haw *haw*.'

Anna shrank back as Gossett opened his surprisingly vast red mouth and roared, jerking his fat, tightly-clad little body about in paroxysms of mirth for the best part of the following minute. 'Quite eligible too,' he gasped, wiping his streaming eyes with a chequered handkerchief, 'although,' he added in a conspiratorial whisper, 'they do say his girlfriend's *quite* extraordinary.'

'*Do* they?' Anna said, not at all sure what he meant. She reeled slightly. Orlando's breath was pure alcohol. One flick of a lighter and . . .

'Yah. Put it this way – Lavenham always says she screws like an animal.'

'But that's rather flattering, isn't it?'

'Not really.' Gossett paused, then nudged her. 'Like a *dead dog*, he says. Haw haw *haw*.'

Anna did not smile. 'Have you met her?' she asked, coldly.

'Not exactly, not in the flesh, no.'

'You have, actually.'

'Sorry?' Orlando looked blank.

'Met her. You're meeting her, in fact. Sebastian Lavenham is my boyfriend.'

There was an exploding sound as Orlando Gossett choked on what Anna calculated to be his seventh glass of champagne. '*Christ*. Oh my goodness. Oh *fuck*. I really *didn't* mean . . . I'm *sure* he was joking . . .'

'Yes. Of course he was.' Part of her refused to believe Seb could ever be so cruel. Part of her, however, feared the worst. 'Excuse me, I really must go and powder my nose.' At least she could get away from him now.

'Well, you won't be alone,' Gossett remarked cheerily. 'Half of Kensington's chatting to Charlie in there. They say there's more snow in Strawberry St Felix's bag than in the whole of St Moritz.'

Seb having completely disappeared, Anna, after a hesitant moment or two, decided to pass some of what promised to be a very long evening exploring the castle.

As she wandered from the thronging hall, ringing with the depressing sound of everyone but her having a good time, Anna wondered where she and Seb would be sleeping that night. And whether it would be the same place. The traumas of the journey were beginning to catch up with her. She longed for a lie-down.

The passage she was walking down was very dark, of a blackness so intense it almost felt solid. Anna inhaled the deep, cool, mildewed smell of centuries and wondered what it would be like to live somewhere so ancient. To have a past of burnished oak refectory tables, tapestries and mullions; Anna, whose own past was rather more semi-detached, G-plan and Trimphones, was fascinated by the air of age and decay.

The darkness was now absolute. Proceeding steadily onwards, Anna stuck her hands out in front of her, terrified of being impaled on something sharp – perhaps one of the intimidating halberds she had noticed festooning the hall. The noise from the hall having long receded, the silence was ringing in its intensity. Yet, straining her ears, Anna thought she heard the faint sound of a door closing. A bolt of fear shot through her as she realised the castle might be haunted. That, of course, was the downside of old places. Say what you like about semis, Anna thought, you rarely saw headless green ladies in them. Unless you'd knocked over one of Mum's china shepherdesses.

On seeing a dim light in the distance, Anna felt weak with relief. Approaching, she saw that the faint glimmer was a large, diamond-paned oriel window, the deep recesses of which held two cushioned seats facing each other. She collapsed on one of them gratefully. A sense of calm ebbed slowly through her as she gazed out into the night.

Directly in front of her, distorted through the ancient and tiny panes of glass, a full moon silvered the vast expanse of loch. The water shimmered and wrinkled like liquid satin, edged with the thinnest of watery lace as it rippled peacefully up the pebbly shore. All was silence.

'Beautiful, isn't it?' said a voice beside her.

Anna leapt out of the seat and tried to scream, but found she could only manage a petrified croak. Yet even in her terror she couldn't help noticing that the voice was less marrow-chilling and deathly than low and well-spoken and shot through with a warm thread of Scots. Anna opened her eyes. The moonlight shone on tumbling dark locks.

'Terribly sorry,' gasped the diffident waiter. 'Didn't mean to scare you.'

'Well, I dread to think what happens when you do,' Anna snapped, immediately regretting it. For some reason she didn't want him to think she was a harridan. As he put a nervous hand over his mouth to stifle a rather forced-sounding cough, she noticed the signet ring that glinted on his finger. Anna stared at it, surprised. But then why shouldn't a waiter wear a signet ring if he wanted? It was disturbing to realise that Seb's values – that only the wealthy and well-born were allowed rings with coats of arms – were seeping through.

'My name's Jamie Angus,' he told her, proffering his hand. It felt cool and reassuring over hers.

'Anna. Anna Farrier,' she mumbled, embarrassed both at how prosaic it sounded beside his own splendidly Caledonian affair and also at the waves of attraction thudding up her arm, down through her stomach and straight into her gusset. I must be drunk, she thought wildly. Guiltily, even, until, suddenly, the memory of Seb's hand on Strawberry's naked back flashed into her mind. Slowly, reluctantly, she withdrew her hand from Jamie's and, looking at him, smiled.

His wide, dark eyes, Anna noticed, were as far removed from Seb's spiteful blue ones as soft malt was from a vodka martini.

'Did you come on your own?'

'I came with my boyfriend, actually.' *Damn. Why the hell* had she said that?

The warm light in Jamie's eyes died away.

'Although,' Anna gabbled, desperate to limit the damage, 'he seems slightly more interested in one of the other women guests.'

'Well, he must be mad,' Jamie said. Silence descended. In an abrupt change of tack, Jamie asked her if she'd ever visited Scotland at the exact same time she asked him if he'd worked here for long. 'No,' was the mutual and simultaneous answer.

'Not exactly,' Jamie elaborated. 'I'm just helping out.'

'I think it's beautiful,' Anna said.

Another pause followed. Unwilling to risk banalities, Anna stared silently out of the window at the moonlit loch. The waves flexed tiny, tight muscles beneath the surface of the water. She stared hard at the stars glowing like Las Vegas in the blackness of the sky and tried to work out which of the constellations she could see.

'Is that a planet over there?' she ventured, pointing at a particularly brilliant star to the west. 'It looks very bright. Is it Venus?'

'No. That's the planet easyJet.' Jamie said it gently but sounded amused.

Anna reddened in the darkness as the star moved steadily through the sky, accompanied by a bright flashing light. Astronomy had never been her strength. Orion's belt was about her level, and she wasn't altogether certain of that. The one she was staring at seemed to have fewer notches than last time. Perhaps he'd been losing weight. Lucky old him.

'I'd better get back,' Jamie said. 'The cake needs cutting. And I think the disco has started in the Great Hall.'

He led her back down the passage and gave her a swift, sweet, farewell peck on the cheek before propelling her through a door which, unexpectedly, opened directly into the cavernous, vaulted room, amidst whose friezes and flagstones the disco was indeed in full swing. Or swinger – a superannuated Ted with a thinning, greying quiff proudly presided over a console emblazoned with the words 'Stornaway Wheels of Steel Mobile Disco'. As the cacophonous blare of 'The Locomotion' filled the air, Anna's heart sank in depressed recognition of the nuptial-attender's ritual nightmare, The Wedding Disco From Hell.

She glanced around the scattered strobe-lit crowd for any sign of Seb. Or Strawberry. Neither was in evidence. Taking care to position herself as far as possible from Orlando Gossett, currently investigating the buffet at one end of the room, Anna headed for the bar and drowned her sorrows in getting to know a group of delicious White Russians. After a while, emboldened by their company, she tottered unsteadily towards the dance floor and sank gratefully into a chair at the edge. The flashing lights made her head spin, as did the jerking forms of about thirty men in morning suits leaping around as the dying strains of 'Love Shack' were replaced by 'Come on Eileen'. Roaring and foot-stomping floated through the speakers. When 'Fever' succeeded 'Mustang Sally', Anna felt the first urge to laugh she had experienced all day. The sight of Orlando Gossett writhing around and assuring some blonde, horsy woman in an Alice band that she gave him Fever All Through The Night made her snort with suppressed mirth.

It was odd, Anna mused with the intensity of the inebriated, how people seemed happy to sacrifice all dignity in the face of really terrible music. Just what *was* it about 'Hi Ho Silver Lining' that got couples leaping up from their tables? Why did 'I Will Survive' prompt mass histrionic role-playing, or 'YMCA' and 'D.I.S.C.O.' have everyone waving their arms about like the compulsory morning workout at a Chinese ball-bearing factory? Most of all, why did the merest riff of Rolling Stones suddenly turn every man on the floor into Mick Jagger (in their dreams)? Even now, Orlando Gossett was prowling plumply around with one arm stuck straight out in front of him, rotating his wrist and imploring the horse-faced blonde to give him, give him, give him the honky tonk blues.

Eventually, inevitably, *The Rocky Horror Picture Show*

got an airing. As the heaving crowd on the dance floor shifted, Anna suddenly spotted her long-absent consort Doing the Timewarp Again. She watched, unsure whether the nauseous feeling in her stomach was because he was doing it a) at all, b) with a willowy, writhing someone bearing a striking resemblance to Brie de Benham, or c) because the effects of the White Russians were by now wearing off. Or possibly wearing on. Unable to reach a conclusion, or indeed anything else apart from the arm of the chair on which she kept a tight, stabilising grip, Anna watched their gyrating figures, oddly comforted by the fact that even the beautiful people looked ridiculous in the context of a really dreadful disco. It was a great leveller. Quite literally, she thought, as Orlando Gossett flicked to the right just a little bit too enthusiastically and went crashing heavily down on his well-upholstered bottom.

'*Desperate*, isn't it?' Anna had been too absorbed in watching the floorshow to notice that someone had sat down next to her. 'Still, it beats LA, I suppose,' added the voice. It belonged, Anna saw, to an extremely pretty girl.

'It does?' Anna stared at her neighbour's glossy tan and radiant teeth. 'But I thought LA was full of beautiful people.'

'It is. All the men are gay and all the women are gorgeous. The competition's too stiff.'

'But you look great,' Anna said. Certainly, the girl smiling back at her hardly looked the shrinking violet type when it came to men. The only thing shrunken and violet about her, in fact, was the tiny lilac cashmere cardigan out of whose casually unbuttoned front a pair of tanned and generous breasts rose like twin suns. Even in the dim light her smile was electric, emphasised by plum-coloured lipstick applied with architectural precision.

'Thanks. As the lady said, it takes a lot of money to look this cheap.' The girl grinned, smoothing a black satin skirt slit the entire length of her thigh over her slender hips. She flicked a heavily mascara'd glance around the room. 'It's nice someone appreciates it. No one else seems to.' A precision-plucked eyebrow shot peevishly upwards. 'Can't say I'm too thrilled about having schlepped all the way up here,' she added. 'I only came because I was told this wedding would be thick with millionaires. But I suppose,' she lit up a cigarette, 'they were right about the thick bit.'

The girl blew smoke out in two streams from her nose. 'And the *women* . . .' She stabbed her cigarette in the direction of Strawberry who had suddenly reappeared and was glaring at Brie and Seb smooching to '(Everything I Do) I Do It For You'. 'Look at *that*. Hair like a badger's *arse*.'

Anna looked determinedly away from the dance floor

and bulldozed a grin across her face. 'Quite. I'm Anna, by the way.'

'Geri. Lead me to the drinks. If I can't bag an heir, hair of the dog will have to do.'

Chapter 3

'Then there was Hugh.' Geri struck the manicured pinnacle of her middle finger. 'Gynaecologist. Met him at a BUPA check-up – it always pays to go private. Said I had the prettiest cervix he'd ever seen. Saved me a fortune on smear tests and breast examinations.'

'Oh?' said Anna, unsteadily. Geri had located a store of champagne behind a curtain beside the blazing hearth in the hall, grabbed three and withdrawn with them and Anna to an alcove. Endless warmish fizz plus endless highlights of Geri's romantic history were proving a potent and anaesthetic brew. Even the sight of Seb grinding his pelvis into Brie de Benham was by now painless. More painless than for Seb probably, as the de Benham pelvis resembled two Cadillac fins and could hardly have been comfortable up close. Seb, however, seemed to be rising to the occasion.

'Commitment problem though, unfortunately,' Geri continued.

'Absolutely,' said Anna, looking resignedly at Seb.

'Yes, except Hugh's was that *I* wouldn't commit,' said Geri, oblivious to the connection between Anna and the couple on the dance floor currently in the throes of '2-4-6-8 Motorway'. 'Wish I had now, really. But at the time, I wanted to play the field. Trouble is,' she rolled her long-lashed eyes, 'if you play in the field, you come across a lot of shit. Like Guy, for example.'

'Guy?' With difficulty, Anna shifted her bovine stare from the disco.

'A very rich banker. Or *was*. Complete ruthless shark. He was on the financial fast track until he got sacked.'

'Insider dealing?' Anna hoped she sounded worldly wise.

'Nothing quite so glamorous as that, I'm afraid. Someone in the office – everyone there hated him – changed his computer screensaver to say Fuck Off Cant. Unfortunately, Cant was the name of his immediate boss.' Geri paused and grinned. 'But we did have other problems, particularly in bed. He could barely raise his eyebrows, let alone anything else.' She paused and sighed.

The disco, it suddenly dawned on Anna, had stopped. Everyone was milling about, many of them making a beeline for the cut-up pieces of wedding cake. This had suddenly arrived in their midst on plates borne by Jamie who looked on with contempt as two wags grabbed handfuls of icing and began to throw it at each other. Anna tried to catch his eye to throw him a sympathetic glance and perhaps experience that delicious frisson again, but, deliberately or otherwise, he failed to notice her. Wresting his wares from the wags, he disappeared into the crowd and was soon lost to sight. Resignedly, Anna tuned back into Geri.

'*Then*,' Geri was saying, 'there was James. Wanted sex three times a night at first. *Exhausting*. Nightmare, in fact. Then, after we'd been together a few months it went down to twice a night. I couldn't decide whether I was insulted or relieved. So I left him for Ivo. An academic. *Hopeless*.'

'Oh?' said Anna, interested. She'd once entertained academic ambitions herself. 'Why was he hopeless?'

'Oh, not academically. He was one of the best in the world at ancient languages. He spoke fluent Aramaic which, apparently, is only of any use if you happen to meet Jesus.'

'So what happened?'

Geri sighed. 'He was skint. And as far as I'm concerned, if there's no dough, it's no go. He could be awkward as well, which is no good either – you do it my way or hit the highway. But in the end it was me who went. Took myself off to LA. But now I've come back. Got offered this fantastic new job in London and there seemed no reason to turn it down.'

A ripple of misgiving slid coldly through Anna's stomach. Her nose twitched suspiciously at the sweet smell of success. *A fantastic new job*. Just as she had started to regard Geri as a soul mate. As someone doing just as badly as she was.

Further questioning was rendered impossible by a sudden commotion in the hall. As everyone began to arrange themselves into pairs, Anna realised that Scottish dancing was about to begin. She shrank back against the hard wooden settle on which they sat. She hated country dancing. There were few people she loathed more than the Dashing White Sergeant, and could imagine nothing less gay than the Gordons.

'A new job as what?' Anna had to shout to make herself heard as the fiddling struck up.

'Executive development,' Geri yelled back cheerfully, lighting up another cigarette. 'Lots of travel, lots of responsibility. Lots of man management. A real challenge. I'm looking forward to it, although I must admit I was hoping to meet someone here who would save me the bother of working altogether. Anyway, enough about me. What do you do?'

'Oh, nothing much,' Anna bawled. 'I'm trying to write a book, actually.' As hesitantly as possible, given the volume required, she swiftly outlined her ambitions.

'That's *brilliant*,' screeched Geri. 'Can I be in it? I've always wanted to be in a novel.'

'I'm afraid I haven't got very far with it,' Anna shouted, feeling her voice beginning to break with the strain. 'The trouble is, I'm not sure whether I'm any good or not. I think I need a bit of professional advice about the nuts and bolts of things.' It was as near as she planned to come to admitting that she had neither agent, publisher, nor reason to believe she could write anything more than a postcard.

On the dance floor, the stomping, clapping and shrieking had intensified. 'Ow,' yelled Geri as hairpins, shaken from their rightful positions by the frantic activity, began to fly in the direction of the settle. Brows streamed with perspiration, women's breasts sprang free from their moorings. An excited-looking Seb shot by with a fetchingly rumpled Brie de Benham, their pupils the size of pinpoints.

'This is dangerous.' Geri was pulling someone's *skean dhu* out of her cleavage. 'Let's get out of here.'

Too late. The unmistakable form of Orlando Gossett, red-faced and polychromatic, was shoving its way purposefully through the heaving crowd towards their alcove like a vast tartan Sherman tank. 'Would you,' he asked, addressing Geri's cleavage, 'do me the honour of partnering me for this dansh?'

Grasping Geri's thin brown arm in his plump, pink palm, he dragged her to her feet. With no time to do more than roll her eyes, Geri tottered after him and plunged into the heaving quicksand of the crowd.

As tiredness crashed over her in huge waves, Anna decided to try once more to locate her room. Numbed by the champagne, she felt too exhausted to mind that Seb – no longer visible among the dancers – would almost certainly not be joining her in it. It took several goes to extract Miranda from the whirling crowd, but Anna eventually secured directions bedwards; her progress through a series of dark corridors this time sadly unimpeded by dark-eyed young men.

Unlocking the door of her room, Anna had a vague impression of high ceilings and a moonlight four-poster bed before passing out with sheer exhaustion. Not to mention sheer alcohol. Hours later, she woke up. It was still dark but something was scrabbling at the door. The empty mattress stretched away beside her. Could it, at last, be Seb? Struggling out of bed, falling over her clothes and shoes on the way to the door, Anna opened it to reveal, not Seb, but Miranda leaning against the lintel. The formerly radiant bride now looked distinctly the worse for wear. Her ivory wedding dress, the epitome of taste and restraint mere hours ago, was now smeared here and there with smudges and stains. Such was the devastation wrought on her once-magnificent white cathedral-length veil that, stunted and blackened, it was now more Methodist chapel. She cast an agonised glance at Anna, muttered something about needing a lie-down and disappeared into the gloomy nether regions of the corridor.

Next morning, at breakfast, Anna was disappointed to see that Jamie was not presiding over the chafing dishes. Instead, a couple of Australian hired helps as wide as they were tall slammed the lids cheerfully on and off dishes of scrambled eggs and mackerel with a clang reverberating round the alcohol-swollen brains of all present.

Seb's brain – or what remained of it following what had clearly been a night of literally staggering excess – was so swollen that he was still in bed. He had appeared with the dawn, thankfully not with Brie de Benham, but inebriated beyond belief and surprisingly, unwelcomingly randy. Happily, his attempts to force his attentions on Anna were interrupted several times by his dashing to the bathroom to vomit – 'drive the porcelain bus' as he called it. In the end, much to Anna's relief, he gave up and spent the rest of the night groaning for reasons that had little to do with ecstasy.

About five chairs away down the long dining table, Thoby slumped over his breakfast looking greyer at the gills than the mackerel he was pushing resignedly round his plate. Eventually, he put his fork down, his head in his hands and emitted something sounding rather like a groan. The memory of Miranda despairing at her door the night before confirmed Anna's suspicions that the wedding night had not been a brilliant success.

Sympathetically, she steered her stare away from Thoby and focused on her surroundings instead.

Dampie Castle seemed to be entirely enveloped in a cloud. The windows of the dining room were long and elegant, though the view outside bore a strong resemblance to that enjoyed by aeroplane passengers five minutes out of Gatwick. Nothing was visible apart from an ectoplasmic mist which pressed up against the panes and extended as far as the eye could see, which was not very far at all. The view inside, on the other hand, was pure old school patrician – towering bookcases, armorial fireplaces and several patricians from Seb's old school whose purity was anyone's guess. Anna was just beginning to wonder whether her boyfriend's condition was terminal when someone suddenly slammed a plate down on the next worn Scenes of Scotland place mat and threw themselves into the chair beside her.

'What a night,' said Geri, whom Anna had not seen since she disappeared to Strip The Willow with Orlando Gossett. She hoped that was all Geri had stripped, but it appeared she had hoped in vain.

'Oh dear.' Anna swallowed hard. It really didn't bear thinking about. 'Don't think about it,' she counselled.

Geri put her fork down, her face as white as her unwarmed plate. 'Well, I'm trying not to, only there are about a million bruises to remind me.'

Anna swallowed. 'He wasn't, well, *violent*, was he?'

Geri stared at her. '*Violent?* The man's a fucking Neanderthal. He practically threw me round the floor, stamped repeatedly on my new Jimmy Choos, knocked out one of my contact lenses and then, *then*, he tried to get me to *sleep* with him. Can you imagine?'

'No,' said Anna, quickly.

'He couldn't understand why I *wouldn't* sleep with him, though. Came over all indignant and said, "I haven't got Aids, you know." "Don't *worry*," I said. "I *believe* you." '

'So how did you get rid of him?'

'Simple.' Geri probed her fish with her fork. 'Told him I was going to the bathroom. I just didn't mention I meant *my* bathroom in *my* room and I had no intention of coming down again.'

'Ah,' said Anna.

'But eventually I decided to sneak back down,' Geri confessed, looking strangely furtive. 'Had rather a good time in the end . . .' Her voice trailed off. 'Anyway,' she added briskly. 'I've had a brilliant idea. About you.'

'About *me*?' Anna felt a vague sense of panic. It seemed rather early for ideas. Hadn't Oscar Wilde said something about only dull people being brilliant at breakfast?

'Remember, management consultancy is what I do,' said Geri confidently. 'I'm paid to advise people on how to run their professional lives better. And I've got just the solution for you.'

'You have?'

'Sure,' said Geri, abandoning the mackerel and flinging her fork down with a flourish. 'What you need is an apprenticeship.'

Dickensian visions of workshops and boy sweeps loomed before Anna. 'You mean long stands and striped paint?'

'Of course not. Stop being so rigid in your definitions. The first principle of management consultancy is creative thinking. I'm talking about a particular sort of apprenticeship. A *bestseller* apprenticeship.'

'But where do they do those?'

'Lateral thinking,' said Geri, tapping her forehead with a fingernail which, for all the night's traumas, remained impeccably manicured. 'You need to find a writer who needs help. Be their dogsbody. Do their errands, take their post, make their life run smoothly. And in return . . .'

'They'll show me how they do it,' said Anna slowly, catching the thread of thought. Her alcohol-sodden brain suddenly sparked into life like a match. 'Or at the very least, I can pick some of it up. Chapter construction, how one gets an agent, the different publishing houses . . .'

Geri nodded. 'Exactly.'

'Oh Geri, that's a *fantastic* idea.'

Just then, Orlando Gossett entered the room and glided swiftly towards the chafing dishes. Having piled his plate high with eggs and fish, he looked for somewhere to sit.

'Head down,' Geri muttered, suddenly taking an intense interest in her Stirling Castle place mat.

'It's all right,' Anna said. 'He's sitting down next to Thoby, who doesn't look very pleased about it. But then, Thoby doesn't look very pleased about anything. He certainly doesn't look like a man who's spent a night of bliss with his new bride.'

'That's because he didn't.' Geri blushed. 'He spent it with me.'

Chapter 4

'Forty-two, two twenty-eight, five fifty-seven.' Cassandra squinted at the list of clothes beside the computerised wardrobe door and entered the numbers of her chosen garments into the keypad, taking great care not to damage her nails. Tyra the manicurist had just left; the fact she cost just over double what most painters of nails and buffers of cuticles charged demanded that her handiwork be shown a certain respect. She was worth it though; did she not count Nicole Kidman, Elizabeth Hurley and the editor of *Vogue* among her clients? Though the fact that they probably paid nothing explained Cassandra's own exorbitant bills.

Still, full battle dress was essential today. Cassandra

was not looking forward to the meeting with her publishers at which she would no doubt be expected to explain the whereabouts of *A Passionate Lover*, her long-promised but as yet unforthcoming new novel. So far, she'd pleaded writer's block, crashing laptop, even periodic bouts of mysterious illness, but now, floating faintly but definitely into her ear was the unmistakable sound of music that had to be faced. Cassandra was unsure how exactly she would break the news that no lover, passionate or otherwise, currently lurked in her laptop, still less in the left-hand side of her brain or wherever the creative part was supposed to be.

A PASSIONATE LOVER, screamed the poster pinned on the wall opposite her desk in bold letters of searing red. They were a searing reminder to Cassandra that her publishers had seen fit to start a poster campaign before seeing a single word of the novel it described. The apparent rationale was that if they proceeded as if the book existed, it might, through sheer force of corporate effort, actually materialise. 'Love, lust and betrayal – with a twist in the tail,' declared the poster. 'The new Number One bestseller from the author of *The Sins of the Father*, *Impossible Lust*, *Guilty* and *Obsessions*,' it went on in smaller letters running across the illustration of a tousle-haired Pierce Brosnan-alike in a frilled shirt performing the astonishing feat of being able to pout and suck his cheeks in at the same time. Cassandra stared at him with loathing.

Love, lust and betrayal – with a twist in the tail. Well, thought Cassandra bitterly, the publishers certainly had a head start on her. She hadn't even begun to think about the plot, let alone start trying to write it. And as for Number One bestseller, well, despite the publisher's best efforts – and often their worst and most underhand ones into the bargain – that, as well she knew, was in the lap of the gods. It certainly wasn't, at this precise moment, in her laptop.

Forcing this uncomfortable and inconvenient fact from her mind, she stared at the electronic display beside the wardrobe door as it processed the numbers she had punched in. The figures were rippling like the destination boards used to do at Waterloo in those thankfully long-ago days when public transport and Cassandra were not the strangers they were now. She tapped her foot as impatiently as she could, given that each tap sank into inches-thick cream carpet.

What had gone wrong? Why had the inspiring spark, so reliable for so long, recently failed to spring into anything approximating a flame? 'Everything I'm writing is shit,' a panicked Cassandra had yelled at her editor recently. Harriet's lack of surprise, indeed the unspoken implication that that was entirely expected, did little to improve Cassandra's mood. But if shit it were, she thought indignantly, it was successful shit. Four bestsellers under her belt in as many years, spawning three mini-series and one talking book read by Joanna Lumley. But lately . . . Cassandra swallowed. The thought of the flint-faced executives she would shortly face around the boardroom table make her heart sink.

She could no longer think of plots. The personalities of her characters vacillated as wildly as their gender, hair colour and motivation; her development and consistency skills had gone, although, she thought, reddening, many of her reviewers had questioned the existence of those skills in the first place. *Bastards*. But far, far worse than the worst reviews (and there had been plenty of those and she never forgot the names and one day the score would be settled) was the fact that Cassandra couldn't seem to write sex scenes any more.

Sex scenes had been Cassandra's stock in trade. Or stocking trade, as more than one razor-witted reviewer had pointed out in the past. Along with the smirking observation, following revelations that Cassandra was celebrated among the commuting classes for her ability to produce erections on the Circle Line at seven in the morning, that 'here was a writer at the peak of her powers'. But for the moment, those powers had deserted her – Cassandra doubted now she'd be able to produce an erection among a gang of footballers being lapdanced in Stringfellow's. Chronicling the most basic sexual encounter seemed beyond her; the leaping breasts with their dark aureoles of nipple consistently failed to spring to mind. Likewise, the piston-like penises, so reliable of old, resolutely refused to come.

Cassandra was at a loss to explain, to Harriet or anybody else, why this should suddenly be the case. It was not, after all, as if her own sex life had suddenly slowed down to a splutter, or that she had lost interest. She had never been interested in the first place. When push came to shove – and she rued every day that it did – Cassandra hated sex, at least, when she was sober. Her husband Jett, unfortunately, did not share her views and continued to press for his conjugal rights, although, admittedly, his requirements had gone down from a daily service to a Sunday one. Cassandra supposed she should be thankful for small mercies, even though there was nothing small or merciful about Jett at full throttle. The only point to sex, as far as she was concerned, was children. And after Zak's birth, eight years ago, Cassandra had dropped even the pretence that she liked it.

From briefly dwelling on the favourite subject of her son, that most gifted, charming and beautiful of children, Cassandra's mind flitted to the rather less comfortable subject of Emma the nanny. Now *there* was a pressure, coping with the latest in that endless line of troublesome girls. *Five* in the last *twelve months*, Cassandra seethed to herself. Did staying power and commitment mean nothing any more? Given what she had to put up with in her domestic life, was it any wonder that her storylines were about as sexy as an orthopaedic shoe?

They were all the same, these ridiculous girls; at least, they all said the same things about Zak. Emma had proved particularly unresponsive to Cassandra's standard line of nanny rebuttal, the argument that a child as brilliant as Zak was bound to be difficult from time to time, gifted children always were. And of *course* he was occasionally – *very* occasionally – disobedient. The respect of a child like Zak had to be *earned*. Cassandra decided not to dwell on Emma's mutinous expression the last time she had tried this tack, still less the pointed way she had turned her back and marched out of the room. She decided instead to concentrate on the matter in hand, which was the meeting and what to wear for it. It was eight o'clock, a blearily early hour for Cassandra to be up, and she was due in the boardroom at nine.

Forty-two, two twenty-eight and five fifty-seven. It had been a difficult decision, but in the end Cassandra was sure she had trodden the sartorial line between professionalism and plunging cleavage with consummate skill. Forty-two was the classic black YSL trouser suit with the big black buttons. Two twenty-eight was her new purple Prada shirt, and five fifty-seven her favourite pair of black elastic Manolo boots.

Boots? Was it, Cassandra thought, suddenly panicking, the *weather* for boots? She looked quickly at a second liquid crystal display beneath the keypad, which helpfully showed the temperature outside so you could pick your clothes to suit: 5°C. Christ, it was practically *freezing*. Amazing weather for June, but then, this *was* England, she supposed. She'd need a coat, too, obviously. It could be the fur's first outing since Gstaad in February. Cassandra scanned the list. Seven hundred and four was the silver-mink ankle-length. If that didn't wow them, nothing would.

There was a grinding sound, a faint rattle, then the door of the wardrobe slid back. Cassandra blinked as it revealed a pair of orange towelling sweatpants, a bright yellow jacket with shoulder pads of Thames Barrier proportions and a bikini top in magenta satin. As Cassandra stared, aghast, a pair of olive-green wellington boots hove into view along the conveyor belt at the bottom. 'Jett!' she exploded. 'Jett!'

'Whazzamatter?' A man in a red satin Chinese bathrobe far too small for him appeared in the doorway between the dressing room and the bedroom. His figure, with its round, protruding belly and long, skinny legs, was reminiscent of a lollipop. 'Whazzup?' he asked, rubbing his eyes and yawning.

'This fucking computerised wardrobe you gave me,' Cassandra almost spat.

'I didn't realise it fucked as well.' Jett lounged against the doorjamb, his heavily bagged eyes narrowed in amusement. 'The miracles of modern science. I'd have kept it for myself if I'd known.'

'Don't be so bloody facetious, Jett,' Cassandra snarled. 'This wardrobe is *shit*.' Losing her temper altogether, she slammed her clenched fists repeatedly against her sides with impotent rage, irrespective of Tyra's recent careful and costly efforts. 'How the *fuck* am I supposed to wear *this* lot to meet my *publishers*?' She gestured furiously at the ensemble before her.

'Looks all right to me,' Jett yawned, loping over and tweaking the bikini top. 'Looks quite rock 'n' roll, actually.'

'Rock 'n' roll my *arse*,' hissed Cassandra.

'No, rock 'n' roll your goddamn *tits*.' Jett thrust out a hairy, ring-festooned hand to grab Cassandra's breasts, half revealed by her flapping Janet Reger peignoir. Twisting deftly out of Jett's way, Cassandra heard the unmistakable crunch of her neck muscles going. Damn. Another fifty quid to the osteopath.

'This stupid sodding wardrobe's suggesting I wear nothing but this disgusting thing,' she tugged the yellow jacket, 'outside when the temperature's more or less zero.'

'Zero?' echoed Jett. 'It's goddamn *baking* out there. Just look out of the window.'

Cassandra turned and screwed up her face against the brilliant light streaming through the greige pashmina curtains, looped with studied artlessness over black iron rods.

It *did* look rather warm outside. '*Sod it*,' she spat. 'I've got to start all over again now. I'm going to be late. I need some help. Where's that useless nanny? Where's Emma?'

'I'm 'ere,' said a northern accent in the doorway. 'And I'm handing in me notice. With immediate effect.'

Cassandra and Jett stared at the solid figure standing at the entrance to the room with two large bags in her hand. Then they stared at each other.

'You've been at it a-bloody-gain, haven't you?' Cassandra shrieked at Jett. 'Trying to screw the sodding nanny. I thought as much when I caught you with her in your library last week. Showing her a few of your favourite *passages*, were you?'

'Well you can bloody well talk,' Jett snapped. 'Getting her to take those goddamn dresses back to the shops and saying they're not suitable, when you knew goddamn well you'd worn them. Poor cow. Sent packing by half of goddamn Bond Street.'

'Well, if she'd ironed the linings properly like I told her, no one would have known,' howled Cassandra, seemingly oblivious of the fact that Emma was still present and shifting from foot to sturdily shod foot. 'And anyway, it's not as if she'd ever go in those shops of her own accord. I gave her an *education*, asking her to take them back. She should be bloody *grateful*. You, on the other hand, gave her an education of a completely different sort. *Why can't you keep your zip up?* Cassandra yelled. 'You're not a rock star being chased by every groupie in town any more, you know. You're not a rock star, *full stop*.'

Jett's eyes flashed fire. Cassandra saw she had hit him where it hurt. 'You haven't released anything for years,' she taunted. 'Apart from that *thing* in your trousers.'

'Well, neither has anybody goddamn else,' yelled Jett, furious. 'You goddamn bitch. Solstice will be back with a bang, you'll see. You wait till the new goddamn album's mixed.'

'Mixed? *Mixed?*' bawled Cassandra. 'The only thing you know how to mix these days is bloody whisky and soda.'

As Jett stormed out of the room, Emma stood aside, then stepped forward. 'The real reason I'm leaving has nowt to do wi' what you just said,' she said in dull Lancastrian tones, 'although I'm not saying they didn't 'elp.'

Cassandra stared at her in contempt. *Nowt* indeed. *Ghastly* northern vowels. She probably thought elocution was what happened if you dropped a hairdryer in the bath.

'Only summat 'appened this morning,' Emma added, unbowed by her employer's freezing stare, 'which made me realise I'd 'ad enough . . .'

Summat. Ugh. And just *look* at that *hair.*

'Zak were complaining about feeling awful, and wanted to stay off school. He said there were summat wrong wi' 'is insides.' Emma paused. ' 'E said his poop were white.'

'Poop? *Poop?*' Cassandra was incandescent. 'We don't *poop* in this house. We *poo.*'

'Course,' Emma continued flatly, her stare concentrated at a corner of the room beyond her employer, 'I tried to find out what were wrong before I got you involved. Zak took me into his bathroom and pointed at his toilet . . .'

'*Lavatory.*'

'And there, bobbing around in the bottom of it, were these little round white thingies.'

'*Really?*' Cassandra was intrigued despite herself at this concrete evidence – *white* poo, of all things – that the sun did indeed shine out of Zak's perfect ivory bottom.

'Well, obviously I were worried,' Emma continued, still addressing the corner of the room. 'Zak were screaming 'is head off saying he were in 'orrible agony and I were just about to call t'ambulance when summat about them white thingies struck me as funny, like.'

'Well, of course they were *funny, like,*' Cassandra barked. 'What's remotely normal about white poop? *Poo,*' she corrected herself.

'So I looked closer and picked one up,' Emma said.

'Picked . . . one . . . up?' Cassandra's face was a mass of disgusted lines. Who did she think she was? Dr Sam bloody Ryan?

'And it weren't poop at all. It were,' Emma concluded with all the flat finality of the *Silent Witness* pathologist, 'a can of tinned potatoes Zak 'ad emptied down the toilet. Suppose 'e thought that were funny,' she added. 'But I didn't. Ta-ra.' She turned on her sensible low heel and left.

Cassandra stared after her, the blood pounding in her temples. Oh *Christ.* She didn't need *this.* Not *now.* Not with this meeting, not with the book problems, husband problems and problems of every other description she had to put up with. Did no one realise she was a *creative artist*? Where the hell would Shakespeare have been if he'd had the kind of poop – poo – she dealt with on a day-to-day basis, white or otherwise? Boy, did she need a *drink.*

Cassandra lunged with the last of her fury at the sweatpants and magenta bikini top, tearing them from their hangers as she sank to her knees. Sobbing, she crawled across the floor, her bony knees cracking painfully against the rubbed beech boards, towards the sustainable rainforest-wood bed draped with its white shahtoush duvet. 'I'm sure I put one there,' she muttered, feeling around underneath until her hand closed over a hard glass object. She pulled out the gin bottle, her nose almost touching the mirrored door of the wardrobe.

Cassandra stared at her reflection. In the harsh light of morning, her skin had all the bloom and smoothness of screwed-up tissue paper. Her hooded eyes, which in her more optimistic moments seemed Rampling-like, today looked more like Rumpole. Cassandra reflected resentfully that, despite the fact that her face was the only well-fed thing about her, the gallons of expensive skin creams she rubbed in each night had clearly done nothing to help. Nor had last year's lift. She looked older even than her forty years. Her heart sank. She clamped a palm to her thin lips, shuddering as she saw the snaking veins on the back of it. Perhaps she could ask for a hand-lift for Christmas . . . 'Bugger them all,' Cassandra murmured as she unscrewed the top of the Bombay Sapphire.

Sometimes it felt like her only friend. The only one who understood the nightmare of her marriage, the challenges of her child and the demands of her publishers. She'd started drinking it to soothe herself, to take the pain away, to give her courage to face and, more importantly, *do* things. Like the book. But lately she hadn't been able to do anything. And the only thing that made her feel better, Cassandra thought, as she put the bottle to her lips, was giving her little glass friend here a big, big kiss.

* * *

When Jett returned to the house several hours later, he found it suspiciously silent. But then, he thought, most things seem pretty peaceful after you've been playing lead guitar at top screaming volume for hours on end. Boy, had he made that axe *weep* this afternoon. *Bleed*, even. Gone up to eleven and beyond. Whatever Cassandra might say, *Ass Me Anything* was shaping up to be a peach of an album; 'Sex and Sexibility' if released as a single, might even make it to number one. What a blast that would be – Solstice's first chart-topper since 'Bum Deal' in 1979. He'd show that bitch. Where *was* that bitch, anyway? Hopefully recovered from that mother of all strops she'd been in this morning. But of course it was the drink talking. Pity, thought Jett, the drink couldn't goddamn *write* as well. Because, since Cassandra had been on the sauce, she could hardly manage a sentence any more.

There was, Jett noticed, a light downstairs in the kitchen. Had the impossible happened and Cassandra had decided to cook for a change? The usual rules of the house were that whatever nanny was currently in residence at the time fed Zak; Cassandra ate pretty much nothing and Jett was left with whatever happened to be in the fridge or on the menu of one of the local pubs. Although fancy bar food didn't always appeal – he'd have traded all the Thai prawn sausages and celeriac and Parmesan mash in Kensington for one steak and kidney pie – the beer certainly did. He'd been thinking of going down there later but, with Cassandra in the kitchen . . . he smiled to himself. At this rate he might even get a shag out of her as well.

Jett put his nose in the air and sniffed like a Bisto kid. He couldn't actually smell anything but then, he reminded himself, he hadn't for about twenty years, thanks to all that shit he'd stuffed up there. In his time he'd snorted the equivalent of an entire fleet of Gulfstreams. Ah well. That was rock and roll for you. He shook his head and smiled ruefully as he dropped jauntily down the stairs.

His benevolent mood instantly disappeared as he entered the kitchen. 'Aaargh!' screamed Jett, terror clenching his heart, which then leapt into his mouth and began to ricochet among the wisdom teeth he had never plucked up the courage to have out. '*Zak!*' he thundered. 'Put that cat *down*.' He had arrived just in time to stop his eight-year-old son putting the neighbour's Bengal Blue into the microwave. 'For Christ's sake, leave that animal alone.'

'But Daddy, you once bit the head off a snake on stage,' protested Zak.

'That's different,' snapped Jett. 'Snakes are two a penny. Have you any idea how much that sodding cat *costs*?'

'But it was *cold*,' Zak whinged, his shiny red lower lip shooting out like a cash till.

'Don't talk *shit*.' Jett felt calmer now. The prospect

had receded, at least temporarily, of having to replace Ladymiss Starshine Icypaws Clutterbucket III, the prizewinning pride and joy of Lady Snitterton next door, an animal with a longer pedigree than the Queen and certainly Lady Snitterton herself, but one which possessed a strong self-destructive streak as well as a replacement price tag of about ten thousand pounds. He drew out a chair and sat down, admiring his long legs in their tight black jeans stretched out before him, but wincing slightly as the waistband cut into his belly.

'Where's your mother?' he asked.

'Upstairs,' snuffled Zak, now occupied with turning the gas hobs of the cooker on and off.

'*Stop* that,' demanded Jett. 'What's she doing?'

'Praying.'

'*Praying?*' Jett was astounded. 'What sort of praying?' He could think of many words to describe his wife, but devout wasn't one of them.

'She's on her knees in front of the wardrobe mirror saying "Oh my God".'

Chapter 5

Anna looked lovingly at the tiny, coloured oblong – ENGLISH GRADUATE SEEKS WORK AS AUTHOR'S ASSISTANT – and blew it a surreptitious kiss as she pinned it to the noticeboard of Kensington Library. 'Good luck,' she whispered to it. In fact, acting on Geri's advice, she had left as little as possible to chance. Geri had stipulated she use hot pink card, neatly and clearly printed in ink, to distinguish it from the other dog-eared and sloppily Biro'd offerings usually found on noticeboards. And the noticeboard Geri had favoured, during her impromptu post-breakfast consultancy the morning after the wedding, was that of Kensington Library.

'Only bestseller-list regulars can afford to live there,'

Geri explained, as they stood in the castle entrance hall knee-deep in bags, most of which seemed to be hers. 'Guess I'd better shoot,' she added as a tense-looking Miranda appeared. 'Before she shoots *me*. See you in London, anyway. Good luck.'

'Here's my address.' Anna thrust it at Geri as she strode in high-heeled boots out of the Gothic arched doorway and disappeared into the mist. The roar of a powerful car engine had been heard almost immediately.

As she turned and left the library, Anna wondered what Geri was doing now. As yet she had had no word from her, although admittedly only a few days had passed since the wedding. She was probably out of town; Anna imagined her reclining in club class on her way to troubleshoot some international management crisis or other, clad head to foot in tailored pinstripes, exciting the discreet interest of a few tanned and handsome businessmen with cryptic smiles. Or sweeping through town in a limo, a mobile clamped to her ear. Or moving swiftly but authoritatively through an open-plan office, a gaggle of executives rushing after her, waving papers and vying for her attention.

Meanwhile, all Anna herself was doing was wandering vaguely down the library steps having stuck a small pink card on the noticeboard and wondering whether she had done the right thing. It seemed pathetic in comparison. But what, as Geri had said, could go wrong?

Anna imagined listening raptly as Julian Barnes read aloud his latest chapter, or hovering helpfully in the shadow of Louis de Bernières' desk lamp. Perhaps her little pink plea might even be spotted by a visiting John Updike or Garrison Keillor and she would be whisked away to the land of white picket fences, clapboard, clam bakes and American literary legend. In the meantime, she boarded the number 10 bus and was whisked away to the land of Seb slouching in front of the television and a kitchen full of empty crisp packets, crusted cereal bowls and dirty coffee mugs.

Staring out of the window as she juddered past Hyde Park, Anna's thoughts wandered due north to a soft-spoken Scotsman with wide-apart eyes and rumpled hair. As they fought through the traffic of Knightsbridge, Anna was lost in her memories of Dampie. The stone-flagged hall, the vast fireplace with carved canopy, the tapestries, the stags' heads, the ancient, misty, standing-stones-and-islands romance of it all . . .

Suddenly, Anna realised she'd missed her stop and was at the bottom of Oxford Street. She'd have to walk almost all the way back up to Seb's South Audley Street flat now. '*Fuck!*' she muttered.

'No need for that sort of language,' snapped the conductor.

* * *

'*Fuck!*' Cassandra threw down her pen and scowled at the Schnabel on the wall of her study. A present from her publishers when her fourth novel went through the five hundred thousand barrier, it only served to drive home the fact that she was getting precisely nowhere with her fifth. She flung herself theatrically back in her zebraskin chair, stretched her hands out before her and tried to raise her spirits by examining the vast and glittering rings on her red-nailed fingers. Some people thought them vulgar, but they were wrong. If you could never be too rich or too thin – and she was hell bent on being both – you could certainly never have jewellery that was too big. She hadn't got where she was today by being subtle.

Cassandra reached for the small gold bell which always stood by her laptop and shook it. 'Lil!' she screeched. 'Lil!'

'Yes, Mrs Knoight?'

A wrinkled apparition with orange-pencilled eyebrows, lips a painted purple bow and hair the chewed yellow of a bathroom sponge poked its head round the door almost immediately. The cleaner, Cassandra realised, must have been next door attending to the latest interiors innovation, a perfume bathroom devoted entirely to scent bottles. *Cleaner* – that was a joke. *Filthier*, more like. Lil invariably left more smears behind her than she found, especially on the scented candles whose black smoky bits she never quite managed to clean off, to her employer's intense irritation. Nor, despite Cassandra's compiling and captioning an album of photographs of each room for her, showing exactly how each cushion, ornament and curtain should be arranged, did the house ever look really up to scratch. But there were always lots of scratches. Cassandra groaned. She felt terrible after the party last night.

'I'd like a large gin and tonic, Lil,' Cassandra ordered, thrusting a cigarette between her violently red lips. She always sat down to work in full make-up. After all, you never knew when a TV station might suddenly appear on her doorstep wanting an interview, or whether a celebrity fan might pop in at a moment's notice. Princess Diana, she'd been told, had loved her books and, as Kensington Palace was practically at the end of her *garden*, Cassandra had always cherished the hope . . . until . . . Tears filled her eyes. '*Diet* tonic,' she ordered, her hand suddenly shaking.

As the door closed behind Lil, Cassandra sucked on her cigarette like a Hoover in those hard-to-get-at corners of the staircase – well, Lil found them hard to get at anyway – and groaned anew at the memory of last night's gathering. The drink had been dreadful; it had, after all, only been warm white wine for the local Neighbourhood Watch co-ordinator's birthday. Admittedly, she'd had a glass or two more than was advisable – assuming any of it was advisable. It had come out of a *box*, for God's sake. In Cassandra's experience, the only good boxes worth opening were pale blue and marked 'Tiffany & Co'.

Still, she'd needed some rocket fuel after that wretched publishers' meeting. It had been tough, but she'd managed to buy more time – and half a case of Bombay Sapphire on the way back to help her recover. But she'd been left in no doubt it was her last chance. She simply *had* to get on with this book.

The thought of it made her feel sick. Compounding her nausea was the memory of last night's conversation with that *ghastly* Fenella Greatorex at number 24 who had banged on practically *all night* about her son getting one of the coveted invitations to Savannah and Siena Tressell's birthday party.

Cassandra's skin had almost *blistered* with the heat of her envy. Zak *had* to, she resolved, simply *had* to get an invitation too. Otherwise her life would not be worth living. And, hopefully, when – not if – Zak was invited, Otto Greatorex's wouldn't be worth living either.

Cassandra ground her teeth. *Then* she'd had to listen to Fenella Greatorex crapping on about her wonderful new nanny. This was doubly infuriating considering Fenella's new one was none other than Emma, Cassandra's old one. *Fuck* Fenella, thought Cassandra; still, she'd looked a lot less smug after Cassandra had pointed out a few home truths to her. 'Oh yes,' Cassandra sneered as the alcohol took hold. 'You bloody well stopped at nothing to get that girl out of my house. Offering her money, cars, paid holidays, her own bathroom, the lot. You ought to be ashamed of yourself. You're nothing less than a thief.'

That, Cassandra thought, had shown her. Only it hadn't. Murderous rage rose within her at the memory of Fenella piously pointing out that money, cars, paid holidays and their own bathrooms were the bare minimum of what most nannies expected anyway and the sooner Cassandra realised that, the better. 'No wonder you can't keep a nanny for more than a month,' had been Fenella's parting shot.

Wheeling round on her chair, Cassandra stabbed her cigarette out in her Matthew Williamson ashtray and seethed. A *month*! She'd kept at least two nannies for *six weeks*; Isabel, that fat one from Wales, had lasted *two months* until that unfortunate business with the flower vase. Cassandra stuck by her guns, even now. That bunch of flowers had been unspeakably vulgar. *Carnations*, for Christ's sake. She'd been firm and unyielding. Isabel's boyfriend may have had every right to *give* her carnations but Isabel had no right – no right *whatsoever* – to expect to display them in Cassandra's house. She couldn't *quite* believe Isabel considered it a resigning issue, but so be it if she did. Cassandra permitted herself a slight sigh of regret. Isabel had been the best of a bad bunch – quite literally, in the case of those carnations – particularly because she had been so reassuringly plump and therefore Jett-proof. Her husband was not a big fat fan, unless you counted the beef dripping sessions he occasionally indulged in to keep in touch with his working-class roots.

At the thought of Jett, a chill suddenly swept through Cassandra. Was she meant to be doing the school run this morning? She scrambled to her feet in panic. Anyone delivering the children late got an automatic black mark in the headmistress's book, and Cassandra had few lives left with Mrs Gosschalk as it was. Last term she had been publicly humiliated when her car had been one of those named and shamed in the school magazine for parking on double yellow lines with the hazards on at dropping-off time. Still, at least she hadn't been on that *dreadful* list taking to task those mothers who turned up at the school gates in *jeans*, which had appeared in the same issue.

'Did Mr St Edmunds take Master Zak to school?' Cassandra demanded as Lil returned with a large cut-glass tumbler. The ice cubes crashed and shook together as Cassandra lifted it to her lips.

'Yars,' rasped the cleaner in a voice so gravelly it sounded as if her oesophagus had been pebbledashed.

Cassandra was relieved and slightly amazed to hear that her husband had managed to perform at least one parental duty. For, despite the staff crises in which he had most certainly had a hand – in the case of

Emma, Cassandra chose not to dwell on exactly where that hand had been – Jett was scarcely displaying Dunkirk spirit at the moment. More bunker mentality as he disappeared for days on end into a studio whose precise location had never been satisfactorily pinpointed.

Cassandra frowned hard at the screen of her laptop. It was a magnificent machine, customised in her trademark zebraskin, with a matching carrycase and special supersensitive keys designed not to break Tyra's nails. When she switched it on, an encouraging electro-musical burst of 'Diamonds Are Forever' greeted her, while each time she completed five hundred words, a little pink cartoon figure appeared at the corner of the screen to blow her a kiss. It corrected the spelling for her, it suggested alternative words for her, it could do practically everything except write for her, something Cassandra profoundly regretted. Still, it did its level best to encourage her – its screensaver swirled with the affirming messages 'Just Do It' and 'Go For It' in about a hundred different typefaces, which, in her present mood, Cassandra found more irritating than motivating. The very fact she was sitting there staring at 'Just Do It' meant she wasn't doing it. The only It she felt like going for now, in fact, was the sort you put in gin.

She decided to go for a walk. A walk would clear her head, Cassandra thought, emptying the last of the Bombay Sapphire down her throat.

'Just going to the library,' she called to Lil, who was now busy bashing the paint off the skirting boards with the Hoover.

'I 'aven't done in there yet,' Lil thundered over the vacuum cleaner.

'No, not *our* library,' Cassandra screeched. 'The *local* library.'

She rarely, if ever, made an appearance in the mock-Victorian Gothic book repository Jett had had built for himself for his fortieth birthday – or what he claimed had been his fortieth birthday – the year before. God alone knew what he wanted it for, certainly not for reading. Jett's idea of quality fiction was the front and back pages of the tabloids. He had never read a single one of Cassandra's novels, although she derived some comfort from the fact that she was up there with Tolstoy and Dickens in that he had never read one of theirs either.

A walk round Kensington Library, Cassandra decided, was what she needed to stir her into action; the sight of all those volumes by other writers would ignite the petrol-soaked rag of her latent competitive spirit. It would also be interesting to see how many of hers were out on loan. All, hopefully.

Cassandra pulled on a shiny zebraskin mac and, conscious of the thick-waisted Lil watching her from the end of the hall, dragged the belt round her thin middle as tightly as it would go. Who cared if she had writer's block, husband problems and a galloping staff crisis? She had the waist of a sixteen-year-old, didn't she? And the bottom of a twenty-year-old – Jett was always telling her she had the best arse in the business. A frown flitted across her face as she wondered for the first time what business he meant, exactly.

Cassandra negotiated the front steps as well as she could in her high-heeled leopardskin ankle boots. She trotted unevenly down the street, glorying, as always, in the fact that it was one of Kensington's most recherché roads and her house one of the most expensive. They can't take *that* away from me, she thought, sticking her scrawny, plastic-covered chest out with pride and trying not to dwell on the fact that if she didn't keep up with the mortgage payments they most certainly could – and would. She simply *had* to get on with this book . . .

And to do that, she simply *had* to sort out a new nanny. The only *slight* hitch was her usual agency's flat refusal to supply her with any more staff. Cassandra twisted her glossy red lips as she recalled that morning's conversation with the head of Spong's Domestics.

'I'm sorry, Mrs Knight,' Mrs Spong had told Cassandra. 'I'm afraid we're unable to recommend you to our clients as employers any more.'

'What the hell do you mean?' Cassandra had raged, embarrassed as well as furious. Spong's was the smartest staff agency in the area. To be treated like this by them was humiliation of the first order, or rather it would be if anyone found out. She'd heard of *employees* being struck from agency books, but never *employers*. Really, this Spong woman had the most ludicrous airs. 'Do you know who I *am*?'

There had been a polite silence before the agency head had, in a tone Cassandra considered downright insolent, informed her that yes, she knew exactly who she was. 'So what's the problem?' Cassandra had demanded.

'The problem, Mrs Knight, is that we have supplied five nannies to you in the last twelve months, none of whom have managed to stay with you – or, more to the point, your son – for a period any longer than two months. It would seem that, ahem,' Mrs Spong cleared her throat, 'perhaps we are unable to supply quite the, um, *calibre* of staff you are looking for.'

'Well, do you have any suggestions as to who might?' Cassandra had demanded. 'I suppose it's back to trawling through *The Lady*,' she had added furiously.

'I think, Mrs Knight,' Mrs Spong had replied, utterly deadpan, 'that you might have more luck with *Soldier of Fortune* magazine.' Cassandra had never heard of this publication, but she liked the sound of it. It must be for rich military types. Another good reason for going to the library. She could save money by helping herself to their copy.

Cassandra swept into Kensington Library and sailed

straight for the shelf with her works on it. She was horrified to see that the whole fat-spined four of them were in residence. Furious, she pulled out *Impossible Lust*, marched purposefully towards the display cabinet at the back of the room, and replaced *Captain Corelli's Mandolin* with it. Who wanted to read about a bloody *mandolin* anyway? Feeling better, Cassandra returned to her shelf and flicked to the front of *The Sins of the Father*, the book that had gone through the five hundred thousand barrier and netted her the Schnabel. She felt comforted by the date stamps tattooing the first and second pages – there had obviously been no shortage of borrowers. Then, absently, she flicked to the back, whose last page, she was disgusted to see, was covered in shaky initials in pale blue Biro; put there, she knew, by old women who couldn't remember what they'd read. Realising that the initials at the back tallied roughly with the number of date stamps at the front, fury consumed Cassandra. If only the old bags would leave her books on the shelf for more than *five seconds*, perhaps some *fashionable* people would have a chance to borrow them.

Her mood did not improve as a stooping old woman with a trembling jaw, thin grey hair and skin like a raisin came shuffling into the room and made the sort of line a shaky, ancient bee might manage in the direction of Cassandra's shelf. Cassandra shrank against the Sidney Sheldons – at least they weren't all out either

– and watched in disgust as the woman took *Impossible Lust* between her liver-spotted fingers and turned to the back page. Apparently unable to decipher her initials, the old woman grunted with satisfaction and shuffled back out with the volume in the direction of the librarians' counter. Cassandra's hand flew up to her skinny throat. She felt violated. Seeing that old woman's filthy old hands over her precious words was, she shuddered to herself, like being *raped.* Bile welled up within her. Cassandra hated most of her readers – the pitiful, pathetic, *poor* masses who bought her books in their hundreds of thousands. But even more despicable were the readers who got her books free from the libraries.

As best she could in her crippling heels, Cassandra rushed dramatically out of the room and into the library foyer, where she paused to catch her breath against the noticeboard. As her hammering heart calmed down, her eyes wandered across the many ruled and drawing-pinned pieces of card offering everything from Opera Camp for musical fives-and-up to wine appreciation courses for under-eights. There was hardly time for a panicked Cassandra to wonder whether she should be sending Zak on the latter before her eye fell upon the bright pink card pinned next to it. English Graduate Seeks . . . Cassandra did a double take. Her eyes narrowed. She read it, then read it again. Finally, she snatched it off the board, slipped it into her plastic zebraskin pocket and left. It was only when she was halfway up Kensington Church Street that she realised she had forgotten to look for *Soldier of Fortune* magazine. But hopefully she wouldn't be needing that now.

Chapter 6

Anna heard the snap of the letterbox and wandered slowly down the long, white-painted corridor to the post lying on the mat. Not *more* wedding invitations for Seb, she thought in amazement, almost buckling under the weight of the thick, cream envelopes.

Over the few weeks since she had moved into his flat, the wedding invitations on Seb's solid Edwardian marble mantelpiece had grown from a mere spinney to a mighty forest. The rather hideous ormulu clock was now entirely obscured by folded cards in Palace script concealing lists from the GTC and directions to receptions – including, once, instructions on how to arrive by helicopter or Gulfstream jet. None of them, however, bore Anna's name. 'And Guest' seemed as far as most of Seb's friends were prepared to go. Given his track record with girls, it was probably a sensible policy; sometimes Anna wondered if he was only with her because he'd been out with everybody else.

Yet soon after they had met – at a wedding party, naturally – Seb had invited her to move in with him, which surely was an encouraging sign. Anna tried not to dwell on the fact that he had more or less had to. Having just lost the latest in the series of post-university, part-time dead end jobs she had taken while trying to get her writing off the ground, Anna could no longer afford to rent a flat of her own and was about to give up on London altogether and go back up north to her family.

It had seemed like a miracle, Seb's offer of free flat space, yet in Anna's more paranoid moments she wondered if he had merely calculated the cost to himself of losing not only her unquestioningly adoring company, but also a free laundress, cleaner and cook. Anna performed these duties in lieu of rent and on the vague understanding that sooner or later she might move out. The feeling that she was living on borrowed time, both in the flat and in his affections, hung heavy. Yet, given that no one else was currently occupying either, squatter's rights didn't seem out of the question.

Anna came to the last of the envelopes. Another frightener. The steady stream of what Anna had come to think of as 'frighteners' – confidence-shattering rejection letters for the many jobs she applied for out of the Monday *Media Guardian* – continued their daily trickle through the front door. Anna swallowed as she bent to retrieve this one. Although it bore no corporate logo and was handwritten, the second-class stamp was a giveaway. Someone obviously thought she was not worth first. Anna slid her nail under the flap, wondering how they had phrased it this time. Overqualified? Underqualified? Overwhelmed by applications?

'I don't believe it,' Anna muttered to herself. She stared at the white piece of paper in her shaking hand, heart thumping. 'I don't *believe* it.' She let out a whoop and rushed into the sitting room where Seb was crouched, fists clenched, in front of the lunchtime racing. Despite his marked and consistent inability to pick a winner, the delusion that he was a keen judge of horseflesh died hard. Perhaps, Anna thought nastily, this explained his attraction to the distinctly equine Brie de Benham. But this was no time to dwell on her, still less on the mysterious, anonymous click-burr answerphone messages that had appeared since the Scottish wedding. 'It's fantastic!' Anna shrieked, jumping up and down in front of the television. 'A writer saw my ad in the library and wants to see me straightaway. I've got to ring immediately. I could go this afternoon. *Wonderful*, isn't it?'

'Not as wonderful as you getting out of the way of the television would be,' Seb drawled. 'Got a hundred on Friend of Dorothy at twelve to one. I could clean up.'

Anna stood aside and watched as Friend of Dorothy started last, reared at the first hedge and finally threw her hapless rider into the water jump. Having rid herself of the unwelcome burden, the horse then galloped merrily down the course, passed the leaders and crossed the finishing line. Seb looked on furiously. 'Bloody useless nag,' he snarled. 'That was the last of my sodding week's allowance. Still, I suppose I can always ask Mummy for some more tonight.'

A 2000-volt electric charge went through Anna. '*Tonight?*' she stammered, the momentous piece of paper in her hand quite forgotten. '*Mummy*?' she croaked.

'Mm, Mummy's coming tonight,' Seb yawned, his eyes still glued to the Newmarket paddock. Swallowing, Anna faced the terrifying prospect of meeting Seb's mother in the flesh. The only contact so far had been her tones, crisp and chill as an Iceberg lettuce on the answerphone, barking out instructions for Seb to call her. 'We're having dinner,' Seb added.

'Why didn't you tell me before?' Anna was panic-stricken in the knowledge that the fridge and cupboards contained little beyond Patum Peperium and a mildewing can of half-eaten Old El Paso Refried Beans.

'Forgot, I suppose,' Seb said, over-casually. 'But you don't have to meet her. Mummy will quite understand if you're out, I can take her to the Ivy or something.'

'But of *course* I want to meet her.' Anna gave Seb a puzzled smile. 'And where else would I go? I *live* here, don't I? There's no need to take her out. I'll *cook*.'

Dinner, it suddenly struck Anna, was a cast-iron if not a Le Creuset opportunity to impress Seb's mother with her cooking skills. Or at least the ones she planned hastily to acquire with the help of a notebook and an hour's browsing in the cookery section of W. H. Smith. 'I'll do the shopping on my way back.'

'Back from where?' asked Seb.

'From here.' Anna waved the letter at him. Surely he hadn't forgotten about her interview already?

Seb looked at Anna blankly.

Anna had been up and down the smart Kensington street three times now. People were starting to appear at the corners of the windows to stare. Anna, however, had no option other than to continue squinting at their houses. For, among the figures painted neatly in black on the white pair of pillars framing each imposing doorway, number 54 did not seem to register.

Where 54 should, by process of elimination, have been, the letters Liv were painted. Liv. Odd name for a house, thought Anna. Then it hit her. LIV. Fifty-four in Roman numerals. *Of course*. A *tad* pretentious for a house name, perhaps; she hoped Cassandra had a classically educated postman. But then, most of the postmen round here were probably out of work ex-students like herself. Post-graduates, as it were.

Despite its number – or was it its name? – the house looked just like the rest of the street. A tall, wide slice of West London real estate heaven, its stucco gleaming white in the sunshine, its shining black railings thick and bumpy with a century and a half of paint. An Upstairs Downstairs house with a basement kitchen and five floors above it, their windows decreasing in size and grandeur towards the top. Anna went slowly up the paved path, jumping as the gate clanged spitefully behind her, and, using one of the many pieces of brass door furniture on offer, knocked.

'Yars?' The black-painted door swung back to reveal an overalled woman with electric yellow hair and a suspicious expression. 'Can I ewp you?' She shook her peacock-blue feather duster inquiringly.

'Er, I've come to see Cassandra Knight,' said Anna. 'I've got an appointment.'

'Carm in. You'll 'ave to wait in the kitchin. Mrs Knoight's busy at the mowment.'

In the kitchen, airforce-blue panelling coated every vertical surface including, Anna was interested to observe, the front of the dishwasher. A single lily stood atop the vast steel fridge. The black stone table was supported by skinny chrome legs fashioned into spirals; arranged in precisely-measured ranks beneath it were two rows of three tractor-seat stools in chrome. Anna heaved herself on to one, aware she had completely disrupted whatever visual concept prevailed.

The emphatic lack of any hint of food provoked a raging hunger in Anna's stomach. But the disproportionately vast antique station clock on the wall was to measure out a further lonely, unrefreshed half hour before footsteps could be heard on the stairs. As Anna sat, paralysed, in her tractor seat, an extremely thin woman with white-blonde hair in a straight, short bob, vast black sunglasses and a white waffle bathrobe wafted through the doorway into the kitchen.

'Cassandra Knight,' announced the woman, sticking out a hand so thin it was practically transparent and as chill as if it had just come out of the freezer. Anna gazed at the bathrobe with admiration. So this was what real writers wore to work in.

She felt instantly disadvantaged by her own hot and sticky palm and not being able to see Cassandra's eyes properly. She could sense them moving behind the sunglasses, as cold and invisible as fish at the bottom of a pond. The lenses were as impenetrable as they were inexplicable. Perhaps, Anna concluded, they were to combat the glare of Cassandra's computer screen.

'Yes, I recognise you from your book jacket photographs,' Anna smiled, hoping to ingratiate herself. Panic flared in her stomach when, instead of looking flattered, Cassandra frowned.

'Which one?' she demanded imperiously.

Anna's mind whirled. She sensed something was at

stake. One false move and all could be lost. 'Er, the one on *Impossible Lust*,' she hedged, plumping for the photograph which, when flicking through the volumes in the bookshop, had struck her as the softest lit, most touched up and generally most flattering. She had guessed right. Cassandra preened.

'Yes, Tony – Snowdon – did quite a reasonable job on that one,' Cassandra purred. 'And he did say I was one of the most *challenging* people he had ever photographed. Let's get down to business, shall we?' she suddenly barked. 'I haven't got all day. You want this job, I take it?'

Anna swallowed. 'I'd love to work for you. It would be a wonderful training for *any* writer . . .' She stopped as Cassandra held up a hand.

'I *am not* offering a writing course,' she snapped. 'In my letter to you I said I wanted a *general assistant*. To assist me, er, generally.'

'Of course,' Anna echoed. 'A general assistant.'

'*Precisely*,' said Cassandra, inhaling so hard on her cigarette her eyes watered. 'An, um, *general* assistant is exactly what I want. I take it you're quite *versatile*?' Two plumes of smoke came flying out of her nostrils.

Anna jerked her head up and down eagerly. 'Absolutely. I can type, research . . . even write,' she added anxiously.

Cassandra nodded curtly.

'How are you with children?' she demanded.

'*Children?*' Anna vaguely recalled from the potted biographies on the book jackets that Cassandra had a son. Anyone working at close quarters with her would of course have to get along with her family. 'Oh, fine,' she stammered, recalling the occasional bout of unenjoyable teenage babysitting.

'Good,' said Cassandra, grinding her cigarette out. 'The job involves quite a lot of contact with Zak. He's, um, between nannies at the moment. You – ahem, I mean, whoever did the job – would have to help with the school run, his supper, that sort of thing.'

'I see,' said Anna, the dimmer switch of her enthusiasm turning down a jot. 'But most of the job would be helping *you*, wouldn't it?'

Either Cassandra was nodding ferociously, Anna thought, or she was tossing that highly flammable-looking platinum bob out of the way as she ignited another Marlboro. 'Absolutely,' Cassandra confirmed. 'You'd be helping me an *enormous* amount.' She paused and pressed her lips together as the smoke poured out of her nose. 'But of course if you feel it's not quite right for you . . .'

'Oh, no, I didn't mean . . .' stammered Anna, panicking. 'I'm absolutely happy to do whatever . . .' One child, after all, surely couldn't be too much trouble.

'*Good*,' said Cassandra, satisfied. She stared at her hands, pushing an amethyst the size of a door handle slowly round her forefinger. 'Well, you seem all right to me. You can start tomorrow, if you like. The sooner the better as far as I'm concerned.'

Anna felt a huge grin split her face. She was just about to stammer her thanks when Cassandra said, 'We haven't discussed pay.' She then named a weekly sum so ludicrously low that Anna gasped.

'I can't possibly live on that.'

'You won't have to. The job is, of course, live-in.'

Of course, thought Anna. That explained the awful money. Living in would be much cheaper for Cassandra. But surely it was unusual for assistants to live in? Nannies, of course, did it all the time. But she wasn't a nanny.

'I didn't realise.' She spoke slowly, but Anna's heart started to slam against her chest like a moth trying to reach a lamp behind a windowpane.

'Well, *obviously* it's live-in,' snapped Cassandra. 'Children are a twenty-four hour job, you know. As is writing, of course,' she added hurriedly. 'You never know when the muse will strike.'

Half an hour later, Anna found herself standing, confused, beside the ready-packed salads in Ken High Street Marks and Spencer. She could not concentrate. Her ears were still ringing from Cassandra's furious reaction to being told she would think about her job offer.

'Most people would give their eye teeth to live for

free in a house like this,' Cassandra had snapped. 'I would, for a start,' she added acidly.

'Of course, it's the most wonderful house and most fantastic opportunity . . .' Anna had stammered.

'So what's stopping you?' Cassandra's eyes, turning from cold fish to lasers, blazed through the sunglasses.

'I need to discuss it with my, um, boyfriend,' Anna had faltered.

'Your *boyfriend*? Can't you make your own decisions? Christ, if I asked my husband what he thought *I* should do with my life, I'd be permanently making full English breakfasts in between giving him blow jobs.'

But Anna, albeit shakily, stood her ground. She would let Cassandra know in the morning. She was not sure she wanted to move out of Seb's so soon. And anyway, there was always the possibility – admittedly remote – that the prospect of her leaving would make him finally lay his cards on the table as far as their relationship was concerned.

She lunged for a bag of Mixed Herb salad, grabbed a box of baby potatoes and headed finally towards the checkout.

'Where the hell have you been?' Seb demanded as she staggered through the door at precisely the same time that the bulging plastic bags, strained beyond endurance, finally burst their flimsy moorings and spilled their contents all over the hall.

'For my interview, of course,' Anna said. 'I got the job,' she added, scrabbling around on the floor in pursuit of several mushrooms making good their escape.

'Did you get any wine?'

'What? Oh, yes, Chardonnay,' Anna told him abstractedly. 'But they want me to live in,' she added, returning to the matter at hand.

'*What?*' said Seb in outraged tones.

'I *know*,' Anna said, relief surging through her system. 'I mean,' she added, 'they *do* live in W8, just off Ken Church Street, and their house *is* enormous, but . . . *oh*,' Anna gasped, gazing rapturously at Seb. 'I'm so *glad*. I thought you wouldn't care . . .'

'Of course I care. Chardonnay's so *naff*, for Christ's sake. Why the hell couldn't you have got Chablis?'

Anna stared at Seb in disbelief. Had he not understood a word she had said? 'So you don't care one way or the other?'

'Of course I care,' Seb snarled, furiously thrusting a long-fingered hand through his unbrushed hair. 'I don't want Mummy to think she's at a hen night in a Peckham wine bar, do I?'

'Did you hear what I just said to you?' gasped Anna. 'I've been offered a live-in job. Do you want me to stay here with you or not?'

'We'll talk about it later,' said Seb. 'There's too much

to do just now.' He disappeared into the sitting room, switched on the television and put his feet up on the sofa arm. Whatever needed doing, someone else was evidently going to do it. Can't imagine who *that* might be, thought Anna, gathering the bags up and heading crossly for the kitchen.

There was something about the way Seb's mother rushed at him as if he were the first day of the Harvey Nicks sale that confirmed Anna's worst fears. Lady Lavenham was, Anna realised, a full-on, fully-paid-up Son Worshipper.

Anna could recognise the breed from a cruising height of thirty-three thousand feet. She had, after all, encountered them before. The boyfriend's mother before last had been one; a Welsh Italian who had made almost nightly phone calls and who had insisted on driving up from Cardiff to college to comfort Roberto practically every time he sneezed.

'Call me Diana,' Seb's mother barked to Anna on arrival. The coda, 'If you dare', hung unspoken in the air of the hallway, air that had suddenly thickened with expensive-smelling scent.

Anna had been expecting trouble. But she hadn't expected it to look like this. Diana was about as far removed from the tweedy battleaxe Anna had been anticipating as Michelle Pfeiffer was from Margaret Rutherford. It wasn't just that Anna felt wrong-footed by Seb's mother. She felt wrong-haired, wrong-make-upped, wrong-dressed and most of all wrong-shoed. Diana Lavenham had the type of long, thin feet that even looked graceful in wellies. A fully-paid-up Fulham blonde, she had thick wedges of expensive hair that shone brilliantly in the light of the hall chandelier, as did the single, polished platinum ring hanging loosely on one long, tanned hand. She had expensive skin too, opaque, glowing and virtually unlined from a rich diet of face cream. Seb, who had suddenly shot into the kitchen, now emerged sporting an apron, a tea towel over his shoulder and an air of cheerful culinary professionalism. 'Anna, will you take Mummy into the sitting room while I get on with supper?'

'Darling, you're *so* clever,' Diana purred at her son as she followed Anna down the hallway. 'Are you sure it's not *too* much trouble for you?'

'No trouble at all, Mummy, honestly.'

That much was true, at least, Anna fumed silently.

Her mouth set rigidly into a smile, Diana regarded Anna with narrowed eyes as they sat at opposite ends of the leather sofa. The silence roared in Anna's nervous ears.

'Tell me about yourself,' Diana said creamily. 'Basty tells me you want to be a writer. I'd love to see some of your work.'

'*Basty?*' echoed Anna, squirming at the thought of a

stranger knowing such an intimate thing. Who the hell was Basty? Damn Seb for telling them, whoever they were.

'Se*bast*ian?' said Diana in the bright voice of a careworker trying to communicate with a senile idiot. 'My *son*?' She blinked repeatedly, her mouth turned up at the corners. 'I call him that because I can't bear the thought of anyone calling him *Seb. Ghastly.* Makes him sound like an *estate agent.*' As opposed to an estate owner, I suppose, Anna thought.

Seb appeared. 'Almost there with dinner,' he said, obviously lying. Anna wondered if he had even managed to find his way into the packets of salmon fillets. Heaven knew what he thought the carton of ready-made hollandaise was. Custard, probably.

'I'll come and have a look, shall I?' She rose to her feet, for once grateful for the chance to slave over a hot stove. Anything to escape from this woman's icy, interrogative glare.

Following Anna's intervention, dinner was soon served. Throughout the meal, Diana chatted tinklingly yet pointedly to Seb about people Anna didn't know. 'Yes, darling, they've just bought a house in what they call up-and-coming Acton but honestly, I ask you. *Acton?* I mean, where *is* Acton? *What* is Acton? Not even on the *A–Z*, is it?'

Anna opened her mouth. Here, at last, was something she could contribute to the discussion. 'It *is* supposed to be getting smarter, I believe. I have a friend who lives there.'

'Oh really?' Diana had still not looked at her once since they sat down at table. She did not look at her now. 'And where do *you* live, Anna?'

Anna watched Diana stab a baby potato with her fork. Surely Seb had *told* her they lived together? She shrank into silence and waited for him to take the initiative. It was up to him to explain their cohabiting arrangements to his mother. Who must, even if she didn't know, at least suspect it.

But the silence remained unbroken. Looking from Anna's flushed face to Seb's suddenly grey one, Diana raised a faintly amused eyebrow.

'*Kensington,*' Seb burst out suddenly. 'Anna lives in Kensington. Just off Ken Church Street, actually. With a writer. Anna's her assistant.'

Diana looked coolly at Anna. Was it Anna's imagination, or did those narrow blue eyes hold a triumphal glitter? Diana smiled. 'How *fascinating*.'

'How *could* you?' Anna screeched at Seb after Diana, who had lingered as long as she possibly could in the obvious hope that Anna would leave first, had finally descended to her Dorchester-bound Dial-A-Cab.

Seb shrugged, unrepentant. 'Well, what was I supposed to tell her? It's not as if we're married, is it? Anyway, I've done you a favour. She owns the place, after all. If I told her you lived here, she'd probably start charging you rent.'

'How *thoughtful* of you,' Anna snapped, having searched in vain for some appropriately reductive retort. She tried to console herself with the thought that even Oscar Wilde would have been stumped with Seb; all the *bons mots* in the world, after all, failed to get Bosie to behave himself.

'But it's probably time you moved out anyway,' Seb muttered, not meeting her eye.

Anna felt suddenly sick. Here it was, then. It had finally come, the moment she had always been expecting, yet never really believed would happen. She was being given her marching orders. Like an employer dismissing an unsatisfactory servant, Seb had sacked her without batting an eyelid. There had been a steeliness to his tone which suggested pleading for clemency would be useless. Not that she felt like pleading. She felt like taking the untouched hollandaise sauce and pouring it all over him. Especially when the mysterious person who refused to leave answerphone messages flickered once more into her mind.

Retreating to the bathroom, Anna slammed the door and set the water thundering from the taps to disguise the sobbing that suddenly overwhelmed her.

It was the humiliation. The helplessness. All made so much worse by the sight of her naked body in the bath. The roll of flesh seemed bigger than ever; her stomach rose above the waterline like an island. An *island*. Anna sighed, the thought flitting into her head and then out again of Jamie and what he might be doing now.

She lay in the bath, hot and shiny with misery and sausage pink with a fury that mixed with the steam rising from the foam-free water. The final insult was that Seb had, at some point during the day, used up the last of the Floris Syringa her mother had given her for her birthday. Her mother would never meet Seb now. But it was unlikely either would have relished the occasion.

One good thing, Anna tried to persuade herself, was that if she wasn't going to be the wife of a sewage millionaire, at least she could take the job with Cassandra. This prospect, though it lacked the platinum charge card, sports coupé and season ticket to Champneys that went with the former career option, at least offered a large and luxurious house in one of fashionable Kensington's chic-est streets. Not to mention an apprenticeship with a successful writer. She'd show Seb. *And* his stuck-up horse of a mother. Anna permitted herself a delicious few minutes imagining their faces when she hit the bestseller lists.

If the job was still available, that was. Anna glanced at the watch on top of her pile of clothes on the loo seat. Just past midnight. Too late to ring Cassandra now. Please God she hadn't found someone else. She'd ring her first thing in the morning. In the meantime, Anna decided, as the silent sobs overtook her once more, she'd just sit in the bath and weep.

Chapter 7

Usually, Cassandra never saw first thing in the morning. She usually hit it around fourth or fifth thing, but this particular antemeridian was different. She'd had to get up *ridiculously* early to do an interview. In the normal course of events, Cassandra loved nothing better than talking endlessly about herself to journalists – friendly *OK!* and *Hello!* ones in particular. But there was nothing friendly about the sharp-faced, skinny woman sitting opposite her on the cowskin sofa with a tape recorder, a notebook and a sceptical twist to her lips. Her eyes intermittently darted round the room, focusing in on, Cassandra was cringingly certain, every surface left respectively undusted, bashed and unwiped by Lil as she had made her morning rounds. That was the trouble with minimalism; there was nowhere to run when it came to hiding dirt.

Lil herself had already been grilled; as Cassandra had clumped down the stripped wood stairs to greet her inquisitor, she had overheard the cleaner being questioned about her mistress's working hours and daily routine. Although not a religious woman, Cassandra had sent a heartfelt prayer heavenwards to whichever benevolent deity had allowed her to appear on the scene before Lil had got on to the breakfast gin and tonics.

A curse on her publishers, though, thought Cassandra, grimacing. The deal that had eventually been hammered out between her agent and the increasingly irascible people who commissioned her books had been that, the continued non-appearance of Cassandra's expected new manuscript notwithstanding, the planned publicity for the novel should continue to go ahead. Hence the presence of this spiky girl in her sitting room.

Cassandra sighed inwardly and gazed glassily at the journalist. The pre-interview nerve-soothing double gin had not only affected her concentration, but had dealt a temporary death blow to her ability to see straight.

'Sorry, can you rephrase that?' she asked.

The journalist looked astonished. 'Er, yes. I just asked you what the name of your son was.'

'Zachary Alaric St Felix Knight.' Alaric St Felix had been the dashing hero of *Impossible Lust*, in whose heady, thrilling, champagne-and-cash-flooded wake (and particularly the latter) Zak had been conceived. Repeating Alaric's name only reinforced Cassandra's awareness that she had so far failed to invent a hero to rival him.

'How do you *cope* with him?' the journalist asked next.

Cassandra's heart skipped a beat. What *exactly* had this woman heard about Zak? Surely she didn't know about the dreadful events of yesterday. 'Theft, madam, is a criminal offence no matter *whose* son you are,' that ghastly little Boots store detective had snapped. 'How *could* you?' Cassandra had furiously admonished Zak all the way home. 'Stealing like a common criminal.'

It wasn't the *criminal* bit she minded – heaven knew, half the squillionaires in the City were crooks and she was fervently hoping Zak might join their ranks one day. It was the *common*. And from *Boots*, for Christ's sake. If Zak *had* to steal, he could at least have chosen Harvey Nicks.

'Cope?' she asked suspiciously. Was this woman trying to catch her out?

'Well, we've talked about your bestsellers and how you write them, but we haven't touched on how you also manage to run a house this size *and* have a family life. Not to mention how you keep yourself in such great shape.'

Relief swept through Cassandra. This was more like

it. 'Oh, well, I find getting up at five and doing a couple of hours on the treadmill generally does the trick,' she simpered. 'I try and read all the papers at the same time.'

The journalist looked astonished. 'But surely you have some help with *something*? Do you have a nanny even?'

Cassandra shook her head vigorously. 'No,' she smiled. 'No help at all.'

'Why on earth not?'

Because that stupid fat Anna girl had had the unbelievable cheek to practically *beg* for the job and then announce, cool as a Decleor face pack, that she'd *think* about it, Cassandra thought viciously whilst training a look of melting sincerity on the journalist. 'I suppose I can't bear to think of my child being brought up by *anyone* else but me,' she said silkily. 'It would be *desperately* sad to miss these crucial years when his character is forming, don't you think? He's so independent, Zak. Such an amazing little personality already.'

The journalist nodded sympathetically; this argument, Cassandra was gratified to see, went down much better with her than it did with Mrs Gosschalk. For Zak had taken full advantage of the interregnum in nannies and had, besides the unfortunate Boots incident, recently been conspicuous by his absence at school. The result was that the headmistress's office had been on the phone again complaining about his behaviour. Cassandra's blustering defence that it was proof of her son's extraordinarily entrepreneurial outlook and incredible creative spirit had cut no ice with Mrs Gosschalk, although she had conceded 'extraordinary' and 'incredible' were accurate descriptions.

'And then of course,' said the journalist, 'you're half of a high-profile marriage.'

Half, thought Cassandra indignantly. If you were talking profile, she was a good *two-thirds* of it, thank you very much. What on earth had Jett done this side of the Boer War? She very much doubted the re-formed Solstice would be a stadium-filler. If the tepid press reaction their reunion had prompted so far was anything to go by, they'd be lucky to be a stocking filler.

'Yes. Jett and I are truly blessed,' Cassandra cooed through gritted teeth, 'because, apart from being lovers, we're such good friends. We're very close. There's hardly ever a cross word . . .'

The sound of the slammed front door interrupted her musings. 'Sandra?' roared a voice. 'Where the hell are you? You've got to get someone else to take that *goddamn* brat to school. He's doing my goddamn head in.'

The journalist stared in astonishment.

'In here, darling,' trilled Cassandra, faking a sudden attack of coughing in the forlorn hope of drowning

Jett's yells. The journalist's thin lips curved slowly upward.

'Hang on, I'm getting a goddamn drink first,' yelled Jett, thundering down the stairs to the kitchen. 'Zak made me park the goddamn Rolls round the corner *again*,' he bellowed from below. 'Said he was embarrassed in case the other kids saw it. And when I told him he should be goddamn *pleased*, not embarrassed, that his father had achieved enough to have a Rolls,' Jett continued, his voice approaching up the kitchen stairs, accompanied by the rattling of ice cubes, 'Zak said he was embarrassed because the Rolls was so *uncool* and *all the other kids' parents had groovy four-wheel drives*.'

Cassandra had now coughed so much her face was red and streaming. That her efforts had been utterly in vain was obvious from the way the journalist was checking the red Record button of her tape recorder and scribbling manically on her pad. As Jett's raddled visage appeared round the sitting-room door, Cassandra was momentarily torn in deciding which of them she wanted to murder the most.

'What's going on?' he demanded, looking from Cassandra to the journalist. 'Not another of your *goddamn* Mystic Meg sessions, for Christ's sake.'

'If you're inquiring as to whether this is one of my metamorphic technique lessons, then the answer is no,' said Cassandra, icily. 'I'm being *interviewed*.'

The revelation that he was in close proximity to a publicity opportunity had a more electric effect on Jett than the famous incident in Athens, Georgia, 1978, when his guitar had been accidentally (or was it? he was still not sure) plugged into the mains. Even by his optimistic lights, the reaction of the music press to the news Solstice were re-forming could hardly be described as ecstatic, with the result that 'Sex and Sexibility' needed more of a push than overdue quadruplets. He could not afford to let golden opportunities like this pass.

'Hi. Jett St Edmunds,' Jett said, stretching out a hand to the journalist. Not bad, he thought. A bit skinny and pasty, perhaps. 'And you are?' he asked, pulling in his stomach and moving closer.

'Brie de Benham. *Daily Telegraph*.'

'Hi, Brie. Know the name,' Jett drawled, chewing on a non-existent piece of chewing gum.

Yes, of course you do, Cassandra only just stopped herself saying. *From the Waitrose cheese counter*. She could spot Jett's thunder-stealing game a mile off. She was aware that 'Sex and Sexibility' was hardly lined up to be the Christmas number one, but she'd be damned if it got publicity, however badly needed, at the expense of her new book.

'How's it going?' Jett asked, fixing Brie with his most charismatic stare.

'Fine,' Brie smirked. 'Miss Knight has been telling

me how she gets up at five and reads all the newspapers while she's working out in the gym.'

Jett stared at his wife, who returned his gaze unblinkingly. 'Gets up at *five*?' he chuckled. 'Oh yes, she gets up at *five*, all right. Five in the goddamn *afternoon*, that is. And working out? The only thing of Sandra's that gets regular exercise is her goddamn credit card.'

In the hall, the telephone began to ring. Both Jett and Cassandra held their ground, locking eyes, neither willing to give up the valuable field of potential publicity to the other. 'Phone's ringing,' smirked Jett at his wife. 'Probably that goddamn Gosschalk chick. She's never off the blower.'

Silently telling herself she was doing it for her son, Cassandra gritted her teeth and stalked out of the room. Jett promptly sat down on the sofa beside Brie de Benham, who immediately rammed her elbows together to make the most of her skinny cleavage.

'*Ass Me Anything*,' he breathed. Might as well get in a plug for the album straightaway.

'OK.' Brie switched on her tape recorder again. 'Is it true that Jett St Edmunds isn't your real name and you're really called Gerald Sowerbutts?'

'*What?* What are you goddamn talking about?'

'You said to ask you anything.'

'*Ass* me anything. Name of the new goddamn album.'

'Oh. Right. Well, anyway, is it true? About the name?'

'Of course it bloody isn't,' snarled Jett. 'I'm called St Edmunds because I come from there.'

'From Bury St Edmunds?' At least, he thought, she'd got off the Gerald bit.

'You gottit, baby.'

This was, in fact, merely the version of the truth preferred by the record company who, having decided to ritz up Jett's Christian name, completed the exercise by surnaming him after the town where their A&R man first discovered him performing 'House of the Rising Sun' *a capella* to an audience of two at a bus stop. Jett had objected to the name at first because he thought the town was pronounced Bury Street Edmunds, but preferred the story, as well as the rest of the tricky subject of his origins, to remain cloaked in mystery. He decided to change the subject.

'And do you ever take your sunglasses off?'

Through the mirrored shades Jett invariably wore to do everything but sleep in, he saw Brie looking at him coolly. 'Take them *off*?' He laughed theatrically. 'Honey, I'm in showbiz.' Brie smirked.

'Is it true what I've heard about you women journalists?' Jett murmured, moving his mouth close to her ear. 'That you keep vibrating pagers in your knickers so you get a thrill when someone calls you?' He placed a hand heavy with silver skull rings on her thin, black-nyloned knee and began to work it slowly up her thigh. Hearing the phone slam back down in the hall, he hastily took it off again.

Cassandra swept back into the room looking triumphant. 'Thank God,' she declaimed. 'That girl's finally seen sense. She's moving in tomorrow morning.'

'What girl?' asked Jett, looking hopeful.

'The fat one who *inexplicably* lives in Mayfair. She's coming to be the nanny.' Joy was not a regular visitor to Cassandra's fearful heart, but now she positively fizzed with it. No more interminable games of Monopoly with Zak, although it *was* gratifying how good he was at it. No more Harry bloody Potter at bedtime. Best of all, no more calls from Mrs Gosschalk.

'The nanny?' echoed Brie, faintly mocking. 'So you're getting some help after all.' Cassandra did not like the tone of her voice.

'Not at all,' she snapped. 'This girl is an Oxbridge graduate. She is coming to be my assistant. It's just that,' Cassandra added in an undertone, 'she's going to be assisting me in rather more ways than she bargained for.'

The following morning, Anna let herself out of Seb's flat for the last time. As she headed for the bus stop and the Kensington-bound No. 10 she worked out that probably the most valuable thing she possessed was an old beaver coat which had a marked tendency to moult. It had been the only thing Seb had ever given her.

Apart, that was, from an inferiority complex the size of Manchester.

Her recent emotional traumas, however, had not remotely affected her ability to be everywhere far too early. It made sense in a way; she had always suspected that her tendency to be unfashionably punctual had sprung from a lack of self-esteem. Following Seb's recent antics, it was surprising she wasn't even earlier – Cassandra had told her to present herself and her belongings at eight o'clock sharp, and here she was at a positively devil-may-care five to.

For reassurance more than warmth, Anna huddled further into the depths of the tatty coat. Seb had told her it gave her a Russian air. Doubtless, she thought sourly, he had meant less Anna Karenina than head-scarved babushka with wrinkles deep enough to abseil down. *Bastard.*

Anna lifted the fountain-pen shaped knocker and let it crash back against the door. Following some vague sounds of shouting from within, it was opened by a man wearing studded black leather boots and a T-shirt bearing the Dayglo green legend. 'My Probation Officer Went To London And All I Got Was This F***ing T-Shirt'. Given its thinness and his age, his hair was longer than seemed advisable; his creased and baggy face was less lived in than marked for demolition.

'Your dog's obviously very fond of you.' He looked pointedly at her upper thighs.

Anna glanced at her legs in mingled panic and fury. The coat had been shedding all over her. Her best Joseph trousers were covered in short black hairs.

'Oh, it's not a dog,' Anna said. 'That's my beaver.' The moment the words were out of her mouth she regretted them.

'Well, I can see we're going to get on splendidly,' the man remarked, a broad grin splitting his stubbly face. He thrust out a hand. 'You must be Anna. I'm Jett St Edmunds, Sandra's husband.' The palm that greeted Anna was as hot and moist as rice pudding. And rice pudding was one of the few – very few – desserts that Anna had never liked.

'Stick your bags in the hall. Sandra's in there.' Beckoning her in, Jett gestured at a door that led off the hall. 'She's not,' he added, with a conspiratorial wink, 'in a very good mood.'

Anna entered the vast white sitting room to be greeted by the sight of a bathrobed Cassandra prone on a chaise longue. She was wearing a sleep mask that failed to disguise that, beneath it, her expression was thunderous. Beside her on the floor lay a copy of the *Daily Telegraph*.

Cassandra raised herself a little. 'You *bastard*,' she hissed. 'How dare you come in here after what you've done. You've ruined *everything*.'

Anna swallowed, scared as well as confused. 'Um, your husband told me . . .'

Cassandra whipped off her mask and stared at her in fury. 'Oh, it's *you*,' she said grudgingly. 'At *last*. I've got to go out to an extremely important meeting.'

Rather like those people who die and come back to life, Anna had a vague impression of lots of brilliant white. Rugs, cushions, curtains – apart from the two cowskin sofas, all was white. The floorboards were pale and interesting, as perhaps they were in heaven, Anna thought. Heaven, after all, was bound to be stylistically unimpeachable.

A small boy suddenly burst shouting into the room and stopped stock still when he saw Anna. He regarded her with approximately the same level of warmth and enthusiasm generally accorded to a heap of dog faeces. *After* one has just stepped in it.

'This,' said Cassandra triumphantly, her *froideur* melting like ice-cream in the sun, 'is Zak.'

The boy wore grey tweed plus fours, a matching short jacket, black boots with buttons on the side and, above his thick white-blond basin cut, a ribboned straw boater. He bore an equally close resemblance to his mother and the pre-Ekaterinburg Czarevich.

'Don't you look wonderful?' smiled Anna, encouragingly. 'Very Railway Children.'

'What's Railway Children?' demanded the boy.

Cassandra smiled indulgently. 'I'm afraid, Anna, that the only railway Zak is familiar with is the first class Eurostar to Paris. But St Midas's uniform *is* splendid, isn't it? *Everyone* recognises it – let's face it, there's no point shelling out four thousand a term otherwise, is there?'

'I suppose not,' Anna agreed, faintly puzzled. She had always imagined high school fees reflected the quality of the teaching rather than the complexity of the uniform. And had Midas really been a saint?

'*One* of the governors,' Cassandra added, 'recently tried to vote to have Edwardian underwear as well but some of us felt that was a little, well, *excessive*. I believe,' she dropped her voice, 'that the gentleman in question is under investigation by the Kensington police at the moment . . . But it's a marvellous school. Very *media*. Half the BBC top brass send their children there, not to mention practically every national newspaper editor.' She flashed Anna a conspiratorial grin. 'The opportunities for *networking* are excellent.'

'That must be very useful for you,' Anna remarked politely.

Cassandra's face froze. 'Not for *me*,' she snapped. 'For *him*. You can never start too early, you know. After all, the children at St Midas's now will probably be shaping the future of the country in twenty years' time.'

Anna shot a glance at Zak who had by now climbed on the cowskin sofa and was jumping manically up and down on it with his boots on. It was not a comforting thought. Aware he was being watched, Zak then leapt down with a clatter on to the wooden floorboards and started kicking Anna's handbag with the tip of his boot. 'I'm Dennis Wise,' he shouted.

'Don't do that, darling,' Cassandra murmured, as Anna bent and pulled her bag out of the way. 'Those boots are very expensive.'

'Is *she* my new nanny?' Zak pouted, looking sulkily at Anna.

'*Yes*,' said Cassandra crisply.

'*Not exactly*,' said Anna at the same time.

'Sort of,' Cassandra compromised, giving Anna a dazzling, don't-argue-with-me smile.

There was an uncomfortable silence.

'She's not very *pretty*,' said Zak loudly, staring boldly at Anna. 'But she's got big tits. So you won't need to send her to the hospital like Imelda, Mummy.'

Another uncomfortable silence. Bubbling under with rage, Anna felt she could not let this pass.

'What does he mean?' she asked. Cassandra had reddened slightly.

'Oh, he's referring to an operation one of his former nannies had,' Cassandra said with a rather forced lightness. '*That's enough, darling*,' she mouthed.

'Mummy wanted to have a tit job but didn't dare,' Zak announced loudly. 'So she made Imelda have one first to see what it looked like and to see if it hurt.'

Anna was so astonished she forgot she was angry. Meanwhile, the unspeakable brat was speaking again.

'Has Daddy tried to shag you yet?' he demanded

excitedly, fiddling covertly with his genitals through his pocket. 'Don't worry. He will. He even shagged Imelda. Particularly after the tit job, even though she looked like Pandora Peaks.'

'*Zak!*' shrieked Cassandra. 'My son has a very lively imagination,' she added hastily. As Zak still rummaged frantically in his pocket, Anna felt her apprehension grow.

'Would you like to see my scab?' asked Zak, his hand emerging from his pocket balancing a matchbox on his palm. A matchbox which, Anna noticed, bore the logo of the Hotel Eden Roc, Cap d'Antibes. With a flick of his pink thumb, Zak pushed it open to reveal a very large, very green and very nasty-looking scab, with specks of blood and mucus still attached. It looked very fresh, although, darting a quick glance at Zak's smooth golden knees, Anna was unable to see where it had come from.

'It looks very painful,' she said. 'You must have been very brave when it came off.'

'Oh, it's not *mine*,' said Zak, faintly contemptuous. 'It's Otto Greatorex's. And *no*, actually, he wasn't *at all* brave. It took three of us to hold him down, but *I* ripped it off.' He grinned at Anna, revealing gappy white teeth set in very pink gums. Behind him, Cassandra let out a light laugh.

'Such a *character* already, isn't he?' she smiled at Anna.

'You can say that again,' growled Jett, suddenly entering the room behind them, the metalwork on his boots jangling irritably. 'Look what he's done *now*.'

The creature straining to be released from his hairy arms was not instantly recognisable. It looked, Anna thought, rather like a very large, very bald and very angry rat. 'This,' said Jett, holding the furious animal up so it clawed wildly at the air, 'is what remains of Lady Snitterton's Bengal Blue after Zak's had a go at it with my Remington.'

Chapter 8

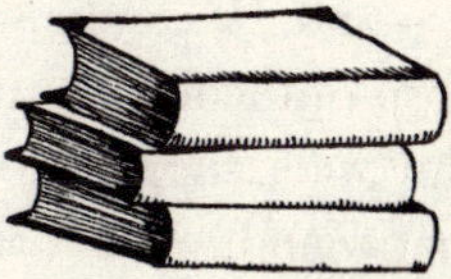

The room contained a desk, a hard chair and a sofabed that had clearly seen better days. Judging from the cracked and peeling paintwork, it was obviously between decorating jobs as well. Anna looked round in admiration. So *this* was where Cassandra did her writing. *This* was the inner sanctum.

'What do you think?' asked Cassandra.

'Wonderfully *plain*,' Anna said brightly. 'I imagine it's a marvellous place to concentrate.'

'*Concentrate?*' Despite her permanent efforts to keep her face as expressionless and therefore wrinkle-free as possible, Cassandra could not prevent a slight frown rippling across her forehead. 'Are you *Buddhist* or something?' she demanded, realising that, once her first, fierce instinctive opposition to anything unusual or foreign had worn off, she rather hoped so. After all, Baba Anstruther was always banging on about her wretched New Age Italian au pair, the sum total of whose duties seemed to be floating around the school gates in white, reeking of essential oils and flirting wildly with the house husbands. Cassandra stared thoughtfully at Anna. Yes, a Buddhist would suit her very well. Very *Absolutely Fabulous* – and, Cassandra wondered, straining her sketchy grasp of theology to its limits, weren't they the ones who were supposed to renounce all worldly goods? That would sort out any remaining ifs and buts over Anna's wages very nicely.

'Oh, you're not a Buddhist,' Cassandra said, disappointed, as Anna shook her head. 'New Age then?' she hedged hopefully. 'Oh well, I'll leave you to make yourself at home,' she announced finally, a petulant note in her voice.

'You mean this is my *room*?' gasped Anna in horror.

'Yes, what did you think it was? A very *comfortable* room this is,' Cassandra said defensively, in the face of all visual evidence to the contrary. She sat on the sofabed and bounced gingerly up and down on it. A hollow rattle ensued. 'One of the best addresses in Kensington.'

'I thought it was your writing room,' Anna said boldly.

Cassandra's reptilian eyelids flickered for a moment. Better not push it *too* far, she realised. Time to concede a point or two; after all, she didn't want the wretched girl leaving. Not now she'd gone to the *enormous* trouble of showing her all over the house. But the sooner she snapped out of the idea of being a bestselling writer, the better. Everyone knew writers didn't look like *that*.

'Well, it's not,' Cassandra said curtly. 'My writing room is just off my bedroom, as it happens.'

What was the creature saying now? Where was her bathroom? *Her* bathroom? What did she think this was, bloody Claridges? 'You use the *downstairs* loo,' Cassandra snapped. 'And there's a shower in the garage.'

'But . . .'

Closing the subject with a wave of her bejewelled hand, Cassandra led the way to the considerably warmer and smarter lower floor where she flung open a door to unleash a blaze of colour.

'Zak's room. Marvellous, don't you think?'

Anna blinked. 'It's very, um, *bright*.'

'Biodegradable, non-allergic paints in serotonin-stimulating primary colours,' Cassandra announced briskly. '*Very* important to have a lot of brightness around – develops a child's senses, increases intelligence. Can't have Zak falling behind at school just because his bedroom is the wrong shade.'

'I suppose not.'

'Naturally, I've checked on what everyone else in Zak's year has, just in case. Otto *Greatorex*,' Cassandra pronounced, as if a rotting kipper had been placed under her nose, 'has a frankly rather *ill-advised* Captain Pugwash theme in his nursery, while Savannah and Siena Tressell – well, of course, their father *is* an architect – have a trendy French thing in primary colours with lots of foam-rubber cubes and tubes everywhere. Mollie Anstruther has a giant Barbie bedroom – *ghastly* – and Ellie Fforbes has an appallingly *vulgar* fairy palace with chandeliers and a four-poster bed. Screamingly camp, but then of course there have always been question marks about which team her father bats for . . .'

'So,' said Anna, looking at the walls and choosing her words carefully, 'what's the theme here? The countryside?' Each wall crawled with animals and sprouted foliage in preternaturally bright colours. Small settlements appeared between gaps in fat blades of grass – here sunny English villages, complete with church spires, there Eastern cities, minarets gleaming in a starry sky. It reminded Anna strongly of a pantomime set. Or perhaps a particularly cheesy birthday card.

'Well, originally it was supposed to be Narnia, as you can probably tell. I'd booked Damien Hirst to do it – he's a friend of my architect – but he had *absolutely no intention* of following my designs.' Cassandra pursed her lips at the memory.

'What a shame,' Anna said. A halved and pickled Zak would have added a certain *je ne sais quoi*.

'The only other bedroom I really rather envied,'

Cassandra said, 'was Milo and Ivo Hope-Stanley's Nantucket-style one; terribly glamorous, all tongue and groove panelling, Navajo blankets, bunks based on ships' berths and Stars and Stripes cushions – very Ralph Lauren. Caroline Hope-Stanley's housekeeper used to be a stylist for *World of Interiors* and she knows just how to arrange it. *Lil*, of course, wouldn't have had a *hope*. But that's all over, thankfully.'

As if the horrors of that morning's *Telegraph* hadn't been enough, Cassandra had, just before Anna arrived, swept into the sitting room to discover Lil had failed to wipe the smoky smudges off the scented candle glasses *yet again*.

'If I've told her once . . .' Cassandra raged as she stormed round picking up and slamming down the black-tipped jars with the Diptyque label.

'Really gets on your wick, doesn't it?' Jett drawled. He spoke in a lightly insouciant tone precisely calculated to cause his wife maximum annoyance. He wasn't a musician for nothing.

Cassandra had stormed out of the room in search of the hapless domestic. She'd had enough. Something had to give. Notice, preferably.

Cassandra tsked now as she snatched down a poster of a grinning Michael Owen. 'Can't *bear* those boy bands, can you? That's Zak's bathroom, by the way,' she added, gesturing at the vast white expanse visible through a door ajar at one end of the room. 'Make sure you clean behind the sink pedestal. It gets filthy there for some reason.'

'Me? *Clean?*'

'Yes, I've had to let Lil go, unfortunately,' Cassandra trilled. 'So if you could just step in for her for the moment, that would be lovely. Oh, and there's a pile of ironing downstairs for you – we iron all sheets and underwear here, I'm afraid – and if you could just run round with the Hoover that would be fabulous. Garden could do with a weed and I'm afraid I haven't had time to go to Waitrose either. To make your first day as easy as possible, Mr St Edmunds will do the school run this afternoon as well – you can take over tomorrow morning. Lunch is at one. Roast Mediterranean vegetable terrine, I thought.'

'Lovely,' mumbled Anna, still reeling from the list of tasks.

'So if you start to cook it at about eleven, that should be fine. Right, I'll leave you to sort yourself out.'

Anna returned upstairs to 'her' room and closed the door. She placed her back against it and slid slowly down into a crouch. Looking hopelessly at the bare and cheerless surroundings, she felt the familiar gulping in her throat. She wondered what Seb was doing now. Still in bed no doubt – it was the crack of half past ten, after all. And probably not alone. As tears stung her eyes and began to roll slowly down her cheeks, she closed her eyes and swallowed hard. From millionheir's

Mayfair apartment to skivvy's boxroom, she reflected. And all in the course of one morning. You've come a long way, baby.

Anna's first night on the sofabed was even worse than she had expected. After the endless fetching, carrying, negotiating and, finally, pleading involved in putting Zak to bed, she had finally turned back the thin and smelly duvet, only to hear a bloodcurdling howl ricocheting wildly around the walls of the room. It took a few seconds for Anna to realise it was her own.

As the ghastly sight sank in, shock shuddered through her. There, on the grey-white sheet beneath the duvet, crouched the stark, black and hideously leggy forms of what looked like at least twenty enormous spiders. Anna *hated* spiders.

'Of course,' Cassandra said, appearing in the room in a baby blue pashmina bathrobe, her eyes round islands of contempt in a sea of face cream, 'had you been to *public school* you would have *instantly* realised that they were the tops of tomatoes, and not real spiders. It's the oldest trick in the book, along with apple pie beds, although I understand duvets have put a stop to those. Really, I'm *amazed* you fell for it. Zak's *hilarious*, isn't he?'

Having been educated through a series of largely benign local state seminaries, Anna's knowledge of public school had come mostly from Enid Blyton and

Seb, neither of whom had mentioned tomato tops. They would, anyway, have failed to register on the Richter scale of prep school nastiness that Seb had suffered – being made to swim outdoors naked in the freezing cold and have Matron smack your penis with a cold spoon were among the more lurid lowlights he had mentioned to Anna. Seen from this angle, it was no surprise Seb had turned out to be the person he was. What was amazing was that he wasn't worse.

'And making all that *ridiculous* noise as well,' Cassandra continued mercilessly. 'Zak needs his sleep, even if *you* don't. He, at least, has to work hard tomorrow morning. All *you* have to do is take him to school.'

'I've done them this morning,' Cassandra announced martyrishly next day. 'But from now on, they're *your* responsibility.' Collected in the hallway was a sprawling collection of extremely smart bags which looked like the personal effects of a visiting potentate. An entire suite of Louis Vuitton; a soft, buttery, buckled leather holdall; dark red crocodile Mulberry and any number of Bond Street carrier bags nestled up lovingly on the floor.

'Gosh,' said Anna, admiringly. 'It looks like the luggage people take on Concorde.' Some of the bags, in fact, had Concorde labels on them.

'*Concorde!*' Cassandra shot her a withering glance.

'*No one* takes luggage on Concorde,' she snapped.

Anna looked puzzled, previously unaware that the celebrated jet was luggage-free. She supposed it made sense – how else, after all, did it go so fast?

'All the luggage on Concorde,' Cassandra explained, a pitying note in her voice, 'is carried *on* and *off* by the cabin staff. Only tourists or the *terminally unsophisticated* take their *own* on.'

'Oh. I see.' Anna resolved to bear the tip in mind next time she flew supersonic.

'*These* are Zak's *school* things.' As Cassandra produced a list and began performing a roll call of the contents and purpose of each bag, Anna's jaw dropped ever nearer to what Cassandra had already told her were the individually peasant-fired Tuscan tiles on the hall floor. Wonderingly, she recalled the one satchel and single gym bag which had got her through her entire formal education.

'Young Futures and Options,' barked Cassandra, pointing at a Vuitton attaché case in the corner. 'Operabugs and Junior Gastronauts,' she added, stabbing at another bag. There was also a fixture for *extra* extra tennis – 'His instructor says he's Wimbledon potential.' Cassandra chose not to reveal that what the instructor had actually said was that, yes, Zak could easily get to Wimbledon, but only if you were talking about the Tube station. There was advanced French and dinner-party Chinese – 'Well, if the bloody Chinks *are* taking over the world, after all Zak may as well learn how to pass them the mangetout.' After being briefed about Madame Abricot's dance class and what sounded like tuition in every single instrument of the orchestra, Anna felt almost sorry for Zak.

Until, that was, he climbed into the brand new four-wheel drive – 'We only got it yesterday and any damage comes straight out of your wages' – and turned Zoe Ball up to window-shattering volume. As Zak began throwing himself about on the front seat to the music, Anna inched through the Kensington High Street traffic uncomfortably aware of the curious gaze of taxi, lorry and double-decker bus drivers.

'Mummy's very cross with Daddy,' shouted Zak suddenly. 'There was an interview with him in the paper yesterday, about his new record. My daddy's a very famous pop star, you know.'

'I see,' said Anna, glancing frantically between the *A–Z* and the back bumper of the car in front.

'The interview was *supposed* to be about Mummy's book,' added Zak. 'But the only bits about Mummy were her shouting at Daddy.'

'You've read it then?' asked Anna. She was surprised until she recalled Cassandra saying that reading and discussing the broadsheets was part of the daily curriculum at St Midas's.

'No, but Mummy read lots of it out very loudly at Daddy.'

St Midas's seemed to be at a particularly tricky-to-get-at end of the Cromwell Road, an area inconveniently plunged into the darkness of the *A–Z* gutter. Panicking, Anna snapped back the book's paper spine and stared fiercely at it for clues. It was only when other people-carriers, their back seats alive with squirming children in boaters, drew up in the lanes either side of her that Anna realised she was on the right track.

'Look, look,' screeched Zak, clambering over the front and then the back seat to bang on the rear window. 'It's Savannah and Siena! They're overtaking!' As the lights changed, a shining people-carrier containing two leg o' muttoned girls sped past.

'Put your foot down, *stupid*,' Zak ordered Anna. 'Catch them *up*!'

Despising herself for being intimidated by an eight-year-old, Anna allowed the speed to creep up a fraction on the dial.

'I'm going to call them.' Zak leant over the front seat, rifling through the Mulberry rucksack and eventually producing a miniature silver mobile phone. He stabbed at the keypad for a few seconds before diving into the bag again. 'Bugger, I've forgotten their number,' he cursed. 'Where's my Psion?'

That contact with Savannah and Siena had finally been established was confirmed a few seconds later by muffled whispering and giggling in the back. Anna swallowed and tried not to listen as 'Yes . . . new nanny . . . I *know* . . .' floated over from the rear.

'No, you *don't* come in with me,' Zak ordered imperiously as Anna parked beside the gates of the handsome pair of Queen Anne houses which, to judge from the boaters pouring within and the sign standing proudly without, was St Midas's School. 'Stay *there*.' Slamming the door behind him with shattering violence, he ran off.

Waiting for her blood pressure to subside from Dangerous to merely High, Anna sat and watched what she assumed to be a collection of St Midas's mothers and fathers milling about the entrance. Sartorial competition seemed stiff, if not positively cut-throat. Pashminas abounded and there were more racehorse legs around than at a Grand National starting line-up. The morning sunshine bounced off gleaming, well-cut hair, shining, straight white teeth and gold and diamond rings. And that was just the men. These people, Anna realised, spent a lot longer preparing for school than their children did.

She stared through the windscreen as she conducted a gloomy résumé of life with Cassandra so far. The word *writing* had not been mentioned once, although the word *nanny* had, countless times. Feeling her spirits slump, Anna leant over and rested her forehead on the steering wheel. The view that met her was the far from uplifting one of her black-trousered thighs spread out like flattened sausages on the driving seat. She sighed heavily.

A sharp rap on the window disturbed her musings. Blearily, Anna looked up to see a grinning dark-haired girl wearing a great deal of plum-coloured lipstick. She fumbled in panic for the window button.

'*Geri!*'

'Hi, babe. Didn't realise it was *you* I was racing down the Cromwell Road in the Bratmobile.'

'I didn't realise you had children,' Anna said, bewildered. She stared at Geri with renewed admiration. Was there no end to her capabilities? Combining high-powered management executiveship with single motherhood and *still* finding time to put her lipstick on properly.

'Oh, they're not mine,' Geri said breezily. 'They're just part of my portfolio of responsibilities. But what about you? That was Zak Knight you had in the car, wasn't it? Surely . . .' her eyes widened, '*surely* you're not . . . his latest nanny. Are you?'

'*Latest*?' Anna tried to keep the quaver out of her voice.

Geri glanced at her. 'Got time for a coffee?'

'Probably not,' said Anna, recalling the Augean list of chores Cassandra had barked at her as she had tottered out of the door en route to her Very Important Meeting. 'But it sounds like I'd better.'

* * *

Cassandra's hands shook as she took her seat at the long wooden table. Despite her distracted state, she could not help noticing that it was, as usual, polished to a mirror-like perfection infinitely beyond the capabilities of Lil. Lil hadn't even been able to polish mirrors to mirror-like perfection. Still, hopefully the new girl would do better. She certainly couldn't do worse.

Cassandra shot a nervous look at the set and determined faces around her, each one of which, she knew, had its own agenda as well as that which, neatly printed and bound, lay before each delegate on the glossy expanse of the table. She cleared her throat, took a swig of still water from the sparkling tumbler before her and clicked the end of the pen which had been laid at a precise diagonal across the jotting pad bearing the letters SMSPA.

'May I call the meeting to attention.' An imposing brunette with thin lips and elegantly understated make-up shuffled the sheets in her perfectly manicured hands, slipped on a pair of rimless glasses and cast a steely glance over them and around the table. 'Item one on the agenda. Funds . . .'

Boring *boring*. Why did they always have to trawl through the money bit first? The backs of her thighs, Cassandra realised, were well and truly stuck to the shining leather seat of her chair. Any movement would result in a ripping of flesh ten times more painful than the most inept bikini wax. She should have worn tights

– but it was so easy to get the shade wrong and, anyway, leaving them off was an opportunity to show everyone else how unscarred, well moisturised and, most importantly of all, *thin* her legs were. No hiding behind thick black opaques for her, thank you very much; it was vital at these meetings that you showed yourself off to the best possible advantage. One false outfit and you were sunk; your stock as irreversibly lowered as if your knickers had fallen down.

'. . . pleased to announce,' enunciated the brunette in crisp tones, 'that the Association finds itself in its best financial position *ever* . . .'

Bugger Polly Rice-Brown, thought Cassandra, glaring at the speaker and wincing as her left outer thigh peeled itself away from the seat. Why *leather* dining-room chairs, for God's sake? Surely that brat of hers wasn't *still* peeing everywhere? It had taken weeks to get rid of the smell of urine after Sholto Rice-Brown had stayed overnight with Zak; an occasion which Polly had had the *bloody* cheek to claim actually marked the *start* of Sholto's loss of control over his bowels. She'd tried to blame Zak, of all people, just because during the night he'd dressed up as a ghost and pretended – not *tried*, as Polly had insisted – to strangle Sholto. Honestly, Cassandra silently fumed. Some people had no sense of *humour*, let alone any appreciation of the exceptionally *imaginative* child Zak was.

No, Cassandra decided, an agonising tug at the

bottom of her right buttock returning her abruptly to the present. She really shouldn't have worn quite so short a skirt; despite its being one of Enzo Boldanzo's signature bold prints (at his signature bold prices). But the computerised wardrobe had been playing up again . . .

She shot a careful glance to her left. Even Shayla Reeves was wearing what looked suspiciously like Prada trousers. *She'd* changed her sartorial tune, Cassandra thought viciously, hoping for the hundredth time that the rumour that Shayla had bagged her Premiership footballer husband whilst working as a lap dancer was true. If it was, Shayla had certainly ratcheted herself up a class or ten since – her son was called Caspar, for Christ's sake. Her interior-designed Notting Hill home, innocent of the merest trace of concrete lions, had recently been opened to *Hello!* magazine and her neatly side-parted hair had lost all trace of Stringfellow's blonde and was now a tasteful fugue of beige and brown stripes not dissimilar to the top of a fine sideboard.

'. . . the St Midas's School Parents Association,' continued Polly, 'would like to take this opportunity to put on record its thanks to Caroline Hope-Stanley for her careful stewardship of our funds . . .'

Cassandra pursed her lips. Just *what*, she thought to herself, is so bloody *amazing* about being a good treasurer when, like Caroline Hope-Stanley, you've been an investment banker for *ten years*. She glanced over at the offending official – lightly tanned, long blonde hair, slim figure in jeans and T-shirt, the latter brilliant white to match those great pearly gates of teeth of hers. Oh-so-relaxed, except that the jeans were Versace, the T-shirt Donna Karan and the teeth the beneficiaries of the latest American bleaching treatment. Caroline's casual look, Cassandra estimated, cost twice as much as most people's smartest – certainly more than Polly Rice-Brown's, who had on what was quite obviously something from Next.

'. . . our Bolivian interests, in particular, have yielded high revenues . . .'

Now of course, Cassandra thought sardonically, Caroline wasn't a banker any longer. She was one of the gym-sleek, Knightsbridge-groomed breed of New Housewives; she'd packed the City in at the age of thirty-two in order to bring up her twins Milo and Ivo. *With* the help of a full-time nanny, a housekeeper and an army of cleaners and gardeners. 'I simply adore being at home,' she had told more than one glossy magazine. 'I now realise what I was missing out on.' Well, the sack for one thing; if Cassandra could remember rightly, Caroline's entire team of fund managers had been made redundant the week after she'd walked off with her golden handshake, due to question marks about the ethics of some of their South American investments. Drugs had been mentioned. Bolivian interests *indeed*.

'. . . some of the fundraising initiatives have been particularly inspired . . .'

Cassandra ground her teeth. She was sick of Polly Rice-Brown's fundraising initiatives. Ruthlessly determined to raise more in her stint as SMSPA chairman than anyone ever had before, she had already organised Himalayan treks, East to West bicycle tours of America and blindfold bungee jumping. And, loath as Cassandra was to admit it, she *had* raised a great deal of money. By the end of it all, Cassandra thought sourly, St Midas's would be able to send up its own space probe.

'The Bring Your Child To Work Day, of course, was a big hit . . .'

Bringing them to work being the only way *some* women ever saw their children, Cassandra thought piously, reflecting on the fact that she saw as much of Zak as possible. Whether she wanted to or not. She'd heard that tale, famous among St Midas's mothers, of how Sholto's final act before going to sleep was to call up his mother at the newspaper plant where she worked as a picture editor and whisper 'Night night' to her on his mobile. Not to mention the poignant rumour concerning Savannah and Siena Tressell, who supposedly spent one Christmas Day feeding turkey to the television, or, more precisely, to their absent TV presenter mother's talking head on the screen.

'For me, of course,' Polly continued, 'Bring Your Child To Work Day was wonderful. Sholto was such a hit with the editor that he was actually given his own newspaper column taking a sideways look at life as an under-nine . . .'

Precocious *brat*. Cassandra had been bored to death already during the pre-meeting coffee about the National Theatre's being Sholto's second home these days, his forthcoming solo violin debut at the Wigmore Hall and the sample chapters of his first novel that were already causing a stir in publishing circles.

'Aren't you a bit worried?' she had asked.

'About what?'

'Well, all this artsy stuff. Doesn't sound very . . . *masculine*, does it?'

'Oh, I see what you mean. Well, that's fine. We're quite happy to have one of each.'

'One of each? But Sholto has a brother, doesn't he?'

'Exactly, one of *each*. One gay and one straight.'

Well, what else did you expect from someone who worked on a bloody *leftie* paper? Cassandra thought. A *tabloid*, at that.

'. . . which of course led,' Polly was saying now, 'to the piece Sholto wrote about the dilemma of how to tell his old nanny about her appalling BO winning the coveted Columnist of the Year award . . .'

Cassandra fumed. Her own efforts having never earned anything other than derision from the literary establishment, it was hard to accept that an eight-year-old had won such an award. With a piece about a *nanny*, of all things. Well, she could give them pieces about nannies until they came out of her *ears*. *Christ* knew what the St Midas's bunch had made of *her* new one. What had all the glamorous nannies everyone else seemed to employ so effortlessly thought of someone who quite obviously had never seen a full-length mirror? Or *any* mirror, judging by that *figure*. More visible panty line than the knicker department of M&S, not to mention tits like *coalsacks*. Cassandra glanced down complacently at her own neat little buds, still standing proud after forty-two years on the planet and a little help from the appropriately named Dr Pertwee. Not forgetting Imelda, much as she'd like to. Shame Zak had brought all *that* up again. Especially after the pains she'd taken to keep Imelda and her family quiet 20,000 feet above the Pacific. Girl had got a free tit job, hadn't she? Even if one *had* imploded, it hadn't *cost* her anything.

Still, the fact that the new girl was plumper than a Christmas goose should at least keep Jett from straying. He *hated* fat women. Mind you, she'd hired Emma on the grounds that she weighed a good twelve stone and look what had happened there.

Cassandra sighed at the thought of her husband. Jett was like a dog on heat at the moment. He was quite *literally* a pain in the arse. Whether it was the absence of Emma or an excess of testosterone generated by the incipient release of his comeback album, Cassandra was not sure. Whatever it was, it wasn't welcome. He'd wanted her in everything from whipped cream to Nutella over the past few days and when, last night, he had asked her to crawl under the glass-topped coffee table, Cassandra had decided enough was enough. 'You pervert!' she had screeched.

'But I'm only asking you to pick up my goddamn lighter,' Jett had protested. 'You know I can't bend down that low with my goddamn back problems.'

'I don't care,' Cassandra had shrieked. 'You've gone too far this time. You're disgusting.'

'OK then, I'll pick it up myself,' Jett had drawled. 'And you can pay the goddamn osteopath's bill,' he had grimaced a few minutes later, clutching his spine in one hand and flicking the tiny silver microphone lighter furiously on and off with the other as he headed through the door to spend the rest of the night in the spare bedroom. Cassandra sighed. Most men Jett's age only wanted sex once a year – and usually not from their wives even then.

'. . . a vote of thanks for Kate,' Polly Rice-Brown was saying when Cassandra tuned back in. Cassandra glanced enviously down the table in the direction of Kate Tressell's flawlessly chic porridge linen Mao jacket. Then there was the Cartier Tank on the narrow wrist, whose thinness implied steely self-control and whose tan hinted at regular trips to the second home in

Tuscany. Trust Kate Tressell always to wear the right thing, as well as have the right job being the nation's favourite current affairs anchorwoman, as respected for her brain as for her shapely bottom. She also had the right husband – happening architect Julian Tressell who combined building Britain's most talked-about edifices – such as his famous Tressell table which sank into the floor when not in use – with presenting popular TV programmes about architecture. Kate also had the right haircut, dark-blonde and expensively tousled. And the waft of discreetly delicious perfume that had just entered Cassandra's nostrils from Kate's direction was, no doubt, the right smell.

'How does Kate manage to be the hottest thing in broadcasting, not to mention being one of the most proactive of St Midas's mothers?' simpered Polly, echoing Cassandra's boiling thoughts. 'Really, she's an example to us all . . .'

The rest of the table sat and listened to Polly's encomium about how, without Kate's determination and, more importantly, her contacts, the school's new state-of-the-art TV studio would never have got past first base. Or off the drawing board of Julian, who had designed it. The TV studio was intended not only to elevate St Midas's facilities for its pupils into an entirely different league to that of even its closest competitors, but also to provide a training ground for the producers and presenters of tomorrow, amongst whose ranks

Kate and Julian's daughters Savannah and Siena were obviously intended to feature.

Savannah and Siena, no doubt, would dominate the chattering classes of the future as easily as they excelled in the Kumon maths classes of today. They and their parents were easily the brightest stars in St Midas's mini-firmament. And it was for this reason more than any other that Cassandra had come to the meeting.

Her mantelpiece – in infuriating contrast to Fenella Greatorex's – *still* being inexplicably innocent of an invitation to Savannah and Siena's birthday party, Cassandra had decided to screw her courage to the sticking place and *force* Kate Tressell to invite Zak. After all, the children certainly *got on*; Savannah and Siena were almost unique among St Midas's pupils for *not* having been the victims of some of Zak's more hilarious pranks. And there had been so many of those high-spirited expressions of Zak's boundless humour and creativity – Cassandra did not have to dig deep in her memory to recall the time Zak had shut Milo Hope-Stanley in the garage overnight. Or when he had helped himself to the foie gras in Fenella Greatorex's fridge that was intended for a client-clinching dinner party. *Then* he had been sick all over the sisal. She quickly lowered her eyes again.

Zak had never done anything remotely like this to Savannah and Siena, although preventing him *had*, Cassandra thought ruefully, taken more persuasion than

Jane Austen. So why, why, *why* had she not been granted dropping-off and picking-up rights to the birthday party? Cassandra clutched her fists so hard under the table that her knuckles turned white. Zak simply *had* to be there. After the appearance of Cherie Blair and the First Kids at last year's celebration had prompted a rash of newspaper articles about Power Children's Parties, the Tressell bash had become the most talked-about children's event since the Pied Piper hit Hamelin.

Cassandra hardly noticed the meeting moving on. Her mind was locked on to the party like a barnacle on a boat. She felt panic rising; had she not, for the past month at least, tried to impress on Zak that if he didn't get an invitation, there would be hell to pay? And there had been plenty to pay already. Zak had been wired up to the Internet on the grounds that last year's summons had been sent out by e-mail – after the man who had installed it observed how appropriate an address for Zak demon.co.uk was, Cassandra had called to complain. Cassandra had heard that this year's was some sort of smart card pass. Surely the invitation, whatever form it took, would come soon? She looked desperately at Kate's smiling face as she acknowledged the applause for her efforts. How on earth could she introduce the subject? Perhaps over a cup of coffee afterwards? But what would she *say*?

Kate's minimal make-up made Cassandra wonder anew if she'd needed *quite* so much lipstick on herself.

But then, some of the mothers coming to these parents' meetings hired make-up artists for the occasion. And why not? St Midas's, after all, was not any old school. It was a power prep of the first order. Which was why securing an invitation to its most sought-after event was so *vital.* Cassandra felt sick. She *couldn't* go home empty-handed. If Zak wasn't asked, they'd have to change schools; there would be nothing else for it, the shame would be too much to bear. But Zak had already changed schools so often due to what Cassandra could only put down to the lack of *imagination* of the head teachers, there were precious few left for him to go to. Landing a place at St Midas's had been nothing less than a miracle – the best evidence Cassandra had yet had that there might be a god. But even so, and without losing her sense of proportion *too* much, the rest of Zak's *life* depended on this party.

She swallowed hard and tried to refocus on the matter in hand. The meeting had by now moved on from the much-anticipated joys of the about-to-open studio – 'Can you imagine, a mini *Question Time*? We could make a pilot and try and get the Beeb to squeeze it in between Blue Peter and the six o'clock news . . .' – to the next item on the agenda. Some group of bleeding hearts, Cassandra noted with scorn, were suggesting that St Midas's set up an outreach link with London's underprivileged – 'Holiday work with the homeless so that the children would gain some understanding of those considerably worse off than themselves,' as the movement's main spokeswoman put it. Cassandra listened with contempt. Who in God's name wanted to understand anyone *worse off*? The whole *point* of St Midas's was to meet as many rich and useful people as possible. But the bitter core of her loathing was reserved, not for these ludicrous sentiments, but the fact that their mouthpiece was that *bloody* Fenella Greatorex. Whose son *had* been invited to The Party.

'I mean, it's the *homeless* I just can't bear to see,' Fenella sighed.

'Oh, *absolutely*,' burst out Cassandra. 'I mean, if they *have* to lie around all over the pavements, why can't they do it in nicer sleeping bags? Those disgusting blue flowery ones are *so* unstylish. They really ought to have more consideration.'

A frozen silence followed. Cassandra smirked to herself. *That* put the bleeding heart lefties in their place once and for all. The shocked expressions round the table reminded her of the time, several meetings ago, when she had admitted to spending Zak's child benefit on Château Lafite.

'Um, well,' Polly Rice-Brown said, after a plethora of throat clearing. 'Perhaps we could think about that while we move on to the next item, the Promises auction. Which, hopefully, will get the fundraising for our next project, the film-editing suite, off to a great start.'

Cassandra's dormant interest in any other subject but The Party was briefly stirred. The film-editing suite would, with luck, encourage Zak's obvious acting ability and get his career as a film star off to a great start as well. Her secret dream, apart from securing The Invitation, was that Zak star as Alaric St Felix in the blockbuster film version of *Impossible Lust*, the only one of her books to be optioned by a film studio and still, as it had been for the past five years, stuck in Development Hell. 'Impossible Film', Jett sneeringly called it.

To demonstrate her devotion to the film-editing project, Cassandra had come up with what she confidently expected to be the most sought-after item in the Promises auction. Surely even Kate Tressell would be impressed with this.

'Well, thanks, everyone, for promising such wonderful things,' Polly Rice-Brown said, half an hour later. Wonderful my *arse*, thought Cassandra sourly. What on earth was the use of Caroline Hope-Stanley's offer of a year's supply of horse manure from their weekend place in Oxfordshire? 'For the garden, of course,' Caroline had snapped when Cassandra had said as much. Or Polly Rice-Brown's wildly over-generous year's subscription to her bloody newspaper? Much as it pained Cassandra to admit it, the detox day at a health farm promised by Fenella Greatorex almost nudged the borders of reasonableness – until one reflected on the fact that Strydgel Grange was, quite apart from being firmly on the health spa B list, one of Fenella's own PR accounts.

Cassandra's own contribution had not quite been the one she had intended. Her original offer of an autographed boxed set of her own works was unexpectedly dismissed out of hand on the grounds that the purpose of the auction was to raise the school's profile, not any of the mothers' (Cassandra had dwelt bitterly but silently on Fenella Greatorex's spa at this point). *In extremis*, she had had to come up with a substitute. VIP seats at the Solstice reunion concert being deemed similarly unsuitable, Cassandra had eventually been pressed into offering to cook a dinner party for eight *at her home*. Or rather, offering Anna to cook for it, and, she resolved, the cheapest way possible. Was pasta and pesto, Cassandra wondered, a socially acceptable dish?

The end of the meeting was now in sight. As the smell of coffee drifted over from the kitchen wing, Cassandra braced herself to buttonhole Kate Tressell – despite the fact that the latter's Mao jacket had no obvious buttons on it. Leaping to her feet, the leather seat ripping from the backs of her thighs, Cassandra stumbled, eyes watering, in Kate's wake as she headed with remarkable speed for the hallway.

'Just one thing,' Polly called, holding up a hand to the half-dissolved meeting. 'Kate's had to dash, but she wanted to suggest the auction be held at Siena and Savannah's birthday party. She thought it would be something for the parents there to do.'

Cassandra's heart sank. Following the rest of the herd into Polly's Provençal-style kitchen, she wondered whether to commit hara-kiri with one of the large knives protruding from the olive-wood butcher's block. The worst had happened. She had secured neither invitation nor word with Kate Tressell. Suicide seemed the only option.

Chapter 9

About the same time as Cassandra took her seat at the highly polished conference table, two men behind the counter of a little French café in Kensington burst into flamboyant and flirtatious life as a curvaceous girl with long brown hair and precisely applied lipstick made her entrance. Geri, Anna saw as she followed in her wake, was clearly a regular.

'So tell me what's going on,' Geri said, as they sat nursing cappuccinos. 'Why have you departed from my carefully constructed, individually tailored personal goal-achieving plan?'

Anna's face stayed frozen. 'I *haven't*,' she said evenly. 'As a matter of fact I'm sticking to it like glue. I'm *supposed* to be Cassandra's assistant. She's *supposed* to be teaching me to write.'

Geri raised an eyebrow and lit a cigarette. 'I see. When did you start?'

'Today's my second day.'

'Which means,' Geri said, 'you've been with her a full twenty-four hours. That puts you streets ahead of some of Cassandra's past nannies. One lasted about ten minutes.'

'How many has she got through?' Anna's voice had lowered to a horrified croak. Her heart thumped against her rib cage and, despite the fact she was sitting down, her knees shook uncontrollably.

'Well,' grinned Geri cheerfully, 'you're the seventh this year, at a conservative estimate. I expect Cassandra just forgot to tell you about the others.'

Anna was silent. It was all very well for high-powered career girl Geri to think her predicament the most enormous joke.

'But the good news,' Geri continued, 'is that you're in a *brilliant* position.'

'I *am*?'

'Yes. All us nannies are.'

'You're a *nanny*?' Anna gawped at Geri in amazement. 'But what was all that about management consultancy and executive responsibility? I thought you were the head of Unilever at the very least. A captain of industry.'

Geri took a bite from her croissant and grinned at

Anna as she chewed. Her other hand still held the cigarette.

'But I *am*,' she said. 'We both are. We're valuable commodities in one of the most highly sought-after sectors of the economy. That of childcare provision.'

Anna snorted. 'You *are* joking? I feel about as valuable and sought-after as yesterday's copy of the *Sun*.'

'Don't you *see*? It's a complete seller's market,' Geri continued enthusiastically. 'Play your cards right and you have the pick of who you work for, you can practically write your own salary cheque, you get glamorous holidays thrown in and get paid for going on them, you don't pay tax or National Insurance, there are no overheads whatsoever and there are plenty of perks. I, for instance, have a company car.'

Anna stared. 'A *company* car?'

'Sure. You have to see the families you work for as companies. Some of which perform well, others not so well. Your job is to help them improve their performance.'

'*Performance?*' gasped Anna, attempting to grasp the idea of the family as a unit floated on the stock exchange of life. 'But how on earth do you *measure* it?'

Geri gave a short laugh. 'Let me count the ways,' she grinned. 'Like any company, through the achievements of its individual members and of the group as a whole. For children, there is a practically endless list of fields in which they are expected to compete and excel.

Some of their timetables are more crammed than their parents' . . .'

Anna remembered the list of Zak's after-school lessons.

'Academic performance, for example,' Geri continued. 'The competition among parents even before the school stage is incredible. I've worked for people whose nursery floors are covered with rough sisal matting so the child will be discouraged from crawling and learn to walk more quickly.'

'*No!*'

'Oh yes. Some of my past employers set up entire pay structures incorporating performance-related bonuses if the baby learned to talk by a certain date. At the moment, for instance, I have to make sure Savannah and Siena can talk about current affairs at their parents' power Sunday lunches. So every night we watch the six o'clock news and discuss it afterwards.'

Anna was speechless. Geri, meanwhile, was anything but.

'The key,' she said, stuffing in the last of the croissant, 'is to identify your role in the corporate organisation and then exploit it. If you don't believe me, ask the others. They've just come in.'

A laughing group were ordering at the counter. Anna recognised them as the same glamorous creatures she had seen milling about outside the gates of the school; a dark girl dressed entirely in white, a lanky man in a tight T-shirt and two blondes – a rangy one who sported loafers, pashmina and bob, and a larger sporty-looking one. 'You see that blonde with the bob?' Geri whispered. 'That's Alice. Worked for Cassandra about three months ago.' As a roar of laughter suddenly convulsed the group, Anna's heart fell out of her bottom and hit the stripped wood floor. The sick feeling in her stomach, she told herself sternly, must be due to her lack of breakfast.

'Hey, guys. Over here.' As the group began to look about them for seats, Geri waved frantically. 'Come and meet the new recruit.'

Chairs borrowed from neighbouring tables were scraped across wooden floorboards as people shoved, exclaimed, giggled and shuffled into position. In the end, everyone was squashed round the tiny marble table, which the waiter then attempted to pile with cappuccinos and croissants.

'This is Anna,' Geri announced. 'She's Zak Knight's new nanny.' A collective gasp followed, then a silence interrupted by a giggle, followed by a snort which, much to Anna's annoyance and intense embarrassment, soon achieved full-blown laugh status. Alice, Anna noted, was laughing hardest of all.

'Well, you've got to, haven't you?' she sniffed, mopping a streaming eye. 'Otherwise you'd cry.' She stopped as she caught Anna's baleful glare.

'Let me introduce everyone,' Geri interrupted hastily.

'This,' she said, gesturing at the large blonde girl who had a perfectly round face the colour of strong tea, 'is Trace. Works for a journalist called Polly Rice-Brown. Cassandra knows her. Zak tried to kill her son once.'

'Wish she bladdy hed,' pronounced Trace in broad Australian tones. 'Wouldda sived me doin' it. Liddle *bastard*.'

'Oh, come on, Trace, you know you don't mean that,' interjected the lanky youth who, besides his rangy figure, had big lips, high cheekbones, a heavy Eastern European accent and subscribed to that variety of sexiness known as brooding. 'You love Sholto,' he continued in the same flat monotone. 'You just won't admit it.'

Trace grinned. 'Well, I suppose I *im* fond of the liddle *bastard* really. When I think what I could have inded up with . . .' She flicked a small-eyed glance at Anna.

'This is Slobodan,' Geri intervened, introducing the lanky youth. 'He looks after the children of someone called Caroline Hope-Stanley, another of the St Midas's mothers.'

'You're a nanny?' Anna exclaimed. 'But you're a *man*.'

Everyone laughed. Slobodan winked at her.

'Male nannies are *terribly* trendy at the moment,' Geri explained. 'Particularly exotic ones. One of the St Midas's mothers has a rather dishy Japanese bloke called Hanuki, who was the first male Norlander. Slob's from Bosnia. Lots of the mothers are starting to want men to look after their children – they're more athletic and brilliant at games.'

'Yes, Caroline loves my games.' Slobodan narrowed his eyes and grinned. He shifted in his seat, drawing attention to the very tight jeans straining across his crotch and pushed back his floppy dark hair with both strong, tanned forearms.

'Slob's a terrible flirt,' Geri said, rather unnecessarily. 'The St Midas's mothers love him, despite the fact he insists on pickled fish sandwiches for breakfast. The Hope-Stanleys' stock has shot through the roof since he came on the scene – they get invited to everything so everyone can flirt with Slob. He's probably been through most of the mothers by now. And a few of the fathers as well.'

'Ees not true, Geri,' Slobodan protested, grinning. He winked at Anna. 'Not *all*. Not *yet*.'

He might be about as subtle as Benny Hill, Anna thought, smiling back, but he was *very* attractive. However, judging by the challenging way the dark-haired waif next to him was looking at her, she wasn't the only one who thought so.

'I'm Allegra,' the girl breathed in an Italian accent of X-rated sexiness. 'How do you do?' She over-pronounced the 'H', Anna noticed, in a way that made her large lips pout even further forward.

'Allegra's even trendier than Slob,' Geri supplied. 'She's one of London's first New Age nannies. She smears her children with oil and makes them take baths with lots of dirt and leaves in them.'

'Oh, Geri,' protested Allegra, pushing her lips out like drawers. 'You know the hoils are hessential hoils, for the calming of the bambini, and they are sage baths with horris root, to promote 'appiness.'

'Allegra ees very good at massages as well,' Slobodan added, grinning. Anna smiled back, feeling slightly better. It was, she decided, like being in a nanny version of *Friends*.

'And this is Alice.' Geri waved at the girl with the blonde bob, whose face, Anna thought, was as long, flat and pale as a new wooden spoon. 'As I explained, she used to work for Cassandra and now works for someone called Shayla, whose husband's a footballer. Now you've met everyone. I've just been telling Anna that being a nanny's the best job in the world,' Geri added, to general murmurs of assent. 'That we've got our employers round our little fingers. Trace has, in any case. Almost didn't take her latest job because of the skiing –'

Anna nodded, feeling it was about time she said something. 'Skiing's not my strong point either,' she told Trace, who looked astonished.

Geri stepped in, grinning. 'Trace *loves* skiing,' she explained. 'The problem was that the Rice-Browns wanted to take her to Val D'Isère with them and Trace never skis anywhere but Aspen.'

Trace nodded triumphantly as she took a large mouthful of *pain au raisin*. 'They daren't even take a holiday without checking with me whether it's somewhere I want to go to and that the dates are convenient for me,' she assured Anna through a bad case of tumble-drier mouth. 'I was saying to Polly only yesterday, do we have to go to Barbados *agin*? Why not splish out and try the Maldives? So thit's where we're going.'

Anna stared.

'Trace gets poached more often than anyone else,' Geri explained. 'The Rice-Browns are desperate to keep her, but she'll go eventually. She gets great offers, all the time. Fighting off half the royal family at the moment, aren't you, Trace?'

'Not that that's saying *anything*,' Alice chimed in. 'I worked for some royals once and they were ghastly. Mean as mouseshit. Wrote the dates on the lightbulbs, for Christ's sake. Rock stars are the best ones – at least I used to think so before, um . . .' Her voice faded into a cough as she avoided Anna's gaze and pretended to splutter on her Marlboro.

'But we're all very jealous of Allegra,' Geri said hastily. 'She's worked for loads of celebrities, from Tom and Nicole to Richard and Judy. She's supposed to be writing a kids-and-tell book about it all, in fact.' Allegra pouted and raised an eyebrow. 'But she's got such a cushy number anyway,' Geri added. 'Her family, the Anstruthers, are so anxious not to lose her, they've given her a Saab convertible and her own apartment with a Jacuzzi bath. She's got them by the balls, haven't you, darling? Quite literally, if all that stuff about you and Oliver Anstruther is true.'

Slobodan sucked his cheeks in thunderously, while Allegra smiled lazily. '*Si*, and I've already 'ad hoffer of hupgrade to Porsche Boxter from someone else.'

Anna was fascinated. She had never thought of nannies as ruthless executives before. Less Mary Poppins, more Gordon Gekko. The only thing Poppins about Geri, Anna noticed, as they all stood up to leave, were the top few silver buttons of the short-skirted blue dress straining to hold back the brown tide of cleavage.

'Is that a uniform?' Anna asked pointedly as everyone started to drift out of the café. After all Geri's self-determinist big talk, the clothes of subservience seemed something of a comedown. 'Don't you mind having to wear one?'

Geri threw back her shoulders, thrusting out her impressive bosom yet further. '*Mind?*' she barked, slipping on a navy blue coat with distinct NHS overtones. 'Far from it. I *insisted* on it, as a matter of fact. Best professional tool I've got. You look the part, no one argues with you when you're in one, and,' she lowered her voice, 'men *love* them.'

'Uh?' Anna was lost again.

Geri flashed her a sly smile. 'Let's just say that at my current employer there are benefits I'm planning to avail myself of when the market situation is right.' She paused and grinned. 'I'm having some very interesting discussions with the CEO at the moment.'

Anna frowned. 'You mean the father?'

Geri nodded. 'He's an architect and works a lot from home.' She paused, and gave Anna the benefit of her dazzling smile. 'You might say the situation's building up nicely.'

Cassandra roared through Kensington crashing her gears and grinding her teeth. The SMSPA meeting had been a nightmare, and not only because of the non-materialisation of the party invitation. As she was leaving, Cassandra had overheard Fenella Greatorex mention that St Midas's was holding aptitude tests at the end of the week; when questioned, she had turned those huge cow's eyes on Cassandra and said, yes, absolutely, and hadn't Cassandra got a letter about it?

Back at Liv, Cassandra hunted high and low for the letter. Nothing. Bugger all in Zak's room, or in the wretched nanny's room, although there was a diary in one of the drawers that looked quite interesting, she'd come back to that later. She spent the rest of the afternoon with *A Passionate Lover* but, somehow, it failed to gell. Three double gins later it seemed to be gelling less. But that was only because the thought of The Tests was dominating everything. If Zak failed, his entire educational future would implode. Her dreams of him breezing through Common Entrance into whatever senior school topped the league tables at the time would have to be forgotten, along with those of his Cambridge First and Blue in everything from jousting to Footlights.

'I don't know what you're worrying about,' Jett said when Cassandra came down for yet another gin and a rare consultation with him on the matter. 'No point him going to university anyway. He can go to Clouds House like I did.'

Cassandra almost choked on her Bombay Sapphire. 'What, you mean the *detox centre*? Where you dried out?'

'Sure,' breezed Jett. 'The way you're spoiling him, he's going to end up there before he's eighteen anyway. May as well make an advance booking now.'

Cassandra exploded. 'How *dare* you accuse me of spoiling Zak? Can you *blame* me? It was *almost ten years* before I could have that child.'

'Only because you wouldn't have sex for nine of them.'

Cassandra stormed out of the room and returned to her study where she stared out of the window, thinking not of her book, but of her son. Her clever, charming son, who said the *sweetest* things.

'It took you *nine* years to have me, Mummy?' he had said when she told him. 'You must have been *very* tired.' Cassandra smiled a watery smile. Zak had such a very *particular* view of the world. He had been such a comfort to her that dreadful day of Princess Diana's funeral; when he had been convinced Princess Di was a mummy all bandaged up in her coffin. 'But it says Mummy on the card,' he had insisted. '*And* Dodi's Egyptian.' Then there had been the time he had seen her getting dressed in the bathroom and rushed downstairs to tell the gathering dinner party, 'Mummy's got hair on her bottom.' Cassandra still blushed at the memory. Along with that of Zak telling the entire school gate set that 'Mummy has been taken away by a policeman because of her straps.' Reassuring everyone that she was not running an S & M brothel but had merely been driving without a seatbelt had been humiliation of the first order.

At half past seven, when Anna appeared through the door with Zak, Cassandra's grey mood had deepened to thunderous black.

'Where the hell have *you* been?' she yelled.

'School run,' murmured Anna.

'Well, what school did you bloody run to?' Cassandra shouted. '*Gordonstoun?*'

Anna could not frame a reply. Waiting outside Zak's endless extra-curricular maths, music, judo and dance classes, she had listened to so much radio news her mind was numb. In the interests of keeping her temper while Zak ground the fistfuls of cereal he had apparently been saving since breakfast into her hair, she had taken so many deep breaths on the way home she was practically hallucinating. She was also desperate for a pee.

'Excuse me, I must just . . .'

'What's that on your head?' Cassandra resumed her disdainful interrogation as soon as Anna emerged from the lavatory.

'Cereal. Zak was shoving it in my hair all the way home.'

'I don't know what you're complaining about,' Cassandra retorted. 'Oatbran is very good for hair. Don't you ever read glossy magazines?' She raked Anna up and down with her chill glance. 'Mmmm. Thought not.'

'The loo stinks of *poo*,' Zak announced loudly as he emerged from investigating it and came back into the sitting room. 'Ugh!' he said, looking directly at Anna. Rage boiled within her. She'd had a pee, that was all. Little *bastard*.

'Darling, do you have a letter for me about some examinations?' Cassandra's voice was pure syrup.

'I don't think so,' Anna began.

'Not *you*. Zak.'

'No,' snapped Zak. 'Can we have a portable video disc player for the car?' he wheedled. 'Siena and Savannah have one. They only cost a thousand pounds and then you can watch pop videos in the people-carrier.'

'If you pass your exams, darling,' said Cassandra tightly. She didn't want to think about Savannah and Siena just now. 'Right, this letter must be somewhere. Let's just look in your pockets, shall we – *ugh*.'

Her face screwed up with revulsion as she unearthed a festering handful of paper, cloying cereal and a substantial quantity of rotting green matter which may or may not have been more of Otto Greatorex's scabby knee.

'I don't know *how* you could allow him to go about with all *this* in his pockets,' Cassandra ranted at Anna as she placed it gingerly on the table. 'It's *disgusting*. Probably *dangerous* . . . ah, here's the letter.' She smoothed out the chewed-up, screwed-up ball and scanned it quickly. 'Oh, it's easy peasy, darling. All you need to be able to do is draw a triangle and a circle and that sort of thing.'

She poked again at the matted mass on the table. Something shiny caught her eye. '*What's* this?' Cassandra's hand trembled as she held up what looked like a silver card. Her eyes blazed feverishly in her face. *Could* it possibly be . . .

' 'Ninvitation,' Zak said casually, his attention absorbed in setting fire to a pile of post with the microphone-shaped lighter which he had unearthed from under the coffee table.

'To *what*?' Cassandra's voice was trembling as well.

'S'vannah and Siena. Birthday party.'

'H-*how* long have you had it?'

''Bout a week. Not going to go, though. All *girls*.'

Cassandra gasped, then dropped to her knees before her child. 'Darling,' she breathed, her voice cracking with emotion, 'you *must* go. It's very *important* to Mummy that you go. Do it for Mummy, darling.'

'Nah,' said Zak, scowling.

'Isn't he wonderful?' Cassandra grinned rigidly at Anna. '*So* independent-minded. But *darling*,' she addressed him again, waving a finger, 'I'm afraid part of being grown up is that sometimes you have to do things you don't want to.'

'Fuck *off*,' said Zak and scampered out of the room.

Chapter 10

After the first week as Cassandra's nanny, Anna found it hard to believe she had ever been anything else. It was impossible, as she crept, back bent, round the house, Hoover in one hand, Harry Potter in the other, to imagine the scale of her past achievements. Neither the fact that she had a university degree nor that she had had a dashing, blond heir – albeit to a sewage fortune – as a lover now seemed possible. Her utter and permanent exhaustion wiped out even the fierce pangs of longing for Seb that had, at first, lain in wait to ambush her when she was at her lowest. But before long she didn't have the spare energy to squander on emotional indulgence. Her entire previous existence – and most sentient hours of her present one – seemed to have been annihilated by the cycle of toil and bone-tiredness otherwise known as looking after Zak. As well as all the housework. Anna had never known a building which required as much attention as Liv. Not to mention its mistress. Several times, since entering Cassandra's service Anna had felt life quite literally to be not worth Liv-ing.

She had heard, of course, that childcare was drudgery – the screaming in the night, the endless demands – but she had always imagined that was the child, rather than the mother. Not in this case. After completing the school run and returning to the house, Anna's first duty of the morning was to go up the three flights from the kitchen to Cassandra's bedroom with a tray containing her breakfast requirements. These comprised one peeled and cored Egremont Russet apple cut into eight identical sections, one slice of dry toast (lightly golden) with the crusts removed, Earl Grey tea in a china cup and saucer served with the merest dash of milk, and a vast number of different vitamin tablets – one each from the serried ranks of bottles kept in the kitchen. So vast, indeed, was the proportion of pills consumed compared to that of food that it seemed a miracle Cassandra didn't rattle when she moved. The gin, which swiftly followed half an hour after breakfast, may, Anna thought, possibly have had something to do with this.

Remarkably, Anna's first attempt at serving Cassandra's breakfast had gone without a hitch. She did not fall upstairs with the large and unwieldy tray, nor did she slip over on Cassandra's wooden bedroom floor and throw boiling hot water over her employer, tempting though it was. Anna went back down to the kitchen feeling ridiculously relieved. Until, that was, the already-familiar screech resonated through the house. Anna raced back up, her mind juddering with ghastly possibilities. Was the toast last season's tan rather than this season's pale gold? Had something unspeakable crept out of the slices of Egremont Russet? She arrived in Cassandra's bedroom to find her propped up against her pillows, her face contorted and purple with fury.

'The tea,' Cassandra roared. 'It's *disgusting*. I can't *possibly* drink such *filth*.'

'But it's weak, like you asked. With a dash of . . .'

'It's not *stirred*,' Cassandra yelled, jabbing a forefinger at the teaspoon lying beside the saucer. '*Deal* with it, will you?

'Perfect,' she pronounced five minutes later when Anna reappeared with a cup stirred so vigorously that, its journey up three flights of stairs notwithstanding, the milk was still swirling around like a flamenco dancer's skirt. 'You're learning.'

Anna was by now beginning to wonder if that was all she was learning. After days in the job, writing had not been mentioned once. There were, however, mitigating circumstances; as far as Anna could see,

Cassandra had not written a line since she had arrived at Liv, and seemed in any case to have been drunk or in a rage most of the time.

Night after night, when she had finished writing up her own diary, Anna would flick, uncomprehending, through the pages of Cassandra's novels, borrowed from the wenge bookcase downstairs that held nothing else, and wonder what the secret was that lay locked behind those tight-set lines of type. How could such bilge have sold in its hundreds of thousands of copies? Hopefully, some time soon, Cassandra would have sobered up or simmered down enough to tell her.

Her days having been spent largely at Cassandra's tyrannical beck and call, Anna's nights, on the sofabed which managed, like an anorexic with cellulite, to be thin and lumpy at the same time, were usually rent with screams from the floor below. Cassandra's violent rows with Jett seemed at their most ear-splitting between midnight and morning, and generally accompanied by the sound of smashing glass or crockery. The day Anna had started, she had been subjected to a lecture on the great care that had to be taken when cleaning the perfume bathroom; seven days later, Cassandra seemed to have destroyed every piece in it by herself and quite deliberately.

Anna chose not to think about the psychological damage the nightly battles were having on Zak; although it seemed unlikely that anything could make him viler than he was now. The fact that, with his blond basin cut, defiant expression and turn-of-the-century school clothes, Zak bore a disturbing resemblance to a photograph of the infant Hitler she had spotted one day in the book review pages of the *Daily Telegraph* hardly came as a surprise.

Having made this connection, Anna immediately dropped all pretence that it was from a sense of despair and powerlessness due to his parents' behaviour that Zak ordered her about, laughed at her clothes and, after she had served his cereal, threw it on the floor because he preferred his Bran Flakes dry and his milk flavoured with strawberry syrup and served in a separate glass. The child was obviously even more of a tyrant than his mother – and was beginning to exhibit some of his father's personality traits into the bargain. On the second day of her employment, Anna had crawled up to her room at bedtime to find him standing over the rucksack which still served her as an underwear respository, sniffing hard at a pair of her knickers.

After he had swaggered back downstairs, and she had reached for her diary to confide the episode to the battered exercise book, Anna noticed it seemed to be at the back of the drawer rather than the front of it. Had Cassandra been reading it? Anna profoundly hoped not; the first impressions of Liv and its inhabitants recorded there were far from flattering. However, the next day Cassandra seemed no more poisonous than usual, and if it had been Zak she was safe anyway as, despite the thousands upon thousands being stumped up for his education, he still had difficulty pronouncing words of more than two syllables. If the grand plans his mother had for him didn't come off, Anna thought, he would still be on course for a brilliant career as a breakfast TV presenter.

One reason at least that Zak's parents rowed mostly at night seemed to be that Jett, thankfully, was rarely around during the day. The few glimpses she got of Cassandra's husband – with his long, patchy, pube-like hair, balloon-like stomach, limbs as wrinkled as left-over sausages abandoned overnight on a dying barbecue and the unmistakable smell of armpit which seemed to fill the house whenever he was around – made Anna profoundly glad she had so far not had to suffer any of his attentions. Particularly the sort of attentions Alice had reported during the post-school-run morning coffee sessions in the café.

Yet one night Anna had woken and thought she had seen – in the bright light from the streetlamps afforded by the room's lack of curtain – the handle of the door slowly turning. Dragging herself up from the sofabed, she had quickly rammed the chair from the desk under the handle. Was it her imagination, or did the sound of retreating soft footsteps, and perhaps the faintest of rattles – as of the many chains, bracelets and rings Jett liked to festoon his wrinkled self with – then drift to her strained and anxious ears? During the day, as far as a thankful Anna could work out, Jett was apparently too busy preparing for a tour with his geriatric rock band and finishing a new album to pay much attention to her. At least, that was the official version of what he was up to. There came a day, however, which illuminated some of his other activities.

It had quickly become a source of great irritation to Anna that Cassandra expected her to take painstakingly accurate telephone messages on which the date, time and person were clearly marked, while evidently feeling no compunction whatsoever to return the compliment herself.

'Who was *that*?' she demanded one afternoon standing, arms folded, a foot away from the telephone after Anna, who had rushed right down from the top of the house to answer it, had completed taking down the message. 'And come downstairs less heavily. Those treads aren't meant to take people who weigh over ten stone.'

'It was The Earl of Wessex.'

A brilliant smile irradiated Cassandra's face. She punched the air in triumph, her grin unwavering even when she sent the Alexander Calder mobile into an unscheduled flat spin.

'*Dearest* Edward! So like him to call in person. *So* unaffected! Such a *shame* we couldn't make it to his and *dear* Soph's wedding . . .'

She paused and sighed happily.

'But I should have known they'd have us round for dinner just as soon as they could. Old friends being like gold and all that. When do they want us?'

'Now,' said Anna.

'Now?' Cassandra blinked rapidly. 'You've obviously got the message wrong,' she snapped. 'People like that book one for dinner at *least* six weeks in advance. What do you mean, *now*?'

'The Earl of Wessex in Golborne Road would like you to get there straightaway and fetch Mr St Edmunds who is apparently,' Anna struggled with her features, 'drunk and disorderly.'

Anna grinned as Cassandra tore, cursing, out of the door. She did not, however, have the last laugh for long.

Returning from the school run one morning, Anna opened the door at the end of the hall and felt instantly that something was wrong. This was partly because the door had collided with something hard, hairy and very strong-smelling. She yelped as the door opened fully to reveal a pair of naked hairy buttocks capering in the direction of the staircase. Unable to tear her horrified gaze away, she watched as they turned at the end to reveal a leopardskin thong. Above the beachball waistline, a vast crucifix on leather nestled in the patchy spaces of a thin-haired chest. A heavily beringed hand held an enormous joint.

Although behind the inevitable mirrored shades his

eyes were invisible, it was obvious Jett was far too high to feel embarrassed. On the contrary, he seemed glad of an audience. He inhaled deeply then breathed out, wiggling the roll-up between his huge teeth and flashing a crazed, Jack Nicholson grin at her. Anna recoiled from the smell. She had never liked cannabis; it reminded her of dates with charmless students in search of easy sex who, having tried and failed to get her drunk on college lager, brought out the cigarette papers and lighter in the hope she would abandon her inhibiting senses. The only abandon that ever ensued was the contents of Anna's stomach – invariably a kebab from the shop on the corner which was her escort's idea of dinner for two.

'Just rehearsing my stage routine.' Jett strutted back up the hall waggling his hips from side to side and pumping his arm in the air. The fanlight flashed in his mirror lenses. 'First gig in a fortnight.'

'Oh really?' Anna gasped, wondering how she could beat a polite retreat. 'Where? Wembley Arena?'

'You must be joking. Mandela Hall, Surbiton University, mate,' Jett said rotating his arm Pete Townshend style, until, hitting it on the banister, he yelped in agony and rubbed it hard. 'We're going straight to the goddamn people this time. No messing about in massive goddamn impersonal stadiums where no one can see you.' His voice held a hint of wistfulness. 'That's where it all went tits-up last time. Got too far away from our fan base. This time we're taking everything that will goddamn have us . . . um, I mean, no chances. Playing small halls and small audiences. Back to our goddamn *roots*.'

'I see,' Anna said, still wondering how she could get away. Suddenly, Jett shot out his undamaged hand and grasped her wrist so hard, his rings cut into her flesh.

'C'mon. C'mon. I wanna show you something.' She hoped, as he dragged her down the corridor, that it wasn't the contents of his thong.

'Wow,' said Anna, a few minutes later. 'It's incredible.'

'Not bad, huh?' agreed Jett proudly.

Anna gazed in amazement at the rows of handsome leather-bound volumes filling every wall of Jett's library. He had hardly struck her as the literary type; more the sort to think *Vanity Fair* was a glossy magazine and Shelley a shoe shop selling platformed soles and silver Dr Martens. This, however, was not the only reason the library was an anomaly; the style, classic Hammer Horror Gothic right down to the red velvet curtains and leaded windows, was utterly at odds with the aspirational minimalism of the rest of the house.

'Glad you like it,' Jett breathed, coming closer. Overwhelmed by the powerful garlic aroma of his breath, Anna hardly dared think of the near proximity of his hairy, unclothed body, least of all his thong. Fortunately, the end of his joint chose just that moment to fall off and disappear into the intensely patterned carpet. 'Damn,' cursed Jett, flicking furiously at the remainder with the silver microphone-shaped lighter. At least, Anna hoped it was a microphone. Just as she hoped that vast pink object in the corner wasn't what she thought it was.

'I see you've spotted Dick,' grinned Jett, waving an expansive arm towards the vast, thick and hideously veined protrusion somewhat at odds with the bust of Shakespeare in the niche above it. 'Ten-foot-tall rubber penis. Part of one of our old stage shows. Kept it out of sentiment – wanted to have it in the front garden at one point but Sandra wouldn't hear of it. Might take it on tour – it'll be good to get it up again.'

Anna cleared her throat and edged away on the pretext of admiring some of the volumes.

'How fantastic,' she enthused. 'You've got *everything*. From *The Idylls of the King* to the complete works of Christopher Marlowe. Amazing.'

'Yeah, and what's even *more* amazing,' yelped Jett, evidently restored after a deep drag or two, 'is that they've got the complete goddamn works of Martin Scorsese underneath them.' He stabbed the shelf beneath the book spines with his beringed forefinger. *Tamburlaine* lurched forward, then, slowly lowering itself to the horizontal, revealed the video of *Mean Streets* fitted snugly behind the leather spine.

Anna stared. 'What, they're all *videos*?'

Jett nodded. 'There's a button beneath each book which activates a spring at the back of the video and pushes it out,' he explained proudly. 'All filed by what you might call free association. Sixteenth-century playwrights equal mobster movies – I reckoned old Marlowe had probably seen some pretty goddamn mean streets in his time – while all those repressed Victorian chicks are the porn section.' He flipped *Wuthering Heights* forward to reveal the lurid cover of *Debbie Does Dallas*.

'Yeah, I've read most of the classics,' he told her. Anna could see her astonished face reflected in his lenses. 'Can't beat 'em for song ideas. Wrote a great one about King Lear called "Bitch Daddy" and then of course you'll remember the *Bloodcastle* album inspired by Macbeth. Number one both sides of the Atlantic. Nineteen seventy-eight,' he added, wistfully. 'What a great goddamn year *that* was. Wrote off the Rolls in the goddamn swimming pool. Jagger was *furious* . . .' He took another long drag of his joint.

Why was it, Anna wondered, that all rock and roll anecdotes seemed to involve Mick Jagger and swimming pools.

'Specially as it was his neighbour's goddamn swimming pool. I'd got the wrong goddamn garden. Say, let's put some *goddamn music on*,' Jett suddenly shouted. He threw himself into a vast, carved, throne-like chair and produced a large gold ingot studded with what looked like vast, different coloured jewels. It was only after he started to stab furiously at it that Anna realised it was a remote control.

One of the walls of volumes on the opposite side of the room slid aside to expose a vast TV the size of a cinema screen. It instantly flicked into life to show a plump dark-haired girl, naked apart from a black leather bustier, whip and cap festooned with chains, thrusting away on top of a skinny, long-haired man wearing sunglasses and an ecstatic expression. He looked, Anna thought, vaguely familiar.

'Oops,' giggled Jett, shoving his joint back between his teeth and stabbing anew at the remote. 'My version of *Emma*. Not quite the same as Jane goddamn Austen's. Let's have some music instead.' As the screen slid away behind the rows of Fieldings and Popes, a vast stereo appeared; what had been an entire wall of Shakespeare slid from sight.

'*You*,' said Jett, jumping about in his seat and pointing the remote in the direction of the stereo, 'are about to be the luckiest goddamn woman on *earth*.'

Anna, catching sight of the sprouts of salty growth under Jett's armpits, doubted it.

'Because *you*,' Jett went on, 'are about to have a private world prem-eer of Solstice's comeback album.'

Anna said nothing.

'*Featuring*,' Jett added, still fumbling with the remote control, 'thanks to the miracles of modern technology, our former bassist Dirty del Amico, the greadest axeman rock and roll has ever seen until he perished in a mysterious gardening accident twenny years ago. *Play that axe, dead boy*,' Jett screamed, leaping to his feet and puffing frantically on his spliff as a head-spinning blast of the loudest music Anna had ever heard suddenly shook the library to its foundations. She tried not to look as Jett, starting to headbang frantically, set all his wobbly bits reverberating like wind chimes in a gale. Suddenly, he rushed over to the stereo and, grinding his buttocks into its buttons while still facing Anna, started to jerk wildly up and down. She swallowed, fearing the worst, until she realised he was attempting to push the volume control up with his bottom.

'*Say, you're a really cool chick*,' Jett screeched. He pulled Anna towards himself and breathed a mixture of garlic, sweat and patchouli in her face. Something hard was pressing against her, somewhere in the region of the thong. '*I can instinctively tell you empathise with creadive people*,' he bawled at her. '*My wife doesn't understand me ad all. Ad all. I'm just a money factory as far as she's concerned. A goddamn trophy husband . . .*'

'Trophy *husband*?'

Anna was suddenly aware the sound had been turned abruptly off. A ringing silence now filled the library.

'*Trophy* husband?' repeated the acid voice that Anna recognised, heart sinking, as Cassandra's. Wrapped in her pashmina bathrobe, Cassandra, barefoot, silently circled the pair. Her eyes were mean and narrow. 'Depends what you mean by *trophy*, I suppose,' she hissed, her glance, now mocking, sliding from Anna to Jett and back again. 'If you mean a *rotting moosehead* someone shot in nineteen fifty-eight, I suppose I'd have to go along with it. *Atrophy* husband, more like. Except when it comes to getting your end away with the sodding nanny. *Bloody hell, you don't waste much time, do you?*' she screamed at Jett, who pressed himself back against the stereo, his thong shrinking visibly.

'And as for *you* . . .' As Cassandra took a step towards her, Anna recoiled. But not soon enough. As Cassandra pressed her face threateningly close, an overpowering smell of gin filled Anna's nostrils. 'I've been waiting,' Cassandra hissed. 'Waiting and *waiting* . . .' Anna felt herself start to shake. Nonetheless, it occurred to her to wonder – if Cassandra had been so certain Jett would try to seduce her, why hadn't she stopped him? 'And *waiting*,' Cassandra continued. 'So in the end I came downstairs.' She paused again, eyes glittering, then struck. 'Where the FUCK is my fucking breakfast?'

'Oh no. That's just too funny! Hope you put *that* in the diary.' As Geri spluttered her café au lait all over her nurse's uniform, the waiters looked at them with interest.

Anna felt both irritated and gratified that someone

found her ordeal amusing. Her legs still ached from the five times Cassandra had proceeded to send her tea back, and she had ironing blisters. The sheer scale of the pile Cassandra demanded she spend the day pressing had had a fairy tale quality – it had made Anna feel pretty Grimm, in any case. Still, it had been good material for the diary, whatever purpose *that* might eventually serve.

'Actually,' Geri confessed, 'she accused *me* yesterday of having a fling with him.'

'*What?*'

'She called me on my private line and told me to fuck off and stop ringing her husband.'

'And were you?' Remembering the aftermath of Thoby's wedding, Anna braced herself for the worst.

'*Of course not.*' Geri looked outraged. 'When I'm *that* desperate I'll stick my mobile up myself. It vibrates,' she explained, catching Anna's puzzled glance. 'No, Cassandra pressed one four seven one. It must have been after I'd tried to call you. When I answered she must have thought I was one of his slappers. So do I take it he *is* on the loose again, then?'

'You could say that,' said Anna, thinking of the thong. 'Last night she flung an entire dinner service at him whilst yelling she was a woman who loved too much.'

'What *she* loves too much is gin,' Geri grinned. 'No wonder she can't write any more.'

There was a silence. Then Anna remembered something.

'Did you say you had a private line?'

'Of course. Naturally the family pay for all the calls . . . even if my bill does sometimes look like an international phone book.' Geri grinned guiltily.

'I can't believe it. Cassandra makes me pay whenever I use her phone. Even if I don't get through.'

'That's ridiculous. She should bloody well give you your own phone. Insist on a digital answerphone as well, and while you're at it, get the stingy cow to give you a mobile. Preferably a vibrating one like mine. Hours of fun, I promise you.'

'Some hope.' The nearest she was going to get to a mobile, Anna thought miserably, was Alexander Calder in the hallway.

'So,' said Geri, a careful look creeping into her eyes. 'She given you any writing lessons yet?'

Anna's heart sank. At the back of the café she could hear Slob, Allegra, Trace and Alice laughing with each other. No doubt because, Anna reflected jealously, they had all probably had two changes of sports car and three pay rises since yesterday. Reluctantly, she shook her head.

'Shall I tell you something?' Geri looked at her. 'I think you're wasting your time with Cassandra. Time for a change of focus. I've been thinking about you, and—'

Anna took a deep breath. Her measured tones, she hoped, gave no hint of the fury suddenly filling her. 'As I recall, you'd been thinking about me when you encouraged me to get a writing apprenticeship in the first place,' she burst out. 'And look where *that's* got me.'

'*Quite*,' said Geri, not batting an eyelid. 'But we need to approach it a different way. It's obvious that you don't want to be a nanny, despite us all spelling out to you the advantages. If you still want to write books, well, fine. But you need more than a great novel to get what you want out of life.'

'I *do?*' How did Geri always manage to completely wrong-foot her?

'Absolutely. What you need is a great *man*. A rich one, so you don't have to work and can write your books without having to wait hand and foot on Cassandra and rush off to Operabugs and junior Cordon Bleu every five minutes. And *I'm* going to help you find him.' She grinned broadly at Anna. 'There. What about it?'

'But I'm a complete failure with men,' Anna wailed.

'Rubbish. You may not be in a brilliant position bookwise, but you're certainly in one manwise.'

'*What?*' The dreadful suspicion that Geri was encouraging her to have a fling with Jett dawned on Anna. She blinked hard to eradicate the memory of his scrawny, hairy buttocks bouncing around in front of her in the hall.

'I mean that when nannies pick the family they're going to work for, they should do it with two things in mind. One is everything we discussed last time. The other,' Geri paused, fixing Anna with her Malteser-brown stare, 'is the man-meeting potential. High-profile, high-earning families, such as the one I work for, attract high-profile and high-earning men to their dinner parties. The type of men no nanny could hope to meet in normal circumstances.' Geri leant forward, eyes glowing. 'You coming to Savannah and Siena's birthday party on Saturday?'

Anna nodded. 'Cassandra bribed Zak with a digital camera to get him to go.'

'Good. Because, let me tell you, it's a man *magnet*. Those kids have so many godfathers, it's not true. Kate and Julian asked practically every mover and shaker in the country to come and move and shake by the font. Establishment, high society, the arts, the lot. You can't *fail* to score.'

'Just watch me,' said Anna, miserably.

Chapter 11

By dawn on the day of Savannah and Siena's party, Cassandra had already been up for several hours struggling with the computerised wardrobe. Denim shirt and jeans for that wholesome, Hope-Stanley, yoghurt-ad look? Or more smart Sloane with the loafers and stand-up collar? Casual yet stylish was what she was going for; you couldn't join in Sardines and Pass the Parcel in Givenchy couture (although Shayla Reeves would probably try to). What she wanted was something scruffy enough for games but smart enough to translate to the Number Ten dinner table, should Cherie suddenly find herself a body short of a *placement* and remember that perfectly charming writer at Kate's children's party.

Cassandra had prepared for the party like a military offensive. Every grooming eventuality was anticipated. By the end of the week, she had had a full-peel facial, manicure and pedicure and even a bikini wax. Well, you never knew. It might be sunny and she didn't want to be sprouting around the gusset of her Versace swimsuit. A bit of hedge-trimming was essential.

The remainder of her time had been spent finding exactly the right presents. Ignoring Zak's insistence that what Savannah and Siena really wanted was a plastic ray gun and a light sabre respectively, Cassandra had rifled the racks of Oilily, Petit Bateau and half junior Bond Street before settling on two fabulously sequinned and frill-festooned party dresses, complete with huge net underskirts, from Please Mum. She was, Cassandra told herself as she left the shop with her bags, now ready for all eventualities. The only thing that remained out of her control was the SMSPA Promises auction to be held at the party.

Cassandra bitterly regretted her offer – well, as much as anything you were *forced into* could possibly be an offer – to cook a dinner party for eight at her home. She quailed at the thought of who might win it and, in order to prevent such ghastly eventualities as having to wait on Fenella Greatorex and friends hand and foot, almost considered bringing Jett along to outbid everyone else. Financial considerations – Jett, after all, was the man who bid ten thousand pounds for one of

Eric Clapton's guitar strings during that dreadful period when he was trying to set up a rock and roll museum – had forced her to abandon the plan. The added risk that Cherie might clap eyes on Jett had been judged worse than Fenella Greatorex's being the highest bidder for the dinner. Cassandra had decided philosophically, that, if Fenella won, she would just have to put Tippex in the sauce.

Anna too had been up for hours. Saturday was glass day – after doing all the windows she had now moved on to the mirrors. She sprayed furniture polish on the vast, frameless one in the hall and rubbed it while trying not to look at her dejected reflection. It was difficult to avoid it – the sheer misery in her eyes drew the viewer. Once sparkling, they were now as flat as week-old Bollinger; her hair looked redder and lanker than ever beside the grey of her exhausted face. The only comfort was that she looked thinner – cheekbones, faint, but discernible, ridged each side of her formerly shapeless cheeks. Her mouth too, though pale and dry, seemed bigger. Anna tried to smile at herself, but the lips didn't move. I don't do smiling any more, she thought.

I must get out of here, she repeated mantra-like to herself with each circle of her duster. God knows how, though. Or *where*. I've no money, nowhere to live and no skills to speak of, especially housework . . . *damn* this polish. Every stroke of the cloth left wild white streaks elsewhere on the mirror's surface. Cleaning, Anna was beginning to realise, was more exacting an art than she had imagined.

Depressing though it was to admit it, Geri was right. Cassandra had absolutely no intention of teaching her anything at all about writing and Zak had no intention of doing anything other than making her life a misery. The only mercy was that the library incident with Jett had thankfully not been repeated – Anna had kept well away from its Gothic portals, especially after having, during one of Cassandra's rants about her being more useless even than her predecessors, worked out who the Emma in the video must be. Less thankfully, Jett had recently taken to squeezing past her in the corridor and, less excusably, in rooms containing sufficient space for two articulated lorries to pass each other, let alone two people. On each occasion Anna had been aware of something large and hard in the region formerly occupied by the leopardskin thong.

'Sue him for sexual harassment,' Geri had urged her. 'I would. I knew a nanny who sued her employer's husband for coming into her bathroom by mistake. She wasn't even in it at the time. *You'd* make a fortune. Jett's famous – or *was*.'

'And be all over the papers?' protested Anna. 'Spend the rest of my life being the woman who was groped by some has-been old celebrity? At least Monica Lewinsky was groped by the President of the United States.'

'Well, he'll be a has-been old celebrity soon,' said Geri.

'Yes, but imagine it all over the *News of the World* – The Rock Star, Me And That Leopardskin Thong.'

'Well, it's got more of a ring to it than that boring old blue dress. I think you should consider it.'

Anna sighed and rubbed her polish harder. The sound of the telephone ringing in the hall was a welcome diversion.

'Guest list for the party's looking *great*,' Geri whispered on the other end. 'Two financiers, three actors, four TV executives, a lord and a couple of national newspaper editors, and that's just for starters. *Your* best bet is one of the financiers. *Stinking* rich and – although admittedly this *is* a drawback – *young*.'

'Why is that a drawback?'

'They're best old, really, then they drop off the perch after the honeymoon and leave you all their money. The good news is, no emotional baggage or, worse, grabby first wife wanting tons of alimony. He's unmarried – never has been, from what I can work out – but *seems* to be straight. Reasonable-looking, as well, apparently, although I've never seen him in the flesh to confirm this.'

'Sounds like a real dreamboat,' said Anna, unable to stop a note of grumpiness creeping into her voice.

'Hey, well, you've got to know what you're dealing with in this game,' Geri said huffily. 'No point me steering you towards some sex god who turns out to be penniless and as gay as New Year's Eve into the bargain.'

'No, *absolutely*,' said Anna, realising Geri sounded annoyed. Alienating her would not be a good idea. Not now, when, however mad her schemes sounded, they represented a better route to escape than any she could think up herself. 'Thanks. Really, he sounds *wonderful*. Just the job.'

'Good,' said Geri, mollified. 'Anyway, get here as early as you can. And don't forget – look *gorgeous*.'

How *amazingly* self-confident, thought Cassandra as she trotted into the entrance hall holding her invitation like a shield. How almost *show-offy* of the Tressells to have the party *in their own house*. Only people with nothing to hide and everything to reveal dared expose their homes to the scrutiny of other St Midas's mothers and fathers, most of whom, when their own children's birthdays came round, preferred to stump up the thousands demanded by Hollywood theme restaurants for a couple of burgers, a shake and a photo opportunity with an Arnold Schwarzenegger lookalike.

'It's very cutting edge,' was all Geri had said to Anna of the Tressell home and current world headquarters of her operations, a converted former prison in Islington. Well, Anna thought, entering in Cassandra's Gucci-heeled wake, there was certainly plenty of glass. Above the transparent hall roof, the grey London sky hung like a giant old grey T-shirt. She wondered what the drill was when, as it occasionally must, a passing pigeon let fly a splatter or two. She glanced at the shattered-blue-glass-effect floor, which Zak trying to shatter further by removing his black patent shoes and using the heels as hammers.

'Stop that *now*.' Geri detached herself from a milling group in the light, circular hall where, stuffed as usual into her plunging uniform, she was rounding up the arrivals and their broods with the efficiency of One Man And His Dog.

Among the throng, Anna spotted Allegra shepherding a child in a pink net tutu. Slobodan shuffled in behind her with a pair of basin-cut boys, looking, as usual, as if he'd just got out of bed; Anna wondered whose. A plump, dark-haired girl who confirmed Anna's worst suspicions about Jett's video, was being clung to by a pale, frightened-looking child with noticeably scarred knees – Otto Greatorex, Anna realised. A delicate and extremely handsome Japanese man was visibly buckling under the weight of a very large, pink-faced child in a – possibly real – tiara, whom he held in his arms; this, Anna realised, must be Hanuki, the first male Japanese Norlander. Well he'd certainly got his hands full.

The parents and godparents, distinguishable by their unhassled expressions, brimming glasses of champagne and complete absence of any children near them, stood chatting happily in a group in the centre of the hall while the nannies and children formed a loose collective at one end. The pink-faced child, Anna noticed, had already thrown up something purple and sticky down the front of Hanuki's white shirt. Beside her, Zak was banging on the floor again.

'Children and nannies in there,' Geri shouted above the chaos, indicating a room in which serried ranks of forms and tables could be glimpsed. 'Parents and godparents this way.' She pointed to where a waitress stood by a door bearing a tray with yet more champagne glasses.

'Not so fast,' Geri murmured as Anna headed automatically after Slobodan, Alice, Trace and the rest of them. 'You're helping me with the nibbles. Best way for you to meet people. I've OK'd it with Kate, so Cassandra can't object. Leave Zak with Trace.'

Zak looked mutinous as the massive Trace, her face set, clasped his fat wrist in her strong grip and whisked him off into the children's room.

'You look very smart, by the way,' Geri said. 'Lost weight, haven't you?'

Anna nodded and grinned. 'All thanks to washing-up liquid.'

Geri stared. Then her face relaxed. 'Oh, I see, the old Fairy Liquid trick. Do that, do you?'

'No, not me,' said Anna. '*Cassandra.*'

Although the housework work-out had no doubt

helped, it had been Cassandra's habit of obliterating temptation by squeezing washing-up liquid over Zak's leftovers and any other cooked food she found in the kitchen that had really made the difference for Anna. A pizza and several sandwiches Anna had made for her own supper had, several times, been rendered inedible this way. She had been furious at the time, but now, given that her trousers hung slackly from her waist and she'd managed to tuck her shirt in without feeling remotely self-conscious, she felt almost grateful to Cassandra. Almost.

'The idea,' Geri was explaining, 'is that the grown-ups have their party while the children have their tea, their games and the party entertainer. Then we all get together for the Promises auction and the disco.' Gingerly, she touched the skin beneath her eyes, careful not to smudge any of her precisely applied make-up. 'I'm *knackered*. I was up more or less all night wrapping forty Pass the Parcels in recycled paper containing Third World-friendly items. Did you realise that these days you have to have a present between *every layer?*'

As yet more sleek parents and sleeker offspring arrived, Geri hustled Anna into a vast kitchen off the main hall in which a production line of chefs was busy making faces from basil, mozzarella, anchovies and olives on a collection of mini pizzas. 'Olives!' whispered Anna. 'I didn't think children liked olives.'

'Well, these ones do,' said Geri. 'What's more, they

can distinguish between about ten different types. Olive oil as well – they spend so much time in Tuscany they think "Like A Virgin" is a song about first cold pressings.'

Anna giggled. 'They're very glamorous, these chefs,' she muttered. Male and female, each one had the heavy eyebrows, lithe limbs and bee-stung lips of a super-model. They smouldered at each other as they arranged the anchovies into smiles.

'They're from some screamingly expensive Italian restaurant by the river, apparently,' Geri hissed. 'But I've got better things lined up for you than them. Take these.' She thrust a plateful of perfect miniature bacon sandwiches at Anna, each complete with heart-shaped dab of tomato ketchup beside it and a plastic skewer bearing the initials SS. 'Make sure you eavesdrop on all the conversations,' Geri warned, as they sailed forth through a sliding aluminium side door which led from the kitchen to a large, light, glass-walled reception room. 'They're hilarious. I once overheard three women talking for hours about vaginal sprays and how much their husbands earned.'

Giggling, they swept into the crowd.

'Why *do* people in England despise success so much?' a woman in violently coloured clothes was saying to a toned, tanned man with close-cropped white hair as Anna and Geri started to circle the room.

'*Who's* that?' Anna mouthed.

'Julian, of course,' said Geri, her eyes fixed longingly on her employer's face. 'Oh, the woman? Son at St Midas's. He's got the concentration span of a gnat. They're hoping he's autistic, I believe. *She's* a happening fashion editor.'

'Looks more like a what's happened fashion editor,' observed Anna, taking in the pink hair, yellow dress and orange tights, topped off with a large black fedora. She looked with interest at Julian Tressell, short-cropped, sandalled and dressed from head to foot in white linen, his only decoration a CCCP Soviet-era Lenin badge in deep red enamel and gold.

'Yes, she is rather post-nuclear.'

'And who's that?' Anna slid her eyes meaningfully at Kate Tressell talking to a pneumatic blonde in a tight white dress and hot pink heels that added at least a foot to her height. Beside her exuberant beauty, Kate's hemp suit, though doubtless eye-wideningly expensive, looked drab and monastic.

'Champagne D'Vyne,' whispered Geri. 'You know, that spectacularly thick society columnist. She's supposed to be getting married next month to an unfeasibly rich landowner called Juan Legge, but it'll never happen. She always trades them in at the last minute for something better.'

'Lucky her.' Anna took in Champagne's ripples of ice-blonde hair, undulating figure and spectacular tan. Netting landowners must be a breeze when you looked like that. She strained to hear the conversation.

'Are you thrilled about the wedding?' Kate was asking.

'Oh yah,' Champagne replied in a bored voice. '*Beside* myself.'

'Will you be wearing white?'

'God no. Dior I thought.'

Anna and Geri caught each other's eye.

'You go that way and I'll go this,' Geri hissed, shoulders shaking. 'Meet you in a minute.'

Anna veered away and headed towards a pair of matronly thirtysomethings in sensible heels.

'. . . well, at the moment we've got what you might describe as a *below stairs* problem.'

'Oh *really*? Does it involve wearing paper pants?'

'No, the *nanny*, silly.'

'Oh. Of course. The *nanny*. Oh, yes please. Bacon sandwiches, how *scrumptious*.'

Anna now bore down on a thin woman with an Anna Wintour crop and a lilac cashmere cardigan listening to a tall, haughty blonde in a lime green lacy dress.

'We know he's a boy, yes, well, if he has my looks and Marco's brains, he's bound to be fine.'

And both of your modesty, thought Anna, proffering her wares.

'*No* thank you.' Both women looked at the food in horror. 'What are we going to call him?' continued the blonde. 'Well, we were thinking about Wyndham, but it sounds a bit *bottomy*, and then Louis, but when you come to think of it, that's rather redolent of lavatories as *well* . . .'

Anna stood as the woman in the cardigan, apparently unable to stop herself, slid out the skewers from a couple of sandwiches, peeled off the bread topping and, without moving anything from the tray, crammed the pieces of bacon hurriedly into her mouth.

'Yes, you've got to be careful,' she agreed, amid much loud sucking of red-tipped fingers. 'You need to steer clear of anything that's going to be pilfered by centre forwards or triplicated in the nursery. We had the most awful time – our first choices were Atlanta or Aurora, both once solidly B1, but now skidding firmly into C2 territory, I'm afraid. We considered Cheyenne, but . . .'

'*So* trailer trash.'

'Mmm, so in the end we called her Doris.'

'*Lovely*. So *millennium*.'

Anna drifted away to where a reed-thin woman in a linen dress with eyebrows plucked into surprised-looking arcs was talking animatedly to an exhausted-looking man. 'Well, of course I went *straight* to my homeopathic doctor, and she said my stomach was like a pond that hadn't been cleaned for years.'

The man paled. They both shook their heads at the sandwiches.

'Vegetarian,' said the man.

The woman's eyes lit up. 'Really? *Are* you? How very interesting . . .'

'That was Frank Gibbons,' whispered Geri as she swung by with her plate of sandwiches. 'Siena's godfather. Edits the *Guardian*.'

'Really? Who's that he's with?'

'His wife. He's so busy that the only time they get to speak to each other is at parties.'

Anna grinned. Geri, she noticed, had got rid of even fewer sandwiches than she had herself.

'Last round before we refuel,' Geri said as they parted ways again. 'We'll need to reheat. I'm not sure your financier has arrived yet, by the way. Probably delayed closing the deal that will make his fortune. Even *more* of his fortune,' she added hurriedly.

Anna moved off in the direction of two more glamorous women in skimpy dresses and the type of strappy sandals that, on lesser mortals, would have been a showcase for bunions and stubbed, square toes.

'. . . unfortunately he's at that stage where he thinks bottoms and poo are *hilarious*,' one was saying to the other.

'Tell me about it,' said the other woman. 'Marcus's hand is practically *welded* to his *you know what*. Dreadfully embarrassing when we were on holiday – there we were, outside the Fairfaxes' wonderful *palazzo*, feasting on hand-reared pasta, when Mango Fairfax suddenly says *what on earth* is Marcus doing? And we all look and – well, frankly, he had his hand on it and was yanking it up and down for all it was *worth* . . . don't suppose we'll be asked there again. No thank you, I don't eat bacon.'

Or anything else by the look of you, Anna thought as she sailed off, almost colliding with Geri who was hurrying urgently towards her.

'Look, look, he's over there. Just arrived. Your financier. Talking to those men,' hissed Geri. 'Grey suit. Quick, girl, get over there with your nibbles.'

Obediently, Anna wove her way through the throng to the other side of the room where a group of smartly dressed men were braying conversationally at each other. She approached the grey back – it seemed rather broad – and hovered. A narrower navy one next to it turned and grinned at her. 'Delicious,' he said, stuffing two in his mouth at once. 'Sandwiches aren't bad either.'

Anna rolled her eyes. The old ones, she thought, were most definitely the old ones. Irritatingly, the grey back was the last of the group to turn and attack the sandwiches. And when he did, Anna wished he hadn't bothered. Not only was he plump, pink-faced and almost bald, he was also Orlando Gossett. Anna threw a burning mortar of a glance over to where Geri stood, open-mouthed, on the other side of the room. Was this her idea of a joke? Her pale face and shocked expression, however, suggested she was as surprised as Anna was.

'Orlando . . . what . . . what on earth are you doing here?' Anna stammered. Gossett looked at her in astonishment. His eyes did not register the faintest hint of recognition.

'You're very *familiar*,' he boomed. 'But, since you ask, I'm one of Savannah's *thousands* of godfathers.'

'Oh, are you?' asked the navy suit. 'Me too.'

'Yah, Julian's an old mucker of mine – built me an outdoor sauna recently, as it happens,' honked Gossett. 'Quite an achievement considering I live in a mansion block in Fulham. Actually,' he said, screwing his small blue eyes up at Anna, 'you know . . . you *are* familiar actually. Didn't we meet at a wedding or something?'

'Yes, in Scotland,' said Anna. 'Thoby and Miranda's.'

'Gosh, your company gets around, doesn't it? Well, the eats here are a damn sight better than they were at Bollocks's. Worst food in the world, that was. Canapés looked like cat sick. Tasted like it too.'

'Can't say I've ever tasted cat sick,' Anna retorted. 'But the food *was* dreadful.' Even if the waiters weren't, she added mentally, a sudden vision of Jamie coming to mind. She was jolted from her musings by what felt like her spine leaping out from between her shoulder-blades. Orlando Gossett was slapping her on the back.

'*I* remember now. Course. Friend of Lavenham's, weren't you?'

Anna nodded.

'Enjoy the other day?'

'What other day?'

'Lavenham's wedding, of course.'

It felt as if a bucket of freezing water had been flung in her face. '*Wedding?*'

'Yah. Whirlwind stuff. You didn't go? Actually, I didn't either. No one did – tiny private do at the Chelsea Register Office, Lavenhams and de Benhams only, and then off to this island – Knacker, I think it's called.'

'You mean Necker,' said Geri, who had just floated up. 'How *ghastly*. Necker's so five minutes ago. Anyone who's anyone's honeymooning in the Maldives. Or going backpacking, like Lachlan Murdoch . . .' The jaunty note in her voice dried up as she saw Anna's white-green face.

'*De Benhams?*' stammered Anna, her tongue moving slowly around her dry mouth. 'Seb's married *Brie de Benham*?'

Orlando nodded emphatically. 'Yup.' His eye caught one of the waitresses circulating with glasses of champagne and he threw back his head to drain his existing flute. Champagne cascaded down his shirt front. 'Yah,' he bubbled, foaming at the mouth. 'Everyone's *thrilled*. Lavenham's mother, particularly. Apparently couldn't *wait* to see the back of the last girlfriend.'

Anna staggered away with her tray and headed out

to the kitchen. It was empty; the chefs were presumably busy with the children. She sat down at the counter and stared, stunned, into space, unable to decide whether the numb feeling inside her was devastation or indifference. Seb married to Brie de Benham. It was so utterly predictable she almost wanted to laugh. So expected – and yet not expected at all. Geri rubbed her sympathetically on the back. 'Never mind. He was a bastard. Treated you like shit.'

Anna's eyes pricked. Her throat ached. She sniffed. No, she told herself. I *will not cry*. She wiped a hand across her nose. 'It's the shock, I suppose. Not that it's that much of a surprise. He was always going to marry someone like her.'

'W*ere* you *in love* with him?' Geri's voice, though incredulous, had softened.

Anna nodded miserably. 'Yes. Yes I was. He was very good-looking. Impossibly handsome. But in the end he turned out to be just impossible.' Geri rubbed her back again. 'Yes, I loved him. But I was very let down.' Anna stopped and forced a smile at her friend. 'Sound like Princess Di, don't I?'

Geri thrust a brimming glass of champagne at her. 'Sounded like a nasty piece of work to me. Looked like one too – that handsome but shifty type. I vaguely remember him from that Scottish wedding.'

'Shame you didn't remember Orlando Gossett as well,' Anna sniffed, mopping her eyes with a piece of kitchen towel. 'I'm amazed you forgot *him*. He more or less smashed you to bits during the eightsome reels.'

'Believe me, I haven't forgotten,' Geri said. 'I've still got the scars. But he never actually told me what he was called. So when I saw his name on the party list, I was none the wiser. I judged solely on his other criteria, although I have to say,' she added, wrinkling her brow, 'my informant who claimed he was reasonable looking has rather low standards. Subterranean, even.'

Anna managed a smile. Geri looked at her. 'Come on. We're wasting valuable man-meeting time. Once more into the breeches.'

By now, miniature bacon sandwiches had given way to tiny vegetarian burgers, each with their Savannah and Siena skewer and a V-shaped blob of mustard on the side denoting their meat-free state. Anna again approached the *Guardian* editor and his wife.

'JJ – you know, the one who has a decoupage shop in Fulham – rang me yesterday,' Mrs Gibbons was twittering. 'Ooh, *thank* you. Look, darling, little *veggie burgers* . . . well, she's just got back from running with the sheep. Ovine alignment therapy, it's called.'

Frank Gibbons, although heavily occupied stuffing in two burgers and balancing another two in his napkin, stared in astonishment at his wife. '*Uuggghhh?*'

'*Terribly* good for you. You go to an Australian sheep ranch, live in a tent and run with the baa-baas all day. Gets rid of all your city neuroses, apparently. Mmm, *may* I just have another one? *So* delicious.'

'*That,*' said Gibbons decisively, 'is a feature.' Placing his burgers down on a nearby construction of plastic and wood whose function was not immediately apparent, he fished out his mobile and started to stab the keys.

'So I might stop having monkey gland injections in my bottom and try that,' Mrs Gibbons was saying. 'I'm not sure they did me much good anyway. But lots of people swear by them. *Ooh*, just one more then.'

'Well, you swore by them when you came home,' Gibbons observed, pressing his mobile to his ear. 'The air was blue until the pain wore off and you could sit down again . . . Hello? Editor here. Get me Features.'

The Gibbons having decimated her supplies, Anna returned to the kitchen. Geri was peering through a porthole in the connecting door to the children's room. 'Entertainer's going down a storm,' she reported. 'He's getting them all to pretend to be animals.'

'*Pretend?*' said Anna with feeling.

'I always find it amazing how entertainers remember the children's names,' Geri mused. 'But then I suppose they're all called either Venetia, Jack or something ending in "o" so it's not that difficult.' She turned back into the kitchen.

'Puddings now,' she announced. 'I'll take the little tartes au citron and you take the miniature jam roly-polys. Don't forget the thimbles of custard.'

As they opened the door into the adult room, the sound of braying voices hit them like a wall.

As Anna took a deep breath and prepared to plunge in, a soft voice beside her said, 'Hello.'

Anna turned. Someone with floppy dark hair and wide-apart eyes looked back at her. Dressed in a smart three-piece suit in Prince of Wales check, Jamie looked very different from his last appearance as the uncertain bearer of a tray full of dirty glasses.

'Er . . . just going to the loo,' trilled Geri, over-obviously making herself scarce.

Chapter 12

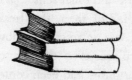

Spreadeagled on the loo seat, Cassandra was feeling distinctly inebriated. She'd had a good four glasses to calm her nerves and had now retired to the bathroom to regroup her forces. After all, the two great challenges of the day were still to come – the meeting with Cherie Blair, *still* not here but expected, and that wretched Promises auction. It was imperative that things went well at both.

Cassandra's head swam. Champagne always had a devastating effect on delicate nervous systems like hers, particularly in the quantities she'd consumed it. She tried to focus on her surroundings, but immediately wished she hadn't. *Damn*, thought Cassandra, looking about her with twisted and envious lips at the blanket-sized taupe towels, the vast greige granite bath, the recycled green glass cistern in which a number of tropical fish glided serenely around and the tiny chrome push-button taps tucked away above the granite sink.

It was all *so bloody tasteful*. It made her own attempts at minimalism look about as stylish and assured as those things they used to make on Blue Peter with sticky-back plastic and toilet rolls. *Loo* rolls, Cassandra corrected herself. But then, the Tressells' converted Islington prison was universally acknowledged to be a modern masterpiece, even though some dissenting voices – Jett's for one – had been contemptuous of its pointed eschewal of obvious luxury. 'Still looks like the inside of Pentonville,' Jett had scoffed when Cassandra had shown him the feature on it in *House and Garden*. She had been so busy condemning him as a philistine that it only occurred to her later to wonder how he *knew*.

It was odd, but Cassandra could not wrest her thoughts away from Julian Tressell. She'd always found him handsome, but today . . . well, she'd initially had trouble identifying the unfamiliar feeling but she felt positively *randy* towards him. But architects *were* sexy, she thought. All that talk about pillars and erections . . .

Standing up, she looked in the mirror that covered the whole of one wall. She looked *stunning* today. This skirt, well, she had wondered if it was a *bit* short, but *no*, how could it be – it showed almost the entire length of her still-excellent legs. No man could resist a really cracking pair of pins and Julian was a better judge of fine structures than most. Cassandra moved closer to the mirror, ran her tongue round her lips and thrust her hips out. Her nipples pinged erect under the thin fabric of her top. Christ, she was a sexy beast.

Cassandra lowered herself with difficulty on to the marble floor. You never knew, it *might* still work, and there were few better ways of relieving tension. Flipping off her knickers – not that there was enough of *those* to seriously get in the way – Cassandra slid a hand between her legs. Christ, it was like a swimming pool down there. Somewhere down here was *that bit* . . . ah, here it was. Cassandra began to rub slowly up and down, caressing her nipple with her free hand, running her tongue around her lips and thinking of Julian Tressell. Mmm. This was *good.* That sort of electric build-up feeling in her legs . . . She raised her pelvis and rubbed harder. Damn, lost it . . . ah, no, here it was again. 'Mmmm. *Mmmmm . . . oh, oh . . .*' Cassandra gasped.

'You OK?'

Cassandra shot upright and stared wildly at the doorway. Peering round the blond wooden door was that *bitch* of a United Nations nanny.

'Can I help at all?' said Geri, struggling to control her facial expression.

'No thank you,' gasped Cassandra. 'Period pains. You know,' she added hurriedly.

As Geri withdrew and audibly exploded with mirth in the corridor, Cassandra lay on her back again. Well, it had worked, in a way. It had relieved her former worries. The thought of the Promises auction and the Prime Minister's wife faded into insignificance beside the thought of Geri telling Julian she'd caught Cassandra wanking in his bathroom.

'You look different,' Jamie said to Anna.

'I'm thinner.' Wonderful to be able to say it as a mere statement of fact. But sad that there had been no joy in achieving it.

'That's it. Thinner. Suits you. Not that you didn't look great before . . .'

Seen in full daylight – or at least under Julian Tressell's concept spotlights – Jamie, too, looked better. Suited and booted, he looked even handsomer than she remembered. Anna had lost no time in telling him she no longer had a boyfriend. Unfortunately, she had not left it at that, not left the door open for a pleasant, ego-boosting flirty conversation. Oh no. Instead she had stupidly ploughed on through the events of recent weeks, told him all about Cassandra, all about Zak and Jett and how miserable she was, becoming increasingly aware as she did so that none of it reflected particularly well on her judgement and intelligence. He probably thinks I'm more stupid than even I think I am, she reflected miserably, drawing the sorry tale to a close.

Jamie looked at her speculatively.

'Anyway, enough of me,' Anna said hurriedly, plastering a vast smile over the exposed cracks in her life. 'How's the wonderful world of waiting?'

Jamie's composure dramatically slipped at this. 'Sorry? *Waiting?* Waiting for what?' His eyes, most unexpectedly, appeared to narrow in suspicion.

'When I met you,' Anna persisted, puzzled, 'you were a waiter at the wedding.'

An unmistakable expression of relief crossed Jamie's face. 'Oh, er, um, yes, well, actually, I'm not a waiter.'

'You're not?' This at least explained why he had been so bad at it. 'You're a student then? Holiday job?' He looked too old for that, though.

'No, I live at the castle, you see. It belongs to my, er, family.'

'*Oh.*' Anna felt her mind ripple with the effort of reassessment. That explained the signet ring still gleaming – she shot it a look – on his finger. He actually *lived* in the castle. Probably owned the island. How *wonderful.* 'So you're a laird?' How *romantic*. 'Skul is so pretty.' As Jamie's expression changed from faint gratification to utter astonishment Anna panicked that she had said the wrong thing. 'Pretty? Do you think so?' he demanded, amazement still tingeing his tone. He smiled incredulously. Anna nodded, relieved. For she *had* thought so. In the few snatched seconds she had been allowed to take her eyes off the map book she had admired from the car window great misty sweeps of grass and heather. Pewter lochs, air as cold and clear as water, Seb cursing that the signposts in Gaelic read like a monkey let loose on a typewriter. 'Bloody stupid language. Like the worst possible letters in Scrabble.'

Jamie shook his head so his hair flopped once again into his eyes. *Needs someone to cut that for him*, Anna thought, longing to reach up a hand to push the errant lock aside. His smile was dazzling now. *Good teeth*.

'And did you like the castle?'

'Loved it,' Anna said, thinking of the view of the moon from the oriel window. Did Jamie remember? she wondered. Blushing. Suddenly, she asked him, 'So how come *you* were handing out the drinks?'

'Well, Dampie gets rented out for weddings sometimes, and I was just helping.'

'How *wonderful* to actually live there.'

'Bit damp sometimes.'

'But I'm sure that doesn't matter, does it?' For how could living in a castle not be wonderful? 'It must be *so* romantic.' As she said this, Geri came past and gave her a huge, encouraging wink.

'Actually, I do rather like it myself, but it's not everyone's cup of tea. Some people find it a bit too remote.'

'Do they?' Anna could see their point, but chose not to say so. Such a shame he was stuck up there in the middle of the Atlantic. That ruled out any taking up where they had left off after the wedding. Although, come to think of it, they had left off almost immediately.

She looked at him again and lowered her eyes. There was silence. Anna was aware, from the other side of the room, of Geri shooting her a concerned gaze. She was also aware of the tray of untouched miniature jam roly-polys in her hands. People were looking meaningfully at her, obviously wanting her wares. Time was running out. If she didn't say something – anything – soon, he could just turn on his shining leather heel and leave, having had no more than a pleasant, meaningless exchange with someone once met at a wedding. Anna cudgelled her brains for a topic. Something to catch his imagination. Something original. 'Er, um,' she finally said, as inspiration struck. 'How do you know the Tressells?'

'Met Kate ages ago when she did some report about Scottish nobility for *Harpers & Queen*. And now I'm Siena's godfather.'

Siena had, Anna thought, more godfathers than the whole of Southern Italy.

'And your firm,' Jamie was saying. 'Do you often get asked to cater . . . ?'

'Oh, I'm not a waitress. I'm a writer. But frankly,' Anna sighed as, out of the corner of her eye, she saw Cassandra picking her way down the spiral metal staircase, 'my writing's been more trouble than it's worth. And that's the reason why.' She pointed out her employer to Jamie. 'My boss.'

Jamie looked hard at Cassandra. 'Christ.'

Anna suddenly noticed Julian Tressell heading towards them. He whirled up and seized Jamie's Prince of Wales checked wrist. 'Cherie's *refused* to do the Promises auction; says it's her day *off*,' he sighed theatrically. 'So Kate and I were wondering whether, as our resident squire, *you'd* get us out of jail . . .'

'See you later,' Jamie whispered, as he was led away.

Every nerve in Cassandra's body jangled. Not because of the recent events in the bathroom – by the look of it, that wretched Geri had kept her trap shut and the story had got no further. But the auction was now about to begin. Just let Fenella Greatorex *dare* bid for the dinner. Cassandra shot her a vicious look from where she huddled on the floor cross-legged. Cross everything, in fact. Chairs, it seemed, were banned throughout the house.

'An enemy to good posture, apparently,' someone behind Cassandra whispered. 'Julian and Kate eat dinner by candlelight on leather cushions on the floor.'

'That sounds like an enemy to good digestion to me,' replied her companion. 'Oh look, the auction's starting.'

Anna watched, impressed, as Jamie immediately got quite literally into the swing of the gavel-wielding.

He had a natural authority – she supposed it went with the territory; aristocrats, after all, spent half their lives in salerooms, buying or selling according to how their luck was going. There was even a wicked gleam in Jamie's eye; like a naughty little boy, Anna thought fondly, until she remembered Zak. Still, at least *he* was next door for the moment. *Pretending* to be an animal.

Bidding for the health club, newspaper subscription and an organic food box delivery service which had mysteriously appeared from somewhere swiftly dispensed with, it didn't take long for the moment Cassandra dreaded.

'Dinner party for eight at the home of, um, Sandra Knight.' Jamie peered at the card in his hand, then brandished the Philippe Starck toffee hammer that stood in for a gavel.

'*Cass*andra,' yelled Cassandra furiously.

'The bidding starts at fifty pounds,' announced Jamie.

Cassandra bristled. *Fifty pounds?* It had better raise more than *that*. She'd be a laughing stock.

'Do I hear a hundred pounds?' said Jamie in his soft Scottish voice, cupping a hand to his ear. 'Wonderful menu. Foie gras to start with, partnered with the most wonderful old Sauternes, then noisettes of Highgrove lamb, served with a Château Margaux nineteen fifty-nine . . .'

There was a stirring of interest. Hands sprouted in the air. Cassandra goggled. *Sauternes . . . Margaux . . .* what was this ridiculous man *talking* about? It would cost a *fortune*. She hadn't been thinking beyond boeuf bourguignon and supermarket plonk. 'Er,' she called, raising her hand.

'No, sorry,' Jamie said, all charming Caledonian firmness. 'You can't bid for your own promise. Dessert is, um, yes, of course, champagne sorbet followed by tarte au citron especially flown in from Fauchon. Do I hear a hundred pounds? The lady over there.'

Fenella Greatorex. Cassandra's spine froze. This was worse than the worst nightmare. She looked desperately at Cherie Blair. Entertaining the Prime Minister would put an entirely different complexion on things; one might well run to the Margaux then. Something château-bottled, at least. But Cherie Blair's hand remained resolutely on the shoulders of her son Nicky. Her large brown eyes swivelled round the room in amusement.

'One hundred and fifty pounds. To the gentleman in the grey suit.'

Orlando Gossett, Anna saw with dismay. For once she was with Cassandra in wanting the bidding to get higher.

'At this point,' Jamie said, grinning, 'I'm going to depart from convention and put a bid in myself. Three hundred pounds.'

There was a surprised murmur, then silence. 'Sold to the Scotsman,' smiled Jamie as Kate rushed up and shoved a note in his fist. 'Now, um, I hold in my hand a piece of paper saying the disco's started. Ladies and gentlemen, everyone into the next room and join the children for the disco.' As the room scrambled to its feet, Anna glimpsed Cassandra sitting, stunned, in the middle of the floor. Then she saw Jamie coming towards her, looking very pleased with himself.

'What on *earth* did you do that for? You know who'll have to cook it all, don't you? *Moi*.'

Jamie looked astonished. 'You surely don't think I'm going to take her *up* on it, do you? Go to her wretched house and have dinner?'

Anna smiled. The disco could now be heard thumping away in the room previously occupied by the forms, trestle tables and pizzas with faces on them. Jamie placed a hand on her bare arm, the shock of his touch shuddering all over her body. He put his mouth close to her ear. 'Did it for you. Call it bribery if you like. Now, I have to go, but perhaps I could take you out to dinner later? What's your address?'

Hoping that he meant it, Anna scribbled Liv's location down in a tiny leather-backed notebook Jamie produced from the inside of his jacket. 'Pick you up at seven thirty. But not a word to *her* about the dinner party. Let her sweat a bit.'

* * *

'You *see*. You *see*.' As Anna entered the disco, someone shot to her side and nudged her hard. It was Geri, looking smugger than Mrs Bennet at the wedding of Elizabeth and Darcy. 'Told you you'd score with someone. Very *nice*, I must say. Actually, I'm rather jealous.'

'Well, there's nothing to be jealous of,' Anna told her. 'He's only asked me out for dinner.'

'*Only?*' teased Geri. 'That's pretty fast work considering you only met him this afternoon. *And* he bought Cassandra's wretched dinner party. I call that gallantry beyond the call of duty.'

'Actually, I *had* met him before. He was at the wedding in Scotland.'

'*Was* he? I don't remember.'

'Yes, well, your memory of that event isn't exactly *perfect*, is it?' Anna prodded Geri as Orlando Gossett took the floor, Savannah and Siena each holding one of his plump red hands. Anna looked about her in surprise. She had been expecting a ghettoblaster with a few infants jumping around it. Instead, a pair of intimidatingly trendy-looking DJs presided over a console and the full complement of flashing lights; the disco was indistinguishable from a grown-up one, and a good deal better than most. Miranda's and Thoby's sprang particularly to mind.

'Now,' boomed one of the DJs, 'we have our first competition. Every child on to the floor, please.'

As a hundred plus parental hands pushed their little darlings forward, Cassandra looked wildly around for Zak. There he was, behind the console, busily pulling the wires out. So technically minded already, Cassandra thought proudly, clawing her way through the crowd to get to him. Within seconds, he had been propelled on to the floor. Zak may not be making his debut at the Wigmore Hall or Pinewood Studios, Cassandra thought fiercely, but here was a wonderful opportunity to display his Madame Abricot dancing skills.

'We're going to play some music,' one of the DJs announced as Fatboy Slim began to pulsate through the room, 'and you're all going to dance like your mummy does.'

As the parents laughed and clapped, the children stood uncertainly in the strobe lights. One or two, Otto Greatorex among them, Cassandra noted furiously, started to sway to the music and move their feet from side to side. Come on, Zak, she urged silently from the sidelines. *Dance*, you *sod*.

'Like your *mummies*, remember.' The DJs turned the sound up until the room throbbed. Anna wondered how loud it had to be before the glass, of which there was plenty, shattered and showered down on them all.

Savannah and Siena, Cassandra saw with panic, were stepping neatly from foot to foot in perfect time, making graceful and economical movements with their arms. Kate Tressell obviously danced as perfectly as she did everything else. Cassandra derived some comfort from the fact that, beside her, Polly Rice-Brown was clearing her throat embarrassedly as Sholto stood swaying his hands from side to side, an ecstatic expression on his face. Otto Greatorex presented a similarly heart-warming sight, galumphing around determinedly off the beat, an inane grin stretching from cheek to cheek. On the sidelines behind him, Fenella looked thunderous.

'Ooh, is *this* how your mummies dance?' mocked the DJs. Cassandra grinned to herself. She was beginning to enjoy this. More satisfactory still was the arrival onto the floor of Milo and Ivo Hope-Stanley, who began to jerk wildly around in a sort of graceless bop that Cassandra did not at all connect with Caroline until she spotted her mortified face through the crowds. She shook with laughter. This really was *hilarious*.

'What on earth is Zak *doing*?' Geri suddenly whispered to Anna. Cassandra's son had suddenly appeared in the midst of the now heaving dance floor, clutching a bottle of champagne he had found somewhere. He proceeded to stick it in his mouth, tip his head back and stagger around the floor, deliberately colliding with as many people as possible.

'Don't ask,' Anna murmured, gazing from between her fingers at the rapidly clearing floor. Zak was now ripping off his shirt and waving the bottle around. As they watched in horror, he rushed up to Milo Hope-

Stanley and began grinding into his pelvis, the hand not holding the bottle now clasped firmly to Milo's behind. Milo squealed in terror and rushed to his mother on the sidelines.

'Look at Cassandra,' Anna whispered, glancing at where the strobe lights sporadically illuminated a mini-skirted, horror-transfixed figure by the edge of the dance floor.

'I can't. I might miss something,' Geri hissed back. Miming that the bottle was empty, Zak now proceeded to strut in an unsteady circle, both hands thrusting his imaginary breasts forward, a lascivious expression on his face. 'But look at Cherie Blair!'

Across the dance floor, the Prime Minister's wife looked on in amazement as, the music fading, Zak slid to his knees then flipped on to his back, spread his legs wide apart and yelled to the assembled company, 'I don't suppose there's any chance of a shag?'

Chapter 13

Anna had never had a date with a laird before. Apart, that was, from a landlaird – Mr McGrabbie, the owner of the tiny, scruffy terrace house in which she had occupied a small room during her last year at university, had practically haunted the place. He had, Anna recalled without affection, been particularly fond of appearing either early in the morning or late in the evening, hours which a cynic might assume to be timed in the hope of finding Anna in a state of undress.

A laird. It was really rather exciting. Admittedly, Seb had been an Hon, but one, despite his own wealth, relentlessly Hon The Make. Anna had not been surprised to see, the once or twice she had glimpsed the *Daily Telegraph* recently, that Seb had been given a racing tipster's column. Seeing that he was married to one of the paper's leading writers, the coincidence was really no less than astonishing. What was more genuinely amazing was that, glancing at his byline picture smirking from the page, Anna felt nothing at all. Seb now seemed to have been part of someone else's life altogether, but then again, most things BC (Before Cassandra) seemed to have that quality.

It had not been easy to extricate Zak from the party and get back to the house in time to get ready for her date. He was not only having the time of his life stabbing the party entertainer hard in the backside with a plastic sword, but unsurprisingly seemed in no hurry to face his mother, who had suddenly found it necessary to leave the party during his dance routine. Anna, for her part, was dreading seeing Cassandra; no doubt she would in some way be to blame for the embarrassing turn the afternoon's events had taken.

For once, united in fear, Anna and Zak entered Liv to find it silent. Neither Cassandra nor Jett was anywhere to be seen. Or heard, even. Zak shot like greased lightning up to his room whence, before too many seconds had elapsed, the unmistakable sound of Warlord Bloodlust II could be heard emanating from the direction of his Playstation. Anna, it seemed, had the house to herself. Or, more significantly, the bathrooms. The shower in the garage – fitful, sulky and invariably occupied by some hideous insect or other –

hardly seemed the place to prepare for a hot date with someone like Jamie. Not least because it was always freezing cold. Anna padded up the stairs silently and approached Cassandra's bathroom with the trepidation of Hercules entering the lair of the Minotaur. Dare she?

Taking a deep breath and ancient toilet bag she slid through the bathroom door, locking it behind her. She turned on the mock-Edwardian tangle of shower head and mixer tap, and looked in wonder at the thundering, warm Niagara pouring into the familiar – and emphatically un-Edwardian – circular bath she spent much of each morning wiping and polishing. Sometimes, admittedly, with her own spit. She burrowed her toes into the thick white carpet which stretched away to the room's distant corners and up the three stairs leading to the platform on which the bath was placed. Cassandra's ablutions, like everything else in her life, had to be a performance.

As the bath slowly filled, Anna, undressing, stared at herself in the mirror. It gave her a distinctly mixed message, the good news being that the wretched swag of flesh had almost disappeared. Even better was the fact that, if Anna raised her arms above her head, she could even see her ribs, although this exercise also revealed the less satisfactory sight of sprouts of russet hair from her armpits. That, plus the unruly thatch between her thighs and the white and flaking expanse of her calves, was the bad news. Christ, thought Anna, surveying with horror the auburn fuzz on her long-neglected lower limbs. I look like a Yeti.

More bad news was that the brilliant light of Cassandra's bulb-and-gilt encircled Hollywood-style mirror only accentuated her pale, dry lips and the exhausted dark smudges under her eyes. As if, Anna thought, she'd gone ten rounds with Prince Naseem. There was no obvious solution to this. Her own stock of make-up had run out weeks ago and in any case it would take more than a quick slick of Boots 17 to reverse – much less repair – the damage she was now contemplating. It called for Polyfilla, at the very least.

The bath was now ready. Stepping in, Anna sank back thankfully among the few bubbles she had dared add. Not that Cassandra was exactly short on unguents – there seemed to be enough royal jelly for a globewide celebration of the Queen Mum's hundredth birthday. Now the excavations could begin: taking her ancient Ladyshave from her washbag, Anna took the first tentative strokes at her armpits, reflecting as she did so that, this being Saturday night, millions of other girls all over the country would be doing the same thing. Men too, very possibly. As she watched the hairs floating on the water's surface, Anna briefly wondered what happened to all the excess fuzz removed from the arms, legs and pubes of the nation during such preparations.

Was there, somewhere underground, a compacted mass of unwanted hair, like the vastest bathroom plug clot ever seen? It was a disgusting thought.

Anna lay back fully now. The delicious and unaccustomed warmth of the water seeped into her bones. She felt sleepy. Exhausted, in fact. That light above the bath was a bit bright; Anna reached for the cord to switch it off, then, a nanosecond later, was forced to stifle a scream as the whole bath erupted around her. Powerful jets of water were pummelling her on every side – in the ribs, under the arms, in the small of the back and, rather enjoyably, a particularly strong and focused one pouring into the space between her legs. As the delicious tension grew, Anna realised that she had stumbled across not only Cassandra's Jacuzzi – so that was what all those tiny holes had been for – but very possibly also the source of inspiration for the racier scenes in her novels. Given that Cassandra and Jett seemed to go in for steaming rows far more than steamy sex, Anna had never really understood what had fuelled her employer's high-octane literary raunchathons. It was now obvious it wasn't Jett, but another jet altogether.

Anna gasped as the water drilled on, pleasurably, painfully, direct into her inner nerve centre. She'd had no idea that a bath could be so much fun. The blood pounded round her head as a slow throbbing spread through her body; simultaneously, the thudding in her brain seemed to intensify. Anna lifted her head slowly from the water. It was as she had feared. The thudding was coming from the door.

'Who's that in my fucking bathroom?' Cassandra's furious shriek was practically glass-shattering.

Anna looked at Jamie over the artificial carnation. The soft glow of the food warmer flickered over his cheekbones as he smiled at her. He seemed to be finding the story of Cassandra and the bathroom extremely diverting. It was almost worth having had her eardrums practically punctured with the force of Cassandra's wrath. Until, that was, Cassandra had thrown a handful of cubes into a glass and topped it up with neat Bombay Sapphire. The resulting stupor had afforded Anna the opportunity to sneak into Cassandra's drinks fridge and help herself to the make-up and perfume that were stored there for reasons Anna had been unable to get to the bottom of, beyond Cassandra's snapped assertion that 'All the supermodels do it.' After all, thought Anna, dragging the ice-cold tip of the eyebrow pencil painfully across her brow, one may as well be hung for a sheep as a Lancôme.

For her first date with Jamie, Anna had imagined someone with a Scottish island to their credit would have come up with something slightly smarter than the King's Cross tandoori Jamie eventually ushered her into. Even if, as he explained, the sag aloo was to die for and it was convenient for Euston, where he was due to catch the sleeper back to Scotland later. The fact that, come midnight, Jamie would be somewhere in the region of Newcastle did at least solve the problem – raised by Geri – of whether to sleep with him on the first date. As it was, the murky-looking vegetable curries currently being deposited by the waiter on the table looked likely to scupper any plans to kiss him into the bargain. Those plans, anyway, were under constant review. Jamie smiled a lot, especially at the bath story; he was perfectly friendly, yet Anna detected a guardedness, a tendency to withhold personal information, yet ask instead a veritable barrage of questions about herself. It was difficult not to be flattered, however – no one, after all, had ever been *this* interested in her before. Seb, certainly, had barely bothered to find out her surname, let alone any family details. Not that Anna had blamed him overmuch for that; there certainly wasn't anything *obviously* fascinating about the fact that her civil servant father had died when she was ten, and that she had no siblings and a polite but distant relationship with her part-time librarian mother. Jamie, however, seemed riveted.

There was no time to ask him questions anyway. Having exhausted Anna's stock of answers, Jamie spent the rest of the evening talking about Dampie, while Anna, listening patiently, tried hard to be fascinated by sheep figures, fishing statistics and dry stone wall replacement programmes and supposed it went with the territory. Quite literally – growing up on a Scottish estate probably did spark a lifelong interest in Tudor oak settles and eighteenth-century portraiture, although growing up in her mother's spotless semi had correspondingly failed to ignite any fascination on her part with MDF and Anaglypta.

Through sheer dogged persistence, Anna managed to extract a handful of facts about Jamie's background. Her eyes pricked, his terse and dispassionate delivery notwithstanding, on being told how, after his parents died in an aircrash when he was fifteen, the young Jamie had divided his time between school and the Dampie estate. Despite his obvious reluctance to talk about it, Anna managed to gather that, due to some complication in his father's will, he had only inherited the estate fairly recently and even now the process was not complete. Something about the right personnel not being in place.

'And do you like the countryside?' Anna nodded, her cheeks bulging with onion bhaji, and wondered why he always managed to ask her a question when her mouth was full. He still hadn't shown the slightest inclination to flirt with her. She was beginning to wonder sadly if getting the right personnel was the point of the evening and he was merely sounding her out as a potential housekeeper. After all, he knew she was acquainted with dusting and could manage basic meals. Perhaps this was why he seemed far more interested in the domestic details of her day than her ambition to be a writer. She hadn't even told him about the existence of the diary, whose entries seemed daily to get longer and more clogged with telling detail. It seemed to be occupying the same role in her life as the bottle did in Cassandra's – as a comforter. She was a diaryholic.

The miserable conviction that Jamie wasn't remotely romantically interested in her grew as the waiter replaced their plates (hers empty, his full) with the extremely modest bill (he paid it) and the complimentary After Eights (he left them). By the time they both stood up to leave – he still banging on about the reroofing needed at Dampie – she felt the distance between them to roughly resemble that between Land's End and John O'Groats. That's it then, she thought, looking her longing last on his rangy frame as she followed it out defeatedly into the rain-slicked, greasy street. Another one bites the dust. The inimitable Farrier line in charm and conversation had reeled in yet another willing victim. *Not*.

It was with astonishment that she heard him mutter, as he pecked her distantly on the cheek, that it would be wonderful to see her again. She spent the whole journey back in the taxi in a state of cautious bliss only slightly punctured by the discovery, when dismounting at Liv, that Jamie hadn't paid for it as she had assumed. Handing over her last ten-pound note, Anna decided that the fact Cassandra hadn't paid her beyond the first week, and not in full even then, desperately needed addressing. Still, what did that matter? she thought letting herself quietly back into the house, skipping silently up to her sofabedroom, taking her pen and opening her diary. I'm through to the second interview.

Cassandra, naturally, seized upon the fact of Anna's having a suitor with a bitchy glee. 'Aren't you going to get changed, then?' she enquired nastily as, early one evening Anna gingerly descended the green glass staircase.

'Actually, I'm ready.' Having done her best to sponge the marks off her faithful black Joseph trousers, Anna felt reasonably respectable in the white cotton shirt she had slipped in among that afternoon's Everest of ironing. The suspicious way Cassandra was looking at it suggested she might well deduct the three minutes not spent ironing Zak's underpants out of her wages, a further half of which had, after much hand-twistingly embarrassed inquiry, just materialised. This had almost created more problems than it solved – Anna had been torn between paying off some of her student overdraft and investing in new make-up. Torn, that was, until Geri had intervened and, rolling her eyes, steered her firmly off to the Ruby and Millie cosmetics counter at Boots.

'Didn't realise you had another job as a waitress,' Cassandra remarked spitefully before drifting back into the sitting room. As Anna, prompted by the taxi honking outside, exited, she heard the unmistakable clink of the Bombay Sapphire bottle; crossing the road to the throbbing black car, she was conscious of Cassandra's laser stare penetrating the sitting-room window. So far Cassandra, despite her hints and questions, had not met Jamie and Anna intended to keep it that way. Thankfully, even her basilisk gaze could not penetrate the gloomy depths of the back of the taxi.

It was their second date and, imagining it would be romantic, Anna had suggested they went to see a film. The intervening several months since her last visit to the cinema had, however, obliterated its universal laws from her mind. Such as the one dictating that, directly after she took her seat, the Person With The Biggest Head In The World would sit down slap bang in front of her. And then that the Person With The Noisiest Sweet Wrappers In The World would arrive to sit directly behind. And that thus situated, Anna would spend the whole of the film stiff with rage and frustration, or cringing with embarrassment during the sex scenes. Meanwhile Jamie, back like a ramrod beside her, didn't as much as move his hand to take hers. The few sneaked sideways glances she dared to steal showed his profile, rigid and tight-lipped, staring stonily at the screen in front of him. The last straw had been that the film – one of the must-sees of the moment – was worse than terrible. Its cheesy plot, impossible twists, gratuitous sex and utterly unbelievable and unsympathetic characters almost, Anna thought, made it comparable to Cassandra's worst.

'I'm so sorry,' she gasped afterwards, as they filed down a back staircase which, like all cinema back staircases, stank of urine. 'That film was *desperate*. You must think I'm a moron.'

'Actually, I didn't notice,' Jamie, all gallantry, reassured her. 'To tell you the truth, I was thinking about the drainage.'

'The *what*?' Had the reek of urine wafted into the cinema as well? She thought she had smelt something else unpleasant, but imagined that to be connected with the bowel movements of the Person With The Biggest Head In The World, from whose direction the smell seemed to be seeping.

'The drainage at Dampie,' Jamie explained. 'It needs replacing.'

Anna sighed. 'Let's go and eat something, shall we?' she said. 'There's a Pizza Express round the corner.'

Clad in the three-piece suit he had also worn for their last date, Jamie looked slightly out of place among the tourists in their pastel polo shirts. He glanced, irritated, down the list of elaborately named pizzas, discounted them all and asked for lasagne. Afterwards, Anna watched as he unenthusiastically pushed a hard disc of individually portioned vanilla ice-cream around his plate. 'Looks like a breast implant, doesn't it?' she grinned.

Jamie looked from her to the ice-cream. 'Does it?' he asked, looking puzzled and faintly disgusted.

'It's a disaster,' Anna wailed to Geri as soon as the other nannies had left the café next morning. 'He spent the rest of the evening talking about flashing.'

'What?' Geri's face darkened. 'You mean . . . *macs* and things?'

'No.' Anna permitted herself a faint smile. 'The lead flashing on the roof at Dampie. Needs doing, along with everything else, apparently. He's obsessed with that place.'

Geri sighed. 'Sweetie, it could be much worse. Better that he's obsessed with something glamorous like his ancestral home than *trains* or *football* or something. Or,' she grimaced, 'DIY. I once had a boyfriend who . . .'

Anna cut in. She wasn't in the mood to hear about yet another of Geri's erstwhile swains. 'Well it is DIY of a sort,' she retorted. 'I'm sure if there was a Do-It-All on Skul, he'd be down there every five minutes. And, from the sound of the place, so would I. Apparently there's one pub on the whole island and the nearest

M&S is in Inverness. Imagine what the clothes must be like.'

Geri looked stern. 'I don't think you're approaching this quite the right way,' she said sharply. 'Is Jamie or is Jamie not the best chance of escape you're ever going to have? Don't you want to get away from Cassandra? Don't you want to get *married*?'

'*Married*?' Anna echoed. 'I . . . I can't say I'd ever actually thought about it. I mean, I hardly know him. We've only had two dates . . .'

'The trouble with *you*,' Geri began, as Anna's back stiffened defensively, 'is that you never think far ahead enough. What's the point of you going out with Jamie unless you've decided what you want from him? Where's your game plan? *Your* problem is that you just drift along. Take life by the balls, or you'll just end up being taken for a ride.'

Anna squirmed. She wished Geri would drop her dictatorial tone. As a matter of fact, the thought of taking Jamie by the balls *had* crossed her mind, although not quite in the way Geri meant.

'You have to visualise the end result you want,' Geri stated firmly, grinding her spoon round and round in her coffee cup. 'Approach each date like a board meeting – ground you need to cover, subjects discussed etc., and make sure you prepare for *every eventuality*. You've slept with him, of course?'

Anna recoiled, shocked. She felt her face flood a

sizzling, mortified red. 'Well, as a matter of fact, I haven't,' she muttered. 'There haven't really been any opportunities.'

Geri was gazing at her in amazement. *What do you mean, there haven't been opportunities?* said her eyes. *You've been alone with him for two whole evenings. What do you think back rows of cinemas are for? People have sex in taxis, you know. What do you need? A four-poster bed and full set of love toys?* In the event, however, Geri confined herself to an emphatic 'Why not?'

'It's just that,' Anna stammered, blushing ever more furiously and tearing the last corner of her croissant fanatically into pieces, 'I'm not very good at sex, you see. Seb told his friends . . . um,' Anna flinched at the memory, 'that I was like a corpse in bed.'

Geri's eyes flashed fire. 'Well, take it from me, sweetie, that there are some men out there who think having a corpse in bed is *very sexy* indeed.'

Anna sighed. She did not feel up to confessing that the corpse in question was a dog's. And what was Geri suggesting anyway – that she target necrophiliacs?

'Look, don't worry about all that,' Geri ordered. 'I've got an idea. When did you say your next date was?'

Anna sighed, more deeply this time. 'I didn't. There isn't one.'

Anna drove home, wondering if Geri was right. Part of her thought that perhaps she *didn't* control her own destiny enough. Part of her thought she'd got into enough trouble already by allowing Geri to, but given that Seb had practically thrown her out, working for Cassandra *had* seemed like a good idea at the time. That, of course, had turned out to be an utter dead end. But perhaps if she had insisted more . . . As Geri was fond of saying, a tad defensively, 'It *was* a good idea. It *might* have worked.' But now it hadn't, Anna felt powerless to do anything about it. She was too exhausted, for one thing. Having the self-esteem of a lugworm didn't help either.

Perhaps Jamie *was* the answer to all her prayers. She was strongly attracted to him, but it was very early days and she hadn't thought – hadn't *dared* think – of him as a potential husband and saviour. But was that symptomatic of her general lack of direction? Perhaps a great opportunity was staring her in the face – although admittedly Jamie seemed reluctant to look her in the eye for too long.

Anna bit a nail on one hand as she absently steered the people-carrier with the other. What exactly had gone wrong with last night's date? The dreadful film with the faint, seeping smell of fart from the stalls in front? The painful scares over the pizza later, when the conversation had dried up to such an extent they had been reduced to discussing the number of regional Pizza Express branches listed on the back of the menu? The way he had, after pecking quickly at her cheek with his lips in farewell, shrugged his broad, skinny shoulders as if to apologise for wasting both their time? It seemed, Anna thought, vaguely conscious of having jumped a red light, as if it was less a case of what had gone wrong. More what had gone right.

Her heart sank still further when she entered Liv to find Cassandra lurking in the hallway. Her eyes were blazing with fury – or possibly alcohol; the difference, after all, was minuscule.

'Hello, Cassandra,' Anna stammered, instantly feeling wrong footed, despite the fact that she wasn't the one wearing a bathrobe who had obviously only just got up.

'Message for you,' she spat, stabbing at a piece of paper by the telephone. Anna tried to walk as composedly as she could in Cassandra's direction. After all, it might only be the bank manager, thwarted by Anna's persistent inability to address her financial problems by mail. Unlikely. There was only one person in Anna's life that Cassandra would be sufficiently interested in to take a message from. Anna picked up the paper. The name, written in wildly veering handwriting – no wonder Cassandra used a laptop – was not the one she had been expecting.

'*Johnny?*' she repeated, puzzled.

'Your . . . er . . . *admirer*,' Cassandra snarled. 'Just called about a minute ago. Wanted your address.'

'My *address*?' But Jamie had picked her up from Liv only last night. 'Here, you mean?'

Cassandra's eyes narrowed. She shrugged. 'No idea,' she drawled. 'He called this morning as well, now I come to think of it. Zak took the message. I heard him telling whoever it was that you didn't live here any more. *Such* a sense of humour, that boy.' She swept off, grinning, into the sitting room and Anna, still standing stunned in the hall, heard the familiar clink of bottles. Cassandra reappeared unsteadily in the sitting-room doorway. 'To Romance,' she announced theatrically, raising her tumbler in the air.

It was two evenings later. Anna, taking the small flight of steps to the left of the garden as instructed, found herself facing a neat little door painted a glowing lavender blue. She pressed the small gold bell and waited.

'Geri! It's gorgeous.' Anna stepped under the recessed spotlights beaming down into the smart, white-painted hallway. 'Is all this really yours?'

Geri nodded nonchalantly. 'It's the granny flat. Only both Kate and Julian have such rich mothers that they don't need it. So now it's the nanny flat.' Walking down the hall, Anna glimpsed both a shining white bathroom and a roomy bedroom with powder blue bedding piled on a white iron bedstead before Geri showed her into a small, neat sitting room with big squashy sofas. The faint scent of lavender drifted over from a scented candle on an oak coffee table whose sturdy little legs nestled into a fat sheepskin rug. On another side table sat the state-of-the-art answerphone, next to a mobile miniature on a charger.

'I can't believe it,' Anna gasped, noting the low lighting and the fashionable slatted wooden blinds at the big windows, and recalling her own stark boxroom with its single bare bulb and curtainless, bird-spattered panes. She sank gratefully into the sofa's comforting embrace. It seemed like – indeed, it had been – ages since she had sat on anything so luxurious. Cassandra's chrome tractor-seat kitchen stools, for all their stylishness, were about as comfortable and supportive as their owner.

'Drink?' At the back of the room, below a large, spotless, frameless mirror, Geri was rummaging in an antique-looking box with brass fittings. 'Birthday present from Savannah and Siena,' she said, seeing Anna looking at it. 'An eighteenth-century tea chest, although I like to keep something a bit stronger than Earl Grey in it. And boy, do I need a drink today. G and T?'

'I'd rather have vodka, if you have it.' Gin and tonic, formerly one of Anna's favourites, was now too reminiscent of Cassandra. 'Why do *you* need a drink? What's up?' Geri rarely, if ever, seemed stressed.

'Slight turbulence at the high tea table.' Lighting a Marlboro, Geri blew smoke from her nostrils like the con trail from a plane. 'Savannah finished everything on her plate. Kate went *ballistic*.'

'What's wrong with that? Isn't that what children are supposed to do?' Apart, she thought, from Zak, who took the view that eating anything she had cooked was tantamount to expressing affection for her and invented excuses not to ranging from 'it looks like dogshit' to 'it's got bugs'. Anna had come to derive a certain comfort from this – there was always the hope he might die from malnutrition.

'They're only ever supposed to eat half of everything,' Geri explained. 'Kate's strict instructions. If they eat everything on their plate they only get half as much at their next meal. She's terrified they're going to grow up fat. She won't let them have any sweets and once even tried to convince them that sugar was salt so they wouldn't develop a sweet tooth. Needless to say, as soon as they're away from the house they're *desperate* for chocolate.'

She inhaled deeply and blew smoke out of her nose again. 'Anyway, enough of that. The main thing is, *he's* called you again.'

Anna grinned. Kicking her shoes off, she hugged her knees excitedly on the sofa. 'Not exactly. I called him.'

Geri frowned. 'That's not in The Rules,' she said. 'The man should always call you. Treat him mean and . . .'

'I *know*. But I didn't have much choice. Zak told him I'd left the country. Thank *God* for one four seven one. I managed to get Jamie's number just before Cassandra staggered out of the sitting room again and caught me.'

'Good thinking.' Geri looked at her approvingly. 'So, down to business. How much time do we have before you're meeting him?'

'Two hours. Pasha at nine.'

'*Pasha?* Hope he's paying.'

'My treat,' Anna said firmly. 'After all, I made the call. And he paid for the pizza.'

'Big fucking deal,' said Geri, looking considerably less approving. 'So, let's get to work. This way to the bedroom.'

Ten minutes later, Anna was beginning to regret having agreed to come to Geri's for a make-over, clothes-borrow and pep talk. It had seemed such a good idea at the time. 'Success is all in the psychology,' Geri had told her. 'You need to have your tactics sorted out. More importantly, you need some sexy clothes.'

Standing in Geri's bedroom, knee-deep in the contents of her wardrobe, Anna was beginning to have second thoughts. Her breasts had been cantilevered almost to chin level by the most aggressive push-up bra she had ever encountered. She looked doubtfully at her rear in Geri's leopardskin-printed trousers. 'Does my bum look big in . . .' she began.

'No,' snapped Geri. 'You look fantastic. More curves than a Rococo balustrade, as Julian would say.' Anna glanced at her suspiciously, wondering when, exactly, Julian would say *that?* Things were obviously going well. Geri had already mentioned that she was accompanying the family on holiday at his special insistence, even though the other family they were going with had two nannies of its own. She turned back to the mirror.

'This shirt is far too tight,' she protested, gazing disconsolately at her reflection. Geri was at least two sizes smaller than she was.

Geri sighed. 'Shirts,' she stated patiently, as if talking to an idiot, 'can *never* be too tight.'

'But I look fat.'

'Rubbish. You look fabulous. And next time you get depressed about your weight – which is nothing, by the way – remember that a ten-stone person weighs seven pounds on Pluto.'

'I don't think this is really Jamie's sort of thing,' Anna ventured as, after half an hour's backcombing, eyelash-curling, mascara-applying and lipgloss-slicking, Geri stood back, said, 'There!' and held up a mirror to Anna's face. The dark-eyed, pneumatic-lipped stranger with the wild red hair staring back at her looked, Anna thought, utterly terrifying. 'I look like Rula Lenska,' she blurted.

'Well thanks a lot,' huffed Geri. 'I turn you into a raunchy sexbabe and this is the thanks I get.'

'But I'm not sure Jamie likes raunchy sexbabes,' said Anna, recalling his set face during the film's more explicit scenes.

Geri put her hands on her hips, exasperated. 'Well, he'll be the first man ever in the history of the universe who doesn't. *Every* man likes raunchy sexbabes. Get *real*, will you?'

Anna's appearance being, in Geri's eyes at least, satisfactory, they then moved on to tactics. 'For Christ's sake look *interested* if he talks about the castle . . .'

'You mean *when*,' said Anna. 'There's no if about it.'

'Well, do you want to be Cassandra's slave for the rest of your life or would you rather be lady of the manor? Doesn't seem much of a choice to me.'

Anna was forced to admit this was true. Nonetheless, she had a sense of events moving out of her control. Did she really want to marry Jamie? Did he want to marry her? 'Mere details,' scoffed Geri. 'Just *make* him want to marry you, that's all. You like him, don't you? If the marriage goes tits up you can always leave him and get half his property into the bargain. It's not what I'd call a great risk. He's good-looking, isn't he? Which ninety-nine per cent of men aren't. And anyway, what other options do you have?'

Put like that, it sounded almost reasonable. Anna, in any case, had barely had a chance to wonder aloud about love, sex and having to want to spend your whole life with the other person before Geri cut in with a single word. 'Guff.'

Anna had no idea why a small part of her still believed that marriage should be for love. Certainly, she had never seen any evidence to the contrary. From her own parents' squabbles – so far as she could dimly remember them – to the vicious battles between Cassandra and Jett, not to mention her own miserable co-habiting experiences with Seb, there seemed no reason to believe marriages were ever idyllic.

'Marriage,' Geri declared, 'is like a tornado. It starts with a lot of blowing and sucking, then it ends up taking your house.'

'Did you make that up?' Anna looked at her admiringly.

'No, James Caan did, as it happens. Told me that at a dinner party once. So stick with Jamie and, whatever happens, you'll get his house. Half of it, at least.'

'Hopefully the half with the roof and plumbing,' grinned Anna.

'Stop splitting hairs and go out there and get yourself one. An heir, I mean.'

Somehow implicit in her tones was the suggestion that if Anna didn't, Geri would. It was this more than anything else – apart from the taxi hooting outside –

that finally propelled Anna out of the lavender front door.

'Remember,' Geri called after her, 'it's all about tactics. Think Premier League. The manager gives the team a pep talk before the game, and again at half time.' There was a sound of running footsteps and then something small and hard was slipped into Anna's hand. 'Take the mobile and call me from the loos before the pudding. Which, of course, you'll have refused.'

Jamie was late. Anna shifted uncomfortably in Geri's tight trousers, trying to relieve the pressure on her bladder. In twenty-five minutes, she'd got through almost the entire bottle of rosé provided by the kaftaned waiter. Her nerves now felt much better, but she was dying for the loo. Two things prevented her from going: the thought of missing Jamie when – *if* – he finally appeared through the carved front door; and, almost worse, the thought of everyone else in the restaurant scrutinising her too-tight clothes as she walked past their tables and descended the look-at-me staircase leading down past the petal-strewn fountain to the loos.

The girls at the next table, she knew, would be merciless in their criticism. There were about eight of them, strappy dresses flopping off their tanned shoulders, spindly, high-heeled ankles poking out in all directions from under the table, taking quick, nervous puffs on their cigarettes as their narrowed eyes flicked speculatively at each other and around the room. They had already cast her a few pitying, been-stood-up-have-you glances made worse by Anna's surmising that, judging from what the ringleader, a naughty-looking blonde chignon with a dirty laugh, was saying, they were a hen party. 'Yah, and the worst thing is that so many people are buying off-list,' complained the chignon. 'I mean, this morning I got sent some *Italian toasting flutes*, for fuck's sake.'

'Is that the same as toasting forks?' asked the very thin dark crop next to her.

'No it isn't. And while we're on the subject of Italy,' added the blonde, 'I'm sick of people ringing me up and asking where it is. *Unbelievable*. I'd no idea my friends were so thick.'

Anna smiled to herself and reached for another piece of pickled carrot. Jamie was now half an hour late. The many scenarios she and Geri had rehearsed – what to say, how to sit, how to look ('Catch his eye, drop yours and then, with a sweeping glance back upwards, look at him directly again and give him a slight, full-lipped smile,' Geri counselled. 'It's called The Flirt. Never fails.') – had not included a complete no-show on his part. She'd give him another ten minutes, thought Anna, pouring the last of the rosé into her glass. Until then, she'd practise The Flirt in the mirror opposite the table and hope the girls didn't think she was trying to pick them up.

The restaurant buzzed with laughter and conversation. Tiny alcoves were let into the walls, each containing a softly radiant oil lamp; from the ceiling above the stairs hung a collection of magnificent brass Moorish lanterns, all of different sizes and heights. Rugs were scattered over the wooden floors, providing a challenge for the waiters as they slid back and forth with huge brass trays of food. It was every bit as romantic as the glossy magazines she had consulted said it was, as well as being deliciously camp – Disney Moroccan – into the bargain. The only fly in the ointment was the food – for someone like Jamie, who had been barely able to cope with a choice of pizzas, Pasha's suggestions of yoghurt chicken, seafood tagine and prawn chermoula would probably be completely unnavigable. But that was a bridge she would cross when she came to it; at this rate, she wouldn't have to bother.

A flurry of interest among the hen party suddenly impressed itself on the daydreaming Anna (the rosé had been more potent than she had thought, the restaurant was deliciously warm and she had finally found a way to sit that didn't make her want to wet herself). Something tall and imposing was walking through the restaurant – and straight to her table.

'Anna, I'm so sorry.' *Jamie. At last.* 'Got delayed, I'm

afraid, and couldn't recall the name of the restaurant. Just came back to me in the taxi – thank God. Rhymed with crasher, I remembered.'

Well, it wasn't the *most* flattering thing he could have said, but Anna decided to make the best of it. Aware that the hen party – and a good many of the waiters – were staring at Jamie in open admiration, she levered herself halfway out of her chair to receive his kiss on both her cheeks. She was surprised to see that he, too, seemed to have made a considerable sartorial effort. His crisp white shirt glowed beneath his wide, dark eyes and Mediterranean tumble of thick black hair to perfection, despite the emphatic crease across the nipples and lower stomach revealing that he'd just got it out of the packet. There were other transformations too. Instead of sitting down, as expected, and glancing suspiciously at the menu, Jamie picked it up enthusiastically. He did not quite say, 'Oh, chermoula, my favourite,' but did make interested noises about the chicken. Anna, encouraged, and clenching her buttocks to strengthen her resolve, tried out The Flirt on him.

Jamie looked back at her. She felt her stomach tense and her lower bowels turn to liquid – which at the moment, was pretty much what they were anyway. Finally, after a long, sexy silence pregnant with possibility, Jamie, still gazing at her, spoke.

'Got something in your eye?' he asked.

Anna buried her face in the menu. Fortunately, the

waiter chose that moment to mince up.

But that was the only wrong note of the evening, apart from when Anna, helping herself to the mixed mezes with more enthusiasm than skill, accidentally knocked her hand against his. As the usual electric shock shot deliciously up her arm, the spoon wobbled and a great dollop of aubergine and tomato splattered onto the glaringly white tablecloth. Anna blushed furiously and, in her confusion, promptly set a spoonful of tabbouleh scattering across the table as well. She felt like a four-year-old. Seb, she knew, would have left the splodge where it was and stared at it meaningfully all evening. Jamie, however, simply moved one of the many terracotta meze dishes over the mark, pressed it firmly down on top and grinned at her.

As they talked – or, rather, as Anna listened to Jamie talking – it struck her that he seemed to be making an effort to charm similar to the pains he had taken to dress well. Neatly side-stepping the subject of himself directly, Jamie related a string of anecdotes about his ancestors. Never had someone talking about their relations seemed so sexy. Or so amusing.

'Yes, Granny Angus was quite a character. She used to stick her teeth in with exactly the same mortar she used to mend the walls – you see, as a family we've always been patching up the old place.' Jamie paused and flashed her a gusset-immolating grin. 'After she had her fifth heart attack, my father was at her bedside thinking she was about to peg it when she opened her eyes, looked straight at him and demanded, "Fetch me my compact mirror." '

Anna giggled, feeling that rare thing, happy. More rosé was ordered, food arrived and plates were taken away. Suffused with wine, glowing brass and the soft light of oil lamps, she felt herself relaxing under Jamie's barrage of charm. Enough even to go to the loo, at last.

There was something different about the table when she returned to it. Anna's stomach did a double loop of nervous delight when she spotted, nestling against the knife blade next to her plate, a small, rather tatty blue box. Sitting down quickly before her knees gave way beneath her, she gazed from it to Jamie, her eyes wide with hope and fear.

'Well, aren't you going to open it?'

Anna put out a trembling hand, hoping he wouldn't notice how bitten her nails were. Inside the box, nestling on a bed of rather moth-eaten cream satin, was a diamond of impressive dimensions. Anna gasped. Inside her, the mezes and prawn chermoula attempted an ill-advised pas de deux.

'It was my mother's.'

'It's lovely.' Never having been one to count her chickens, Anna could not yet be sure he hadn't just brought it along as a Dampie curio to show her, rather as some people got out their holiday snaps.

'Aren't you going to try it on?'

'Do you think I should?' Her heart beat a tattoo as she gazed unsteadily at him. His face was fading in and out of focus. Its strong, well-defined edges disappeared in places into a watery mass. As she bent her head, something wet and warm trickled down her cheek. She blinked hard.

He rolled his eyes to the ceiling. 'Well, of course it's up to you, but it might be an idea as I'm asking you to marry me.'

Anna stared at him. She was conscious of feeling nothing beyond being perfectly stunned and immobile. Opposite her, Jamie, as if in slow motion, smiled, gestured, and, finally, picked the ring out of its box and slid it on to her hand. In the watery world of utter shock she now inhabited, Anna was dimly aware of the cold metal sliding up her finger, of the hen party at the next table staring in unadulterated envy.

'. . . know it seems sudden . . . thought you would be perfect,' Jamie was saying in a slow, gloopy, surreal voice that didn't sound like him at all. She tuned out again in panic. '. . . share all the same interests, love of old buildings, the countryside . . .' he was mouthing at her as she picked up his voice again. She felt her head, heavy as a rock, moving slowly up and down in assent. '. . . saw no point in waiting for years to ask you . . . one just knows, doesn't one . . . important to have a wife who shares one's interests . . . very happy,' Jamie was adding, a hint of concern now creeping into his wide eyes at her lack of response. 'Thought you could come back to Dampie with me . . . going up in a couple of days . . . sooner you move in the better . . . can plan the wedding from there . . . chapel in the castle grounds . . . are you all right?'

There was a crash. Waiters rushed to the scene as Anna fled in the opposite direction, leaving a trail of the glasses she had swept from the table as she leapt up. She was conscious both of Jamie's concerned stare and the laser hatred of the hen party as she rushed, heedless of her heels, headlong down the tiled staircase beneath the lanterns, past the fountain and into the sheltering space of the lavatory cubicle. Hanging over the shining enamel hole, she realised she didn't want to be sick after all. It was exultation rushing up her throat, not half-digested couscous.

Suddenly, the mobile in her pocket buzzed. 'Half-time team talk,' hissed Geri. 'Decided whether you're going to shag him or not?'

'I'm not sure,' Anna said slowly, 'that I'm going to have to bother. Yet, at any rate.'

The next day was Sunday, yet Anna and an unusually grumpy Geri were drinking coffee together as usual. Operabugs, the junior appreciation society designed to ensure St Midas's pupils shone in the Covent Garden corporate boxes of the future, had been moved to

Sundays, there no longer being space on the weekday timetables to give it the attention it was felt it deserved. Puccini was currently under the microscope, and 'One Fine Day' was pouring out of the St Midas's windows into Cassandra's rain-spattered people-carrier, where Geri and Anna sat side by side like a couple of Bank Holiday coach drivers awaiting their cargo of pensioners. Their usual café being closed, they cradled plastic cups of distinctly inferior coffee from a fourth-rate builders' café round the corner and watched the water run down the windscreen.

'Geri,' said Anna finally, 'how long do I have to hold my cup like this before . . .'

'Omigod!' Geri, beside her, shot upright on the seat, her eyeballs large, rigid with excitement and clamped, mesmerised and unwavering, on the vast and glittering gem on Anna's finger. '*Christ*. It's colossal. That's *incredible*. I mean, from what you said when I called you, that you weren't going to sleep with him, I thought the whole thing was off. Was quite cross, actually,' Geri suddenly grinned at her. 'After all the advice I gave you and everything . . .'

So that explained the grump. Anna pressed her hand. 'Well, I couldn't have done it without you. You were brilliant.'

'So, can I be bridesmaid?'

Anna smiled at her nervously. 'Course you can. But the wedding date's not set yet – I'm supposed to be moving up to Scotland with him and sorting it out from there.'

'When are you going?' Geri's face suddenly fell. 'I'll miss you.'

'And I you.' Anna squeezed her hand.

She felt a tremor of fear course through her intestines. The wedding, certainly, was an intimidating prospect. In the back of her mind was the worry that she had not done the right thing by accepting, had allowed herself to be carried along on a tide of reckless romance at the expense of common sense. But it wasn't this that had caused the tremor. The fear was caused by something else altogether.

'Well,' Anna said slowly, 'I suppose I'd better tell Cassandra.'

'Zak! ZA-AA-AAK!' Having scanned the envelope's contents, Cassandra had bounded up the stairs two at a time, oblivious for once to the damage the Gucci spikes inflicted on the treads. She burst into his nursery to find her son slinging what looked like a dressing-gown cord over the hook on the back of the door. The vague, dreadful suspicion of what he might be up to – she, like all the other mothers, had read the reports of the Eton Strangling Game – stirred in Cassandra's mind, but there was no time for that now. Besides, everyone knew that dicing with death one way or another, be it sadistic prefects, capital punishment or initiation rites involving everything from buggery to bogflushing was an occupational hazard at public schools. It was part of what you paid for.

'What the hell is all this about?' she shrieked, waving the letter with the St Midas's crest at Zak whose spoilt face faded from pampered pink to haunted grey. He had never seen his mother so angry. He had never, really, seen her angry at all.

'It says here,' Cassandra said in the low, dead voice of one forced to accept that their worst fears have become reality, 'that you failed the mid-term exams. *How has this happened?*' Cassandra's voice sank to the agonised whisper of Macbeth at the point it dawns on him that life's but a walking shadow. 'It says here that you failed at *drawing*. How *could* you? After all that *work* I put in. I spent *weeks* showing you how to do a triangle . . .' Tears rose in her eyes.

Zak nodded, his eyes slits beneath his thick blond-and-honey-striped fringe.

'So why the hell *didn't* you draw a triangle?'

'Because,' Zak said contemptuously, 'they wanted me to draw a *circle* in the exam.'

Cassandra howled, smacked her head with the base of her palm and waved the letter again. 'And apparently you were asked to draw a woman.'

Zak nodded. 'I *did*.'

'But you drew one *with one leg*.'

Cassandra glared at her son, torn between murderous fury and blind despair. Then, most unexpectedly, an idea occurred to her. It really was a good one, Cassandra thought. Rather *brilliant*, actually. She tottered to the telephone and dialled the school's number.

'But Mrs Gosschalk, did Zak not tell you about my *amputation* . . .?'

Five minutes later, Cassandra put the phone down, her face magenta with fury. Not only had Mrs Gosschalk not believed her – Cassandra could tell from her tone of voice, despite the sympathetic noises, although, come to think of it, they had not been *that* sympathetic – but she had mentioned The Party. Cassandra had cherished the wild hope that Zak's behaviour at Savannah and Siena's birthday had been brushed under the sisal – after all, it had not been mentioned since. The reason for this, it now turned out, was because the school – which took a keen interest in its pupils' behaviour both on and off the premises – had been deliberating on what action to take. It had, Mrs Gosschalk had just informed Cassandra, decided to hold a kangaroo court on Zak's future at St Midas's, at which the entire SMSPA (apart from Cassandra) would be present. She would, Gosschalk had said, be informed of the results of its deliberations in due course. Cassandra's blood boiled. That *bloody* Fenella Greatorex would be sitting in judgement on *her*. A woman whose property was at best borderline where the St Midas's catchment area was concerned. Borderline in every other respect as well. The *humiliation* of it.

Things, Cassandra thought, could not get any worse this morning. But that was before Anna dropped her bombshell.

'*What?*' Only her spike heels, anchored firmly if ruinously in the kitchen floor, stopped Cassandra from collapsing. She glared at Anna with blazing loathing. '*What* the *fuck* did you just say?'

'Jamie says he doesn't want to take you up on the dinner party. He just, um, wanted to make, um, a donation to St Midas's.'

'No, not that,' Cassandra snapped. 'The *other* thing you said.'

Anna swallowed. 'And, um, he's asked me to marry him.'

'Oh my *God*. I've got to sit down.' Cassandra collapsed dramatically into a chair and stared at the delta of thin blue veins in the heel of her hand. Should she end it all now?

'*Give me air*,' she yelled at Anna as she fired up a Full Strength Ultratar. Hot tears began to flow over her foundation like lava over the cragged face of Etna. Her mascara – part of a new range called Rock Star she was celebrity test-driving for one of the few glossy magazines still aware she existed – began to run in black streams down her face.

'So I'm afraid I'll have to be leaving rather sooner

than I had planned,' Anna muttered. She genuinely felt almost apologetic. She'd seen earthquaked cities look less devastated than Cassandra at that moment. 'Jamie wants me to move up to Scotland with him.'

Anna spent her last night in Liv hearing Cassandra and Jett screaming more violently at each other than they ever had before. Unable to sleep, she was red-eyed and exhausted when Jamie came round in the morning to pick her up in an enormous hire car specially rented for the occasion. Doubtless he had thought, Anna realised as, embarrassed, she stuffed her one piece of luggage into the boot, that she had slightly more possessions than was the case. Or even the rucksack.

'What time will we arrive at Dampie?' she asked him, over-brightly, as they headed up through Hampstead.

'Oh, about midnight, I should think.' At least, Anna thought, he knew his way there; there would be no repeat of Seb's cold fury at her inability to tell right from left.

'We'll be starving.'

'Don't worry. Nanny will have left something for us to eat.'

'*Nanny?*' Anna sat upright in her seat. 'You've still got a *nanny*? You never mentioned *her* before.'

'Oh, didn't I? Oh yes, she still lives at Dampie. She's, um, well, sort of the housekeeper now – been in the family for ever. *Great* old character. You'll *love* her.'

There was a silence as Anna tried to suppress a sense of rising panic. She gazed out of the window, unseeing, as Golders Green flashed past.

'What's Nanny like?' she asked, as they turned on to the M1.

'Mm?' Jamie was absorbed in indicating to move into the middle lane.

'*Nanny*,' repeated Anna. 'Tell me about her.'

'Oh, Nanny. She's wonderful. You'll love her. Actually,' he added smoothly, 'you might find her quite useful as well. Thought you could talk to her about the wedding. Organising it and all that . . . Nanny's very good at organising things.'

It was a while before Anna spoke again.

'Are you very close to her?' she eventually asked, choosing her words carefully.

'Well, she looked after me after my parents died. Used to knit me scratchy jerseys.' Jamie laughed fondly as they sailed past Northampton. 'Still does, as a matter of fact. Bright yellow. Keeps the fleas off, she says.'

'*Fleas?*'

'And always a bit tight,' Jamie continued.

'What? Gin?' Not another dipsomaniac, Anna hoped. Cassandra had been bad enough. But bad enough, thankfully, to still be in bed when they left.

Jamie's shocked jerk sent the car spinning into the fast lane. Quickly, he pulled it back into the centre of the middle lane. 'God, no. Nanny never drinks. She knitted the jerseys a bit tight, I mean. She's always been a bit funny about clothes. She thinks T-shirts are very scruffy and once drew a collar and tie on a picture of me in one. I looked rather strange beside the rest of the school cross-country running team.' He grinned uncertainly at her across the handbrake. 'But I'm sure you girls will have a wonderful time planning the wedding.'

Girls. Even at best, Nanny would hardly qualify as a twenty-something. Difficult to imagine giggling over the wedding dress with a white-haired pensioner, however twinkling the eyes, apple-like the cheeks and benevolent the smile.

'Did she spoil you?' If Nanny was generous, that at least would be something. They could giggle over the lavish menu and champagne instead.

'*Spoil* me?' Another amazed swerve. 'Oh no. Nanny was *very* firm. She thought running water was immoral and used to make me break the ice on the horse troughs before I could wash. Even in summer. And long after we'd stopped using horses.'

As far as Nanny was concerned, Anna quickly decided, what remaining ignorance there was was bliss. She made no further inquiries and spent the rest of the journey either dozing or listening to Jamie describe the various repairs to the castle he had planned. From what he said, the place seemed to be falling apart; the weather since she had been there must have been appalling. She didn't remember it being so bad at Thoby's wedding. Although, come to think of it, it had been a bit cloudy.

By the time they reached Dampie, Anna realised there was a lot she didn't remember from Thoby's wedding. Such as the drive being a moonscape of yawning holes with the castle lurking glumly at the end in a cloak of swirling mist. The moss-slimed steps leading to the cracked and peeling front door had also slipped her memory. Indeed, so far removed was Dampie from being the Disneyland palace of light she remembered that Anna wondered if the wedding had been somewhere else altogether.

Anna gripped Jamie's hand tightly and tried not to shudder as something unimaginably ancient opened the door and thrust a battered, kerosene-scented lantern almost in their faces. The light blazed on the brimming red rims of the creature's rheumy eyeballs and caught the slimy stumps of its teeth. Flecks of phlegm were speared on the unshaven wastes of its chin like cuckoo-spit on grass, and a strong smell of whisky clung to the shabby layers of its clothing. It took all Anna's self-control not to recoil in disgust.

'MacLoggie!' exclaimed Jamie, much to Anna's relief. The unshaven chin had been a hint but hadn't necessarily ruled out the possibility of this being Nanny.

'Hame safely,' the ancient retainer gasped at Jamie, apparently deeply affected, although whether by alcohol or by emotion, it was impossible to tell.

'D'ye want anything ta eat? Nanny's left you some stovies in the kitchen.'

Jamie brightened. 'Nanny's stovies,' he informed Anna, 'are a force to be reckoned with.'

Anna had no idea what stovies were, except that they sounded like something you presented to your doctor in a glass jar for examination. 'Too late for me,' she muttered. 'If you don't mind, I think I'll turn in.'

'I'll take ye up to bed then,' the ancient heap growled.

Anna swallowed, trying to stifle the almost unimaginable thought of snuggling down with such a creature. She lifted her ring finger half in protection. The diamond glimmered dully in the lamp light. But MacLoggie showed no signs of noticing it.

'Take Miss Farrier to Dr Johnson,' said Jamie.

'Dr Johnson?' echoed Anna. 'But I feel perfectly all right. I *was* slightly carsick around Scotch Corner but I'm fine now.'

'The Dr Johnson *suite*,' said Jamie. 'He slept in it when he visited Dampie on his tour of the Highlands. Thought that might appeal to your literary side. He really enjoyed himself here,' Jamie added. 'Wrote in his diaries that Dampie was "a most impressive ruin . . . the first sight of which weighed very solemnly on me." '

'Oh.' It didn't sound like a five-star recommendation to Anna.

The weak light from MacLoggie's lantern had faded to a pinprick in the all-absorbing gloom of the back of the hall. Stumbling in his wake, Anna found a far more reliable guide to be the strong smell of whisky trailing after him. Endless passages and stairways were negotiated. Anna wondered which of the many dark passages contained Nanny.

'Hae we are,' MacLoggie said as they finally emerged on a red-carpeted landing where a number of low, wide white doors with brass handles were set deep into their respective frames. He unlocked one of them and, turning on his heel, disappeared into the darkness without another word. The blackness descended on Anna with the intimidating suddenness of a kidnapper's cloak.

As she felt for the bedroom door and opened it, the chill air hit her like a fist. She fumbled and found a light switch, revealing a room vaguely similar to that she recalled occupying with Seb. This was, however, much larger and presumably much grander, so vast were its proportions, so impressive in size if possibly not in comfort the large four-poster bed which stood in the centre of it. There was a slight smell of mildew and mothballs. A honeymoon suite for the Addams Family, thought Anna, peering closely at a murky oil which hung between two deeply recessed windows and depicted what looked like a soldier dying in the arms of a tragic-looking woman. A spaniel apparently also breathing its last lay nearby; the picture was entitled 'The Double Sacrifice'. A door in one wall of the room led to a cavernous Edwardian bathroom with a rust-scabbed container of Ajax standing on the bathside where the Crabtree and Evelyn ought to be.

Anna returned to the bedroom, knelt in the recessed window and squinted out through the diamond panes. One was missing, and the draught shot through her thin Ghost dress – a good luck present from Geri – like a bullet. She shivered, hoping it was the only Ghost in residence and remembering her suspicions from the wedding that the castle was haunted.

A hideous and heavy mahogany piece of furniture, seeking to combine the functions of desk, dressing table and decorative object and failing singularly at all three, stood against the faded floral paper of one wall. Anna debated whether to put her underwear in it, but having taken one sniff at the damp and dusty interior, decided not to. The flat, wide drawer just below the mirror in the centre would, however, be the perfect place for her diary. After she had written today's entry, of course. Fishing the small exercise book out of the front pocket of her bag, Anna crouched on the end of the bed and scribbled her account of leaving the vibrancy and crowds of London – never had she thought of them with such affection before – for a land where both the warmth and the light seemed permanently switched off. She shivered as she scribbled, noting at the end of her entry that she seemed to be further from writing a novel than ever. But perhaps the silence and space of the castle might prove an inspiration. After all, hadn't Dr Johnson stayed here?

Anna unpacked quickly and thrust her clothes into the dank and icy wardrobe. After finally screwing up the courage to get between the sheets – just as cold and old-smelling as anticipated, and very possibly the very same the eminent lexicographer had slept in – Anna lay and waited for Jamie. As the fatigue of the journey overcame her, she drifted in and out of dreams where she was being chased up an endless and ever-shrinking staircase by a large, bewigged and whisky-scented creature who may have been Dr Johnson. Or Nanny.

Chapter 14

The doctor put his pen down on his desk, sighed and looked at Cassandra.

'Mrs Knight. Is there anything in Zachary's past, any experience he may have had, that could have left a deep and abiding impression on him?'

'Certainly not,' snapped Cassandra. 'Zak's very resilient. Nothing ever makes an impression on him.'

'Yes,' said the child psychologist. 'That's roughly what I'd heard from Mrs Gosschalk.' He sighed, picked up his pen again and tapped it on the desk. Mont Blanc, Cassandra noticed crossly. *And* the desk looked antique. Probably bloody Chippendale with the fees she was paying him.

'Children are very sensitive, you know. It could have been something minor.'

'Zak's never met a miner. I try and keep him away from *that* sort of person.' Cassandra narrowed her eyes and hoped the psychologist – all too obviously *that* sort of person himself – would get her drift.

'So, no trigger that you can think of?'

'Well, he does have a number of guns piled under his bed.'

'He *does*, Mrs Knight?'

'All toy ones, of course. *Almost* all, at any rate.'

Still, she had had no choice but to come, such had been the verdict of the St Midas's parents in that *bloody* extraordinary general meeting held after Zak's performance at the Tressell birthday party. Cassandra boiled inside at the memory of that *wretched* Fenella Greatorex, now risen to chairman of the SMSPA, telephoning her afterwards and telling her in a voice *saturated* with sugary condescension that, given his obvious degree of mental disturbance, Zak needed to be referred to a child psychologist, on the basis of whose report Zak's future at St Midas's would finally be assessed. Stay of execution, then. But executions there would be, Cassandra was determined. Eventually.

'Never mind, darling,' Cassandra had reassured her son. 'What goes around, comes around, and when you're head of MI5, you can have them all stabbed to death with poisoned umbrellas.' Zak's eyes had lit up;

Cassandra had tried not to notice when, several hours later, she spotted him looking with interest at the inhabitants of the Jade Jagger umbrella stand in the corner of the hall.

Great though the relief that Zak could – at least temporarily – stay at the school had been, the expense of fulfilling the conditions had been greater. Cassandra had been amazed to discover the waiting list for a child psychologist was almost as long as that for a Hermès Kelly bag. She'd virtually had to found a whole ward before she could leapfrog it. But it was unthinkable that Zak lose his place at St Midas's.

'So.' The psychologist looked up at Cassandra from his notes. 'As far as you are concerned, Zachary's childhood has passed entirely without any violent or emotionally upsetting incident?'

'Yes.'

'Sure?'

'Well, there was a *slight* scene on the Ghost Train at Chessington when he was about six years old, but I never managed to find out whether it was Zak or his father who burst into tears during the ride.'

'Mmm.' The psychologist raised an eyebrow. 'Is that all?'

'And I suppose I was a *bit* cross with him when he only came second in the hundred metres sprint at the school sports day last year. But I *was* entitled to my view – after all, I'd won the mothers' race only after *months* of intensive daily training with a former Olympic athlete. I felt Zak was rather letting the side down.'

'Ah.' The psychologist brightened. 'Now we're getting somewhere. You must beware of ambitious parent syndrome, Mrs Knight.'

'*Tell* me about it,' Cassandra sighed dramatically. 'The parents at St Midas's are so pushy it's *embarrassing*. One of them is talking about getting his child selected to stand as a Labour MP at the age of twelve. He says if William Pitt can do it, so can Mungo, although I suppose William Pitt must be at another school somewhere. I don't think he's at St Midas's.'

The psychologist's eyes boggled slightly. He rippled his fingers repeatedly on the desktop as if playing an overture. 'Zachary, Mrs Knight, is a child. Not a racehorse.'

It was Cassandra's turn to stare. 'Dr Leake,' she said, flaring her nostrils, 'I find it hard to believe that I am paying good money – and rather a lot of it at that – to be told my son is *not* a racehorse. Do you think I wouldn't have noticed when he was born?'

'You misinterpret my meaning, Mrs Knight. What I am trying to say is that parenting is not a competition. Pushing him too hard can result in burnout syndrome. You don't want him to win cups at eight only to drop out at sixteen.'

'No, of course not. I want him to win cups at sixteen as well.'

The psychologist sighed. 'Mrs Knight. Like many parents you are over-anxious that your child should be a success. You are perhaps expecting too much of him. Parents who want their children to be MPs at ludicrously early ages are not really doing them any favours.'

'I agree. The very least they should expect is Prime Minister. Aim high, that's what I say.'

'Thank you, Mrs Knight. I think that's quite enough for one afternoon.'

Put *him* in his place, Cassandra thought triumphantly as she drove home. How dare anyone suggest Zak was anything other than an angel?

'I mean, really,' she declared to Jett on arriving back at Liv. 'How could anyone possibly take any of that party business *seriously*? Just because Zak's a chip off his father's old performing block and has a powerful stage presence. What's happened to everyone's sense of *humour* . . .?' Her voice tailed off as, having finished flinging off her pashmina and checking her make-up in the hall mirror, she turned and caught Jett's expression. It was one of unbounded fury.

'Yes, well, the little *bastard's* done more than demonstrate stage *presence*,' snarled Jett. 'He's been demonstrating some of the goddamn *props* as well.' He shook a fist at the ceiling from where lengths of wire dangled like beheaded flower stems.

Zak, Jett furiously, and at considerable volume, proceeded to disclose, had discovered a broadsword from the forthcoming Solstice stage show under the chaise longue in Jett's study and, with the aid of judiciously-placed chairs and tables, had immediately set about hacking every ceiling light in the house from its flex on the pretext that he was playing at pirates.

'Well, quite right too,' yelled Cassandra, determined to defend her son. 'Everyone knows ceiling roses are hopelessly passé. Zak's just taken the first step on the road to uplighters.'

'Trust you to take his side,' roared Jett. 'You let him get away with goddamn *murder* – almost literally in the case of that poor bastard Otto Greatorex. Zak gave his goddamn arm so many Chinese burns yesterday he nearly burst into goddamn flames. What sort of example are you setting him?'

'*You fucking hypocrite!*' shrieked Cassandra. 'If we're talking examples, just hang on in there while I get the lawyer on conference call. What about you and that Yugoslavian *slapper*?'

'Ethnic Albanian, actually,' huffed Jett. 'She lost her entire family in the Kosovo war.'

'And then she came here and got screwed by *you*. I wonder which was worse.'

Svetlana, the East European nanny, had seemed manna from heaven the day, almost a week after Anna had left, that Cassandra had spotted her ad in the local freesheet. She had been irresistible to Cassandra because she was cheap; to Jett she had been merely irresistible.

Just as Zak could not pass over the opportunity to call her Sweaty instead of the approved diminutive of Sveti, Jett could not pass over the opportunity of making a pass.

'I didn't screw her.'

'Oh no? What about all those scratches and squeeze marks on your back?'

Jett's protestations and excuses that Sveti had been a dermatologist before the war in Kosovo and was giving him some free treatment cut no ice with his wife.

'A *dermatologist*?' Cassandra hissed. 'She's got a face like a *pizza*. Probably thinks cathiodermy is an *Irish barmaid*.' She was, Cassandra suddenly decided, *sick* of playing host plant to a parasitic philanderer. The last strumpet had sounded. She'd had enough.

Seeing the genuine light of battle in her eyes rather than just the drunken rage he had privately come to think of as the Warninks signals, Jett panicked. A large house in Kensington and a lavishly subsidised lifestyle seemed to rise up before him and disappear out of the window.

'Um,' he stuttered. 'I can explain . . .'

Cassandra held up a hand. 'And besides,' she spat, 'what the *hell* do you want with dermatology anyway? You've got skin like an old teabag that's been buried for years. Just *look* at you.'

Jett bristled. He stared at his wife with a mixture of fear and loathing. Finally, squeezing through the decayed and dripping cells of his brain came the dimly remembered instruction that attack was the best form of defence.

'You're jealous,' he hurled back. 'You can't bear to think another woman finds me attractive.' As Cassandra stared at him in disbelief, he wondered whether he had got it wrong. Perhaps defence was the best form of attack. 'So what harm does it do?' he wheedled. 'It's not as if *you* give two hoots. I'm not *hurting* anyone.'

'*That*,' snapped Cassandra, 'depends whether you're wearing your Five Gates of Hell penis strap or not. I imagine that could hurt quite a lot.'

'How do you know about *that*?' What colour there was in Jett's face drained out of it. 'Been opening my post again, I suppose?'

'Never mind how I know. The point is,' Cassandra said, feeling suddenly exhausted, 'it's over. Our marriage. I've had enough.'

'I'd say you haven't had anything *like* enough,' Jett said bitterly. 'That's the problem.'

'You're a dead loss,' snarled Cassandra. 'Or, to be more specific, you look dead and you make a loss. I can't afford to have a sponge like you hanging round me any longer.'

'Dead loss?' expostulated Jett. 'What about the band getting back together? The TV deal?'

'TV deal?' snorted Cassandra. 'You mean that cowboy outfit wanting to make a fly on the wall documentary about your shitty band re-forming and going on the road? Hardly your own *chat* show, is it? And fly on the wall documentary my arse – fly on the *fly* is what they should make about *you*.'

Desperate, Jett produced his trump card. 'So what about Zak? How's he going to feel when he finds we're splitting up?'

'Delighted,' Cassandra returned triumphantly. 'I've already discussed it with him and he's thrilled. Very keen it should go through as soon as possible, in fact.'

'*Bastard*.'

'Sadly, no,' Cassandra said. 'I wish he was but, unfortunately, my child *has* a father. *You*.'

'Worse luck,' said Jett, to whom it had now become evident that resistance was useless.

'For *you*, yes,' spat Cassandra. 'Zak, as a matter of fact, was the one who alerted me to your antics in the first place.'

'*What?*' Jett's hands clenched and unclenched as best they could while sporting a row of rings like knuckledusters.

'Oh *yes*,' Cassandra said. 'Asked me why does Daddy have Sweaty in bed with him when you're not there, Mummy? I had to tell him it was because Daddy was frightened of the dark. He thought that was pathetic and that I should divorce you.'

'I bet he did,' Jett snarled. 'He's set the whole thing up. I *knew* it.'

'How *dare* you?' shrieked Cassandra. 'Typical! You'd blame your own eight-year-old son rather than take responsibility for your inability to keep your trousers zipped.'

'Yes, because as far as he's concerned, us splitting up means two lots of Christmas and birthday presents for *him*. Can't you *see*?'

'Don't be *ridiculous*,' snapped Cassandra, recalling that, now Jett came to mention it, Zak *had* raised the matter of presents during the divorce discussions she had had with him. Quite frequently, in fact.

Chapter 15

It hadn't been – *absolutely* it hadn't been – Jamie's fault; he was obviously *completely* exhausted by the drive and, well, if the expected first night of passion had boiled down to nothing more than him dragging it in and out a few times, at least, Anna thought, he'd made some effort to mark the occasion of their homecoming. If not the bedsheet.

'I'm sorry,' he had the grace to say as they lay, silent and several feet apart, in the darkness. 'I'm afraid I wasn't really in the mood.'

Anna reached across and squeezed his hand. 'You're tired.'

'Yes, and I was just reading the most depressing report about how the curtain walls are going to need completely rebuilding. I'm afraid,' he added, 'that the wedding probably can't be as lavish as we'd hoped.' Anna said nothing. 'Still,' Jamie concluded brightly, 'you need to discuss all that with Nanny. You'll see her at breakfast.' So saying, he turned over and went to sleep.

Anna woke up alone. Jamie, she imagined, had gone to inspect some decaying part of the castle or other. She hugged her knees to her chest beneath the covers as she tried to preserve the precious pocket of warmth between her thighs and her stomach for as long as possible. In the cold air outside the bed, she could even see her breath.

Thin grey light divided the curtains, and as Anna stared at it, she noticed that the line didn't seem to be increasing much in brightness. If anything, it was fading slightly, as if the day had dawned, thought better of it and gone away again. And what on earth was that odd noise? That strange, wailing sound, like a soul in torment, coming from the direction of the window. The wind trapped under one of the panes? As the ghastly yowling seemed to reach a peak of high-pitched, hopeless misery, Anna, suddenly deciding not to go and check, took the boldest action she was capable of and stuck her fingers in her ears.

A few minutes later, she reluctantly peeled back

the covers and shuddered as the cold rushed to embrace her like a long-lost relative. Perhaps she would brave the plumbing first, and have a bath to warm up . . .

After wandering aimlessly about the seemingly endless corridors in search of the breakfast room, Anna found Jamie in what, to judge by the long oak table in its centre and heavy, dark, carved sideboards against its walls, was a dining room. It seemed to be a different room to that where, over breakfast, Geri had confessed to taking Miranda's place on Thoby's wedding night, but without the milling people, deafening clang of the chafing dishes and, most of all, the electric light which had *definitely* been on then, it was hard to say. The silence was absolute, interrupted only by the bad-tempered spatter of rain against the windows. Outside, nothing could be seen but fog. *That* much, Anna thought, she could remember.

Jamie sat calmly at one end of the table blowing the dust off a pile of ledgers, documents and receipts. 'There you are,' he remarked distantly, noting something down in a margin. Somewhere in his tone, Anna felt, lay rebuke.

'What time is it?'

'Ten past nine.'

'Christ. I had no idea. *Sorry.*'

'Didn't MacLoggie wake you up?'

Anna started. The thought of the bent old man

creeping into her bedroom to lay a clammy, whisky hand on her sleeping arm . . . she suppressed a shudder. 'No, he certainly did not.'

'But surely you heard the pipes.' Jamie looked at her with surprise.

'Oh yes.' Come to think of it, she had heard some rushes and rattles and gurgles, counterpointed by the occasional distant explosion, immediately after their abortive lovemaking. Still, noisy plumbing was preferable to no plumbing at all. And the eccentric-sounding pipe layout may have had something to do with her recent experiences in the bathroom, experiences she intended to bring up with Jamie. But in the meantime she was determined to put a brave facecloth on it.

'Oh, and there was the most *appalling* yowling noise an hour or so ago,' Anna added. '*Horrible* row. Like a cat being tortured to death.'

Jamie looked annoyed. 'Yes. That's what I mean. The *bagpipes.* When the laird is in residence, MacLoggie plays under the windows every morning at six. Has done for centuries. His family has, I mean.'

'*Oh.*' Anna blushed furiously. So *that* was what the ghastly noise had been. Dr Johnson's sudden flight was starting to make sense.

'Yes. The MacLoggies have been pipers to the Anguses for as long as anyone can remember. Far back into the mists of time.'

Mists was right, Anna thought, glancing at the grey cotton wool beyond the windows.

'But darling,' Anna said, 'does he *have* to do it so early?' She wondered where she might get a cup of tea or even, luxury of luxuries, a slice of toast. The rack in front of Jamie was empty.

'Early!' Jamie sounded indignant. 'He *usually* does it at six. This morning he did it at eight as a special favour. You were very honoured.'

Anna plastered what she hoped was a suitably awestruck expression across her face, and drew out a chair to sit down. She promptly jumped about seven feet in the air as she suddenly became conscious of something massive and frightening in the doorway behind her.

'Nanny,' Jamie said as the figure moved slowly forward like a juggernaut. 'This is Anna. My fiancée.' It was difficult not to notice the apprehension in his tone.

'How do you do,' stammered Anna, whose tongue suddenly felt as dry and rasping as a piece of biltong. Call her a scaredy-cat, but there was something ever so slightly intimidating about the large, thickset, late-middle-aged woman before her. Perhaps it was the huge and hairy mole nestling beside the thick boxer's nose. Perhaps the eyes, like ice chips behind glasses as thick as a crateful of bottle bottoms. Perhaps it was the line of her mouth, as flat and unrelenting as that on a switched-off life-support machine; perhaps the few strands of hair scraped back to expose the huge and pouchy face. Perhaps it was the way the very dining room seemed to shrink in her presence. Because *this* woman came from the other end of the childcare spectrum from the apple-cheeked, lavender-scented, *Brideshead Revisited* variety of cradle-rocker. Nanny looked as if she could bite the bollocks off a brontosaurus. And frequently did. In an act of instinctive self-protection, Anna spread her fingers out across the table, so the ring shone as best it could in the gloom. But if Nanny saw it, she showed no sign.

'Nanny's an extraordinary woman,' Jamie said appreciatively as the vast figure, armed with the order for a cup of tea which was as much as Anna dared ask for, left the room.

'Yes, she looks it.' Feeling the colour slowly start to return to her face, Anna realised Nanny also looked like the last person on earth she wanted to discuss her wedding with.

'She can see things we can't. Fairies, ghosts, images from the past and the future. She's got second sight,' said Jamie admiringly.

Just as well, thought Anna. Because if those glasses are anything to go by she obviously hasn't got first. She lapsed into depressed silence. Jamie, meanwhile, returned to perusing his papers. Anna watched him as, handsome brow furrowed in concentration, he ran his finger slowly up the page.

'What are you looking at?' It seemed reasonable to try and strike up a conversation with her fiancé on their first morning in their future home.

'Just checking the figures for the deer herd.'

Looking round the dining room, it seemed a miracle there were any deer left. The walls bristled with antlers. Above some large dark oblongs which she imagined must be paintings, hundreds of stags' heads ran like a frieze round the room. She jumped as Jamie abruptly closed the deer book. Her hopes of engaging him in discussion were swiftly dashed as he instantly opened another.

'What's that one about?'

'Refurbishment.'

'Can I help?' Anna asked eagerly. At last, something she knew about. The annual university ritual of rolling white paint over the walls of dingy student rooms would prove to be useful experience after all. She could come to Jamie's emulsional rescue.

'Any good at roofing?' asked Jamie, a shade sarcastically. 'And there are a few walls that need rebuilding as well.'

By the time Nanny returned with the tea, which was tepid and thoroughly stewed, silence had descended once more. Seeing Jamie turn to yet another ledger, Anna tried again. Third time lucky.

'Er . . .'

'Tenants' complaints,' rapped out Jamie before she could get the words out. He did not sound as if he wished to discuss what they were.

Silence. As Anna replaced her cup in its saucer, the noise seemed window-shattering. Perhaps that was why so many of them were broken.

'Um, about tenants' complaints,' she ventured.

'Yes?'

'Well, I've got one. There's something very wrong with the water supply.'

'What do you mean?' She'd got his attention now. His head had lifted, at least.

'When I ran my bath this morning, it was absolutely filthy.'

'*Filthy*?' Anna was conscious of both Jamie and Nanny staring at her in amazement. 'It can't be,' Jamie said. 'It's as fresh as a daisy. Comes straight out of the local burn.'

'Well, this looked as if it came straight out of the local pub. Horrible dirty brown. Looked just like beer.'

A fork clattered dramatically and possibly deliberately to the floor. Nanny bent to retrieve it. A faint creaking sound accompanied her efforts, and Anna cast an awed glance in the direction of her corset. Evidently a triumph of civil engineering, it was probably holding back as much raw force as the wall of the Aswan dam.

'*That*,' said Jamie, casting a nervous glance in

Nanny's direction, 'is because all the water here runs through peat. There's nothing wrong with it. On the contrary, it's some of the best and freshest around.'

Not for the first time since arriving at Dampie, Anna wanted the floor to swallow her up. Still, there was one saving grace. At least she hadn't mentioned she'd flushed the toilet several times as well, unable to understand why the pee wouldn't go away.

'Oh dear,' she said, grinning apologetically. 'I can see I've got rather a lot to learn about Skul. Perhaps you could tell me a few things.'

'Absolutely,' said Jamie, recovering his equilibrium instantly. 'Skul is a fascinating island. Besides the castle, there's the Old Man Rock, the Mount O'Many Stanes, the Cairns Of Bogster and Mad Angus Angus's Burn.'

Was that like a Chinese burn? Anna wondered, trying not to notice Nanny's massive red hands as she cleared the last of the plates away. 'How interesting,' she said.

'Yes, well you should certainly explore the lie of the land a bit. 'After all, you're about to become mistress of the place.'

A strange feeling – as of her heart soaring and stomach sinking simultaneously – gripped Anna. Then a stray ray of light, bolder than its fellows, suddenly shot through the gloomy dining-room window and scored a direct hit on the ring on her finger. The stone may have been old and slightly yellow, but it still packed a considerable punch. Both she and Jamie gazed at it,

Anna in a kind of dazzled delight; Jamie slightly more speculatively.

'Yes, that would be lovely.' Anna beamed. A walk with Jamie round the island would be absolutely the most romantic introduction to her new home. Perhaps, she thought, they could even take a picnic. One glance at the weather brooding outside the windows, however, and even one of Anna's newly optimistic bent was forced to admit that looked unlikely. She glanced away from the grey mist pressing up pleadingly against the panes as if wishing to be let in to get warm. Some hope. In the space of a single breakfast-time it was already evident to Anna that Dampie's most testing social challenge was the ability to hold a conversation whilst suppressing one's teeth from chattering with the chill. It could, she reasoned, hardly be colder outside than it was inside. 'When shall we go?' she asked.

'We?' Jamie looked astonished. 'I'm awfully sorry, but I've got a few things to sort out this morning. Turns out that yet another section of roof caved in last night, this time over the old wine store.'

'Oh no.' Anna looked at him, her eyes wide with concern. 'Does that mean all the drink for the wedding . . .?'

'Well, actually, the cellar was empty. The point of it is that the wine store connects to the kitchen and we don't want the roof there collapsing in on Nanny.'

Aware that Nanny was clearing up the rest of

the breakfast things as slowly as possible with the obvious intention of listening to every word of their conversation, Anna tried hard to look as if this was absolutely the last thing she wanted. Not that Jamie noticed.

'No,' he was musing. 'I think the last wine in there was taken out for my father's twenty-first birthday party, as a matter of fact. For the wedding we'll most probably get in some boxes of plonk from Tesco's in Inverness . . .' His voice died away as his glance once again settled on Anna's diamond ring. 'Because unfortunately we won't be able to afford champagne. Not unless we sell something . . .'

Seeing what he was looking at, Anna closed up her fingers into a fist. 'I'll go on my own, then,' she said, trying, more for her own benefit than his, to sound as if she felt this to be an attractive prospect.

'Perhaps someone else could show you round,' Jamie said vaguely. 'MacLoggie, for example. Or . . .' His glance fluttered speculatively towards the wide doorway through which Nanny's almost equally wide back was at that moment retreating. 'Perhaps . . .'

With a deafening scrape of her chair, Anna stood up. 'No, really, I'd rather go by myself.' It was clear, in any case, from the sudden acceleration of Nanny's back through the door that Nanny felt as eager as Anna about the prospect of taking a walk together. So they could agree on one thing, at least.

'Oh well, if you're sure. Thought it might be an opportunity for you to talk to Nanny about . . .'

Jamie's voice was drowned in a sudden deafening clatter from the corridor. Nanny, by the sound of it, had consigned most of the breakfast service to the stone-flagged floor. Anna's nerves jangled wildly, both at the noise and the prospect of discussing something so intimate with such a terrifying creature. As the sound of Nanny scraping up china drifted into her ears, it occurred to her that here was another subject on which they probably held identical views.

'Yes, I must get round to doing that,' muttered Anna.

'Yes, and I must get in touch with the vicar,' muttered Jamie, as if to himself. 'The whole thing should have been done and dusted by now. If it wasn't for the fact that the whole bloody place is suddenly collapsing.'

His eye flickered towards Anna's ring again. 'I'll go for my walk, then,' said Anna.

Once outside the front door, the first thing about the lie of the land she discovered was that the land didn't as much lie as desiccate in wiry tufts. Each was surrounded by a sticky sauce of black and oozing mud, over which Anna had to pick her way carefully as she headed automatically towards the loch which, grey and bloated this morning, lapped the rocks on which the castle was built. The waves made a slapping sound which, for some reason, immediately reminded Anna of Nanny. She shuddered. Nanny and the wedding were fast fusing into the same thing, and she was starting to dread the one at the thought of the other.

Glancing back at her new home-to-be from the shore, Anna saw with surprise that the ever-present clouds had parted sufficiently to allow her first proper look at Dampie in daylight. It was not a sight to lift the heart. The rocks leading down to the water from the castle were slimy and rather brutal-looking. The building itself was a long, thin construction, its sheer sides punctured with slitty, sullen-looking windows. Any romantic effect the turreted top may have had was undermined by the walls being coated with a grey pebbledash and concrete mixture across which the dampness spread in a huge unsightly stain. So unprepossessing and prison-like was its aspect that, as the softening mists embraced the building once again, Anna felt almost relieved to see it go.

Her left hand clasped comfortingly round the Panasonic in her pocket that Geri had given her along with the Ghost dress as a farewell gift. 'Think of it as an early wedding present,' she had said. The 'w' word again. Geri, of course, would be in the People's Republic of Tuscany now. Probably at this moment lying by a palazzo poolside sipping Prosecco, nibbling Parma ham and chatting to Tony and Cherie, who had apparently been due to drop by.

Picking her way with difficulty along a soggy glen on either side of which the hills rose sheer as walls, Anna determinedly quashed the frisson of envy that contemplation of Geri's probable lot provoked. Skul's beauty, admittedly, was not of the *obvious* Mediterranean sort. It was a more subtle variety altogether. Very subtle, she thought, scanning the horizon and noticing the threatening grey clouds squatting sullenly atop each twisted hill. As one suddenly, bomber-like, dropped its load of hail straight in her retinas, Anna closed her eyelids hard. Opening them again, she looked once more on the desolate scene, noting that the bumpy spines of the hills reminded her of stegosauruses and trying not to dwell on how strongly their particular shade of bilious green resembled mould. More depressing still was the collective effect of the jagged hills ringing the grey sky above her – making her feel as if she were trapped inside a giant, just-cracked, soft-boiled egg.

The grey mists on one of the summits suddenly drifted sufficiently for Anna to glimpse a tall, thin rock in profile on its upper slopes. Its very particular shape, combined with the 45 degree angle at which it leant from its fellow rocks, reminded her irresistibly of a penis. She smiled before reflecting, rather sourly, that it was the nearest thing to an erection she'd seen so far on Skul. Could this, she wondered, be the Old Man Rock?

The hail began again, and put an end to her curiosity.

Visions of steaming baths drifting before her – which she already knew better than to expect to be realised – Anna set off back towards the castle, hoping fervently she was going the way she had come. The mists were fast closing in, and it was becoming impossible to tell. After spending several worrying minutes skirting the edge of a large and very troublesome bog, she recognised, through the now almost opaque swirls of fog, Dampie's familiar, damp-stained walls rising gloomily up before her, albeit from a slightly different angle to that expected. She was much lower than she had thought. Practically in the loch, in fact. No wonder it had been boggy.

The slippery remains of what had once been a stone path stretched up before her. Gritting her teeth and grasping at clumps of grass to support herself, Anna slowly ascended, eventually emerging through a thicket of extremely wet bracken to what could almost feasibly have been, long ago, part of a garden. There was even some sort of building there, small and squat, lurking behind the vegetation. Moving forward through knee-high grass, Anna used both arms to heave aside the lolling fronds of an enormous rhubarb plant and reveal a half-ruined pile of stones whose relatively imposing arched entrance seemed to hint at some ecclesiastical function.

It could not, thought Anna, the cold hand of panic gripping her stomach, surely *not* be the chapel Jamie had mentioned. The chapel he had marked out for their wedding ceremony? But surely, when Thoby and Miranda had got married . . . ? Obviously, she now realised, they had been married in the castle itself. A room must have been adapted for the occasion, which had passed at the time for a chapel. The wine store, most probably. At least they'd tied the knot before the roof had caved in. She and Jamie, Anna thought, looking at the sodden pile of stones, would have no such luck. Just to recap, Anna thought miserably, I'm getting married in a ruin, toasting my good fortune with wine box plonk and arranging the whole thing with Hagar the Horrible's twin sister because my husband-to-be is too busy trying to prop up our collapsing home to do anything about it. *Marvellous.*

Turning her back on the chapel, Anna walked in what she imagined to be the direction of the castle, now invisible above her. A loud rushing sound, accompanied by a steep downward movement of her path, alerted her to the possibility that she might be about to slip. Parting more fronds of vegetation, Anna suddenly realised in terror that she had stopped just short of certain death down a deep and profoundly gloomy chasm, at the bottom of which lay a voracious-looking river flowing into the loch. The rushing noise was now explained. Deafening now, it came from a waterfall thundering, spitting and spraying over the glistening rocks just to the right of where Anna was standing.

Anna jerked in shock. Her feet slithered nearer the treacherous edge. 'MacLoggie!' she exclaimed. She had not quite framed who she thought had suddenly crept up directly behind her, but she was relieved nonetheless that it was not Nanny. So relieved, in fact, that it did not occur to her to wonder what the ancient retainer was doing here, wandering about in the wet, abandoned garden. MacLoggie did not react. Nor did he make the slightest noise of apology. Instead, he fixed her with his rheumy eyes and demanded to know what she was doing by Mad Angus Angus's Burn.

'Oh, is that what it is?'

'Aye. It's said that it was the only thing that calmed him down. He had a dreadful temper,' MacLoggie explained. 'He especially liked to listen to it at night. In bed.' His watery eyes glistened unpleasantly. He was, Anna thought uneasily, being unusually friendly. His mouth was stretched in a way that, on someone resembling a human being to a slightly greater degree, might almost have passed for a leer.

'I see.' Jamie would be impressed. Two of the island's hotspots before lunch. Not bad going. The weak sun that had finally deemed it safe to come out glanced against her ring. There was no doubt, this time, that MacLoggie had spotted it.

'But this is nae place for a woman engaged to be married,' MacLoggie growled.

'No, I'm sure you're right.' Relieved, Anna grabbed the chance of escape with both hands. 'I'd better go then.'

'Too late.' MacLoggie grinned at her evilly. Anna suddenly felt rather ill.

'What do you mean?'

'Tradition is that the unmarried woman who walks down to Mad Angus Angus's Burn before noon marries the first man who claps eyes on her.'

Anna glanced up nervously at the steep wall of the castle. A mean slit of a window could just about be seen through the dripping fronds of the trees. As MacLoggie strode off, cackling, she hoped fervently, that sometime in the last twenty minutes Jamie had looked out and seen her here.

'Total *bollocks*,' Cassandra stormed.

Twisted old bitch, she seethed. What did Gosschalk *mean* about the psychologist's report confirming her own impression that Zak's unstable parental background affected his attitudes and aptitudes? Call herself a *headmistress. Head case*, more like.

'I'm sorry, Mrs Knight?' Mrs Gosschalk looked sternly over her bifocals.

'*Absolute shit.*'

True, she'd had a gin or three before coming here,

but Saddam Hussein would probably need Dutch courage before facing this shrivelled-up old blue-stocking. On second thoughts, Gosschalk was probably a stranger to stockings. Blue *tights*, more like, the thick, knitted sort with the gusset you can't get above your knees.

'I read a survey only recently,' Cassandra spluttered, 'in fact,' she rummaged in her bag, 'I have it *right here*,' she produced a crumpled piece of *The Times* over which foundation from her make-up bag had liberally leaked, 'which says that parents with, um, *volatile* relationships are the best thing that can happen to a child, and that there's nothing like seeing your parents scream blue murder to kindle the creative spirit. For *Christ's sake*, Jett and I are doing Zak *a favour*.'

Mrs Gosschalk took the piece of newsprint between finger and thumb – *bloody cheek*, thought Cassandra, as if it was smeared with old chip fat and not my best MAC foundation.

'My dear Mrs Knight,' she said in a voice so cutting it could have given the de Beers machinery a run for its money, 'you are no doubt aware that newspapers are full of surveys of questionable value on the subject of education. Only yesterday I read one claiming that giving your child a ludicrous name guaranteed its future success, as the struggle it would have to overcome the teasing in the playground would teach it independent habits of mind. *Obviously* ridiculous.'

'*Absolutely*,' burst out Cassandra. 'Teasing in the playground?' she added scornfully, relieved to have found a theory both she and the headmistress could agree to despise. 'There *is* no teasing of that nature in the playground at St Midas's. *Everyone* has ludicrous names.'

'Quite,' said Mrs Gosschalk. Why were the corners of her mouth quivering like that? Cassandra wondered. Nervous tic, obviously. The mad old bat was obviously off her rocker. 'So naturally you will understand when I fail to take the dysfunctional parent theory quite as seriously as you seem to.'

Mrs Gosschalk's lips were, Cassandra noticed, resolutely lipstick-free. Perhaps she should have held back on her own facial ensemble; the startling Ruby Tuesday lipstick from the Rock Star range was, she was aware, possibly visible from Venus, but the cashpoint was boringly refusing to play ball at the moment so visits to the Harvey Nicks make-up counters were, for the moment, on hold.

Mrs Gosschalk stood up. Cassandra's heavily made-up eyes – well, she'd had to balance the lipstick somehow – flicked over the sensible suit and crisp shirt which seemed miraculously free of creases. Everything everyone else was wearing seemed miraculously free of creases at the moment; Cassandra, for the first time in her life having to grapple with an iron on a regular basis, was constantly frustrated by the fact that whenever she tried to use it, her clothes looked worse than they had to start with.

She was aware that the grey linen trousers she was wearing looked as if they had spent the last fortnight buried at the bottom of the garden; also that their greyness was more the result of a spin-cycle confrontation with one of Jett's new tour T-shirts than a conscious attempt to look businesslike before Mrs Gosschalk. Jett, thank God, was finally away on Solstice's 'Back From The Dead' tour, promoting the *Ass Me Anything* comeback album. Comeback *indeed*, thought Cassandra. The thought of Jett coming back from anywhere but the pub was almost hilarious enough to cheer her up. Although, maddeningly, he was going for half of everything they had in the divorce. Or half of everything that was left after the man from Mishcon de Reya had been paid. Yet Jett had at least put up no resistance whatsoever to Cassandra's claim for custody of Zak. One would almost think – *ha ha* – that Jett didn't want to see his son at *all*.

'I'm terribly sorry, but I'm afraid I cannot allow your son to remain in the school,' said Mrs Gosschalk. 'That is my final word. Now, if you'll excuse me, good afternoon, Mrs Knight.'

'But you can't do this,' Cassandra gabbled as Mrs Gosschalk showed her firmly to the door. 'Zak is autistic, he's got Tourette's syndrome, he's got special needs *and* he's a gifted child.'

'I'm sorry, Mrs Knight. I wasn't going to mention it, but there is also the additional matter of the school fees. As you know, your payments lately have not been as regular as they might have been.'

Cassandra's eyes blazed and a lump rose up her throat. Her week had hardly been enhanced by the demand of the publishers that she pay back her advance for *A Passionate Lover* on the grounds that no manuscript of any description had neared her editor's desk and it was a good six months past the deadline. For the moment at least, money was tighter than a gnat's arse. The fact that Gosschalk probably knew it made her blood boil.

'Have you thought of sending Zachary to boarding school?' Mrs Gosschalk suggested. 'There are ways of getting help with the fees, you know.'

Reduced fees. The horror of it. Something in Cassandra suddenly snapped – something quite apart from the bra strap currently hanging on by a thread. 'Why don't you stuff your school up your leathery old *arse*?' Cassandra yelled. 'And yes, I might well send him to boarding school. You'll be laughing on the other side of your raddled old face when Zak comes out top of his year at Eton.'

'Come the glorious day, no one would be more delighted than me, Mrs Knight. When he's the right age, of course. Although, given your recent remarks and his general attitude I see no reason in keeping from you the fact that the only boarding school I can see Zachary getting a place at is Borstal.'

Chapter 16

'Midgies.' The word hung in the damp, heavy air.

'Sorry?' Anna whirled round to see who had spoken. A cloud of tiny black insects half obscured the unedifying sight of the ancient retainer MacLoggie, grinning malevolently through his tooth stumps.

Her heart sank. She had been avoiding MacLoggie for ten days since the Mad Angus Angus's Burn encounter, the memory of which still made her shudder. She had not mentioned it to Jamie – partly out of suspicion that he was far more likely to have been inspecting a septic tank than looking out of the window at the time, and partly because, given his obsession with Dampie and its traditions and legends, he might just hold her to it.

'What did you say?'

'Midgies. Those wee black flies there. They bite like *bastards*.'

'*Really?*' Disbelieving, Anna flapped her hands half-heartedly in front of her face. 'They don't look big enough to.'

MacLoggie smirked. 'Ye'll see.'

'Well, thanks for the advice, MacLoggie. I'm sure there are lots of things I've yet to learn about living up here.'

MacLoggie snickered. 'Ye can say tha' again.'

'Well, then, perhaps you could tell me how I get to the nearest town.'

Her inquiry was rewarded by yet another glimpse of the ancient creature's slimy stumps. ''Orrible's over there. That way.' MacLoggie pointed vaguely beyond the end of the loch and staggered off in the opposite direction. *Horrible*? Anna echoed, silently. There couldn't, not even *here*, be a village called *that*. Could there?

She walked off at a brisk pace in the direction indicated, along the side of the loch. The pewter platter of the water, bordered by the rust and sodden green of the heather, reflected a chill, white sky. The only signs of life were a few Highland cattle in the distance and a group of sorry-looking sheep limping over the rocky hillside. A slight stinging sensation she had noticed earlier continued; looking down, she saw that small red marks like strawberry-juice stains had appeared on her wrists.

Some time later, quite a long time later, long after she had left the loch behind and had continued onward without even as much as a signpost to confirm she was headed in the right direction, Anna wondered if she should perhaps have pressed MacLoggie for more details. A steel-keen wind began to slice at her across the rock spurs, skimming over the heather like a Stealth bomber. Surely MacLoggie would not have let her set off alone and directionless if the village really were a long way? She looked at her ring for reassurance. It gleamed dully back at her. Far more vivid was the memory of MacLoggie's insolent leer. *Would* he?

By the time she gained the village – not the cheerful cluster of white-painted cottages she had imagined, but a sullen, sodden huddle called, not Horrible, but Oribal – the rain was lashing down like stair rods and bouncing off the deserted street. Shivering in the bus stop, Anna looked speculatively across the road to the only establishment in the immediate vicinity that seemed to feature electric light. The low, grey-white pebbledashed building with frosted windows looked as if it might be a pub.

Though desperate for a vodka and tonic, Anna decided to give it a miss and, taking advantage of a hiatus in the deluge continued her explorations. A damp wooden hut had 'Village Hall' in rotting letters above the door. Before it was a glass-fronted noticeboard containing a Met Office declaration that Oribal had had the most rainfall and least hours of sunshine of any place in the British Isles in the previous year. It was difficult to shake off the impression, fostered by the prominent position the notice commanded on the board, that the village was rather proud of this distinction.

Another notice offered the services of a Mrs McLeod and her ironing board at what Anna considered to be the extremely reasonable rate of a pound per ten items, 'discretion assured'. From this she divined that either people round these parts wore things they didn't want others to know about, thought Anna, or to be suspected of not doing one's own ironing in Oribal was to be suspected of sin beyond redemption. Perhaps both.

Rather grudgingly displayed at the board's bottom was a card advertising evening classes in flower-pressing and the bagpipes. Neither appealed to her much; having failed so far to spot a single bloom she doubted the feasibility of the former, and the idea of learning how to make the sort of ghastly row that woke her every morning similarly held few attractions. MacLoggie, on the other hand, could clearly do with a lesson or two. Perhaps she'd suggest it to Jamie when she saw him at lunchtime; the thought of which reminded her that it was probably time that she was heading back to the castle.

Just then a vibrating sensation somewhere around her lower pelvis announced that either she was having an unexpected orgasm or someone was attempting to make telephonic communication. The latter seemed most likely. Dragging the mobile out, Anna stabbed frantically at the buttons and slammed the instrument against her ear several times before finally the voice came through.

'Hi, babe.'

'*Geri!*' Anna shrieked in delight.

'So, life is bliss, is it? Set a date yet? I'm desperate to get my bridesmaid dress – I've seen just the thing in Gucci. White, tight and with a huge slit up the side.'

'Sounds amazing,' said Anna truthfully. 'We're still sorting the date out, as it happens – *what?* No, nothing's wrong.' Anna crossed her fingers behind her back, keen to get off the tricky subject. 'So how are *you*? Your voice sounds funny. *Deeper*.'

'All that screaming at those *bloody* kids,' said Geri with feeling.

'*What?* But I thought Siena and Savannah were supposed to be angels. Wasn't the holiday good then?'

'Absolute fucking *disaster*. Mostly because their cousin came with them – ghastly brat called Titus. Fought *all the sodding time*.'

'Oh dear.' Yet Anna felt a faint sense of relief that even a take-no-prisoners nanny like Geri was powerless in the face of a truly intractable child.

'And so bloody *noisy* – had a scream that could shatter glass. *Could*, but didn't have to – he managed very well at that with just his hands. Looked like Kristallnacht in the kitchen when he'd been looking for something to put his pomegranate juice in.'

'What a shame. And the place looked so peaceful.' Anna remembered the snaps Geri had shown her of the magnificently well-appointed and stupendously expensive-looking palazzo that Julian Tressell had restored to its former glory after many years serving as a rural bus station.

'Was until Titus got there. Then we became the cabaret for the entire village – walking through these *completely* silent old squares with all the kids screaming and hitting each other with their Barbies.'

'Did Titus have a Barbie as well then?'

''Fraid so. His parents are against sexual stereotyping. Which in my experience has one of two results. Either he becomes a complete wuss who embroiders his own bookmarks, or he turns into Attila the Hun. Titus is the latter. Obsessed with bums, willies and toilets. Loved nothing better than watching himself pee in the bath.'

'Didn't know Attila the Hun did that.'

'Ha bloody *ha*. Well, anyway, I'm thinking of suing retrospectively for mental distress. Had a long discussion about it over lunch with a gobsmackingly rich barrister who has a place out there as well. He agreed it would make an interesting test case, and said he'd be only too happy to take the brief. Except I think he had other briefs in mind.'

'But what's wrong with that?' asked Anna. 'A rich barrister with a place in Tuscany?'

'And a face like a basket of fruit. Rotten fruit, at that,' said Geri with her trademark crushing frankness. 'Even *I've* got standards, sadly. But enough of me. Any gossip?'

'Gossip?' The last gossip on Skul, Anna imagined, was when Flora MacDonald dressed Bonnie Prince Charlie as a woman to help him escape. That rumour was probably still doing the rounds. 'Not as *such*. What's going on down there?'

'Oh, the usual. Otto Greatorex has got a place in the choir of St Paul's and Fenella is beside herself.'

'I bet she is.'

'But not for the reasons you'd think. It's a nightmare, apparently. She's got choir school mother's bottom, sitting on a hard pew for hours every week, and has Otto under her feet all the time because he's not allowed to go out in case he gets a cold and loses his voice. But she says the worst thing is that all that time sitting in cathedrals contemplating the Almighty means she's getting rather worried that He might actually exist.'

'Oh dear. I see.'

'Yes, the parents are rather suffering at the moment,' Geri said breezily. 'The Rice-Browns are mortified because their new nanny drives around in an Audi while they make do with an old Volvo. Polly said to Kate the other day how ghastly it is when your nanny is so much richer than you are. Then Hanuki – you know, that Japanese male nanny you met? Well, he's won the nannying equivalent of the Lottery. The Pottery, I suppose you'd call it. People have tried to poach him so often he's on double pay, works no more than thirty-six hours a week and gets his breakfast in bed. It's rather gone to his head. He refuses to come anywhere near the kitchen until the dishwasher has been unloaded nor anywhere near the children until they've been washed and dressed.'

Dishwashers! Anna determinedly suppressed a pang of envy. Even the thought of Liv seemed suddenly tempting – it was warm, if nothing else. Downstairs, at least. 'I can see now that I never quite got the hang of nannying,' she sighed. 'I practically had to wash and dress Cassandra as well as Zak. Particularly after she'd been at the Bombay Sapphire.' Anna shuddered. Yes. *That* was what it had been like.

'Oh, that reminds me. Cassandra's divorcing Jett.'

'No! Why?'

'Cassandra realised he was shagging her new nanny when she saw someone else had been squeezing the spots on his back.' With a sense of cliffhanger-endings that episodes of *The Archers*, Anna thought, would do well to emulate, the mobile abruptly cut itself off.

As Anna put it away and prepared to return to Dampie, something caught her eye. Something typewritten, white and tucked right into the edge of the board. 'Robbie MacAskill. Poet. Creative Writing Classes Given.' Anna gazed at it in astonishment. A *poet*? The only man of letters she'd imagined ever braving this place was the postman – and Dr Johnson, of course. As the rain began again, she scribbled down the number with one of the family of leaky Biros that seemed to have a member in the pocket of every coat she had ever owned.

Jamie was nowhere to be seen when Anna returned, sodden and demoralised, to the castle. Thanks to her non-existent breakfast, her stomach felt as if it were almost touching her backbone, but she resisted the temptation to seek out the kitchens for fear of encountering Nanny. She made do with some furry, age-softened Polos from the bottom of her bag and spent the afternoon blowing on her purple fingers in the bedroom and trying to write up the morning's events in her diary. The thought of there being a poet in the area intrigued her. She determined to ask Jamie about it at dinner – it was a topic concerning the island, so hopefully she'd get a response. And then perhaps she could tackle the increasingly tricky subject of who was organising the wedding as well. Why couldn't Jamie speak to Nanny about it? After all, he'd known her since birth. Then again, that probably was precisely the reason the task had been delegated to her.

Dinner came and, more thankfully, went with Jamie, as usual, distant and absorbed in paperwork; muttering, this time, about damp proof courses. So when a window of conversational opportunity presented itself during coffee in the upstairs sitting room, Anna seized it.

The sitting room stretched the entire length of the second floor of the castle. Outside the three long deep-silled windows along one wall, the sulky grey of day had sunk into the coma of night. Inside the cavernous chamber, a few inadequate lamps made it gloomier still. There were a few gilt-framed and watery Highland scenes on the walls, a number of small, padded chairs, a couple of battered sofas and a rather experienced-looking china tea set on a side table. The most arresting item in the room was a large portrait opposite her chair. Suddenly it became obvious what her opening gambit should be.

'Is that the Angus tartan?' she asked, wondering if she should be wearing eclipse glasses to view the blazing yellow and orange of the kilt being worn by the large, hostile-looking bearded gentleman with the extremely red face who was the subject of the canvas. Despite the considerable degree of age and fading, the tartan glowed as retina-fryingly brightly as the day it was first painted.

'Absolutely. Yes. That's Mad Angus Angus wearing

it.' Jamie, as predicted, looked up eagerly from his books. As in Burn, thought Anna. She looked at the picture again. 'Why was he mad?' she asked.

Jamie's head shot up again. 'He had what would probably be called an anger management problem today.'

'Oh, I see. Mad as in cross.' That figured. The very portrait looked ready to explode with rage. 'The tartan's very, um, yellow.' There was no polite way of saying it was the most hideous pattern she had ever seen – yellow, orange and brown shot through with bilious green. It was a tartan, in short, that not even Vivienne Westwood could love.

'Oh. Yes.' Jamie was now happily back on track. 'Yellow, yes. There's rather a funny story connected with that. The family motto is Hold Fast. Unfortunately, for many years that did not extend to the colours of the tartan. Ran horribly in the wash.'

Anna decided to change the subject, but did not feel confident enough yet to tackle The Subject.

'Gosh, that's huge,' she remarked presently.

'*Magnificent*, isn't it?' Jamie said proudly.

'I've *never* seen one like *that* before.'

'Glad you appreciate it. Mad Angus Angus's lucky war axes are the pride of the Dampie collection.'

'Unlucky for some, I should imagine,' Anna observed, thinking meanly that they were probably the only thing in the Dampie collection.

'Yes, he killed fifty Englishmen in battle with those,' Jamie said proudly. 'Sharp as a knife, even now. Nanny keeps them in tiptop condition.'

'Does she now?'

There was a silence.

'Very impressive suits of armour you've got over there in the corner,' said Anna.

'Yes. In actual fact they're terribly rusty and not really very valuable at all,' said Jamie. 'Don't know why I bother keeping them. Should throw them away really.'

'Oh, it's probably worth hanging on to them,' said Anna flippantly. 'You never know. You might get called up.' *Oh why had she said that?*

The look Jamie gave her as he opened his ledger again quelled further discussion. Now was obviously not the time to ask about the poet. Or, for that matter, the wedding. After an hour or so's silent contemplation of sheep figures (Jamie) and a mildewed 1962 edition of the *People's Friend* found behind a cushion and fallen on as if it were the latest *Vogue* (Anna), they went to bed.

As she undressed, Anna saw with horror that her neck, arms, shoulders and cheeks were covered in violently red, itching spots. They looked disgusting, red at the bottom and yellow and hard on top, mini volcanoes against the whiteness of her skin. 'My God, what are they?' she shrieked, showing an ankle bearing at least five of them to Jamie who, already in bed, was sitting up with plans of the castle spread all around him.

He looked up. 'Midgies.' He looked down again.

'What, those tiny black flies? I can't believe it.'

But she had lost his attention already. Still, Anna thought as her fingers ran over the hard, painful lumps, at least the midgies fancy me. There was a gap in the bed large enough to drive an articulated lorry down between Jamie and herself. It was almost as if he were trying to avoid a situation where he had to have sex with her.

But *why*? Anna fretted. Her appearance had not changed for the worse since arriving at Dampie almost two weeks ago; on the contrary, the atrocious food and long walks through the mist had resulted in her losing yet more weight. She could feel her rib cage all day long now, not just first thing in the morning when she was flat on her back. So what was the problem? Anna had read enough 'When Sex Dies' magazine stories to realise keeping the sensual spark alive in a relationship was a challenge to most couples. But even in the direst of these tales the spark hadn't disappeared immediately, as it appeared to have done with them. Why was Jamie so much more interested in making walls than love? All she had managed to glean from him today was that he'd spent the afternoon repairing rotten fencing. Did that account for the barrier now between them?

'Look, you can tell me if there's a problem,' she ventured gently as they lay side by side in the darkness. Like two marble sarcophagi, she thought, only without the passion and commitment that implied.

'Oh, there's a problem all right,' Jamie said. 'Several, in fact.'

'Is there?' Anna hadn't expected such frankness. Suddenly fearful, she wondered if she was ready to be told.

'Yes. Well, for a start, the guttering's rotten and the roof on the old guardroom is—'

'Not *that*. Not the bloody *building*. Us.'

'Us?' Jamie sounded surprised. 'What's the matter with us? Aren't you happy? We're getting married, aren't we?'

Anna felt an odd mixture of relief and fear. 'Call me paranoid,' she said, 'but I can't help noticing that you don't seem to like having sex with me.'

Jamie was silent for a few moments. Then he said, 'No. I don't.'

'He said *what*?' Geri demanded.

'He said *no*, he didn't,' Anna shouted into the mobile first thing next morning, crouching unsteadily behind a rock as the wind hurled a spiteful spatter of rain in her direction. 'He said that I wasn't to worry though, it was nothing personal.'

In normal circumstances, Anna thought longingly,

she and Geri would have been having this conversation in hushed whispers in the darkened corner of a wine bar, fuelled by large glasses of chilled Chardonnay. Normal circumstances, however, were now a thing of the past. As was normal anything.

'*Sounds pretty personal to me*,' shouted Geri. 'Sounds about as personal as it gets.'

'He said he'd gone off sex at school. Apparently he was bullied very badly, frequently beaten and buggered on a regular basis.'

'But I thought that was the whole *point* of public school,' Geri yelled. 'That's what every boy in St Midas's has to look forward to. And the girls when they get married.'

'I know. But it seems to have turned Jamie off sex for good. He says he's still getting over the horror of having to do it when we first got to the castle.'

'He really knows how to make a girl feel good, doesn't he?' shouted Geri. 'Sure he's not gay?'

'Well, I did wonder, of course.' Anna pictured Geri in the people-carrier with the entire Tressell school run's ears out on stalks. 'But I couldn't see why he would have bothered asking me to marry him if he was. I mean, why drag me all the way up here?'

There was silence for a few minutes. 'Hello? Hello?' yelled Anna in a panic. Please don't cut me off again, she prayed.

'*Just thinking*,' Geri bawled. 'Basically, you need to

awaken his interest in sex again. Take the initiative. Come up with a love strategy.'

'A *what*?' The wind whipped by Anna's ear, as if trying to eavesdrop on the conversation.

'*A love strategy*,' Geri screeched. 'Seduce him. Wear suspenders. Buy some red underwear and bonk his brains out. That *always* works.'

At this point, the phone cut out and Anna sat back on her heels on the sodden grass wondering dully where one got suspenders on Skul. No doubt Nanny had on more rigging than your average tea clipper, but it seemed unlikely Jamie would find it a turn-on. As for red underwear, the only possibility of that, she imagined, would be if something ran in the wash.

Chapter 17

Cassandra slammed the front door in fury. The girl had to be *joking*. A new Mégane coupé in a colour of her choice – *to keep*! Paid-for membership of the Harbour Club *and* the Met Bar! Tickets for all the best shows in town! On top of this, a salary approximately *ten times* what she had ever paid a nanny before. Cassandra seethed as, from a corner of the window, she watched Ivanka or whatever her bloody name had been sashaying nonchalantly down the street, apparently confident that if Cassandra would not meet her requirements, some other family would be only too pleased to. Judging by the reaction she got from a passing Matthew Rice-Brown, whose keen appreciation of her breasts resulted in an almost fatal wobble of his bicycle, her confidence was not misplaced. Those tits *had* to be fake, thought Cassandra. So pneumatic-looking – you probably had to stick a pressure gauge on the nipple every four weeks to check the air.

Cassandra grimaced as a bilious intestinal twinge almost bent her double. But was it any wonder she had stomach problems? She'd been stuffing herself lately – she'd eaten a whole lettuce sandwich and a ricecake yesterday before reading the fortuitous *Daily Mail* article about how skinny women in New York kept their weight down by eating naked in front of mirrors. Seizing another ricecake, Cassandra had straightaway gone into the bathroom, stripped off and sat with her legs apart. It certainly removed the urge to eat. The problem was, contemplating her dry patches, thread veins, incipient turkey gobble and wrinkled labia in the mirror almost removed the urge to live as well.

Unfortunately, it didn't bring back the urge to write. Since being dumped by its publishers, *A Passionate Lover* was currently as high and dry as a hallucinating bone. Of late, the only occasions Cassandra had ventured into her study were to rifle her gin fund to satisfy Zak's incessant demands for money. On these visits, she had tried not to notice the dust thickening on the laptop lid. Her writer's block had become an entire thousand-foot-thick barrier; the Great Wall of Writing China. Her agent was getting frantic.

'Try anything,' he urged, whilst privately wondering

if he should dump Cassandra. Half literary London was calling her the day before yesterday's woman; having her on his books was getting embarrassing. Not that it hadn't always been, but at least she used to make money. Perhaps, he suggested, colonic irrigation might help unplug the flow.

Cassandra liked the idea of recharging her creative batteries with alternative therapy. Especially if it meant charging Jett's platinum card.

'I want to feel *inspired* again,' Cassandra told a New Age therapist in Hampstead, who advised 'the all-over spiritual spring clean approach. You wash yourself from the *inside*,' he explained. Ugh, like those bristly things you put inside bottles, Cassandra shuddered. The white witch in Camden she consulted next advised flushing out the system by sticking her bottom in cold water and her feet in hot. Or was it the other way round? But sitting with her buttocks in a warm sink with her feet dangling in the loo didn't feel very inspiring.

By the time the crystal therapist in Crouch End advised she stick crystals up her bottom, Cassandra was beginning to doubt alternative therapy could do the trick. On the other hand, the engagement ring Jett had given her could scarcely meet a more suitable fate. She'd try anything once.

Once. Having placed the sapphire in her sphincter, Cassandra quickly became aware that her writer's block had suddenly changed from being a metaphoric to a literal condition. She would have sued the therapist had she not been fearful of all the publicity that would, given her celebrity status, no doubt follow. As it was, she was not entirely convinced that her regular Harley Street doctor had believed her protestations that she had fallen over in her bedroom and landed on her jewellery box. Had she not known better she would have sworn that, as she was leaving, the bellow of loud laughter following her down the corridor had definitely come from Dr Monson's surgery. From now on, she vowed, the only crystal I'm prepared to take internally is the sort with Louis Roederer on the label.

The end finally came when the Tufnell Park thalasso-therapist told her not to 'sweat the small stuff'. Cassandra had indignantly pointed out that she didn't sweat *any* stuff, thank you, she'd had the botox injections to close up any glands of *that* nature, and swept out. She decided to return to the Bombay Sapphire.

Bloody nannies, she thought, sloshing another measure furiously into her glass. Her thoughts returned to the Mégane-coupé-demanding one she'd just seen. Bloody *cheek*. And there'd been plenty of *that* on show as well – Ivanka, had been wearing a miniskirt practically up to her *pubes*.

Cassandra sighed. As if the Nanny Question wasn't enough, there was the continued and worsening matter of finding a school that would take Zak. It was hardly surprising she hadn't written a sentence for weeks. Every ounce of her literary ability was currently employed in restricting to a few scant paragraphs the wonders of her son in letters to boarding school headmasters.

The clang of the letterbox alerted her to the arrival of the post. Cassandra ground her teeth as she opened the usual fistful of rejection letters from schools. Until a thought occurred to her. Why not educate Zak at home? Much cheaper, for a start. And talking of starts, there was no time like the present. She tripped up the stairs to his room.

'Oh, *Mum*.'

'*Mama*. Come on, darling.'

'Only if you buy me a mini CD player.'

'Yes, all right then, darling. Come on. Let's count up to ten in French.'

Around two hours was the approximate time it took Cassandra – and Zak – to realise that she had forgotten every French phrase she had ever learnt, with the notable exception of *haute couture*. Switching subjects to maths, she realised she had never, in the first place, grasped the principles of long division. Similarly, the only geographical fact she was in possession of was that a by-product of the Australian sheep industry was lanolin for lipstick and the sort of moisturisers that gave you a hairy face. Even Cassandra realised that this probably wasn't going to get Zak very far.

Finding a boarding school was, therefore, of the

utmost urgency. For Zak was beginning to get out of hand in other ways as well. Only last week he had threatened to sue her retrospectively over his unsatisfactory Christmas presents and there had been ugly scenes just yesterday when the tooth fairy had left only ten pounds and not the twenty pounds Zak had apparently been expecting. Adore him as she did, it was beginning to dawn on Cassandra that the costs of keeping him at home were astronomical, psychologically as well as financially.

Anna's love strategy had not got off to the most brilliant of starts. Taking the initiative, as Geri had suggested, she had arrayed herself in her best underwear, used the last of her Chanel No. 5, fanned her hair out across the pillow in approved bra-model-ad fashion, put a candle by the bedside – and waited. And waited. And waited. And, eventually, fell asleep.

She woke to find the candle out and Jamie snoring gently beside her. *Damn*. She'd missed the opportunity. Take the initiative, she urged herself.

Taking a deep breath, Anna stole a hand across the customary foot of uninhabited sheet that separated her from her husband-to-be. As usual, Jamie was wearing thick flannel pyjamas, but she deftly circumnavigated the folds and ties to slip her hand through the gap in his bottoms. Running her hand swiftly over the bristle of his pubic hair she at last gained what she was seeking:

his warm, soft, sleeping penis. To her astonishment, it was rigid. More than that, it was as thick and as hard as an oak.

A thrill ran through Anna as she lay on her back in the darkness. Had her underwear had the desired effect after all? Smiling, she circled the warm, wet and rubbery tip of his penis with her finger. She stroked his hot, swollen bristly balls and was gratified to hear the steady breathing interrupted by a faint but distinct groan of pleasure. As she increased the pressure of her fingers, the groans increased. Without giving herself time to worry about the consequences, Anna slid down under the covers and pushed her face straight into his salt-scented pubic hair.

His penis was almost too big for her mouth; it seemed the approximate size and solidity of a cricket bat handle as she began inexpertly to circumnavigate it with her lips and tongue. Still, as she was buried beneath the covers, Jamie would be unable to hear any slurping sounds and anyway, from the still louder moans of pleasure she could hear from above the blankets, she was having roughly the effect she was intending. As matters quite literally seemed about to come to a head, Anna pulled herself up, over and on to her fiancé's body. Wet with excitement herself, she slid him inside her just as he came.

'*Aaaargggh*. Uuugghh. Headmaster! Headmaster! *What's going on?*' Jamie, wide awake now, was thrashing around wildly in terror. For a few seconds, Anna held on as if to a bucking bronco, hoping for an orgasm, but she realised she might as well hope for a miracle as the engorged muscle inside her shrank to proportions she was more familiar with.

'*What's happening?*' The night being blacker than the inside of a Highland cow, it was impossible for Anna to see Jamie's expression but his voice still held traces of genuine fear.

'Oh, nothing,' said Anna bitterly. She swallowed hard to keep down the choking in her throat. The love strategy had been a dismal failure. Everything about coming to Dampie had been a dismal failure. *She* was a dismal failure.

As soon as, after breakfast, Jamie had headed off muttering something about drains, Anna had gone outside with the mobile and called Geri.

'He was definitely thinking about someone. Another woman.'

'Doubt it,' said Geri. 'He was probably fantasising about a lovely stretch of releaded roof.'

'Can't you come up? *Please?*' Only Geri, Anna was certain, was capable of sorting out the mess she had got herself in.

'Mmm. As it happens, this is a good time. Savannah and Siena are off to Opera Camp for a week and I could do with a change of scene. What are the men like up there? I rather fancy getting my hands on something big, hairy and Highland.'

'Well, there's plenty of that about,' Anna said. No need to tell Geri she meant cattle.

'*Fantastic*. I'm *desperate*. I've even started doing yoga classes,' Geri continued, 'hoping I'd get the chance to do the lotus position with some supple young sex god. But everyone in my class is either pregnant, gay or has nasty toenails.' Geri sighed. 'So here I am with this lovely flexible pelvis and no one to flex it on.'

'Poor you.' Anna tried to sound as if she wasn't smiling. Funny how Geri could cheer her up even in the most wretched of circumstances. 'But at least you must be full of inner calm.'

'Funnily enough, I've never felt so ratty as I have since starting yoga classes. But that's probably a lot to do with the nasty toenails. We're always being told we need to keep our anuses soft as well, which as you can imagine makes for some rather ripe results. Which tend to interfere with one's contemplation of the immortal.'

'But at least it explains levitation,' Anna said. 'There's plenty of fresh air up here, anyway.'

'Right. That's settled then. I'll come up on the plane. After all this jetting around with the family I've got enough air miles to practically get to Pluto.'

'Oh Geri,' Anna breathed in relief. 'That would be fantastic. I'll go straightaway and get Nanny to sort out a room for you. The best one the castle has, promise.'

'Well, that's not saying a lot.'

Re-entering the castle, Anna firmly squashed the qualms of marrow-freezing fear that the thought of an encounter with Nanny provoked. She marched with as authoritative a step as she could muster down the stairs, back down the corridor and into the stone-flagged kitchen beyond. Nanny was nowhere to be seen.

From an open door leading to an outhouse, the murmur of voices could be heard. Loud and vaguely obscene noises seemed to be punctuating the conversation. As she crept nearer it sounded, to Anna's quailing ears, horribly like naked flesh being slapped.

'Do ye think she's worked it out yet?' The man's voice, Anna realised, was MacLoggie's. Slap. Squelch.

'Nae idea,' Nanny said in her slow, deliberate monotone. 'She's nae too bright, ye know.' Slap.

Anna stood frozen to the spot. She would have been in any case, given the plunging temperatures of the kitchen passage, but the realisation that they were talking about her sent an additional chill down the cord of her spine.

MacLoggie snorted. 'Surely even someone *that* stupid must hae realised by now,' he drawled in a contemptuous tone accentuated by his Scots accent. 'After all, why else would someone as bonny as him want to marry someone like *her*?'

Nanny snorted. Anna flamed with indignation. *That*

was rich, coming from MacLoggie, who even in a good light looked as if he'd been pile-driven into a brick wall. As for Nanny, the only good light was no light at all. She looked as if her idea of sartorial effort was to shave the hairs off her moles.

'All because the old laird put that clause in saying the young maister had to have a *wife* before he could properly inherit,' MacLoggie observed laconically. *Slap slap slap*.

Anna breathed in deeply and slowly. Her knees had gone weak, and something seemed to have stopped her from moving. Something else, however, was slipping slowly into place. Was this the reason Jamie wanted to marry her?

'Well, ye canna blame the old laird for wanting to make sure there'd be an heir,' Nanny pronounced. A strange flubbery noise like the breaking of wind accompanied her remark.

'Well, and *will* there be, do ye reckon?'

'Well, not if ye're judging by the bed,' Nanny cackled. Anna's stomach hit the flagstones. 'I've looked every morn and there's ne'er anything on the sheets.' *Squelch*.

Anna ground her teeth; her fury now overtaking her surprise. The thought of Nanny on the loose in their bedroom – as, to judge by the rigidly tucked-under sheets, she was on a daily basis – had never been a comfortable one. But never in her worst, most paranoid moments had Anna imagined Nanny checking the bed for stains of activity.

'Aye, bu' that might not be the lassie's fault,' cackled MacLoggie. 'There've always been a few question marks over the maister in that department. That's wha' comes o' sendin' him to public school in England.'

Anna decided she had heard enough. She gave a loud cough and stepped forward. As she entered the outbuilding, the far door was still swinging in the wake of MacLoggie's sudden departure. Yet the slapping noise continued and was explained by the fact that Nanny was noisily rinsing something wobbly and bloody in a shallow stone sink. She turned her heavy face to Anna. 'Can I help you?'

Anna boiled at Nanny's level tones, salted with just a hint of insolence. To think that Jamie had wanted her to discuss a wedding with this termagant. Well, the old battleaxe had asked for it. She'd make her squirm. Anna took a deep breath. 'I couldn't help overhearing . . .' Yet, somewhere along the lines the words came out differently. 'I'd like you to get the best room in the castle ready please, Nanny.'

The slapping continued. Looking around her, Anna saw that a deer carcass hung from one of the hooks in the stark white walls. Near the sink, a vast wooden block on which lay a hatchet, several knives and a considerable quantity of blood confirmed that Nanny had recently been indulging in a little light butchery.

'Did you hear me, Nanny?' Anna was aware that her voice had gone up an octave or two.

'Aye.'

Suddenly, Anna realised that the bunch of unidentified organs hanging from a hook on the wall were the bowels of some unfortunate deer. She knew this because she could see a passage protruding from the organ mass in which small, round black pellets of deer poo were held in their own separate sacs, like the French sweets sold in long ropes of individual plastic packets. Looking at the unexpunged faeces, Anna had an overwhelming sense of life and all its natural rhythms suspended.

'I'd be grateful if you could do it immediately,' Anna said tightly. 'I have a friend coming to stay.'

Chapter 18

Geri's eyes flicked open. Something strange was going on. It wasn't *just* that she was slammed into the nasty-smelling grey carpet wall of her bunk every time the train rounded a bend, or grappled with the wrong sort of rail. It wasn't even that the lid of the cabin's tiny sink, theoretically held up by a catch on the wall, kept being loosened from its moorings by the locomotive's wilder lurches and slamming down with the force and violence of a maniac's fist. Nor was it that the cabin was so airless she could barely breathe, and small enough to satisfy the most rampant agoraphobic. She could barely turn round standing up; lying down, on the other hand, had involved a different set of challenges altogether. When first entering the sleeper, Geri had laughed aloud at the size of it. Now, in the shaking, rattling watches of the night, it didn't seem nearly so amusing. Anna, she thought. The things I do for you. The opportunities I set you up with, and the minute I take my eye off the ball . . . Fancy not even having managed a *wedding date* yet. Still, hopefully it wouldn't take long to get everything back on track. After all, she hadn't bought that Gucci dress for nothing.

Irritating though her inability to get on a flight to Scotland had been – when *was* she going to use all those air miles? – the news that the quickest way up had been by sleeper had not worried Geri unduly. There was, after all, something very romantic about spending the night on a train. Geri's fond visions of walnut panelling, lamplit buffet cars and steam trains puffing gracefully across northern uplands in the sunset had, however, reached the end of the line rather sooner than she had anticipated. At Euston, in fact. Before the train had even set off.

For Geri, any romance the journey might have held was quickly obliterated by the sound of the couple next door going at it hammer and tongs before the rear engine even pulled away from the buffers. 'Didn't even *bother* putting my knickers on this morning,' gasped a woman's voice. 'Didn't see the point – you *always* want it the *minute* we get on.' Brief encounter, thought Geri, it wasn't. Literally.

The rest of Geri's Orient Express-inspired expectations met with much the same disappointments. There was no walnut panelling; the only thing in sight even coming close to resembling a walnut was the short and intensely wrinkled old steward who asked her if she wanted tea or coffee in the morning (and quickly gave up on his attempts to elicit the same information from her neighbours). The lamplit buffet car had turned out to be an ordinary carriage filled with the sort of drunken, disappointed, rootless and downright strange human flotsam and jetsam one might expect to find in a sleeper bar on a weekday evening.

Having secured herself a paper bag containing two miniature bottles of gin and two tins of tonic, Geri headed back to her telephone-box-sized compartment and locked the door, intending not to emerge until the train reached Inverness. She did not even intend to make the long, cold trek in her nightclothes to the loo, having decided on an impromptu but, she suspected, by no means infrequently employed system involving an empty plastic cup and the sink.

One blessing at least was that the couple next door had temporarily ceased their activities, having reached something of a crescendo at Stevenage. Geri downed her second gin and tonic and, having prised apart sheets so firmly tucked together they made opening an oyster with bare hands look easy, determinedly attempted to sleep.

Something in the compartment on the *other* side,

however, seemed just as determined to stop her. Something that shouted, screeched and banged itself periodically against the very wall – against the very section of the very wall, in fact – that Geri's face lay closest to in quest of slumber. As the noises increased in volume and the thuds in violence, she half expected the interconnecting door between the compartments to open and a madman with a carving knife to loom above her. The madman, however, did not seem to be the only person in the cabin. Someone else was shrieking as well. *Two nutters.* Finally, Geri stuffed tissue paper from the complementary toilet bag in her ears and pulled the blanket over her head. Celia Johnson, she reflected, had never had these problems.

But now something had woken her. Not a noise, but a smell. Geri sniffed hard. Something was burning. She gasped and sat up, visions of a rolling fireball filling the corridor outside springing terrifyingly and irrepressibly to mind. There was another scent besides, something heavy, slightly acrid. Geri had never smelt burning flesh before, but . . .

Flinging the compartment door open, Geri stuck her head out into the corridor. No fireball in sight, no nothing, in fact. But the smell here was definitely stronger and coming from the compartment next door, the one with the nutters in it. Geri hesitated for a nanosecond before rapping hard on the door. As shouts within greeted her knock and the door eventually opened to allow the throat-punching fumes within to escape, Geri saw she had not been wrong about the inmates. The person standing before her was, without a doubt, the most insane she'd ever seen.

'*Cassandra!* What the hell are you doing here? And *what on earth* is that stink?'

Cassandra gasped. Her eyes boggled and her mouth fell open. *Was there no escape?* Here she was, trying to leave everything behind her. Trying to forget the theatres of humiliation and degradation otherwise known as Kensington, Jett, St Midas's, Mrs Gosschalk and most of all the Tressells' *wretched party* which had started it all. And who should be in the carriage next to her but the Tressells' ghastly nanny whom she had last encountered whilst in a very compromising position on the Tressells' bathroom floor.

'Got a body in there or something?'

'As it happens, I've got Zak in here.' Cassandra spoke with as much hauteur as she could muster. Was the creature *spying* on her? Would the shameful truth – that she had been reduced to travelling in a second-class sleeper, and a pre-booked, reduced-price Apex one at that – filter back to W8? But now that the divorce was underway and the mortgage payments had fallen behind, did it much matter if it did? The Mrs Curtain-twitchers down the road had had a field day as it was; Cassandra knew she would never be able to hold her head up in Kensington again. Or her hand up either;

taxis were, temporarily at least, a thing of the past. She and Zak had suffered the ultimate indignity of coming to Euston on the Tube, a shattering experience for both of them. Having to actually *hold* those *disgusting* yellow poles that a million filthy commuter hands had gripped before her had turned Cassandra's stomach like a skipping rope.

'So what's the smell?' asked Geri. 'I thought the carriage was on fire.'

'South American Sage Stressbuster, since you ask,' said Cassandra, as haughtily as she could. For she had salvaged one item from the wreck of the luxury liner of her life. The last of her scented candles. Not only did the smell remind her of happier – well, *wealthier* – times, it also reminded her of the joyous fact that Fenella Greatorex had recently burned her entire house down by leaving a scented candle alight while out at a parents' meeting.

'Oh, I see. Well, I am surprised to find you here, Cassandra,' Geri said. 'Didn't have you down as a user of public transport. Unless it's the sort that flies.'

Cassandra swallowed. 'Yes, well, it's really for Zak's benefit, of course.' Over Cassandra's bony shoulder Geri could see him lurking on the top bunk, computer game in hand, watching her malevolently.

'How do you mean?'

'Well, as he'll be going to a Scottish boarding school and they're supposed to be *terribly* basic, I thought it best he got used to travelling rough straightaway. As a matter of fact,' Cassandra tittered hysterically, 'I took him to Euston on the *Underground!*'

'Heavens above,' drawled Geri. 'You'll be throwing caution to the winds and going on a bus next. So which school is Zak going to? Excuse me for saying this, but I thought he hadn't got a place *anywhere*.'

'Of course he had,' Cassandra snapped. 'There were plenty of offers.'

'Well, I'm glad to hear it,' said Geri, unable to resist turning the knife. 'I've obviously been getting the wrong information. Last I heard, you were looking into Christ's Hospital.'

Cassandra's lip curled in a snarl. 'Yes, well, I wouldn't have sent Zak there anyway.'

'Why not?' asked Geri. 'The academic standards are supposed to be excellent, aren't they?'

'Well, it can't have been a very good *hospital*,' Cassandra barked. 'Didn't do Christ much good, did it?'

She shifted forward into the doorway so less of the cabin behind could be seen. The last thing she wanted was for this wretched creature to see the handful of headmasters' letters scattered over the bed behind her, grudgingly agreeing to see Cassandra and her son for five minutes despite there emphatically being no possibility of a place. 'And what are you doing here?' she asked Geri. Time they got off this subject.

'Well, I'm going to see your old nanny as it happens,' Geri said, recognising another opportunity to rub Cassandra's nose in it. 'Anna. At her *castle*.'

'Oh. Yes. You must give me the address.' A light went on in Cassandra's eyes. Or was it, Geri thought, merely the fact that they were drawing into a station? They were stopping, at any rate. Rather abruptly, as well. As the train shuddered with screeching suddenness to a halt, she turned behind her to the window and looked out.

'How bizarre,' Geri said. 'We seem to be stopping in the middle of nowhere.' She grinned at Cassandra, unable to resist the urge to tease her. 'Zak's not pulled the communication cord, has he?'

Cassandra glared. 'Of *course* he hasn't. Zak would *never* do such a thing.' She darted a nervous glance over her shoulder, threw a startled look back at Geri and disappeared inside the cabin.

Geri slipped back into her own compartment just as the train guard strode as furiously up the narrow passageway as his well-built frame would permit.

'How *dare* you say that about my son?' she heard Cassandra yelling as she fitted the tissue paper back in her ears. 'He's just *curious*. A sign of very high intelligence. He pulled it because he thought it was something to do with the air conditioning.'

'But what *did* MacLoggie mean about your father's

will?' Anna was trying to get Jamie to meet her eyes, but so far hadn't even managed to set up an appointment. This made her angrier than ever.

'Here, have some of Nanny's shortbread,' Jamie said quickly, proffering a plate of thick-cut brown blocks. 'She's spent all morning making it.'

Staggered by the inadequacy of the diversionary tactic, Anna took the plate anyway. As her wrist plunged floorwards, she bit back the urge to inquire whether a concrete mixer had been employed in the construction of the shortbread and if so, why didn't Jamie prop up the crumbling curtain wall with it? She looked for the smallest piece possible. None seemed less than a foot across.

'Nice, isn't it?' said Jamie, chewing away so violently his eyes watered with the strain.

Thanks to Nanny's lurking in the shadows all through dinner, it had been impossible for Anna to bring up the subject of what she had overheard in the kitchen. Her chance had, as usual, only arisen during after-dinner coffee – and shortbread – in the castle's upstairs sitting room.

'Let me put it another way,' Anna said when Jamie's jaws had finally stopped moving. '*Why did you ask me to marry you?* You don't *love* me, do you?'

Jamie did not respond immediately. 'We-e-ll . . .' he hedged.

'Well *what*?' A frigid calm, far more disturbing than

anger, spread through Anna. She was, she knew, emotionally anaesthetising herself against what was to come.

'Well, of course I *like* you,' Jamie murmured, crossing one yellow-corduroyed leg slowly over the other. 'But I'm not really sure what *love*, such as it is, really *is*.'

'Oh *really*,' Anna snapped. 'You sound like Prince bloody Charles. You know what I mean.'

There was a pause.

'Well, love's never really, um, been an issue in our family as far as, er, marriages are concerned,' Jamie said, still avoiding her gaze. 'There's an estate to consider. Anguses usually marry for a reason.'

'Yes, so I heard. Your father put it in his will that you had to have a wife in order to make the inheritance final.'

'Yes, um, well, there *is* that,' Jamie said.

'But why? That's not normal, is it?' Anna felt furious, yet oddly detached. Like a cross-examining barrister. A very cross examining barrister.

'No,' Jamie admitted, turning his wide dark eyes on her almost pleadingly. 'But my father realised that, after being beaten and buggered by the other boys at school, I wasn't either. At the start of one term, I begged him not to send me back and told him what was happening. He was worried about the effect it would have on me and my future relationships with women.'

'But that sounds very enlightened,' Anna remarked.

'Not really. He told me it hadn't done him any harm, thrashed me senseless and went straight round to his lawyer and stuck in that clause.'

'Oh. Oh dear.' For a few moments, sympathy for the crushed little boy Jamie must have been welled up in Anna. Then she remembered what they were supposed to be talking about. 'That explains why you want to get *married*, but not why you want to get married to *me*. I'm not remotely grand.'

'Which is why we were the perfect match.'

'Sorry? Am I missing something?'

'Simple.' Jamie darted a look at her. 'You had no money and nowhere to live and were desperate to get away from that boss of yours. I needed someone to come here and marry me in order to properly inherit the estate. What better arrangement could there possibly have been?'

Anna stared at him for a few seconds. 'None, I suppose,' she said, slowly. 'Except for the fact I was the only person – on this entire island, by the sound of it – who didn't realise it *was* an arrangement.'

Jamie cleared his throat. He sounded almost bored now, so distant had his tone become. 'Well, that didn't seem necessary,' he drawled, 'because you seemed to find me rather, um, attractive when we met.'

Anna blushed furiously. 'But I *still* don't understand why you picked me,' she hit back. 'Surely half the smartest girls in Scotland would have been *desperate* to marry you.'

Jamie closed his eyes – a brief but eloquent gesture implying that this was an extremely unpleasant business he heartily wished was over. 'It's true that in the past there *have* been some women – some rich, some beautiful, some even both – who thought they wanted to marry me,' he muttered. 'But they all changed their minds.'

How rich? *How* beautiful? More to the point, *how dare he*? Anna gazed at him indignantly. 'Why?'

'I'm not sure,' Jamie said, not entirely convincingly. 'I think when they came here they realised that perhaps living in an isolated castle in the middle of nowhere wasn't their idea of heaven.'

You mean they didn't realise they would have to play second fiddle to a pile of old stones, Anna thought. She glanced at the engagement ring. *Belonged to his mother*, indeed. His mother and God knew how many other women since. Like an upmarket Pass the Parcel.

'I see what you're getting at,' she said with just a trace of sarcasm. 'It's not so much a matter of not being able to get the staff these days as not being able to get the ladies of the manor.' So this is what he had meant in the tandoori about not having the right personnel in place.

Jamie wrinkled his brow slightly. 'Something like that. But another advantage you had was that you had at least been up here and knew what it was like.'

What I *thought* it was like, thought Anna. Dampie dressed up with flowers and laughter for a wedding and Dampie in its everyday habit had turned out to be very different places. God, she'd been a fool.

'So to a certain extent you knew what you were taking on,' Jamie continued.

'So it's all my fault, is it?' Anna felt the anger rise again.

'To a certain extent, well, um, *yes*.'

Anna stared at him hard. There was something, she felt, that Jamie wasn't telling her. Something wasn't quite adding up. Plenty of women, after all, willingly married into remote estates. There must be some other reason why only someone poor and desperate would want to marry him.

'This is just a thought,' she said slowly. 'Just an idea. But did they, did *any* of these beautiful, rich women happen to meet Nanny?'

Jamie looked away quickly.

'*Thought* as much,' said Anna, as triumphantly as she could, given the circumstances.

Chapter 19

Officially, it was morning, yet as the light stayed that way all day, it could be any time at all. Jamie once had tried to persuade her that the failing light was a consequence of their position in the far north, a sort of Grey Days of Skul answer to the White Nights of Scandinavia. Anna's private theory, however, was that there was only so much light to go around and what there was simply didn't stretch as far as Dampie.

As she walked away from the castle, Anna clenched her fists and stared desperately into the grey half-darkness. Dawn rambles were getting to be a habit with her, as was not sleeping. She had stayed awake almost the entire night after Jamie's bombshell, first pouring out her battered heart to her diary and then lying sleepless in the darkness. She was alone – Jamie had gone off to a bedroom somewhere else. As soon as ashen-fingered dawn appeared between the crack in her curtains, Anna had got up. A walk might clear her head, as well as give her some idea of what the hell to do next. Jamie had asked her not to make any sudden decisions, but to think about things. He'd refused even to take back the ring which she had yanked painfully from her finger and hurled across the mouldering carpet at him. Eventually she had been persuaded to pick it up again; this time, however, it was going in her pocket.

But . . . *think about things*? What was there to think? She must, of course, leave the castle. But go where? In the not-so-broad light of day, the idea of returning to London struck her as lamer than a sheep with foot rot. She was, Anna dolefully told herself, unemployed, unskilled, impecunious and effectively homeless. She was back to square one, square minus one now she'd failed at being engaged as well as everything else. As the mist rolled over her like steam from a kettle, gathering her into its ethereal embrace, Anna let out an agonised howl.

It was a howl of hurt, of betrayal. Of fury with herself for having been so easily taken in. Having failed even at *writing* romantic novels, how had she ever thought it possible to *live* them? She felt exploited, more used than an old five-pound note. And lurking darkly behind all the sound and fury of her disappointment was the maddening knowledge that Jamie had had a point. It *had* suited her to agree to marry him at the time. No one had forced her. She had only herself to blame.

Anna stumbled blindly onward, heading she knew not where and caring less. She felt as if the earth had given way beneath her – which, given the muddy ground and the careless way she was negotiating it, was more or less the case. The violent jolts of her ankles as they twisted and slid onward over the uneven humps of marshy grass were intensely painful; throwing back her head, Anna howled again, investing in the sound all the indignation, betrayal, remorse and shame one might have expected to find given the circumstances. It was a howl that reverberated with perfectly understandable panic and pain. Only one thing about Anna's howl was a surprise. It was answered.

At first, she thought the sound was an echo bouncing off the rocks and drifting back across the water, except that the water she saw before her, she suddenly realised, was the sea. She must have stumbled for miles and did not now recognise the shore she found herself standing on, heels sinking into an expanse of sand as white as bone. She listened in awe as the full aural expression of her agony was borne thunderously back to her on the waves. It was impressive. Terrifying, even, a wild, abandoned shriek, the cry of a banshee, the scream of a soul in purgatory. As she listened, it came again. Exactly the same but with the crucial difference that this time she had not yelled first. Someone else was howling by the shore.

Anna's first instinct was to duck out of sight behind one of the rocks and wait for her fellow hollerer to reveal himself. Yet, as the minutes went by and no one appeared, Anna started to wonder whether what she had heard was, in retrospect, merely MacLoggie at the pipes again. Failing that, a howling dog.

'And you are?'

Anna's throat contracted with terror before she could fully release another scream. A strangled yelp emerged, like an indignant puppy. Having focused all her attention on the shore in front of her, she hadn't heard anyone coming up from behind.

'Come on, you can do better than that,' said the voice. 'I heard you. Very impressive. You were doing a much better job than I was.'

Anna felt her back crunch as she whipped round to find herself staring at a tall, broad-shouldered and very untidy-looking man of about thirty. She was suddenly intensely aware of being a woman alone in the last landscape on earth; easy prey for any psychopath who happened to be passing. Perhaps she was jumping to conclusions, but this strange man, given that he was the person she had heard emitting terrifying howls a mere few minutes before, hardly struck her as particularly normal.

'Oh. You heard me then?' Anna spoke steadily and quietly. *Better not do anything to agitate him.* But it was just her luck. Even on the remotest beach on the remotest island she'd not only ended up engaged to Mr Wrong but meeting Mr Possibly Extremely Dangerous into the bargain. Five minutes ago, she had wanted to die, but was now acutely conscious that she hadn't meant it *really*.

'Yes,' he replied. 'You see, I've been out yowling all morning as well.'

It was fatal, she knew, to make eye contact with lunatics, but there being just the two of them, it was difficult not to. Anna drew a measure of relief from the fact that his pupils seemed warm rather than blazing insanely and that the grin looked more full of friendly inquiry than murderous intent. Yet complete peace of mind was prevented by the fact that, standing like a hedge between herself and reassurance was – a beard.

Anna had read enough of Cassandra's glossy magazines to know that beards, hitherto firmly beyond the style pale, had recently experienced a renaissance. She was aware that, when cut and shaped, they could even be fashionable. But there was nothing trimmed about this one. It was an out-of-control leylandii; large, abundant and the sort of thing neighbours complain about. It was firmly of the variety favoured by geography teachers, vicars and lunatics. Free range, to say the least. And very possibly organic.

'Why were *you* yowling?' she asked him.

The bearded youth smiled again. Looking at his extraordinarily strong-looking white teeth, Anna tried to banish all thoughts about *The Silence of the Lambs*. She also noticed that, apart from the bad hair day at the end of his chin, he had some distinctly deranged-looking clothes on. Torn and faded jeans that seemed to have been attacked by a wild animal and a cotton jumper that had more holes than a string vest peeped from under the wrinkled flaps of an ancient Barbour. 'Yowling helps me in my work,' he said. 'When I'm really letting it all out, I feel as if I'm communicating with a higher, creative force. With the Great One.'

That rules out the geography teacher then, thought Anna. Which left only vicar or lunatic. Could be either, except that he'd mentioned his *work*. Vicar then. Must be of the happy clappy variety judging by all that Great One stuff.

'An unusual approach to work.'

'Not to mine.'

'Really?' Some island parishes, Anna knew, adhered to practices considered extreme and unusual by those of more liberal beliefs and downright bizarre by those of no beliefs whatsoever. But those island priests, the ones who forbade even heating up tins of beans on Sundays on the grounds that it counted as work hardly struck her as likely to go in for screaming on hillsides. Perhaps, Anna thought, the man before her was some sort of charismatic prophet, marrying people on clifftops and baptising others in the freezing real-ale coloured waves breaking ever closer up the shore behind them.

'But what do your congregation think?'

It was his turn to look wary. 'Congregation?'

'Aren't you the vicar?'

'No, I'm a writer. My name's Robbie MacAskill. I'm the—'

'*Poet!*' Anna finished. 'Oh, it's *you*. I read about you on the noticeboard. You give classes in creative writing. I'm *so sorry*.'

'Well, they're not *that* bad.'

Anna had not expected to return to the castle feeling calmer than when she had left it. It was amazing how a few hours' talking about writing soothed the nerves. Robbie was impressively passionate about it. The hilariously trite diktats he had invented for his creative writing classes had made her laugh for the first time in weeks.

'You have to take the *fear* out of it,' he explained as they walked slowly back over the sodden heather.

'Most people would rather show you their bottoms than their writing.' He turned to smile at her, his large teeth glinting in his beard. '*You* write, of course?'

Anna nodded, flushing with both embarrassment and gratification. 'In theory. How did you know?' Was it her eyes? Her hands? The creative aura around her?

'Well, *everyone's* a writer,' came the rather less flattering reply. 'I tell everyone at the start of my course that a book is like an arsehole. Everyone's got one in them. And most of what comes out is, of course, usually . . .' He cleared his throat delicately.

'*Oh.*' Anna wasn't sure what she thought of this. Then Cassandra came to mind and she smiled.

'But the point is,' said Robbie, helping her negotiate a shallow stream which would otherwise have flooded all over her shoes, 'it's better out than in. Most people feel a lot better afterwards, anyway. It helps them work out their frustrations. I'm a great believer in the therapeutic value of writing things down. If everyone did it, the world would be a better, calmer, less hysterical place. And if that means there are a few more bad novels about, so what?'

With surprise, Anna saw that they were already approaching the castle entrance. She stopped and smiled at him. 'This is where I live.' This, she decided, was as much as she would tell him.

'I know.' Anna felt her former sour mood returning. Everyone on this island knew everything. Apart from her.

'Come in for a coffee . . . or a drink?'

'Thanks, but I'd better be getting back. I have a class to prepare. Mrs McLeod has given me another chapter of her novel and I need to have read it with comments by tomorrow afternoon.'

'Mrs McLeod? The one who irons with discretion?'

'The very same. And writes the raunchiest stuff I've seen this side of a Soho porn parlour. All that steam must go to her head.'

'Not to mention all that underwear.'

They said their goodbyes. 'Come to my class,' Robbie told her. 'Come tomorrow afternoon, if you feel like it.' He strode back down the drive with a swinging gait, and without looking back. But then, if he had, Anna realised, he would have probably broken his neck in a pothole.

She stepped, heart sinking, into the flagged chill of the hall and wondered what on earth to do with herself. Where exactly did she go from here – in every sense of the word? But as she paused at the foot of the stairs, a strange, faint and entirely new sound greeted her. A sound she had not heard since coming to Dampie. Someone, somewhere, was laughing.

It seemed to be coming from somewhere upstairs. As Anna mounted the wide treads with their rotting red runner, she wondered who on earth it could be. Kate Tressell just passing through in the BBC helicopter? Or had one of the girls who had jilted Jamie dropped in for old times' sake? The laughter rang out again down the second-floor passage. It seemed to be coming from the sitting room. Anna rounded the corner to the sitting-room doorway, and gasped as Nanny, looming terrifyingly out of the gloom like the Hound of the Baskervilles, rolled on past her down the corridor with the force of a juggernaut and a face like thunder.

Whoever was laughing had made Nanny livid, which must by definition be good news. And, if Anna was not mistaken, before she had surprised her, Nanny had been bent double in the corridor with her ear shoved against the door. Which, come to think of it, seemed rather a good idea.

'Is that the Angus tartan?' a woman's voice was asking as Anna put her ear to the keyhole. *Geri*. It was *Geri's* voice. *Christ, she'd completely forgotten she was coming.* Even though, given the recent developments, her mercy dash now seemed largely pointless, Anna still felt glad she was here.

'*Absolutely*.' Jamie sounded almost incoherent with enthusiasm.

Fools rush in, Anna told herself, taking her hand away from the doorknob she had been about to turn. What a heaven-sent opportunity to let Jamie reveal his true colours to Geri – in every sense of the word. *Not* that *bloody* tartan story again.

Chapter 20

Cassandra had had no idea she had such *resilience.* Driving around in a *hire* car. And by no means the biggest available at that. And actually *surviving* the experience. She'd rather have died than do this in Kensington, yet here she was just west of Inverness in her Weekend Bargain Class A three-door 'Disco' with its denim-effect seats and tan plastic trim, and the God of Style had not struck her down. Not yet, anyway.

It was, Cassandra reflected, *amazing* what the human spirit could bear. A fortnight ago, failure to get a table at the Ivy or an on-the-day appointment with Jo Hansford would have seen her booking straight into the Priory. Were she to go to Jo Hansford now, Cassandra thought, the celebrated colourist might need a spot of trauma counselling herself, given the state of her highlights. At the base of each platinum coloured hair shaft lurked a good one and a half black and sinister inches. Cassandra ruffled them ruefully in the driving mirror. Talk about back to one's roots. For the time being she would have to go cold turkey on blonde. Gold turkey, if you liked. Cassandra didn't, but she hadn't really had much choice.

She hadn't had much choice about the car, either. It had been impossible to book a flight to Inverness for herself and Zak. How was she supposed to have remembered, with all the *millions* of other things she had to worry about, that Zak had been banned by BA after an incident involving an injured member of staff and unlocked central emergency doors eight miles above the Atlantic several months before? Those sorts of things just slipped one's mind, although in this case they had been forcibly helped back into it by the bookings clerk.

Honestly, Cassandra thought. Some people were so *petty*. It wasn't as if anyone *important* had been injured. Admittedly that *ridiculous* hostess Zak had been playing catch-the-gin-miniature with *had* ended up requiring plastic surgery, but quite frankly she'd needed that anyway. Face like a baboon's *bottom*. Anyway, Cassandra thought indignantly, was it *her* fault they'd been stuck on the tarmac for at least ten minutes before take-off waiting for Air Traffic Control to relent? Which had hardly helped with the Zak situation.

Harmless fun was all it had been – the door incident itself was merely the result of Zak *playing* at being an air steward. He'd only wanted to see what his emergency mask looked like when he pulled it down, just as he had only wanted to play at being a pilot when the captain – somewhat *reluctantly*, it had to be admitted – had allowed him into the cabin. Best draw a veil over *that* one, Cassandra thought. The memory of the sudden plummeting of the Boeing 747 made her blood run cold, just as it had made her Bloody Mary run cold all over her white Sulka shirt at the time.

Still, hiring the car and booking the sleeper had worked out very well – not to mention *cheaply*. Once Cassandra had got over the shock of realising that the box on the train she had thought must be her wardrobe area was actually the *entire cabin*, the journey had passed without too much incident. Apart, of course, from that ludicrous nanny of the Tressells' occupying the next door cabin and Zak's ever-curious and inquiring mind bringing itself to bear on the communication cord.

Bumping into Geri had proved useful, however; she'd now got Anna's address and fully intended to use it. It had been obvious from the way Geri had so determinedly talked Dampie Castle down, dismissing it as freezing, tiny and so damp it was practically *wringing*, that the place was vast, luxurious and ramblingly romantic, probably complete with Jacuzzis and aubergine guest bathrooms. And, quite apart from the weight it would take off her bank account, staying at Dampie would, Cassandra decided, prove a useful source of ideas. In the last few days she had been thinking the previously unthinkable – moving out of London. Property was so much cheaper in Scotland; hopefully there'd be enough left after the divorce from Jett for a *starter* castle, at least. Reluctantly, Cassandra recognised she had to get out of her Kensington mindset. She soon wouldn't be able to afford anything more than a shoebox in W8 any more. Location, location, location was all very well. But not if it was broom cupboard, broom cupboard, broom cupboard.

And there were other reasons for being in Scotland. No school in England having been prepared to rise to what Cassandra, in her letters to the headmasters called 'the particular challenge of Zak', the virtues of north-of-the-border education were now being explored. Chief among these virtues, Cassandra decided, was instilling in the pupil the appropriate degree of fiscal ambition. She had little on which to base this conviction other than the names of some of the places – but how, after all, could anyone at school in Stirling have anything other than a healthy respect for cash in all its forms? Unfortunately, the headmaster hadn't seemed interested in any of hers. The school called Dollar Academy had also struck, so to speak, the right note with Cassandra, and so it had been devastating to receive a letter pleading a waiting list longer than an M1 Bank Holiday traffic jam. In the end, Cassandra had decided she had no option but to take the headmasters by the horns and come up and sort things out herself. So far, her in-person surgical strikes on the schools had failed to make much difference – it had, incidentally, been *amazing* how many of them knew Mrs Gosschalk. Bloody woman got everywhere.

Cassandra had now moved on to the north-west Highlands, although getting around the place was driving her mad. These *ridiculous* little single tracks full of even more ridiculous people expecting her to *stop* for them, for some reason. Now she'd finally persuaded Zak he didn't need to get out of the car to pee, be sick or be bought things every five minutes, Cassandra had no intention of stopping for anyone. Zak had latched on with greater interest than she had anticipated to the idea of relieving himself into a plastic cup, although Cassandra had correctly assumed that anything to do with his willy would fascinate him.

'It's a good job you're a boy,' Cassandra observed, hearing the gushing of urine into the receptacle behind her. Unusually, Zak had insisted on sitting in the back seat.

'Why?'

'Because you can aim straight.'

'Can't *bints* aim straight?' demanded Zak, thrilled to be at last discussing his beloved subject. 'Why don't *birds* have cocks and balls?'

Cassandra sighed. Buttock-clenchingly uncomfortable though she found sexual organs herself – both literally and metaphorically – she knew it was vital to be as patient as possible with Zak. His young mind, after all, was still forming and misunderstandings in this very delicate area – *very delicate area* – could result in lifelong psychological maladjustment. Everything had to be explained very carefully and accurately. 'Ladies have whiskers and gentlemen have tails,' Cassandra said. 'I told you on the train.'

'But why don't blokes have *cunts*?' yelled Zak with relish. 'After all, everyone has *arseholes*.'

Cassandra swallowed. 'Darling, you know we call them front bottoms and back bottoms,' she said faintly, almost grateful for the sudden distraction of the frantically flashing headlights of a car in her driving mirror. A few minutes later, Cassandra, forced, finally, to a reluctant halt, was faced with a furious dental supplies salesman from Aberdeen who had just received an unscheduled golden shower through the air conditioning system of his car. It suddenly became clear why Zak had insisted on being in the back seat.

'When I said you could aim straight,' she said as she got back in the car having spent a fortune on mouthwash, enough dental floss to last the rest of her life and a state-of-the-art laser toothbrush apparently developed aboard a space shuttle, 'I didn't mean throwing the contents of your cup at any car that happened to be following us.' Sometimes, she thought ruefully, Zak really took the piss.

Zak did not reply.

Fearing one of his Olympic level sulks, Cassandra turned to see her son sitting rapt with the mobile glued to his ear. 'Darling, give me that. I've told you before about dialling those 0898 numbers.'

Cassandra wrested the mobile out of Zak's grasp and decided to call the London answerphone again. You never knew. Of late, she had become addicted to dialling the Knightsbridge phone number and listening with bated breath as the pitiless woman on the other end informed her 'you have *no* new messages'. Yet Cassandra could still not shake off the conviction that in her absence, every glossy magazine and national newspaper in Britain had called, leaving urgent messages about interviews. Sooner or later, obviously, *Parkinson* would get in touch, and there was always the possibility of another publisher ringing with a huge offer.

Cassandra stabbed the autodial and listened. *Fifteen messages!* Clearly, her fortunes had undergone a transformation more dramatic than Jocelyn Wildenstein. Hand shaking, Cassandra pressed two.

Her dreams had come true. The *Guardian*, the

Independent, the *Daily Telegraph*, *The Times*, the *Daily Mail* and the *Express* had all called wanting interviews. *Vogue* wanted to set up a photoshoot and *Harpers & Queen* wanted to do an At Home. Radios One, Two and Four had called, as had the long-awaited *Parkinson* researcher and about three representatives of prestigious publishing houses. It was overwhelming. In the bright blue sky of Cassandra's happiness, there was but one cloud. None of the messages were for her.

The phrases 'ironic', 'cult' and 'the real-life Spinal Tap' were repeated again and again. 'Jett St Edmunds,' the Radio One researcher breathed reverently, 'you are, quite literally, the new black.' Slowly, Cassandra worked out that not only was Jett's nationwide tour of student halls proving a massive success, but 'Sex and Sexibility', the first single released from the *Ass Me Anything* comeback album, had gone with astonishing speed to number one. 'With a bullet,' some of the journalists added, whatever that meant. She wouldn't mind pumping a few bullets into Jett now. *Number one*. Cassandra's heart plummeted faster and colder than a block of frozen urine from a plane.

She slammed the mobile back into the glove compartment. Damn Jett. It was just so *sodding typical* of him to become successful now she was in the middle of divorcing him. Having sat on his *arse* doing *fuck all* for the past ten years at least, he would choose *now*, of all times, to get his act together and become famous.

And, no doubt, rich. *Bastard*, thought Cassandra furiously. No wonder she was divorcing him.

Geri, Anna considered, was proving something of a disappointment on the moral support front. So far, she had failed to detect any of the expected *froideur* between her faithful friend and her conniving fiancé. On the contrary, they were getting on like a castle on fire, Geri drinking in every detail about Dampie as enthusiastically as she was downing the gin and flat tonics Anna had been relegated to preparing from the rudimentary contents of the drinks tray.

'You know,' Geri said, 'you should really think about promoting this place more. It's so romantic and interesting. Have you ever thought of opening it to the public?'

Anna was unable to suppress a snort. Jamie shot her an indignant look.

'This place is a tourist gold mine.' Geri looked around decisively. 'You've got turrets, towers, suits of armour, Dr Johnson and Mad Angus Thingy's romantic whatsit, and that's just for starters. You've even got a monster.'

'*Have* we?' Jamie looked amazed.

'Yes. That woman who showed me up to the sitting room was just about the scariest thing I've ever seen.' There was a silence. Anna looked keenly at Jamie. 'You mean Nanny?' Jamie's voice was noncommittal. Then, confounding all expectation, his mouth moved up at the corners. 'I suppose she is a bit fearsome,' he admitted.

Anna almost fell off her – admittedly rickety – chair. Jamie had never said anything before that implied Nanny was one whit less beautiful than Kate Moss.

'Any dungeons?' Geri enquired briskly. 'Tourists love a good dungeon.'

'How come you know so much about it?' Anna asked.

'Actually,' Jamie interrupted, looking hurriedly at his watch, 'I think we'd better go down to dinner. Nanny will be very cross if we're late.'

'I was a hotel PR for years,' Geri confessed once they were seated at opposite ends and in the middle of the long dining table. 'I quite enjoyed it, until . . .'

'What?' asked Anna.

'Until it all went horribly wrong when A.A. Gill was supposed to be going to one of the restaurants I represented. Everyone got in such a state because they didn't know what he looked like that they made me do a drawing of him and fax it through.'

'No!' said Jamie. 'How ridiculous.'

'Yes, and it all went more pear-shaped than a Belle Hélène. They ended up making the most *tremendous* fuss of someone who looked exactly like my drawing but turned out to be Jimmy Tarbuck. Adrian Gill got completely ignored, was really pissed off and slagged off the restaurant all over the *Sunday Times*.'

Anna laughed. It was impossible not to find Geri funny, despite her abject failure to find Jamie as appalling as she was supposed to.

'Then I decided to go into travel PR, but I left it when I found myself.'

'Found yourself?' Jamie looked nonplussed. 'But isn't that a good thing?'

'Found myself halfway up some mountain in Grenada with some old git from the travel pages looking up my skirt and asking for my room number, I *mean*,' said Geri. 'After that, I decided to pack it in. Gosh, what's this?'

Nanny had arrived in the dining room, her large, reddened thumbs firmly pushed over the rim into whatever was piled on the pitilessly large plates. A teaspoonful of grey flakes that might have been some sort of fish cowered at the foothills of an Everest of pulverised vegetable.

'Yummy,' said Geri. 'I love mashed potato.'

'Champit tatties, you mean.' Jamie glanced nervously into the shadows where Nanny lurked.

'Do I?'

'Yes, and that orange stuff next to it is bashed neeps.'

'Oh well, never mind. I'm sure they taste just as good as ordinary neeps, whatever they are.'

'Actually,' Jamie said hurriedly, 'Nanny's cooking is renowned the length and breadth of the island.'

'I bet it is,' giggled Geri. 'Well, nobody's perfect. I

expect there are lots of other things she *can* do.'

Anna was not in the least surprised when Nanny turned massively in her shadow and stomped furiously out of the room. What was amazing was that Jamie did not immediately scuttle after her. Instead he shrugged his shoulders and raised an apologetic eyebrow at Geri.

Past one in the morning, they were still all in the sitting room. Egged on by Geri, Jamie had returned to the subject of Dampie and had even dug out some mouldering and ancient leaflets about the island. Anna had felt compelled to stay through a mixture of masochism and curiosity. Geri was up to something, it was obvious. But what?

'And this is Old Man Rock.' Clouds of dust wafted from the pamphlet Jamie waved at Geri. 'It's supposed to look like an old man.'

Anna recalled the penis-shaped rock she had glimpsed fleetingly in the mist. No doubt the keen-to-impress-Jamie Geri would think of a more suitable way to describe it.

'Looks exactly like a penis to me,' said Geri, staring at the grey, grainy picture.

Anna muffled a giggle.

'*Well . . .*' began Jamie, doubtfully.

'But don't you see?' said Geri. 'That's a great *asset.* If you think about how many people go and look at a lump of stone shaped like four presidents, just think how many will come to see a rock that's shaped like a *willy*.'

Jamie did not look entirely convinced. 'I *suppose* I see what you're getting at,' he muttered.

'And what's this?' Geri reached for another pamphlet and sneezed as she prised apart its long unopened pages. 'The Mount O'Many Stanes?'

'A construction in the island's west comprising concentric circles of stones on a hilltop,' supplied Jamie instantly. Both women looked at each other, and then at Jamie, in astonishment.

'Various guesses – graveyard, remains of extraterrestrial settlement, early form of calculator – have been hazarded through the centuries,' Jamie added, 'but no one really knows what the stones really represent. The latest research thinks it has something to do with working out the best time for planting crops.'

'Fine,' said Geri, breezily. 'You're looking at the world's first Filofax in that case, aren't you? The cake-and-a-crap crowd will love it.'

'*Sorry?*' said Jamie.

'*Cake-and-a-crap crowd*,' Geri repeated emphatically. 'Tourists, in other words. They like to have a look at something before going to what they really came for – the café and the loo.'

As Geri and Jamie proceeded to discuss Dampie's potential as the Alton Towers of the North, Anna found following the conversation increasingly impossible.

Quite by themselves, her thoughts kept drifting to a smiling poet with big teeth. She resolved to add every detail of her encounter with Robbie to tonight's diary entry, especially her impression that she had met someone with a heart almost as big as his muscles. 'Come to my class tomorrow if you feel like it,' he had said. *Such* a shame he had a beard. But even given that rather considerable drawback, Anna was surprised by how much she felt like it.

Chapter 21

When Geri failed to appear at breakfast, Anna seized the opportunity to take it up to her. Doubtless after a night on one of Dampie's rock-stuffed mattresses, she would have an altogether different view of both the castle and its laird. At last they'd be able to have the heart to heart she'd been longing for.

'Ugh, that smells *disgusting*,' groaned Geri, turning her face away from the plate of tepid egg on toast. Anna tried not to mind the ingratitude – following Geri's comments the night before it had taken the diplomatic skills of Kofi Annan to get any breakfast at all out of Nanny this morning. Only by pretending the eggs were for him had Jamie acquired them at all. Anna had stepped in before he could take them upstairs himself, but not before hearing about little other than Geri all breakfast-time. 'So positive,' Jamie kept repeating. 'So full of good ideas.'

'*Oh my head*. Someone's tightening a rope around my brain.' Geri, Anna noted, and not entirely without pleasure, looked less than positive this morning. Her usually tanned face was almost as sludge green as the blankets. 'It was that fish we had last night. I'm sure it was off. I've had,' she added, 'what you might call a long dark night of the sole.'

Anna suspected there might be another reason for Geri's condition and wondered guiltily whether she really should have compensated for the flatness of the tonic by adding twice as much gin.

'And I'm sure this horrible seventies paper's not helping,' grinned Anna, nodding her head towards the vast orange and brown flowers crawling all over the walls. To her surprise, Geri refused to pick up the ball.

'Well, I wasn't expecting Claridges. And if you think this is bad, you should have seen the room I got last time.'

'I think it's probably the room I've got now,' sighed Anna. As the familiar drone of MacLoggie started up outside the windows, she looked at her watch. Three hours later than usual – Jamie must have asked him especially to serenade Geri. It wasn't having quite the effect he was intending.

'*What the hell is that?*' Geri shot up in bed like a

scalded cat. 'Christ, my head. My brain's slamming around in there like a squash ball.'

'Since the dawn of time,' Anna intoned dramatically, 'MacLoggies have lived and died as pipers to the Anguses.'

'Died, by the sound of that,' Geri groaned. 'One's heart rather goes out to the Anguses.'

As MacLoggie's attempts to launch into 'Scotland The Brave' collapsed into a cacophony of choking coughs, Geri covered her ears. 'I'm not sure about the bagpipes,' she groaned, 'but he does a great catarrh solo.'

Anna stuck her fingers in her ears. 'See what I have to put up with?'

'Oh, the poor old boy's in a bad way,' Geri chided. 'When he showed me to my room last night, his knees were cracking like a firing squad.'

'Oh Geri, I wish I'd never seen this place.' Anna, suddenly overcome by despair, dramatically buried her head in the musty-smelling quilt on Geri's bed. 'Come for a walk with me?'

'I couldn't. The only walk I'm capable of making is to the bathroom to throw up.'

'But I need to talk to you. My life's fallen apart at the seams.'

'Bit like these sheets then.'

Something in Anna suddenly snapped. Why did Geri have to be so bloody flippant about everything? She rounded on Geri with fury. 'All very well for you to come up here and find the whole thing side-splitting,' she snapped. 'I thought you were supposed to be my *friend*.'

'I *am*. But I feel slightly as if I've been dragged up on false pretences.'

'*False pretences?*'

'Well, you made it sound as if you were more or less rotting alive in a dungeon, helpless in the grip of an evil and ruthless brute of a fiancé and his stone-hearted female accomplice . . .' Geri held up a hand as Anna tried to interrupt '. . . and I arrive to find you in the company of nothing more disturbing than a slightly preoccupied and really rather sweet Scottish aristo and his nanny who, though admittedly not at the front of the queue when looks were given out, isn't exactly Frankenstein. In other words, I think you might have things *slightly* out of proportion.'

'*Well*.' Anna's mouth opened and shut like a guppy catching flies. 'There's nothing much in proportion about Nanny, for a start.'

'Nanny's easily dealt with. She just needs showing who's boss. Take the piss out of her a bit, like I did last night. Better still, just sack her.'

'And what,' demanded Anna furiously, 'is so wonderfully in proportion about Jamie only wanting to marry me so he'll inherit the estate? What about the fact that he lured me up here on *false pretences?*'

'*Darling*,' Geri sighed ostentatiously, '*every* husband, to some extent, lures his wife on false pretences. If every woman knew exactly who and *what* she was marrying, there wouldn't be any weddings at all.'

The blood pounded in Anna's head. Her brain whirled. How *dare*, how *could* Geri make light of her situation – a situation she was only in, after all, largely thanks to Geri. Right, well, she'd let her have it with both barrels.

'What about Jamie not wanting to have sex with me?' There. Get out of *that*.

There was a pause. *Got* her, Anna thought, triumphant.

'Well, sweetheart,' Geri eventually remarked, 'I suppose you have to look on the bright side.'

'*Bright side?*' Anna was staggered. 'What *bright side*?'

'Well, a lot of wives would give their eye teeth for a husband who doesn't want to have sex with them. Kate for one. Julian gives her cystitis practically every time. She has to sit on the loo for *hours* pouring water on her clit from a milk bottle.'

'But this was practically an arranged marriage,' blustered Anna. 'Except for the fact that no one ever got around to arranging it,' she added.

'Well, in that case perhaps you should get on with it, Jamie's very good-looking. Just get real, will you? You could have ended up with a lot worse.'

Anna felt she was about to hyperventilate with shock and disappointment.

'OK, so your sex life isn't exactly electric,' said Geri, 'but you *can* be friends. Lots of couples are and have affairs on the side. It would be rather fun. *Very* French.'

'But I don't want to have affairs on the side,' wailed Anna. 'I wanted to marry for love. I thought I was *going* to.'

Geri looked at her with a mixture of exasperation and pity. 'Your trouble is that you're a fully paid up, hearts and flowers romantic, aren't you?'

'And what's wrong with that? Surely better than viewing every relationship as a business opportunity,' she snapped, immediately regretting it.

There was a silence.

Anna's top lip quivered, her throat ached and her eyes brimmed with tears. *She would not cry.*

'I just don't understand,' Geri continued, 'why you seem incapable of seeing what a brilliant position you're in.'

Anna closed her eyes. 'You've lost me.' The only position she was aware of was sitting in a rickety armchair from which entire handfuls of smelly stuffing were making a bid for freedom.

'The castle, of course. Absolutely *bursting* with opportunities. Wake up and smell the coffee – not to mention the tearoom, the conference dinners, the five-star restaurant specialising in local produce – you name it. Just stop being so *bloody sensitive*. You could really make a go of this place.'

'*Well, why don't you then?*' sobbed Anna, simultaneously reaching the end of her tether and her ability to hold the tears back. 'As you've got so many brilliant ideas for it. Personally speaking, I'm finding it less than wonderful to be stuck in a rotting pile in the middle of nowhere with a fiancé who literally doesn't give a fuck.' Tearing out of the room, Anna headed for her bedroom. Her first instinct was to go straight to her diary and confide to its unconditionally sympathetic bosom every shocking detail of Geri's shameless betrayal.

She lay on the musty quilt and flicked back randomly through the pages, reliving the humiliation of the overheard conversation between Nanny and MacLoggie and the misery of Jamie confessing he was marrying her for a reason. *Get real* indeed. Was there something wrong with her that she didn't immediately feel able to pick herself up, dust herself down and channel her frustrations into a tourist boutique? Or head straight for the kitchen and plunge her dreams of romance into passion cake for the Wallace Arnold set? Reading on, however, she suddenly felt self-conscious. She imagined Geri's mocking tones. 'To paraphrase Oscar Wilde, it would take a heart of stone to read the diaries of Little Anna and not laugh.'

The battered pad, its pages covered with her

embarrassingly large and juvenile-looking scrawl, suddenly seemed the essense of futility. What was the point of writing things down in a filthy old book when no one but herself would ever see them? What had happened to the wonderful writing career – *real* books – that she had promised herself? Anna contemplated the creased and battered old notebook with sudden loathing. It seemed less a repository for observations, dreams and ambitions than a chronicle of abject defeat.

Grasping the diary by its cover, Anna walked slowly out of the room, down the stairs, out of the front door and down the pitted and scabby drive, pausing only at the bottom to stuff the entire volume firmly into the dustbin that stood by the peeling and half-unhinged gate for collection. Rubbish to rubbish, she thought.

'Her nipple pinged erect under the urgent rasp of his flickering tongue. She groaned as, tracing her long, red-painted fingernails down the matted hair on his chest, her hand touched the thick, insistent swell of his tumescent and throbbing cock . . .'

Cassandra switched off her Dictaphone and paused. Could cocks be both throbbing *and* tumescent? She wasn't even sure she knew what tumescent meant. Was it a bit like *fluorescent*?

Whichever way you looked at it, it certainly put the dick into Dictaphone. Which her machine wasn't really, not in the strictest sense of the word; but cassette recorders were all they had had in Ullapool, the point in the journey where Cassandra realised the floodgates of literary inspiration were opening once more. Like a glacier in the sun, her writer's block seemed to have melted. She was beginning to have ideas again.

This was a relief, as it explained the persistent and rather unpleasant erotic fantasies that had coloured her dreams over the two preceding nights. As it was, she certainly intended to use the scene involving the horse, the dog and the masturbating hermaphrodites in *A Passionate Lover*, although, as she had left *him* in a Knightsbridge office block, it was difficult to see exactly where, so to speak, they would all fit in.

Although in no circumstances could the new flow of ideas be described as a torrent, Cassandra was nonetheless as puzzled as she was pleased by its advent. Perhaps the long hours she had spent driving the denim-seated Disco and poring uncomprehendingly over maps had used up her conscious mind and freed up her id for creative activity? Maybe books conformed to similar physical principles as a watched kettle; a constantly monitored steamy novel never got to the boil either. But this couldn't be right – all the driving had, after all, cut her off from the gin bottle. The fact of her precious son's being in the car with her had stopped Cassandra drinking anything stronger than the occasional Perrier or Diet Coke ever since the

Scottish trip had started. Oddly enough, it had been around that time she had first been aware of the occasional plot idea struggling to get through. But that, Cassandra reasoned, *must* be impossible. Gin was the source from which all her inspiration had traditionally flowed. Wasn't it?

Pulsating cock, Cassandra suddenly thought. She whipped out her Dictaphone and, still keeping one hand on the wheel, whispered fervently into it, whilst casting a nervous glance in the driving mirror to make sure that Zak was still asleep in the back. She thought she saw his eyelids flicker, but no, he was sleeping like a baby, bless him. As he had been, interestingly enough, ever since she'd started working this way. She'd never known him to be so tired. It seemed all she had to do to keep him quiet was get out her Dictaphone; something in the cadences of her voice, something redolent of the womb, probably, lulled him to sleep. At first, she'd been afraid he was listening but he'd assured her he wasn't. And Zak was always a *very* truthful boy.

Oh *yes*, thought Cassandra as she bowled merrily past a passing place and forced yet another approaching farmer to reverse for miles to the last one. Some writers would find muttering erotic scenes into a tape recorder while driving around some island off the coast of north-west Scotland something of an eccentric way to go about one's business. But it was working very well for *her*.

Time to celebrate, Cassandra suddenly decided. Non-alcoholically, of course. But it would be nice to be *near* some real drink. Just to *look* at it. Smell it, even. The small and rather ugly little village she was driving through – Orrible, it seemed rather aptly to be called – did not, on the face of it, have much in the way of hostelries. But Cassandra could smell booze a mile off and, unless she was very much mistaken, that building by the side of the road that looked rather like a loo was in fact a pub. Deciding to leave Zak in the car – he looked so peaceful – she closed the door of the Disco as quietly as she could and tottered across the road in her tight ponyskin jeans and leopardskin high-heeled ankle boots.

Cassandra had not, from the moment she had arrived in Scotland, seen any need to drop her standards of dress. If Scottish women's idea of style was something that didn't show the cat hairs, that was fine by her, so long as she wasn't expected to follow suit. Especially if the suit was tweed, a fabric hideously reminiscent of Mrs Gosschalk. Cassandra was prepared to go as far as cashmere, but no further. Unless you were talking shahtoush.

She pushed open the toilet-glass door. A fug of smoke, twenty hostile stares and a deafening silence greeted her. Cassandra had never clapped eyes on such a collection of inbreds – at least, not since the last St Midas's sports day.

Letting the door slam loudly behind her, Cassandra crossed the thick, dusty and hostile space between the threshold and the bar. 'A glass of mineral water, please,' she commanded. From beneath brows so protruding they seemed in need of scaffolding, the landlord shot her a suspicious look. Unbowed, Cassandra met it with a freezing stare.

'We daen't have *mineral water*,' he growled. 'This is a pub. Nae a *health farm*.'

'*That*,' Cassandra snapped back, 'is obvious enough.' She fixed the landlord with a gimlet eye, aware that this was a trial of sorts, a test of nerve. *High Noon*, albeit that her current Cooper aspirations were rather more Jilly than Gary.

'*No* mineral water – that's *ridiculous*.' Cassandra's eye did not move from mine host's. 'You're missing out on a potential *gold mine*. Only last week I took my son to a restaurant where there was a mineral water *menu*. You could,' Cassandra blasted, 'mix two or even *three* different waters in the *same glass* to make a *cocktail*.'

The landlord looked stonier than ever, but Cassandra did not flinch. Mine host indeed. *Mean* host, more like. She recognised this belligerent, macho, brazen-it-out stare. It reminded her of Jett, which, free association being what it is, also reminded her of Jett being so *bloody inconsiderate* as to hit number one at the precise time she had chosen to divorce him. The memory packed her backbone with ice and her voice with fire.

'Well, as you haven't got any *mineral water*,' she hissed, 'I'll have a *Diet Coke*.'

Somewhere in the depths beneath the bar counter, mean host separated the tab from a can with a venomous rip.

A few minutes later, as she tottered, drink in hand, across the rickety, sawdust-strewn wooden floor, Cassandra stopped dead. The room, which had started to murmur to itself again, immediately fell silent. The ice cubes clanked belligerently together in Cassandra's glass as she turned and hit the landlord straight between the eyes with a glare like a laser.

'This is *not* Diet Coke.' She stalked back to the bar and slammed her drink down on its sticky surface. Mine host took an involuntary step back. '*This*,' Cassandra snarled, brandishing the glass, her face a mask of cold fury, 'is *fat* Coke. Which means,' she leant over the bar, pressing her face as close to the alarmed landlord's as she could, 'that you have *knowingly* force fed me a total of *one hundred and twenty calories* I had not allowed for. *Force fed* me. *Without my say-so, permission or go-ahead*.' She waited, then delivered the coup de grâce. 'For all you know, I could be a *diabetic*,' she roared at the by now quite openly cowering landlord. '*I could sue you*.'

She'd forgotten how good it felt to reduce a man to rubble. Ten minutes later, Cassandra sat, satisfied and reflective, in an inglenook by the pub's fire – a rather sorry-looking blaze that seemed to be burning strips of lawn. But nowhere near as sorry, Cassandra thought triumphantly, as the landlord had looked when she'd finished with him. After the magic word 'sue' had been uttered, he'd showered Cassandra with every gin bottle in the house in an attempt to placate her.

Cassandra had decided to limit herself to one sip only. Just for appearance's sake. Just to be polite. It was the least she could do; after the way she had humiliated him, the landlord would certainly have to sell up and leave, or bear the tale's constant repetition for the next thousand years or so. Probably nothing so exciting had happened since Mel Gibson had dropped by in the thirteenth century to raise his troops.

She took a sip. And then another. Was there anything *quite* like that powerful shot of juniper-infused spirit ricocheting round one's empty intestines? It was, Cassandra thought, finishing her third double in as many minutes, like the blissful reunion of lovers after many months apart. Like herself and *A Passionate Lover*, in fact. With his *pulsating, throbbing, tumescent, fluorescent cock* – no, *no*, that couldn't be right. Perhaps *pulsating* wasn't really the right word after all. If only she had a tyrannosaurus to look it up in. Funny how she couldn't seem to think any more. Again.

Plastering on her best grin, Cassandra leant over and shook the ancient, shrunken character slumped the other side of the inglenook, a white trickle of saliva running steadily down into his beard. '*Shcuse* me,' she boomed in a loud, shrill voice as MacLoggie lurched, terrified, back into wakefulness. Silence dropped like a stone on the rest of the bar. 'Wonder if you could help me. Could you tell me . . . have you notished . . . Doesh your penis ever pulsate, throb, swell and *tumesh* all at the shame time?'

Chapter 22

Stretching away on all sides, the wiry russet grass made the island seem like the broad back of a massive Highland cow. Anna had been walking for hours now, higher and higher, striding furiously so the pounding of the blood in her brain would be louder than the cacophony of her thoughts. She paused, panting.

Below her, the loch opened up like a giant silver oyster; beyond, the sea stretched into misty infinity, the horizon hidden by a grey stretch of storm cloud. It was, as usual, raining. Anna sat down at the summit and peered into the distance. She could see the village from here, the odd person – very odd person probably – moving about, and wondered if what Robbie had told her the previous day was true, about the island being cut off from civilisation for the first half of the century and its inhabitants having to mate with whatever came to hand. 'They screwed anything. Animal, vegetable or mineral.' Anna had wondered aloud what mineral Nanny's mother had screwed. Robbie's claim that she had been a Gloucestershire Old Spot didn't quite ring true.

She twisted her lips in what was half-smile, half-grimace. Geri's lack of sympathy made her feel both vulnerable and foolish, her despairing stride round the island seemed increasingly the act of a drama queen. Lear, of course, had strode the blasted heath in a much more convincing manner, but he *had* lost a whole kingdom and he *did* have Shakespeare arguing his case, which obviously helped. He'd never had to cope with Geri telling him to pull himself together and concentrate on the business opportunities.

But there was no doubt Geri was right. Nanny *was* an annoying old monster but she was hardly life-threatening, even if she undoubtedly represented a higher than usual risk of salmonella. Even more irritatingly, Geri was right about Jamie. He hadn't deliberately lied to her, there had just been facts he hadn't bothered to reveal. Economical with the actualité, if you liked. As well as everything else. She hadn't felt warm since she'd got here. And there had been bottles on that drinks tray whose only known exact contemporaries were in the wreck of the *Titanic*.

And it was probably just as well she had found out that she was about to plight her troth to a pile of old stones before she did so. The love of Jamie's life was undoubtedly Dampie; last night, he had been wildly excited by Geri's increasingly drunken suggestions – about the castle, of course – especially her recommendation that he try and turn Dampie into the Glastonbury of the north and promote it as a rock venue. 'Imagine,' Geri had shouted up into the chilly rafters of the sitting room, which no heat had penetrated since the great summer of 1538, 'you could have floating stages in the loch. Floodlight the castle in pink and purple. Have fireworks. It would be *amazing*.'

And then there were Geri's other suggestions. The ones she had made to Anna over the cold egg on toast. It might be possible to stay at Dampie with Jamie and just be friends. But could she really settle for so little?

As for the taking lovers proposal, well, that really *was* foolish. Only someone, like Geri, who had been on the island a mere matter of hours could have failed to notice the howling absence of suitable partners on Skul. The bearded poet suddenly slipped into her mind; yes, Robbie *might* have been a possibility. Witty, sensitive, poetic; she could tick all those boxes, but there was the problem of what lurked on the end of his chin. Try as she might, Anna could never love a man with facial fungus, especially grown to that extent. It was impossible to imagine kissing him – she'd probably come out in a rash with the friction. Still, it was probably very useful for scouring pans.

Yes, thought Anna, looking over the wide, low-lit, sea-girt land around her, I should definitely stick to writing books rather than trying to live them. Somewhere along the line she had, quite literally, lost the plot. Whatever spanners Fate had thrown in her works in the past, at least she had always had her writing. It had comforted her through Seb, encouraged her through Cassandra. But since becoming engaged to Jamie, it had disappeared altogether. She thought ruefully of the diary buried in the rubbish bin.

Once she was writing again – and this time she planned actually to finish the wretched thing – everything else would fall into place, even if she had doubts that that place was Dampie. But that all lay in the future. Time now to get herself back on track. She would write, she needed to write; all she required was a little prod in the right direction. She looked at her watch. She'd been here *hours.* But if she hurried, she could get to the village hall in time for Robbie MacAskill's afternoon class.

'*Fuck me. Fuck me.* I want you to come inside me, big boy. Fuck me *hard*.'

Anna, about to push open the door of the village hall, drew back in embarrassed astonishment. The voice was a woman's. Soft, Scots and urgent with lust.

'That's *fantastic*, Mrs McLeod. Don't stop.' *Robbie*. Anna's stomach plunged with disappointment. For some reason, possibly the beard, it had never occurred to her that there might be a woman in Robbie's life. Yet here he was with Mrs McLeod, going at it like a steam train. A steam iron, even. It might only be – Anna glanced at her wrist – a quarter to two, but presumably on Skul one had to get one's kicks where, and with whomsoever one could.

'I'm *wet*,' the voice continued. Anna felt white-hot knives of jealousy plunging into her stomach. There was, she realised, nothing like competition to make you realise you liked someone. 'Just *feel* how wet I am,' Mrs McLeod panted. 'I'm a *river* down here. Taste it, here, lick it off me. Oh, *fuck* me. *Harder*. I want you to come *like a fire hose*.'

Well, it certainly gave a whole new meaning to ironing board cover, thought Anna. What on earth did Mrs McLeod look like, she wondered – a wild-haired Hebridean Carmen, no doubt, full-breasted, with a lusty glint in her eye. I should go, Anna thought as the Hebridean Carmen began once again to speak.

'Panting, running her tongue round her wet lips and staring at him through hazel eyes glazed with lust, she ripped off her shirt. Her breasts sprang out like dogs let out for a walk—'

'Hang on a minute, Mrs McLeod. I'm not sure that's working. The image of dogs being let out for a walk is *slightly* at odds with the rest of the passage. And I'm not too wild about that fire hose either.'

'Are ye not, Mr MacAskill?'

'No, well, the whole point of this exercise is to read aloud to see what works and what doesn't,' said Robbie, completely matter-of-factly. 'The problem with very erotic passages often is that they can sound slightly, well, *excessive*. The trick is to err on the side of believability. Otherwise you end up being awarded things like the *Literary Review* Bad Sex Award, which I don't think you'd appreciate, Mrs McLeod. Not least because you'd have to go to London to receive it, and you know what you think of England.'

'Particularly when you lie back,' Anna murmured as, feeling vastly relieved, she pushed the door wide open.

'Sorry I'm late,' she said, 'but better to come late than never to come at all. As I'm sure Mrs McLeod would agree –' she stopped short in amazement. '*You've shaved your beard off.*'

He looked so much *better*, she thought, admiringly. Years *younger*. The excavations revealed a firm jaw and a wide, sensual mouth in the context of which the tombstone teeth looked considerably less fearsome. Rather than a handsome face, Robbie's was a strong and a rather heroic one. The sort that remained set in the midst of the most violent hail or blizzard. The sort rocks bounced off.

Robbie clamped a hand to his naked chin and grinned sheepishly. 'Yes. Thought it was getting a wee bit out of control. Any longer and I'd have needed a chainsaw to do it. Used up the village shop's entire stock of Gillettes as it was. No one's going to be able to shave their legs for a week until the new delivery comes over from Inverness. Sorry about that, Mrs McLeod. Oh, have you met Mrs McLeod, *Anna* . . .'

Hearing his warm voice pronounce her name was unexpectedly delicious. Suddenly aware she was gawping at Robbie like an idiot, Anna turned to shake hands. Mrs McLeod was not the expected hair-tossing femme fatale, thrusting of breast, flashing of eye and bent on removing local underwear for purposes entirely other than ironing, but a small, neatly-dressed woman, the only flashing thing about whom were small mauve-rimmed glasses. Similarly the only hint of Carmen about her was her hot-rollered, home-permed hair; to Anna's amazement, she looked well over sixty. Her prose, it would seem, was just as blue as her rinse. And, far from being an avid leg-shaver, her lower calves were covered with thick stockings. In short, Mrs McLeod looked as if she thought a leg wax was something one did to the nether regions of a dining table. She was also blushing violently.

'We're just going through Mrs McLeod's new chapter,' Robbie explained.

'So I heard. I thought it was wonderful,' Anna said sincerely. '*Very* sexy.'

Mrs McLeod looked traumatised. Anna stared at her carefully. What on earth could this timid creature know about breasts bursting forth like dogs let out for a run and ejaculations like fire extinguishers? Certainly it made one keenly curious about *Mr* McLeod.

'No, but I mean it,' Anna enthused, as Mrs McLeod shook her head. 'You should be proud of it. I thought it was terribly good. And for what it's worth, I *adored* the bit about the fire hose.' Anna had forgotten how one could discuss the most extraordinarily intimate things under the flag of literature. Her university days had included a number of racy tutorial sessions, including a particularly graphic one on the Metaphysical poets which had certainly put the semen in seminar. She would not have imagined that could be so spectacularly eclipsed by a discussion of firefighting equipment in a church hall on a Scottish island.

'Mrs McLeod is very shy about her work,' Robbie said, somewhat unnecessarily. 'But she shows enormous promise.'

Anna was touched and impressed by Robbie's determination to encourage what was possibly his only student. No wonder, with attendance like this, he had been so keen that she should come. But was that, it suddenly, miserably occurred to her, the *only* reason?

'As now, being three, we constitute a crowd,' Robbie

declared, gesturing Anna to one of the hard wooden chairs scattered around the bare and rather cheerless hall, 'I'm going to give a reading from another work. I thought it would be valuable for Mrs McLeod to hear how another author has handled sex.'

Anna swallowed. Her lower bowels seemed to be in a constant state of excitement; either Nanny's champit tatties had had a deleterious effect or, suddenly, she fancied Robbie like mad.

She watched him as he rummaged in his battered leather briefcase, watched him clear his strong throat and run his deliciously clean-looking pink tongue over his lips before proceeding. She liked the way his mouth curled upwards when he spoke, as if he was constantly amused. Most of all, in profound contrast to Seb for example, she liked the way he didn't seem to take the subject of sex too seriously. The main amusement Seb seemed to have got out of it, Anna recalled, was laughing at *her*.

As Robbie began to read, Anna wrinkled her brow. The words sounded oddly familiar. As his voice rumbled, soft and low, never stumbling on or mispronouncing a single word, horror began to grip her. *They were her words.* Robbie was reading *from her diary*. Blushing furiously, she gazed at the surface of the table at which she sat with Mrs McLeod. *How the hell had he got hold of it?* And did he know *she* had written it?

She sat in stupefied silence and listened, unsure of

what, exactly, the etiquette was when hearing one's most intimate and private thoughts read out in public. It was a miserable experience, not least because Robbie had picked a passage dating from a particularly unhappy period of her relationship with Seb, in which Anna had reflected on her own sexual inadequacy. She had, she remembered, originally written it in a self-deprecating way, trying it out as a possible comic passage for future use. Listening to it now she was struck only by the pain in the words, the sadness and the sense of humiliation and betrayal beneath the thin surface of wry humour.

As a contrast to Mrs McLeod's fire extinguisher, it could not have been more profound and, as she listened, Anna felt the remembered misery welling up inside. Seb had been so *unbelievably* nasty; listening to this rawly autobiographical account of their worst time together, Anna doubted whether her self-esteem would ever recover. No wonder, having gone through this, she had submitted meekly to Cassandra's excesses and leapt for Jamie as a drowning man might seize a lifebelt.

'*Brute*,' gasped Mrs McLeod, blowing her nose loudly as Robbie finished reading.

'That,' he announced, 'is the work of an extremely talented writer who understands completely that comedy and tragedy are often almost the same thing.' Anna was amazed to see that Robbie's eyes, too, were shining slightly brighter than before.

'Who wrote it?' squeaked Mrs McLeod timidly, dabbing at her eyes with an embroidered handkerchief.

There was a silence. Anna, puce with embarrassment, looked determindly downwards as Robbie darted a glance at her. Was he waiting for her to admit it? She hesitated.

'I shay,' demanded a loud, unsteady, shrilly patrician voice at the back of the hall. 'Ish thish Mishter Robbie MacAshkill's creative writing clash? I was told I'd find him here.'

Anna froze to the spot. *Those horribly familiar tones. It could not be. Surely.*

It was. 'Eckshellent,' pronounced Cassandra, eyes rolling as she advanced, swaying wildly through the hall.

Anna leapt to her feet. The chair crashed to the floor behind her. '*Cassandra*. What on earth are you doing here?'

Cassandra clomped up, gyrated wildly to keep her balance, buckled suddenly on her leopardskin heels and collapsed on the floor.

'I want to talk to someone about penishes.'

Chapter 23

'Friend of yours?'

As Cassandra lay crumpled and comatose at their feet, Robbie raised an ironic eyebrow at Anna.

'Not exactly. I was rather hoping I'd never see her again.'

'Well, you probably won't from the look of her. I'd better call an ambulance.'

'Och, there's no need to do that,' piped up Mrs McLeod. With surprising strength, she dragged Cassandra's prone body across the dusty floorboards and deftly manipulated it into an upright position against one of the radiators. Propping the lolling head up straight, she began to slap Cassandra's cheeks. 'Mr McLeod comes home from the pub like this all the time.'

Anna grinned to herself. This, at any rate, completely scuppered the theory that Mrs McLeod's sexual fantasies were autobiographical. Or at least, that they were inspired by her husband.

Through gritted teeth, Anna offered to put Cassandra up at the castle. If nothing else, it would annoy Nanny. But because, in her present state, it seemed likely that the rough roads up to Dampie might well finish Cassandra off altogether, it was decided she should go first to Mrs McLeod's cottage, conveniently just round the corner from the village hall. Once the long, slow process of moving the body was completed, Robbie was dispatched to track down Zak. Cassandra, slipping in and out of lucidity thanks to Mrs McLeod's face-slapping, had rather mysteriously revealed him to be in a disco somewhere in the area.

'But there isn't a disco anywhere on the island,' Robbie said, puzzled.

As he left Mrs McLeod's cottage – a pin-neat, shining haven of order that could not have been less suggestive of her blatantly erotic prose style – Robbie brushed against Anna. She shuddered at the charge of desire whilst trying to tell herself that the contact might have been accidental. The cottage was, after all, so tiny that only dwarf anorexics could have negotiated each other without colliding.

Listening to Mrs McLeod sluicing down Cassandra in the bathroom, murmuring sympathetically as she did so, Anna tried to make sense of the afternoon's events. Neither Cassandra's sudden appearance, nor the means by which Robbie had got hold of her diary seemed to have any explanation whatsoever.

'I eventually tracked him down at the police station,' Robbie reported, returning half an hour later dragging a thunderous-looking Zak who, once inside the cottage, immediately started to pick up and look at Mrs McLeod's large, immaculately dusted collection of ornaments.

Anna tried, like a victim at a human rights trial, not to flinch at the sight of her former torturer. For Zak looked more evil than ever. His prep-school-perfect basin cut looked straggly and wild, its former white-blondness noticeably darker. It occurred to Anna to wonder whether Zak's platinum locks were at root no more natural than his mother's; could Cassandra have really had her son's hair coloured to match her own? Could she really be so vain? Was the Pope Catholic?

'What was Zak doing?' she asked.

'Sitting in a cell. He'd tried to drive the car – called a Disco, by the way, so that explains that – but ended up smashing it into the postbox. Car's a write-off.'

'The postbox? So at least he hadn't got very far then. The postbox next to the village hall, you mean?'

'No, the one on the other side of the island.' Robbie passed a palm ruefully through his hair. 'The police were alerted after someone coming out of the pub saw a small boy driving a car at a speed in excess of one hundred miles per hour through the village. They would have got him sooner, only the person coming out of the pub was MacLoggie and, given his condition, his evidence was considered unsafe.'

'I see.'

'When they caught up with Zak, he was apparently sitting in the front seat listening to a woman talking dirty on a cassette recorder. Turned up full blast.'

'Ugh.' Anna tried not to remember the knicker-sniffing incident on her second day at Liv.

'How did you get him out of the police station?'

'Amazingly, they didn't seem too sad to see the back of him.'

'*I* want to be a policeman,' Zak interrupted defiantly, one hand holding an ornament while the other fiddled excitedly in his pocket. '*I* want to put people in prison.'

'They'll want a word with Cassandra when she comes round.' Robbie continued, ignoring him. 'Fortunately – for him at least – Zak's too young to have a criminal record.'

'A record?' Zak's voice was scornful. 'As if I'd want one anyway. No one has vinyl these days.'

'Shut up,' Robbie snapped at him. There was a smash as one of Mrs McLeod's china shepherdesses collided with the tiles of the fireplace.

* * *

Driving back to the castle in Robbie's rattling old Land Rover, Anna tried to stop her thighs shooting across the metal seat and cannoning into Robbie's every time they rounded a corner, which was hair-raising, sudden and surprisingly frequent. Either Robbie was a very bad driver, Anna thought, as her legs slammed into his rock-hard thighs, or . . .

'Hope Mrs McLeod can cope with both Cassandra *and* Zak,' she remarked, looking out of the Land Rover's broken window across the camouflage-coloured landscape. 'But she did insist she'd have them until Cassandra gets . . . um . . . better.'

'Mrs M's a tough old bird,' Robbie said. 'We'll pick them both up tomorrow in any case. She probably wants them for material.'

'Talking of material,' Anna turned her head away to disguise the deepening vermilion of her face, 'how *did* you get hold of my diary?' She unenthusiastically regarded the sodden, rendered walls of Dampie Castle as they jerked into view across the windscreen.

'Oh, so you're admitting it was yours?' Robbie threw her an amused glance as the Land Rover lurched up the Dampie drive like a bucking bronco. 'I wasn't sure if you were going to. As it happens, I found it in the castle dustbin only this morning.'

'*Dustbin?*' She remembered putting it there, of course, but what was *Robbie* doing rummaging in the castle refuse? Poetry paid badly, she was sure, but all the same . . .

'Yes, the dustbin. One of my jobs is to collect the local rubbish. You don't think I make a living being a poet, do you? Or through my creative writing classes, although I must admit that if I were a literary agent I'd probably be retiring on Mrs McLeod.'

'Are you *really* a poet?' Suddenly, the idea of a dustman who gave creative writing classes and was a poet into the bargain struck Anna as rather strange.

There was a silence. Robbie looked at her, then looked hastily back at the windscreen as the Land Rover plunged into another pothole.

'No, of course I'm not a poet,' he confessed easily. 'As a matter of fact, I'm a novelist. Trying to be, at any rate. I'm writing a comic murder mystery set on a Scottish island.'

'Oh.' Was anything on Skul, Anna wondered, what it seemed?

'I'm here researching my characters, and being a poet was the only thing I could think of that wouldn't attract too much suspicion. Islands like this are packed with hawk-eyed old bards with beards. I managed the beard, as you saw, only I never felt it was quite me.'

'It wasn't. It was a personality in its own right.' Anna furrowed her brow. 'But I don't understand why you felt you had to give creative writing classes.'

'They were supposed to help convince people I was a

poet. I never expected people to actually *come* to them. When, one night, the village hall door opened and Mrs McLeod trotted in, I almost fell over with shock. When I heard what she'd brought with her, I almost died of it. Having said that, I think she'll have a great future as an erotic novelist once she's got a bit more, er, *front*.' As his glance flickered, *possibly* involuntarily, towards her breasts, Anna's stomach lurched, in perfect synchronity with the Land Rover.

There was a silence, punctuated only by the grinding of the Land Rover's engine.

'Yes. My character research has been rather more, er, *interesting* than I imagined.' Their eyes met, briefly, before Robbie's swung suddenly back to the windscreen just in time to stop them smashing into a tree.

'Especially if you go through everyone's rubbish,' said Anna. 'I suppose that was part of your research as well.'

'Oh yes. There's a pivotal scene in my book where the maverick detective—'

'Unhappily divorced?'

'Yes, and with a drink problem of course.'

'Of course. Smokes too much? Loves classical music?'

'Absolutely. Anyway, in this pivotal scene he's going through the dustbins in search of the murder weapon, so of course I had to know what the average islander puts out for the binmen. You wouldn't believe some of the things I found.'

'Like my diary.'

'Yes. I hope you didn't mind me looking at it, but once I'd started reading it, I couldn't stop. It was so well written . . .'

Anna blushed again. It occurred to her that, although she knew next to nothing about Robbie, he was now familiar with her entire recent history. The humiliation of life with Seb, the near slavery of life with Cassandra, the boredom and disappointment of life with Jamie, he knew it all. Leaning very close to her, close enough for her to smell his aftershave and the faint mint of his breath, Robbie murmured softly, 'You're not very lucky in love, are you?'

Anna shook her head. *Until now*, she thought, crossing her fingers behind her back. She was just closing her eyes and parting her lips when, with impeccable timing, Robbie's mobile rang.

After several minutes' terse conversation, Robbie snapped the telephone away. 'That was Mrs McLeod. She wants me to come and get Zak at once. Apparently he's sprayed a fire extinguisher all over her wooden floor. Mr McLeod's just come in from the pub and gone flying.'

Cassandra hadn't felt so dreadful in *years*. Someone, somewhere was plunging red-hot needles into her brain. When, oh when would she remember *cheap* alcohol disagreed with her? One never felt like *this* on Bombay

Sapphire. Possibly because one could only afford *one* bottle of that at a time.

She narrowed her eyes as she took in her surroundings. Where the *hell* was she? Some poky, ghastly little bedroom, by the looks of it. Was it a nightmare? *Must* be. But only in the very *worst* of nightmares, thought Cassandra, cringing with disgust as her toenails scraped against the fabric, did people have *aquamarine nylon sheets* on their beds. *Or* wear baby pink bed jackets *with ribbons*, she thought, tearing frantically at her throat. Exhausted with the effort, she lay back and tried to make sense of the fuzzy images of herself rolling past the back of her eyes.

Dancing on the tables in some appalling pub – now *that* bit obviously was a nightmare. So difficult to work out what had really happened and what hadn't, but such, Cassandra thought, was the burden of the creative imagination. Some muscular man folding her tenderly into his arms – nothing remotely surprising about *that*, though. She could have sworn that wretched ex-nanny of hers Anna, had been in the room as well – that *must* have been a nightmare too, even though she fully intended to drop in on her for at least a week's full board and en suite bathroom. A hideous thought suddenly struck Cassandra – perhaps this poky, chilly, ugly little room actually *was* in the castle. If so, she'd request a transfer to the master bedroom without delay.

What time was it? Cassandra raised herself on one

elbow and peered at the bedside table, where she was gratified to see a number of her own paperbacks piled up. She was less delighted when her vision focused enough to reveal the plastic jackets and typewritten numbered labels of the public library – although this one said mobile library. Cassandra had not previously been aware one *could* borrow mobiles from a library. So that was what she'd been paying her bloody taxes for all these years. *Ridiculous.*

And what was *this*? Cassandra reached out and grabbed a handful of paper by the bed. Typewritten. A story by the looks of it. Someone had left it, perhaps by mistake. That ludicrous Anna, no doubt; she was so obsessed with writing she probably carried manuscripts round in her knickers. Well, Cassandra thought viciously, there'd certainly be plenty of room.

She may as well give it the once over; if nothing else it would send her back to sleep. Yawning, Cassandra pressed the papers close to her nose and began to read.

Five minutes later, she was sitting bolt upright, her hangover forgotten. This stuff was *sensational.* As her eyes moved greedily over the unevenly typed lines, Cassandra felt awe seeping slowly through her; either that, or she'd wet herself with excitement. She hated to admit it – in fact, she never had before – but there could be no doubt whatsoever that she was in the presence of a truly great writing talent. Someone who could knock herself, Jilly, Danielle and even dear departed Dame Catherine into a cocked beach bag. Could this really be *Anna's* work?

Damn. Damn. Damn. Cassandra rolled her bloodshot eyes to the ceiling. *What* an opportunity missed. How *could* she have been so *stupid*, so pig-headed as to have had the girl actually in the bloody house with her and have *no idea* she was capable of this? When a soft Scottish voice suddenly inquired whether she was all right, Cassandra leapt a foot into the air and looked furiously at the small, timid-looking woman who had appeared at the foot of her bed. Doubtless one of the castle servants.

'Do you always creep up on people when they're reading?' she snapped at the woman, looking in disgust at the rollers and tartan apron. Really, Anna needed to take a firmer hand with the appearance of her domestic staff.

'I'm very sorry, Mrs Knight. I didn't mean to wake ye up. But ye were so *quiet* . . .' Mrs McLeod touched her rollers in panic. She'd just wanted to titivate herself up a bit; one didn't, after all, get the great author Cassandra Knight staying every day of the week. Not that she had intended the legendary creator of *Impossible Lust* to see her in her Carmens; given Cassandra's condition when she and Anna had stuffed her between the sheets, Mrs McLeod had not expected her to see anything for several days. 'I just wanted to bring ye a couple of notes that have been left. Your son has been taken up to the castle and you're invited to stay there when you feel well enough to go. I'm very sorry to disturb ye . . .'

'Quite all right, quite all right,' snapped Cassandra, relieved that this hideous little room wasn't in the castle after all. The hideous little woman, however, was appalling – not only one of the servant classes, but a fan of hers as well. These grovelling old crones could be so *tiresome*. She knew the type – hideous old crumblies who crowded to her periodic bookshop appearances by the ambulance load and gathered dribbling and twitching round her table while she signed 'To Edna' as quickly as she could before the reek of mothballs and Parma violets overwhelmed her. *Ghastly*.

Cassandra waved the paper in her hand impatiently. 'Was quite enjoying this, actually. Rather well written. *Quite* impressed.'

'Oh, Mrs Knight, do you really mean it?' Mrs McLeod's eyes shone even brighter than her polished purple spectacles.

'Do I mean it?' Cassandra gazed dramatically up in the air. 'Well, yes, actually, I rather think I *do*,' she drawled, patronisingly. 'Must say, wish I'd known this was the sort of thing on offer. Could have written half of my books for me, ha ha.' Anna bloody *could* have done too, with all the spare time she'd had on her hands, seethed Cassandra silently. Could have knocked off entire sagas between school runs. *Damn*. All that time she'd been suffering from writer's block herself and there'd been the literary equivalent of colonic irrigation just up on the next landing.

'Mrs Knight . . .'

Really, the old girl was getting very excited. Gone quite red in the face.

'Yes, Anna certainly kept her light under a bushel,' Cassandra continued. Really, it was *infuriating*. What a team they could have been. I, Cassandra thought wistfully, could have supplied the name and the reputation. All Anna would have had to do was bash out the books.

'Anna didna write it.'

'Yes, well, I must say I found it hard to believe myself – plump, plain sort like that knowing about steamy stuff like this. Still, the ugly ones are supposed to go like the clappers aren't they – so *grateful*. That's been my downfall really. Being born beautiful means you don't *have* to try and so you don't tend to bother. Not that you'd know much about *that* of course, Mrs, er, um, but—'

'McLeod. Actually, *I* wrote it . . .'

'*As I was saying*, there are positions in here I wouldn't have dreamt possible – and the *language*. Very, *very* racy. If this doesn't get the gussets of Gloucestershire moistening, nothing will. And it's those gussets,' Cassandra raised herself on both elbows and looked aghast into Mrs McLeod's blazing eyes, 'that I need to tap into. *What did you say?*'

'I wrote it.'

'You wrote it? *You?*'

'Yes.'

'*Fuck me.*' Cassandra fell back on her pillows, gasped and stared at the ceiling. The answer to her prayers had just walked through the door in rollers and a tartan apron. 'Mrs McLeod, please sit down. Does the term *ghostwriting* mean anything to you?'

'Christ. *What* a day.' At approximately the same time Mrs McLeod tremblingly drew a chair to Cassandra's bedside, Anna pushed open the door of the castle dining room. 'Oh, *Geri*. Wonderful. You're still here then. Thought you'd have given up on me and be halfway back to London by now.' Was she imagining things, or did Jamie and Geri spring apart almost guiltily as she entered? Their heads certainly had been *touching* as they pored over the maps spread across every possible surface of the room – but had anything else? On the surface of it, Jamie seemed to be midway through a drain tutorial. But *that* didn't explain, Anna thought, why they both looked so flushed.

'I'll get you some coffee,' said Jamie, hastily beating a retreat.

Geri gave Anna an apologetic smile. 'Sorry I was so vile to you this morning. I had the mother of all hangovers and I'm afraid you rather got it in the neck. Whatever I said, I didn't mean it. I take it all back.'

'Oh, there's no need.' Anna swallowed. 'Quite useful, actually, some of it. What are you doing with all these maps?'

'Thought I'd try and give Jamie a hand. You know how I love to organise things.'

'And *has* she *organised* things,' Jamie exclaimed, returning with a coffee cup trembling violently in his hand, his wide-apart eyes shining. 'She's been on the phone all morning ringing up rock stars to try and get them interested in coming to play up here. She talked to Robbie Williams for *ages*.'

'Really? I didn't know you knew Robbie Williams.' But much more amazing than that, Anna considered, was that Jamie knew who he *was*.

'Oh yes,' said Geri casually. 'He's one of Savannah and Siena's—'

'*Godfathers*,' finished Anna. 'Don't tell me.'

'Yes, but he wasn't at the party because he was on tour. And sadly, he's on another one at the moment so won't be able to come and play Dampie for ages. But he's definitely interested.'

'Meanwhile,' Jamie was barely able to control his excitement, 'we've had a breakthrough. Tell her, Geri.'

'Oh yes, well, as Jamie said, I've been phoning round, and one of the people I called was Solstice. You remember – Jett St Edmunds . . .'

Anna grimaced. Would the memory of him prancing around in a thong, she wondered, ever fade?

'But you know Solstice are really huge now.' Geri's eyes were wide with enthusiasm.

'They *are*?' Certain aspects, Anna thought, were pretty huge then.

'Yes. Amazing, I know, but they've become a massive ironic student hit.'

A sense of impending doom started to seep through Anna's veins.

'They're really famous,' Geri pressed. 'They've revived heavy metal single-handedly. They're on every chat show going. You can't open a paper without reading about them – and Champagne D'Vyne, of course.'

'Champagne D'Vyne?' Anna racked her brains. The name was familiar – the blonde, tanned girl with the hot pink heels from the Tressell children's party, wasn't she?

'Jett St Edmunds's new girlfriend. She dumped her last fiancé – one of the Manchester United squad she'd been engaged to for about forty-eight hours – to get in on the act with Jett. Self-publicist like her couldn't let an opportunity like *him* go to waste. He's massive, you know.'

'So he used to keep telling me.'

'Yes, well, it's great you know him, because he's coming to stay.'

'*What?*'

Geri and Jamie nodded eagerly. 'Most amazing coincidence,' Jamie gabbled. 'Geri called him on his mobile and it turned out that he's just come to the end of an extensive tour of British universities—'

'His Wold Tour, as he called it,' Geri interrupted. 'It was a sell-out.'

'And he's just, er, been playing at the, um, University of Achiltibuie, just over on the mainland. Better still,' Jamie stuttered, plainly trying to recall the unaccustomed vocabulary, 'he's doing a live, um, album of all his concerts—'

'Which his record company want released as soon as possible.' Geri regained the narrative while Jamie looked at her in open admiration. 'But he now needs to shoot a cover and mix the tapes of all his live gigs. He's had a lot of trouble finding the right place to do it. So I told him all about the special acoustic effects of the dungeons here, and also that the castle not only looks stunning but also sits at the junction of every known ley line and is filled with cosmic forces.'

'And is it?' Yet another fascinating fact about Dampie that's passed me by, thought Anna.

'May well be, for all I know,' grinned Geri. 'Anyway, Jett was thrilled and said he'd be right over with the boys.'

'The boys?'

'The engineers,' said Geri. 'The rest of the band have gone back to London.'

'But there's the girl,' added Jamie.

'Oh yes, the girl.' Geri smiled at him conspiratorially.

'*What* girl? *Not* . . . ?'

'Champagne D'Vyne. Sure. They'll be here,' Geri looked at her watch, 'within the hour.'

'Perfect timing. Considering Jett St Edmunds's soon-to-be-ex-wife is at this moment throwing up in a bathroom very close to us,' Anna remarked grimly.

It was Geri's turn to look amazed. 'Oh Christ, *yes*,' she said, slapping her forehead loudly with the palm of her hand. 'Meant to tell you. I met her on the sleeper. Completely went out of my head.'

Anna looked at her searchingly. So *that* explained Cassandra's sudden advent. 'Shame my address didn't then.'

Geri had the grace to blush.

'Well, she'll be here at some stage as well. We should,' said Anna, 'be in for an interesting evening.'

Chapter 24

Jett St Edmunds was delighted. His two engineers, Bill 'Newcastle' Brown and Tommy 'Vindaloo' Jones, had finally finished setting up the mixing equipment in the dungeons and disappeared to the pub. The time had finally arrived to put his secret cover concept into action. Alone at last. Devising a way to get the rest of Solstice back to London so he could be photographed gloriously solo had used up practically every megabyte in his brain for the past few days.

Geri's sudden offer of a castle had been the answer to his prayers. Her assurance that Dampie was a glorious combination of Abbey Road Studios and Balmoral had failed rather spectacularly to deliver the former, but had not disappointed with the latter. The castle fitted the photographic bill – which Jett would do his best to get out of paying – superbly. Even as he lurched up the drive, Jett was planning how magnificent he would look against the battlements, aquiline profile silhouetted before a savagely beautiful sunset, storm-tossed tresses lifted in the wind, cloak thrashing as if possessed by the devil. Jett was very proud of his cloak, a sequinned, hooded affair in midnight blue bought in a rock auction in the belief that it had belonged to Marc Bolan; a conviction Jett persisted in despite his subsequent discovery of the legend 'Walberswick Amateur Dramatic Society' embroidered on the inside of the collar. He had not previously realised that Marc Bolan was a member.

All that remained to be sourced for the cover shoot were the pair of devil horns he intended to have protruding from the storm-tossed tresses. Plus, of course, some blood to drip from his hands and run in gory rivulets across his cheekbones. It had not been easy to brief the photographer on a dodgy mobile from the back of the tour bus, but he'd finally got the message, despite sounding doubtful about precisely where to obtain the blood and the horns. Typical bloody photographers, thought Jett. Everything was too much goddamn trouble for them. Anyone with a camera thought they were goddamn Mario Testino these days.

He'd never been in favour of Seven des Roches, Solstice tour photographer and self-billed rock 'n' roll snapper extraordinaire; after all, what had been so wrong with Annie Liebovitz? But the record company's budget had been tighter even than Jett's own trousers and had ruled out practically everything apart from an art student with an Instamatic. Which was more or less what Seven seemed to be. Still, Jett was confident of success. His visual concept was so strong it was practically foolproof. The title was rock and roll perfection; an idyllic fusion of the theatrical with the threatening, the light with the dark, the poetic with the diabetic – or was that diabolic. *Spawn of Satan*. It had a ring to it. Ten at least. Jett admired the array of gold skulls, snakes and wolves' heads ranged along his fingers like knuckle-dusters. Unable to pick just one for the shoot, he had worn the lot.

Call him a sentimental old fool, but something about the fistful of metalware reminded him of his wife. As he left the studio to make the rendezvous with the photographer, cloak billowing about him and sending out powerful wafts of patchouli, Jett wondered how Cassandra was getting along. He hadn't heard from her for ages, not since the night Solstice had been playing the Enormodome in Portree and his mobile had gone off mid-set. Dragging it out of the bulge in his pants before a crowd of at least fifty had been bad enough; far worse had been Cassandra screaming at him about school fees and accusing him of being homeopathically disturbed. He had put the phone away conscious that he almost missed her. As he almost did now. This was a pretty spooky goddamn place to be alone in. After three laps of the ground floor, including a terrifying encounter with a huge bruiser of a woman with a face like a road accident, even a seasoned performer like himself was beginning to feel a little self-conscious mincing round in a sequinned cloak.

Not least because it was so goddamn dark – he could barely see a thing through his sunglasses.

'Mr St Edmunds? Over here.' Having just managed to find his way out of that spooky goddamn castle and into the yard, Jett almost leapt out of his cloak at the unexpected voice. He whirled round to see Seven des Roches sticking his head out of an ancient, stone-built shed set slightly apart from the main castle building. As he approached the photographer, his relief turned to surprise and then to terror. Seven's hands were dripping blood and there was a maniacal grin on his face.

'Gore galore,' enthused Seven. 'And guess what? I've found some horns as well.'

Jett followed him into the building. The interior was gloomy, a sink at the murkiest end of it piled high with glistening organs. Some kind of big, hairy thing was hanging on the wall; beneath it, on the floor, was a bucket of what looked horribly like blood. Jett felt the gorge rise in his throat. 'Fucking hell,' he exploded. 'What is this? Sweeney Todd's goddamn fucking sitting room?'

'It's a deer larder,' said Seven, who had once had a girlfriend whose father owned a shooting estate. Although the relationship hadn't lasted more than a week, its enduring legacy was his name losing its T in a bid to sound more glamorous than the Steven he had been born, even if everyone assumed it was either a misspelling of Sven or he was a big Brad Pitt fan. His original surname, Stone, had gone through the same glitzification process with slightly more success.

'Look at this incredible stag.' Seven directed Jett's gaze to the hairy thing on the wall. The vast, gutted carcass dangled rather abjectly against the roughly whitewashed stone, the cavern that had once contained its entrails gaping forlornly the entire length of its trunk.

'Horns on tap,' grinned Seven. 'We just pull them off and stick them on your head with a few bits of gaffer.' Jett grimaced. The thought of pulling off the antlers made him retch. He could imagine the fur tearing, the sickening rip of muscle off bone. *Ugh*. 'Or just hack the whole thing off,' Seven continued cheerfully. 'I've got a machete in my bag from when I was shooting the Nolan Sisters' comeback tour of Uganda.'

'No fucking goddamn *way*.'

It took the photographer a further five tense minutes to hit on the inspired idea of Jett actually getting *inside* the stomach cavity of the deer carcass and standing facing front so its shoulders rested on his, its legs dangled down his back and its head balanced atop his own, antlers soaring outwards. 'Fantastic. Very His Satanic Majesty,' Seven pronounced admiringly as Jett stood trying not to notice the still-wet insides of the animal and hoping it was water that was seeping into his clothes. At least the cloak was safe – Seven had thrown it over the back of the deer. 'Looks awesome, I tell you. *Fantastic. Great.* Now just hang on while I pop on a bit of blood.' Seven dipped a rag in the bucket and slapped it, dripping, across Jett's face.

'Hey, watch my goddamn sunglasses.'

'*Fabulous.* You look *gorgeous.* Now we're almost ready to roll. Just come outside, *that's* right, take my hand and *don't* try looking from left to right – it'll all fall off. Thought we'd just shoot you with the castle in the background. *Awesome.*'

'Make sure you get my goddamn good side,' Jett mumbled, feeling oddly helpless and vulnerable as he slowly emerged, clutching Seven, blinking and covered in blood, into the daylight. He could look only in one direction – straight ahead. One unscheduled jerk of the head and the whole precariously balanced construction would collapse.

'Sure, *sure.*' Seven rustled in the plastic bag beside him, producing a plate and arranging something Jett could not quite see on it. 'Now here. Just take these prawns. That's right.'

'Prawns?' Jett was pleasantly surprised. 'Great. Could do with a snack. Got any mayo?'

'Ha *ha*. Now *just* hold them in both hands and look satanic.' He picked up his camera, thrust forward his hips, then swayed them from side to side in a grinding motion. '*Great*. Let's go. Wow. Fantastic. *Awesome*. Now we're *really* cooking with gas.'

Jett stared at him from under the antlers and behind the ever-present sunglasses. 'This is for the Polaroid, right? You're checking the position of the goddamn dripping dagger or whatever it is I'm really gonna to be holding.'

'*Great*. You look *well* scary now.' Although his pelvis was as eloquent as ever, Seven's face was now invisible behind his lens. 'Polaroid? No, this is for the shoot.'

'*Whoa*. Hold on just one *minute*.' Jett tried to hold up a hand, but the deer carcass swaying on his shoulders prevented him. 'Remind me again,' he said in a dangerously level voice, 'where the prawns come in?'

Seven lowered the lens. His hips stopped jerking. 'You're joking, aren't you? They're the title, aren't they? *Prawn of Satan*.'

Behind his mirror shades, Jett's eyes bulged with fury. '*Prawn of Satan?*' he gasped eventually. '*Prawn?*' he spluttered. 'If anyone's a fucking goddamn prawn it's *you*. Of *course* it's not called fucking goddamn *Prawn* of fucking goddamn *Satan*.' The deer carcass lurched and began to list dangerously to the left. Seven hastily put his camera down, rushed forward and pushed it back on again.

'Well, it was very hard to hear what you were saying on the mobile,' he said testily. 'It sounded *exactly* like prawn to me. Thought you must be doing a tie-in with Iceland. You know, free kilo of crevettes with every CD. Lots of people do that sort of thing now, you know. Anyway, *anyway* . . .' he added hastily, catching Jett's murderous glare, 'being a professional, I have a contingency plan. There is an alternative.'

'So I should fucking goddamn *hope*,' exploded Jett as Seven scuttled back inside the deer larder to emerge, a few seconds later, with a long, thin orange plastic device. A length of twine dangled out of the front of it. Jett glanced contemptuously in its direction before swivelling his reflector-lensed glare back to the hapless photographer. 'And what the goddamn fucking *fuck* is *this*?'

'A strimmer,' said Seven.

'May I,' asked Jett in even more dangerously level tones than before, 'ask *why*?'

'Well,' gibbered Seven, 'I thought what you'd actually said might have been *Lawn of Satan*. As I believe I mentioned,' he blathered helplessly on, 'it wasn't easy to understand you on the mobile. I thought I could have you standing on some grass smeared in blood with your horns on, strimming with an evil expression . . .' His voice trailed away at the sight of Jett's face. Never had Seven seen an expression more evil. The problem was, he knew if he snapped it, he'd never live to tell the tale. Let alone develop the film.

Jett's anger dropped several hundred degrees below freezing hatred. He took a few steps closer to Seven so the dead stag's nose pressed almost into the photographer's face. '*Lawn of Satan?*' he hissed. '*Lawn? Lawn?* When did you last see someone looking like the goddamn Antichrist mowing their goddamn *lawn*, for Chrissakes?'

'Well, take Haselmere any Sunday afternoon—'

'The name of the *album*, you *fucking moron*,' Jett cut in viciously, 'is *Spawn of Satan*. *Spawn*. Not *lawn*. Not *prawn*. *Spawn*.'

For a few seconds, Seven looked downcast. Then he brightened.

'There's a loch over there,' he said eagerly. 'We could borrow a jam jar from the kitchen and get some frogspawn. You could hold the jar up to the camera . . .' His voice trailed away again as he realised Jett was no longer listening to him. His furious expression had been replaced by one of terror. Seven whipped round to see the largest, widest, biggest, ugliest and angriest woman he had ever set eyes on stomping towards them from the direction of the kitchen. In her wake floated the vilest of cooking smells.

'And what exactly,' boomed Nanny, striding up to Jett and prodding the carcass with a forefinger as thick as a tree branch, 'do you think you are doing with tonight's dinner?'

* * *

Jett stormed back into his bedroom feeling rawer than a sushi makers' convention. The cover shoot degenerating into farce had been bad enough without that terrifying old bag bearing down on them into the bargain. Seven's offering her the prawns as a starter had only made things worse. Jett was not looking forward to the evening's planned big dinner party, despite being flattered that Geri and Jamie had decided to throw one in his honour.

The door, slamming shut behind him, echoed his feelings.

'Is that you, Wobblebottom? In here, darling.' Jett's heart sank as he heard Champagne's voice issuing shrilly from the bathroom. In the three hours he had been absent, Champagne had managed to progress from the bed to the bath, a distance of a full ten feet. He stuck his head round the bathroom door to see her immersed in bubbles.

Champagne pushed her hands into her hair and pouted at him. As her breasts travelled gloriously upwards at the movement of her arms, Jett was conscious of a tightening around his groin area hardly due to his skin-tight black jeans alone. Champagne's body was the most generously luscious he had ever seen, even if being first in line in the Looks queue meant she'd gone straight to the back of Brains. He'd heard that her beauty could drive men mad; but hadn't, until recently, appreciated in quite what way.

'Darling, I'm relaxing, yah?' Champagne beamed at him and raised a tanned, pink-toenailed foot from the foam. 'Had an unbelievably exhausting afternoon. Waited *ages* for the maid to come and unpack my bag and in the end had to go down and drag someone up here to do it. Annie, I think she was called. Bloody useless, anyway. Hung my Gucci up *all wrong*.'

Jett's heart sank. 'That,' he said evenly, 'is the castle owner's fiancée. *Your* hostess.'

'*Oh*. Well, I must say she was *very* unhelpful over doing my washing for me. Can you *believe* there's no laundry service here? She said she always washes her knickers in the *sink*.'

'Well, that won't be a problem for you. You don't wear knickers. Anyway, you better get ready,' said Jett impatiently. 'Dinner's in half an hour.'

'Oh, *Wobblebottom*.' The special voice Champagne put on for wheedling purposes set Jett's teeth on edge even more than the maddening pet name. His bottom emphatically did *not* wobble. 'You know I *never* eat in public,' she purred. 'Can't you get them to send me up a *tiny* vegetable consommé followed by a *minuscule* white truffle risotto and – oh, perhaps a *tiny* bottle of Krug as well? I *hate* to put anyone out, of *course* . . .'

For a moment, Jett flirted with the delicious idea of ordering room service from that terrifying bruiser of a cook. Better still, of getting Champagne to. 'Well, come down for a drink at least. Be rude not to.'

'Oh, if I *must*.' As Champagne rose, pouting, from the bath, water running down her breasts, hips and pubic hair, Jett struggled to keep his erection under control. If Champagne saw it, all would be lost and he really wasn't in the mood. Her voracious sexual appetite could have left Casanova on his knees weeping and begging for mercy.

Galling though it was to admit it, Champagne was getting too much of a handful for him. His hands, at any rate, were getting too full of her rather too much; Jett wondered, quite literally, how much longer he was going to be able to keep it up. The years between his first flush of fame and recent revival had not seen an increase in stamina to match the decrease in hair. And besides, girls seemed to be getting more difficult to satisfy; Jett had no memories of sixties chicks being as goddamn demanding as their millennium counterparts. Girls today seemed to expect more, and Jett had never met anyone who expected as goddamn much as Champagne did.

In his defence, Jett knew his decline had been less spectacular than that of the rest of the band. Talk about the Mild Ones. By Solstice's former hell-raising standards, the pre-gig dressing-room conversations during the Wold Tour had been embarrassing. Less sex and drugs and rock 'n' roll than gardening, mortgages and children. He was the only one even getting *divorced*, for Christ's goddamn sake . . .

Jett gazed out moodily into the impenetrable black beyond the windows. Say what you like about Cassandra – and he had, many times – at least she didn't want five orgasms a night. Didn't want any at all, in fact. Recalling the deep, deep, unmolested peace of the marital minimalist double bed, Jett sighed almost wistfully in the direction of the emerging stars.

'*Dah-dah*, yah?'

Jett was jerked out of his daydream to see Champagne standing in the bathroom doorway, arms raised in triumph and wearing a pair of snakeskin pants that must have been looser on the original snake.

Champagne wriggled her shoulders. 'Like my bustier? Very rock chick, yah?' She tugged out a breast to expose the tip of a nipple and pouted at him again.

Jett stared at the complex structure of underwiring and cantilevering necessary to support and contain the flowing flesh of Champagne's cleavage. 'Looks like something by Isambard Kingdom Brunel.'

'Never heard of him, darling. This is Westwood.'

Jett gritted his teeth. Champagne's obsession with fashion had been the one flashpoint of the Back From The Dead tour. Deriding their blow-dried, tight satin and studded leather look, Champagne had attempted to shoehorn the whole of Solstice into Prada. At this, the Mild Ones had finally seen red. As Champagne ordered him into a leather sarong, Nigel 'Animal' Gurkin, drummer, father of five, resident of Tunbridge Wells, builder of dolls' houses out of matchsticks, and the Mildest One of all, had snapped. 'We're a heavy metal band, you know,' he had remonstrated, placing his glass of orange juice down on the table with slightly more emphasis than was strictly necessary. 'Not *Boyzone*.'

If only we *were* Boyzone, thought Jett longingly. For the money if nothing else. While it was true that 'Sex and Sexibility', the first single released from the *Ass Me Anything* album, had gone straight to number one on a rip tide of ironic revivalism, the unhappy consequences for him personally had been the unwelcome attentions of that slumbering lion, the Inland Revenue. Then of course there was the yawning pit otherwise known as divorce into which he was pouring thousands despite a settlement seeming light years away. Talk about *nisi* goddamn work if you can get it, Jett thought sourly.

Last, but by no means least, was Champagne's conviction that, as a much-publicised, relaunched rock star in regular receipt of lavish amounts of publicity, Jett was rolling in money and it was her duty to get through as much of it as possible. His pleadings that a Solstice Wold Tour brought in significantly less than a Madonna-style World one completely failed to make an impact. Champagne had, Jett eventually realised, absolutely no idea of the multimillion-dollar difference between ironic and iconic.

At first he had thought she was joking when she'd asked him what she should wear to the Number Ten celebrity party this year. The thought of Champagne in Downing Street was an arresting one, especially after she had confided her belief that the Gulf War was caused by people queue-jumping at the Gulfstream factory. Even Cassandra had more of a grasp of foreign affairs than that, although she had once mortified him by insisting they stayed in the Hôtel de Ville on a trip to Paris on the grounds that it was larger and more impressive than the Crillon.

Jett sighed. He had passed from being an enthusiastic admirer of Champagne's frontage to looking forward to seeing the back of her. What had been initially good for his cred was proving disastrous for his bank balance. A Champagne lifestyle was not all it was cracked up to be. Yes, he was definitely missing Cassandra.

Zak stuck his fork in his glass and clanked it loudly backwards and forwards. Tendrils of venison stew sauce unravelled from the prongs and floated slowly in the water.

'Zak darling?' Cassandra smiled vaguely and beatifically at her son. 'That's *such* a wonderful noise, but—'

'*Shut up*,' snarled Jett as Zak, tiring of glass-banging, started instead to smash the silver cutlery hard against the polished surface of the table. In the shadows, Anna felt Nanny stiffen, yet couldn't help noticing that Cassandra, most uncharacteristically, failed to fly like a wildcat to her son's defence. She seemed very calm. Probably still drunk, thought Anna. Yet, for someone recovering from an industrial-strength hangover, Cassandra seemed in an amazingly good mood. Even more amazingly, a whispered conversation with Robbie had revealed that it was something to do with Mrs McLeod.

Anna shot an amused glance across the table to Robbie, intercepting an amused one from Geri to Jamie. *Those two*, thought Anna with a twist of the lips. Obvious enough what was happening *there*. They'd bonded over the tearooms and toilets – talk about lav at first sight. Just as well she wasn't the jealous type. Besides, discussing books with Robbie made such a welcome change from Jamie banging on about drains.

Robbie looked so handsome in his dinner jacket, the miraculously white and crisp collar of his shirt – could she detect the skilled hand of Mrs McLeod here? – contrasting with the high, outdoor colour of his face. Looking at his eyes, shining large, amused and amber in the candlelight, Anna felt for the first time in her life that here was a man she could trust. Except for keeping the dreaded beard at bay – his five o'clock shadow was now edging rather more towards midnight.

'Darling, what are you doing *now*?' Cassandra's

urgent whisper suddenly cut across her thoughts.

'Willy tricks.' Zak, smirking ostentatiously, was busy pressing down hard on his leeks with a fork so the white centre shot out at a distinctly penile angle.

'Behave your goddamn self,' snapped Jett, raising an eyebrow and grinning apologetically at Cassandra.

To Anna's amazement, Cassandra not only grinned back but, in addition, shot Jett a coy look from under her eyelashes. In Jett's mirrored lenses, the candlelight glowed softly in reply. What *was* going on there? The expected hysterical scenes following Jett and Cassandra's discovery of each other in the castle had not taken place. And that was *before* Champagne D'Vyne had appeared.

Champagne had arrived at the dining table forty-five minutes late. 'Sorry, yah?' she trilled, tossing her long blonde hair back over her shoulders. 'Had to write my column.' She rolled her brilliant green eyes theatrically. 'Deadlines. *Such* a bore.'

'You're telling me,' muttered Jett. Champagne's weekly newspaper column, in which she chronicled her dizzyingly glamorous social life and in which Jett had recently made his debut portrayed as the author's adoring lapdog, had done his street cred almost as much damage as Champagne herself had done his bank balance.

The rest of the company exchanged looks. Along with everyone else in the Sunday newspaper-reading universe, all those present, apart, perhaps, from Jamie, were aware that Champagne did not write the society column that appeared weekly under her name. It was well known that the only person for whom Champagne's deadlines were a bore was the unfortunate hack on the paper whose job it was to extract the eight hundred words or so from her.

Having arrived for dinner fashionably late, Champagne soon found herself in the considerably less chic situation of facing Jett's ex-wife across the table. 'Is this some kind of *joke*?' she had, after a freezing silence, demanded of the hapless Jamie who was doing the introductions. Stamping her metal heel so hard it drew sparks from the flagstones, Champagne treated the assembly to a display of explosions worthy of the millennium celebrations and a stream of eye-watering expletives that would have left a battleship crew gasping but left Zak in raptures.

By way of a finale, Champagne stormed off as best she could given that at Dampie storming off anywhere involved waiting in the hall for the one local taxi for up to three hours. And there was another curious thing, thought Anna. Jett had seemed almost relieved to see the back of her, even if the two engineers he had brought with him had looked rather regretful. In the end, it had been they who took Champagne off in their gaffer's van, thus freeing up three portions in total of Nanny's venison stew to be divided among those left behind. This had not been a blessing. The rule that each mouthful must be chewed thirty-two times could have been invented for Nanny's cuisine. Then doubled.

'I can't eat any more of this crap.' Zak suddenly spat out a mouthful of venison casserole on to the table. Jett immediately cuffed him across the basin cut.

'Gosh, the wind's getting up, isn't it?' Geri said loudly and distractingly, as Nanny smashed plates together on the pretext of collecting them. Outside, the gale was slapping itself against the windows almost as hard as Jett had just smacked his son. And, no doubt, almost as hard as Nanny would like to smack Geri.

'Nanny'll soon fix that,' said Jamie, grabbing the chance to make amends with both hands. 'She's amazing. Full of ancient lore. Whenever there's a storm, it always calms down after Nanny goes to the shore and throws a pudding into the sea.'

'I beg your pardon?' Cassandra, evidently glad of the excuse, put her fork down in surprise. Anna blinked. Even *she* had never heard this one.

'Ancient tradition,' Jamie added. 'Feeding the waves, she calls it.'

'Eat *up*,' Jett ordered Zak, who immediately stuck his tongue out even further.

'Tummy ache,' he muttered.

'Oh, Nanny's got a cure for that as well,' Jamie burst

in eagerly. 'She'll have you hanging upside down like a shot.'

'*What?*' Cassandra and Jett peered into the shadows, where Nanny lurked, with awe and interest, as if observing a strange and wonderful beast.

'That's her cure for stomachache,' Jamie gabbled, clearly relieved that Nanny was receiving the respect she deserved from some quarters at least. 'Hanging people upside down by the heels.'

'Really?' Cassandra looked impressed. A speculative light shone from Jett's eye. A few moments of silence followed, during which it was hard not to notice that Zak was the stillest and quietest of all.

Chapter 25

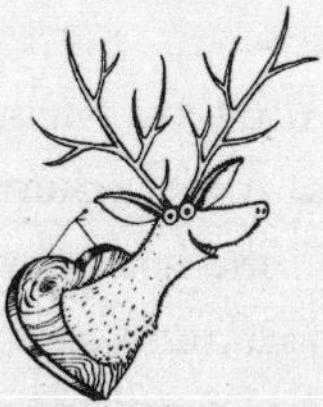

'Will you . . . ?' Jamie looked apologetically at Anna. The question, raised after dinner in the sitting room while Geri had gone down to the kitchen to, in her words, 'put a bomb under Nanny with the coffee', was not entirely unanticipated.

Anna had been expecting it for days, ever since she had caught Jamie kissing Geri in the ruins of the wine store. After which Geri had studiously avoided her – that had been Anna's interpretation, at least, of the fact Geri had suddenly been rushing back and forth to London on 'urgent business'.

'Would you mind very much giving me back the, um . . .'

'Ring? Not at all.' Anna delved frantically in her

pocket to produce the small box. It was, more than anything, a relief to hand it over. Apart from all its other unfortunate associations, the responsibility of carrying it around all the time had been onerous. She passed the ring to Jamie not entirely convinced it would reach its next rightful recipient. The wine store roof, after all, had yet to be replaced.

'You don't mind?'

'Of course not. You'll be much better off with Geri.' The odd thing was, Anna believed it. Even before the wine store incident, she had caught a number of looks passing between Jamie and Geri that were of a far more incendiary nature than anything she personally remembered. Perhaps it was because they were such opposites – fiery, capable, earthy Geri, dreamy and romantic Jamie. Although the dreamy bit might be in for a shock; Geri, Anna knew, would not stand for any shirking in bed. Jamie would be expected to stand and deliver.

'Thanks.' Jamie swiftly pocketed the ring. 'I'm glad you think so. She *is* wonderful, isn't she? So capable and full of energy.'

Anna nodded, looked around the room and reflected that it was just as well. Her gaze fixed on the telltale black sweep of fungal damp on the wall behind the sofa.

Its disintegration was a grim reminder that at Dampie decay was not a slow, gentle, faintly melancholy process, but a vital, thrusting affair. Less a case, Anna thought, squinting at the fat black beads against the whiteness, of watching paint dry than watching it warp, bubble up, split and eventually slide defeated off the damp walls. She shuddered. Call her spineless, but all her previous sense of abject failure had disappeared, to be replaced by the profound relief of knowing she was not spending the rest of her life in this place.

'I hope you'll be very happy,' she told Jamie.

'I'm sure we will,' Jamie assured her, his gaze following hers to the wall. 'Geri's fantastic at DIY, you know. I've never seen anyone handle a grout gun like her.' His eyes shone with mixed adoration and admiration. 'And she loves the traditions – all the history . . .'

'Yes,' said Anna. 'And that's all great. But you know you've got to sort out one thing. Once and for all. Otherwise it will never work.'

Jamie swallowed and dropped his gaze. 'I'm going for sex counselling, if that's what you mean . . .'

'Good,' said Anna. 'But I *didn't* mean that, actually.' As Jamie looked at the floor, Anna pressed on, suddenly feeling this was the best and ultimate service she could do her friend. After all, Geri had in a roundabout sort of way, rescued her from an untenable situation and provided an extremely neat, if unorthodox, solution. She wanted, Anna decided, to give Geri the best wedding present possible, one that owed nothing to the GTC and decoupage waste paper bins.

'I mean Nanny,' she said.

* * *

'What will you do now?'

Anna, face buried in the thick, salty matt of Robbie's chest hair, heard his question reverberate powerfully through his rib cage. She raised herself slowly until she was sitting up on top of him, pushing aside her tousled hair so she could see his eyes. He looked serious.

'I don't know,' she replied truthfully. In view of where careful plotting had got her before, she had decided not to have a plan for her future. 'I'm taking things as they come,' she smiled at him. Inside her, Robbie's just-spent penis stirred inquiringly. She'd already had three orgasms, each one longer than the last. And miraculously, so far, no sign of cystitis.

Although it applied to every other encounter she had had, Johnny Rotten's famous pronouncement that sex was 'two minutes of squelching', was a glorious misrepresentation of Robbie. Unlike all who had come and gone before him Robbie did not thrust immediately into her, dragging a host of delicate, dry and protesting internal organs with him.

Robbie's – surprisingly expert – method was to slowly raise her to a pitch of wet and gasping expectation, guiding her with flickering tongue and precise, circling, lust-slicked finger through hoops of quivering delight to the brink of back-arching ecstasy. Only then were her vaginal muscles allowed to clamp the great rod of his penis. Only then, as she swayed poised on the cliff of juddering delight, did Robbie finally fire into her and combine with her yelps of pleasured pain his groans of discreetly profound ecstasy.

But his greatest skill of all was that he managed to do it all without making her feel for one second self-conscious. Merely conscious of the fact that he found every inch of her, every ridge of cellulite, every careless bruise, every soft white swell of excess flesh, every split nail quite literally delicious. He had an earthiness about him, an unbounded, unabashed joy in the carnal.

'Will you come and live with me?' he suddenly asked her, clamping both strong, warm hands around her waist. Anna luxuriated both in the question and the feeling of strength and security. It was tempting. And she knew there was only one answer. No.

'I'd love to. I really would,' she mumbled. 'But I just couldn't stay here, I'm afraid.' Before coming to Dampie, Anna had never really considered herself a city girl. Now, however, even the thought of the Circle Line with signal failure filled her with eye-misting nostalgia.

Robbie pushed both hands through his thick hair. At the sight of the abundant hair in his armpits, Anna felt the familiar, dizzying plunge in her pelvis. *Oh God.* Was she making the right decision?

'Of course we wouldn't stay here,' Robbie muttered, sitting up and sucking at her nipples. 'We'll go back to London and write.'

'But where will we live? I haven't got a flat. Or any money.'

'Don't worry about that. I have. Rather nice one in Belgravia.' Beneath her, he was grinding gently up and down. Anna gasped as the red waves began to rise in her once again.

'*Belgravia?*' she murmured into his salt-tang hair as he pulled her head down to kiss her. She winced as the Brillo Pad brush of his bristle scraped hot and rasping against her cheek.

'Family flat. But only I ever use it.'

Anna spat out Robbie's tongue and looked at him in dismay. This had a horribly familiar ring to it. She shot a suspicious look at his naked little finger. At least *that* didn't.

'Family flat? So your father is . . . ?'

'An earl.' Robbie looked at her shamefacedly. 'I'm awfully sorry. I didn't want to tell you. I gathered from your diary that you weren't too keen on the aristocracy.'

'So you are?' Anna gazed at him stonily.

'The Hon. Robbie Persimmon-MacAskill. But don't hold it against me. I'm all right really, I promise you.'

Anna looked searchingly at him. Then she grinned as she felt his penis, formerly growing limp with despair, begin to swell within her once more. 'Talk about an ingrowing heir,' she whispered.

'So will you move in with me?' Robbie gazed anxiously at her.

Anna's breasts bounced wildly as her shoulders shook with laughter. 'I guess I'm Hon for it,' she spluttered, grinding herself down on him once more. 'Get to it, big boy,' she shouted joyfully. '*I want you to come inside me like a fire extinguisher.*'

'Will you come back to me?'

Jett saw the windscreen plunging towards him as Cassandra, shocked at the question, jerked her foot suddenly down on the accelerator. The car plunged forward almost into the back of a swaying beige Volvo with a sticker in the back window proclaiming 'It's Hard To Sit Down When You've Been To Harrow'. Cassandra stared at it and said nothing. For possibly the first time in her life she seemed to be choosing her words carefully.

'I've missed you,' Jett persisted. It was true. Without Cassandra exploding every five minutes, his life had seemed flat and without drama. He had not realised until now how addicted he had become to their screaming rows and steaming exchanges of vicious insults. How addicted to the wonders of W8 as well, as many weeks of crummy tour hotels, student digs and B&Bs had helped remind him. The particular horrors of a bed and breakfast in Grantham run by a couple called Ken and Flora and called Kenora still had him waking sweating in the night.

Nylon sheets. As slippery and electric as an eel. Jett

had not realised until skidding up and down that single bed, albeit in the birth place of the blessed Margaret Thatcher, how largely Provençal lavender-scented sheets of Irish linen had previously loomed in his life. And who was to say, if they persisted in going through with this stupid and expensive divorce, that both he and Cassandra wouldn't be condemned to nylon sheets for ever. Catching their toenails for the rest of their lives, sliding around on seas of tequila sunrise orange, aquamarine and bright purple. Breathing their last on sheets alive with static.

'We suit each other, you and I,' he added persuasively. Funny how a master lyricist like himself, from whom choice phrases usually flowed like the cleansing swirl down a lavatory, found it so hard to express himself in real-life situations. Cassandra was the same – celebrated author, and yet unable to utter a word about what was really important. Mind you, Jett thought, nothing new there.

'Come on, Sandra,' he urged. 'You know I've got a bit more wonga now after the tour. And there have been,' he plucked a figure from the air, '*ooh*, a good half million orders for *Spawn of Satan* already and it's only been goddamn released today. I can keep you in the manner to which you used to be accustomed.'

He looked at her hopefully. There was silence.

'Actually,' Cassandra said regally, drawing herself

up at the wheel, 'now I've hammered out the deal with Mrs McLeod, I'll be quite nicely off myself, thank you. We've got the summer paperback market stitched up well into the millennium.' She beamed through the windscreen. Getting Mrs McLeod to write her books had been an infinitely more satisfactory arrangement than having to bother doing it herself. Far better to become a brand and just slap her name on whatever McLeod produced. Her writer's block may have lifted slightly, but not enough, she knew, to power her through another 600-page Lanzarote beach special, and certainly not at the speed McLeod could write. The old bag could leave a jet ski lagging behind. How *clever* she had been to find her, Cassandra thought. How *inspired* of her to turn up at that ridiculous, rustic creative writing class. Suddenly, Cassandra's satisfied smirk twisted into an unbecoming scowl. 'Though if anyone's been stitched up it's *me*,' she added bitterly. 'That *bastard* Robbie MacAskill got McLeod a shit hot agent and she's getting a straight fifty per cent cut. Bloody cheek. After all, it's *my* name the books go out under. *My* reputation at stake.'

'Well, she *is* doing all the work, isn't she?' Whoa, Jett warned himself, seeing Cassandra's furious face. You're almost there. Don't fuck it up now. 'But yes, I quite see your point,' he added hurriedly. '*Your* reputation, absolutely.'

Cassandra's stony profile softened, although how

seemed a miracle, given the amount of plastic surgery it had undergone.

'Come on, Sandra,' Jett wheedled. 'You know you've got a soft spot for me.'

'I've certainly got a spot for you,' said Cassandra levelly. 'And don't call me Sandra. You know I hate it.' Her lips tightened. Cassandra loathed being reminded of her real name.

'Aw, baby. You know you're the only one for me.' Jett's voice began to take on a desperate tone as the outer darkness of rootless drifting and grubby groupies beckoned. As the image of Champagne D'Vyne raised itself terrifyingly before him, he cringed inwardly. The day she had walked out of his life had been better than jamming with Hendrix. Not that he *had* jammed with Hendrix. But he had once judged an organic lemon curd competition with Paul McCartney.

'But what about Zak?' demanded Cassandra suddenly. 'You were so horrible to the poor darling before.'

Behind them, Zak was too busy carving up the cream leather of the hired Rover's back seat to listen. He sat back to admire his handiwork. 'SHAMPAIN.' *What* a woman. He almost regretted now finding her phone number and writing it in every service station telephone box they stopped at with the words 'FOR FREE SEX FONE' scrawled above it. He sniffed loudly. That funny white powder he had found on the top of the loo in

Champagne's bathroom after she had gone had really made his nose run.

'*Listen* to him,' Cassandra declared dramatically. 'He's *terrified*. And there's the problem of his school as well. We can't live in London – no one will, um, *rise to the challenge* of him. Every London prep school I tried,' Cassandra's voice rose, 'said there was a basic problem with home discipline and they couldn't help until that had been rectified.'

'Which means a good nanny,' said Jett.

'Exactly.' Cassandra pressed her foot down in helpless fury. The Harrow sticker on the back of the Volvo came into focus again. Even if she took Jett back and – miracle of miracles – they managed to find a good nanny, the old problems were bound to come back. She sighed. It was a vicious circle. Good day school meant good nanny which meant Jett trying to jump on them which meant goodbye nanny which would now mean goodbye school as well. Talk about Catchment Area 22.

What she wanted was someone who could control Zak to the standards demanded by the strictest schools whilst being completely without charm for Jett. What we need, she thought, is a battleaxe. A nanny of the old school. Of the old *everything*. Damn. She could have *sworn* she'd met one of those lately . . .

What we need, Jett was thinking, is someone who will be as firm as a goddamn Gucci heel with that brat. Someone who will put the fear of God into him and give the goddamn little *sod* the hard time he deserves. *Christ*, but his memory was bad. He was *sure* he had seen the fear of God in Zak's eyes recently, but *goddamn* it if he could remember where. He had a vague memory of someone very big and frightening looming out of the shadows . . .

'Do you think,' Cassandra said suddenly to Jett, 'that we could somehow persuade—'

'That old nanny of Jamie Angus's?' finished Jett. They looked at each other in wild – and in Cassandra's case reflected – surmise.

In the back, Zak, who had suddenly tuned into the conversation, yelped in terror.

'Don't worry, darling,' Cassandra beamed, turning round. 'Everything's going to be all right.'

Pastures Nouveaux

Wendy Holden

From SW7 to rural heaven . . .

Cash-strapped Rosie and her boyfriend Mark are city folk longing for a tiny country cottage. Rampantly nouveaux-riches Samantha and Guy are also searching for rustic bliss – a mansion complete with mile-long drive and hot and cold running gardeners.

The village of Eight Mile Bottom seems quiet enough, despite a nosy postman, a reclusive rock star, a glamorous Bond Girl and a ghost with a knife in its back. But there are unexpected thrills in the hills. The local siren seduces Guy while a farmer fatale rocks Rosie's relationship. Then a mysterious millionaire makes an offer she can't refuse. But should she?

Praise for *Pastures Nouveaux*

'Delicious mayhem. With this updated version of *Cold Comfort Farm*, Holden has pulled it off yet again. Simply divine' *The Times*

'Pacy pastiche of city dwellers gone country . . . an entertaining novel which will no doubt delight' *Daily Mail*

'Clever, naughty, affectionate and good-natured . . . a comic romp engineered with aplomb and dash' *The Sunday Times*

'People will adore this book' *Independent*

'Hilarious look at townies who move to the country' *Mirror*

'Holden at her funniest and most perceptive . . . spot on' *Mail on Sunday*

0 7472 6616 6

headline

Fame Fatale

Wendy Holden

Unbridled lust. Unlimited excess. Unbelievable egos . . .

Ruthless hack Belinda wants a rich and famous man. Her problem is her job: interviewing Z-list celebs for a tabloid's Tea Break slot means zero opportunity for megastar-bagging.

Unassuming Grace just wants a quiet life. Her problems include an egomaniac boyfriend, a matchmaking mother and a publishing job with the authors from hell.

Scheming Belinda finally finds fame, while Grace has it thrust upon her in the shape of a handsome film star. But life among the A-list is anything but easy. Amid unbridled lust, unlimited excess and unbelievable egos, the girls' lives spectacularly collide. And then the real problems begin.

Praise for *Fame Fatale*:

'A hilarious, touching romp through stardom, sex and addiction to celebrity' *Cosmopolitan*

'A frothy, naughty, Evelyn-Waugh-on-speed take on literary and media life, pulled off with great aplomb by a writer firing on all cylinders. A real hoot' *Daily Mail*

'Wicked wit . . . totally fun' *Mirror*

'High-speed satire . . . perfect' *Glamour*

'Holden is on delicious form . . . needle-sharp and witty' *The Sunday Times*

0 7472 6615 8

headline

A Married Man

Catherine Alliott

When Lucy Fellowes is offered a dream house in the country she leaps at the chance. It's hard enough living in London on an uncertain income, but when you're widowed with two small boys it's even harder. And anyway, a rural retreat will bring her closer to Charlie. Charlie? The only man in four years to make her heart beat faster. Perfect. Or it would be. If only he didn't belong to someone else . . .

A wickedly witty new novel about how complicated relationships get when you grow up, from the best-selling author of *Rosie Meadows regrets . . .* and *Olivia's Luck*.

'Alliott's skilled handling of such delicate, difficult and deep material marvellously counterpoints the Cotswolds comic archetypes and provides psychological depth and shadow to the sparky surface action. Sensitive, funny and wonderfully well-written.' Wendy Holden, *Daily Express*

0 7472 6722 7

headline